THEY FIRED THE FIRST SHOT 2012™

By

A Friend of Medjugorje

THEY FIRED THE FIRST SHOT 2012™

By

A Friend of Medjugorje

SPECIAL STATEMENT
Medjugorje Status
December 1, 2011 A.D.

No attempt is intended to pre-empt the Church on the validity of the Medjugorje Apparitions. They are private revelation waiting the Church's final judgment[1]. In the interim, these private revelations **are** allowed by, and for, the faithful to have devotion to and to be spread legally by the Church. Devotion and the propagation of private revelations can be forbidden only **if** the private revelation is condemned because of anything it contains which contravenes faith and morals according to AAS 58 (1966) 1186 Congregation for the Doctrine of the Faith. Medjugorje has not been condemned nor found to have anything against faith or morals, therefore it is in the grace of the Church to be followed by the faithful. By the rite of Baptism one is commissioned and given the authority to evangelize. *"By Baptism they share in the priesthood of Christ, in his prophetic and royal mission."*[2] One does not need approval to promote or to have devotions to private revelations or to spread them when in conformity to AAS 58 (1966) 1186, as the call to evangelize is given when baptized. Caritas of Birmingham, the Community of Caritas and all associated with it, realize and accept that the final authority regarding the Queen of Peace, Medjugorje and happenings related to the apparitions, rests with the Holy See in Rome. We at Caritas, willingly submit to that judgment. While having an amiable relationship with the Diocese of Birmingham and a friendly relationship with its bishop, Caritas of Birmingham as a lay mission is not officially connected to the Diocese of Birmingham, Alabama, just as is the Knights of Columbus.[3] The Diocese of Birmingham's official position on Caritas is neutral and holds us as Catholics in good standing.

1. The Church does not have to approve the apparitions. The Church can do as She did with the apparitions of Rue du Bac in Paris and the Miraculous Medal. The Church never approved these apparitions. She gave way to the people's widespread acceptance of the Miraculous Medal and thereby the Apparitions to St. Catherine.
2. Catechism of the Catholic Church 2nd Edition
3. The Knights of Columbus also are not officially under the Church, yet they are very Catholic. The Knights of Columbus was founded as a lay organization 129 years ago, with the basic Catholic beliefs. Each local council appeals to the local Ordinary to be the Chaplain. The Knights of Columbus is still a lay organization, and operates with its own autonomy.

Foreword

This foreword contains two parts. The first part is the "Story in Brief" and the second part is "An Important Read."

THE VILLAGE SEES THE LIGHT is the title of a story which "Reader's Digest" published in February 1986. It was the first major news on a mass public scale that told of the Virgin Mary visiting the tiny village of Medjugorje, Bosnia-Hercegovina. At that time this village was populated by 400 families.

It was June 24, 1981, the Feast of John the Baptist, the proclaimer of the coming Messiah. In the evening, around 5:00 p.m., the Virgin Mary appeared to two young people, Mirjana Dragičević* and Ivanka Ivanković*. Around 6:40 p.m. the same day, Mirjana and Ivanka, along with four more young people, Milka Pavlović*, the little sister of Marija, Ivan Ivanković, Vicka Ivanković*, and Ivan Dragičević saw the Virgin Mary. The next day, June 25, 1981, along with Mirjana, Ivanka, Vicka and Ivan Dragičević, Marija Pavlović* and Jakov Čolo also saw the Virgin Mary, bringing the total to six visionaries. Milka Pavlović* and Ivan Ivanković only saw Our Lady once, on that first day. These six have become known as and remain "the visionaries."

---

* Names at the time of the apparitions, they are now married with last names changed.

These visionaries are not related to one another. Three of the six visionaries no longer see Our Lady on a daily basis. As of June 2013, the Virgin is still appearing everyday to the remaining three visionaries; that's well over 14,271 apparitions.

The supernatural event has survived all efforts of the Communists to put a stop to it, many scientific studies, and even the condemnation by the local bishop; yet, the apparitions have survived, giving strong evidence that this is from God because nothing and no one has been able to stop it. For over thirty-one years, the apparitions have proved themselves over and over and now credibility is so favorable around the world that the burden of proof that this is authentic has shifted from those who believe to the burden of proof that it is not happening by those opposed to it. Those against the apparitions are being crushed by the fruits of Medjugorje — millions and millions of conversions which are so powerful that they are changing and will continue to change the whole face of the earth.

An Important Read

Many who will read this book have been following the writings of A Friend of Medjugorje for over twenty-five years. His original and unique insights into the important events of our day have won credence in millions of hearts around the world. His moral courage in the face of so many leaders caving in to the pressures of a politically correct world is not only refreshing, but according to tens of thousands of written testimonies, has helped to deeply strengthen those who desire to live the fullness of Christianity. His insights, that are often prophetic, have their source in the apparitions of the Virgin Mary in Medjugorje. Deeply and personally influenced by a Biblical worldview and the events surrounding Medjugorje, he gave himself to the prayerful study and application into his life of the words that the Virgin Mary has been speaking over the past quarter of a century. He discovered that She has come to speak to mankind in this time because the dangers we face are on a scale unlike any the world has ever known. Millions have been deeply affected by his writings.

While reading this book, one is free to ignore the happenings of the phenomenon of Medjugorje, but in doing so, one would be choosing to ignore over 30 years of scientific testing, from 1981 until the present. The most recent comprehensive study was conducted by a team of French scientists in 2005, with the most modern means of testing available from the scientific world. Those findings affirm that while science cannot say it is the Virgin Mary appearing, science **"can support the absence of deception."** The scientist teams have determined that these occurrences are of supernatural origin. Over 30 years of testing, evaluation, and the proof of changed lives are a testament to the reality that God is speaking to the world today through Medjugorje.

For those who approach this writing with skepticism concerning the apparitions of the Virgin Mary, whether you are of a faith that is inclined to reject such apparitions or a nonbeliever, we suggest that you not let that deter you from reading this book, but simply read the messages of the Virgin Mary as comments such as a pastor would make. We say this because there are a great many things that are threatening our nation's future and that knowledge is important for all men to understand, especially Americans because of the position God has placed us in the world. The truths contained within this writing have an important contribution to make in the ongoing national dialogue that will determine whether America will continue on the path of destruction it has been on for the past several decades or will find the will to return to the ideals and the vision of their founding fathers. <u>They Fired the First Shot 2012</u>_™ places in the hands of the reader the answer by which <u>all</u> our woes can be corrected, when each Christian accepts to change his life and live according to all the precepts given to us by God. In doing so we will be contributing more to the future peace and security of the United States of America than any government, military, agency or program. For as the author often writes, "a people are not so much protected by their armaments as they are by their way of life." In the United States of America, the way of life of *"we the people"* has always been based in the living of Christian principles, even for non-Christians. If we wish to have the protection of God that we have always enjoyed in this nation, if we wish America to be saved from all of the impending evils that are surrounding us, then America must return to living Christianity in its fullness. By doing so, we will become God's children of light again, and He will reach down from the Heavens and save us. We thank God for allowing Our Lady, the Queen of Peace, to be with us in these trying times, as His ambassador from Heaven. May we heed Her words to return to the Father, who is waiting for us that He may once again bestow His blessings upon us.

—The Publisher

ACKNOWLEDGEMENT

God alone deserves the credit for the publication of this book. It is from Him that the messages are allowed to be given through Our Lady to all of mankind. He alone deserves the praise and honor.

Table of Contents

What you are about to read has been prayed about for years. A great deal of discernment through Our Lady's messages and the Holy Spirit has gone into its contents. In our books and newsletters, we have often recommended praying to the Holy Spirit for understanding; however, the following should not even be begun until it can be read slowly, in a contemplative way, and without interruptions. As you read it, become part of it. Find some quiet time or place such as in front of the Blessed Sacrament or some other place of solitude. If you are a Protestant, you may wish to meditate and pray to the Holy Spirit for several moments. If you are not sure of God, pray in your heart to the God you do not know. He will manifest Himself to you. Also, this book was not written to be read one time only. It is to be read several times and each time it is read, you will gain more understanding than the previous reading. It would be wise to put off reading this material until after much prayer. The Holy Spirit will provide the necessary enlightenment and strength to understand, and even to endure, the truth, which was masterfully hidden from us but is now exposed to the light by Our Lady through Her messages. Remember, the following should only be read slowly, after prayer to the Holy Spirit, and from the heart to grasp its full meaning.

CHAPTER ONE

"There are no devils left in hell."

Medjugorje visionary, Ivanka, stopped receiving daily apparitions from the Virgin Mary on May 7, 1985. Our Lady told her at that time that she would receive a yearly apparition on June 25th for the rest of her life. Throughout these years, on June 25th, Our Lady has often spoken to Ivanka about the secrets. *Ivanka has received all ten secrets, the 10th given to her the second to the last day of her daily apparitions. What follows is a very significant apparition that Ivanka experienced that has ramifications for all of mankind.*

On this anniversary apparition, June 25, 1993, and Ivanka's once a year apparition, she entered the room in her home where Our Lady would appear to her as usual — very happy and blissful. But the way the apparition ended was anything but blissful. How could that be if Ivanka was seeing the Virgin Mary, the Queen of

---

* Our Lady has given three of the visionaries ten secrets, while the other three visionaries have nine secrets and are waiting for the 10th. Three of these secrets are admonitions or chastisements. Their purpose is for purification and the correction of the conscience of man. They will take place in the present generation. It will be a final proof of God's sending the Virgin Mary to warn man that without Christ, there is no future.

1

Peace? What Ivanka sees is not what one sees as on
a TV or movie screen. It is not theatrical. It is real.
Scientists have proven through the most advanced and
highly sophisticated scientific measurements of the
brain that what the visionaries of Medjugorje see during the apparition is more real, there is a heightened
reality, than what they experience when they are in
their "normal" state of human perception. When they
see Our Lady, they literally "fall" into a deeper state
of being. What is more real is more in the fullness of
truth. The visionary moves into a world of truth. As
the apparition ends, they enter back into a lesser reality, which is their normal state of being. Repeated
scientific tests and studies from 1983-2005 conclusively
prove the six visionaries are seeing something supernatural and not of this world. The group of scientists,
however, say they cannot say "what" they are seeing.
That relies on the testimonies of the visionaries and the
way they conduct their lives.

This particular apparition of Ivanka's, as it ended,
not only brought her back to normal life reality, it also
left her distraught, even near panic-stricken. Our Lady,
over several annual apparitions to Ivanka, spoke to
her about the secrets—admonitions to the world, yet
none of these apparitions, as is known publicly, created

within her the reaction as what happened after the apparition of June 25, 1993. On June 25, 1993, Our Lady gave more than words. Our Lady showed Ivanka the near future of something the devil would incubate for the next nine months until birth. The scene Ivanka saw would be recorded into world history. The name of the child to be born would be 'hate.' Of what Ivanka saw nine months before it happened, secular *Time* Magazine's cover of May 16, 1994 said, **"There are no devils left in hell,"** and then continuing in the article itself, **"...actually they brought hell with them."**[1] Amazingly this referred directly to what Ivanka had seen months before—a view of hell spilling out onto the earth. Ivanka was so distraught after her encounter with what Our Lady showed her, that she was inconsolable. One who attended the June 25, 1993, apparition in Ivanka's home gave an eyewitness account of Ivanka's reaction:

"Ivanka came into the crowded room and knelt down to pray the Rosary in anticipation of Our Lady's apparition. Ivanka was poised as one would be as if they were about to meet the greatest personage of their lifetime. She had a nervous smile, but one could see in her joy and desire with a thirst that only could be quenched by seeing Who was anticipated. Suddenly Our Lady was

there in front of Ivanka and all became silent. After a few moments, Ivanka's lips moved in conversation without sound coming through them. Ivanka stared with head raised, looking towards Our Lady, and then silently began speaking again. It was a beautiful scene mirrored through her face and eyes what someone would look like who is literally watching the fullness of love.

But something happened; I witnessed Ivanka go from experiencing the fullness of love, to the extreme opposite, experiencing the fullness of satanic hatred. If Ivanka's countenance did not define these two extremes during the apparition, signaling to those present that something unusual was happening, after the apparition it was clear. I have been present during several annual apparitions when Our Lady spoke to Ivanka about the secrets, but never did I witness what I saw that day after the apparition.

When the apparition ended, Ivanka jumped up saying, "Horrible, horrible…horrible scenes," *all the while moving rapidly through the crowd of people, seemingly oblivious to their presence. Ivanka's husband followed her, presumingly asking what was wrong, obviously disturbed by her anxiety. Ivanka ran into the hallway, then moved rapidly from room to room, still loudly saying,* "horrible scenes." *Confused at what was happening, her husband tried to talk to her. Not responding clearly to him, Ivanka had grabbed her light coat, coming back into the hallway, and then ran out the front door, followed now not only by her husband, but her small daughter who also ran after her. Ivanka ran into the front yard, then to the left side of the house, jumped down a wall, and hurried off. Her little girl was by then laying down partially in the grass, crying at her father's feet while Ivanka disappeared down the trail that led to the church."**

What had Ivanka seen? What had Our Lady shown her? Why did it upset her so much? Ivanka saw a truth of the fullness of hate and its fruit that was soon to be born. She saw hundreds of thousands of bodies floating down a river, bodies everywhere, bodies mutilated, not only of men, but many who were women and children and even babies.

What Ivanka saw, she saw as a truth, not as a TV report. This was a very potent reality, a reality that the

---

* A Friend of Medjugorje was in attendance at Ivanka's June 25, 1993 apparition in her home and gave this testimony.

—The Publisher

world came to see itself on April 6, 1994, nine months after Ivanka peered into the future. This truth physically manifested into the horrible, horrible scenes, seen by her on June 25, 1993.

As already stated, *Time* magazine's May 16, 1994 cover told of it after the fact:

"There are no devils left in hell. They are all in Rwanda."

Then turning to the beginning of the May 16, 1994 article, it says:

"...Actually they brought hell with them."

Time quoted Daniel Bellamy, a freelance journalist, who encountered these killers eye-to-eye at several road blocks:

"There is something there that is not in the eyes of normal people."

Time asked the question: *"How can so much hate have accumulated?"*[2]

In Africa, Rwanda consisted of two major ethnic groups, the Hutus and the Tutsis. There are many things in their history which could explain reasons for what happened, but only one is necessary; that which

Ivanka experienced, a satanic event that resulted
from the full maturity of hatred. The Hutus decided
to eradicate the Tutsis. The Hutus, typically a darker
skinned people, could be easily distinguished from the
lighter-skinned Tutsis. Along with being able to easily distinguish a Tutsi from a Hutu, the Hutu plan of
genocide was well organized,[3] with representatives
in each neighborhood. Hutu businessmen imported
581,000 — literally, five hundred eighty-one thousand —
machetes for the Hutus to kill the Tutsis.[4] If any Hutu
refused to kill Tutsis, the Hutu would also be killed.[5]
The killings were organized nationwide, with one killer
for every ten families in the neighborhood.[6] Planned
in cabinet meetings, one cabinet member said she
*was personally in favor of getting rid of all Tutsis. All
Rwanda's problems would be over."*[7] Genocide planners included members of the militia, village mayors,
police officers and many other respected members of
society, which led great numbers of Hutus to organize
and incite to kill their Tutsi neighbors. The moderate
Hutus, who resisted killing Tutsis were also massacred
and amounted to ten percent of those killed.[8]

How was such hatred conceived? The Hutu genocide planners knew they could easily incite the people.
Easily manipulated, the organizers capitalized on this

trait, propagandizing the Hutu people to go savagely
tribal against the Tutsis. Hatred towards the Tutsis was
promoted constantly through the state Hutu-controlled
newspaper, *Kangura*.[9] Some of the individuals behind
the newspaper also produced a leaflet picturing a machete with a question, *"What should we do to complete
the social revolution?"* Another use of media that was
key to inciting violence, was two different radio stations which worked to build up tensions of hate, sus-
picion, paranoia, fear, mistrust, and victimization to a
point that a spark could explode the Hutus hatred and
release a satanic fury against the Tutsis.[10] And when
this spark ignited, it resulted in the death and mutila-
tion of 1,170,000 men, women, children, and infants,
according to government reports. Seven people killed
per minute for just over 100 days. Ivanka's reaction
of running to the church, not even stopping to explain
to her husband what she had seen or to calm her little
daughter, can now be understood. Ivanka carried the
weight of knowing what no human on earth knew—not
even those who were in the midst of already planning
the eradication of the Tutsis, while Ivanka, in June of
1993, was actually seeing it. The only place Ivanka
knew to run was to the church, where she could bear
her heart to Jesus.

While the planners of Rwanda's genocide could not see what Ivanka was seeing as they planned it, they also could not see their own fate either. In the late 1700's, the French Revolution planners were all killed soon after the revolution began. This is usually the fate of those who plan evil. Likewise, one of the Hutu genocide planners, who through Hutu businessmen ordered the 581,000 machetes, was President General Habyarimana. The genocide planner president would be the first to be killed along with others.

His death provided the spark that ignited the explosion of instant mass killings, just as a dam broken by flood water destroys everything in its path. The plane of Rwanda's President General, the man who ordered the machetes, was shot down April 6, 1994. Thus the massive attack on the Tutsis began on April 6, 1994, while TV, radio and newspapers blared that the Tutsis were responsible for the downing of the airplane. A later investigation blamed Hutu extremists for the crimes.[11] In January, 2012, a French investigation confirmed that the missile which shot the plane down *did not* come from Tutsi rebels, but from a Hutu military camp.[12] The blaming of the Tutsis provided the spark needed for those who were so keyed up with hatred to become fully possessed with demons to commit the sa-

tanic killings and many other unmentionable atrocities.
The two radio stations placing blame upon the Tutsis
fueled the hatred for the next 100 continuous days. The
international research center, *"Hate Media in Rwanda,"*
conveyed what happened. The Hutu controlled media...

> *"repeatedly stressed the need to be alert to Tutsi*
> *plots and possible attacks. It warned Hutus to*
> *prepare to 'defend' themselves against the Tutsis.*
> *After April 6, 1994, authorities used Radio Rwan-*
> *da to spur and direct killing specifically in areas*
> *where killings were initially resisted* (Hutus who
> resisted, who did not want to kill Tutsis). *Two*
> *radio stations were used to incite and mobilize*
> *populations followed by broadcasters' specific*
> *direction for carrying out the killing."* [13]

They did so with over half a million machetes.

World history was made on April 6, 1994 and continued for the next 100 days until mid July. World history, before it happened, was shown in one small room
on June 25, 1993. Medjugorje is bigger, much bigger
than can be understood in the moment. What does all
this tell us of the future? Prophecy or Revelation is
given not to forecast the future, but to move us to deci-

sions which must be made in the present in order to mitigate, even avoid altogether a dangerous future, just as when Jonah went through the city of Nineveh warning of its coming judgment, and listening to him, the king down to the lowest peasant repented, sacrificed and ultimately avoided what was to be forecasted for their future. Abraham, looking for righteous souls to save the city, was not so successful in Sodom.

12   <u>"There are no devils left in hell."</u>

CHAPTER TWO

Pride has Come to Rule

What do the incredible, yet horrible events you just read about say about our own future? To know, we must observe the present to see the path the world is taking. Do you think, "Well, Our Lady is here. Everything is going to be fine?" Do you think that apparitions every day for 31 years, as of June 25, 2012, are for 'in'significant reasons concerning the future of the world? Can we say, "Well, Our Lady is here. She will take care of everything?" Then why does Our Lady say:

March 21, 1985

> **"Dear children, I wish to keep on giving messages and, therefore, today I call you to live and accept my messages...I call on you - accept me, dear children, that it might go well with you..."**

Did you know that before the Rwanda massacre, Our Lady was there, appearing in the small village of Kibeho in Rwanda? Do you think when Our Lady

13

of Kibeho appeared in 1982 to seven visionaries, and gave a warning to pray and repent, repeatedly warning them of the blood bath coming, that She did so to save everyone physically? Did you know the Catholic Church approved these apparitions, yet three of the seven visionaries were killed in the genocide? Being a visionary did not spare them. Did you know that Our Lady, during the Kibeho apparitions taught one of the visionaries a song, and when she got to one part of the song, Our Lady stopped her to teach and emphasize the following words? Our Lady made her repeat the following words seven times:

> *"There will be fire that will come from beneath the earth and consume everything on earth…The day You will come to take those who have served You, God, we beg You to have mercy on us…"[14]*

Fire did come out of the ground, the fire of hell by the sword. Do you think this song just applies to Rwanda? Will it also apply to a world now gone mad? Stop and seriously consider the following words Our Lady gave in Medjugorje:

August 2, 2011

> **"...As individuals, my children, you cannot stop the evil that wants to begin to rule in this world and to destroy it..."**

You will read the above message several times in this book, applying it to various situations. Do you think Our Lady of Medjugorje's above words are referring to a different evil than what savagely infuriated hearts and ruled in Rwanda? What do you think, what do you make of the following words Our Lady gave in Medjugorje?

January 25, 1991

> **"...satan is strong and wishes not only to destroy human life but also nature and the planet on which you live..."**

Do you think that because Our Lady's above words were said 21 years ago, as of 2012, that it therefore means satan no longer has an evil design to rule? The words of Our Lady given on August 2, 2011, are worth repeating here:

> **"...you <u>cannot</u> stop the evil that <u>wants</u> to begin to rule in this world and <u>to destroy it</u>..."**

Just over six months later, remarkably, Our Lady tells us:

February 2, 2012

"...pride has come to rule..."

Who is pride? Who fell like lightning from Heaven for birthing pride? Rwanda became hell on earth. Pride, satan, was the leader that brought hell there. But this cannot happen in our western Christian society, can it? Can you comprehend that the majority of Hutus and Tutsis, in particular, were Catholic! A shared religion in which murder is considered a sin that can lead a soul to damnation, did not prevent genocide. These people were not only of the same Church, but they were neighbors. The *Rwanda Crisis History of Genocide* states:

> *"Most of the victims were killed in their own villages or in towns, often by their neighbors and fellow villagers. The militia typically murdered victims by machetes, although some army units used rifles. The Hutu gangs searched out victims hiding in churches and school buildings, and massacred them. Local officials and government-sponsored radio incited ordinary citizens to kill their neighbors, and those who refused to*

kill were often murdered on the spot. Either you took part in the massacres or you were massacred yourself." [15]

Can it be said that this cannot happen in families? A quarter of all Rwandans, Hutu and Tutsi, have great grandparents from both sides. [16]

Does all this weigh you down? Depress you? Scare you? Then just think—all Ivanka did was see it. Can we now see why Our Lady keeps saying:

May 2, 2009

"...My poor children, look around you and look at the signs of the times..."

Our Lady's messages are supposed to get our attention in order that we would pay attention to what paths to take so that She can help us in the future.

Our Lady warned both the Hutus and Tutsis in Rwanda, through Her apparitions in Kibeho, telling them not to hate. It was foreshown by Her in the Medjugorje apparitions...but Our Lady could not help them. On April 25, 1994, 19 days into what would be more than 100 days of the Rwanda genocide, Our Lady gave Her monthly message to Medjugorje visionary Marija. Our Lady said:

"...if you do not pray and if you are not humble and obedient to the messages I am giving you, I cannot help you..."

In fact, despite the fact that world leaders, including the United States, knew the genocide was taking place, no one intervened to help. Rather, United Nations peace keeping forces were actually recalled from Rwanda, leaving the victims without any hope of rescue. President Clinton actually made a public apology at the airport in Kigali, Rwanda on March 25, 1998, for his lack of response and that of other nation's leaders. The might of the United States military against a militia whose primary weapon was a machete would have quickly brought the genocide of over a million people to an end. And yet no help came. Nor could Our Lady help them because they were deaf and blind to where everything was going. Ask yourself, and be honest with yourself: which way is the world going? Our Lady said:

February 2, 2012

"...You continue to be deaf and blind as you look at the world around you and do not want to see where it is going without my Son..."

CHAPTER THREE

Chapels into Stables

What sort of period are we entering into, in the way the world is going? Many believed the year 2012 would be an important and significant year in history. Some cite ancient prophecies foreshadowing 2012, such as the end of the Mayan calendar, falling at the end of the year on December 21, 2012. It, of course, is also an election year in the United States, and the war between two opposing ideologies in a battle for sovereignty over the nation is heating up more and more as the November elections grow closer.

The beginning of 2012 has proven to be significant, in that actions by President Obama concerning mandates in his healthcare bill sent shock waves through the nation as the thinly veiled threat to religious freedom, specifically singling out the Catholic faith, became apparent. This action polarized the Catholic Bishops, and in an unprecedented response, it was reported that all 191 bishops,[17] in a united body, vocally and authoritatively denounced the Obama administration's attempt to coerce Catholics to go against their con-

sciences and their beliefs to conform to unjust government mandates.

In this period of time, the United States Bishops
called for action, led by New York Cardinal Timothy
Dolan, president of the United States Conference of
Catholic Bishops, against a law by President Obama's
administration that would force Catholics to pay for
abortion, sterilization, birth control, etc. In every parish of every diocese in the United States, a letter was
read to the parishioners that was written by their respective bishops stating that Catholics will not comply
with such a law. Following is an excerpt from the letter
issued in the Diocese of Birmingham, Alabama, but the
wording of the bishops was the same or similar around
the country, demonstrating that the United States Bishops stood in solidarity behind the statement:

> *"We cannot, and we will not, comply with this
> unjust law. People of faith cannot be made sec-
> ond class citizens. We are encouraged that mem-
> bers of all faiths and many other people of good
> will have joined us in this vital effort to protect
> religious liberty in our country. Throughout our
> history as a nation, the Church has always been
> able to count on its faithful members to stand
> up and protect her sacred rights and duties...*

religious liberty in our nation (United States) is
under attack..." [18]

Many of the United States Bishops are stating that,
"religious liberty in our nation is under attack!" This
has been known for a long time by many, but many
others did not recognize the assault, under its disguise
of healthcare, until Obama finally forced the issue. The
assault has grown to such a point, that now the United
States Bishops have publicly come forward and acknowledged it. Are we to keep our heads in the sand
and wake up when it's too late? Chicago's Cardinal
Frances George said in 2010, of these times:

> *"I will die in bed. My successor will die in pris-*
> *on. His successor will die a martyr in the public*
> *square."[19]*

On February 10, 2012, Bishop Daniel Jenky of Peoria, Illinois, said in regards to the present and what is
unfolding for the future:

> *"The intensity of hatred against Catholic Chris-*
> *tianity in elements of our culture is just astound-*
> *ing." [20]*

In regards to where this is headed, he said, **"We are**
under assault," and makes a comparison between

Obama's actions and his present illegal law, and the 20th century atrocities. He said:

> *"I am a Holy Cross religious and my own community had six colleges in France and they (the Nazis) turned our mother house chapel into a stable."* [21]

In regards to Communist dictator Joseph Stalin, Bishop Jenky said Stalin would, *"admire the uniformity of the American press…"* [22] The press is filled with *intentional* wickedness, slander, calumny, misleading statements and untruths, for the purpose of forming and indoctrinating the thoughts of the population with a liberal agenda. The media is constantly in violation of the Commandment: ***"Thou shall not bear false witness."*** There is no grace in the old secular media, which includes even some religious media. In regards to the Church, it purposely distorts what Pope Benedict says and what the Catholic Church teaches, and indoctrinates the population in teaching that anything moral is actually immoral, because moral principles put restraints on unbridled behavior and passions, thereby violating and injuring the rights of certain individuals. However, since history proves that moral principles are essential for preserving true liberty, attacking the moral fabric of a nation directly attacks that nation's liberty.

The media presents religion as the culprit, as the oppressor of freedom. The media constantly purports that true freedom can only be discovered through the encouragement of every kind of immorality and perverse behavior. The voices that denounce such behavior are labeled 'oppressors' while those displaying the behavior become 'victims,' just as the Hutus painted themselves. Tyrants understand that religion must be removed for tyranny to rule. Remember, it was the press which was a key factor to the Rwanda genocide. Rwanda's massacre was built over time with the press helping at each step, aiding those in power. It was only after the massacre when the world asked, "How could this have happened?"—that the role of the media was recognized for what it was—a propaganda machine against the Tutsis. **There is a propaganda machine working also in our nation—against believers.** We, as Christians, need to be aware of the world around us. As Our Lady said:

February 2, 2012

> **"...And you, my children? You continue to be deaf and blind as you look at the world around you and do not want to see where it is going without my Son..."**

Our Lady is calling us to use truth as the measure to look at the world and its voices, to see how untruth is leading the direction of the world.

CHAPTER FOUR

Defy the Law? Is it Law?

The following points were discussed on the February 16, 2012, Caritas *Radio WAVE* * program after Obama, responding to the United States Bishops' outcry that this law was an attack on religious liberty, tried to delude the Bishops further by saying the health insurers and not the religious organizations themselves, would cover the costs. Excerpts from this radio show entitled, *"The Battle Begins Here, the Moment is Now,"* are included in the following six chapters, with additional wording included for clarity.

* * * * * * * * * * *

And so we are facing at this moment something that's been building for several decades. The momentum is being built that at some point in time, the goal is to take charge and to take over, and it is very evident it

---

* *Radio WAVE* broadcasts around the world through sponsors of the *Radio WAVE* programs and Medjugorje.com. Hosted by A Friend of Medjugorje, these programs have become a major source of insight to help the culturalization of the Medjugorje messages into one's life, especially on the 2nd and 25th of each month. WAVE stands for Worldwide <u>AVE</u>.

is happening now to force us into positions that we will
find ourselves in, just as the early Christians did. Will
we accept Christ and His principles, or will we deny
Him? Will we give our life for that? How far will we
go? Even the most liberal bishop is speaking out. It is
the Bishops, who in union are saying, **"We cannot, and
we will not, comply with this unjust law."**

What does that mean? That means we need to look
at this situation and ask, "Where do we go from here?"
I know people say, "Call your congressmen." But we're
not going to get either party to fix this because **'evil has
come to rule.'** It's not going to go away that way. The
moral order is going to come back only by repentance
and by living our faith with our lives. Our Lady said on
January 25, 2012:

> **"...with your lives witness faith..."**

**If we cannot and we will not comply with this unjust
law,** as the United States Bishops have stated, what are
the consequences at the stated point of defiance? What
will be our next step? We need to think it through, because Obama is not going to change or rescind this law,
which is without authority, that will force us to pay for
abortion, sterilization, etc. For him to state that these
procedures will be free because the insurance compa-

nies will have to pay, shows Obama thinks Christians
are mindless. It is perfectly clear that this was just a
shell game. We've given up our religious liberties. But
now we also have been given a green light because
bishops across this land, both liberal and conservative,
as well as moderate, are all speaking out saying, "we
will" defy this law.

So, what does it mean to defy this law? We need
to look for guidance in our nation's Declaration of Independence. The Declaration is the perfect guidance
for this crisis today, but few recognize this because the
indoctrination of the media and educational systems
intentionally hide and cloud these truths from you.
Many have been taught that the Declaration of Independence is just a historical document. Many more
have been taught doctrines conflicting with the "great
landmarks" found in the Declaration of Independence.
But how could something from over 200 years ago apply to our situation today? One hundred years after
the Declaration of Independence was written, Abraham Lincoln obviously did not see it as just a historical
document, but rather it had value for his day. We also
for our day should see it as guidance for us, especially
in restoring Christian principles to our land. The Declaration cannot be viewed only as a historical document,

rather it is pertinent to this crisis we are faced with to-day—the assault against the Catholic Church and other Christian faiths, and all people of good will.

The revisionists are the ones who have taught, in-doctrinated, and led people to believe the Declaration of Independence is only of historical value. But Lincoln's own words, stated nearly 100 years after the Declaration was written, called for the people to come back to the truths of the Declaration. He stated:

> *"Our fathers established these great self-evident truths that posterity might look again to the Declaration of Independence, and take courage to renew the battle which their fathers began, so that Truth and Christian virtues might not be extinguished from the land."* [23]

Our Lady appeared in the beginning months of the apparitions in Medjugorje and said:

January 21, 1982

> **"...don't you see that the faith begins to extinguish itself and that it is necessary to awaken the faith among men?"**

Think about that. You are hearing incredible things, thoughts from significant people of the past wedded to incredible words of Our Lady. This moment, in which Our Lady has been preparing us for over thirty years, is materializing. You are in the moment. Are you going to seize it? Or are you going to lose it? Abraham Lincoln's statement about the Declaration demonstrates that it had relevancy one hundred years after it was written when applied to his day, and it still is relevant and can be applied to our day. He says, *"take courage,"* *"renew the battle"* your *"fathers began"* so, ***"Truth and Christian virtues might not be extinguished from the land."*** Lincoln continued in his statement:

> *"Now, my countrymen, if you have been taught doctrines conflicting with the great landmarks of the Declaration of Independence...let me entreat you **to come back...come back to the truths that are in the Declaration of Independence."*** [24]

What are the truths of the Declaration? The document confirms truths already in existence, that men are created equal with rights... unalienable rights... rights which cannot be taken from man by the government because they are not given to us by the government, but given to us by God. These unalienable rights are laws of nature. You cannot change laws of nature because they are made by nature's God. Lincoln said to come back to these truths, because evil doctrines are being

spread by those who want you to believe that your
rights come from the government, and once you accept
these doctrines of untruth, you will accept that the government can take rights away from you, believing it was
the government that gave you them to start with. These
doctrines conflict with the truths that the Declaration
of Independence itself states. Why is this so important?
It is important because we will not be able to defy the
imposed law of Obama unless we understand that he
has no authority to impose the false law. Obama has
given Catholic organizations and other Christian groups
until August, 2013, to comply with paying for abortions,
sterilizations, contraceptives, etc., but other religious
non-Christian organizations, as well as non-religious organizations and the individuals that work for them who
might have a conscientious objection to the law have, as
of August 2012, been forced to comply.

The Declaration of Independence gives the basis,
gives "we the people" **legally, gives us lawfully**, the
means and moral high ground to impose upon any and
all perpetrators who wish to impose false laws on the
citizens of the United States, consequences for the steps
they take to lead this nation towards tyranny. The Declaration of Independence follows in the next chapter.
Read it as though you are studying it word for word and

through prayer. **You do not have to be a lawyer to know and comprehend** your unalienable rights in order to act upon, and follow the guidance given in the Declaration of Independence. Nor do you have to be a lawyer to comprehend the truths in the Declaration that we are to come back to, for our direction of what we are to do when facing an assault against our religious liberty. The Declaration spells out what we can do <u>lawfully</u> when forced into a position to say, *"we cannot, we will not comply"* with this unjust law. Read the document in the next chapter for this moment of time of what we are face to face with.

CHAPTER FIVE

A Document that is a Directive for Our Times

It is important not to speed through, or skip through the Declaration, as understanding it is crucial to grasp what we must know for the future security of the United States. Upon reading the latter part of the grievances against the King, the parallels of abuse of which we are now suffering from today are striking.

The Declaration of Independence

When in the Course of human Events, it becomes necessary for one People to dissolve the Political Bands which have connected them with another, and to assume among the powers of the Earth, the separate and equal Station to which the Laws of Nature and of Nature's God entitle them, a decent Respect to the Opinions of Mankind requires that they should declare the causes which impel them to the Separation.

We hold these Truths to be self-evident, that all Men are created equal, that they are endowed by their Creator with certain unalienable Rights, that

*among these are Life, Liberty, and the Pursuit of
Happiness — That to secure these Rights, Governments are instituted among Men, deriving their
just Powers from the Consent of the Governed,
that whenever any Form of Government becomes
destructive of these Ends, it is the Right of the
People to alter or to abolish it, and to institute
new Government, laying its Foundation on such
Principles, and organizing its Powers in such
Form, as to them shall seem most likely to affect
their Safety and Happiness. Prudence, indeed,
will dictate that Governments long established
should not be changed for light and transient
Causes; and accordingly all Experience hath
shewn, that mankind are more disposed to suffer,
while Evils are sufferable, than to right themselves by abolishing the Forms to which they are
accustomed. But when a long Train of Abuses
and Usurpations, pursuing invariably the same
Object, evinces a Design to **reduce them under
absolute Despotism, it is their Right, it is their
Duty, to throw off such Government, and to
provide new Guards for their future Security.**
Such has been the patient Sufferance of these
Colonies; and such is now the Necessity which
constrains them to alter their former Systems of*

Government. The History of the present King of Great-Britain is a History of repeated injuries and Usurpations, all having in direct Object the Establishment of an absolute Tyranny over these States. To prove this, let Facts be submitted to a candid World.

HE has refused his Assent* to Laws, the most wholesome and necessary for the public Good.

HE has forbidden his Governors to pass Laws of immediate and pressing Importance, unless suspended in their Operation till his Assent should be obtained; and when so suspended, he has utterly neglected to attend to them.

HE has refused to pass other Laws for the Accommodation of large districts of People, unless those People would relinquish the Right of Representation in the Legislature, a Right inestimable to them, and formidable to Tyrants only.

HE has called together Legislative Bodies at Places unusual, uncomfortable, and distant from the Depository of their public Records, for the sole Purpose of fatiguing them into Compliance with his Measures.

* The expression of approval or agreement; to give in; yield; concede

*HE has dissolved Representative Houses repeat-
edly, for opposing with manly Firmness his Inva-
sions on the Rights of the People.*

*HE has refused for a long Time, after such Dis-
solutions, to cause others to be elected; whereby
the Legislative Powers, incapable of Annihila-
tion, have returned to the People at large for their
exercise; the State remaining in the meantime
exposed to all the dangers of Invasion from without, and Convulsions within.*

*HE has endeavored to prevent the Population
of these States; for that Purpose obstructing the
Laws for Naturalization of Foreigners; refusing to pass others to encourage their Migrations
hither, and raising the Conditions of new Appropriations of Lands.*

*HE has obstructed the Administration of Justice,
by refusing his Assent to Laws for establishing
Judiciary Powers.*

*HE has made Judges dependent on his Will
alone, for the Tenure of their Offices, and the
Amount and Payment of their Salaries.*

HE has erected a Multitude of new Offices, and sent hither Swarms of Officers to harass our People, and eat out their Substance.

HE has kept among us, in Times of Peace, Standing Armies, without the consent of our Legislatures.

HE has affected to render the Military independent of and superior to the Civil Power.

HE has combined with others to subject us to a Jurisdiction foreign to our Constitution, and unacknowledged by our Laws; giving his Assent to their Acts of pretended Legislation:

FOR quartering large bodies of Armed Troops among us:

FOR protecting them, by a mock Trial, from Punishment for any Murders which they should commit on the Inhabitants of these States:

FOR cutting off our Trade with all Parts of the World:

FOR imposing Taxes on us without our Consent:

FOR depriving us, in many Cases, of the Benefits of Trial by Jury:

FOR transporting us beyond Seas to be tried for pretended Offences:

FOR abolishing the free System of English Laws in a neighbouring Province, establishing therein an arbitrary Government, and enlarging its Boundaries, so as to render it at once an Example and fit Instrument for introducing the same absolute Rule into these Colonies:

FOR taking away our Charters, abolishing our most valuable Laws, and 'altering fundamentally' the Forms of our Governments:

FOR 'suspending our own Legislatures,' and declaring themselves invested with Power to legislate for us in all Cases whatsoever.

HE has abdicated Government here, by declaring us out of his Protection and waging War against us.

HE has plundered our Seas, ravaged our Coasts, burnt our Towns, and destroyed the Lives of our People.

HE is, at this Time, transporting large Armies of foreign Mercenaries to compleat the Works of Death, Desolation and Tyranny, already begun with circumstances of Cruelty & Perfidy, scarcely paralleled in the most barbarous Ages, and totally unworthy the Head of a civilized Nation.

HE has constrained our fellow Citizens taken Captive on the high Seas to bear Arms against their Country, to become the Executioners of their Friends and Brethren, or to fall themselves by their Hands.

HE has excited domestic Insurrections amongst us, and has endeavoured to bring on the Inhabitants of our Frontiers, the merciless Indian Savages, whose known Rule of Warfare, is an undistinguished Destruction of all Ages, Sexes and Conditions.

IN every stage of these Oppressions we have Petitioned for Redress in the most humble Terms: Our repeated Petitions have been answered only by repeated Injury. A Prince (the president and his administration), whose Character is thus marked by every act which may define a Tyrant, is unfit to be Ruler of a free People.

NOR have we been wanting in Attentions to our British Brethren. We have warned them from Time to Time of Attempts by their Legislature to extend an unwarrantable Jurisdiction over us. We have reminded them of the Circumstances of our Emigration and Settlement here. We have appealed to their native Justice and Magnanimity, and we have conjured them by the Ties of our common Kindred to disavow these Usurpations, which, would inevitably interrupt our Connections and Correspondence. They too have been deaf to the Voice of Justice and of Consanguinity. We must therefore, acquiesce in the Necessity, which denounces our Separation, and hold them, as we hold the rest of Mankind, Enemies in War, in Peace, Friends.

WE, therefore, the Representatives of the UNITED STATES OF AMERICA, in GENERAL CONGRESS, Assembled, appealing to the Supreme Judge of the World for the Rectitude of our Intentions, do, in the Name, and by Authority of the good People of these Colonies, solemnly Publish and Declare, That these United Colonies are, and of Right ought to be, FREE AND INDEPENDENT STATES; that they are absolved from all Allegiance to the British Crown, and that all political Connection between them and the State of Great-Britain, is and ought to be totally

dissolved; and that as FREE AND INDEPEN-
DENT STATES, they have full Power to levy
War, conclude Peace, contract Alliances, establish
Commerce, and to do all other Acts and Things
which INDEPENDENT STATES may of right
do. And for the support of this Declaration,
with a firm Reliance on the Protection of Divine
Providence, we mutually pledge to each other our
Lives, our Fortunes, and our sacred Honor.

END

When a government elects to take away an unalienable right, as it is planning to do with religious freedom
through the healthcare legislation, then tyranny rules.
We must underscore again, unalienable rights do not
come from the government but from God. Abraham
Lincoln said, come back to *"the **truths** that are in the
Declaration."* What is truth? God is Truth. Lincoln
said to come back to the Declaration that *"Christian
virtues might not be extinguished from the land."* The
extinguishing of Christian virtue is exactly what is happening in our present time. Have you been taught
doctrines conflicting with the Declaration of Independence? This law that is being imposed on us by force
is against nature's law. By virtue of the truths in the
Declaration of Independence that are rooted in the

Bible…this cannot happen. The Declaration affirms
that liberty is given to us by God, **"endowed (to us) by
their (our) Creator with certain unalienable rights, that
among these are Life, Liberty and the Pursuit of Happiness…"** The government has not given us our liberty.
When we let government think it is theirs to give to
us, we will lose it, because what the government gives,
it can take away. Before leaving this critical point,
thoughtfully breakdown the government's present
plans and actions vs. the United States' principles of
liberty and what truths the United States must function
by if it is to continue as a nation.

The Declaration of Independence Our Founding Fathers' Principle Doctrine that Power Flows from the Consent of the Governed The Right of We the People.	vs.	The Declaration of Dependence The Obama Administration's Principle Doctrine of Government Rights and Rights it Bestows Upon the People.

Founding Fathers	vs.	Obama Administration
We hold these truths to be self-evident that all men are endowed by their Creator with certain ...Unalienable rights that among these are Life *(Life)*...	vs.	We hold these truths to be self-evident that all rights of men are endowed by the government and can be given and taken away at the discretion of the government. It, therefore, is the right of the government to impose tyrannical tactics forcing Catholics and Christians of other denominations to pay for the "right" of free abortion for all *(death)*
As "Religious Liberty" is an unalienable right endowed by the Creator, men have the right to exercise conscientious objections to unjust laws, laws against nature.	vs.	It is the right of the government not to "give" liberty to conscientious objections.

Founding Fathers	vs.	Obama Administration
It is an unalienable right to pursue happiness and con- tentment and is the will of the Creator for us to have religious freedom in the public square and through- out society protected by civil laws indissolubly bonded to Christian principles.	vs.	It is the right of government to impose mandates which encourage the pursuit of any and all of the most debase actions and behaviors in the name of freedom. The right and entitlement of these behaviors are to be paid for by all, regardless of consci- entious objection to them. Those who claim rights to pursue happiness according to their conscience, based in Christian principles, cannot be allowed this right at the expense of discriminating against those who in their pursuit of happiness desire free choice healthcare, of which the Christian consci- entious objection takes such rights away.

Founding Fathers	vs.	Obama Administration
That to secure these Rights...governments are instituted among Men, deriving their just Powers from the Consent of the Governed.	vs.	That to secure the right to force believers to pay for abortion, sterilization, etc., the government instituted among men must derive its powers from the consent of those in government office who are governed by the seduction of power, influenced by the 'powers that be,' and in league with the powers of Non-Governmental Organizations (NGO's) with the same agendas.

Founding Fathers	vs.	Obama Administration
That whenever any Form of Government becomes destructive of these Ends… "…men…endowed by their Creator with certain unalienable rights…Life, Liberty (religious), the Pursuit of Happiness" "…it is the Right of the People to alter or abolish it, and to institute new Government, laying its Foundation on such Principles, and organizing its Power in such Form, as to them shall seem most likely to effect their Safety and Happiness.	vs.	That whenever any form of religious and/or conscientious objection arises against government mandates and the imposition of its laws to re-order the moral order of the nation which is destructive to its ends (government standards vs. moral standards) it is the right of the government to alter or abolish the right of conscientious objection in order to establish newer forms of government and rights through regulations and laws to form new methods for compliance and to organize its powers under totalitarian forms, so to achieve its goals to the dictate of its ends.

Founding Fathers	vs.	Obama Administration
That Governments long established should not be changed for light and transient Causes; and accordingly all Experience hath shewn (shown), that mankind are more disposed to suffer, while Evils are sufferable, than to right themselves by abolishing the Forms to which they are accustomed. But when a long Train of Abuses and Usurpations, pursing invariably the same Object, evinces **a Design to reduce them under absolute Despotism, it is their Right, it is their Duty, to throw off such Government, and to provide new Guards for their future Security.** Such has been the patient Sufferance...(of the present)...and such is now the Necessity which constrains them to alter their former Systems of Government. The History of the present government, political and administrative is a History of repeated Injuries and Usurpations, all having in direct Object the Establishment of an absolute Tyranny over these States and its people.	vs.	That government long established will not be changed or challenged by a people who are indoctrinated with the idea that they have not the right to throw off the political bonds that oppress them. Believing it is not within their right, they then can be forcibly disposed to suffer any and all evils, rather than to exercise a right not granted by the present bonds which hold them, despite a long train of abuses over decades of time. Usurpation against the people's consciences and religious beliefs, even unto despotism, conditions them to abide and comply.

CHAPTER SIX

What the Government Tells Us is Illegal, We the People can make Legal

What we need to learn is to unlearn what we have been conditioned to believe in regards to the steps we are "allowed" lawfully to take. History shows that our forefathers took action which the British Crown held as illegal, and changed the action to be legal through the Declaration of Independence, when it became apparent that tyranny ruled, and there was no alternative. Nothing will change through a call to vote, calls to your congressman, by passing a law, protesting in a march or filing a lawsuit, because none of these actions work in the long run once tyranny reigns and begins its assault against liberty. The voting box will be controlled. The Legislative Branch and Judicial Branch will be under the thumb of despotism's power.

In regards to what the Bishops said, we really should say, *"We cannot, we will not comply"* with an ordinance against nature's law, instead of as worded, **"unjust law."** Legally it is not an "unjust law." In fact, it is not to be recognized as a law at all. A 'law' recognized as going against nature's law is a law against nature's God. As already stated, but must be reiterated—you cannot change nature's laws because they are made by nature's God. This is the basis of laws in general. We, Christians, and all lovers of liberty, must be **'educated'** to what is law and what is not valid as law and, therefore, not to be obeyed. In the introduction of William Blackstone's <u>Commentary on the Law</u>, it states that Edmond Burke, on March 22, 1735, rose to his feet in England's Parliament and explained how *"this education in the law among the colonies had contributed to a 'fierce spirit of liberty' in America."* Burke states:

> *"In no country perhaps in the world is the law so general a study...But all who read, and most do read, endeavor to obtain some smattering in that science. I have been told by an eminent bookseller that in no branch of business, after tracts of popular devotion, were so many books as those on the law exported to the plantations. The colonists have now fallen into the way of printing them for their own use. I hear that they have sold nearly as many Blackstone's Commentaries in America as in England."* [25]

We, Christians, as well as people of all faiths, must understand the basis for the revolution which began this country, in order now to understand how to reset the United States of America back on its foundation of liberty, through the recognition of the unalienable rights endowed to us by our Creator. In, "Foundation of Moral Law," it states that William Blackstone's,

> *"...compilation of the common law with an emphasis on God-given rights and liberties unintentionally inspired a revolution and brought him a great deal of criticism in Great Britain... nevertheless, in the first paragraph of the Declaration of Independence, Blackstone's views, that certain God-given rights were unalienable, and that no civil authority could usurp those rights, were adopted as truths upon which the revolution was based."* [26]

How are we to know and understand this about the actions of Obama and his administration? Blackstone gives the answer for now, our time in 2012, as he gave the answer to the founders, who themselves were enlightened by it and founded a nation. Blackstone states in his commentaries:

> *"This law of nature, being co-eval* * *with mankind and dictated by God Himself, is of course*

* Co-eval means of the same age, beginning to exist at the same time; of equal age.

superior in obligation to any other. It is binding
over all the globe, in all countries, and at all times:
no human laws are of any validity, if contrary to
this; and such of them as are valid derive all their
force, and all their authority, mediately or imme-
diately, from this original... [27]

William Blackstone stated that the revealed law,
which is found within Scripture, is really a part of the
laws of nature, though superior to them. Blackstone
went on further to state that all human laws must be
in conformity to both the revealed law (The Bible)
and the laws of nature, otherwise the human law is not
valid. Therefore, the human law in conflict is not to be
obeyed, because it is in conflict with the revealed law
and the laws of nature. Blackstone writes:

"...upon these two foundations, the law of nature
and the law of revelation (The Bible), depend all
human laws; that is to say, no human laws, should
be suffered to contradict these... if any human
law should allow or enjoin us to commit (violate
God's law) it, we are bound to transgress that hu-
man law, or else we must offend both natural and
the divine..." [28]

Blackstone went on to state that even when human laws may reinforce God's law, they in fact do not add anything to them, as God's law is superior to all laws.

"...no human legislature has the power to abridge or destroy them (God's law)... the declaratory part of the municipal law has no force or operation at all, with regards to actions that are naturally and intrinsically right or wrong..." [29]

To state clearly again, God's laws are to be the foundation of all human laws. No human laws which contradict God's law are to be obeyed, but instead, they are to be defied...defied by whatever means within the bounds of Christian principles, especially according to just war principles.

Obama and the present rulers of the United States are rearranging the moral order, imposing an unnatural standard of law, therefore, invalid law. They, thereby, are giving the <u>legal basis</u> for action to not only disregard, but to defy the ordinances just as the truths of the Declaration of Independence remind us of the right to do so, because the ordinance of Obama has no authority to be made law.

CHAPTER SEVEN

Will You Go to Jail Rather Than Violate God's Law?

What does this mean, as the Bishops said, to *"not comply?"* Rick Warren, well-known pastor and author of the book, A Purpose Driven Life, put out a statement that he'll stand with his Catholic brothers. He said he'd go to jail for this. Well, let's take this to another step because Obama just did another shell-game. On February 10, 2012, he said Catholics could let others pay for the abortions, contraceptives, etc., thinking we would fall for his line, *"We're going to give you Catholics a loop-hole."* What is the loop-hole? There isn't one. He doesn't even understand our principles, even though he claims to be a Christian. He thinks that we will say, *"Oh, okay, we'll do that."* So who is Obama to Christians? As the United States Bishops stated, *"this assault against religious liberty"* means there is an enemy at play against Catholics and all Christian faiths. We must accept that we all are facing an enemy; otherwise there is no *assault* but rather only a misunderstanding. The Bishops officially spoke of the **"assault**

on our religious liberty." This is what we must recognize, what we are face to face with—there is a foe that is threatening our right to live our Catholic faith, a foe against all Americans of goodwill. Evil on the move, unchecked, <u>will</u> eventually move under the roof of our church steeples. Some have not wanted to accept Obama as an enemy, but it is he who has led the attack, a war on our religious liberty. Many Catholics, including some bishops, wanted to be friends with him. We cannot be friends if there is an action of assault against our core religious beliefs. Do not delude yourselves. The second to the last paragraph of the Declaration of Independence ends with:

"Enemies in war, in Peace, Friends."

How can one assault our most basic unalienable rights and we not be in war? We must be wise and understand our circumstances. **We are face to face with an enemy**.

To know your circumstances—first, you've got to understand who your enemy is in war. But, only understanding your enemy is not enough to defeat this action. Sun-tzu was a Chinese warrior from 2,500 years ago, who all military academies still study to this day. Sun-tzu said that you must know your enemy as one of your principles to defeat him. He had three principles about defeat and victory:

1. If you do not know yourself and you do not know your enemy, you will lose every battle.

2. If you know yourself but not your enemy, you will win only half your battles.

3. If you know yourself and you know your enemy, you can win a hundred battles without a single loss.

This is how Obama deceived several bishops about healthcare, while other Catholics and Christians were warning not to pass the Obama healthcare legislation. Some Catholics and other Christians understood the intention of the heart of their enemy. How do we discern our enemy's intention of heart? Our Lady of Medjugorje said:

November 7, 1985

> **"...I am calling you to the love of neighbor and love toward the one from whom evil comes to you. In that way you will be able to discern the intentions of hearts..."**

We must not hate our enemies even though we must fight them, as we are commanded to love our enemies. But, by doing so, we will not be unaware of his, the enemy's intentions. We need to understand that we have an enemy against Christianity that is in some ways unseen, but seen—a group of people that are bent on Christianity's destruction in this day, just as in the days of Stalin and Hitler. Do we need to pray for Obama and those in league with him? Do we need to ask for their conversion? Yes. Is it going to happen? It could. But they have to have good will. We are dealing with people of bad will. Peace to men of good will, conversion to men of good will. Not everybody's going to convert, so don't get hung up on that level. Pray for them, but recognize them as an enemy.

So where do we go from here? Rick Warren thinks it's worth going to jail over. I don't think it's worth going to jail for. We need to look at and realize what authority the Declaration of Independence gives us. To live our faith means we've got to stand up against ordinances not having any authority to be made into law, which force us to violate our consciences. Why? Because it is unnatural law, because it's against nature's law. When the government of Spain ordered Catholics, through laws against nature, to adopt children to abominables, Pope Benedict XVI gave a directive to the whole Church in Spain through the President of the Pontifical Council for the Family, Cardinal Alfonso Lopez Trujillo, that they not only are not to comply with it, but they are obligated to defy it. On April 25, 2005, Cardinal Trujillo made the following statement in regard to the new law just passed in Spain:

> *"Because it is an evil law, the Church urgently calls for the exercising of freedom of conscience and the duty to oppose."* [30]

When we become educated that laws against nature are not to be obeyed, which is the basis of why the Bishops have declared, *"we cannot, we will not comply with this"* ordinance against nature's law, then we can ask the question: *"So, who is breaking the law?"* By not obeying, we are not breaking the law if we don't comply with this. We, as Christians, are obligated to defy it. This is where we need to go to the next level. It's not, *"Call your Congressman."* This is over. We don't want to take the wind out of the sail of what the Bishops are doing, but we're dealing with evil. We must understand the enemy's intentions of the heart. Our Lady told us how to discern this, and the warrior Sun-tzu has shown the principle of why this is important. You think we're going to call our congressman?

We're beyond the Democratic Party. We're beyond the Republican Party. We're beyond any party out there.

Evil has come to rule. Heaven, on February 2, 2012, told us it was so. For evil to secure itself, its ability to continue to rule, it must make radical moves now while it has its foot in the door. The intention of those on the verge of consolidating their power is to push for it now, knowing that once their evil intentions are exposed, to retreat is to face defeat. Evil must make its moves now because Christians are waking up. Those who possess evil intentions which rule in their hearts, have a limited time to make radical moves. The more moves they make, the more naked their intentions become and, therefore, the quicker they must move to the next step, in order to bulldoze resistance before it builds any momentum to resist and stop them.

This false law has put the Church in the crosshairs of the 'powers that be,' through Obama's office, as the best moment to take down the Church. Whether one is hunting for deer, or making plans for war, strategy is always at play to act at the most opportune moment for the strategist and put the deer or the opponent of war at the maximum disadvantage. If it's a hunter, as he watches a buck coming down the trail, he doesn't just shoot. He waits for the most advantageous shot to bring the deer down. Would a cougar not do the same—lying in wait for a doe to get within its grasp, so as to have the best advantage to capture its prey? Does one who plans an attack not strategize and launch his attack at the exact moment to the disadvantage and defeat of who is being attacked? Do not think for a moment that each and every step Obama has made is not without being calculated and strategized. He initially deceived the Bishops, making them think he was in tune to their concerns in order to gain their support of his healthcare bill in 2011. He then turned the tables on them with his announcement in February 2012, that Catholics would be forced to pay for abortions, etc. He then made a "concession" to allow the target date for compliance to be scheduled to August, 2013, in order to buy time and wear the Bishops and people down before the enforcement date, in order to minimize and cancel out resistance.

Evil's every move and countermove is well planned, anticipated and pre-played out in order to guide all the events to a predetermined outcome. Obama just needed time to wear down the conscientious objectors, normalize the law, weaken Catholic resistance, and then go for its implementation. Obama played with the Bishops, and they trusted him. Trust is not a factor the warrior Sun-tzu would teach you to use in dealing with your enemies. Jesus identified and knew who His enemy was.

> *"... 'for Herod wants to kill you.' And He (Jesus) said to them, 'Go and tell that fox, 'Behold, I cast out demons and perform cures today and tomorrow ...'"* Luke 13:31-32

In other words, the enemy is clever in evil. If you want to outfox a fox, get another strategy. First, cure the Church, by casting out the demons in the Church. Then, in union with God, form your plans and strategies.

Obama and his minions have laid out "the paths" he wants us to follow. Vote, file lawsuits, call congressmen, etc., all under the management of evil. We must not play the game of the fox, when he is clearly identified as a 'Herod,' who not only is for killing babies in the womb, but wants us to pay for it; a fox who wants to repeal the Defense of Marriage Act (D.O.M.A.), to rearrange marriage; a fox who is the first president ever, without shame or blush, to publicly endorse abominables. You cannot title yourself Christian when the tenets you embrace say the opposite. **No, President Obama is not a Christian.** There are requirements to being a Christian. Your life and witness must correlate with Christian beliefs and principles. All Christians are sinners and fall short in their witness at times, but to be Christian, one cannot believe contrary to the Commandments of God and His precepts, nor can one wear the title Christian if they are doing what Obama is doing. He not only is not a Christian, but by his actions he has proven himself to be an enemy to Christianity. When we understand who he is, we then can defeat him, not by his own game but by our game. Jesus said:

"For the children of this world are more prudent in dealing with their own generation than are the children of light." Luke 16:8

The children of light must not be naïve in dealing with the children of the world, rather we must be more astute, more prudent, so as not to fall into their claws. Learn their tactics and adapt what we morally can. We must not let satan play with us. Our Lady said:

March 25, 1992

"...you have gone away from God and from me because of your miserable interests...satan is playing with you and with your souls and I cannot help you because you are far from my heart..."

To look at this point from another analogy, many have been lulled by the cat in the yard, who charms the bird with its tail in order to eat the bird. But the bird has great skill to fly, to stay free and out of the grasp of the cat. There is no reason for it to be captured and eaten. The Church can fly. It is the power. It cannot be defeated, except when it stays on the ground, handled and charmed into calling our congressmen, going to court, fighting for our lives while on the ground with an enemy, the cat, even though we have the ability to fly, really fly out of 'their' claws. Don't play out your strategies on their ground. Don't land in the cat's backyard when you can be sitting in the trees, safe from everything and all dangers. They want you to call your congressman. No, this is not the answer! They want you to file lawsuits. No, this is not the answer! They need you to expend all your energy to pass a new law to protect our religious conscientious objection. No, this is not the answer! We will not be given protection with a new law when protection is already law. You think another law is going to work? No, this is not the answer! It is a band-aid, and band-aids always fall off. The wound itself must be healed. They have strategized that you will take this path which is their path for you. They need you to walk down their sidewalk into the cat's backyard, because their power is not yet completely

consolidated. The throne of power is not yet secured.
Every new law won for us will actually strengthen them
and will give them more power and us less liberty because their strategy is to wear us down. They want us
to think we have achieved protection with new laws we
have fought for, where they know a court can strike the
laws down later. That is why Obama and his gang lied
to the Bishops—to minimize resistance until the time
becomes favorable to take control. Everything is very
close in its prime moment to seize total power now.
Radical moves must be made now. Repeat the following thought and understand it. <u>Evil cannot retreat
or it will be defeated, because the Church is waking
up</u>. Evil cannot stand still, its momentum must move
swiftly, with disregard of anything in its way. You think
you have rights, civil liberty? You think they cannot
go so far as to take "your" rights away? This is laugh-
able. Do you think confronting this assault on religious
liberty through going to court or trying to get a new
law passed, such as the new introduced law, HR 1179,
S 1467, "The Respect for Rights of Conscience Act,"
will stop them, when for decades they slaughtered tiny
infants in the womb? The introduction of "another"
new law is a defensive position by us, offering victory
to them. The attempt of a new law is evidence of Sun-
tzu's principle that we do not know our enemy. We

must act offensively not defensively. Don't go where they expect us to. It is a trap. Do not play them on their home field. Force them to play on our home field. Their's is the court, congress, voting—ours is the Declaration of Independence and the legal right to throw off tyranny.

Who are you, that they would not hesitate in trampling over not only your unalienable rights, but your very right to life? What are you to them, that you can reason with them or debate your Constitutional points to the courts? Are you deaf and blind to what is going on around you? They own the courts. They own the verdict you will receive. It is already predetermined. One of our founding fathers, John Adams, writing of the new United States of America and the United States Constitution, said we would not hold onto liberty if our government ever abandoned religious principles and morals. Nor, he believed, could the Constitution be used to protect immorality and an unreligious people without it leading to the destruction of our nation, just as we are seeing today with the Constitution being used to redefine marriage and give the right to abortion with Roe vs. Wade, among a thousand, thousand in-betweens. Adams wrote:

"Statesmen…may plan and speculate for liberty, but it is religion and morality alone which can establish the principles upon which freedom can securely stand." [31]

Adams, in writing again of the Constitution, said that it cannot work if it is put in the hands of immoral and unreligious people. He said:

"Our Constitution was made only for a moral and religious people. It is wholly inadequate to the government of any other." [32]

Adams wrote that if we allow for the Constitution to be used for protection of immorality and irreligious people, we will lose our liberty. He stated:

"The only foundation of a free Constitution is pure virtue; and if this cannot be inspired into our people in a greater measure than they have it now, they may change their rulers and the forms of government, but they will not obtain a lasting liberty. They will only exchange tyrants and tyrannies." [33]

It should be stated here again, that most have been duped into believing that the Constitution "gives" us rights. The Constitution does not "give" us any rights per se, but rather, affirms the unalienable rights which already exist from God, as explained earlier. The Constitution cannot, therefore, be interpreted for immorality, since the Constitution affirms only those rights which come from God.

Forget the avenues laid out before us as our weapon of battle. We must create and choose our own way to battle.

Our Lady tells us on August 2, 2011:

> **"...with my Son, you can change everything and heal the world..."**

It's not going to come through the congressmen or through the presidents, or a new introduced law. We already have protection by law for our religious liberty. Another one will advantage the enemy, giving them the ability to overturn it in court, making precedence to further nullify original Constitutional protection of natural rights for conscientious objection that was common law even before our nation's founding and placed in our founding documents. Our Lady gave the following message:

December 31, 1985:

"...You will not have peace through the presidents, but through prayer."

Is it important who we get as president? Yes. But, that comes through God. That's a secondary thing. It is the living of our faith, living the Ten Commandments — in particular, keeping the Lord's Day holy, all through prayer, these are the means to overcoming evil. By these means we are empowered to stand up. To win against our enemy, we must know ourselves, and we, as Catholics and all Christians, must acknowledge that we ourselves are at fault for not living fully the Commandments. Expect no victory if we do not repent and live God's Commandments.

CHAPTER EIGHT

Will You Be Fed to the Lions?

The question remains: So is it worth going to jail for?
No, it is not. It may be a noble thing Rick Warren is
saying. But what we need to say back in return, and
where we go with this is to use the authority the Declaration of Independence gives us. It is of legal use today,
as Lincoln's time, as in our founding fathers' time. We
have the power and legal authority as one people to
lawfully overthrow the illegal mandating regime and
change this surrogate system which supplanted the
principle of the "consent of the governed." With evil
intent, the "consent of the governed" was changed to
the consent of a surrogate, who has circumvented our
republican form of government. Our forefathers had a
legal right 236 years ago to start this nation through the
Declaration. We have a legal right now to correct this
grave tyrannical oppression that is forcing the breaking
of our conscience with a law against "nature's God."
Drill this into your heart so to counter the wrong thinking of what so many institutions have drilled and sup-

planted into your heart for decades. Repetition in this book is necessary to <u>learn</u> what you are reading.

The Declaration states:

> *"When in the Course of human events it becomes necessary for one people to dissolve the political bonds… and to assume among the powers of the earth, the separate and equal station to which the **Laws of Nature and of Nature's God** <u>entitle them</u>, a decent respect to the opinions of mankind requires that they should declare the causes which impel them to the separation…. whenever any Form of Government becomes destructive of these ends, it is the Right of the People to alter or to abolish it, and to institute new Government… it is their Right, it is their Duty, to throw off such Government, and to provide new Guards for their future Security…"*

So the question must be posed, and this is where we need to develop to, with this thinking, if I'm saying it's not worth…and we all should possess this thought…it's not worth going to jail for; we need to be asking <u>them</u>, who are imposing this invalid law upon us the question, *"Is it worth it to <u>you</u> to go to jail for?"* We, as Catholics and all Christians and all others of good will, do not need to go to jail for this. We don't need to stop our "non-compliance" nor shut down Catholic institutions,* as we are legal and within natural law. There is no valid law forcing us to pay for abortions, etc. that has to be obeyed. So don't recognize or concede that we can go to jail for this. That is where we stand. We cannot concede the high ground to lawbreakers, that it is Catholics or other Christians who are breaking laws.

These tactics being used by these tyrannical people are exactly how the Hitlers took over. Tyrants in the past have done the exact same thing. Fr. Eric Flood, FSSP, in his February 2012 Fraternity Newsletter, writes about the confrontation the Catholic Church now faces, and the seeking of a legal means to silence Her. Fr. Flood writes:

"...An example of how this loss of respect for the Church can occur may be seen in Germany in the mid-twentieth century.

"In his book, <u>Christ in Dachau</u>, Fr. John Lenz, who was arrested for being a Catholic priest in

---

* We must be honest in asking ourselves how could 106 Catholic Universities not escape judgment of God in being shut down or vacated as Catholic institutions since these 106 Catholic Universities have been highly praised and identified as abominable friendly and in promotion thereof. See "Thirty Years of Apparitions" by a Friend of Medjugorje, http://www.medjugorje.com/download/booklets/326-30+Years+of+Appari tons.html.

*Austria and subsequently imprisoned in Dachau,
has profound insights for our consideration. He
begins by saying that evil does not just spring up
in a nation overnight and without reason. Rather,
he says, that 'if our Catholic Faith had really been
something living, something vital to our very existence, it is doubtful whether even a portion of
our people would have fallen prey to the Nazi
pseudo-religion. We had been too lukewarm, and
many had become blind to truth.*

Fr. John Lenz writes:

*"The lukewarmness of faith produced a coward-
ice in resisting, and for those who had rejected
their Catholic Faith or stopped practicing it, the
emptiness in their lives made them easy prey to
Hitler's new religion of power…*

*"Only those who lived in the light of Faith could
recognize the danger behind the Nazi propaganda, **harmless enough though it might at first
appear.'** As 'no one in his senses could expect
good out of evil, or happiness and prosperity at
the hands of a man who denies God…even 'good
Catholics' were led astray, for their religion had
long ceased to be something which really inspired*

*their lives and they had lost sight of the truth. Put
to the test, their faith simply folded up.'*

*"Hence, the dark Nazi regime serves as a warn-
ing to future nations to maintain faith in Christ.
The demise of a nation easily begins at the basic
level of people rejecting Christ as their true King
and Leader. Without His governing right hand,
the lack of belief among the people can quickly
spread throughout society and unto its leaders.*

*"Thus, it is imperative that Christ and His
Church be unified with the State for the well-
being of a nation."* [34]

The Church must awaken because this 'is' the
battle. We, the faithful, must repent and turn from
our lukewarm Christian life. Then we must wake up
to what we are founded upon. Tyranny has not completely rooted itself yet, but is close. We need not cow
down to atheistic, humanistic secularization that is
threatening our nation's existence, nor do we need to
stand by and allow for tyranny to bring the Church into
compliance. We have examples of the French Revolution, two World Wars, among many other tyrants in history that point to where this is going. If we do not rise
up now, head to head, to win this battle coming to us on

August 1, 2013, to comply—no battle, no victories will
come afterwards. We would have lost this opportunity
and will enter into the period when we will have to go
to jail, lose our property and be martyred in the public
square, as Cardinal George proclaimed in 2010. Then
victory will come only through the blood of the mar-
tyrs. Our Lady said of your Christian duty:

November 25, 1997

> **"...Today I invite you to comprehend your
> Christian vocation. Little children, I led and
> am leading you through this time of grace, that
> you may become conscious of your Christian
> vocation. Holy martyrs died witnessing: I am a
> Christian and love God over everything..."**

We must wake up now. Our Lady said:

May 25, 2010

> **"...God gave you the grace to live and to defend
> all the good that is in you and around you..."**

I'm going to tell you, if we lose this, we will be
weaker in the 2nd battle, the 3rd, weaker, and the 4th,
totally defeated. This is the line in the sand. Black and
white. We don't cross this. We don't do it. And they
go to jail, including Obama as a president if he imple-

ments this violation against common and natural law.
He will be in violation of nature's law, made law by nature's God, Who authored the law into nature as natural law. Keep repeating this truth in your mind, at every step, so that the Church will not stay on the ground,
but fly. No one, nowhere, no power can change nature's law. They can only violate it. It is by nature that
it cannot be changed and against the law of nature's
God to do so. They're breaking natural law. We are in
the right. We are in the moral right. It is Church teaching. It is a Christian principle. It is in the Constitution.
Archbishop William Lori of Baltimore, in an interview
with Raymond Arroyo on March 17, 2012, said:

> "…Religious liberty is endowed from our Cre-
> ator. Our founding documents state this. The
> Church teaches this." [35]

He also said:

> "We are going to defend tooth and nail, to do
> everything in our power, to win our God-given
> rights." [36]

We're not at the point where we have to be standing helpless while being carried into the Coliseum and
eaten by the lions fed to them by those who are against
Christianity. We have the legal authority and the power

now to do this and everyone better educate themselves to the legal authority we have, because if they don't, we will soon find ourselves standing helpless, fed to the lions.

CHAPTER NINE

How Far Will You Go Letting Your Conscience be Violated?

Every corporation has incorporating documents. Every corporation has its by-laws. The act of incorporation of the United States is the Declaration of Independence. Its by-laws are the Constitution. Enlighten yourselves with prayer to the Holy Spirit. We will be doomed to the errors of the past if "we the people" do not throw off the chains before the tyrants bind them to our hands and feet. We have the words of Patrick Henry who said, **"Give me Liberty or give me death."** Liberty was that sacred to Patrick Henry. What is the fuller meaning behind his statement than what history tells us? What was Patrick Henry's thought process? First, he and other Christian men of the time thought from a Biblical worldview. *"Give me liberty or give me death,"* is a statement based in Biblical thought. The founders of the United States thought liberty was more precious than life, just as did the early Christians who chose death rather than give up the liberty to profess belief in Christ. They would not allow their conscience to be violated. Those Christians are the great, great grandfathers times a hundred generations ago who gave up their lives rather than lose the liberty to profess belief in Christ and His truths, His principles of life. Many other Christians through the ages did not simply walk into the Coliseum as did these first Christians. They fought in the crusades to liberate and protect the sacred places in the Holy Lands. They fought the Turks in the battle of Lepanto. Had Catholics not fought, the situation would have resulted in countless Christians being martyred. There were many other holy and just causes fought for throughout history. Whether one is shackled and led to the public square or fights in a just cause, 'liberty' at its core is a religious cause, as the loss of liberty always results in the loss of religious liberty. Why? Liberty, by virtue of being an unalienable right from the Creator, can be nothing less than Biblical.

> *"...where the spirit of the Lord is, there is liberty."* 2 Corinthians 3:17

If Liberty is an unalienable right given by God, what are we to think of those who take away our religious liberty? Those who will deny us the right to follow the principles of Christ, our Liberator, can be no less than tyrants. We can now understand the fuller meaning of Patrick Henry's *"Give me liberty or give*

me death!" We then can face the assault against our
religious liberty and say, *"Give me the liberty that I do
not have to pay for abortion, or give me death!"* Do
you understand where we are? We stand today in the
same place Patrick Henry stood. But he, like us, was
not shackled yet, and was not intending to go to the
gallows. Patrick Henry knew he and his fellow patriots
still had time to fight. If they did not, they soon would
be shackled. Hence, he'd rather live with liberty or
rather die if he lost it. He still had time to fight. Neither should we be content that we are going to the
Coliseum to be eaten by the lions of a pagan-minded,
secular, humanistic group of people suffering from the
spiritual disease of liberalism, who are in deep need of
conversion, but who are bad-willed. We will fight. We
will not comply. We will not go to jail, and we will die
for liberty if it comes to that. A serious question now
arises. Even if we are commanded to be just and to
love our enemies, that does not stop us from defending
our liberty. For you who would take our liberties away
unlawfully, we address a question to you: Are *you* willing to go to jail? Are *you* willing to die? We will not
be idle while you dismantle our nation and take from
us our right to follow our true Liberator. So my call
today to those who deny me my right to exercise my
belief in following Christ, my Liberator, I say:

"Give me my Liberator or give me death!

Tyrants' reign will always end in disastrous defeat, ours in glory. We willingly give our life, while they unwillingly pay with theirs."

CHAPTER TEN

Stirring the Pot of Hatred

It is known that repetition is the best teacher. The repetition you will read throughout this book is written with intent that you learn what you are reading. For decades, we have been repetitiously taught, forming wrong mentalities and beliefs. These mentalities must be changed in order to see clearly our path out of the looming crisis coming our way. Therefore, avoid the temptation of skipping over quotes you have already read. We have repetitiously been taught doctrine in conflict with our nation's founding documents and our Christian morals and principles. As these documents and principles are what our civil law must be rooted to, we find we must now relearn them.

Many people for years have said what now the United States Bishops are saying. Cardinal Dolan, in a letter dated March 2, 2012, warned the United States Bishops that given this current anti-church climate, we have to prepare for tough times.[37] God always will warn His people to be ready. So how do we prepare? First thing—don't wait to fully transform Our Lady's messages into every aspect of your life. For just as She foretold the future by showing Ivanka the Rwanda genocide, we understand that we are advancing hourly towards the setting into motion of plans to force us to comply with evil in the future. We are not only speaking of healthcare, but a whole train of abuses are heading in our direction. Our Lady's plans are to save the world. Our Lady said:

February 17, 1984

> **"...The world has been drawn into a great whirlpool. It does not know what it is doing. It does not realize in what sin it is sinking. It needs your prayers so that I can pull it out of this danger."**

In this message of 1984, Our Lady knew why She was coming and what the Church would face here in the United States as well as the world in 2012 and the years to follow. For those who follow Our Lady's plans, to whom, as a Mother, Her Son has entrusted Her to represent Him to the world, to save the world from itself, you will recognize a message that in and of itself, makes this connection of the present crisis of liberty. It is why we must pay attention to Her guidance now. Our Lady's own words speak of a time of lamentation coming soon.

August 25, 1997

"...soon a time will come when you will lament for these messages..."

These messages of Our Lady, not acted upon now, while there is still time, will be the cause of great lamenting and regret of what we could have done, yet did not. The media and radio stations in Rwanda stirred the pot of hatred. We must learn to recognize the tactics of satan so as not to fall into the trap of being incited by evil who clothes itself in "victimhood"—leading people to believe they are victims of other people. The Catholic Church is being made the culprit, denying 'rights' to those seeking abortion, contraception, etc., making those who want them free, through Obamacare, the victims. We must understand Christ was the only Victim. We, because we are sinners, deserve whatever befalls us. So repentance is where every Christian must start in order to enter the future. Prayer, fasting, penance and living peace within ourselves must follow with repentance. When we do these things, we experience conversion. When we convert, we see with greater depth our need of repentance. When we continue in our daily repentance/penance, prayer, fasting and peace, we continue in our conversion. This, in turn, gives us the spiritual vision to see with clarity what things of the present satan is throwing into the pot to stir up hatred until it is boiling over. This spiritual vision gives you the ability to see with honest eyes where Our Lady desires to lead us. Our Lady said:

December 2, 2011

> **"...implore the Father to forgive you your omissions up to now. My children, only a pure heart, unburdened by sin, can open itself and *only honest eyes can see the way by which I desire to lead you...*"**

Can we identify now what satan is brewing in the present? If you look with honest eyes, you will see as it happened in Rwanda. You will see how tyrants captured power and authority. The media and many in the government are fostering class warfare today in our nation. The haves vs. the have nots. The have nots are being conditioned to hate the haves. This is against every Christian tenet. The media and a small radical group responsible for the creation of Occupy Wall Street among other things, paint a picture that the have nots make-up 99% of the population. This is a highly exaggerated percentage purported by the radicals, but they use it to paint an equally false picture that the haves make up only 1% of the population. Therefore, the 99% have nots become the victims of the 1% haves, and suddenly it is as in Rwanda. satan is trying to build a division. This victimhood mentality also can be transferred into those who supposedly cannot afford their contraceptives, etc., such as Sandra Flukes testified as a 30-year old college student who claimed she needed her contraceptives paid for by others. They are being conditioned to believe that these are rights that no one should be denied and therefore, should be paid for by the haves, and the haves, again, are the 1% as taught by the media and Occupy Wall Street Movement.* As stated, this percentage, is grossly inaccurate and reveals the desired results—that everybody should be against those who have, even moderately, which is fostering and brewing class warfare. Just as hatred was bred in Rwanda, class warfare is a growing danger to everyone in our nation and around the world—the rich, the middle class, and the poor. If you are poor, you are not to envy those who have more than you. Proverbs 22:2 says:

---

* This concept of 99% vs. 1% is adopted and taken by many other voices. That contraceptives must be paid for by the haves is from a radio program transcript of Sean Hannity's interview with Miss Jehmu Greene. Jehmu was quoted as saying that 98% of Catholic women use contraceptives, of which is a blatant lie. That leaves only 2% who Miss Greene says follows the virtue of the Church's teaching on contraception. These numbers of 98% vs. 2% runs in tandem with the theme 99% vs. 1%.

*"Rich and poor have a common bond: the
Lord is the maker of them all."*

Likewise, if your needs are met or if you are well off,
you have a Christian obligation to help those who are
not. Proverbs 22:9 states:

*"The kindly man will be blessed, for he gives of
his sustenance to the poor."*

Nowhere in Scripture, nowhere in Our Lady's messages can justification be found to resent others, be
they rich, middle class, or poor. Nor is there given any
justification to even draw a line between the haves
and the have-nots, which will polarize into mutiny and
then into that hatred which always destroys those who
harbor and foster such. To hold such resentment in the
heart is a violation against the Commandment, *"Thou
shall not covet thy neighbor's goods."* The breeding
and inciting of people to be against those who have,
evolves into a belief that one has the right to covet
a neighbor's goods. Even if someone receives their
goods through unjust gain, that does not justify the
taking of the goods of another. God will rectify those
who have been unjust. Even if one does not take a
neighbor's goods, but holds *envy and/or desire* for a
neighbor's goods in the heart, this can be compared to

"adultery in the heart," which is sin. Though it is not carried out physically by stealing, envy and/or desire of the heart to covet what belongs to another is still sin.

Christians are to dissipate all efforts to pit one class against another. If we do, we win the future. If we do not, we will all lose the future. The issues in Rwanda may be different from the class warfare which evil is trying to birth now in our nation and in the world, but the results in the end will be the same — division, hatred, anarchy, bloodshed.

This hatred will not just spill out against a few that are very rich, but spread to any who have even a little more than someone else, destroying your right to property and peaccful living. Abraham Lincoln wrote:

> *Property is the fruit of labor;*
> *Property is desirable;*
> *It is a positive good in the world;*
> *That some should be rich*
> *Shows that others may become rich,*
> *And hence is just encouragement*
> *To industry and enterprise.*
>
> *Let not him who is houseless*
> *Pull down the house of another,*
> *But let him labor diligently and*

Build one for himself, thus by
Example assuring that his own shall
Be safe from violence when built.

Abraham Lincoln
March 21, 1864 [38]

Lincoln's sound principles apply not only to your house and your property, but also to other unalienable rights, because when one or another liberty is threatened, it **'also leads'** to the loss of religious liberty. This is the progression of evil.

CHAPTER ELEVEN

If the Enemy Wanted to Take Over, How do They Make you Defenseless?

In his March 2, 2012 letter to the United States Bishops, Cardinal Dolan warned:

"We have made it clear in no uncertain terms to the government that we are not at peace with its invasive attempts to curtail the religious freedom we cherish as Catholics and Americans...We did not ask for this fight, but we will not run from it."[39]

Since Cardinal Dolan writes, *"We have made it clear in no uncertain terms to the government that we are not at peace...,"*[40] then the thought process must follow through, if we are not at peace, then where are we? If God is peace, and God is removed from the public square, then there is no peace in the public square. If there is no peace in the public square, then there is war. **We are at war. They Fired the First Shot.** Medjugorje visionary, Vicka, said that Our Lady told her that war starts in the heart first and then manifests physically.

The Catholic Church is in the crosshairs of its enemies. While it can be said the Church has always had its enemies, it is important to grasp they have been held at bay in America by our religious liberty, maintained by our living a virtuous life. But because the Church, as a body, has not been living what we should, now that barricade has fallen, and we are finding that what has been in the hearts of our enemies is manifesting out in an attack of physical war against us. We, as Catholics, with our brother Christians, have yet to engage and we will lose the war if we do not do so now. Again, as Cardinal Dolan stated, *"we did not ask for this fight, but we will not run from it."[41]*

Some think guns are always bad. But what does one think when they are used in defense against those whose evil schemes are to commit genocide, erase moral principles, etc. What of Croatians breaking away from Communism? The date was June 25, 1991, the 10th anniversary of Our Lady's apparitions. The nation Our Lady Queen of Peace was appearing in daily was birthed on the 10th anniversary of Her apparitions! It obviously was a grace interceded for by Our Lady. But for Croatia to break loose, they had to rise up in battle and fight with their weapons against their communist oppressors.

When evil wants to reign it knows the people must be made defenseless. Evil attacks the morality of the people, the churches, and also the right to protect oneself to insure that people have no means of defense. The fact that there is a great amount of attack today against the Second Amendment of the United States Constitution to bear arms is a **warning** that the moment to gain total power by evil-minded men is at hand.

Why do we as Catholics, as Christians, as well as all those who are good-willed, not question why, after 236 years since our nation's founding, there is now great pressure, great efforts being orchestrated to override the Second Amendment and the United States Constitution, and to take away the right to bear arms through the introduction of treaties, regulations, etc.? In the book Look What Happened While You Were Sleeping_{TM}, it states:

> *"The U.N. passes non-binding treaties to get policy in place and then immediately begins to work on making them tighter and legally binding. Hence, by graduating slowly by degrees, most enactments of treaties are falsely imposed with negative consequences against the United States. Several tactical plans of the U.N. have been to move forward in the implementation of policies*

and treaties from the 1970s, one little step at a
time, building on each accomplishment." [42]

Efforts and strategies from outside and inside
of our nation have been put forth to introduce non-
binding treaties that in time will slowly become binding to disarm all Americans. However, this is false. In
a later chapter, we will show you that treaties cannot
override the Constitution, and it will be a very big
surprise to most Americans and a shock to those who
have believed this to be so. For now, ask yourself, with
the wisdom of what the forefathers possessed, why did
they see it so necessary to write the Second Amendment as a Constitutional right for every American to
bear arms? Why did the founding fathers spell it out so
clearly into the foundation of the United States Constitution? One should contemplate those who are pushing, not to change the United States Constitution by a
legal amendment, but rather by stealth through an international treaty to unlawfully circumvent the Second
Amendment. Why do they care so much about this?
If you investigate the ones calling for this, you will discover they are the same people who are assaulting our
religious liberty.

One should ask oneself, why do they want to disarm
the citizens? This in itself is a telling sign. The 'powers

that be' are so scared as to what the people would do to them if it was found out what their real plans and agendas are, it's no wonder they want to get rid of guns. A true picture emerges when reviewing these efforts to remove, negate and/or restrict the Second Amendment. One can clearly discern their intentions of the heart, not only over this one issue, but over their entire agenda hidden in their hearts. Could a Rwanda genocide have taken place where a people had such rights as to bear arms and exercised that right? The forefathers' main reason to include the Second Amendment was that if tyranny begins to rule in the government, the people could protect themselves against it. The Declaration defines this. If there is no case in which we should ever accept genocide, there is no case where we should accept an assault on our religious liberty, nor forfeit our right to defend ourselves as given to us in the Second Amendment. These are questions we all must ask, as well as contemplate, if peace is to be preserved. Our Lady said:

February 25, 1991

"...God is peace itself..."

If God is peace, and God is being removed to 'desacralize' our nation in order to 'secularize' it, how will we be in peace? We cannot be. In Washington D.C., the following inscription can be found on General William Sherman's monument:

> *"War's Legitimate Object Is More Perfect Peace."*[43]

For the preservation of peace, it is necessary to understand the preservation of life. The Catechism of the Catholic Church states:

> *"...The act of self-defense can have a double effect: the preservation of one's own life; and the killing of the aggressor... the one is intended, the other is not."*

> *"Love toward oneself remains a fundamental principle of morality. Therefore it is legitimate to insist on respect for one's own right to life. Someone who defends his life is not guilty of murder even if he is forced to deal his aggressor a lethal blow.*

> *"Legitimate defense can be not only a right but a grave duty for someone responsible for another's life. Preserving the common good requires rendering the unjust aggressor unable to inflict harm. To this end, those holding legitimate authority*

have the right to repel by armed force aggressors
against the civil community entrusted to their
charge." [44]

This is not just talking about calling 911 for your defense. It is doing whatever you have to do to protect your own life and those entrusted to your care. Those in legitimate authority include those in charge of the smallest part of the civil community, which is the family. Whether it be a father or mother, or older brother in charge while the parents are away for a few hours, you have not only a moral obligation, but a grave duty to the defense of those entrusted to your care that clearly applies to the greater local community and the larger community, your nation. It is the plan of darkness to take that moral obligation away from you so you can be left defenseless. This has bred the mentality that the only thing someone can do is call 911. But the reality is that only with the clear right of protection of life intact, can there be peace. And yes, defense against the government is what the Second Amendment was written for. No one should be deluded about why this is necessary and fundamental to preservation of peaceable living. The Catechism of the Catholic Church continues:

"If a man in self-defense uses more than necessary violence, it will be unlawful: whereas if he

*repels force with moderation, his defense will be lawful **(but)**... Nor is it necessary for salvation that a man omit the act of moderate self-defense to avoid killing the other man, since one is bound to take more care of one's own life than of another's.*

It is important to place all the above in proper context of the civilization of love Jesus taught. Did the early Christians rebel against Rome to establish Christendom? Jesus taught to establish His Kingdom on earth, first, within the heart. Even while Jesus was still alive, He had the admiration of some Roman pagans. He did not do this by violence. Rather, Jesus taught to behave as a holy people before the ruling authority. When a people act in this way, they convict those over them to come to truth and they win them through their witness, rather than through violence. A holy people will sanctify authorities, turning them away from pagan ways and leading them towards Christianity, with many becoming Christians. To suffer under authority is to be sanctified, to be sanctified then will lead to sanctifying authority. That will happen through patience and virtue, allowing a holy people's witness and example to penetrate the heart of those in authority. It is a long term work but as history has shown, many times it is a successful work. We are never excused from obeying authority, being good and obedient examples to them, even when authority seems oppressive. A holy people will always succeed. A people who are chosen and called to holiness, but who do not live holiness will never succeed. For such people, rebellion is of no use, for when one becomes unholy and rises up in disobedience to authority, he will fail. Obedience is one of the Christian principles we must cling to. We must abide by it. We are to sanctify and change it to a Christian authority by first respecting it.

There is only one exception to obedience to authority. It is when authority, our rulers, those who govern over us, require what is noxious and damaging to our own souls. It is then we are to remain and can remain holy in God's eyes in defying authority's sinful edicts. We must grow holy, sanctify ourselves, repent, and only then can we be successful in rejecting what is now before us by the authority of the 'powers that be' in forcing Christians to do that which can kill our souls. We have before us not rebellion but obedience to God. A just battle we will fight, if necessary, but only can win with holiness turning our society into a kingdom of love. Our Lady said:

March 25, 1986

"...Dear children, pray, so that in the whole world may come the Kingdom of Love. How mankind would be happy if love reigned!"

To help in understanding the context of which everything in this writing is to be understood, the words of Pope Benedict, spoken from the Consistory Hall, on January 19, 2012, are enlightening. Pope Benedict was addressing the United States Bishops who were making their "ad limina" visit. Pope Benedict told them:

*"One of the most memorable aspects of my Pastoral Visit to the United States was the opportunity it afforded me to reflect on American's historical experience of religious freedom, and specifically the relationship between religion and culture...America...as enshrined in your nation's founding documents, was grounded in a worldview shaped not only by faith but a commitment to certain ethical principles deriving from **nature and nature's God**. Today that consensus has eroded significantly in the face of powerful new cultural currents which are not only directly opposed to core moral teachings of*

the Judeo-Christian tradition, but increasingly
hostile to Christianity as such."[45]

Benedict states the Church is not to be silent, but to
boldly proclaim to those hostile elements the truth of
which we shall not turn away from. The Pope continued:

> *"The Church in the United States is called, in*
> *season and out of season, to proclaim a Gos-*
> *pel which not only proposes unchanging moral*
> *truths but proposes them precisely as the key to*
> *man's happiness and social prospering..."[46]*

Benedict sees America's move toward diminishing
God and His mystery as moving toward the script for
'totalitarianism.'[*]   Benedict told the United States
Bishops:

> *"When a culture attempts to suppress the dimen-*
> *sion of ultimate mystery, and to close the doors to*
> *transcendent truth, it inevitably becomes impov-*
> *erished and falls prey, as the late* Pope John Paul
> II *so clearly saw, to reductionist and* **totalitarian**
> *readings of man and the nature of society."[47]*

---

* Totalitarianism means the centralized control by an autocratic authority; it is a political concept that the citizens should be totally subject to
an absolute state authority.

Benedict continues in saying the Church must counter this danger, promoting freedom and liberty derived from moral truth, defending our reasoning based on natural law. Pope Benedict continues:

> *"The Church has a critical role to play __in countering cultural__ currents which, on the basis of an extreme individualism, seek to promote notions of freedom detached from moral truth...*
> *The Church's defense of a moral reasoning based on the natural law is grounded on her conviction that this law is not a threat to our freedom, but rather a 'language' which enables us to understand ourselves and the truth of our being, and so to shape a more just and humane world. She thus proposes her moral teaching as a message not of constraint but of liberation, and as the basis for building a secure future."[48]*

Obama's idea in regards to our founding documents is that constraints on what the government cannot do to you is negative. Contrast his view to that of the moral order of things seen as Benedict stated above, that moral teaching is not a message of 'constraint but of liberation.' This thought process of Obama's compared to Pope Benedict's, highlights the condition our time suffers from — a condition in that you have Obama standing upon relative truth vs. Pope Benedict standing upon absolute truth. The Church has constraints, just as does our Declaration and Constitution, put there by our forefathers to foster liberty, while what Obama proposes is freedom *from* moral constraints, which will foster the loss of liberty. Natural law vs. unnatural law.

Pope Benedict goes further, calling Catholics to enter into the public square without being silent, but rather to proclaim truth. He stated:

"Separation of Church and State cannot be taken to mean that the Church must be silent on certain issues, nor that the States may choose not to engage, or be engaged by, the voices of committed believers in determining the values which will shape the future of the nation."[49]

Benedict then strongly and directly addressed the violation of using unnatural laws to take away our religious freedom in the United States:

"...it is imperative that the entire Catholic community in the United States come to realize the **grave threats** *to the Church's public moral witness presented by a radical secularism which finds increasing expression in the political and cultural spheres. The seriousness of these threats*

needs to be clearly appreciated at every level of ecclesial life. Of particular concern are certain attempts being made to limit that most cherished of American freedoms, the freedom of religion. Many of you have pointed out that concerted efforts have been made to deny the right of conscientious objection on the part of Catholic individuals and institutions with regard to coop- eration in intrinsically evil practices. Others have spoken to me of a worrying tendency to reduce religious freedom to mere freedom of worship without guarantees of respect for freedom of con- science."[50]

Our Lady wants to enlighten you, to make you aware, to educate you, in union with Pope Benedict, of what She is doing in this special time in which the world is rejecting Christ. Our Lady said:

June 22, 2012

"...I desire to lead you, to teach you, to educate you—I desire to lead all of you to my Son...Put Him in the first place in your life..."

In light of these words, all Christians must be educated from a Biblical worldview, and with that perspective, articulate with strength the views of the Church, confronting agendas that harm the Church so that the Church will not be diminished in the public square. Christians must fight so the truths of the Church be considered in everything before any laws are passed where there may be something that conflicts with our Christian principles. There is to be nothing in the law that violates Christ's teachings or His statutes. Benedict said to the United States Bishops:

> *"Here once more we see the need for an engaged, articulate and well-formed Catholic laity endowed with a strong critical sense vis-à-vis the dominant culture and with the courage to counter a reductive secularism which would delegitimize the Church's participation in public debate about the issues which are determining the future of American society. The preparation of committed lay leaders and the presentation of a convincing articulation of the Christian vision of man and society remain a primary task of the Church in your country...maintain contacts with Catholics involved in political life and to help them understand their personal responsibility to offer public witness to their faith, especially with regard to the great moral issues of our time...the secular sphere must also take into consideration the truth*

that <u>there is no realm of worldly affairs which</u> <u>can be withdrawn from the Creator and his do-</u> <u>minions.</u>"[51]

As Cardinal Dolan said on March 2, 2012, *"We did not ask for this fight, but we will not run from it."* The apostle John taught as Jesus taught him. His writing in the Gospel shows very clearly that love is best displayed by obedience, but obedience also to natural law. Natural law cannot be compromised, rationalized, or given away. We must begin a new way of life, away from the direction of the present culture.

CHAPTER TWELVE

You Must Decide Today for a Future With God or Without Him. The Consequences will Commence Accordingly.

The previous chapters make it clear. History shows by the present steps we are taking, where we are headed. The door is further opened now—that when enough people believe falsely they are victims, particularly victims of the Catholic Church, they will begin to believe the Church is their enemy. The reversing tactic—the Hutus are the victims, the Tutsis are the culprits—is the tool of tyranny. The world is growing in an evil spirit of victimhood. The media propaganda machine continually teaches that you are owed recompense for everything. There is always someone else to blame for your unhappiness, discontentment or bad luck. The mentality of victimhood will next progress to look upon the Church as part of the 'haves' group. They will grow to 'covet' her riches and eventually demand their rights to 'redistribute' her wealth. Victimhood's mentality will be, *"We have a right to her riches."* This is why we have the Second Amendment. You think this is unthinkable? A people who have been indoctrinated that they are victims can, as in Rwanda, be manipulated into thinking, *"The Church has taken from the people."* If you reject this, you know not history, nor the present actions of the Catholic Church's enemies. As already quoted, please consider once again these fresh words from Heaven. Our Lady said:

February 2, 2012

> **"...You continue to be deaf and blind as you look at the world around you and do not want to see where it is going without my Son..."**

Where does all this end? Read history, learn from it and you will see. At the same time, we must understand that what we are inheriting has come from our failure of not living fully the Christian life. We have indulged in comfort of self, we have disregarded God's commandments and have made light of our sins, and in the midst of this, waned in our morality, allowing religion to be removed from the public square. How then can morality prevail without religious principles undergirding it? In our comfort, we have grown lazy and fallen asleep, while evil never sleeps. The Father of the United States, George Washington, stated:

"Of all the dispositions and habits which lead
to political prosperity, religion and morality are
indispensable supports. In vain would that man
claim the tribute of patriotism, who should labor
to subvert these great pillars of human happi-
ness, these firmest props of the duties of men and
citizens...let us with caution indulge the suppo-
sition that morality can be maintained without
religion...reason and experience, both, forbid us
to expect that national morality can prevail in ex-
clusion of religious principles." [52]

It is time to wake up and teach virtue while we
can. God is to be your provider, not the government
or some other entity or person. But God's provision
is contingent upon your cooperation with Him. You
must work virtuously, be industrious, a good steward
of His provisions and forsake all laziness. If malady
befalls you, your holy way of life and God's help will
be your protection, but virtue is necessary. Yet, practically everything that befalls a person today is blamed
on someone else. It is always another person's fault.
Christian principles of responsibility are fading in society. The following example takes this to the extreme
but perfectly illustrates how this thinking has become
so pervasive in our society. On Christmas Day, Decem-

ber 25, 2007, a man crashed, at a high rate of speed, into the back of a family car that was stopped at a red light, killing three people. David Belniak, of Spring Hill, Florida, pleaded guilty to three counts of manslaughter while Driving Under the Influence and was sentenced to 12 years in prison. Four years later, in December, 2011, Belniak incredulously filed a lawsuit against the estate of the deceased driver of the car he crashed into, stating that the crash was the victim's fault. Even while he sits in jail for his drunken manslaughter, he is demanding the victim's relatives pay for his "pain and suffering...mental anguish...loss of capacity for the enjoyment of life" and to pay for his medical bills he got because of the accident.[53] This "everybody is a victim" mentality prevails in the world today. What must God think when He looks upon the earth and sees what our nation and our world have become? How much longer can God tolerate this?

Our Lady of Medjugorje said on November 6, 1982:

"...Go on the streets of the city, count those who glorify God and those who offend Him. God can no longer endure that."

Are we in the throes of His turning us over to ourselves? We, in the times in which we live, can certainly be identified as a corrupt society as described in Romans, Chapter 1, verses 18-32 in which it is stated that, ***"God gave them up to themselves."***

The breeding of widespread mentalities of victimhood doesn't happen on its own, but is part of the strategy to create class warfare. The people themselves, easily swayed by the propagandist media, are used to help bring in the reign of tyranny. Lenin reportedly called them the "useful idiots."

Some may think we are still a long way into the future of what is manifesting on the horizon, but think of things now happening in the present that just 10 years ago, we could not imagine would happen in our lifetime.

Our Lady did not give Ivanka the scenes of death that resulted from uncontrolled hatred in Rwanda to entertain her. She was shown these scenes for a purpose. Reason and meditate on this purpose. This present moment is a 'now time' for us to alter our future. Are there negative things, in the present, along with issues, and circumstances that 10, 15, and 20 years ago we could have altered and, thereby, today be experiencing a different life than what we have inherited in the present? If you do not like the present, you most certainly will not like the future. Now is the moment to at least alter somewhat our present circumstances and change our future. If enough people change, greater will the future change by our decisions today. This is a grace period for us as Christians. Our Lady comes to tell us to alter our future now in the present. Our Lady said:

June 15, 2012

> **"...Put...(God) in the first place in your life and in your families and together with Him, set out into the future...through this upcoming time of grace..."**

Christ is the only way, the only path, not just for eternity, but for the world and its earthly future for peace. Reject Jesus, as the world is now doing, divorcing itself from He who sustains it, and the result will be as we are already experiencing it, life on earth radically changing as we have known it.

December 25, 2008

> **"...comprehend that, without Him (Jesus), you have no future..."**

CHAPTER THIRTEEN

Verbicide
The War is Won

The definition of verbicide is:

1. deliberate distortion of the sense of a word

2. one who distorts the sense of a word

The war is won—a "verbicide" war that changed
what our nation once believed itself to be. Today in
our nation, the people believe our country is a democracy. Many may say, "No, we are a republic." Yet, by
their thinking and actions they demonstrate that they
believe and live out a contradiction, that we are a democracy, not a republic. We must re-educate ourselves,
our families, our friends, and our schools of the difference between a democracy and a republic. The forming
of our thoughts through decades of efforts by verbicide
revisionists, has literally changed even what we accept
as lawful. Once we understand the difference between
a democracy and a republic, then we can once again
know what it is we are—a republic. We must become
active in changing back our nation to a republic in our

understanding, in our speech and by our actions. We all
must do our part to re-educate those around us, be they
teachers in public or private schools, home schoolers,
CCD teachers, those in our work places, or wherever
else you can get into a position of opportunity that en-
ables you to instruct, teach, correct and to guide people
to this truth. We have been slowly conditioned through
the media and the educational systems—from the university level down to kindergarten, even preschool classrooms—that we are a democracy. Even great patriots of
recent decades, such as President Reagan, would refer to
our nation as a democracy, not realizing the significance
in saying so moulded our thinking into believing such.
This fundamental change of thinking through "liberalism," that Pope Benedict XVI named as the wind of bad
doctrine (liberalism), has been used to make us believe
the United States is a democracy, causing us to slip into
being one. **This new mentality, developed over recent
decades, that we are a democracy has actually led us into
the situation we now find ourselves in with the highjacking of the Judicial System.**

Our forefathers believed that a democracy would
not last long and that it was a very bad form of government, more bloody than a monarchy or aristocracy. In
a democracy, the voting majority can force their will on

others. Why should 10,000 people be forced to have their unalienable rights taken away by 10,001 people? A democracy rules by *feeling,* a very unstable form of government. A republic rules by law, thereby, a very stable form of government. David Barton relays that in a democracy, if the majority of the people decide that murder is no longer a crime, murder will no longer be a crime.[54]   So, the source of law for a democracy is the *popular feeling* of the people. If that is so for a democracy, then what is the source of law for the American Republic? According to one of our founders, Noah Webster:

> *"Our citizens should early understand that the genuine source of correct Republican principles is the Bible, particularly the New Testament and the Christian Religion."*[55]

A democracy's source for law is popular feeling. A correct republic's source for law is the Bible. The foundation of the *American Republic* was the Bible. Therefore, murder will always be a crime because it is a crime as written in the Bible. Not so with a democracy. Hence, change a nation by indoctrination through educating the people to believe they live in a democracy, and you can pass laws and advocate that killing in the womb or starving someone, as in euthanasia is not murder, along with a host of other criminal actions which can be made legal. Not so in a correct biblical, Christian principled republic, which its laws cannot operate legally outside the perimeters of the Bible, the Divine Law, 'nature's law, nature's God.' This is true not only for our nation, but for all nations. Now do you see how our Judicial system, approving abortions, etc., was highjacked by this simple work of the distortionists utilizing verbicide and revisionism? We have been made to believe the word Republic is interchangeable for the word Democracy.

Early law books of our Republic foundationed the United States on teachings that government was free to set its own policy only if God had not ruled in an area. For example, Alexander Hamilton, a signer of the Constitution, said:

> *"The law…dictated by God Himself is, of course, superior in obligation to any other. It is binding over all the globe, in all countries, at all times. No human laws are of any validity if contrary to this."*[56]

On the other hand, Thomas Jefferson said:

> *"A democracy is nothing more than mob rule, when fifty-one percent of the people may take away the rights of the other forty-nine percent."*[57]

Does our Republic give us the right to live in a culture of life? Yes. Does the democracy we have become give us the right to live in a culture of life? No. The culture of death is flourishing. This cannot be if we set out to place our Republic back on its correct foundation of Divine Law, the Bible, first in our hearts and then in the law, in our institutions, and in the public square.

In a Republic, everyone has rights. You are protected as individuals. Our Constitution guaranteed a republican form of government—a government where men are free from civil government constantly interfering with their lives. In a Republic, government is greatly restricted in its reach into the affairs of its citizens and their liberty to self-govern their affairs within the perimeters of Christian principles. The citizen's liberty was only restricted when one stepped out of the perimeters of Biblical principles, which are the source of our republic's law, or where municipal law ruled where Divine Law had not. In other words, if you live the Christian tenets, there is not really any need for more laws except for municipal laws such as the setting of speed limits, etc.

Alexander Hamilton said, *"Real liberty is never found in despotism or in the extremes of democracy."*[58]

The word "democracy" does not appear anywhere in the U.S. Constitution because the United States is not a democracy.

James Madison—1787 Federalist Paper #10:

> *"Democracy is the most vile form of government...Democracies have ever been spectacles of turbulence and contention: have ever been found incompatible with personal security or the rights of property and have in general been short in their lives as they have been violent in their deaths."* [59]

John Adams, 1815:

> *"Democracy...while it lasts is more bloody than either **aristocracy or monarchy**. Remember, democracy never lasts long. It soon wastes, exhausts, and murders itself. There is never a democracy that did not commit suicide."* [60]

John Marshall—Chief Justice of the Supreme Court:

> *"Between a balanced Republic and a democracy, the difference is like that between order and chaos."* [61]

Why? Because in a correct republic, you are bound by
the order of law which cannot be changed on a whim;
while a democracy, by mob rule, can change the current
of the nation by popular feelings. Jedediah Morse, one
of the authors of the Bill of Rights said:

> *"A simple democracy is the devil's own govern-*
> *ment."* [62]

What is Jedediah Morse's statement based on?
Why did he say the "devil's own government?" Indeed,
the angel of "light," lucifer's first action of dissent before war broke out in Heaven was to rally other angels
to get the votes to rule by numbers, not by the ways of
God. lucifer, the devil, placed himself beyond God's
sovereignty by popular feeling and mob rule, utilizing
the angels' rebellion to try to establish a democracy
in Heaven. Pride was born, and Our Lady's words of
February 2, 2012, confirms he, pride, has come to rule...
on the earth. To do what? To turn to chaos this "democracy" he helped to establish, thereby, making the
ground fertile to usher in pride to rule over and destroy
the world. Our Lady said:

August 2, 2011

"...As individuals, my children, you cannot stop
the evil that wants to begin to rule in this world

and to destroy it. But, according to God's will, all together, with my Son, you can change everything and heal the world..."

Fisher Ames, author of the words of the First Amendment said:

"A democracy is a volcano which conceals the fiery material of its own destruction. These will produce an eruption and carry desolation in their way." [63]

All American youth, just a few short decades ago, knew these truths. Our youth were required to memorize the Declaration of Independence. Why? So these truths would not be forgotten, lest we lose our nation in a generation.

The influence bishops have across this nation over Catholic schools to institute and make sure the minds of our youth are not indoctrinated with doctrines conflicting with the truths of the Declaration of Independence and of the United States founding is immense. All the Bishops have to do is exercise their authority, break through the curtain of power and committees that surround them and become personally involved. They should review periodically what is being taught, not through committees, but by personal

involvement. They could even write teaching papers
for their diocesan schools, not complicated theological
teaching, but simple teaching as what has been read in
this book. The Bishops righting the errors that came
through verbicide and revisionism that have rooted
themselves in our school systems, both in private and
public schools, alone can play a major part to rechart
the United States back to the wisdom of our founding
fathers. Across our land, most citizens do not know
what is at stake concerning our liberty and the attacks
being leveled against United States citizens. For decades, the verbicide revisionists have been unopposed
in their efforts.

A legal maxim which gives reason why there is a
prohibition of democracy in the United States, states:

*"The multitude of those who err is no protection
for error."* [64]

A multitude of people in our nation presently believe
the error that we are a democracy, but just because the
majority believe this does not mean our nation is not
in serious error. We are. We must distinguish between
the fact that we use a democratic process of voting, but
that is not to be confused with democracy as a form
of government. We cannot vote against nature's law

made by nature's God, except if we are a democracy. We have covertly slipped into being a democracy.

In a republic, free men are protected from over-bearing civil authority, by the U.S. Constitution, Article 4, Section 4, which guarantees to every inhabitant a republican form of government. You pledge allegiance to a republic, not a democracy:

> *"I pledge allegiance to the Flag of the United States of America and to the Republic for which it stands..."*

David Barton writes in <u>Original Intent</u>:

> *"The founders understood that Biblical values formed the basis of the republic and that the republic would be destroyed if the people's knowledge of those values should ever be lost.*

> *"A republic is the highest form of government devised by man, but it also requires the greatest amount of human care and maintenance. If neglected, it can deteriorate into a variety of lesser forms, including a **democracy**; a government conducted by popular feeling; an **anarchy**; a system in which each person determines his own rules and standards; an **oligarchy**, a government run*

*by a small council or a group of elite individuals; or a **dictatorship**; a government run by a single individual. As John Adams explained:*

'Democracy will soon degenerate into an anarchy, such an anarchy that every man will do what is right in his own eyes and no man's life or property or reputation or liberty will be secure, and every one of these will soon mould itself into a system of subordination of all the moral virtues and intellectual abilities, all the powers of wealth, beauty, wit, and science, to the wanton pleasures, the capricious will, and the execrable (abominable) cruelty of one or a very few.'"[65]

By what you have just read and now learned, Jedediah Morse's words can now be clearly understood.

"A simple democracy is the devil's own government."[66]

Everyone must counter this by declaring war, to de-verbicide decades of subtle indoctrination by revisionists who have, through creeping gradualism, literally changed what this nation believes itself to be.

You, as an individual, must engage and fight against this war of verbicide. Make a battle promise right now and say,

* I will never 'say again' that the nation of the United States of America is a democracy.

* I will never 'refer' to it as a democracy.

* I, when hearing others say or refer to the United States of America as a democracy, will 'correct' them and not remain silent, but rather will courageously address even those who are teachers, lawyers or any other who it may be difficult to do so.

* I will not remain silent when I hear others saying that we are to spread democracy to other nations.

* I will respond instead, "No, you and I are to spread liberty and liberty is the fruit of Christianity, and the tree of Christianity is from the seed of the Cross. I, therefore, will spread by my witness, Jesus Christ, Who is the author of liberty, and Who through liberty will bring about the fruit of peace."

* I will learn more about my moral republic and those who want to destroy it.

CHAPTER FOURTEEN

Give us Our Rights...We Beg Pretty Please

Why do we, as Christians, sit on the sidelines letting atheists and humanists subjugate us to their impositions and restrictions on our faith? These two diametrically opposed worldviews — Christianity and secular humanism cannot co-exist in our public policies, court systems and public offices, while we all hold hands singing Kumbaya. There is only one way that will win out: either Christian principles or secular humanistic atheism. Both will not share the seat of power without one struggling against the other, trying to conquer. Christians have been too passive, too compliant. The very nature of Christianity cannot accept tolerance by the world's definition of live and let live, leaving things as they are, but rather Christianity commands believers to witness to the truth of the Christian faith with their lives. Christians are to convict, not with force, but by witness. A proper witness convicts, and often those who are being convicted will change, but just as often those who do not want to change will be greatly agitated by being convicted. This is why living a convicting witness of your Christianity, as Christ taught, will bring persecution, especially when after a long sleep, we begin to wake up to the secularism that has prevailed over the Catholic Church and all other Christian denominations. And now that secular atheism has come knocking on the doors of our Church, we find ourselves begging for concessions, "Pretty please put on the table of negotiation that we not be forced to violate our consciences." We falsely think we will be granted religious liberty through this means, when it is God we are to answer to and beg protection over our liberty after recognizing our need to repent. So, it is that the Catholic Church and all Christians today, find ourselves prevailed over, begging for rights. What will it be, Christianity or secularism? We must realize one will guide the other. One will prevail over the other and *will rule*.

Obama, on February 10, 2012, had just finalized his "rule" to force compliance to his invalid law. Indeed, **pride has come to rule**. Obama declared the invalid law would be "without change." His only concession was to delay the enforcement of his atheistic law, for Catholic organizations and other faith-based groups. They will still be forced to pay for abortions, etc., but compliance was deferred until August, 2013.

We need a new strategy against these advances. The attacks against our liberties and our faith are no longer being made just yearly or monthly or even daily, but now by the hour they march against us. These strategies we have been engaged in have been ineffective, and if we continue down this path, we will see the last vestige of Christian principles in our law and our way of life disappear, forcibly taken from us. Atheists have the free will not to believe in God. The Catholic Church and all of Christianity accepts and recognizes the freedom of will. What they do not have is the right, either constitutionally or by exercise of a so called Constitutional freedom, to strip Christianity from the land and replace it with secular humanistic atheism. This must be defeated. We have within our right to deny them this unconstitutional right they have invented through humanism. To defeat this assault Catholics, Christians and all people of good will, should have strategies to prevail in our faith and principles which are simple. No need for a complex formula. One goal, one aim. A strategy, like the heroic Christians of the past:

We win. They lose. Nothing less.

This is what caused the proverbial saying of the Indians, *"If you can't beat 'em, join 'em."* When Christianity began, this is what the early Christians did, though small

in numbers. Their strength was so mighty that others
who fought them left the caesars to join them. The
Christian ranks swelled, throughout history, when they
were strong, and they decreased when they were weak.
Emperor Constantine came to know this, and pagan
Rome became strong again through becoming Christian Rome. Fr. Eric, quoted earlier in his commentary
of Fr. John Lenz's book, Christ in Dachau, explained
this in his newsletter for what makes a great nation:

> *"Fr. John Lenz goes as far as saying that 'those
> who did not encounter Christ in the depths of the
> misery and horror of Dachau missed the most
> wonderful experience of all...It is a triumph of
> good over evil, of truth over falsehood.'* Christ
> in Dachau *proclaims the victory of God and His
> Church. Souls were tried in the crucible of suffering, and many found Christ.*

> *"The Nazi regime which rejected Christ collapsed. The Catholic Church united to Christ remained. Hence, the strength of a nation is dependent upon the faithfulness of its people to Christ.
> When the people are strong in the Faith, the government will likely be strong; when the people are
> weak, the government will naturally follow suit.*

"Belief in the Catholic Faith cannot be considered a threat to the life of a nation; rather, it is necessary for its survival." [67]

Our nation became weak by our not living our faith. Tyranny is rising up to fill the void that formerly was filled with followers of Christ. So where do we start to win? First, with deep repentance, then amend our lives with fasting, prayer, peace and penance. We must awaken our faith, deep in our hearts and in our families. We must have both a strong daily structured and a spontaneous prayer life. Next, we look at where evil began to win and where we began to lose. And isn't this exactly what Our Lady did with the parish of Medjugorje? She led them to repentance, then into the spiritual life and then the confrontation of atheistic communism where they prevailed against it and became a free nation. Our Judeo-Christian principles are to be applied into the very fabric of our institutions, governments, and public offices. They are what makes this country the beacon of hope for the world. And through this nation, the whole world will fall into tyranny or will rise up in a new springtime that will renew both the Church and the nations of the world. The United States of America is the wall evil must knock down in order to flood the earth with evil. But do not mistake what is written here, that the United States can be saved by any other way or method than by Christ being in the heart of its people, and thereby, in the heart of the United States as a nation. It is Jesus Christ, the King, whom we recognize as the reason for our being a great nation. We are entering a period that apart from Christ, there is no future. As already stated, Our Lady of Medjugorje said on December 25, 2008:

"...without Him (Jesus), you have no future..."

No revival can come without repentance and conversion, and repentance and conversion must happen to become strong in God again. We must parallel this revival with educating ourselves, our families, even every church to the beliefs and dreams of our founding fathers that were formed before the United States was even formed, and that was taught and handed down from generation to generation, right up to the 1950s. Among your discoveries, you will find that no atheist could testify in a court of law, take oaths, hold public office, or sit in the jury box. Why? Because Christian principles prevented him from doing so. Christianity was not passive and tolerant, but believers knew to put guards up in order to protect the foundations of our nation's founding documents. Yes, there was tolerance for one's free will to be atheist, but to put him in a position to rule—No! We have sat on the sidelines as secular humanistic atheism has supplanted Christian principles in the United States. Remember, one will rule over the other.

John Locke believed that atheists should not be allowed to hold office. In 1685, he wrote an essay on toleration, which exempted atheists from civil protection of toleration. He wrote:

> *"Lastly, those are not all to be tolerated, who deny the being of God. Promises, covenants, and oaths, which are bonds of human society, can have no hold upon an atheist. The taking away of God, though but even in thought, dissolves all, beside also, those that by their atheism undermines and destroys all religion, can have no pretence of religion whereupon to challenge the privilege of toleration."* [68]

Our Lady said June 16, 1983:

"I have come to tell the world that God is truth. He exists ..."

We do not have to apologize for truth, even if it offends.

In the book <u>Look What Happened While You Were Sleeping</u>_{TM}, it illustrates clearly that for our modern day

the same principles as above can be applied in regard
to atheists:

>*"In essence, an atheist would not have a proper*
>*conscience to be credible in upholding the oaths,*
>*testimonies, decisions, and judgments rendered.*
>*This shows us that no one needs to be sensitive*
>*to an atheist's belief or accommodate them on a*
>*level constitutional playing field. This statement*
>*of not accommodating atheists on a 'level con-*
>*stitutional playing field' may stun many mentali-*
>*ties. If it does, you must change your mentality,*
>*adapting back to the old mentalities that guided*
>*this nation right up to a few decades ago. God is*
>*God. He exists, and for a professed atheist to be-*
>*lieve that He does not exist, does not cause God's*
>*existence to cease. So who do we honor? The*
>*atheist or God? Who do we respect? The athe-*
>*ist's belief that God doesn't exist or those who*
>*believe He does exist? Both cannot be accom-*
>*modated equally. One will offend; one will be of-*
>*fended. It is one way or the other. So whose way*
>*is to win out? Throughout the last decades, it has*
>*been the atheist's mentality. However, it is time to*
>*make all things right. An atheist does not have*
>*an equal right to prevail in his views or to be ac-*

commodated in law. He has the right to excuse
himself, nothing more. The Christian attitude
toward the atheist or non-believer is to be one
of love and respect. The atheist has a free will to
choose not to believe. He does not have a right
nor the liberty to impose his belief and mentality
*into our laws or institutions." *[69]

Why? Because for an atheist to impose his belief is
to violate nature's law, which was expressly declared
law by God Himself, "Nature's God." He, the atheist,
cannot, therefore, be accommodated. It may surprise
some because they never thought about it, but even the
devil is not an atheist. He believes more in God's existence than all of us put together. When Jesus walked
the earth and demoniacs came up to Him, Jesus would
order the demoniacs to be silent, and the demoniacs,
being believers in God, knew they had no choice but to
obey. Why then, should we give hearing in the public
square to allow humanistic atheism a voice or power
to drive our society? Christ Himself would not even
allow the demoniacs who said, "You are the Christ,"
to speak. We are not speaking of those who are non-
believers, pagan or agnostic, because they are ignorant
or they just do not know any better, or those who do
not know the love of God and therefore, do not know

Him. We, instead, are talking about the humanistic atheists who, with purpose and intention, are implementing their beliefs into our system. The irony of atheism is that they have to have God to be atheist, otherwise who would they not believe in? Is it not humanistic atheistic principles that are being implemented and forced upon our Catholic institutions with the healthcare mandate to pay for sterilization, abortion, etc.? Atheistic views imposed upon us are prevailing over Christian principles. Which power will rule? One will win out over the other. Again, we will not be singing Kumbaya together. One will prevail.

We must go back to the principles which protected our unalienable rights of liberty. Both the atheist and the pagan fare far better, as well as all people of the United States, in a Christian principled society, than in a humanistic atheist society. Hence, this is why there are many atheists who keep their beliefs out of the public square and are quite comfortable to live in a culture where Christian principles thrive. Many Jews, prominent and otherwise, have acknowledged that nowhere have Jews fared better than Christian America. Everyone fares better under Christian principles. Our Constitution does not require God to be stripped from law. Atheism has imposed this into the legal system, and for years Christians, operating under the false premise of toleration, sat on the sidelines and did nothing.

For our founding fathers, oaths were sacred. If you did not believe in God or were irreligious, how then could you take an oath for public office, to testify, to be on a jury and so forth? One cannot because oaths are taken upon the Bible for all these positions of public office, courts, judges, etc. Since an oath cannot be accepted by an atheist or a wiccan, pagan, irreligious person, etc., can he take a secular oath? No. To do so would be to take an oath to self, as he would be his own god, answerable to his own determined boundaries, to his own truths.

In *Life and Letter of Joseph Story,* as cited by David Barton in <u>Original Intent</u>:

"A man cannot be his own measure to truth." [70]

In the book <u>Original Intent</u>, it explains:

"This is why atheists were never allowed to testify in court. Oaths were sacred, witnessing to the authenticity of God. How could an atheist take an oath? For an atheist, every man is his own god. Secular Humanism says, 'Man is the measure of

all things.' He never prays, 'So help me God.'
As a result, United States Supreme Court Justice,
Joseph Story, observed "infidels and pagan men
(were) banished from the halls of justice as un-
worthy of credit." [71]

So it is now Catholics and other Christians who are banished more and more from exercising our principles in office and the public square, and this will continue until we say to this push against us, against our religious liberty... NO MORE! We, just as our founding fathers did, must impose into law the principles of Christianity without consideration of offending the humanistic atheists and pagans whose ideologies we presently are being forced to subjugate our faith to. You cannot live under both principles. The two ideologies do not, cannot have equality, as they are in conflict on a public level. If you, as a Christian, cannot accept this, then Obama prevails and you must pay for abortion. If you do not accept to be ruled over by secular humanistic atheism, then we are not to walk down the path they offer us, but must choose our own path.

Choose for yourself whom you will serve.

"As for me and my house, we will serve the Lord." Joshua 24:15

CHAPTER FIFTEEN

Hostilities Against Only One Group

What is our path? Our path is to go back to the truth of the Declaration of Independence, and reset our nation upon it, going back to its founding principles. How? We must:

Invoke the Declaration of Independence

When? At the most opportune moment. When might that be? You must ask yourself these questions: Do you believe Heaven just told us, through the Virgin Mary, on February 2, 2012, that **"pride has begun to rule,"** or do you deny it? If you are unsure of the authenticity of the apparitions of the Virgin Mary in Medjugorje, looking at the situation today, is this still a fair statement to make: "pride has begun to rule?" If you choose to deny it, then wait. But be forewarned that what was seen in the period of time when totalitarian regimes ruled nations, such as in Germany or Russia, during and after World War II, that we will see the same happen to us. First, they came for the Jews, then for the Catholics, then the Protestants, until there was no one else to stand up. It will be the same for you. If you choose not to deny, but accept and believe that **"pride (evil) has come to rule,"** then you can understand there should be a serious look at invoking the Declaration sooner rather than later. This chapter was written on March 15, 2012, when many still naively believed that the November 6, 2012 election was the big hope to remove the Obama administration from office. With the undeniable actions displayed by this president as an enemy to the Catholic Church, and to all Americans who cherish religious liberty, can you really believe he will be leaving the presidency, even if someone else is elected… when in a time evil has come to rule? To know your enemy is to know that everything and anything, legal or illegal, will be done to keep Obama in office. But even if somehow Obama is removed from office, do not think that evil will pack up and go home. If one prays and is in deep prayer, it is impossible to believe that evil will just simply vacate its throne, a throne which doles out edicts in a complete assault against religious liberty. It will not. To know your enemy one must understand the enemy's intentions of the heart. Do you not understand the time we live in? We must look at Scriptures:

Matthew 16:3-4:

> *"You know how to interpret the appearance of the sky, but you cannot interpret the signs of the times."*

Are we to be so trusting, so naïve to believe that
the November 6, 2012 election will be an honest election? Obama is so intent on implementing the mandate, yet why is he so comfortable in putting off the
mandate for religious organizations until August 2013?
Does he trust that the next administration will keep
the healthcare mandate? Why would he risk it being
turned over to another administration? He could have
said August, 2012 instead of 2013. One could argue he
did not want to cloud the chances of running for re-
election, so he put it off until after the election. If he
was worried about continuing as president in the next
term, why in this moment did he do something so damaging as to disregard the Catholic Church by pressing
for unconstitutional mandates without giving conscientious objections a way out? Why is he so comfortable
doing this and in postponing its implementation for
one year and six months from his decision? You need
to ask and answer these questions to understand your
enemy and his intentions. Will Obama just leave office
if he truly does not get the votes? That is the big question. Will he, through hook and crook, get the votes
no matter how many votes another candidate gets? To
fly you have to have a pilot's license. If stopped for
a traffic violation, you must show a photo ID driver's
license. If you rent a car, a boat, or rent an electrical

tool from your local equipment store, you have to show
a driver's license. If you go to Sam's Club or Costco's
Wholesale to get their photo ID card, you have to 'first'
show them your photo ID driver's license. No one has
a problem with this. It is normal practice to show and
prove that you are who you say you are. It is constitutional. Go to the airport, they only will accept a government issued photo ID, as is the case with all official
functions of government where identity is important.
Try going to get anything through the government and
show your power bill saying, "See my name on it." It
is the same thing for your air travel, going to cash a
check at your bank if it is over a certain amount, and
there are a hundred more examples that could be cited
where a photo ID is required. Because voting is a serious civic duty, it is also a serious duty to insure voters
are who they say they are, and so you must prove it.
In fact, voter fraud and intimidation in the last presidential election was witnessed in several places and, as
a result, voter identification has been one of the hot-
test topics in state legislatures over the past few years.
Thirty-four states introduced Voter ID legislation in
2011, and by June of the 2012 sessions, legislation was
already pending in 32 states. Since the 2008 election
when voter fraud and intimidation were so flagrant in
order to elect Obama, 13 states have passed new voter

ID laws or strengthened existing laws. Roughly half
of the 13 new laws strictly require photo ID, and most
of the other half require photo ID except for very limited special exceptions. [72] Who, with honest intentions,
would object to this? Who is foolish enough to accept
that with something as important as voting, that it is
wrong and too restrictive to ask for government issued
photo IDs, such as a driver's license, a passport, etc.?
Obama's Attorney General! Why? You ask why?
Obama's Attorney General, Eric Holder, through the
Justice Department, declared war on several states
which require a photo ID. Holder is attempting to
strike down the new state laws by <u>any</u> way possible.
Only one reason can explain Holder's aggressiveness
to stop verification identification. There was blatant
fraud in the last election. What, therefore, will happen
in November 2012?

Think about the November 2012 elections. Do you
think if the opponent who runs against Obama wins,
that it is beyond the 'powers that be' to come up with,
through whatever means possible, the votes for Obama
over what the opponent received? After reading of the
tactics of Eric Holder, and those of Obama himself, acting without any moral conscience, does this not lead you
to the conclusion that a whole machine, at the time of

this writing, is being assembled with strategies and cal-
culations of how and what to do to win the coming election no matter how outvoted Obama will be? By what
Obama is doing, and seeing the actions of those who
support him, do you not think every effort will be put
forth to do whatever has to be done to keep the present evil in power? How can these questions be raised?
By knowing your enemy. This present evil knows fully
it cannot retreat or even temporarily vacate its hold on
power or it will be defeated. Those who are diametrically opposed to everything America stands for, who want
to remake America, who now sit in the seat of power
over this nation have never been this close to taking
over. In February, 2008, Michelle Obama was speaking
in Milwaukee, Wisconsin. She stated:

> *"...for the first time in my adult life I am proud
> of my country because it feels like hope is finally
> making a comeback."* [73]

What do the Obama's believe America is, to say
such a thing? The Obama Idea is what is manifesting.
This is their biggest opportunity, their one and only
shot to take over the United States. This is one of the
biggest bucks evil has ever had in its crosshairs to destroy the United States, and this is the shot they don't
want to miss. War starts with a single shot and they

fired it; first against the Catholic Church. They pre-
planned to seize control over religious liberty and conscientious objection. They must win now or they know
they will be defeated. They—know—this.

The question is not do *they* know it, but rather do
you know it. They are strategizing that you do not.
This is their moment. They have gotten too close to
totalitarianism to let an honest election remove the
evil, the pride that rules. Do you think Catholics paying for abortion, sterilization and contraception, the
reversal of the Defense of Marriage Act, the reversal
of "Don't ask, don't tell" to destroy the cohesiveness
of the military, among many, many more other things
that Obama has initiated of murderous immorality, that
these atrocities would be subjugated in seriousness, as
a lesser offense to voter fraud or to whatever can be
done to keep in power? He is killing babies, holding to
the most extreme positions that if a baby is born alive
after a botched abortion, that baby should be left to die
without any assistance to help keep it alive. His views
on this is just as notorious as any tyrant. One may object that the statement, "He is killing babies" is going a
little too far. After all, he is not actually doing the act.
But it is he who is mandating and promoting the right
to abort. Did Hitler not do the same thing? After all,

others were running the gas chambers, Hitler was only indirectly involved. Is Obama only indirectly involved? Reason it out. If one can, with a cold heart, be for killing a baby, and then forcibly mandate that Catholics must pay for it when it goes against their most fundamental beliefs, is it possible to have a troubled conscience in committing a much lesser offense of doing whatever is necessary to rally up a false vote count to hold onto the office? In Jesus' time, a scene played out that Luke writes about in his Gospel where crowds of people listening to Jesus were so thick that they had to lower a paralyzed man through the roof to be in Jesus' midst. Jesus said to the man, ***"Your sins are forgiven,"*** and the teachers of the law who were listening to Jesus who were filled with bad will began to reason in their hearts that He was a blasphemer because who but God can forgive sins? Jesus **'knew'** their hearts. The situation being tense, Jesus posed a question for them to think about. Jesus asked, ***"Which is easier to say, your sins are forgiven or say to this paralyzed man, rise and walk?"*** We do not know how long Jesus let them ponder in silence the question, but in those moments, you most likely could have heard a 'pin drop'. Jesus then did the more difficult of the two things he did that day, saying ***"rise, pick up your mat, and go home,"*** and the man did.

Ask yourself the question, which is harder to overcome in violating one's conscience as Obama is doing: (1) to publicly mandate that Christians are to
be forced to make payments of 'murder for hire' for
someone to perform abortions, OR (2) to get elected
by any means? Which of the two crimes is the lesser?
Again, is it to force others to pay for abortions against
their will or to, by any means, get others to get votes
or arrange for votes that will assure your re-election
by whatever means? And if you are willing to do the
more heinous, it is much easier on the conscience to
commit the lesser. It is easy to see which of the two is
far lesser of an offense. If one can arrogantly deny the
guaranteed rights of Americans that are clearly drawn
out in the Constitution by forcing them to pay for
murder of which their faith teaches is a sin that can
lead a soul to damnation, why would one think, come
election time, that integrity and moral character will
suddenly come into play? Which was the easier thing
for Jesus to say and do? "Take your mat and walk" or,
"your sins are forgiven?" Which is the easier thing for
Obama's conscience to do? Murder babies or voter
fraud? Jesus proved who He was. And as Jesus proved
who He is, and what He is capable of, Obama proves
who he is, and what he is capable of.

Are these moves beneath the principles and the character of Obama and those who placed him in power? He mandated with cold callousness: You...will... pay...for other's abortions... You...will...pay...for... other's contraceptives...and therefore, you...will... support...many...illicit relationships. Do we want to deny this is tyrannical? We know clearly what our founding fathers would say today about this invalid law by what Thomas Jefferson said 226 years ago:

> *"To compel a man to furnish contributions of money for the propagation of opinions which he disbelieves and abhors, is sinful and tyrannical."*[74]

After we are forced to pay for other's sins, etc., there is nothing that will stop tyrannical evil from going to the next atrocity. Evil has no integrity and has no scruples. Evil defines its own values—that making free abortions, contraceptives, etc., available to all is not only a good, but is a "right" that the government is responsible for protecting—a "dreamed-up right." It will become obvious when we arrive at the point when Americans everywhere will be ready to invoke the truths of the Declaration of Independence.

CHAPTER SIXTEEN

Action

Is this thinking out of bounds? Are these questions unethical to even be asked? From numerous multi-million dollar vacations at the tax payers expense to mafia tactics to force healthcare passage, and a hundred in betweens, there is nothing ethical in Obama or his administration. If Obama has, through an invalid law, doled out mandates that assault the liberties and freedoms of all members of the Catholic Church and all Christian faiths, then we are forced into being, by no choice of our own, his opponent in this battle. *"Enemies in War, in Peace, Friends."* We are in war. To win, questions need to be asked and answers need to be found to "know better your enemy and his plans" if you want to win not only this battle, but the war, for peace to ensue.

To answer these questions about your enemy, let's step back and look at just four of many actions Obama has taken as president to understand what those who assault our religious liberty are thinking about.

- Obama has not only helped propagate abortion, but even as a United States Senator was the most far left liberal in place, desiring absolutely no restrictions upon abortions and their providers. He repealed the Mexico funding ban for abortion in Mexico and Latin America through the signing of an executive order on January 23, 2009. [75]

- Obama is aggressively doing everything he can to repeal the **Defense Of Marriage Act**, known as **D.O.M.A.**, which was made law to protect the most important institution in existence, the family, despite the fact that the vast majority of Americans believe it is necessary to protect marriage and family, which is based in Biblical truth. [76]

- Obama repealed the "Don't ask, don't tell," policy (don't tell us you are abominable, and we won't ask), within all the military branches of the United States, despite overwhelming factual evidence as well as common sense that this action would severely damage the cohesiveness of the military. Obviously cohesiveness is crucial for the military to operate. Without it, we will become second rate, and defense of the United States National Security will be greatly compromised. This will destroy our military, just as did the judgment against Sodom. [77]

- Obama rammed through, using every devious trick possible, to pass the healthcare legislation. There are many terrible aspects of this invalid law, including the violation of conscience, forcing Catholics and Catholic institutions, along with other Christians, to pay for abortion, contraceptives, and people's sterilizations. All of this has set the stage for the assault on liberty, with the loss of all other liberties following suit.

- It is not an exaggeration to say that Obama is devious. He and the 'powers that be' worked behind the scenes with no moral bounds, with mafia tactics, to get the healthcare legislation achieved. Just to give one example, a November 22, 2009 Washington Post article titled, "Sweeteners for the South," reported that Louisiana Senator Mary Landrieu was wavering on whether to vote for or against the healthcare bill, seemingly fishing for concessions. The 'powers that be' re-wrote the bill to give Landrieu at least $100 million. A section of the bill was added just for that, with a loophole that would allow only Louisiana these funds. In the November 19, 2009 article titled, "The $100 Million Vote," ABC news writers Karl, Khan and Wolf stated, "the bill spends two pages describing what could be written with a single

word: Louisiana." Landrieu's state of Louisiana
is full of Catholics, yet she supported the bill. Her
vote was outright purchased. Would it be unjust to
call that devious? You may decide.

These four major points tell us who Obama is, but
there are many more which help to illustrate clearly
the ideals, thoughts and plans of this man who holds
the most powerful secular position in the world. Just
recently we have Obama selling out the National Security of the United States and Europe to the Russians.
Our defense with missiles in Europe is vital to United
States security. Our defense missiles will stop dead a
missile attack on the United States by Russia. Russia
has never liked the European 'defense' missiles and has
done everything to get them removed. And, Obama
seems bent on dismantling the United States Defense
System. Without Obama's knowledge, he was caught
on a microphone telling Russian president Dmitry
Medvedev on March 26, 2012, to pass a message on
to the incoming Russian president Vladimir Putin.
Obama's message to Putin through Medvedev 'Quote':

> *"On all these issues, but particularly missile de-*
> *fense, they can be solved, but it's important for*
> *him to give me space…This is my last election.*
> *After my election I have more flexibility."* [78]

Obama, knowing that the "flexibility" he would give the Russians would harm his re-election, as it would be seen as undermining United States Security, asked for patience. He shows no qualms in this exchange of damaging the United States of America's security.

For a sitting president to tell the Russian president to wait until after the elections to give up missile defense in Europe that could protect against a Russian attack is an unconscionable, impeachable offense. This, a few years ago, would have been easy grounds for treason and should be today. This is more serious than American spies giving away secrets of the military to Russia. What it tells us is that Obama's plans are to wholly, radically, and fundamentally not just change and transform the United States of America, but weaken our influence and might to clear the path for internationalism to be the influence and might that rules the world. This has been the goal of the United Nations for decades and they have aggressively struggled to accomplish it. Totalitarianism can then take hold of the whole world. Before internationalization of the world can happen, Christianity must be diminished to nothingness. This would be the breakthrough in the wall that would give the 'powers that be' the ability to move forward unrestrained and destroy America's might

for an anti-christ system to fully reign. The following
are other evidences of Obama's war against Christianity. These are only some of the items we know about.
Do not be tempted to skip some of them as reading
the list in completeness is a study of understanding
the mindset of who is battling against you. Know
what your enemy is thinking. Jesus proved who he is.
Obama proves who he is.

**Obama Administration's Attacks Aimed at People of
Biblical Faith**

> **April 2008** — With disdain for Christians, Obama
> says they *"cling to guns or religion or antipathy
> to people who aren't like them."* [79]
>
> **February 2009** — Obama announces he plans to
> revoke a rule put in place by the Bush admin-
> istration that would protect healthcare workers
> who will not participate in medical activities
> that violate their consciences. [80]
>
> **April 2009** — When speaking at Georgetown
> University, Obama orders that a monogram
> symbolizing Jesus' name be covered when he
> is making his speech. [81] A Georgetown Uni-
> versity official in defense of Obama stated the
> administration wanted a simple presidential

backdrop, and the symbol of Christ "IHS" and cross was not deemed appropriate to be in the background, even though he was speaking at a Catholic University. Our Lady said:

December 25, 2005

"...decide for Jesus..."

To cover up Jesus for whatever reason except for reverential intentions is to decide against Jesus. That goes for Georgetown University officials and Obama as well.

April 2009 — As a "calculated insult to the Holy See," Obama nominates three pro-abortion ambassadors to the Vatican. The Vatican, not surprisingly, rejected all three ambassadors. [87] Be thoughtful about the action to understand the mindset and where this group is going with their plans and agendas.

May 2009 — Breaking with years of tradition from the Bush Administration, Obama refuses to host an official service in the White House for the federally established National day of Prayer. The National Day of Prayer was first established in 1952 by President Harry Truman, and every president since Ronald Reagan has participated in it. Obama is the first president to refuse participation.[83]

October 18, 2010—Though passed off as a "mistake" by the White House press, when quoting the Declaration of Independence, Obama intentionally excludes the phrase "the Creator." This is revisionism in the war related to verbicide. Obama revised the Declaration of Independence:

> *"We hold these truths to be self-evident, that all men are created equal, that **each of us** are endowed with certain unalienable rights…"* [84]

The Declaration of Independence states:

> *"We hold these truths to be self-evident, that all men are created equal, that they are endowed by **their Creator** with certain unalienable rights…"*

Obama has intentionally excluded **the Creator**, rephrasing it with **each of us** in several public speeches and presidential proclamations, counting at least seven times, all of which fits in line,

that unalienable rights come from the government, not the Creator and, therefore, can be
taken away by the government.

November 2010—Obama uses revisionism with
the National Motto, saying it is "E pluribus
Unum," which means "Out of many, one," rather
than "In God We trust" **as established by federal
law.** [85] Who is breaking the law?

January 2011—Clearly in a move to reject the
cross, the Obama administration ignores a law
passed by Congress and a U.S. Supreme Court
decision in refusing to cede a piece of land to
the Veterans of Foreign Wars organization,
thereby preventing the veterans from rebuilding a cross that was originally erected there in
1934 in memory of fallen soldiers. [86] Obama has
repeatedly ignored Congress, and courts are the
next branch to make insignificant. Who is im-
peding the law?

February 2011—After more than two years of
neglecting to fill the post of the Religious Freedom Ambassador, who works to address religious freedom issues around the world, and only
after receiving heavy criticism from religious

leaders and politicians did Obama fill the post in February 2011. [87]

February 2011—Obama fulfills his intention announced in February 2009 by changing a Bush administration rule that protected conscientious objection for medical activities that violate religious beliefs. [88]

April 2011—Obama openly supports passage of a non-discrimination law that would remove most all conscience protections in hiring in both the public and private work force. This is most obviously damaging to religious organizations whose hiring frequently includes selection of individuals whose lives are consistent with Christian principles and teachings. [89]

August 2011—The Obama administration promulgates new healthcare regulations, in particular relating to abortion and contraception, that clearly violate our God-given and Constitutionally protected right to conscientious objection to practices that violate the tenets of Christianity.[90]

November 2011—Obama objects to adding President Franklin Roosevelt's prominent D-Day prayer to the World War II Memorial.[91]

December 2011—In a public release from the
Secretary of State's website, the Obama administration stated that people's deeply held
religious beliefs in the United States and around
the world **are "obstacles standing in the way**
of protecting the human rights of" those living
abominable lifestyles. The administration's desire is to introduce radical abominable "rights"
into all countries and cultures through legislation. [92]

January 2012—The Obama administration con-
tends that churches and synagogues receive no
protection under the First Amendment to dis-
criminate against those living contrary to Judeo-
Christian Biblical principles when hiring pastors
and rabbis. [93]

February 2012—The Obama administration announces a change to the existing student loan
forgiveness program whereby student loans are
forgiven in exchange for public service. Under
this administration's new rule, student loans will
no longer be forgiven in exchange for public service if that public service is related to religion.[94]

Obama-led Military Attacks Aimed at People of Biblical faith:

> **June 2011** — The Department of Veterans Affairs censors prayers during funeral services at Houston National Cemetery by banning the names "God" and "Jesus". [95]
>
> **August 2011** — The United States Air Force cancelled a nuclear missile training course at a base in California taught for more than 20 years by military chaplains because the course included Christian religious content such as the Just War theory of St. Augustine and other Biblical passages and principles. The Just War theory has been taught for centuries in civilized nations around the world and is part of the ethos of the U.S. military taught to all incoming soldiers until now.[96]
>
> **September 2011** — Air Force Chief of Staff issues memorandum titled "Maintaining Government Neutrality Regarding Religion," in which he states commanders cannot notify airmen of religious programs provided by chaplains. [97]
>
> **September 2011** — The Commander of the Walter Reed National Military Medical Center

issued guidelines stating, "No religious items
(i.e. Bibles, reading material, and/or artifacts)
are allowed to be given away or used during a
visit." Congressional Representative Steve King
denounced the guidelines on the House floor, in
union with several other Congressmen, and the
guidelines were rescinded the next day. [98]

November 2011—In response to a complaint
that Operation Christmas Child is run by a
Christian organization and gifts handed out
through the program contain religious messages,
the Air Force issued an apology for promoting
it and withdrew its support of the program that
sends Christmas gifts to children in 100 different
countries.[99]

November 2011—In an opposite way, the Christian religion is being stopped. The Air Force
Academy in Colorado Springs, Colorado, spent
$80,000 to construct a "small Stonehenge-like
circle of boulders" as an outdoor worship center
for "earth-based" religions - pagans, wiccans,
druids, and witches. [100]

February 2012—Retired Three-Star Army General and outspoken Christian, Lieutenant Gen-

eral William G. "Jeffy" Boykin, withdraws from
his speaking engagement at the West Point Military Academy after the Academy received intense pressure to disinvite this highly decorated
war hero because of his public and unabashed
presentation of his Christian views. [101]

February 2012—The Air Force removes the
Latin phrase "Opus Dei," which means "Work
of God," from the patch of the Rapid Capabilities Office. [102]

February 2012—The Army orders Catholic
chaplains not to read a letter at Catholic masses
that their Archbishop instructed them to read
from the pulpit. [103]

Words alone do not speak in completeness, for another
word with two syllables must be added. The word is
"action." Obama is implementing, with "action," what
he said he would do.

CHAPTER SEVENTEEN

What the Federal Government must do for You, it is not Supposed to do

As the preceding chapter shows Obama's mindset, it also tells us the why behind his actions. We need to understand Obama and those in league with him in order to learn how they are strategizing so that we can better predict where he is leading this nation. Knowing more about what is behind Obama's intentions is essential for discerning our own strategic actions. You need to know what does he truly think of your liberties and especially, specifically, about your Christian faith. If you knew what his views are concerning your unalienable right to liberty, you could then better know why he, without hesitation or scruples, thinks nothing of taking them away from you. Obama is radical in his thinking and we need to know this to know our enemy. His radicalism is showing up more and more in his actions. He thinks the founding fathers' constraints in protecting the liberties we enjoy, constraints that they placed in the Constitution, must be broken away from. In particular, he wants to break away from the idea in the Constitution that citizens have the right to be protected *from* the government, and that the State's overreaching into their affairs should no longer apply. Obama believes what the Federal and State government cannot do to you, according to the Constitution, like take away your liberty, are "negative" rights and that courts now need to radically overturn the restraints of these founding government principles that our nation was birthed upon in favor of what Federal and State government "must do on your behalf," termed positive rights by leftist radicals. As you read the astounding quote from Obama from which you will also draw these same conclusions, be thoughtful of every word. Ask yourself why is he thinking this way? What is it in his thought process that makes him state something so un-American? You will then know your enemy better and why healthcare legislation is not about healthcare, but a part of a larger scheme that Obama is planning to rearrange the foundation of the United States of America. Read carefully.

Obama stated:

> *"...but the Supreme Court never ventured into the issues of redistribution of wealth and a sort of more basic issues of political and economic justice in this society. And to that extent as radical as I think people tried to characterize the Warren Court, it wasn't that radical. It didn't break free*

from the essential constraints that were placed by the founding fathers in the Constitution, at least as it's been interpreted, and the Warren Court interpreted it in the same way that generally the Constitution is a charter of negative liberties. It says what the states can't do to you, it says what the Federal Government can't do to you, but it doesn't say what the Federal Government or the State Government must do on your behalf..." [104]

Obama was not discussing whether the redistribution of wealth is right or wrong. Rather, he was discussing how to achieve this goal. These words of Obama give greater understanding of not only knowing your enemy, but also understanding his plans, agendas, strategies and his ultimate goal to radically change America by breaking away from the very foundation it was formed upon.

Jesus Christ's redistribution of wealth called upon the hearts of believers to care for their brothers in need and is called charity. Charity is to be a virtue of the heart, to use what blessings God has shared with you, and share these blessings with others in need. But you, as a believer, are charged with this virtue. Obama sees this as a negative, believing it is not you, the believer or the body of believers in league with or through the Church that should do this for your brother, but rather Big Brother, government, is to take the wealth of everyone and redistribute it. Christ saw it as the believer's responsibility. Obama sees it as the government's responsibility. This is a problem for enemies of Christ because our charity is given in Christ's name to not only meet the needs of the poor, but to spread and evangelize God's Kingdom through our witness and charity. Darkness, therefore, erases Christ right out of the equation by means of the government taking the money from citizens with the ruse of giving to those in need. The healthcare provided by the Catholic Church that has grown to cover 25% of all healthcare needs in the United States, was established because of Christ. With the healthcare take-over the government grows, and the political machine and bureaucracies driving it grows, and with it greater corruption and secular humanism grows and suddenly man has no need for Christ as government becomes god. These preceding thoughts, in the spiritual realm, are the goals of darkness. Obama's idea of redistribution of wealth is not economic justice, rather it is "coveting thy neighbor's goods." The government has no right to take away your right to choose how, when, and what you should spend your hard earned money on. Nor is it in its jurisdiction to decide that you aren't being charitable enough. That is the individual's right of liberty alone.

If that liberty is taken away from you and the government takes from your pocket to give to others, taking a big chunk of what you earn, when it passes through government hands—it is not charity; it is socialism. These are the steps the Stalins, Lenins and Hitlers rose to power on. What happens to all the Church under tyranny? When wealth is taken by the government to be redistributed, who gets it? In the end, when government achieves its agenda—using the masses who are in need, of which many are those who put forth no effort toward meeting their own needs as they are solely dependent on the government's provisions—no needs will be met adequately through Obama's redistribution. As stated, what Christ taught concerning charity, when a church talks about redistributing wealth, it is called charity and is freely and peaceably given, begetting virtue. When government talks about redistribution of wealth, it is called socialism and is forcibly and unpeaceably taken, begetting vice. Christianity teaches love and virtue to the poor and the rich.

> *"The poor must not envy the rich and the rich must not cause hatred through display of wealth and hardness of heart."* [105]

This is fundamental to understanding Obama's philosophy that is leading to class warfare. He and the 'powers that be' are creating tensions between people that will eventually erupt in our society in some type of event as what happened in Rwanda. Beware when you hear the words, "you are owed something," "you are a victim," or words such as what Obama stated above, "... *what the Federal government or the state government 'must' do on your behalf...*" [106] This is only a ruse to take power. It is easy to discern the intentions of evil. Since we stated earlier that the Constitution does not give us any rights, but rather affirms unalienable rights which find their foundation in God's law, any effort to usurp or overthrow the Constitution is an effort to overthrow and usurp God's law; a telling sign that these plans are from darkness. What can the government do on your behalf that you cannot do better? Whether it be you and your doctor, you and your construction project, you and your buying products of your choice, or you judging and choosing who are the ones most in need of your help. You do not need the government to be a middleman between you and your doctor. Do you want your doctor to have to go from you to the government in his decisions on how or what treatment you can receive? This is what the healthcare bill will do. This intrusion of government will grow and reach into every aspect of society and will foster the culture of death to avenues unknown to us at this time. Government can never do better for an individual than what the individual himself can do. The individual is the better administrator of his own affairs, his needs and the distribution of what he has to help others. This is why the Catholic Church and its institutions, the most extensive private healthcare delivery system in the nation, has hospital expenses of over $100 billion for all those they serve, taking a leading role in providing services to patients, many times without profit, for those who do not have insurance or the means to pay.[107] Here in the deep South, in the early 1900s, in Birmingham, Alabama, which at that time was far from being a Catholic "welcoming" center, nuns were sought out by Birmingham political office holders to come and establish a hospital. They knew well they could not do what the church'ed' could do. The churches, Christian hospitals and charities, etc., rose up to meet a need that could be met better and more efficiently through the living out of Christian principles than any government entity ever could. Do not be deceived. Know thy enemies and you will know their plans. Government passed healthcare legislation because it is part of their plan for control to, thereby, gain more authority for agendas that will become clearer as you read on.

During his inaugural address, Ronald Reagan said:

> "...government is not the solution to our problems; government is the problem..."[108]

With pure and honest hearts, we must examine our consciences. Is darkness taking over what we spiritually vacated? Catholic healthcare, as well as healthcare offered by other Christian denominations, have allowed a great deal of secularization into their facilities. So, is what is happening a judgment against us? It is a just question to ask. A little spiritual emptiness allows darkness to fill it. Our Lady says:

September 5, 1988

> **"...satan desires you and is looking for you! A little spiritual emptiness in you is enough for satan to work in you..."**

The first question we must ask is why have we fallen under oppression and are losing our liberty? It is because of our sins. Just as Israel's sins led to the Assyrians rising up and oppressing them because of their failure to keep God's statutes, we are urgently in need of "the one tear of repentance" that will return us to God's favor and the grace to receive His mercy. In other words, we must be in prayer enough to see that the calamity upon us is one that we have brought upon ourselves. Therefore, we must pray, repent, and seek God's grace, before we can be restored.

CHAPTER EIGHTEEN

Forward

Are you asking yourself where is all this leading? What is the big picture? Before Obama became President of the United States, his campaign organizers published what was entitled, *"The Blueprint for Change: Barack Obama's Plan for America."* Obama wrote in the opening paragraph:

> *"I believe it's critically important that those of us who want to lead this nation be* <u>*open, candid, and clear*</u> *with the American people about how we will move* **forward***."* [109]

In his victory speech after winning the presidential race, he said:

> *"I will always be honest with you about the challenges we face."* [110]

What do you think of those statements? Do you feel Obama and his administration have been open, candid and clear in expressing their objectives? He promised to be honest with the American people.

Do you feel he has met that promise? Over the past
months of researching and studying the speeches, policies, activities and actions of Obama, it can be deduced
that he has been true to his words. He is doing exactly
what he promised he would do, all the way down the
line. What was discovered, however, is that Obama
and most Americans are speaking two different lan-
guages, though using the same words. For instance,
when Obama uses the words "service," "responsibility,"
"citizens," "forward," "transformation," "middle class,"
"volunteerism," "democracy"—what many Americans
believe he is speaking about is not, in truth, what he is
saying. Yet, by *his* definitions of the above words or
terms, he *is* speaking the truth of what he intends.

   In an essay by a French lawyer, Jean-Hugho
Lapointe, the case is made that socialism has become
more and more accepted, even among nations based in
the free market, through the corruption of words and
language. For instance, most everyone knows that the
term "redistribution of wealth" is socialist terminology
and carries a negative connotation with those who believe in the capitalist system. The challenge becomes,
for socialists who want to move **forward** their ideas
and policies, to find a more accepted way of saying the
same thing, avoiding terminology that would be out-

right rejected because of knowing the meaning behind it. Lapointe says:

> *"Leftists realized early that liberty may be the only value shared by each and every human being, and that it may be their dearest. Leftist philosophers were at the same time well aware that their ideas, which all involve the coercive power of the state, were not reconcilable with political freedom and that for both to exist, the latter needs to be reduced for the benefit of the former. Some leftists and socialists thus simply began to use the word freedom as if it was compatible with leftist policies, while some others put **forward** a new concept of economic freedom."*

> *"To allay these suspicions and to harness to its cart the strongest of all political motives—the craving for freedom—socialism began increasingly to make use of the promise of a 'new freedom.'...The demand for the new freedom was thus only another name for the old demand for an equal distribution of wealth."* [111]

Lapointe pointed to the word "social" and said that no other word has been used as often in political debates for whatever purpose is being debated on either side

so that now the word has been rendered meaningless.
Lapointe further states:

> *"I would suggest that a word that can be used to
> any purpose and in any context has no meaning
> by itself, just like water can be used in so many
> recipes because it is tasteless."*

> *"The most reprehensible and damaging use of
> the word 'social' is in the now universally ac-
> cepted phrase* **'social justice.'** *By corrupting the
> word 'justice' with their deceptive language, left-
> ists have managed to use this noble word in their
> call for wealth redistribution…* **'social justice** *is
> nothing more than the language fraud that leftists
> have invented to avoid using 'wealth redistribu-
> tion.'"*

> *"I firmly believe that political abuses of lan-
> guage…have contributed much to help socialist
> policies gain much more popularity than they
> deserve. By hiding themselves under the cover of
> the very principles and values which they actu-
> ally intend to fight against, they are allowed to
> constantly deceive unwary citizens towards and
> convince them of the worth of their attractive but
> erroneous solutions."* [112]

This **verbicide** abuse of language becomes more and more apparent the more exposure you have to what is actually being said by Obama and his administration. Just one example of how words are being redefined in Obama's rhetoric follows, but it is enough to help you realize the deception that is being perpetrated in plain sight, in full view while he speaks "his" truth.

On the eve of May 1, 2012, Barack Obama announced his new campaign motto for the 2012 election season. It is a simple motto, a single word: **"Forward."** It was an interesting day that he chose to announce it, on April 30, because May 1, also called May Day, is well known as a day associated with displaying communist arrogance. Also interesting, is that **"Forward"** was a theme song of Hitler's Youth. **"Forward"** has also been used as a magazine title by Marxists. Lenin had a publication called "Vpered" or **"Forward."** China's Mao gave a motto to his economic plan calling it, "Great Leap **Forward**." You could say that the word **"Forward"** has become a generic name for socialist publications. It is defined in a political sense as follows:

> *"The name **Forward** carries a special meaning in socialist political terminology. It has been frequently used as a name for socialist, communist*

*and other left-wing newspapers and publica-
tions.*"[113]

What is the meaning behind the word? Those who
believe in Marxist philosophies think it's just a matter
of time before nations will leave capitalism behind to
embrace socialism and communism. For them it is "the
march of history," moving "**forward**" towards what they
see as an inevitable event. To know this history, it was
a startling revelation when Obama released a 7-minute
campaign video stating his intentions to be re-elected
President in November. They chose a one-word title
for the video, **"Forward,"** and it was first aired on the
eve of "the" major communist "nationalist" day. With
this knowledge, researching through some of Obama's
speeches during his first campaign for presidency and
as president, patterns began emerging. What was
discovered was much more than what would be expected to be found. Of course, forward is a word we
all use. However, "**forward**" has been in the thoughts
of Obama from the beginning, and a running theme
throughout all his discourses when speaking about the
direction he is moving the United States of America.

"The Blueprint For Change," as already mentioned,
was published in 2008 to inform the public what
Obama's objectives would be if he became president.

The subtitle states, **"Barack Obama's Plan for America."** Re-reading the opening lines in the opening paragraph, Obama states:

> *"Thank you for taking a look at this booklet. I believe it's critically important that those of us who want to lead this nation be open, candid, and clear with the American people about how <u>we will move **forward**</u>..."* [114]

On February 5, 2008, after winning the Democratic nomination to run for the presidency, **"forward"** is used again in his speech. Read with special attention the whole statement and especially the whole paragraph context that surrounds the word "forward" to get its fuller meaning. The following is not just political rhetoric:

> *"...there is one thing on this February night that we do not need the final results to know.* **Our time has come. Our time has come.** *Our movement is real. And* **change is coming to America...** *This time must be different. This time we have to turn the page. This time we have to write a new chapter in American history. This time we have to seize the moment...We owe the American people a real choice. We have to choose between*

change and more of the same. We have to choose
between looking backwards and looking for-
ward. We have to choose between our future and
our past."[115]

A very disconcerting statement, and Obama has been
true to his vision in what he has done in his first term of
presidency. Obama says, **"We have to choose"** between
looking backwards or looking forward. In other words,
"choose" between our future or our past. Pope John
Paul II said if you want to renew your religious orders,
go back to the founders and what they began. If these
religious orders grew and flourished from the founding
principles, they can be renewed by returning back to
their roots to grow and flourish anew. This principle of
returning to the founder's principles works for nations
as well. What, therefore, is Obama saying that we must
choose between? Looking back to our nation's foundation, the Declaration, our founding fathers and the
Constitution—or looking **"forward"** to Marxism? Socialism? Communism? Or worse? In fact, in this same
speech, Obama spoke cynically about those who were
looking to the past.

"The Republicans running for president have al-
ready tied themselves to the past. Those Republi-
cans are running on the politics of yesterday. And

that is why our party must be the party of tomor-
row. And that is the party that I intend to lead as
president of the United States of America." [116]

Ironically, it was Obama himself and his election to
the presidency that sparked and started a whole spontaneous movement of Americans looking "back" not
"forward," to the United States' foundational documents. Americans began seeing Obama's forward
direction and decided not to go forward with Obama,
rather many Americans began turning back to the
only direction they know that can 're'birth our nation.
As John Paul II said, to be renewed, "go back to your
founder(s)"; in that way Americans are turning back
to what first sparked the nation's birth. They turned
'backwards' to the words and philosophies of our
founding fathers of which, to Obama's credit, helped
give birth to the movement named from the past: The
Tea Party. Despite Obama's promise to be the president for everyone and that he would listen to everyone,
he showed only contempt and disdain for the Tea Party
movement in his determination to move the United
States "**forward**."

On January 12, 2009, before Obama officially took
the seat of authority in Washington, a new television
advertisement was run to initiate his directives in en-

couraging all Americans to make a year-round commitment to "community service." The name of the public-
service announcement was **"<u>Step Forward</u>."** Former
Secretary of State, Colin Powell, commenting on this
initiative said,

> *"What we really need are Americans to come **<u>for-
> ward</u>** ..."* [117]

Within days of this statement, Powell again used this
same verbiage in another interview:

> *"People are losing their jobs. Let's come **<u>forward</u>**
> to serve our fellow citizens and to serve our na-
> tion."* [118]

It's almost as if **"forward"** is a watchword, informing those around the world who know its clear but hidden meaning that their plans are on the move. From
Obama's January 21, 2009 Inaugural Address come the
following statements:

> *"...But in the words of Scripture, the time has
> come to set aside childish things. The time has
> come to reaffirm our enduring spirit; to choose
> our better history; to <u>carry</u> **<u>forward</u>** that precious
> gift, that noble idea passed on from generation to
> generation..."* [119]

*"The question we ask today is not whether our government is too big or too small, but whether it works…Where the answer is yes, <u>we intend to move **forward**</u>…"* [120]

*"To the Muslim world, <u>we seek a new way **forward**</u>, based on mutual interest and mutual respect…"* [121]

On March 27, 2009, speaking of his new policy for Afghanistan and Pakistan, Obama stated:

*"Going **forward**, we will not blindly stay the course…"* [122]

On the night of December 31, 2011, Obama stealthily signed the "National Defense Authorization Act," N.D.A.A., which gives unprecedented power to the office of the President to take away the rights of American citizens. The time it was signed, "New Years Eve," speaks volumes as to Obama's devious intentions of moving **forward** in transforming America. The watchword surfaces again, as Obama said:

*"<u>Moving **forward**</u>, my Administration will interpret and implement the provisions described below in a manner that best preserves the flexibility on which our safety depends…."* [123]

"Safety depends?" Americans have fallen head long into a mentality of "keep me safe at all cost, even take my liberty, just keep me safe." A man who believes it is not worthy to die for liberty will be worthy only for chains and shackles. Because of the serious implications of the National Defense Authorization Act, it will be discussed at greater length further in the book.

Strangely, just five days later on January 5, 2012, Obama undermines his own stance concerning the "flexibility for our safety" by announcing major cuts to the military budget. Yet, Obama confidently states we will be "moving forward from a position of strength:"

> *"But the question that this strategy answers is what **'kind of military'** will we need after the long wars of the last decade are over. And today, <u>we're moving **forward**</u> from a position of strength."* [124]

On the very same day of announcing strategy for "what kind of military we will need," January 5, 2012, Obama's administration announced a new government program. This program, titled *Opportunity Youth,* targets low-income, disconnected and unemployed youth and was put into effect by yet another danger to liberty—an executive action without Congress' consent. In the following chapters you will learn the significance and the connection of these two announcements made on the same day. Again, **"forward"** found its way into the script when the new program, *Opportunity Youth,* was announced. The White House spokesman stated:

> *"Today's announcement is the latest in a series of executive actions the Obama Administration is taking to strengthen the economy and move the country forward because we can't wait for Congress to act."* [125]

"Can't wait for Congress" is a slogan Obama's administration is using more and more with the desired effect to get the idea accepted among the general populace that it's okay to bypass Congress. This reflects Obama's mentality to use executive orders to unconstitutionally go around and bypass a branch of government that was created to keep in check the Executive office from taking exactly the steps Obama is taking now as president. Normally, done with more stealth, Obama is becoming more bold in simply disregarding Congress. At the same time, through these "series of executive orders" among others already passed, he is amassing for himself total control and total power to "interpret" and "implement" all that "moving forward" involves.

On July 2, 2008, just a few months after winning the Democratic nomination for President, comes this disturbing statement, when Obama sends out a call to all Americans that every American will be asked to serve their country. Keep in mind that the socialist idea of "**Forward**" is the "march of history." Remember as you read Obama's following statement that he said he would always tell us the truth:

> "...*We need your service, right now, at this moment—**our moment**—in history. I'm not going to tell you what your role should be; **that's for you to 'discover.'** But I am going to ask you to play your part; ask you to stand up; ask you to **put your foot firmly into the current of history**. I am asking you to **change history's course...**"* [126]

When Obama says, **"that's for you to discover,"** this should be understood that it is part of the strategy to make you believe it's your choice, all the while, the path to discovery is laid out purposely to lead you to "discover" what the plan is in your regard.

With the template of the communist/socialist definition of "Forward" laid over Obama's remarks, what is he really saying here? *"Change history's course..."*— away from the Constitution, away from a free society, and away from the history that has made this country great? Now, take a look at what Obama said just after making the statement above:

"...And if I have the fortune to be your President, decades from now—when the memory of this or that policy has faded, and when the words that we will speak in the next few years are long forgotten—I hope you remember this as a moment when your own story and the American story came together..." [127]

Obama often uses the phrase, *"when your own story and the American story came together."* [128] What does it mean? Isn't "your own story" already a part of the American story? It's a puzzling statement unless you think of it in terms of what socialists believe, which is that the individual's rights are secondary to the rights of the collective group, and that the American story won't be fully lived until America is brought into a socialist state. In that respect, what policies, specifically, may Obama be referring to as fading from our memory decades from now? Policies based on our Constitution that make this a free nation? The policies of the protection of liberty that guarantee protection of our God-given rights of life, liberty and the pursuit of happiness? Are these the "policies" Obama is referring to when he says, *"when the memory of this or that policy has faded, when the words we speak are long forgotten."* [129] Are we coming into a time when the founding documents of our nation will be only memories, a nice thought, a dream in the minds of Americans who are old enough to remember what freedom felt like?

Though not a direct quote from Obama, the following is one example of how the Obama administration is working to wipe from America's memory important events in our history as a patriotic nation. Through Obama's vehicle to change America "towards" a socialistic mindset, the Corporation for National and Community Service, in 2009, had Congress name September 11 the National Day of Service and Remembrance. Every American is asked to spend this day not in prayer and reflection, but rather in "service" in some way. From the government's website, Serve.gov, it is explained that the National Day of Service and Remembrance, on September 11 is a culmination of those:

> *"... who worked to establish the charitable service day as a **forward-looking** way to honor 9/11 victims, survivors, and others who rose up in service in response to attacks."* [130]

"The worker" is a Stalinist term. We're suppose to work to honor September 11? Become "the worker" is the way to honor 9/11? The charitable service day for 9/11 in lieu of prayer and reverence honoring the dead caused by the attacks? To exchange the traditional way of honoring the dead by becoming a service worker is a very stupid notion to accept. It is absurd. "Let's make a service day to honor an attack?" And notice the last words in the quote, *"response to attacks."* It doesn't give reference to the specific horrendous attacks on the World Trade Center and the Pentagon, but rather generically speaks of "attacks" as if there was nothing particularly defining about the attacks made on 9/11. Lastly, isn't it an odd choice of words to say, ***"forward-looking** way,"* to describe this new initiative?

When you think of September 11, do you think "charitable service day"? Is that what it will evolve to? What is the real agenda here? Using the **Communist/Socialist "forward"** template and placing it over these words and this initiative to make 9/11 a day of "service and remembrance" with the emphasis on "service" and not "remembrance," the idea is to get Americans to "think more" about service. In that way, they will "think less" about what caused such an outpouring of love amongst us and the love of country on that tragic day. America was attacked, and Americans were killed *because of who we are and what we stand for as a free nation.* Those thoughts, those remembrances build American pride and patriotism in the hearts of Americans and, therefore, greatly threaten the development of a socialist state and mentality. And so September 11 must be erased from our memories, and the most effective way to do this is to distract us from "remembering" by getting us busy serving; assign a different meaning to 9/11. Eventually, September 11 will come to be known only as the National Day of Service. And in fact, this is already happening. On the Philanthropy News Digest website, posted on June 24, 2009, it speaks of Obama's initiatives to encourage "volunteerism," and in particular mentions the 9/11 day of service. It states:

> *"Scheduled to run through September 11, which has been designated a <u>national day of service</u>, the initiative will target four key areas in which President Obama has said sustained volunteer work can have a continuing effect on communities: education, health, energy and the environment, and community renewal."* [131]*

---

* Energy and environment is promoted to such a degree as to deceive and consume our attention. This has bred an inordinate "attachment" **to the** earth itself. Our Lady said on May 25, 2012:
  "...but you, little children, are still far away (from God) — <u>attached</u> to <u>the earth</u> and to earthly things..."

In the above Philanthropy News Digest article, September 11 is a day designated only for "Service," as <u>Remembrance</u> is now omitted. Also omitted is an explanation as to why September 11 was designated for this Day of Service and Remembrance. The events and meaning behind 9/11 are already eroding, being replaced by the entire focus on volunteerism and service to make the god-State—not to the ideals of which our nation was founded and upon which it was attacked. This is just one example, but you will begin seeing this more and more. More revisionism in the making right before our eyes!

There is no doubt that serious inroads have been made in leading Americans away from the foundation laid by our Founding Fathers, our Constitution, and freedom. From decades of indoctrination in our schools, to communist-laced propaganda throughout today's movies, television, music, and the news media, to socialist government programs saturating all our "social" "services" and so many other agendas that are moving **"forward"**—a divide of what Americans believe America is all about, to what it has become,

---

Education, health, community renewal are also promoted to such a degree as to deceive and consume our attention. This has bred an inordinate "attachment to these **things** of the earth".

Of course, Obama's education, health, etc., are diversions to aid in his and the 'powers that be' implementation of an agenda.

has taken place. Looking at all the moves the Obama administration and the 'powers that be' are currently making, we would have our heads in the sand if we do not see that a great battle is looming before us. Communism aims to overthrow capitalist systems, usually by revolutionary means. It wants to destroy social classes as a protection to keep everyone equal and eliminate private property. Communism demands the loss of the person in favor of the state. Though Communism purports to desire a utopian society, the reality is that when everyone's property is confiscated, it is held in the hands of a communist elite, a tyrannical group, that has forced its way upon the backs of the people—making the government all powerful, and the people without any way to defend themselves from the 'powers that be.'

We began with the question, where are we headed? Although many in the United States are succumbing to the Pied Piper's socialist tune, a great many Americans are awakening to this danger, are educating themselves, are finally articulating what has made America great in the past, and they are fighting back. So with Obama and the 'powers' associated with the **"forward"** march of their own agenda, do you begin to see that there is a confrontation arising? Do you believe that the citizens of this nation will peacefully stand by while American society is dismantled? In his inaugural address Obama stated:

> *"To those leaders around the globe who...blame their society's ills on the West, know that your people will judge you on what you can build, not what you destroy."* [132]

Obama has often spoken about "rebuilding" America. But before you rebuild, you have to tear down. Do you think it is premature to question if we are soon going to be facing a takeover? What follows in the book reveals what plans Obama and the *'powers that be'* must implement because they do not believe Americans will willingly allow such radical societal changes. There are indicators that do more than suggest that there are plans underway to make sure their agenda continues to move **"Forward"** whether the American people accept the change or not. These plans, in their own words, reveal that they will do it through the people's resignation in allowing it, or by force. Plans are being made ready, with back up, for a bulldozer-type move **forward**, aiming to effect change that will fundamentally transform America. The lining up of three significant facts cannot be coincidental:

1. Obama chose for his motto, a single word, **"For-ward,"** for his 2012 Presidential bid.

2. **May Day, May 1**, is an officially declared Com-munist day, hailed to the "glories" of commu-nism, declared so in 1899 by the Communist World Congress. The worker is held up as the cause of honoring this day, a ruse in that the worker is actually enslaved by Communism. May Day is celebrated by communists around the world to honor Communism and its father, Karl Marx. In the former Soviet Union, it was accompanied by huge spectacular parades of military armaments and a show of strength, a strength that savagely murdered tens of millions of people. On this day they are recognizing publicly, and sometimes covertly, the humanist philosophy that they abide by: that man is all sufficient in providing for himself and for the needs of "humanity," discounting God's exis-tence and His Sovereignty. It is a rejection of God and the understanding that man works in cooperation with God and His laws over man, and has been condemned numerous times by the Church. President Barack Hussein Obama chose on the eve of May 1, this communist hon-

ored day, to announce his new Presidential campaign, the socialist motto, **"Forward."**

3. **"Forward"** is a code word for identifying Marxist
   and Communist publications and past dictators
   and tyrants—from Hitler to Communist China's
   Mao Zedong—have used the word "forward" for
   their own programs and in their own propaganda.

Why did Obama choose April 30 instead of May 1st,
for the release date of his motto? If you understand
your enemy, you will know that in no way this is a coincidence, rather it is a signal to all who are on the march
forward to usher in tyranny. Christmas Eve is what it
is. 'Eves' have significance. When Medjugorje visionary Marija was in Alabama for the Consecration of
the United States for the 4th of July, Our Lady on July
2, 2008 said in Her apparition that the next day, July
3, She would appear in the evening at 10:00 p.m. for
the 'vigil' of the 4th of July and in preparation for the
Consecration of the United States of America to Her
maternal care. Yes, the eve of events are important,
especially if you are moving forward to **"tomorrow,"** in
Obama's case the **next day**. Obama's announcement
on the eve of Communism's most decorated day, with
a motto that has Karl Marx's thumbprint all over it,
speaks clearly in knowing what your enemy is doing.

Special Note

This chapter title, "Forward," was finished at the point above. After the book had gone to press, on August 15, 2012, the following was added. This additional information that follows was not known when the above was written in June. What this displays is the principle of knowing your enemy. These principles applied can lead you to a deeper understanding of his motives. The following is very clear that the action written above in the "Forward" chapter concerning Obama's moves in releasing his re-election motto, was indeed for May Day, which is clearly proven in the following addition to this chapter.

The Publisher

During Obama's adolescent years, he became associated with a black man named Frank Marshall Davis in Hawaii. As Obama grew up in a home without a father, Davis became for him a father figure.[133] How influential was Davis in imprinting his own mindset and worldview upon Obama in these formative adolescent years? Obama mentioned "Frank" in his memoirs no less than 22 times,[134] but he comes up many more times that number through various forms of references. What Obama does not say in his memoirs is what Frank Marshall Davis was. What he was, is why Obama only refers to him discreetly, as "Frank," as to do otherwise would be too damaging for Obama. Yet Frank's impact on his life, his beliefs, and his principles was so strong, Obama could not keep himself from mentioning Frank, even though it was a risk to do so. Who was Frank? What was Frank to Barack Hussein Obama?

Frank Marshall Davis, unquestionably, was a hardcore Marxist communist. Frank Marshall Davis, unquestionably, was Obama's main mentor. Obama seems to be possessed by the spirit of Frank Marshall Davis, whose hatred for the United States was caustically vehement. F.B.I. records show that Frank was a member of the Communist Party USA (CPUSA),[135] therefore, he would have taken the following oath:

"I pledge myself to rally the masses to defend the Soviet Union, the land of victorious socialism. I pledge myself to remain at all times a vigilant and firm defender of the Leninist line of the party, the only line that insures the triumph of Soviet Power in the United States."[136]

Frank wanted the United States overthrown and changed to a Socialist state. He wanted the Soviet Union to triumph over the United States as he swore his allegiance to it, and worked to fulfill his oath. K.G.B. secret files of the Soviet Union that are now open, revealed that the United States Communist Party, from the year 1919, when it began, to 1989, when the Soviet Union collapsed*, was funded by and was under the control of the Soviets. F.B.I. files were also released on Frank Marshall Davis. Obama, before meeting Frank, was already surrounded by liberal and leftist thinking through his mother. His African born biological father was extremely anti-colonial, anti-American and held to far left philosophies as well. Though Obama had only met his father once when he was in 6th grade, Obama's mother glorified and behailed Obama's father to her son, despite the fact that he had abandoned their family and left her to raise Obama alone. Obama's maternal grandparents were also very liberal, as were their friends. When Obama's atheist mother left him to seek a degree in another country, Frank is who Obama turned to. Obama's soul was fertile ground for the devilish hatred Frank spewed out

---

* Our Lady said in Fatima that Russia, if not consecrated, would spread Her errors throughout the world. Although the communist Soviet Union collapsed, its residue of errors still live on and are corrupting the United States today.

against the United States of America. As an open vessel, Obama further absorbed Frank's infectious hatred for the United States. Frank also rejected Christ, believing that Christianity was the white man's religion.[137]

How deeply did Frank imbed Obama with anti-Americanism? What can be said of Obama's beliefs and his ideology can be traced back to when Obama was at Occidental College in California. So much of Obama's life, including his college days, are shrouded in shadows and mystery. But one fellow classmate came forward and agreed to be interviewed. John Drew was an angry Marxist at the time he knew Obama as a student at Occidental College. Drew, who abandoned Marxism and is now a Professor, was interviewed by author Paul Kengor for his book, The Communist, about Obama's mentor, Frank Marshall Davis. Drew stated:

> *"Obama was already an ardent Marxist when I met him in the fall of 1980."*[138]

Confirming what Obama himself admitted to in his autobiography, Dreams from my Father, Drew said Obama,

> *"attended 'socialist conferences' and 'hung out' with Marxist professors, but what Obama did not*

explain, or clarify…is that he was in 100 percent,
total agreement with these Marxist professors."[139]

Drew also states of Obama:

"I recall, Obama repeatedly used the phrase,
'When the revolution comes…(or)*'There's going*
to be a revolution,'"[140]

Drew, in a later interview with Kengor, expressed
his thoughts in regard to the question, "Has Obama
changed these Marxist ideologies and his desire to
implement them?":

"Young Obama was looking forward to an im-
minent social revolution [Class warfare/Hutus
vs. Tutsis], *literally a movement where the work-*
ing classes would overthrow the ruling class and
institute a kind of socialist utopia in the United
States…I mean, that's how extreme his views were
his sophomore year of college."[141]

John Drew said Obama looked to a revolution of
the working class to overthrow the wealthy class. We
need to ask ourselves, do we not hear in his speeches, a
soft, glib echo of Rwanda? Do we not hear it through
Obama's own words across the flat lands, the mountains, and the coasts and borders of the United States?

Hutus vs. Tutsis. Drew, knowing the terms Marxists use, having been a former one, stated of Obama speaking as president:

> *"I think whenever he talks about people clinging to their guns and their religion due to economic stress, that is just the standard Marxist argument. In fact, that is the argument of alienation and class-consciousness that **Marxists** hold to..."*[142]

But could not Obama change just as John Drew did? Drew was asked this by Kengor. Drew answered:

> *"I see evidence of **continuing commitment** to Marxist ideology every time President Obama traces the furor of the public to underlying economic conditions and inevitable changes taking place in society."*[143]

Yet, still the question remains, is Obama still intent on the revolution "to fundamentally transform the United States." Drew says to Kengor:

> [Now as president, Obama is] *"still using the Marxist mental architecture in the way he talks about things, and I really think he's surrounded by people that share that mental architecture."*[144]

Drew said he and Obama got into a lively debate
one night at dinner while at Occidental College about
the "revolution" and Drew told Obama it would
not come through a revolutionary overthrow, rather
through a political overthrow. *"Politics,"* Drew relayed,
"would be the road to the overthrow."[145] Drew believed
he changed Obama's mindset in this exchange and
stated:

> *"At that time, the future president was a doctri-*
> *naire Marxist revolutionary, although perhaps –*
> *for the first time—considering conventional poli-*
> *tics as a more practical road to socialism."*[146]

Obama himself has never repudiated his radical Marxist philosophy, while John Drew has.

On a last note, regarding whether or not Obama left
his Marxist philosophy…it can be easily discerned by
the following: What if you were told Obama marched
in the Communist May 1, May Day parade during
his college years at Occidental College? This day being remembered, honored and celebrated around the
world by Karl Marx's followers, whose actual birthday
lands just four days later on May 5, is the antithesis of
the birth of Christ, celebrated by Christians around
the world on Christmas. Would that convince you of

Obama's Marxist ideologies? Or could it still be ar-
gued when Drew knew him as a Marxist communist,
that Obama may have changed sometime between
those 1980 college days to now?[147] A future president,
marching in a parade celebrating a national holiday for
the Communist world!! However, Obama **did "not"
march** in the May Day parade while attending Occidental College, as far as we know. But what we do
know is the future President of the United States of
America, just 30 months before being elected President of the nation that Communism wanted crushed,
did march on May Day, on **May 1, 2006,** in a parade in
which Communism was celebrated and honored. He
not only proudly marched in the May Day celebration,
he did so as a United States Senator!! Yet, this is still
not all. Further pouring salt on this shameful wound,
Obama most amazingly and brazenly, just 16 months
ago,[*] as acting **President of the United States of America**, made a presidential proclamation, proclaiming this
communist day, May 1, May Day, as **'Loyalty Day!'**
This can be checked at the White House website, Office of the Press Secretary, April 29, 2011, *"Presidential
Proclamation – Loyalty Day."*

---

[*] It was 16 months ago from this writing which was first printed in August, 2012.

Does the question still persist within you, has
Obama changed from who Drew knew him as, an ar-
dent marxist? Evidence shows he has not. But what
has changed is our nation, to Obama's hope. With
all his being, he has hoped to change it to what he
believes — **'his hope, your change.' Hope and change,**
his 2008 motto now achieved, he then turns to his 2012
election motto released on May Day's eve, **"Forward."**
He hoped, and he changed America, now he is going to
march forward with his agenda. He is clearly moving
forward with his radical revolution to achieve Frank's
dream of which possesses Obama. When one looks at
Obama's rise, prayerfully analyzing his climb, his formation, one cannot discount the spiritual element of
darkness looming around in his thoughts as he moves
forward. How can light dwell in such a darkened
heart? We are in a very dangerous moment. We have
at our nation's helm a vessel who is open to the father
of atheist communism, Karl Marx, whose father of such
godless ideolgy, was satan.

Is there more salt to put in this cut? One more
thing, but it is not salt; it is a gorging of the wound,
making the salt penetrate deeper. Obama, in this May
1st tribute to Communism, in his proclamation, begins
the invocation using, as Kengor says, "the language of

our Founding Fathers." Is May 1st America's new 4th
of July? His proclamation uses words that could be
used for the 4th of July. But therein lies the cover-up
which could be used for his defense. But why another
4th of July on May 1? Is it because he sees himself as
founding a new nation? Obama declares this honor
for all future May Days to be celebrated yearly by the
United States of America—beginning with calling to
mind the Declaration of Independence. Paul Kengor
writes of Obama, as if Frank is speaking through him
from the grave:

> *"Obama...*(marched) *as a U.S. senator for May
> Day 2006. And speaking of loyalty on May Day,
> it is uncanny that, as president, Obama issued
> a formal presidential proclamation declaring a
> national 'Loyalty Day' for 'May 1 of every year'
> —that is, every May Day.* **In an almost creepy
> Frank-like way**, *Obama presented his procla-
> mation in the language of the Founding Fathers,
> their Declaration, and their Constitution. The
> very first words of the proclamation are:*
>
> *'When our Nation's Founders adopted the Decla-
> ration of Independence...'"* [148]

Obama said February 5, 2008:

"Change is coming to America."[149]

Know your enemy; know yourself. We have been
guilty of not knowing either our enemy or ourselves. If
we know Obama, we know he is a gift, a gift of purification over us as the Assyrians were placed over Israel
to purify them of their sins. If we know ourselves, we
know Obama is where he is because we are the cause.
Until we know ourselves, his removal will not come,
because first there must be a removal of our sins. Without that, there will be no victory. Through more than
enough clear evidence, we have a covert, identified,
radical, Marxist socialist as President of the United
States and we wonder how could such a thing happen?
If you know yourself, you would have the answer. We
Christians are "guilty as charged."* Go on your knees
now, don't just shed a tear, but a pail full for what we
have brought upon ourselves and our poor nation.
Spend some moments in prayer and repentance and
more so through the next weeks and months.

---

* Words of Dan Cathy of Chick-fil-A saying "Guilty as charged," in answer to his belief in the biblical principles of marriage.

CHAPTER NINETEEN

Life-supporting or Life-sustaining But What of Authority Choosing Not to Support and Not to Sustain?

Ominous wording shows up sprinkled throughout the healthcare legislation. What does Section 9006 of H.R. 3590, the "Patient Protection and Affordable Care Act,"* have to do with healthcare? Nothing. But it has a lot to do with greater control and tracking resources. Section 9006 glides in under the unassuming section heading of *"Expansion of Information Reporting Requirements,"* and yields an expansion of IRS reporting requirements that will cripple many businesses and also give the government the ability to minutely track the transfer of goods and resources within the nation to an even greater degree. Gold and silver dealers have been one of the strongest voices of opposition to this section of the healthcare law, as the nature of their businesses and transaction structure will mean a very heavy burden for them and deeper intrusion into the privacy of the financial holdings of Americans, of which is none of the government's business, so long as people

---

* Healthcare legislation was accomplished with two separate bills—H.R. 3590, "Patient Protection and Affordable Care Act," signed into law by Obama on March 23, 2010, and H.R. 4872, "The Reconciliation Act of 2010," signed into law by Obama on March 30, 2010.

pay their taxes. What you legally buy with your money is your Constitutional right. Whether you choose to let the government know or not know what you legally buy, is your choice not the government's.

The change in law of section 9006, *"**Expansion** of Information Reporting Requirements,"* is a great expansion of the power of government intrusion and will require a much more frequent filing of 1099 forms with the IRS for a much broader range of transactions. The government <u>now</u> will know who is buying, selling, and holding the precious metals, gold, silver, etc. Precious metals are important for storing one's wealth into a medium with intrinsic value. The government has no Constitutional right to track your after tax dollars when there is no criminal action involved. What was once unthinkable has become reality. It's a ruse, a disguise, and devious trickery. By removing this thin veil one sees more clearly another of the poisons sprinkled throughout the law to 'inwardly' lasso a huge increase in control, the ability for confiscation, etc.

It is part of the larger picture to bring, by rule of law, everything under the management of the government. By the time this plays out, it of course, will have already metamorphosed into tyranny and will expand its power further. This tactic is essential in understand-

ing your enemies' intentions who are tireless in working
to take away all forms of liberty. When a law contains
thousands of pages of compliance, there is nothing that
cannot be touched in the land it rules over. Thus, in one
sweep of healthcare legislation not one aspect of our
lives is protected from the reach of the government. Its
control is to a point where totalitarianism can be instituted like turning on a light switch, and suddenly liberty
is vanquished. The great question that no one knows the
answer to is who wrote the 3216 pages[*] of the healthcare
law? We are not asking who sponsored it or who supported it, but rather, specifically, what are the names of
the people who put the words together? Who are these
people? Who are they associated with? Who paid them
will reveal this has nothing to do with healthcare. They
had to have an issue — healthcare — to get the legislation passed, but hidden within the law, one can find its
true purpose, all of which this book is about. Any aspect
of the healthcare bill that is not acted upon in the current moment does not mean it goes away, rather it is
still there, asleep in union with other Executive Orders
and laws, to be activated at the most opportune time for
evil to expand its rule. The wording is often so open, so
vague, so broad in its interpretation, so convoluted, that
in the hands of evil it will be easily used for evil as it can

---

* As noted earlier in the book, the healthcare legislation was accomplished with two separate bills. These two bills totaled 3216 pages.

be interpreted to be whatever those in power want it to mean. Do not be deluded, the healthcare legislation is fatal to our liberty. Liberty <u>will</u> die as a result of these bills and executive orders, not just over the concern of the conscientious objection violation, but many more poisons sprinkled throughout the countless pages will move to control every aspect of our lives. Christians are concerned specifically about being forced to pay for abortions, etc., but most do not grasp a greater danger. The healthcare bill will open the doors into areas, now unforeseen, that will expand the culture of death in un-imaginable ways. When a pro-abortion bill is passed and is called healthcare, you can guarantee this will give the 'powers that be' a legal avenue over health issues which will not be looked at, as Christians would look at the law. Their mindset will be one of euthanasia, afterbirth abor-tion (already happening), assisted deaths, elimination of unfortunates, human experimentation, and cloning among many other scenarios. Literally, things we have never heard of before will soon be seen on the horizon. We, with this bill, have allowed the government to exer-cise the taking and deciding of life or death in every and all situations.

Just as tracking of gold and silver are hidden in the healthcare legislation, another hidden part relates to

Radio Frequency Identification Devices, referred to as
R.F.I.D., that are implantable into the human body. Here
again, the language relating to these **R.F.I.D.**'s is sprinkled
throughout the document and given in a way open to
broad interpretation. When the pieces are brought together, it becomes clear that given a state of emergency
in the nation, forced implantation of these devices into
people could be required in the "interest of public health
or safety." But even in normal times outside of an emergency state, an evil heart could very easily interpret the
language within the healthcare law to require forced implementation of **R**adio **F**requency **I**dentification **D**evices
in individuals. In other words, a computer chip.

A study of the **R.F.I.D.** issue within the healthcare
law would be too lengthy to go through the full development of those portions of the law here. The following
wording from the law, H.R. 4872, "The Reconciliation
Act of 2010," follows to see concrete examples of what is
there.

SEC. 1401. COMPARATIVE EFFECTIVENESS RE-SEARCH.

*"(E) encourage, as appropriate, the development
and use of clinical registries and the development
of clinical effectiveness research data networks*

*from electronic health records, post marketing drug and **medical device surveillance efforts**, and other forms of **electronic health data**.*

SEC. 2521. NATIONAL MEDICAL DEVICE REGISTRY.

"National Medical Device Registry

*"(g)(1) The Secretary **shall** establish a national medical device registry to facilitate analysis of postmarket safety and outcomes data on each device that—*

*"(A) is or has been used **"in"** or **"on"** a patient; and*

"(B) is—

> *"(i) a class III device; or*

> *"(ii) a **class II device that is implantable**, life-supporting, or life-sustaining."*

If your enemy is already aligning with the culture of death, what will they do with total authority given over health? They will do exactly what they have been doing, with the exception that now they will be expanding into all areas.

Do not believe those who say chip implants will not be forced. Today, stored health information in an implanted chip is considered **life supporting and life-sustaining**. If you are in a car wreck, that information can be interpreted to be "life sustaining." This, however, is the justification of why government will force such requirements. No amount of medical good can compare to the result of evil that will come through forced compliance with required **R.F.I.D.** chips, and how it will aid and foster the culture of death, much less restrict one's liberty.

Other examples of language within the law also show the mentality of reaching for a very broad scope of authority. The Secretary of the Department of Health and Human Services is given great leeway to exercise his judgment in certain circumstances as he deems *"necessary,"* and/or *"appropriate,"* or *"necessary...to protect the public health."* [150] This concept of very broad *"discretion,"* the freedom to act or judge on one's own without restriction, appears plainly in other recent actions implemented as part of Obama's control machine.

If the above is not enough to convince you what technology in a R.F.I.D. chip can do in keeping tabs on you, consider the following: General David Petraeus, former head of the allied forces in Afghanistan and now Director of the CIA, which most respect as an important agency for our nation's security, spoke at an intelligence summit on March 1, 2012 about the transformational shifts currently happening in surveillance technology. In his talk, General Petraeus spoke on the next generation of connecting, how we are moving from an internet of personal computers, *"toward an 'internet of things'—of devices of all types, 50 to 100 billion of which will be connected to the Internet by 2020."* [151]

What "things" is he referring to? Really anything digital that can contain a chip.

> *"In the digital world, data is everywhere...Data is created constantly, often unknowingly and without permission. Every byte left behind reveals information about location, habits, and, by extrapolation, intent and probable behavior."* [152]

So what does that lead to? Petraeus continues:

> *"In practice, these technologies could lead to rapid integration of data from closed societies and provide near-continuous, persistent monitoring of virtually anywhere we choose."* [153]

From door bells to your flat screen TVs, the door is opening to unwanted surveillance in your own home of what you are doing and what you are saying. The Electronic Frontier Foundation warns how the 'internet of things' can be misused as more and more devices connect and multiply. CIA director David Petraeus ended his talk thanking the firms who have helped build this new generation of 'internet of things,' stating:

> *"Thank you for what you and your firms do in helping the agency to be 'diabolically clever'... "[154]*

While this may have been a good natured statement, unknowingly, evil will eventually use such power, turning it into a misused power, power used against American citizens. What does this have to do with healthcare? The inclusion of Radio Frequency Identification Devices in the healthcare bill reveals that there is a broader plan being put into effect through the bill that will be bad for America. Our Lady says:

January 25, 2001

"...the one who prays is not afraid of the future and the one who fasts is not afraid of evil..."

Why did Our Lady say that on January 25, 2001, except that when She said it, She knew all this was leading to a time when evil would come to rule. "But this is our trustworthy CIA," you might say. Yes, that is true, but it is not that agency in particular that one may be concerned with, but rather the 'powers that be' and how will that power be exercised, and what happens when you have that much potential for misuse of power in these hands. What if, for instance, they decide they want to rid society of Christians as the Hutus decided against the Tutsis? The Catholic Bishops have stated, "We didn't' ask for this fight, but we're not going to run from it." What happens when more infringements upon our liberties begin to happen and the Church makes its voice heard of the injustices of these actions? Evil will want to rid society of those who stand in the way of its rule. If they are trying to rid society of our Catholic and Christian belief that it is not right to force citizens to pay for abortions, etc., will they not eventually see the situation in the same light as those who were present at the Hutu cabinet meeting, in which one of its members said she *was personally in favor of getting rid of all Tutsis. All Rwanda's problems would be over?"* [155]

CHAPTER TWENTY

Detained?

Mr. Obama reveals what his next steps will be by what he is placing in action now. Another very alarming set of new laws paralleling the rise of the healthcare legislation sheds more light on the stage that evil is setting. The following two new laws that are discussed in this chapter stop lawful objection to edicts like the January 2012 healthcare mandate imposed upon Catholics and other Christians. If enough people object and the situation grows and heats up, this creates a crisis. Obama's former White House Chief of Staff, Rahm Emanuel, who resigned from his position in 2010, said just months before he initially took up his post in the White House, *"You never want a serious crisis to go to waste."*[156] What was meant by this? Moves are being made to keep us "safe" at all cost, no matter how much our liberties are eroded as a result. But crisis caused by cowardly acts of terrorism is being used to take from law-abiding citizens, their liberty. American citizens are growing in a mentality of "keep me safe, whatever you have to do," without considering what kind of oppressive life this is leading towards. We, as freedom loving Americans with liberty, are surrendering that same liberty in the name of "keep me safe at all cost." This in the end will result in no safety at all. As we give up our liberty, we in turn will give up our security.

Founding Father of the United States, Benjamin Franklin, said:

> *"They who can give up essential liberty to obtain a little temporary safety, deserves neither liberty nor safety."* [157]

How is that? We the people have always trusted those in power when they were bound by Christian principles and morals. We knew they would not use a crisis as an opportunity to take away our liberties at every step. Remember John Adams, already quoted, said:

> *"Our Constitution was made only for a moral and religious people. It is wholly inadequate to the government of any other."* [158]

On the other hand, if those in power are not bound by Christian principles, as has already been proven, measures will be taken that will strip our liberties from us in crisis that avails the opportunity.

Our war against terrorism is a just cause and is rightfully to be carried out. But laws Americans are accepting in order to fight the crisis of terrorism are taking from us an alarming amount of liberty, and once in place, these laws will endanger the freedom of America. These new laws are empowering those already in power to use them adversely in the name of a "crisis" of terrorism under the justification of security. Obama is putting new laws into place which usurp the provisions of due process which is in the Fifth Amendment of the Constitution. This provision gives you a right of a fair trial by jury. There are several grassroots organizations that are keeping tabs on the stealth actions of the president. One such watchdog reported on January 17, 2012, how the National Defense Authorization Act makes an illegal bypass of the Fifth Amendment:

> *"For months leading up to the passage of the National Defense Authorization Act (N.D.A.A.) opponents of the legislation vehemently argued that it usurped, among other fundamental laws of the land, 5th Amendment provisions of due process of law, essentially allowing for the detainment of American citizens without charge or public trial. To remedy the political fallout, President Obama included a signing statement when he approved*

the bill over the New Year's weekend to the effect
that he would only use his newly appointed pow-
er to detain foreign nationals — not Americans. [159]

However, unknown legislation was already being
moved forward alongside the N.D.A.A. that would
make Obama's statement that the law would not be
used to arrest Americans completely meaningless.
Evidently all was pre-planned in league with Obama
to cancel any objections of usurping the 5th Amendment by doing a run around the original law to include
Americans. Many congressmen do not realize what
they are voting for, except thinking they are protecting
America. Continuing the quote above in commenting
on this "amendment":

"...legislation that would completely bypass that
signing statement was already in the works...to
introduce a scant but very powerful amendment
to the Immigration and Nationality Act that out-
lines a 'list of acts for which U.S. nationals would
lose their nationality.'

*"Dubbed the **Enemy Expatriation Act (HR***
***3166)**, the amendment would essentially grant*
*the United States government, **perhaps through***
anonymous military tribunal or by secretive

Congressional super panel, the power to brand Americans as hostiles for 'engaging in, or purposefully and materially supporting, hostilities against the United States, where the term 'hostilities' means any conflict subject to the laws of war.

"As is typically the case, the language is vague and allows for broad interpretation of what is or is not considered a 'hostile' act." [160]

The work around amendment, the Enemy Expatriation Act, would allow "hostile" to be defined by those in power—not our representatives in Congress. As of the beginning of June 2012, the Enemy Expatriation Act had not yet passed through Congress, but it reveals clearly the intention of those in power to gain the ability to squash all resistance. If all else fails with the law, will a Presidential Executive Order create a run around congress maneuver? Will the United States Bishops, starting with Cardinal Dolan, saying and carrying out the actions of not complying with the invalid healthcare mandates be labeled as performing a hostile act? And what when millions of Catholics and others join the United States Bishops? Will we all be labeled as instigating 'hostilities,' a terrorist act, and be stripped of our citizenship?

"An American can first be detained for engaging in or materially supporting <u>ambiguously defined terrorist activity</u> under the Patriot Act, determined to be hostile by a secret panel, stripped of their citizenship, and then, conveniently, detained indefinitely without trial under the National Defense Authorization Act.

"The recent trial of <u>Bernard von NotHaus</u>, who coined his own 'Liberty Dollars' manufactured of pure gold and silver, was accused of terrorism by the Department of Justice for a crime that, for two hundred years, was known simply as 'counterfeiting.' U.S. Attorney Tompkins said when pronouncing the verdict against von NotHaus:

*'Attempts to undermine the legitimate currency of this country are simply **a unique form of domestic terrorism**. While **these forms of anti-government activities do not involve violence, they are every bit as insidious and present a clear and present danger to the economic stability of this country**, she added. We are determined to meet these threats through infiltration, disruption, and dismantling of organizations which seek to challenge the legitimacy of our '<u>democratic</u>' form of government.*

The statement continues:

> *"From teenagers engaging in typical adolescent behavior and protesters fighting for their right to be heard, to a guy buying survival food or joining in a heated debate on the internet, a semantic change for words like terrorism, terrorist, **hostilities**, and domestic extremist is taking place in the social and political spheres.*
>
> *"Soon any activity deemed contrary to the ideas, purposes and principles of the ruling class and the plutocratic elites will be grounds for detainment, imprisonment and expulsion."* [161]

Is this radical thinking? Remember Obama said:

> *"...And to that extent as radical as I think people tried to characterize the Warren Court, it wasn't that radical. It didn't break free from the essential constraints that were placed by the founding fathers in the Constitution..."* [162]

This law, to detain and declare Americans as hostile is breaking away, as Obama said, from the constraints of the 5th Amendment for due process. Yes, it is radical and dangerous to life, liberty and the pursuit of happiness. Under the 5th Amendment, all Catholics, all

Christian denominations and other people with conscientious objections who will not comply with Obama's mandates are exercising their unalienable right within the law. Under the National Defense Authorization Act and its slyly added "deceive the Indians" (Obama saying we won't use it against Americans) Amendment, the Enemy Expatriation Act, H.R. 3166, the 5th Amendment is usurped. Which law will be used, which law will be trampled, as they can be used in contradiction of each other, by one who has made it known he is an enemy to Catholics and other Christians and people of the same principled thoughts and beliefs?

The 5th Amendment to the Constitution

Or

The National Defense Authorization Act and Enemy Expatriation Act

All must decide by August 2013. The latter gives the government the ability to strip you of your United States citizenship.

Is this all the bad news? Wait until you read the next two chapters. It is as shocking as it is stunning. You will not want to believe it, but you will have to.

CHAPTER TWENTY-ONE

Shocking and Stunning
Great Authority

March 16, 2012. It was like any other Friday afternoon.
Everyone was thinking about the weekend, getting off
from work, heading home or heading out. For most
people, Friday is a break from their normal routine
and a disconnection from what most do through the
week—if not completely, at least to some degree. This
shutting down at work, change of pace, or different
routine for the weekend affects even the news cycle. If
you want something known and you know the headlines will generate the selling of a lot of newspapers or
will keep people tuned into the news channels, you release it at the beginning of the week, Monday being the
best day to get the rest of the week's run. If you want
to bury the news that must be put out, you not only
release it on Friday, but the later on Friday the better,
with the hope that it will pass unnoticed by most of the
people and to let the steam it can produce cool down
by being old news by Monday morning.

As you have read several chapters back, it was stated that part of the book "is being written on March 15, 2012." This is important to understand, because much of what you have read in this book, showing that a war has been declared on religious liberty, against the Catholic Church in particular, was written before March 16, 2012. Why is that important? Because on Friday, March 16, 2012, a very important piece of news was released that will negatively impact every single American across our country, and the major—major news item came and went with very little notice. It is without doubt that the Obama administration strategized not to release this information on the White House website until Friday, March 16, at 5:00 p.m. Five o'clock p.m., Friday evening. It came after the news cycle, so as little notice as possible in the news could be achieved.

That release date, Friday the 16th, alone reveals the hidden motives. While legally, it must be released publicly, it was released at the most opportune time to slide it in by stealth and to kill or at least greatly reduce any resistance of an uproar. This very important news release on Friday was nowhere to be found in the news on the following Monday, March 19th. No clarifications, no letters to the editors. No pros or cons discussion. However, just as the deer hunter calculates the buck in the crosshairs and shoots only at the most opportune time to take the deer down, Monday morning's news story completely saturated all the news, keeping Friday's story buried without difficulty. The Friday news story was shut down by another news story that was driven by the media and everyone fell for it. One must ask oneself why an event that happened on February 26, 2012, suddenly came out of nowhere and became headline news on Monday, March 19, staying in the news for entire weeks, on into months.

Every radio news program and TV program echoed the story, and even some of the media reported their surprise of how big the story became of the shooting of Trayvon Martin by a neighborhood watchman, George Zimmerman. The story and the issues raised from this event is not the reason for bringing up this topic. An investigation of the timing and the explosive manner the Martin-Zimmerman story broke out of nowhere three weeks after it happened, coming on the heels of Friday's release, shows that the news story was chosen and packaged to be made so big as to help bury what happened Friday, March 16, 2012. A very good move for the 'powers that be,' searching for a perfect news story that could be strategized for a cover-up of Obama's actions. The manifesting of the story clearly

points to guilt and makes suspect that the media drove
the story.

But evidence also shows that this story was purposely catapulted into the public square. For what
reason? The way the media drove the story lends itself
for Obama's cover-up. Much of the media will deny
and decry this statement, countering that many conservatives also spoke about this. It is true, but it still was
driven for the purpose of using everyone. Evidence
shows that NBC,[163] ABC,[164] and others doctored videos
and the 911 calls, making the story bigger and extend-
ing its shelf life to the public's infatuation. The question must be asked, "Why, along with being manipulated, did the media do this? Why? What's the motive?"

Investigating this story, from the time it happened
in February, shows it received little media attention
until it exploded on Monday morning, March 19, 2012.
Everyone, and again even some media, were commenting on how it got so big and why it continued to stay so
strong in the mass media. Recall the Rwanda media
and what was incited by the 'powers that be.' What is
the motivation for several cases of doctoring by major
media networks? Why are they not being investigated
for the doctoring? What would depositions show and
what would it uncover?

What you are about to read in this chapter, of which section was written in March 2012, clearly proves what has already been written and helps you know your enemy and their intentions. Shocking and stunning, you won't believe it because you won't want to. Remember to read it with the knowledge that this was intentionally released on Friday evening, March 16, after the news cycle. If this is supposed to be a wondrous good for our nation, to be used for the good of all America's defense, it would have been released Monday, in a Presidential news conference, with much fanfare. The fact that just the opposite occurred speaks loudly of the motivation behind what an enemy to religious liberty would cunningly calculate and strategize through repeated meetings with a thought process of how to bring every 'thing' under authority. Even *your* authority…or your neighbor's.

Revelation 13:2

> ***"The dragon gave him his power, his throne and <u>great authority</u>."***

Does Obama have the authority over a pond or lake on your land, or your neighbor's lake or pond or one in the countryside?

Does he have authority over the fish in your ponds if he decides to take them from you?

Does Obama have authority to forcibly install government owned equipment in plants, factories, or other industrial facilities owned by a private person against their will?

Does Obama have authority for expansions or modifications of any privately owned production processes or factories, even small industries, and warehouses, against the will of the owner?

Does Obama have authority to employ you, who are an expert or consultant, in any given area, you who are of outstanding experience or ability or even your entire organization?

Does he have the authority to induct you into forced labor of national service, against your will? As there is no draft, does Obama, without passing any law, have the authority to induct you into the military or into a civilian service?

Does he have the authority to distribute that labor wherever his designees decide?

Yes or No?

Yes to all the above and more.

How?

By taking the authority and giving it to himself, by signing it to himself by an amended Executive Order. It is
an order that obviously was not thought up on a whim
but strategized for a long time, strategized with a lot of
planning to take power under the banner of National
Defense.

But this sounds like Martial Law, didn't we do this
for WWII? Martial Law was never declared in WWII.
The patriotism of the people rose up to fill whatever
was needed. The free market met, without centralization, war time production. People accepted gas rations,
food rations, and factory changeovers to making tanks,
weapons, supplies, etc. The whole nation cranked up
during this time of war. But how Obama is taking authority, great authority, tells much about this man, as
does the fact that his amassing of power is not just in
wartime, but **'peace time'** and **any time** he thinks to.

But how will Obama, in Washington, be able to
reach, for example, so far as to confiscate the fish in
your or your neighbor's pond or to take over the production of your business and make you cancel any contract you have, even in peace time? Through his Ex-

ecutive Order, he will *invest his presidential authority in people* of his choosing to head over departments. He then will build infrastructure behind them that will enable others to be delegated with presidential authority. The heads of these departments will further have the power to invest authority in other "heads"—all who will act with **full presidential authority**. This authority can be re-delegated successively all the way down to your neighborhood watchman if need be.

You may be oooed and awed that your neighbor or someone down the road could be given headship to act in full **presidential authority** on the dictates assigned to him by Obama, a head who can successfully re-delegate presidential authority, especially if they are your friends who get this assigned authority. But what if they are not a believer and you are a Christian? What if one of these presidential invested heads is placed in your neighborhood or in rural areas for every 10 families, like what happened in Rwanda? Would that be wonderful? It might be if you are a Hutu, but what if you are a Tutsi? Do you think, "Come on, this is not Rwanda?" No, it is not. But, nonetheless, with this March 16, 2012, Executive Order the structure is in place for someone to tell you he is over the water resources on your property, and your water in a little pond or stream will no longer be able to be used by you for your garden, or even for your faucet water for drinking, etc. Why? Because according to the Executive Order, it is considered storage capacity water reserve, and/or a food source which is part of the peace time infrastructure being built up in preparation for a stronger national defense, or in case of a national or local emergency. And on top of that, the executive order gives authority to deem your favorite fishing hole to be illegal to fish in because you will be in violation if a ban was put into effect by a person with presidential power.

Obama gained that power not by election, but by self-appointing authority to himself, and he can pronounce an edict just as a King, who on a whim can decide, at his own "discretion," or the discretion of those delegated the authority, that your fish are part of the food source to be used in time of peace or just to strengthen the National Security's Resources or because of a National Emergency, etc. Though this may sound ridiculous, the authority is there. It is there because it is there to be used. If Obama, or any of his designees, declares such an edict, it must be obeyed. The great authority is there to put into action, on any whim, any mandate. In this example, the mandate could be ordered for the preservation of food reserves of fishing lakes on both public and private property. [165]

This Executive Order gives Obama the ability to assign Presidential authority to anyone, over anything, in peace time, for national defense, in national emergencies or non-emergencies. That essentially means any time, anyone, anything. We wrote at the beginning of this chapter that you won't believe this. But it is there in the Executive Order, called "National Defense Resource Preparedness," released Friday afternoon, March 16, 2012, and buried by Monday, March 19, with an explosive long-term driven story. The Executive Order is law, no matter how unconstitutional it is. Other laws surround it, support it and insulate it. If you try to resist it, you become a target of the National Defense Authorization Act and Enemy Expatriation Act (if it passes), stripped of your citizenship and given no trial, all because your local "president," the "designated authority," decided it is so.

Now you know why it was said to you that you won't believe it because you won't want to believe it. What Obama released from the White House on March 16th is a reality. This was not passed by Congress, not given clearance by the Judicial system or voted on by the people. When you know the facts, you will realize that you, we, are had. Catholic Bishops saying, "we won't comply," in the eyes of the present government, can be the cause of a national crisis, and therefore, can be dealt with severely by the Executive Order as well as through other edicts that have recently passed. Tyranny is in place to deal with any who are **"hostiles"** to what the government dictates, including those who rally with the Bishops. But this is America, the land of the free. This is not Stalin's time. Nevertheless, the infrastructure is there for it to be so. Others could rationalize the Executive Order away, that it cannot do that. But in the hands of evil, it falsely takes on the appearance of being Constitutional. In truth, it is unconstitutional.

Christians nationwide not complying with, but rather defying the Presidential authority of Obama's mandate to pay for abortions, etc., can easily be declared a national emergency because of a threat to Homeland Security. If a man can be tried as a terrorist for what was considered counterfeiting for over 200 years, what other "offenses" will be arbitrarily defined as terrorism? The counterfeiter only "copied" the image from the Liberty dollar, basically breaking what would amount to a copyright violation, though it is considered counterfeiting. The "counterfeiter," however, in truth, minted real gold which has the intrinsic value of any other one ounce gold piece, yet he is tried as a terrorist.

Will we begin to see other crimes, even small violations, labeled as terrorism on an increasing level? Do you not think so? Then contemplate how instead of counterfeiting, the judge redefined the crime by calling it **"a unique form of domestic terrorism."** [166]

Once you see the aims of your enemy, you can put yourselves in a position to understand how they would strategize and, thereby, anticipate that this can happen to Catholics, then to all Christians, and then to all the rest. As in Germany, it won't stop. And who will be left standing to defend you? As a unified group, evil's rule will know no bounds. And we must remember, Heaven has told us pride has come to rule. If you have trouble believing that was said by the Virgin Mary, that is okay, we have had more than enough other "signs of the times" to prove evil/pride has come to rule. It is interesting to point out that between Obama's Executive Order, released March 16, 2012, and the unknowing cover up by the media driven news story of Martin-Zimmerman, Our Lady in Medjugorje gave a message:

March 18, 2012

> **"...I desire to take you by the hand and walk with you in the battle against the impure spirit..."**

What we could not have known behind the scenes, She did.

What are we to make of all these radical moves of Obama? It is very clear he is initiating what he cannot implement in his first term. All these Executive Orders, regulations, authority grabs, healthcare laws, the ignoring of Congress that will eventually lead to the ignoring of the United States Supreme Court, and many more actions will be used in Obama's second term, hitting the United States of America so hard with tyranny and oppression that Hurricane Katrina will seem to have been a nice cool breeze in the southern summer afternoon in comparison. Obama, or rather the 'powers that be' that put him there, are using this first term to put into place what they plan to implement in the second term. There are no plans for Obama to be defeated in his second bid for the White House—again— no matter the vote. Steve McCann, writer for "American Thinker," a conservative media outlet, wrote an article on May 8, 2012, titled, "Obama's Second Term Transformation Plans." In his article McCann writes:

> *"The overwhelming majority of all Americans do not understand that Obama's first term was dedicated to putting in place executive power to enable him and the administration to fulfill the*

campaign promise of 'transforming America'
in his second term, regardless of which political
party controls Congress."[167]

McCann continues,

"The most significant accomplishment of
Obama's first term is to make Congress irrel-
evant...and, in a second term, a potential dictato-
rial presidency."[168]

In Obama's 3216 page healthcare law, there are 700
dictatorial "shall do's," and 200 "may take at their sole
discretion's." This means all at the sole discretion of
one person who will be in charge of the healthcare of
310 million people in the next term. Another law, 2,319
pages long, entitled the Dodd-Frank Financial Reform
Act, was written so large and so open, that it will mean
whatever Obama dictates through the agency head of
his choice. No oversight by Congress will be provided
in how it will be interpreted or if additional regulations are added to it. It takes the appearance of law,
but is not law according to our Constitution. This same
scenario is repeated in several other laws and Executive Orders giving the Executive Branch untold control by Obama and his leftist, socialist friends. Among
Obama's departments, new regulations are daily

passed, as well as the modification and changing of laws for radical agendas. These modifications, in essence, rewrite the law, enacting changes never approved by Congress. Why Congress fails to act against these obvious overreaching actions of the Executive Branch is a mystery. When these actions have been challenged by Congress, it has been done so weakly.

Obama's ignoring of Congress sets the stage for exercising the authority he is amassing, even if both houses are taken over by Republicans in the next election. It will be insignificant because of so many volumes of large wordy laws and in his Executive Orders with daily created regulations. It would be extremely difficult for Congress to reverse these. Even while Obama is building his dictatorial system for his next term, Congress is already being stone walled by Obama's Eric Holder, the head of the United States Justice Department. He has for months thwarted Congress' power of oversight.[*]

---

[*] Eric Holder was finally held in contempt. He is in contempt of Congress for not providing documented evidence to which is believed, would be very damaging to Obama's administration. The plan was called "Fast and Furious." The plan was to allow weapons to be sold illegally through gun stores, in the border states of Mexico. They then would claim the need for gun control because guns were being sold for drugs, gangs, etc. However, the government's plan backfired and was exposed for its real purpose which is believed to go all the way back to Obama. Holder has evidence that is believed to prove this cover-up. He has refused congressional orders to turn over these papers, placing himself above the law, along with being in contempt.

* * * * * * * * * * * *

We are foolishly observing what Obama is taking in authority and not seeing that his re-election efforts will be filled with abuses of our electoral process. Who can doubt that there will be massive fraud in the election process to keep Obama in a second term when the first term set him up to have dictatorial power? Will he then have the ability to stay in office after his second term and the power to do whatever he wants done to go into a third term and if not stopped, his executive orders, laws, regulations and his actions can allow him to take a permanent term? This is the mindset seen in those that surround Obama, and those who have appointed him as their stool pigeon. Obama already displays he is not concerned about re-election.[*] Does he believe he will have consolidated his power and will reign unchallenged by then? This is not said in regard to any other candidate, rather, he has amassed enough power to act, if he chooses, before the election to keep power. And, he has amassed enough power to act after the election to hold power. In his taking of power, Americans believe in "goodness" too much to believe this is planned by Obama. They believed and still believe that Obama is good. But good does not deliver evil. Obama, as an Il-

[*] As of April/May 2012

linois State Senator, after voting against the Illinois Born
Alive Infants Protection Act in committee, went on to
be the only senator to speak on the floor of the Senate,
advocating **against** babies being given medical assistance
if they are born alive after surviving an abortion. He
also, as an Illinois legislator, supported "comfort rooms"
where babies who survive an abortion can be taken to
die, unassisted medically, rather than allowing the baby
medical treatment that could help the baby to survive.
[169] A 'sweet little' nursery room was created for these
babies to be rocked to death.

   Jill Stanek, a registered nurse in Illinois who
worked in the labor and delivery department at Christ
Hospital in Chicago, started fighting against live-birth
abortions after coming upon a situation she was unaware of. While working one night at Christ Hospital
she passed one of her co-workers in the hall as the
co-worker was taking a tiny baby to a soiled utility
room to die after having been intentionally aborted,
but then was born alive. The term the "Christian" hospital gave for this "sanitized abortion procedure" was
"early induction of labor." Most babies will die in the
early delivery process, but some do not and are born
alive. Not wanting the baby to die alone, Stanek took
him from her co-worker and held him, a live aborted

baby, until he died 45 minutes later. After unsuccess-
fully approaching hospital management privately about
the practice, Stanek took the issue public, and her story
was picked up everywhere. Because of the publicity,
she was invited to give her testimony in front of the
Illinois State Congress in support of the Illinois Born
Alive Infants Protection Act. Stanek testified in 2001
of how these babies were basically put on a shelf in a
dirty utility room to die, amidst *"dirty linens, bloody
and biohazardous waste, and a urinal."* [170] Four months
before her initial testimony in 2001, Christ Hospital
created a "Comfort Room" in a move to protect themselves against backlash from Stanek's going public. She
testified before the Illinois Senate Judiciary Committee, of which Obama was a member, and stated:

> *"We now have this prettily wallpapered room
> complete with a First (baby) Photogragh ma-
> chine, baptismal gowns, a footprinter and baby
> bracelets, so that we can offer keepsakes to par-
> ents of their aborted babies. There is even a nice
> wooden rocker in the room to rock live aborted
> babies to death."[171]*

Stanek stood before the Senate Judiciary Committee,
again in 2002. Though she did not bring up the "Comfort Rooms" again that year, Obama did, and in doing so

he made an eerie statement saying **he** was the one who
had come up with the idea of the "Comfort Room." Jill
Stanek was interviewed for this book and shared her
story as well as her personal encounters with Obama,
shedding more light about the seriousness and state of
mind of Obama. She thought it strange that he took
credit for the idea of the comfort room because the comfort room, as already stated, went into effect long before
the issue went before the Illinois legislature.

FOM*: Obama said "we" came up with the idea of the
comfort room. He was not ashamed of taking credit
for this "great" idea, which was worse than the linen
closets, because at least people were putting these babies there, by an admission of guilt, that this was griev-
ously wrong.

Jill: Yes, Obama said to me:

> *"**We**' suggested that there be a comfort room or
> something to that nature be done."*

FOM: Do you see any difference in Obama's being for
the comfort rooms or voting against the Infant Protection Act and thereby being indirectly involved in these
babies dying without medical help? What's the difference in what he is doing than someone's holding their

* A Friend of Medjugorje

baby while being led into the gas chambers that Hitler
was indirectly involved in?

Jill: There's no difference. There's none. I suppose the
only difference would be that at Christ Hospital, setting these babies aside to die is not overt killing, it's
just covert killing, and the difference would be in the
gas chambers they were overtly killing. They were doing something to actually cause people to die. In the
case of Christ Hospital, they weren't actually killing the
baby, the baby was going to suffocate to death. That's
how they die.

FOM: So you would say it is evil?

Jill: Yes, it is definitely evil. I call it a whitewashed
tomb. Like the Comfort Room is a whitewashed tomb.
And like what Barack Obama said, "We suggested the
Comfort Room," a whitewashed tomb.

FOM: Would you say Obama is evil then?

Jill: I would. I do. Yes. People get uncomfortable (with
stating that), but there's something maniacal about
him. Furthermore, he said in his book, The Audacity
of Hope, that he understood that his rise to power, he
called it "spooky," in Audacity. I watched it here in Illinois. He shouldn't have been elected to the Illinois
State Senate. They counted votes, they did underhand-

ed things to get him elected in the Illinois State Senate. The ways he wins aren't normal, they are supernatural, getting back to this evil, maniacal. We understand from the Bible that God allows, He's in control of all the rulers in all the world, rise and fall; everything. For whatever His purposes are, God has allowed Barack Obama to rise. It's certainly, I think it's some sort of justice.

FOM: Would you say it's diabolical?

Jill: I don't know what the difference is between maniacal and diabolical, but diabolical is demonic, you mean?

FOM: Yes.

Jill: Yes. I would say as far as Barack Obama goes, there's something that sets him apart, and I'm speaking now to the abortion issue, that I can't put a finger on it. I can't understand why he would be so pro-abortion. I don't get it. He's so nice and it's just so creepy…He understands that some of the races he's won, where he is today, is spooky. [172]

End of interview.

The tongue of the wickedly wicked is silver coated, glib, pleasant in words. Cunningly compassionate in delivering the most vulgar atrocity, that would be obscene,

even for the most beast of a man. Obama displays this
in his address, turning on Stanek as if she were the one
performing the wrong. When she appeared before the
Senate Judiciary Committee for the second time to give
testimony in March 2002, Obama addressed Stanek by
saying:

> *"Miss Stanek, your initial testimony last year*
> *showed your dismay at the lack of regard for*
> *human life. I agreed with you last year, and*
> *we suggested that there be a Comfort Room or*
> *something of this nature done. The hospital ac-*
> *knowledged that and changes were made and*
> *you are still unimpressed. It sounds to me like*
> *you are really not interested in how these fetuses*
> *are treated, but rather not providing absolutely*
> *any medical care or life to them."[173]*

Even the far most liberal democrats stopped short at
this point and dared not disagree that babies who survived abortion should be helped medically. Obama
was the extreme farthest left of the leftists. With a
heart so cold, would it be anything but a statistic to
kill tens of thousands of Americans if necessary for his
continuance in office? He is willing to do this to innocent babies. What is in Obama's character that can
deceive so many?

How does he cross over to assume so many natures? In David Kupelian's article, "Understanding Why Obama Lies," Kupelian quoted a blogger who wrote:

> *"He is Muslim, he is Christian, he is a capitalist, he is a socialist, he is black, he is white,…he is a constitutional professor, he is an average collegian…, he is a foreigner, he is American-born, he is 'EVERYMAN.'"*[174]

Obama has no moral character, that he is not willing to assume, so nothing would prevent him from making a decision to achieve his plans, and the plans of those with him, no matter how murderous they may be. He has achieved a great collection of power in his first term. He will implement and exercise it in the second. He will not be stopped because evil powers this presidency. Only God's intervention will stop it. But will God intervene? The answer can be found in our own hearts. Our Lady said:

August 2, 2007

"Dear children! Today I look in your hearts and looking at them my Heart seizes with pain. My children! I ask of you unconditional, pure love for God…Through this unconditional and pure

love, you will see <u>My Son</u> in <u>every person</u>. You will feel oneness in God..."

What is in our hearts?

It is not an option for us as Christians whether or not we must pray for our enemies. It is not an option whether or not we must pray for the one who persecutes us. It is not an option whether or not we are to love the one who evil comes to us from. It is not an option whether or not we must, as we love our very self, must equally love our enemy. To do these things is to be the cause of the smile of God to come down upon us, offering the greatest and highest holocaust[*] that can come from our individual hearts. There is no gray area. We will be victorious, we will be defeated, according to how we loved or did not love. We do not have to like what Obama does. We do not have to be fond of him. We have to love his soul that he might be saved. Our Lady said:

November 7, 1985

"Dear children, I am calling you to the love of neighbor and love toward the one from whom evil comes to you..."

---

[*] For Catholics, the Holy Mass is the highest form of prayer. This statement is addressing what we make in a decision to do in regard to love, emulating from our hearts. It is not stated in the sense of being above the Mass.

CHAPTER TWENTY-TWO

The Setting of the Stage for a Dictatorship

The following is only partial samplings of what the National Defense Resource Preparedness Executive Order No. 13603 authorizes. The entire Executive Order is confusing, complex, and difficult to grasp. Not because you are not smart enough, rather because these documents are designed not to be grasped in the fullness. It has been said a genius is someone who can explain something complex in a simple way that all can understand. Those who wrote the executive order for Obama are not geniuses. They are cunning, but not geniuses. The Order cites past Executive Orders and other documents and goes back and forth between them, which makes it very difficult to keep track of what has been cited, and what is being cited; from this source to that source like going through a maze. It is hard to sort through and to remember the numerous sections and parts, numbers and letters. All of this is designed so one will not fully grasp what the Executive Order will do. So for this chapter, it is simplified and some examples are broken down to make it easier to see tyranny for what it is.

As stated, the Obama Executive Order includes many alarming aspects. However, one cannot understand the Executive Order's meaning unless you know how it defines the words it uses. These definitions are inconveniently tucked in, not at the end, but just before the end of the document. However, for this writing, the definitions are uncovered first so as we go deeper into some examples of the Executive Order, you will have some understanding of how Obama's gang defined these words. By reading the definitions first, you can see and get the advantage right from the start, how broad and far-reaching the Executive Order will stretch. In the Executive Order, they list these word and phrase definitions as (a) through (n). There are 14 definitions. These definitions stand alone in what they tell. And what do they tell? As an example, the title of the first one is given here: (a) "Civil Transportation."

In simplicity, Obama's Executive Order is about the highjacking of all authority, wherever there is authority. Whether we are speaking of the authority of a Catholic bishop, or of a foreman on a job, or of a man's authority over his home and lands to the use of his car. Executive Order No.13603 gives Obama unprecedented authority. So great an authority that the Bible verse, Revelation 13:1-2, comes alive.

Revelation 13:1–2

"And I saw a beast rising out of the sea, with ten horns and seven heads, with ten diadems upon its horns and a blasphemous name upon its heads…and to it the dragon gave his power and his throne <u>and 'great authority'</u>."

It cleverly docs this by granting presidential authority over defined aspects of what the nation is made up of: water, transportation, mineral resources, distribution of people labor and horse labor, etc., etc., etc., and authority anywhere it is exercised. Most amazingly, in the Executive Order the number of heads given great authority amounts to seventeen—**ten horns and seven heads*. All people and all things can be subjugated to Obama with dictatorial power through these 17 divisions or heads.* Obama's presidential authority is exponentially and immeasurably expanded.** Hence, this is why it was released on the White House website on a Friday and a news story, Martin/Zimmerman, covered it up on Monday. The Executive Order states:

"…The authority provided in the act (act means the Executive Order) *shall be used to <u>'strengthen'</u> this base…"*

* Sec. 701, 1–17 of the Executive Order

"Strengthen" in reality means "gargantuan expansions" of Obama's authority over this base. "This base" is referring to everything—domestic,* industrial and technological—for national defense preparedness. National Defense Preparedness is the excuse, or perhaps the 'ruse,' used to take authority or control, being that all Americans want a good national defense.

Already covered, but made more clear because it is critical to grasp, the Executive Order signed by Obama on March 16, 2012, greatly expanded presidential authority for himself in the name of National Defense Preparedness. For example: according to the order, full presidential authority over civil transportation is delegated to his Secretary of Transportation. How does this expand Obama's authority if he is delegating his authority to the Secretary of Transportation? By **defining the scope** of civil transportation under the secretary's authority in an all encompassing way, by granting the secretary to regulate, allocate, make standards, set procedures, etc.

Basically anything and all things are placed at the secretary's discretion, "as he deems appropriate in the name of National Defense." In this way, Obama, thereby, broadens his own authority. This works in a back-

* Sec. 102 policy

wards way, back to Obama. In granting his presidential authority to a head, then by expanding everything imaginable under that head, Obama is giving himself great authority. For example, through his Secretary of Transportation, Obama spreads his reach to everything defined under civil transportation. Obama even has total power of "direction and walking" as defined in the definition of "civil transportation" in the Executive Order. As the Executive Order states this law is binding under both emergency and <u>non-emergency conditions,</u> under "peacetime" and "gradual mobilization" conditions, etc. By giving the Secretary of Transportation presidential authority over civil transportation, Obama expands his own authority into detailed areas across the United States of America.

With each head of a department, Obama also gives the same presidential authority. So as you read each definition, read it as Obama has complete and total authority over what is defined under each definition, (a) through (n). You will understand that tyranny can decide in a moment's notice a national crisis, a national emergency, a peacetime initiative, even a non-emergency, a gradual mobilization, or a created crisis to take tyrannical control over what his Executive Order defines in the following. The title (a): "Civil Transportation" was the above example for Obama's huge power grab. The title can assume one or multiple jurisdictions under the authority of a department head with full presidential authority. To be clear about this, invested authority by Obama into a department head boomerangs back, after being newly expanded, as defined, giving greater authority to Obama. '<u>If</u>' we have a different president somewhere in the future, he still can use the Executive Order and other insulated unconstitutional laws to bring in full tyranny.

Section 801 Definitions

(a) "<u>CIVIL TRANSPORTATION</u>" includes movement of persons (walking) and property by all modes of transportation in interstate, intrastate, or foreign commerce within the United States, its territories and possessions, and the District of Columbia, and related public storage and warehousing, ports, services, equipment and facilities, such as transportation carrier ship and repair facilities. "Civil transportation" also shall include **direction**, control and coordination of civil transportation capacity **<u>regardless of ownership</u>**. "Civil transportation" shall not include transportation owned or controlled by the Department of Defense, use of petroleum and gas pipelines, and coal slurry pipelines used only to supply energy production facilities directly.[*] (Coal pipelines, etc., do not really escape Obama's grab, as they are listed under energy.)

(b) **"ENERGY"** means all forms of energy including petroleum, gas (both natural and manufactured), electricity, solid fuels (including all forms of coal, coke, coal chemicals, coal liquefaction, and coal gasification), solar, wind (Obama's authority can regulate use of wind!), other types of renewable energy, atomic energy, and the production, conservation, use, control and distribution (including pipelines) of all of these forms of energy.

(c) **"FARM EQUIPMENT"** means equipment, machinery, and repair parts manufactured for use on farms in connection with the production or preparation for market use of **food resources** (Food Resources is defined in "e". Overlapping definitions are used to insure nothing escapes total dictatorial control.)

(d) **"FERTILIZER"** means any product or combination of products that contain one or more of the elements nitrogen, phosphorous, and potassium for use as a plant nutrient.

---

[*] Part VIII, Section 801 Definitions for A-N.

(e) "FOOD RESOURCES" means <u>all</u> commodities and products, (simple mixed, or compound), or complements to such commodities or products, that are capable of being ingested by either human beings or animals, irrespective of other uses to which such commodities or products may be put, at all states of processing from the raw commodity to the products thereof in vendible form for human or animal consumption. "Food resources" also means potable water packaged in commercially marketable containers, all starches, sugars, vegetable and animal or marine fats and oils, seed, cotton, hemp, and flax fiber, but does not mean any such material after it loses its identity as an agricultural commodity or agricultural product.

(f) "FOOD RESOURCE FACILITIES" means plants, machinery, vehicles **(including on farms)**, and other facilities required for the production, processing, distribution, and storage (including cold storage) of food resources, and for the domestic distribution of farm equipment and fertilizer (excluding transportation thereof).

(g) "FUNCTIONS" is defined to include powers, duties, authority, responsibilities, and **discretion**. (Of special note: discretion gives the individual who holds presidential authority the power of "personal" discretion. His opinions, his biases, his personal views can be doled out, under whatever functions his duty falls, to pronounce his edicts as law. Whatever he says is law).

(h) "HEAD OF EACH AGENCY ENGAGED IN PROCUREMENT FOR NATIONAL DEFENSE" means the heads of the Departments of State, Justice, the Interior, and Homeland Security, the Office of the Director of National Intelligence, the Central Intelligence Agency, the National Aeronautics and Space Administration, the General Services Administration, and all other agencies with authority delegated under section 201 of this order.

(i) "HEALTH RESOURCES" means drugs, biological products, medical devices, materials, facilities [your doctor's office], health supplies, services and equipment required to diagnose, mitigate or prevent the impairment of, improve, treat, cure, or restore the physical or mental health conditions of the population.

(j) "NATIONAL DEFENSE" means programs for military and energy production or construction, military or critical infrastructure assistance to any foreign nation, homeland security, stockpiling, space, and any directly related activity. Such terms include emergency preparedness activities conducted pursuant to title VI of the Robert T. Stafford Disaster Relief and Emergency Assistance Act, 42 U.S.C. 5195 *et.seq.,* and critical infrastructure protection and restoration.

(k) "OFFSETS" means compensation "practices" required as a condition of purchase in either government to government or "commercial" sales of defense articles and/or defense services.

(l) "SPECIAL PRIORITIES ASSISTANCE" means action by resource departments to assist with expediting deliveries, placing rated orders, locating suppliers, resolving production or delivery conflicts between various rated orders, addressing problems that arise in the fulfillment of a rated order or other action authorized by a delegated agency, and determining the validity of rated orders.

(m) "STRATEGIC AND CRITICAL MATERIALS" means materials [including energy] that (1) would be needed to supply the military, industrial, and essential civilian needs of the United States during a national emergency, and (2) are not found or

produced in the United States in sufficient quanti-
ties to meet such need and are vulnerable to the
termination or reduction of the availability of the
material.

(n) "WATER RESOURCES" means all usable water, from all sources, within the jurisdiction of the
United States, that can be managed, controlled and
allocated to meet emergency requirements, except
"water resources" does not include usable water
that qualifies as "food resources." [The only water
excluded under "water resources" in the United
States "is water that qualifies as food resources,"
which does not slip through Obama's net. It is
captured under his authority in letter (e) of definitions.]

The Management and Centralization of All Goods, Services, and Resources

As one navigates through the Executive Order,
there is a mindset threaded throughout that shows
a great void in understanding how the free market
works. When caverns are formed from water, washing
away deposits, stalagmites begin to form to fill back
in the void. When the human body gets an infection,
white blood cells attack the infection. When nature

is healthy, when the body is healthy, these physics and laws are at play, automatically triggering in the self-correcting laws of physics. It is the way God made nature to operate. Where there is a need, that need is met. A natural free market does the same. When a demand for a product is needed, people will produce, create, enhance existing production, provide services, consult, etc., each man meeting the demand. How? Because in a free market, unregulated man will go into avenues where he can make income to provide for his family's well-being, or as in the case of World War II, rise up to meet the threat. Just as the cave fills itself in over time, just as the healthy human body provides its healing, so also the free market is in constant motion, self-corrects, changes itself without being guided centrally, and thereby meets what is needed. And through this competition it reaches maximum efficiency.

But just as the human body, when it is unhealthy, cannot cure itself, the free market, when made unhealthy through regulation, forced production, restrictions, centralization, etc., cannot meet needs by demands. Shortages mount, production is stymied and everything begins to go lame. Just speak to any elder Russian who stood hours in line to receive a couple of pounds of hamburger each month. Centralization, central control, socialism, and other similar Marxist principles, work only in a fantasy of a beginning promise to get the masses to accept it. It does not work after it manifests and over the long term. By the evidence given to us by history about centralization, we know healthcare's centralization is destined for catastrophe, even aside from its immoral violations. The Executive Order will infect the free market, creating an unhealthy environment, growing a new surrogate over the economic order, killing the free market's great ability to meet needs for goods and services by demand. Where demand creates a void for goods and services, it is quickly filled in a free market. Being in Rome on a clear day, you will find very few umbrellas to buy. In the afternoon, when a storm comes on, you will suddenly see 1-3 people on every corner selling umbrellas.

This is either not understood or purposely not understood in the Obama Executive Order. The total arrogance and communist style management of centralization threaded throughout the Executive Order will birth a complex, choking bureaucracy and will oppress the ability to meet national defense needs. The Executive Order, Part III, "Expansion For Production Capacity and Supply," shows those heads who are delegated presidential authority will be given authority to make policies, make guarantees for loans, create rules, establish stockpile managers, and on and on. As Ronald Reagan said:

> "...*government is not the solution to our problems; government is the problem...*"[175]

There is a void of wisdom, an absence of common sense in the Obama Executive Order. One could say it is filled with stupidity. Yet, it is dangerous. It is in reality stupidly dangerous. For example, in Part V, Employment of Personnel, Obama's Executive Order states that the heads of agencies with full presidential authority are to 'employ' in the time of peace, non-emergency, or disaster or declared emergency, etc., experts, those who are uniquely qualified. This would include many fields, such as surgeons, other doctors, scientists, service technicians, specialized equipment operators, engineers, actors, oil drillers, CEO's, <u>anybody</u> — **"persons of outstanding experience and ability"** — to aid in national defense, whether or not it be during peace time or just preparing for national defense. You can be pulled as head of your business, organization, or out of any outstanding position you may hold, at a whim of a government presidential agency head who **"under this order is delegated the authority of the president to employ persons of outstanding experience."** And with Obama's

Executive Order to employ the best and "uniquely qualified" for positions, what if you are chosen? What will you be paid? Section 502 tells how much those of outstanding experience and ability, consultants, experts, and even organizations will be paid. The following from the Executive Order is a direct quote. It states:

> *"The head of each agency otherwise delegated functions* ['functions' is defined under definition (g)] *under this order is delegated the authority of the president to employ persons of outstanding experience and ability **without 'compensation'** and to employ experts, consultants, or organizations."*

Yes, what you just read and thought, "Did I really see correctly what I read?" are the exact words of Obama's Executive Order. He does not even give an option if you want to be employed. Can you guess how the 'powers that be' and Obama plan to get you employed to use your experience, leave your position, company, business, profession, without you being compensated? The answer can be found in the **"pride has come to rule"** arrogance in the Executive Order that is threaded throughout the document. But before you receive the answer, you are probably already thinking, "I won't accept to be employed." While the Executive

Order is filled with stupidity in regard to not understanding how demands are met best through a free
market and other aspects, it is not stupid in the way
it was written. It is cunningly evil in what it plans. In
regards to the ones who think, "I absolutely will refuse
not to be employed," the Executive Order has thoughtfully planned for your refusal. Just **after** the **"without
compensation"** statement, Part VI[*] states:

> "...the Secretary of Labor shall...assist the Di-
> rector of Selective Service in development of pol-
> icies regulating **the 'induction' and 'deferment'
> of persons for duty in the armed services."**

The bypassing of Congress by using regulations,
"policies regulating the **'induction'** and **'deferment'**...,"
is Obama's law to bypass law. So employment of outstanding individuals without compensation is slyly written in the Executive Order, through a selective service
draft. Are they really calling for a draft into the **armed
forces**? **No, they are not.** They are calling for a draft
into the **armed "services".** A clever change of words
from armed forces (military) to armed 'services' (civilian).

---

[*] Sec 601, Secretary of Labor (head)

Obama's plans, as you will read later, call for extensive national <u>service</u>. There is a clear display of indifferent pride he shows here, not being in a declared war, to draft into "service" professionals, CEO's, and others who have sacrificed and worked years to build their lives, only to be placed in a government service job without consideration for their work obligations, their company's obligations or having to put their positions on hold, etc., and...no compensation. One other item – if your job is under contract, the Executive Order stipulates it is null and void, as government contracts and positions take precedence. These 'inducted' (drafted) experts and professionals will not be able to afford beans to eat.

The Executive Order also entails several other violations of the United States Constitution, one of which has not been violated in over 200 years. The Third Amendment. The Third Amendment is a protection for citizens, that no soldiers in time of <u>peace</u> or <u>war</u> could stay or be stationed on private property or in homes, barns or other private buildings. This meant no soldiers or their horses, nor their cannons, their supply wagons, their administrator's tents, ammunition production, etc. Obama's executive order states very clearly, the 'set up' for a blatant violation against the

3rd Amendment, that the military or government, in our time, can quarter, in peace time, equipment which essentially could mean from anything to everything wherever, whenever they please.

Section 102 Policy of Obama's Executive Order states:

> *"The United States must have an industrial and technological base capable of meeting national defense requirements...***in peacetime and in times of national emergency.***"*

This also includes the maintenance of national defense equipment during peacetime. Few Americans would disagree with this need. However, what the Executive Order carries out is what everyone who loves liberty would object to. The above policy of Obama's Executive Order establishes this is military action in peace time, war, or any national emergency. Private property cannot even be used in conflicts. The only time this can take place is for Congress to declare war**, and then in addition,** after the declared war, it must pass another law that equipment and troops could be stored or held on private property.

In an article titled, *"The Third Amendment,"* published on *Revolutionary War*, a site devoted to American history and our Founding Fathers, it is stated that

the Third Amendment says that troops cannot be
quartered on private property at all during peace time.
"Quartering" means that the government cannot 'quarter' troops in your home or on your land. The Founding Fathers of the United States believed the Third
Amendment was extremely important because they
believed that use of one's private property without
consent was detrimental to the security of the citizens.
The article continues:

> "Standing armies were viewed as threats to
> freedom because they could quickly and easily
> overpower the common person. So the colonists
> rightly viewed the presence of a standing army in
> their midst, without their consent, as a threat to
> their freedom." [176]

Thomas Jefferson wrote that one of the grievances of
the colonists against the government in the Declaration
of Independence was:

> "For quartering large bodies of armed troops,
> among us." [177]

As for us today in 2012, "The Third Amendment" article continues:

"As a result of this experience with having their private property used by the government, without their permission, the founding fathers wanted a guarantee that they would be protected from abuses in the future by the new government they were creating..."

"Many people were skeptical that the new Constitution adequately protected their rights and they demanded that a Bill of Rights be added...a list of rights that specifically mentioned that the government has no rights to interfere with...so there would be no room for government officials to 'weasel' their way into tampering with them." [178]

The Third Amendment would not allow in peace time, nor in a 'national emergency,' nor even in battles when a war was declared by Congress, if Congress did not pass an additional law that would allow the quartering of cannons, supplies, manufacturing of military needs, etc. on the private property of citizens. Section 308 of Obama's Executive Order states that government property for military and national defense, whether "in peace time and national emergency," can be quartered on your private property according to Section 102 of the Act. Repeatedly, the Executive Order states government is to have priority over civilian use of their own private property. Obama's Executive Order forces the government procurement of your facility by the hands of those who are given presidential authority to quarter on your property. Be it your barns, lakes, lands, business, privately owned warehouses, privately owned factories, everything you can name, <u>nothing</u> is untouchable, including the water you drink.[*]

Section 308 of Obama's Executive Order states quite clearly and plainly...

<u>Sec. 308. Government-Owned Equipment</u>. The head of each agency engaged in procurement for the national defense is delegated the authority of the President under section 303(e) of the Act, 50 U.S.C. App. 2093(e), to:

> (a) *procure and install additional equipment, facilities, processes, or improvements to plants, factories, and other industrial facilities owned by the Federal Government and to procure and install Government owned equipment in plants, factories, or other industrial facilities <u>owned by private persons</u>;*

Obama can even modify your private, "whatever you own," to his dictates and use. Executive Order Sec. 308 B states:

[*] Sec 201 (a) 5 and Sec 801 (n)

(b) *provide for 'the'* <u>*modification*</u> *or* <u>*expansion*</u>
   of <u>*privately owned facilities,*</u> *including the*
   modification or improvement of production
   processes, when taking actions under sections
   301, 302, or 303 of the Act, 50 U.S.C. App. 2091,
   2092, 2093; and

Remember, all this is still unconstitutional even if
it did not violate the 3rd Amendment, however, it does,
as it quarters in times of undeclared war by Congress,
without the required Congressional passage of an additional law. Obama's Executive Order clearly states in
Sec.102 of its policy:

   "...(a) base capable of meeting national defense
   *requirements...of its national defense **in peace***
   ***time** or **national emergency**."*

So which is it? The 3rd Amendment – government
<u>cannot</u> quarter on private property? Or Obama's Ex-
ecutive Order—government <u>can</u> quarter on <u>any</u> private
property? And this means quartering whatever the
delegated entity with presidential authority decides.
When a constitutional crisis arises between the two,
one of the above will be violated. Obama makes clear
which it will be. Obama's Executive Order unconstitutionally can order the quartering of government

equipment on your property, forcing you to even buy the equipment or have it transferred to your personal business or farms. It includes anything the government wants to place on your property with no restrictions to how small or large. Obama's Executive Order 308 (c) states:

> (c) *sell or otherwise transfer equipment owned by the Federal Government and installed under section 303(e) of the Act, 50 U.S.C. App. 2093(e), to <u>the owners</u> of such <u>plants</u>, <u>factories</u>, or other <u>industrial facilities</u>.*

Sell...to the owners?

A factory can be a company producing images on a t-shirt out of a small building. Farms are 'plants,' producing for the food resources. It is up to the head's sole discretion to decide. One may think this will not happen. After all, who will interpret it this way? You say that because you are judging by what you would do, based on your Christian principles. No. You must judge not by your principles, but as one who has no moral principles.

Obama's Executive Order has staged the usurpation of the Third Amendment. One man is erasing all previous laws, rules and orders by his sole combination of decrees. Obama's Executive Order states:

> Sec 803: Authority (a) Executive Order 1219 of June 3, 1994 and section 401 (3) (4) of Executive Order 12656 November 18, 1988 are **revoked**.
>
> **All** other previously issued orders and regulations, rulings, certificates, directives and other actions relating to any function affected by this order shall remain in effect **EXCEPT as they are inconsistent with this order**

"This order" is specifically referring to Obama's Executive Order. In one sweep of the pen, total control usurping the United States Constitution, the Third Amendment, many other amendments and anything that contradicts Obama's Executive Order, blew away with the wind, on March 16, 2012. Amazingly, no one noticed, covered up by the explosion of the Trayvon Martin/Zimmerman story, driven by several unethical actions of the media.

* * * * * * * * * * * *

Obama's Executive Order 'in peace time' or any national emergency declared so, requires the **acceptance of authority of the President** over all the following. That which is bolded is directly from Obama's Executive Order, Section 201:

"In peace time"..."acceptance of authority of the president"** over the whole United States of all."

Sec 201 (a) (1) agriculture with respect to food resources, food resource facilities, livestock resources, veterinary resources, plant health resources, and the equipment and commercial fertilizer.

Agriculture including food sources, facility, livestock, *domestic distribution* of farming equipment, etc.

"In peace time"..."acceptance of authority of the president"** over the whole United States of all."

Sec 201 (a) (2) All authority over energy

"In peace time"..."acceptance of authority of the president"** over the whole United States of all."

Part VIII Sec 801 (b) wind, solar (sun)

Yes, power over your use of wind and sun which God gave man, not government.

Obama, very strangely and god-like, referencing his rise to the presidency, said on June 3, 2008, *"...this was the moment when the rise of the oceans began to slow and our planet began to heal..."* [179] So why should he not have authority over wind and sun?

"In peace time"…"acceptance of authority of the president" over the whole United States of <u>all</u>."

Sec 201 (a) (4)   All authority over civil transportation

"In peace time"…"acceptance of authority of the president" over the whole United States of <u>all</u>."

Part VIII Sec 801 (a) "…includes movement of persons and property by all modes of transportation…"

Your car, **your movement**, even your direction (as mentioned, the Executive Order states this), any and all personal property that can move you; your fork lift in your privately owned warehouse, as the Executive Order states… *"<u>regardless of ownership</u>."*

"In peace time"…"acceptance of authority of the president" over the whole United States of <u>all</u>."

Sec 201 (a) (5) All authority over water

Part VIII Sec 801 (n) All your usable water from all sources on your private property to be controlled or allocated by any head so delegated according to his "functions." The definition of "functions" in the Executive Order includes the word "discretion." Of which gives the delegated authority, which is found under Part VIII, Sec. 801g, the authority that his opinions are law in regard to "your right to water." If you are Christian and he despises Christianity, will his "discretion" go to your favor or disfavor as what happened in the 1927 Mexican persecution of Catholics, which will be explained later?*

Much more could be cited but one can see clearly a move of a Biblical nature of **"great authority"** has been accomplished to do anything and everything. To allow this much authority into the hands of a man chosen by the 'powers that be,' who has made his/their intentions very clear in this Executive Order, is not foolish on his/their part, but on ours, that we have allowed this.

---

* A persecution in Mexico where many Catholics, along with priests, were killed and bishops were exiled.

CHAPTER TWENTY-THREE

Tyrants

In 1933, the Enabling Act, first known as the *Law for Removing the Distress of the People and the Reich,* was passed in Germany. Tyrants rise to power as the saviors of "the distressed" people. But who gives tyrants the ticket to power? The irony is it comes from the ones who end up suffering the most "distress" at the hands of tyrants. The Enabling Act, which gave the power to "remove the distress of the people" to Hitler and his cabinet, also gave Hitler the right to make laws without the consent of Parliament. It even allowed for laws to be created that were in opposition to their constitution, just as Obama is doing now with his Executive Orders and regulations which are unconstitutional. In effect, the Enabling Act gave the legal means for Hitler to establish a dictatorship over Germany. The Enabling Act directly followed the *Reichstag Fire Decree* that passed a month earlier, taking away fundamental civil liberties from German citizens. In the beginning when these laws were being passed, few paid attention to such acts until they started using them.

When the Nazis were firmly in power, they then began to use this legislation to imprison anyone who was opposed to the Nazi regime as well as suppress publications that did not bow to the Nazi propaganda. Just before the Enabling Act was voted on, Hitler made a statement **promising restraint** **in using the power given** in this Act. He said:

> *"The government will make use of these powers only insofar as they are essential for carrying out vitally necessary measures...The number of cases in which an internal necessity exists for having recourse to such a law is in itself a limited one."* [180]

Hitler's promise was accepted at face value, but it was an empty promise made just to pacify and quell the opposition of the few who even took notice. In the end, the power was given to Hitler to do whatever he wanted without any checks and balances, and he used it mercilessly and without restraint against the citizens of his own country.

Likewise, on December 31, 2011, Obama signed into law H.R. 1540, the National Defense Authorization Act, already discussed in a previous chapter. This law is causing grave concern around the country by the few who take notice because, as covered previously,

it establishes the right of the government to seize an
American citizen and imprison him without due process, which includes being denied a trial by jury, if the
government deems he is a terrorist threat to the nation, just as happened with Hitler's laws. The language
in Obama's signed law is vague, especially in defining
who could fall into the category of "terrorist." Knowing that a potential firestorm could be raised against
this law's ability to imprison Americans without due
process, Obama admits, just as Hitler did, to having
"serious reservations" about it— but signed it anyway.
Obama stated after signing it:

> *"The fact that I support this bill as a whole does
> not mean I agree with everything in it. In par-
> ticular, **I have signed this bill despite having se-
> rious reservations with certain provisions that
> regulate the detention, interrogation, and pros-
> ecution of suspected terrorists...**"* [181]

Then why did Obama sign it? Reread Hitler's
"reservation" with Obama's "reservation" in the use
of their respective laws. Obama and Hitler's tactics
are clearly in union so that in seeing what happened
in Hitler's day, we can anticipate the same can happen
now. Obama signs the law, then takes on a reassuring
tone, stating, like Hitler did, that he would never use

this law against American citizens, or at least, he would use it only with reserve. However, even while he says this, he admits that his administration will have to "interpret" the law, because the law is vague in where the lines will be drawn. In an amazing statement, Obama shows clearly that he understands how this new law he signed will be used against American citizens. But how can it be said, "will be used?" By knowing your enemy! Obama further stated:

> *"Moreover, I want to clarify that my Administration will not authorize the indefinite military detention without trial of American citizens. Indeed, I believe that doing so would break with our most important traditions and values as a Nation. <u>My Administration will</u> **interpret** section 1021 in a manner that ensures that any detention it authorizes complies with the Constitution, the laws of war, and all other applicable law." [182]*

Ask yourself, "Why didn't he/they just take out section 1021 of the law that allows American citizens to be arrested, indefinitely detained, denied a trial, etc.?" When a man goes to his chicken coop and meets a fox who tells him, "I will watch your chickens for you," would you trust the fox's word? Obama has been given watch over the chicken coop. Will he keep

his word? He is the one who said, *"**My administration** will not authorize the indefinite military detention
without trial of Americans,"* which is a self-admission
that this law gives him the power to do what he says he
won't do! Then why is it law? Alarmed? You should
be, especially the more you understand the mentality
of one who already has gone against Christians repeatedly.

As the German people trusted Hitler not to interpret his law as it was written, do you trust Obama *not*
to interpret his law as written, even though as written
it *can* be used against Americans? The law says what
it says. Obama's words are just that, words. We know
the enemy not just by words but by what he has shown
he will do. Obama told the United States bishops he
would not violate conscientious objection, yet without
a second thought, he did exactly what he promised he
would not do. Obama can say what he wants, but the
reality is the above law gives him and the 'powers that
be' throughout the government the right to do that
which he said he won't do. We have now moved into
a dangerous phase. Citizens' rights are no longer being protected by law, rather only by Obama's word
and anyone who takes the seat of power that follows
him. We are being asked to trust Obama's *interpreta-*

tion not only of the law, but his and the 'powers that
be's' interpretation of it, according to, as he said in
his above quote, *"the Constitution…and all other applicable law."*[183] We now must ask what is *"all other
applicable law?"* The ones that Obama has spent the
last four years amassing through his Executive Orders
and by other avenues? That means thousands of pages
worth of regulations in which American liberties are
threatened by any one of the interpretations of the
'powers that be.' Why pass all these laws? To render
the United States Constitution powerless in preventing
their radical socialist agendas from moving **"forward."**
History is the best indicator of where we are heading
from here. We will discuss in later chapters plans that
are progressing to completely have the Constitution be
'reinterpreted' to mean something else by 2020.

Hitler's Youth Brigade

Of everything that Obama is doing right now, the
scariest and most disconcerting is that he has put his
crosshairs on the youth of our nation. In studying what
Obama has been saying and doing just over the past
five years, there are obvious parallels in what Hitler did
in forming his Youth Brigade in the 1920's and 1930's.
What follows in this chapter is a comparative look at
Hitler's actions and Obama's.

Many leaders give only a nod to the youth when they speak of their importance as the future leaders, the inheritors of the nation. But Hitler fully believed the success of his super state rested on the youth. He built intricate and extensive programs to fully mold and form every young boy and girl into his radical socialist mindset, starting at the age of 10 and going through middle school, high school, college and beyond. The final goal was to have 100% participation of all the youth of Germany enrolled in these youth programs. And amazingly, in just 10 years, that goal was nearly achieved. The educational process is described below in Hitler's own words:

> *"When these boys enter our organization at the age of ten, it is often the first time in their lives that they get to breathe and feel fresh air."* [184]

At home and at play, they were aggressively pursued by individual Hitler Youths and also through neighborhood propaganda marches, and meetings for parents, etc. Hitler continued:

> *"Then four years later, they come from the Jungvolk (Young People Organization) into the Hitler Youth, and we keep them there for another four years, and then we definitely don't put them*

back into the hands of the originators of our old
classes and status barriers." [185]

Who were the originators of the old classes and status
barriers? The children's parents, relatives, religious in-
structors, priests, nuns, old teachers, etc. Philip Gavia,
in his article entitled *"Hitler Youth,"* stated:

> *"The Nazis capitalized on the natural enthusiasm*
> *of young people, their craving for action and*
> *desire for peer approval hoping, ultimately, each*
> *young person would come to regard his 'Hitler*
> *Youth' or 'Bund Deutscher Mäde'—meaning*
> *'League of German Girls' unit as a home away*
> *from home, or perhaps as their real home."* [186]

The first goal was to get the children away from
their parents' influence, secondly, indoctrinate them
with the Socialist Nationalist agenda, and last, train
them for their placement in the military or society.
Even though the 14-18 year olds went through intense
indoctrination, Hitler and the powers he surrounded
himself with were still fearful that after leaving school
the youth would drift back to old ways of thinking, and
so this door of possibility was never opened. Hitler
said, *"rather, we take them straight into the Party or*
into the Labor Front." He continued on by saying that

youth were also directly sent to the *Sturmabteilung*, the name of the Nazi militia started by Hitler, or the *Schutzstaffel*, known as the SS—which literally means 'protective squadron', or another group called, the National Socialist Kraftfahrerkorps, which was the Motorcycle Corps, and so on. [187] Speaking of college students and post college graduates, etc., Hitler continued to explain the Nazi youth plan:

> *"And if they are there for another two years or a year and a half and still haven't become complete National Socialists, then they go into the **Labor Service** and are polished for another six or seven months, all with a symbol, the German spade. And any class consciousness or pride of status that may be left here and there is taken over by the 'Wehrmacht' (the Armed Forces of Germany) for further treatment for two years, and when they come back after two, three, or four years, we take them straight into the Nazi Militia, SS (Hitler's elite paramilitary force), and so on again..."* [188]

For these special cases where any youth were still not fully formed, they just put them back in the system again. The above statement concludes with a chilling sentence, the end conclusion of the education of the Reich:

"...so that they shall in no case suffer a relapse, and they will never be free again as long as they live." [189]

What Hitler wanted to prevent was any of the youth returning back to prior ways of thinking and believing, especially in regards to how they were raised, their religious faith, their German heritage before the 3rd Reich took over, etc. These ideologies were in direct conflict with Hitler's. Therefore, Hitler made sure that those raised in his youth organizations would never again "be free" to think anything other than what the Party line indoctrinated them with. Any youth that was resistant to this indoctrination would continue to be placed in government organizations and agencies that would work to deliberately conform them to the proper way of thinking. Hitler and his administration knew that though they could force adults into compliance through intimidation and terror tactics, to be successful in establishing a pure race, it was imperative that the next generations be "true believers" in their cause and be ready to carry on the work to replace those who would step down or be forced to leave their positions because of not supporting the regime's agenda. Very early on, the programs Hitler initiated were at first voluntary, but gradually, became compulsory.

Dr. Jutta Rudiger, who was the leader of the League of German Girls in 1937, explained what the main objective was in the training of girls:

> *"The task of our Girls League is to raise our girls as torch bearers of the national-socialist world... We want to raise girls who believe in Germany and our leader, and who will pass these beliefs on to their future children."* [190]

The boys' organizations centered on military training that included weapons and assault techniques. They began, as did the girls, with fun camps, exciting activities, competitive sports for 10-14 years old, etc., in 1932, but by 1939 they were already being trained for combat. A special division was created for them, called the 12th Panzer Division SS, and they were sent into combat towards the end of the war when Germany lines were collapsing. Though most of those in this division were still very young, they fought so savagely that it was a shocking sight for those who came against them. As soldiers, there was no thought to their own safety, or to what they could realistically do in combat to the oncoming enemy. Many of them threw away their lives without consideration. So crazed they were in the battle, some even violently threw their bodies up against moving tanks. Those who watched them in battle had never experienced anything like it. But it was an ill-fated fight. The vast majority of the 12th Panzer Division were killed, most refusing to surrender, but violently fighting to their deaths. This trait of the Hitler Youth being cruel and violent was seen in both boys and girls:

> *"While at first these younger soldiers were put in less dangerous positions, as the war increased, their role increased also, until Hitler had even young teenagers fighting for the Reich. Trained sometimes from the age of 10, they were known for cruelty... The Hitlerjugend (Hitler Youth) trained leader-worship and unquestioning obedience to authority. Brought up as sons and daughters of a cruel state, they were themselves cruel..."[191]*

Social psychologist, psychoanalyst, sociologist, and humanistic philosopher Erich Fromm, was born in Germany but fled his country when the Nazis rose to power. While the war was still going on, he wrote about the training of the youth in Hitler's programs in his book, Escape from Freedom, published in 1941. He identified eight basic needs that were cleverly filled in the lives of millions of youth through Hitler's programs. These programs were structured masterfully in positive ways that appealed to youth, but psychology was also used in luring the youth to embrace the ideologies being taught to them. Hitler captured virtually all the German youth. By capitalizing on their human needs as described in the following eight fundamental categories listed below, the youth were manipulated by Hitler for his evil purposes, according to Erich Fromm.[192]

1. Relatedness—having relationships with others, care, respect, knowledge.

2. Transcendence—creativity, developing a loving and interesting life.

3. Rootedness—a feeling of belonging.

4. Sense of Identity—seeing oneself both as a unique person and part of a social group.

5. A frame of orientation—understanding the world and our place in it.

6. Excitation and Stimulation—actively strive for a goal rather than simply respond.

7. Unity—a sense of oneness between one person and the "natural and human world outside."

8. Effectiveness—the need to feel accomplished.

It was through the family, the first created social
structure, that God ordained these needs to be met in
the lives of youth, and then through the church and
community that surrounded the family. However, in
the case of Hitler's Youth, these primary bonds were
purposely weakened, while the life of the youth became centered around government programs, not family life. Slowly, the above needs began being filled by
the "Party" or the "State," through activities, sports, and
other programs to capture youth, rather than the family and the Church having the primary influence over
them. Instead of emphasis being placed upon serving
God, family and country, the obligation of "service"
was aimed at the "State" and the Fuhrer. This was
made possible because in general, Germany's society
was riddled with the deterioration of family life. The
passion for the faith had waned, and so the moral fabric of the nation was unraveling. In its void, Hitler was
able to take control of the nation's youth, which resulted in the transferring of their allegiance to him and
to the goals of the Third Reich—the master race that
would rule the world. Erich Fromm provided an explanation of how the youth made this transfer to total
loyalty to Hitler:

"...(when) people have lost those ties which gave them security, this lag makes freedom an un-bearable burden. It then becomes identical with doubt, with a kind of life which lacks meaning and direction. Powerful tendencies arise to escape from this kind of freedom into submission or some kind of relationship to man and the world which promises relief from uncertainty, <u>even</u> if it deprives the individual of his freedom." [193]

Fast forward to our present time. The very same dangerous situation is happening today. We are in a perfect moment of a 'dysfunctional family' built soci-ety and for the incubation of a parallel plan 'moving forward' with our youth. The families of our nation are fractured and broken. Divorce has risen above the 50% mark for all marriages. So many young people who have been denied the security of a loving home are searching for something meaningful to belong to, to give purpose to their lives. Now we have extended families, many youth living through several divorces of their parents. Where do these youth feel they belong? Where is their sense of belonging met? This need for a sense of belonging is what Hitler seized upon. Obama, himself, comes from a broken home. On July 2, 2008, during a campaign speech in which much of what he

was saying was addressing the youth of our nation,
Obama said the following:

> "...Through _service_, I found a community that
> embraced me; citizenship that was meaningful;
> the direction I'd been seeking. Through _service_, I
> discovered how my own improbable story fit into
> the larger story of America." [194]

Obama's father abandoned him when he was still
a baby. Obama's mother left him to the care of his
grandparents at the age of 16 to pursue a college degree in Indonesia. Obama said though his grandfather
was good to him, he was _"both too old and too troubled
to provide me with much direction!"_[195] Where, then, did
Obama find direction for his life? He found it in "service" as taught by radical communists who befriended
Obama, such as Frank Marshall Davis. In the void created by his family situation, he became a protege of the
radical ideas that were planted and formed in him for
the role he was to assume in bringing down the United
States and fundamentally changing it into something
else.

Given the history just covered of Hitler's Youth, it
will now be clear why red flags are rising up from the
words and actions of the present President regard-

ing America's youth and how they are now in the crosshairs. Obama himself is a product of such indoctrination. A scary, difficult situation... Yes!

Our Lady of Medjugorje said on August 15, 1988:

> **"Dear children, from today on I would like you to start a New Year, the Year of the Young People. During this year pray for the young people; talk with them. Young people find themselves now in a very difficult situation. Help each other. I think about you in a special way, dear children. Young people have a role to play in the Church now. Pray, dear children."**

CHAPTER TWENTY-FOUR

Civilian National...What?

Many things are coming to light in terms of a very radical agenda that we see unfolding through Obama, his administration and the powerful ones that are stealthily hidden behind him. What follows is a very important aspect of the plan to seize total control of our nation. It may seem exhaustive and exhausting, but this will show you more clearly just how strategic, coordinated, and exhaustive evil has **set out** in furthering this objective. This chapter and the next two will show you with more clarity why it is stated that, unless interrupted, Obama and the 'powers that be' will see their plans fulfilled in taking control of our youth just as Hitler made use of Germany's youth for the fulfillment of his plans.

Civilian National Security Force

As already discussed, many of Obama's Executive Orders raise the fear that the government is readying for a massive crisis which they can declare even in peace time to create a national emergency to help Obama grab power. **"Be Ready"** is the slogan for

Homeland Security Preparedness programs. It is not hard to imagine, for example, an economic meltdown that would lead to food shortages, pillaging, thievery, murder and anarchy. In fact, the Obama administration has created several public service announcements, sponsored by Homeland Security that can be heard and seen regularly on radio, TV, and other media outlets. They sound very ominous. What follows is a transcript of just one commercial, with what sounds like canon shots going off in the distance, and slow eerie music playing. Remember this is produced by the United States Government :

What if a disaster strikes without warning…?

What if life as you know it has completely turned on its head…?

What if everything familiar becomes anything but…?

Before a disaster turns your family's world upside down,

*It's up to you to **be ready**.*

Get a kit. Make a plan. Be informed today.

Learn how at ready.gov. [196]

The effect is disturbing, fear inducing (justly so) and ominous—but it's made more so because it's our government that we do not trust, and it's our government who wants us to "be ready." Be ready for what? Sure it could be rationalized by thinking, "Oh, come on, this commercial is talking about a hurricane or something of the sort." That is true, but when you know your enemy, you know how he will deceptively condition you to accept him as your savior, running to him in crisis. That is the plan — to bring you into compliance. That is why it is not "your plan" in the kit, it is "their plan," as stated: *"Get a kit. Make a plan. Be informed"* — to be conditioned. How much will the government be behind the using of a crisis, so to lead to the pre-determined outcome as has been traced throughout <u>They Fired the First Shot 2012_{TM}</u>? As has been said, even by Obama's administration, never let a crisis go to waste. All this is necessary to understand to see how the commercials were produced to not just inform, but to condition the public to be prepared for an emergency crisis that *is* coming. But the question that seems most relevant is how will the government plan, or rather what is it planning to condition you to accept their remedy for the coming massive crisis? satan always mimics God's call in order to divert people from God. The point is not to trust government's call to **"be ready."** This is not said to criticize or lead to the conclusion that it is not important to prepare for whatever may happen in the future. It is important to "Be Ready," and in fact, Our Lady said this, Herself:

February 16, 1982

> **"satan only says what he wants. He interferes in everything...'be ready' to endure everything. Here, many things will take place. Do not allow yourselves to be surprised by him."**

April 2, 2010

> **"... I pray for you to return to the right way to my Son—your Savior, your Redeemer—to Him who gave you eternal life. Reflect on everything human, on everything that does not permit you to set out after my Son—on transience, imperfections and limitations—and then think of my Son, of His Divine infiniteness...'Be ready,' my children..."**

Our Lady also speaks of our time:

April 25, 1983

> **"I will pray to my Son to spare you the punishment. Be converted without delay. You do not know the plans of God; you will not be able to know them. You will not know what God will**

send, nor what He will do. I ask you only to be converted. That is what I wish. Be converted! 'Be ready' for everything, but be converted. That is part of conversion. Goodbye, and may peace be with you."

So, the question is not whether or not we should "be ready," rather in what way should we be ready.

When the government says to **"be ready,"** one should have a general mistrust of government, just as our forefathers had, because it may be our government that we need to be ready against and in caution of. It was Obama's own words that first alerted people to an ominous foreboding. Obama said during his campaign for presidency several things that are not only noteworthy, they are critical in understanding his thought process and mentality and that of the powers behind him. Many have forgotten these statements or were never even aware that he said them. On July 2, 2008, Obama was in Colorado Springs and gave a very defining speech in regards to what his goals would be if he was elected President of the United States. This is the same speech brought up at the end of the last chapter in which Obama revealed that it was through "service" that he found *a community that embraced me.*[197] There is much to disclose about this speech, but one particular comment sets the tone for all the others. Obama was reading off of the teleprompter a speech that had also been pre-released. In the middle of the speech, he suddenly deviated from the script and the teleprompter and made this shocking statement:

> *"We cannot continue to rely on our military...*
> *We've got to have a **civilian national security***
> ***force that's just as powerful, just as strong, just***
> ***as well-funded.***" [198]

Three incredible revelations were stated here of a plan that Obama blurted out unscripted, without the teleprompter, but known enough in his thoughts that he could rattle them off, giving evidence of strategies that had taken place in back rooms. A Civilian National Security Force that is equally on par with our military in that it will be:

1. Just as powerful!

2. Just as strong!

3. Just as well funded!

It is an astounding revelation. Notice Obama did not say, we cannot continue to rely '*just*' on our military. He said blatantly, *"we cannot continue to rely on our military..."* [199] The United States Military is no longer satisfactory, no longer reliable? The most powerful military force in history?   Obama wants to create a *civilian* force that is just as powerful, just as strong, and just as well-funded as our military today? At the time he said this, it caused a big puff of a ruckus in the media, but the story was suddenly dropped. The uproar went away. The statement by and large was forgotten. This wasn't just a light switch statement in Obama's brain that was turned on, a sudden spontaneous thought during his speech such as, "Oh, by the way, I've got a good idea!" Obama *deviated from the prepared script* as projected on the teleprompter and he spilled the beans of the 'powers that be.' You don't just come up with an idea like this. Common sense, with wisdom, tells us that no one is going to spontaneously say, just off the cuff, "Hey, wouldn't it be great to have a civilian service?" When Obama said this, he revealed something of what was being discussed behind closed doors, and it is very doubtful that Obama is the one coming up with these ideas and how they are to be implemented. Look beyond the words he said. Think about these words. Analyze them through prayer.

Is Obama's call to build a civilian service force which will match our military on all three of these levels stated because he and the 'powers that be' know that U.S. soldiers will face in the future a Constitutional crisis when they will be ordered to detain fellow Americans on American soil, of which a civilian service will not have such constraints? The following will help you answer these questions.

All soldiers and officers swear a military oath to uphold the Constitution. When there are flagrant and blatant actions trampling the Constitution by the Commander-in-Chief, a choice must be made to either fulfill the sacred duty of their oath or follow unconstitutional orders of the Commander-in-Chief.

On March 22, 2012, the Associated Press reported on an article about Marine Sgt. Gary Stein. Stein had first posted on Facebook a page criticizing Obama's overhaul of healthcare in 2010. Sgt. Stein's superior cautioned him and Stein *"volunteered to take down the page while he* (Stein) *viewed the rules at the request of his superiors."* [200] Stein, after reviewing what he had written said he *"was not in violation and re-launched the page."* [201] *

After a March 8 review, Stein was discharged. He responded:

---

* Stein had also made a statement in an online debate about NATO allowing U.S. soldiers to be tried for burning several Korans, which were used by terrorists to pass written messages to other terrorists, while Bibles have been ordered to be burned by U.S. troops in Afghanistan.[202]

"I'm completely shocked that this is happening…
I've done nothing wrong. I've only stated what
our oath states that I will defend the Constitution
and that I will not follow unlawful orders. If that
is a crime, what is America coming to?" [203]

According to Stein, he was discharged for standing by his oath to protect the constitutional rights of American citizens. In his statement he said he would not follow orders from the president if those orders included detaining U.S. citizens who were denied due process or doing anything else that would clearly violate their Constitutional rights. [204]

There is a growing dissension among members of all branches of the military because of flagrant and blatant violations of the United States Constitution by the Commander-in-Chief, President Obama. When a soldier is placed between a Commander-in-Chief's order vs. the United States Constitution, a Constitutional crisis is created. Those who have sworn an oath by their life to defend that "Constitution" are forced to decide which one they will obey. They are cornered in the integrity of their oath. They must choose whether or not to follow orders based in unconstitutional, therefore, unlawful directives or laws. If confronted with a situation like this, there is only one course of action to choose: follow truth. It is just the same with the assault against the Catholic Church and the bishops. Catholic teaching commands obedience to authority, the president and law, **except** when cornered into a forced decision, between obeying a law in line with nature and nature's God or in obeying a president who is in violation of nature's law and nature's God.

The book, <u>SEAL Target Geronimo</u>, about the Navy SEALs taking down Osama bin Laden, was authored by Chuck Pfarrer, a former Navy SEAL. In his book, Pfarrer touches on the growing discontentment of the Navy SEALs towards Obama. In 2009, pirates from off the coast of Somalia attacked and took over a U.S.-flagged ship, *Maersk Alabama*, which was bringing relief supplies to Kenya. An American captain was taken hostage. The Navy SEALs were called in. When they were in a position to act, they had to wait for orders from President Obama. Navy SEAL author Pfarrer writes:

> *"The SEALs waited. Almost two days passed*
> *before a decision came down from President*
> *Obama, and when it did it was excruciatingly*
> *vague. The SEALs and the crew of Bainbridge*
> *were authorized to take action if they deemed*
> *that the hostage's life was in immediate danger.*
> *It was a political shrug. Succeed, and you'll be*

heroes. Mess up, and we'll disavow that you were given any orders to act." [205]

This growing discontentment is going to, somewhere down the road, cause a constitutional crisis. So again, is this constitutional crisis already being anticipated by the 'powers that be' and Obama? Have they foreseen and strategized about this inevitable confrontation? Is this the purpose of developing a civilian force of service that is just as powerful as our military?

"We've got to have a civilian national security force that's just as powerful, just as strong, just as well-funded..." [206]

Can a civilian service force that does not require its members to take an oath to defend the Constitution and that is not bound by law as the U.S. military, but that is "just as powerful as the military," be ordered to strike against American citizens?

Military members, Catholics, Christians of other denominations and people of good will are willing to suffer a long train of abuse:

*"But when a long Train of Abuses and Usurpations, pursuing invariably the same Object, evinces a Design to **reduce them under absolute***

Despotism, it is their Right, it is their Duty, to throw off such Government, and to provide new Guards for their future Security." [207]

In reading the National Defense Resources Preparedness (N.D.R.P.) Executive Order of how Presidential authority will be transferred down through a chain of authority, reaching to our own backyards, and how the military will be used to implement its policies, it becomes apparent that the military **will** be put into a constitutional crisis. The Executive Order uses the military against American citizens, which is a flagrant violation of the Constitution. The military constitutionally <u>cannot</u> be used against United States citizens, but can be as deemed and prescribed in the Executive Order and the N.D.A.A. (National Defense Authorization Act). Both actions cannot be complied with simultaneously. It has to be one or the other.

There is practically nothing our military cannot do. Why duplicate what is the greatest, most powerful military in the history of the world? Again, is it because there <u>is</u> one thing our military <u>cannot</u> do? They <u>cannot</u>, by law, be used against American citizens. A civilian force, however, could. Think real hard.

Thoughtfully look at the quote line by line:

"...We cannot continue to rely on our military..." [208]

There is no military in the world that comes close to matching the capabilities of the United States military. The Navy SEALs finding and eliminating Osama bin Laden and the daring rescues of U.S. hostages from Somali pirates are riveting stories of just how impressive our military is. The capture of Saddam Hussein in which many branches of the military successfully worked together is another example. The technological advances coupled with the superior training and heroism of our American soldiers is outstanding and in a class of their own. It has been 11 years since 9/11 and despite repeated attempts to attack the United States again, every plan has been thwarted by our military and intelligence agencies. The United States Military has always been able to meet the challenges put before them, through the grace of God. And yet, Obama says we cannot continue to rely on our military? Is it perhaps that *Obama and the 'powers that be' can't rely on the military for what they want to accomplish?*

"We've got to have a civilian national security force..." [209]

Why a civilian force? As already mentioned, is
it because the United States military can't be used
against the American people? Because of the very
same issues that are being presented in this book, more
and more members of the military are seeing that there
are potential conflicts arising between what the President is commanding them to do and what they know to
be right constitutionally. They made an oath to defend
the Constitution, <u>not</u> the president, even though he is
the Commander in Chief. As written about previously:

> *"We've got to have a civilian national security
> force <u>that's just as powerful</u>..."* [210]

How do you like the thought of having government
trained civilians exercising authority over you, authority as powerful as our military, but who would not be
required to take an oath to the Constitution to defend
your rights?

> *"We've got to have a civilian national security
> force <u>that's... just as strong</u>..."* [211]

In the domestic United States, a force, just as strong as
the most powerful military in the world? From numbers based on Department of Defense data from 2010,
the United States military is made up of more than
2,300,000 officers and soldiers and could be greatly

increased. This number is all inclusive of those on active duty, the Army Reserve, Marines, Navy, the U.S. Coast Guard, etc. Obama wants a civilian force just as strong? Again, we must scratch our heads and ask ourselves, for what purpose is Obama calling for a civilian army that matches our current military in strength. What is he preparing for? Where will he get such a number of volunteers? How does he plan to train them? What model will he use?

"We've got to have a civilian national security force that's... just as well-funded..." [212]

At the time Obama made this statement in 2008, the Department of Defense's actual spending was $667 *billion* dollars. The defense budget for 2012 is $671 billion. What is in the mind of Obama and who put it there that could conceive the need of this kind of funding for a civilian force? Are the red flags raising? It's no wonder that this comment was quickly removed from the news when Obama first said it. And even when you search resources, most of the sites that have the transcript of the July 2, 2008 speech astoundingly have washed away this statement. You have to dig to find it. This scrubbing of Obama's words does not decrease the credibility of what he said, rather it increases and proves he revealed secrets of the 'powers

that be' that he was not to speak of when he wandered
from the teleprompter. But could it be it was scrubbed
from his speech because Obama has, perhaps, changed
his mind? No. It is apparent that this is still very much
in Obama's plans as section 5210 of healthcare bill,
H.R. 3590, shows. This section calls for **"Establishing a Ready Reserve Corps."** The bill states that the
purpose of this reserve corps is *"for service in time of
national emergency."** For what kind of national emergency would you need to have a civilian army that is
just as powerful, just as strong and just as well-funded
as our current military and why is a "Ready Reserve
Corps" in **a healthcare** bill? When Hurricane Katrina
hit and devastated the Southern coastal states, those
who made the greatest impact in cleanup, bringing
needed supplies and rebuilding were churches from
across the United States. Even F.E.M.A. admitted to
this, while the government was greatly criticized for
their lack of organization. So are you beginning to get
the picture?

After four years of being in office, Obama has set
the stage publicly for initiating this civilian force, while
actively pursuing it behind the scenes for years. It
is a call of multiple factions, hidden throughout sev-

* Sec. 203 (a) (1)

eral various bills, in speeches and program creations. Obama is building an army through **a call to service**. He knows he can't speak openly and outright about a civilian force, so he cloaks what he is saying behind key words—and in this way he can say he has never lied to the American people. Everything is presented right before our eyes. The word **"service"** is a key word. Just as **"Forward"** is the key word for speaking of the *radical socialist agenda* that those in power are trying to overtake the United States, the word **"service"** specifically is linked with the building of a civilian force. The first step was to begin getting the word and the idea of **"service"** into the consciences of the minds of Americans, especially in the minds of the youth. And so, **"service"** came up often in Obama's speeches and continues to do so. In his July 2, 2008, speech, after stating the need for a civilian force, he said concerning the **"call to serve"**:

> *"...I'm determined to reach out—not just to Democrats, but to Independents and Republicans who want to 'move in a new' direction. And that is why I won't just ask for your vote as a candidate—I will ask for your **service** and your active citizenship when I am President of the United States. This will not be a call issued in one speech*

*or one program—this will be a **central cause of
my presidency**. We will ask Americans to **serve**.
We will create new opportunities for Americans
to **serve**. And we will direct that **service** to our
most pressing **national challenges**." [213]*

Are national "challenges" the same as declared national *"emergencies"?* Ask yourself, "Why is Obama
wanting to build up a civilian force while at the same
time reducing the military, slashing away 80,000
troops[214] and making other cuts, weakening the military?" If we are cutting one thing, why are we building
another, just as strong, powerful and well-funded? Answer your question with a common sense answer.

In this call to **service**, the youth of our nation are
being specifically targeted with this message. The
Obama administration took a low key approach in
his first term concerning the civilian force, but he has
voiced it enough times now that in a second term,
"service induction" will be bulldozed into being at full
force. As shocking as it was to learn that the National
Defense Resources Preparedness Executive Order allows for the induction of uniquely specialized experts
into selective services without compensation, now we
can be just as shocked and can see just as clearly how

this can and will be used for the youth of the nation. Obama's Executive Order mandates:

Section 601 a(2): The Secretary of Labor, in co-ordination with the Secretary of Defense and the heads of other agencies, as deemed appropriate by the Secretary of Labor, shall:

> *(2) upon request by the Director of Selective Service, and in coordination with the Secretary of Defense, assist the Director of Selective Service in development of policies regulating the "induction" and "deferment" of persons for duty in the armed services;*

Is the "induction" referred to above what Obama was referring to when he said in his July 2, 2008 campaign speech in Colorado, *"We will create new opportunities for Americans to serve"*?[215] True to his word, there have been many such programs created in his first term—and a significant number of them specifically target our youth. To study what is behind these programs, individually and collectively, is to again raise red flags that something very ominous and dangerous is amiss. In answer to the question, from where does Obama plan to raise his civilian army? From the same place Hitler did, from our own youth—our children.

Obama wants to make an ideological shift in our nation and to do that the youth must be "converted" to this ideology. Therefore, you've got to go from the ground up, to the generations that have not yet been formed and are malleable to those in whom they learn to place their trust. This is what Hitler did and this is why red flags are popping up everywhere Obama is speaking about the youth of our nation—in particular, when he speaks about **"service"**.

CHAPTER TWENTY-FIVE

Service Programs or Indoctrination?

You may be thinking service programs sound good and that we're making a mountain out of a molehill. In the book <u>Look What Happened While You Were Sleeping</u>_{TM}, written in 2007, it was reported that <u>many</u> government school programs have targeted the most gifted and talented youth around the country for enrollment. The programs cover a wide array of topics, from leadership, to music appreciation, to career guidance seminars, but these topics were only a cover for indoctrination programs to lead youth away from their traditional Judeo-Christian, family and American values and lead them into the radical socialist culture of death agenda. The following excerpt comes from <u>Look What Happened While You Were Sleeping</u>_{TM}:

> *"If a fisherman knows how to use the best lure*
> *to catch the prize fish, satan, who is not dumb,*
> *but rather has a superior intellect, will 'lure' the*
> *best minds with attractive tactics to capture and*
> *transform the minds of our youth. These groups*
> *have an agenda, and they are purposely picking*

the top crème of our youth to indoctrinate and
change their thinking. They are very clever and
mostly successful in doing so. In September, 2006,
a mother and father from out of town decided to
visit our mission at Caritas, spending some time
before picking up their daughter from the National
Young Leaders State Conference held at the Hil-
ton Hotel in Birmingham, Alabama. They told
us it was sponsored by the Congressional Youth
Leadership Conference. They, of course, were
honored that their daughter was invited. All that
faded when they picked her up. She was confused
in what once was her firm beliefs, formed by strong
Christian teachings. In the next days the parents
found out the three topics of discussion were:

1. *Cloning*
2. *Abortion*
3. *The Right to Die* [216]

Is it even necessary to ask what cloning, abortion and
the "right" to die have to do with congressional youth
leadership skills? While they have nothing to do with
these issues, they have everything to do with manipulating
the minds of impressionable youth because, as Hitler said:

   "He alone, who owns the youth, gains the fu-
ture." [217]

Take note that the seminar covered only a five day period. Five days was enough to shake the foundations
of a young girl raised in a strong Christian, traditional
American home. What of those youth who had no
moral foundation set for them previously? What kind
of impact are these government programs having on
them, as well as the entire left-leaning educational establishment that the majority of American children attend? As also reported in Look What Happened While
You Were Sleeping **(2007):**

> *"Dr. Dan Smithwick, head of the Nehemiah In-*
> *stitute in South Dakota tested 20,000 students*
> *in over 1,000 high schools in four worldviews:*
> *Christian theism, moderate Christian, secular*
> *humanism, and socialism. The results alarmingly*
> *show that a plunge downward toward hard-core,*
> *secular humanism and socialism is taking place*
> ***in Christian schools**, as well as public schools.*
> *The downward plunge just moves a little slower*
> *for Christian schools. He says the Christian stu-*
> *dent **in the public school** system in the United*
> *States of America will fall to socialism in 2014*
> *while modern day Christian school students will*
> *land there four years later, in 2018."* [218]

The Nehemiah Institute is a Christian organization that did this independent study to trace the inroads socialism is making in the minds of not just American youth, but in particular, *Christian* youth. As you just read, their data showed that the year 2014 would be the year Christian students attending public schools would fall to socialism. This year, 2012, an onslaught of new government programs targeting America's youth have been introduced. If an independent organization can follow the progression of students succumbing to socialist mentalities, then certainly government agencies who enacted the agenda in the first place had a projection of the same year. The indoctrination has already been happening, but now with Obama's very aggressive integration of **"service"** with education, the floodgates have been opened. Now, it's not just the top cream students for leadership positions being sought out, but thousands of youth across the nation.

Strongly emphasized in several of these programs for the youth is the element of **mentoring**. A mentor is a trusted guide, one who is more knowledgeable and experienced than the student. A mentor helps to shape a person's worldview. As trust and confidence develops in the relationship, a greater influence is exerted over the one being mentored. Mentors can be for the good or for the bad. It is obvious that great abuse and manipulation can take place in a mentoring relationship with impressionable youth. Doesn't it seem strange, even out of line, that "mentoring" programs are being funded and provided by the United States government? [219] Do you want the government providing mentors for your children?

Obama knows the power of mentoring, because he himself was shaped by many mentors that made it possible for him to ascend the ladder to the presidency of the United States. As mentioned earlier, Frank Marshall Davis, a radical member of Communist Party USA, had a profound impact upon Obama, both in Hawaii and later when Obama went to Chicago.[220] From there, many names pop up in Obama's past who he admits to having been very much influenced by—so many of them were confirmed Communists with important and influential connections. What did Obama say about the years in Chicago? On his 2008 Campaign website a document exists that gives "Barack Obama's Plan for **Universal** Voluntary Citizen Service." Under the subtitle, "Integrate Service into Education," it states:

"Barack Obama calls his years working as a community organizer in Chicago's South Side the best education he ever had." [221]

Obama was hand-picked to be a front man for a very radical and evil agenda. He was befriended, taken in, formed, schooled and then created to project the answer to all of America's problems—through a radical, leftist agenda that would "fundamentally transform" America from a free-nation to one based on a theory that has not only failed time and time again, but has done so through great upheaval and great suffering and death of hundreds of millions of people.

In his book, <u>The Audacity of Hope</u>, Barack Obama describes how he had come to a point in his political career where he was having serious doubts as to whether to continue or not because he seemed to be stagnating.

> *"I decided to challenge a sitting Democratic incumbent for his congressional seat in the 2000 election cycle. It was an ill-considered race, and I lost badly...for the first time in my career, I began to experience the envy of seeing younger politicians succeed where I had failed, moving into higher offices, getting more things done... I began to harbor doubts about the path I had chosen...Denial, anger, bargaining, despair—I'm not sure. I went through all the stages prescribed by the experts. At some point, though, I arrived at acceptance—of my limits, and, in a way, my mor-*

tality…And it was this acceptance, I think, that allowed me to come up with the thoroughly cock-eyed idea of running for the United States Senate. An up-or-out strategy was how I described it to my wife, one last shot to test out my ideas…."[222]

There's a lot missing between 'A'—Obama's "acceptance" of his limits, and 'C'—his "cockeyed idea" of running for the U.S. Senate. If anyone accepts that Obama came up with the idea on his own to run in the senate race, you are naïve to say the least. In today's politics, money makes politicians. Against all odds, unknown and inexperienced Barack Obama won in a race against six other Democratic candidate contenders, and then against the Republican candidate. Concerning his own meteoric ride to the U.S. Senate, Obama, himself, called it "spooky."

"My campaign had gone so well that it looked like a fluke. Political observers would note that in a field of seven Democratic primary candidates, not one of us ran a negative TV ad. The wealthiest candidate of all—a former trader worth at least $300 million—spent $28 million, mostly on a barrage of positive ads, only to flame out in the final weeks due to an unflattering divorce file that the press got unsealed. My Republican opponent, a handsome and wealthy former

Goldman Sachs partner turned inner-city teacher,
started attacking my record almost from the start,
but before his campaign could get off the ground,
he was felled by a divorce scandal of his own.
For the better part of a month, I traveled Illinois
without drawing fire, before being selected to
deliver the keynote address at the Democratic
National Convention—seventeen minutes of un-
filtered, uninterrupted airtime on national televi-
sion. And finally the Illinois Republican Party
inexplicably chose as my opponent former presi-
dential candidate Alan Keyes, a man who had
never lived in Illinois and who proved so fierce
and unyielding in his positions that even conser-
vative Republicans were scared of him.

"Later, some reporters would declare me the
luckiest politician in the entire fifty states…there
was no point in denying my almost **spooky** *good*
fortune. I was an outlier, a freak; to political in-
siders, my victory proved nothing."[223]

Everything lined up so perfectly to bring about Obama's
long-shot, underdog victory—a victory that "proved
nothing" according to political insiders. All a coincidence? Just a fluke? Yet, the very same things were said
after his winning the election to the presidency. Who

could understand it? How could it have happened? It was, indeed, **spooky**, in Obama's own words. It was not Obama's victory, as much as it was the ones who created the image and the myth of the larger than life man, his mentors, who promised to fundamentally change the United States of America upon his election. "The best education" Obama said he ever had was a step-by-step process—through the mentoring relationships of men and women dead set against everything that America stands for and is foundationed upon. Mentoring is a powerful tool. The government wants to create more Obama's. Your children are in its crosshairs.

It doesn't stop there. Along with mentoring, another named objective from one of Homeland Security's new programs is to *"promote an **ethic** of national service and civic engagement."* [224] The word "ethic" is defined as the discipline of dealing with what is good and bad and with moral duty and obligation. In other words, government agencies have set an objective to teach the youth who enter their programs what is "good" national service and what is "bad" national service. They are going to define for our children what their "moral duty and obligation" is in regards to national service. *"Ethics"* is a set of moral principles or values or a theory or system of moral values. Another form of the word is *"ethos,"* which means the distinguishing character, sentiment, moral nature, or guiding beliefs of a person, group, or institution. In other words, a main objective of the government is to inculcate their own morality and philosophy of "service" into our youth through their government programs. This is both alarming and scary for millions of unsuspecting youth, as well as for parents. We know that the view of morality in this present government is far from the Judeo-Christian worldview. In fact, in great pride, much of the Obama Administration holds this worldview in contempt and disdain. We also know that they do not accept the Christian foundation upon which our nation was established, and they are working, in great pride, to re-interpret the Constitution to fit their own leftist agenda to complete America's transformation. Again, the Virgin Mary's words contain this:

February 2, 2012

"...pride has come to rule..."

Obama's administration makes no apologies for exposing and indoctrinating America's youth to their own ideologies, and through moves they are making in at least some of the youth programs, it is apparent. Some of the youth programs of service oppose the right of the youth to practice their faith while they are involved in govern-

ment programs. Alarming? Yes, very. What follows
are some of the specific programs that Obama has initiated. It should come as no surprise that among the many
concerns that are arising, religious freedom of youth is
attacked, as the first step to transform the youth in their
thinking. What is becoming more and more apparent is
that Obama and his administration believe "religiously"
that their ideology is the only "true faith"—and therefore,
it must be accepted and forced upon all Americans. This
is what the 1st Amendment is supposed to protect us from.

Getting Specific

As already shown in a previous chapter, incredibly
Hitler himself was quoted outlining a whole systematic
plan of taking over the minds of the German youth population. In the speech given in Colorado Springs, Colorado, on July 2, 2008, five months before being elected president, Obama outlined plans for his own youth brigade:

> *"...we need to **integrate service into education**,
> so that young Americans are called upon and
> prepared to be active citizens."* [225]

Recall that "Integrate Service into Education" was the
subtitle on Obama's 2008 campaign website under the
larger title, "Obama's Plan for Universal Voluntary
citizen Service," If it's "universal," how can it be volun-

tary? What we discovered is that it is not voluntary. As with Hitler's model, Obama would start out incrementally. Obama continued:

> *"When I'm President, I will set a goal for all American middle and high school students to perform 50 hours of service a year, and for all college students to perform 100 hours of service a year. This means that by the time you graduate college, you'll have done 17 weeks of service."* [226]

What right does the government have over college students attending private colleges? By a sort of blackmail bribery. These hours, like the model that was successful, would only increase in the amount required after Americans are conditioned to accept this path. Keep in mind that it would not just be hours of service that would be a concern, but the "ethic of service," the indoctrination that each child and all young people would be exposed to that is frightening in reading Obama's plan. To show how serious he was about this plan, Obama planned to force schools into compliance by threatening to take away their federal funding. Obama said on the same date of July 2, 2008:

> *"We can reach this goal in several ways. At the middle and high school level, we'll make fed-*

eral assistance 'conditional' on school districts developing service programs, and give schools resources to offer new service opportunities. At the community level, we'll develop public-private partnerships so students can serve more outside the classroom."

"…For college students, I have proposed an annual American Opportunity Tax Credit of $4,000. To receive this credit, 'we'll require' 100 hours of public service…"[227]

Is this why Obama was pushing so hard for every young American to attend college, because it's essential for his indoctrination program to be complete? He gives and dangles a carrot to help everyone digest and swallow his plan. Obama continues:

"And we will not leave out the nearly two million young Americans who are out of school and out of work. We'll enlist them in our Energy Corps, so that disadvantaged young people can find useful work, clean polluted areas, help weatherize homes, and gain skills in a growing industry. And we'll expand the Youth Build Program, which puts young Americans to work building affordable housing in America's poorest

*communities, giving them valuable skills and a chance to complete a high school education. **Because no one should be left out of the American story.*** *228*

Remember — Obama said being a community organizer was the best education he ever had. What should this say to you? Is Obama's plans for these youth about service or re-education? Is it about service, or indoctrination? Or does "service" actually mean the same? Obama has given a name to these youth, and the program in which he wishes to "enlist" them into "service," called **"Opportunity Youth."** The White House, Office of the Press Secretary announced on January 5, 2012:

> *"While young people who are currently disconnected from school or work are not contributing to our economy, we see these young people as 'Opportunity Youth' — because of the untapped potential they bring to the Nation...Opportunity Youth need social supports and access to relevant education, **mentoring** and training.*" *229*

But to capture the minds and hearts of the youth, they must be banned from church programs which would help them to resist such influence. Apparently the idea is for Obama's program to prevail over the Christian influence.

How strongly does Obama feel about his program, Opportunity Youth? He budgeted $1.5 **billion** dollars to this program, with a goal of creating **250,000 employment opportunities for the start of the summer 2012,** for a program called Summer Jobs. But the program failed to pass as law in Congress. That did not stop Obama. He simply made his own law and announced an executive "action," as the White House blog stated:

> *"Today's announcement is the latest in a* **'series'** *of executive actions the Obama Administration is taking to strengthen the economy and* **move the country 'forward'** *because we can't wait for Congress to act."* [230]

Remember that it was stated a few chapters back that this announcement concerning Opportunity Youth's new program, with its $1.5 billion dollar budget, was made the very same day Obama announced major cuts to the military budget. We remind you again of the words Obama said that day, January 5, 2012:

> *"But the question that this strategy answers is what* **'kind of military'** *will we need after the long wars of the last decade are over. And today, we're moving* **forward**...*"* [231]

Obama speaks of a different kind of military, as he slashes the military budget, and on the same day institutes the program, Summer Jobs, under <u>Opportunity Youth,</u> which targets upwards of two million youth out of school and out of work. He makes this move despite the fact that Congress did not pass the law.

No president has usurped Congress as Obama has. Yet, with impeachment power, they do nothing to stop him, as if Congress is under a spell. Many of these programs and jobs that have been lined up for "Opportunity Youth" are coming from government departments and organizations that are promoters of the White House agenda. Half of the "opportunities" aren't even actual jobs, but programs to help youth find where they could get placed according to what their skills are, etc. Others are in-service programs. Remember that many of these youth are on the margins of our culture, coming from single parent and broken family homes. The program calls for them to be "mentored" and to be given "access" to "relevant education." This is a scary prospect knowing that so many of these youth are on their own, do not have good parental guidance—making them easy targets for government manipulation. "Opportunity Youth" is one of a series of youth initiatives that the government has mandated starting this year, 2012. In

Obama's own words, "America's youth can't wait for Congress to act." As you will see, there is a push to get youth involved, right now, in Obama's initiatives.

One program, in particular, is most unsettling because it seems to be designed right from a Hitler Youth rule book. It is part of Homeland Security, announced in March 2012, and its first members will begin serving in August 2012. The program will reach full capacity within 18 months—showing again, an aggressiveness on the part of Obama's Administration to "move forward" these youth initiatives. Under the Federal Emergency Management Agency (F.E.M.A.), a new unit has been created entitled **"F.E.M.A. Corps"** and will be made up of 18-24 year old youth. These young people will be trained for leadership positions and will be given authority to act in emergency situations and any "threat" to the security of the nation. F.E.M.A. Corps was created from the partnership between the Department of Homeland Security's **F**ederal **E**mergency **M**anagement **A**gency and the **C**orporation for **N**ational and **C**ommunity **S**ervice known as C.N.C.S,. to *"establish a F.E.M.A.-devoted unit of 1,600 service corps members within AmeriCorps National Civilian Community Corps, known as N.C.C.C."*[232] The announcement of the new program came just three days before the release of Obama's Executive Order

H.R. 13603 that was thoroughly discussed, in Chapter 21, known as the National Defense Resource Preparedness Executive Order, which as you have read, gives Obama unprecedented power in times of peace as well as war. Those who are thoughtful will see this Executive Order as Peacetime Martial Law. In a statement made by the Secretary of Homeland Security, Janet Napolitano, a window is provided as to what this youth corps will provide:

> *"We know from experience that quick **'deployment'** of trained personnel is critical during a crisis. The F.E.M.A. Corps (18-24 yr. olds) will provide a pool of trained personnel, and it will also pay long-term dividends by <u>adding depth to our reserves</u> — individuals <u>trained in every aspect</u> of disaster response..."* [233]

Trained in <u>every aspect</u> of disaster response? Adding depth to our reserves? What kind of reserves? New crisscross Executive Orders and programs bridge back and forth over the healthcare bill. What do you find in this crisscross web? The ***Ready Reserve Corps*** that is mandated in the healthcare bill. As already asked, what does healthcare have to do with a Reserve Corps? In what situations will the F.E.M.A. Corps members be trained to respond? This is a full time residential program in which the young people will serve for 10 months, with a minimum of 1,700 service hours, with an option to stay for a second year. F.E.M.A. has made a 5-year commitment to train 1,600 youth leaders by the end of the 5th year. More than 500 were enrolled in the first program that started this August, 2012, in Mississippi. This is not just a short-term experience that F.E.M.A. is planning on, rather, they are hoping to…

> *"inspire a generation of young people to take up careers in emergency management."* [234]

A generation of young people? That's a lot of numbers. Thinking back to what we learned about Hitler Youth, once the youth went through the various programs, they were sent on into government programs— mainly for the purpose of keeping them away from influences that could cause them to question the "national ethics" that had been drilled into them from the time they were 10 years old. Another quote from F.E.M.A:

> *"This partnership will give thousands of young people the opportunity to serve their country and gain the skills and training they need to fill the jobs of today and tomorrow."* [235]

Recall Obama's own words spoken on July 2, 2008:

> *"I'm not going to tell you what your role should be; that's for you to discover."* [236]

Will pressure be applied to the youth in these programs to fill these "emergency management" positions? Is this what Obama is indicating here? Or with the indoctrination, will no pressure be needed? Remember, it took only five days to begin confusing a young Catholic girl who had been raised in a strong Catholic home to think differently about cloning, abortion, and the "right" to die. The answer is in Obama's words. Once trained, among their responsibilities will be to provide support to disaster recovery centers, to share with the public "valuable disaster preparedness" information.

On March 13, 2012, when F.E.M.A. Corps was first announced, Robert Velasco, acting CEO of the Corporation for National and Community Service, gave input into what this new "branch" of F.E.M.A. brings. Not surprisingly, all the "key" words are found in his statement:

> *"**This is a historic new chapter in the history of national service** that will enhance our nation's disaster capabilities and **promote an ethic of national service**..."* [237]

F.E.M.A. Deputy Administrator Richard Serino, in discussing the importance of F.E.M.A. Corps, stated:

> *"As we continue to **move forward** and...look for opportunities to get young people involved in*

*government, to get young people involved in **ser-vice** to their country, we will make a difference... so we have the opportunity to bring this talented, young, will-be-trained workforce to help our staff.*" [238]

Serino echoes Velasco's statement, repeating how F.E.M.A. Corps will:

"*...really help **the ethos of national service**.*" [239]

All of this national emergency "stuff" was not in place during Katrina. For those who were involved in responding to Katrina, this service force would have only gotten in the way, adding another layer of bureaucracy.

When reading the following, remember, F.E.M.A. Corps is the cover excuse to indoctrinate. While F.E.M.A. Corps is targeting 18–24 year olds, another F.E.M.A. program, also initiated in the spring of 2012, targets 12–17 year olds and is known as the "**F.E.M.A. Youth Preparedness Council.**" The purpose of the program under the ruse of "emergency preparedness" is to bring the philosophies of the Obama administration into the homes of all Americans using our own children as "**CHANGE** agents. " These are the actual words F.E.M.A. uses. Dictators in the past have used youth to

change, watch, even report on what is going on politically in their homes. A search for *"a select set of youth
leaders"* from each of the F.E.M.A. districts around
the United States took place earlier this year in order
to place these youth on a council. What follows is information found on F.E.M.A.'s website, that explains
the purpose of this council. To refresh your memory
before reading on F.E.M.A.'s call to youth, look back
on page 285 and read again the eight specific needs of
youth that Erich Fromm identified and that Hitler's
Third Reich manipulated in order to draw youth into
his programs. F.E.M.A. documents state:

> *"F.E.M.A. is looking for youth leaders who are
> dedicated to public service, who are making a
> difference in their community, and who want to
> expand their impact as a national advocate for
> youth preparedness. Are you a 12 to 17 year old
> who wants to make a difference in your commu-
> nity that could help **save lives**? F.E.M.A.'s Youth
> Preparedness Council is a unique opportunity
> for a select set of youth leaders to serve on a
> highly distinguished national council, to partici-
> pate in a community preparedness roundtable
> event in Washington, D.C., and to voice **their
> opinions, experiences, ideas, solutions**, and*

questions on youth disaster preparedness with the leadership of national organizations working on youth preparedness." [240]

What youth wouldn't feel flattered to be a part of this *"highly distinguished national council?"* The Washington roundtable event will include *"National partners engaged in youth preparedness work, Council members, Regional Community Preparedness Officers, and selected federal officials."* [241] There will be twenty 12-17 year old youth council members, two from each F.E.M.A. district, nominated by someone or nominating themselves through a specific application detailing their experience in preparedness work. So, only the cream of the crop will be selected from hundreds, if not thousands of applicants. For many reasons, this is very dangerous. And did you catch the bait of using exaggerated self-importance in the statement of F.E.M.A. — 12 to 17 year olds, voicing their opinions, expressing their ideas, save lives, all of which those who initiated these programs for F.E.M.A. could care less to hear from 12-17 year olds who have yet to go through life's experiences that would give them wisdom. This is called a hook to capture these youth, a baited hook to actually capture and change their opinions, change their ideas, form their solutions and give them experiences, moulding to their agenda.

Council members will be expected to take the information shared in these meetings back home to their own states and local F.E.M.A. districts. F.E.M.A. explains why they have taken this approach:

> *"Children are positive influencers. Children involved in youth preparedness programs can effectively spread important messages about preparedness to their family members. (or send valuable reports back for family and neighborhoods)* ***They can be 'change' agents.*** *Participating in emergency preparedness activities…****empowers children*** *but also educates adults about preparedness."* [242]

Why not educate adults directly? Is it because it is easier to influence youth, 're'educate them in order to plant a seed to weed out in the garden of the family home to change it? Do you realize how dangerous this infrastructure now being built will be in the near future? **Change agents**…to educate parents and/or to monitor them? F.E.M.A. **actually states** that through this program, as children learn about everything having to do with "preparedness," you will see a **"behavioral shift"** in the family, that "preparedness" will become a priority in every family. The operative word is "preparedness." What does Obama's government mean by this? Does it simply mean making sure you have extra water and canned goods, candles and blankets in case of an emergency? Or could it mean being "prepared" for a monumental change that the government seems to be expecting to take place in society? To that effect, our children are being targeted as **"CHANGE AGENTS"** to be trained to assist in this transition within their homes, their schools and their communities. This again, **and brace yourself**, is a quote directly from F.E.M.A.:

> *"As children are learning about preparedness and bringing the information to their families, **A BEHAVIORAL SHIFT WILL OCCUR**, making family preparedness a priority."* [243]

In Hitler's Germany, what began as volunteer service programs later became all but mandatory for every German child and young adult through great pressure applied from teachers, leaders, and especially from youth within the system. This pressure was placed on children not only to participate in the programs, but to take on the mindset of the Hitler Youth. Why was this so important to Hitler that he would go to such extremes to institute the indoctrination of all the youth of Germany? Again, in his own words, he said, *"He alone, who owns the youth, gains the future."* [244]

A young teenaged German boy, Walter Hess, who was a member of the Hitler Youth turned in his own father when he heard his father call Hitler, "a crazed Nazi maniac." The Gestapo arrested his father, sending him off to the Dachau concentration camp.[245] The young boy was commended for his loyalty and good example, and was then raised to a higher rank. Is this the kind of **"behavioral shift"** that awaits us in our own homes?

Why is it important to the Obama administration that family preparedness becomes a priority? What kind of "behavioral shift" can we expect? F.E.M.A. doesn't give any specifics here. We **do know** that they will be teaching **"ethics"** of preparedness, their belief system. We know that in the healthcare bill Obama calls for a Ready Reserve Corp. We know in this healthcare bill religious beliefs of Christians are violated, as are our 1st Amendment rights. We also know older people in a crisis are expendable, and this will apply to babies, as well as the handicapped, the unproductive, and on and on, who all will fall on the list as it evolves in expanding the culture of death. And again in F.E.M.A.'s own words describing their star programs, children will become **"change agents,"** that through emergency preparedness training children will become **"empowered to become leaders"** and they will help to create a **"behavioral shift"** in their own families.

Among other enacted programs at Obama's disposal to tie youth into service is the **"Public Service Loan Forgiveness Program."** As an incentive to draw recently graduating college seniors into government and public service fields that are typically low-paying positions, the program offers forgiveness of a portion of the student loan if they meet the requirements. They must be employed full-time in an approved service position. Out of their salary, they are to make minimal payments each month on their loan. Loan forgiveness will not be considered until after 120 minimal monthly payments are made. At the point 120 payments are made, the worker can apply for loan forgiveness of what is left of his school loan. What does the government get from this arrangement? It guarantees that thousands of **unsuspecting youth** will be placed in service fields, with full exposure to the socialist agenda. And even if they are not happy with their job, the hope in having their loan forgiven over time will be enough to keep them there. One hundred twenty monthly payments equals at least 10 years of being tied to the government's promise, and the promise is not even guaranteed. You still will have to apply for forgiveness of the loan after 10 years and at that time, the government could say they're broke.

What kind of jobs qualify for this program? Any government organization or agency at the federal, state

and local levels, a non-profit, tax-exempt organization, or a private, non-profit organization that provides
specific services detailed under the loan forgiveness
program. Do you think any of the non-profits could
be religious missionaries, etc.? There is one significant
stipulation that would **dis**qualify a particular organization. If you wish to choose a religious non-profit organization in which to serve, *"you may not include time
spent in participating in religious instruction, worship
services, or any form of proselytizing."*[246] Government's
sentiments would interpret evangelizing under "any
form of proselytizing." In effect, this would disqualify
any religious group, regardless of the service it is providing to the community, if the religious belief is central to their mission statement. Christians and those
of other religious faiths are therefore excluded from
participating in this program if they wish to serve in
an organization that coincides with their religious beliefs. One result of this will be that many unsuspecting
youth, though they would prefer to work for a religious
organization, will choose a secular service position because of financial pressure. And as a fly caught in fly
paper, they will likely be trapped and thereby exposed
to socialist, humanist philosophies, which over time will
have an impact on their way of thinking.

In April 2009, just **three months after Obama's inauguration**, his agenda was exposed further when he signed into law the "Serve America Act," H.R. 1388. This law authorizes expansion of the number of approved national service positions to 250,000 by the year 2017, which would manage upwards to eight million volunteers. These service positions are managed by the Corporation for National and Community Service, a government corporation responsible for administering the national service laws programs. A stipulation was also included in this law for **ineligible** activities and organizations. Incredulously worded, it states for those working in public service they are to be banned from religion and God.

"SEC. 132A. Prohibited Activities and Ineligible Organizations.

Prohibited Activities—A participant in an approved national service position under this subtitle may not engage in the following activities:

1. (7) Engaging in religious instruction, conducting worship services, providing instruction as part of a program that includes mandatory religious instruction or worship, constructing or operating facilities devoted to

*religious instruction or worship, maintaining
facilities primarily or inherently devoted to
religious instruction or worship, or engaging
in any form of proselytization…"*

[AND]

*(11) Carrying out such other activities as the
Corporation for National and Community
Service may prohibit. [This means they can
decide to add whatever other activities you
cannot participate in that they hadn't thought
of or foresaw at that point.]*

You might think, they can't mean this. They must
mean these are prohibited activities during their work
hours in these service positions. If that were the case,
it still greatly violates the religious freedom of U.S.
citizens. But in studying the law, it says what it says. It
does not stipulate whether the worker is on or off duty.
It says, "A participant…may not engage…" Period.

Essentially, through this law the government will be
spending a lot more money on public service positions
and opportunities, but because of the above prohibition
none of it will be spent on supporting religious activities or by religious organizations that are aiding society.
Evil's interpretation and spin on this law will not allow

those involved with these programs to be associated with Christianity while in service. Time and again, the fruitful work of Christians is killed, which "as" the work of the nuns starting a hospital in Birmingham proved, is the most beneficial and the most effective in providing special needed services that government cannot do on the same level.

And so again, people with an honest desire to serve in a religious capacity or in a religious organization will be led into Obama's secular programs and influenced by their conditioning. The Serve America Act is a law that left the door open for the government to prohibit anything else they have not thought of yet, or they are afraid to say at this time, that does not fit their agenda. This tactic gives the government the ability to prohibit participants from engaging in *"other activities as the Corporation* [for National and Community Service] *may prohibit."* What these last two initiatives show is that there is an increasing boldness by Obama and the 'powers that be' to attack the rights of believers that are guaranteed in the Constitution. When Obama challenged the Catholic bishops over the healthcare bill, it was not a sudden move on his part, but rather he has been moving towards this for some time through other executive actions.

In 2008, it was reported that Obama, if he won the presidency, planned to:

> *"double the Peace Corps' budget by 2011 and expand AmeriCorps, USA Freedom Corps, VIS-TA, YouthBuild Program, and the Senior Corps. Plus, he proposes to form a Classroom Corps, Health Corps, Clean Energy Corps, Veterans Corps, Homeland Security Corps, Global Energy Corps, and a Green Jobs Corps."* [247]

Lee Cary of American Thinker, in his article titled *"Obama's Civilian National Security Force,"* stated:

> *"Senator Obama aims to tap into the already active volunteerism of millions of Americans and recruit* **them to become cogs in a gigantic government machine grinding out his social re-engineering agenda."** [248]

Many of these objectives have already been met. The "Serve America Act" accomplished expanding the capacity of funded service positions to 250,000 by 2017, which would include the promise he made in 2008 to expand the AmeriCorps, Peace Corps, Senior Corps, and YouthBuild, etc. The act also identifies the development of new "corps," such as the "Education Corps," "Healthy Futures Corps," "Clean Energy Service Corps," "Veterans Corps," and "Opportunity Corps" and more to come that must receive funding under the law. Many of these corps heavily involve placement of or service to youth.[249]

The Serve America Act was first known as the "GIVE" Act, "Generations Invigorating Volunteerism and Education Bill." In this bill, the government wanted to make "volunteering" <u>mandatory</u> for all 18-24 year olds for a three month period, in which, as stated, there would be strict prohibitions upon the religious freedoms of these youth having to participate. At the time this was being discussed and planned, White House Chief of Staff, Rahm Emanuel, stated:

> *"It's time for a real Patriot Act that brings out the patriot in all of us. We propose universal civilian service for every young American. Under this plan all Americans between the ages of 18 and 25 will be asked to serve their country by going through three months of <u>basic training</u>, <u>civil defense preparation</u> and community service."[250]*

In Emanuel's statement, he specifically names what the youth will be volunteering for—basic training and civil defense. The bill didn't pass as written. It was later changed to the Serve America Act and the "mandatory" three months service for all young Americans was dropped from the bill, but again, it reveals the thoughts and goals behind Obama's administration.

Note, most importantly, all these different national service corps have a prohibition that there can be no religious ties whatsoever with those who fill these positions. The fact is that government has no business having these types of service corps in the first place. This has always been territory covered by the Church and other private entities. The alarm goes off when government begins these initiatives. **Is this why the Catholic Church is being forced to comply to the healthcare mandate so as to get it out of these service oriented fields? If you know your enemy, you would answer "yes." If you do not, you would answer, "well maybe, maybe not." Knowing we will not comply, is the government anticipating that we will, therefore, resign these services to a godless government who will foster the culture of death through their corps? In the void left by the Catholic Church and other Christian churches and organizations the government is free to step in and fill the gap with no competition. It will be much easier then to move forward their socialist agenda. This is why the Catholic Church cannot close up shop, nor comply, but must defy.**

CHAPTER TWENTY-SIX

An Important Review

The last chapter is important not only to be informed of but to learn. Would you allow a person to specifically start stalking your child or a child in your neighborhood? Of course not. Then this review will drive home the fact that the 'powers that be' have their eyes on our youth and their futures, and they are no less darker than a stalker's. This review of parallels comparing a past time when youth were used for a sinister purpose to what is happening now brings further clarity to where we are traveling.

A Striking Review of Parallels Mentioned in the last Chapter

- To summarize the ground that has already been covered, there are many apparent similarities between how Hitler used the German youth to build a civilian force, and the actions of Obama who clearly stated that it is his intention to build a civilian force just as powerful, strong and well-funded as the U.S. military. Hitler began building his youth program years before the war began. The Nazis capitalized on the natural enthusiasm of young people, their craving for action and desire for peer approval, ultimately, hoping that each young person would come to regard his Hitler Youth or League of German Girls unit as a home away from home, or perhaps as their real home. Hitler led Germany to initiate the war, creating the crisis himself that then utilized his already trained youth. We are being warned of an impending crisis by Obama, while our youth are being initiated in "emergency preparedness training."

Both Hitler and Obama passed laws that greatly threatened the rights of citizens. Both promised that they would not use the law against their own people. Hitler broke his promise. We have only Obama's word that he won't do the same, but the laws giving him the power have been signed by him, just the same. Obama promised the U.S. bishops a conscientious clause in the healthcare bill. After they helped him get it passed, he backed out of his promise. Obama's word, obviously, is not to be trusted. Obama shares Hitler's view that the youth are key for a "fundamental transformation" of a nation to be successful. They both developed a very methodical and structured educational program to insure that their ideologies successfully passed to the

youth. Though Obama has not yet been able to mandate his plan, the laws he is implementing indicate that
this is still part of his plan unfolding. Hitler strongly
advocated the importance of "service" to the Party and
State, and to him as Fuhrer—while de-emphasizing
the importance of family and church in the lives of the
youth. He aimed to build a superior race to control the
world. Obama also has an "ethic of national service"
that is part of his educational and service agenda. He
also de-emphasizes the importance of God, family
and traditional American values while emphasizing
the importance of service to the State; service being a
key word for socialism. Outside of what has already
been covered, there are still more parallels that can be
pointed out.

Other Parallels Between Hitler Youth and Obama's Youth Programs

- **Both Hitler and Obama Used the Youth to Help Bring them to Power**

  On September 10, 1938, Hitler stood before
  a gathering of 80,000 youth and after speaking to them about his own years as a youth,
  identifying with them about painful adolescent experiences, with smooth talk, Hitler
  said to them:

*"You, my youth, are our nation's most pre-
cious guarantee for a greater future, and you
are destined to be the leaders of a glorious new
order under the supremacy of National Socialism. Never forget that one day you will rule the
world."* [251]

In a speech Obama gave on July 2, 2008, in which a large portion of it addressed the plans being formulated for the youth of our nation with his administration, like Hitler, he spoke about his difficult adolescent years so to make a bridge to the youth that he understood their difficulties:

*"As some of you know, I spent much of my child-
hood adrift. My father had left my mother and
me when I was 2 years old. My mother remar-
ried and we moved overseas for a time. But I
was mostly raised in Hawaii by my mom and my
grandparents who were from Kansas. And growing up, I wasn't always sure of who I was or where
I was going. That's what happens sometimes when
you don't have a father in the home."* [252]

Like Hitler, Obama's shared experience resonated with many youth, and through his calls to them to get involved, thousands did—in helping to elect him to the presidency. On the official web page for Obama's "Organizing For America," the objective is made quite clear:

> *"Generation Obama/GO is a locally-based but nationally coordinated grassroots movement led by young activists with a simple goal: electing Barack Obama the next President of the United States of America through field work, political organizing and fundraising. With a few committed activists and the savvy to reach thousands of people in your community, your GO chapter can play a powerful role for the Obama campaign."*[253]

There is only one problem with the "led by youth activists." How did they get organized? Where did they get the funds? The question proves they are not led by youth, as stated above, but by something much more powerful than they. When Obama won the election, he specifically mentioned the role the youth played in bringing about this victory, with smooth talk, Obama said:

> *"I will never forget who this victory truly belongs to. It belongs to you. It belongs to you...It grew strength from the young people who rejected the*

myth of their generation's apathy who left their homes and their families for jobs that offered little pay and less sleep…This is your victory." [254]

- **The Hitler Youth Brigade grew incrementally year by year, as will Obama's in a second term.**

The Obama administration has an aggressive plan to incrementally increase the numbers of people in their service programs with a heavy emphasis on youth involvement over the next six years, from 2011 up to 2017. According to the "Serve America Act," the Corporation for Community and National Service, that administers the national service laws programs, SHALL (shall means " must"):

"(1) develop a plan to—…

(A) establish the number of the approved national service positions as 88,000 for fiscal year 2010;

(B) increase the number of the approved positions to—

(i) 115,000 for fiscal year 2011;

(ii) 140,000 for fiscal year 2012;

(iii) 170,000 for fiscal year 2013;

(iv) 200,000 for fiscal year 2014;

(v) 210,000 for fiscal year 2015;

(vi) 235,000 for fiscal year 2016; and

(vii) 250,000 for fiscal year 2017; [255]

The "Serve America Act" under Obama provides not an option, but a legal mandate, "shall," for the same incremental steps as Hitler's program. But make no mistake. It will not stop at 250,000. Though these numbers include more than just 18–24 year olds, the youth are targeted in many of these service programs.

Nineteen thirty-three was the year the Nazis came into power; all other youth groups in Germany were then abolished, exploiting more than two million youth who were forced into Hitler's group over the next two years. Obama's youth corps, at any point, can be made compulsory and like Hitler's, the numbers can jump into the millions.

In 1936 one of Hitler's officers, as a gift for Hitler's 47th birthday wanted to enroll all 10 year olds throughout Germany into the Hitler Youth. It was called "the

Year of the Hitler Youth" and great pressure was put
on these children to join the organization. They were
always methodically working towards enrolling more
and more students. By 1939, over seven million youth
were inducted both voluntarily and mandatorily. That's
seven million youth in a period of only six years from
1933 to 1939. Obama hasn't yet made enrollment in
service programs mandatory, but read on. Obama also
seems to have goals set to gradually achieve increasing numbers in his programs. With F.E.M.A. Corps,
when it was announced in March, 2012, they said that
they would have the first corps members established
by August of the same year, working up to full capacity
(1,600 members) in 18 months, which would be February, 2014.

- **Hitler made it law that all youth must become
  members of his organizations. Is Obama creating the pathway to do that here in America?**

Hitler Youth numbers grew substantially when a
law was passed making it mandatory for all youth to
establish membership in his youth programs. Though
it did not make it into the final law, the initial House of
Representatives version of the "Serve America Act"
contained a provision instructing Congress to explore
*"whether a workable, fair and reasonable **mandatory***

service requirement for all able young people could be developed, and how such a requirement could be implemented..." [256] No, it didn't become part of this law, but it was in Obama's vision before becoming president and was <u>put on the table without any attempt to hide it</u>. That fact that this provision was proposed is clear evidence the 'powers that be' want to make regular induction into service mandatory. If you're thinking, "There's no way I'll let my 12 year old join any of these service corps," you must remember that mandatory service induction is part of the Executive Order:

> "...the Secretary of Labor shall...in coordination with the Secretary of Defense, assist the Director of Selective Service in development of policies regulating **the 'induction' and 'deferment' of persons for duty in the armed services.**" [257]

If the Secretary of Labor, Secretary of Defense, and the Director of Selective Service decide your kids will be called to mandatory service, you will have no choice. Your children will have to participate. You may ask where in the Executive Order does it say they are referring to youth? It says, *"the induction and deferment of persons."* All of Obama's laws are written this way so they can be interpreted any way the 'powers that be' want to—youth, middle aged, even those of old age.

But, only the youth have the numbers and abilities needed to build a Ready Reserve Corp and Obama's programs are already in place for this. Obama cleverly and intentionally uses the term *"armed **services.**"* Many youth and others will be forcibly inducted into this service force. And don't be deceived. This isn't just about a service force that mentors youth and assists in times of disasters. By the words in the Executive Order itself, *"armed services,"* it is clear that this contingent will be armed. Did you know the Department of Homeland Security entered into a contract in March of 2012 to purchase up to 450 million rounds of 40 caliber hollow point ammunition over the next 5 years?[258] What could Homeland Security possibly need 450 million rounds of ammunition for? They are not even a police force!!

Homeland Security employs 199,500 people.[259] No small amount of those are administrative. If you divide 450 million rounds of ammo between them, that averages to 2,255 rounds per person. One-third of all Homeland Security personnel are employed under Transportation Security Administration (TSA), or rather, airport security. Not a lot of need for ammunition there. Other divisions under Homeland Security's Americorps include Youth Build Program, Peace

Corps, Green Jobs Corps, Opportunity Corps, Global
Energy Corps, etc. These are service corps organizations. Why would service corps need to be "armed"?
Homeland Security also covers border control, Secret
Service, and the Coast Guard which on occasion has
use for ammunition, but 450 million rounds is well out
of the ballpark in what is needed there. Compare the
numbers: Just before 9/11, all military branches together used only 700 million rounds of small caliber ammunition in a year[260] and we have Homeland Security
made up of primarily service corps organizations buying 450 million rounds? What are they preparing for?
Why? Is it perhaps, as brought up in an earlier chapter,
because by the Constitution our military can't be used
against the people? Or because many of our military
members are dissatisfied with Obama and would not go
along with being used against the people? Or is it because the 'powers that be' know that all across America
"we the people" are arming themselves as never before? Obama knows this...remember he spoke of
those Christians who *"cling to guns or religion."* [261]

As has already been disclosed, one of the tactics
being used to push unconstitutional laws through is
to write laws that are hundreds of pages long, in hard
rhetoric to read, but in language that sounds official.

Fill these laws with massive amounts of regulations. Crisscross laws upon laws, with the same agendas. What happens is that it creates confusion and takes on the appearance of Constitutional law that can then be interpreted by the 'powers that be' to obtain their goal.

In Conclusion

The parallels between Hitler's Youth and the actions of Obama and his administration regarding America's youth are too striking to dismiss. Our children are in the crosshairs. And as happened in Germany, when the parents and the Church finally became aware of the diabolical plan that was aimed at taking over the minds of their children, it was too late to act. The government's slogan for their "Preparedness" programs is "Be Ready." What moves behind these agendas is a worldview that opposes the belief in a Supreme Being. It is a humanist philosophy, a system of thought that rejects religious beliefs and centers on humans, but without God as the point of reference. Man, therefore, cannot have any unalienable rights to life, liberty or the pursuit of happiness because the state becomes the point of reference and human life is held under the state's control. Remarkably, Our Lady gives words addressing this very specific manifestation that is now arising of an anti-god system that seemingly is unstoppable at the rate that it is building. Our Lady says:

April 2, 2010

> **"Dear children; Today I bless you in a special way and I pray for you to return to the right way to my Son—your Savior, your Redeemer—to Him who gave you eternal life. Reflect on everything <u>human</u>, on everything that does not permit you to set out after my Son—on transience, imperfections and limitations—and then think of my Son, of His Divine infiniteness. By your surrender and prayer ennoble your body and perfect your soul. <u>Be ready, my children</u>. Thank you."**

In Obama's July 2, 2008 speech he states that there are *"people of every age, race, and religion who want to come together to renew the American spirit."* [262] He then reveals how that renewal will happen. It is a spiritual statement, one that aims at fundamentally answering what is needed to rediscover the way. Obama states:

"Renewing that spirit starts with   ? ."

Can you guess? Is Obama's answer, God? Prayer?
Going back to what the United States was founded
upon? No. According to Obama,

> *"Renewing that spirit starts with **service**."[263]*

He goes on to define what he means by this:

> *"Make no mistake: our destiny as Americans
> is tied up with one another...That's the bet our
> Founding Fathers were making all of those years
> ago—that our individual destinies could be tied
> together in the common destiny of democracy;
> that government depends **not just on the con-
> sent of the governed, but on the service of citi-
> zens**... We need your service, right now, at this
> moment—our moment—in history."[264]*

Did you get that incredible statement? Obama per-
forms revisionism that it is not just the "consent of the
governed," but he adds it is the service of citizens?

This was not the dream our Founding Fathers held
for this nation. They founded a "republic," not a democracy. And though we are all Americans, we all have
the freedom to seek out our own individual destinies
holding in "common" the protection of rights guaran-
teeing to every man, life, liberty and the pursuit of hap-

piness. Two worldviews are coming head to head in confrontation of each other. One, in order to conquer and rule, must take the free will and freedom away from every individual in order to create what they promote to be a utopian life for all of man. It has never worked in history, and it won't work now. What it leads to, instead, is slavery under a merciless dictatorship. But as Our Lady said, **"...you cannot stop the evil that wants to begin to rule in this world and to destroy it..."** In 1 John 3:8, it states:

> *"The reason the Son of God appeared was to destroy the works of the devil."*

This is why He sent the Virgin Mary. She said:

August 2, 1981

> **"...A great struggle is about to unfold. A struggle between my Son and satan. Human souls are at stake."**

Our Lady has been sent by God in this, Her time, to expose and destroy the works of the devil by bringing us back to Her Son, a battle between the Woman and the dragon. She is raising up Her own army of "children" to gather under the Standard of the Son of God, Her Son, conceived by the Holy Spirit. And as the

Commander of this Army, She calls to us, **"Be Ready."**
Our Lady said:

March 17, 1989

> **"...Prepare yourself to look at Jesus 'eye to eye.'..."**

CHAPTER TWENTY-SEVEN

Move Fast so not to get Resistance

Government is necessary. Government is good when it serves the good of the people. It can only serve good when it is based in the principle of what Thomas Jefferson is attributed with saying:

> "The government that governs least, governs best."

Limited government was the basis of the foundation of our nation. The Alabama State Constitution echoes this thought and states very plainly:

Section 35 – Objective of government

> "That the sole object and only legitimate end of government is to protect the citizen in the enjoyment of life, liberty, and property, and when the government assumes other functions it is usurpation and oppression." [265]

What is government when it tells its citizens you must financially support and then propagate abortion? What is government when it assaults the Church, denies unalienable rights, and removes vestiges of Christianity from the public square, and because we resist, labels Catholics and others of the Christian faith as extremist? When this happens, tyranny begins its reign. In tyranny, liberty fades. As this happens, people begin at first to be concerned about the government. As this concern grows, the reality of what is materializing grows into fear of the government. John Basil Barnhill, a publisher and writer in the late 19th and early 20th century, said:

> *"Where the people fear the government, you have tyranny. Where the government fears the people, you have liberty."* [266]

The leftist and liberal ideologues are attempting to paint and vilify anyone who disagrees with the government as anti-government extremists, many who are simply standing up for their unalienable right of freedom and liberty. In an interview given in 2009, Richard Mack, former Graham County Arizona sheriff, quoting Senator Barry Goldwater, said:

> *"I know this sounds radical. Standing for freedom has always been labeled as radical, but '**extremism in defense of liberty is no vice.'"** [267]

U.S.A. Today has shown itself for years to be, in its articles, a pawn for leftist and liberal ideology. From articles promoting the world is going to end because of global warming, to articles favoring radical environmentalism, to slanting the news to paint Christians as backward and narrow minded, while socialism is utopia, etc. *USA Today's* March 30, 2012 headline is a classic example, which spotlighted a man who has been a hold out on his homestead for 12 years because of a scrap with a state trooper in which he was charged with a felony. Through four terms, all the county sheriffs decided it was best to just leave him and his family alone. The sheriffs did not want a repeat of Waco, Texas and of what happened there, where women and children were unnecessarily killed by federal law officers. Aside from the issues of the Texas man, the headlines read, *"Texas Standoff is Emblematic of the Nation's Growing Anti-Government Sovereign Movement."* [268] The article acknowledged that there are those who do not like the bank bailouts and other things the government has done, but then used an extremist to be representative of this whole group. The *USA Today* article created a stereotype that if you are not in union with what the Federal government is implementing via Obama and his executive orders and directives, then you are called **'a sovereign'**. It is the same old verbicide games the so-

cialists use to make wicked what is good. Sovereignty
is good for nations, when the government is beholden
to the people, but it is not possible under socialist policies. Speaking of the Sovereignty of America as a nation, separately from other nations, is a different matter
than the federal government believing that government is sovereign in opposition to the individual. The
perception of the State is that it is sovereign, whereas,
the belief of the founders was that it is the individuals
who are sovereign, because "we the people" are the
government. Knowing that America's sovereignty is
a good and that the individual's sovereignty resonates
deep in the heart of Americans, the word **"sovereign"**
must be demonized. Enemies to individual unalienable rights and limited government, lump everyone
who simply does not like big government intrusion into
this category, negatively stereotyping this group "the
sovereigns." This includes all those who do not believe
the federal government has a right to force Christians
to do things against very well known Christian beliefs and principles, as well as anyone who fights back
against the government's encroachment on citizen's
freedom and liberty. We are firm in our belief that one
of those foundational Christian principles is the virtue
to respect government authority and abide by the rule
of law based in natural and common law, by which a

government serves the people by protecting their God-given right of liberty. However, respect is not owed if government is ruling over and trampling the very law we are bound to obey by the Constitution. Make <u>no</u> mistake, **this book is not about believing there should be no government,** nor in any way being violently opposed to it. It is about the same problem the nation's fathers had, which impelled them <u>legally</u> to throw off such government that was trampling over the rights of the citizens:

> "*when a long Train of Abuses and Usurpations, pursuing invariably the same Object, evinces a Design to* **reduce them under absolute Despotism, it is their Right, it is their Duty, to throw off such Government, and to provide new Guards for their future Security.**" [269]

In the United States, the early settlers came seeking religious freedom. Built on these same principles, the founders of this Great Nation were anti-big and intrusive government. The move by Obama's Executive Order is unconstitutional and he, and the 'powers that be,' know this. It is their strategy to paint anyone against these executive orders and unconstitutional policies as anti-government, thereby giving them the ability to come down on law-abiding citizens, even labeling them terrorists simply for their protecting their unalienable rights to liberty. Everyone can reason, we need "limited" government. We need military. We need "limited" local authority, police, sheriffs, etc. At the same time, anyone who loves this nation does not want state and local authority, including police and sheriffs, to be used by the federal government as their extended hands fostering federal localization. What federal localization means is the implementation of federal policies at the local level. It certainly can be said that evil helped set the stage, before Obama's presidency. But now, Obama's strategizing is greatly enhancing tyranny's ability to take root with his sudden rush of enacting executive orders, regulations and policies, more and more our government is turning into a tyrannical power lording over our states, our cities, our towns, down to our neighborhoods and homes. A growing government which has been expanding for decades is now reaching a point where Obama can sweep in at the most opportune moment for evil to rule and bring destruction to the United States and thereby, to the rest of the nations of the world. No, Obama does not think he is destroying the United States. But neither did others whose path he is following. Even Hitler said on March 23, 1933, before passing the Enabling Act:

"The national government sees in both Christian denominations the most important factor for the maintenance of our society. It will observe the agreements drawn up between the Churches and the provinces; their rights will not be touched." [270]

All tyrants do not seem to be such when they begin. People think of them as saviors, only to realize later that many cannot handle power without wanting more. This leads to the proverbial saying that power corrupts and absolute power corrupts absolutely. Few men had the attributes of George Washington who had at hand, as president, great power, but was self-measured in his use of it.

It is also important that one not be swayed by the "nice talk" of Obama. As already mentioned before, just because one calls oneself a Christian does not make one a Christian. Obama is not a Christian even though he may state that he is. Even though Hitler made harsh pronouncements against the Church, he also stated:

"The church is necessary for the people. It is a strong and conservative element." [271]

Hitler's close friend Albert Speer stated that:

"Even after 1942, Hitler went on to maintain that he regarded the Church as indispensable in political life…he sharply condemned the campaign against the Church calling it a crime against the future of the nation…He too would <u>remain a member of the Catholic church</u>, although he had no real attachment to it. And in fact he remained in the Church until (his death)…"[272]

The exception, Albert Speer stated, was that Hitler said that the churches would learn to:

"adapt to the political goals of National Socialism (Nazi) in the long run, as it had always adapted in the course of history." [273]

Was Hitler a Catholic just by the fact that he said he was? Church membership means nothing without the living out of Catholic/Christian beliefs and principles in one's life.

So, where are we in the course of history? Churches of today, you do not agree with the healthcare mandate that you have to fund abortions? Churches of today, you do not agree that you have to violate your conscience in funding contraceptives? That's okay, Obama is giving you until August 2013, to *"adapt"* to his political goals, just as Hitler believed the Church would do in his time.

The following is the fast and furious[*] time line of Obama's most recent actions of consolidating total supreme authority and unprecedented power for the President of the United States, with ability to overtake the other two branches of government. Some of these **have already been covered in previous chapters**, while others have not. However, read them again and learn them to be able to know your subject when you inform others or speak of their dangers. Keep in mind all these following plans were well thought out as written by the 'powers that be,' and clearly show a monumental amount of planning, strategizing and conniving. Yet, all have been instituted <u>over a span of only a short five months.</u>

---

[*] Eric Holder headed a plan called "Fast and Furious." The plan was to <u>allow</u> weapons to be sold illegally through gun stores, in the border states of Mexico. They then would claim the need for gun control because guns were being sold for drugs, gangs, etc. However, the government's plan backfired and was exposed for its real purpose which is believed to go all the way back to Obama. Holder has evidence that is believed to prove this cover-up. He has refused congressional orders to turn over these papers, placing himself above the law, along with being in contempt.

2011

- **November 9, 2011**

First ever nationwide test of Emergency
Alert System conducted by **F**ederal **C**om-
munications **C**ommission, the **F.C.C.**, along
with the **F**ederal **E**mergency **M**anagement
Agency, known as **F.E.M.A.** The test of the
Emergency **A**lert **S**ystem, known as **E.A.S.**,
is an alert and warning system the president
can activate during emergencies to provide
information supposedly to the American
public. This can be used to alert Americans
that there is a crisis of which the government
could make use of to fully activate Obama's
Executive Order No. 13603, as well as the
following policies, executive orders and/
or laws. We already have local emergency
warning systems, and to have a federalized
system capable of alerting all 50 states, from
Hawaii to Miami to Alaska, is questionable
as to its purpose. The present local warning systems are very effective and not under consolidated federal control. With the
E.A.S., a crisis can be created and used for a
purpose that tyranny creates.

- **November 18, 2011 National Continuity Programs Expanded – Overstepping the Constitution**

    A **F**ederal **E**mergency **M**anagement **A**gency (F.E.M.A.) document dated November 18, 2011, that contains information about the agency's "National Continuity Programs," was posted on a federal website. The document was quickly pulled from the website when a separate private website drew attention to it. Programs include activities involving **C**ontinuity **O**f **O**perations, labeled **C.O.OP.,** and **C**ontinuity **O**f **G**overnment, labeled **C.O.G.,** which generally refer to minimizing the disruption of and maintaining essential government operations, both federal and local, in times of national crisis or emergency.

    C.O.G. is not a new concept, as the United States government first began to establish **C.O.G.** policy and activities in response to the Cold War with Russia. However, the release of this most recent **C.O.G.** document, taken in consideration with Obama's National Defense Resource Preparedness Executive Order discussed in past chapters

and other elements of takeover and control
covered in this book, is yet another piece of
the puzzle. It's a piece that reveals aggressive focused efforts to align and coordinate
all possible authority to consolidate power,
thereby, controlling every aspect of American life.

The **C.O.G.** document also identifies the use
of the most advanced civilian and military
technology to aid in continuity efforts, such
as the military technology, "Blue Force Situ-
ational Awareness," a technology used to
identify and track friendly and enemy forces
on the battlefield. Again, taken in context
with the rest of the subject matter discussed,
it becomes disturbingly clear that in the eyes
of the federal government, Americans who
voice opposition to the encroachment of
government in their lives are now the ones
who will be considered the hostile "enemies"
from within.

John E. Peters, a senior analyst with the
RAND Corporation, an independent research firm whose national security research

groups are federally funded,[274] stated the following about C.O.G. operations:

"At the state and local level, COG operations can facilitate the quick restoration of civilian authority and essential government functions and services. This can greatly reassure citizens and can minimize the risks that military support to consequence management activities is **_misperceived as an imposition of martial law_**. *It also can reduce the undesirable burdens that can be imposed on the military in attempting to carry out traditional civilian functions, ranging from law enforcement to garbage collection."* [275]

Why would people perceive such military support in the domestic United States as imposition of martial law? Why is this thought even in the minds of the 'powers that be,' to the extent they feel the need to openly address it, unless, of course, martial law or something like it is what they are aiming for? Citizens will:

"misperceive as an imposition of martial law."

If it looks like Martial Law to citizens, if it feels like Martial Law, if it smells like Martial Law—then it is, in fact, Martial Law.

- **December 1, 2011**

    The **N**ational **D**efense **A**uthorization **A**ct,
    called the **N.D.A.A.** bill, passed in the Sen-
    ate on December 1ˢᵗ, and after cleared The
    House of Representatives and was ready for
    the president's signature by December 15,
    2011.[276] Mid-December is a very convenient
    time to move forward controversial acts by
    stealth while the nation is preoccupied and
    busy with the Christmas season. Recall
    that the bill contains a provision to use the
    United States military for indefinite detain-
    ment of, *"a person who was a part of or*
    substantially supported Al Qaeda, the Tali-
    ban, 'or' associated forces that are engaged
    *in **hostilities** against the United States..."* [277]
    Many, including experts reading this law, are
    extremely concerned about the law's ability
    to give power for indefinite detainment to be
    used against American citizens. Naturally,
    there are those saying this will not be ap-
    plied to American citizens. Yet again, as al-
    ready stated but necessary to the point, why
    then would Obama himself say he would
    not interpret it that way, which means he

recognized that it could be interpreted that way. When tyranny reigns, any "potential" will be exploited for what serves its purpose. Yet still, a workaround to make it clearly applicable to American citizens is in the works. Recall also the "Enemy Expatriation Act," is currently under consideration (as of August, 2012) in Congress that works around the N.D.A.A. It can be applied to American citizens by effectively stripping them of their citizenship for engaging in *"hostilities against the United States."* [278] The rapidly broadening and increasingly ambiguous definition of terrorist activities or hostilities, defined by none other than those who are behind these laws, make this a most dangerous addition to Obama's arsenal. **United States' Bishops and those who stand with them, stating, "We will not comply," can be considered hostile by the National Defense Authorization Act (N.D.A.A.).** If one says not so, then the "Enemy Expatriation Act," if passed, could be applied to change not only the Bishop's, but other like-minded people's expression of civil disobedience into an act of terrorism. They then could be treated as domestic terrorists threatening the stability of the nation. However, knowing your enemy you can conclude that the efforts to pass the Enemy Expatriation Act reveals the intent and how they will interpret the N.D.A.A. to detain "hostiles," if the law passes.

- **December 8, 2011**

  The White House releases the "Strategic Implementation Plan for Empowering Local Partners to Prevent Violent Extremism in the United States." The plan document states the purpose is to coordinate national and local efforts to *"counter violent extremism."* [279] The coordination of "local partners" with the federal government makes it possible to implement federal mandates locally. These partners could include local law enforcement agencies, schools, community groups, businesses, service organizations, etc. The shifting and ambiguous defining of terms like "extremism" presents a great danger to those who will be labeled as "Tutsi" extremists, or rather, as "sovereigns" in keeping with the latest terminology being assigned to those who honor religious and unalienable rights. Or, in other words, anyone disagreeing with the "Hutu" government, or those who take away religious and unalienable rights.

- **December 31, 2011**

    Remember Sun-tzu's rule, "Know your enemy." Obama covertly and intentionally waited two weeks after the passage of the **N**ational **D**efense **A**uthorization **A**ct, **N.D.A.A.,** in Congress to sign it into law (see December 1). He signed it into law on New Year's Eve, December 31, 2011, so that as few people as possible would pay attention to it and so it would receive as little media coverage as possible, given that most of the nation was busy ringing in the New Year.

2012

- **February 14, 2012**

    Obama signed into law H.R. 658. Always with nice and acceptable names, the "Federal Aviation Administration Air Transportation Modernization and Safety Improvement Act of 2012" is now law.[280] This law authorizes "government public safety agencies" to fly unmanned drones in the United States airspace, giving the government ability to execute detailed and constant surveillance of Americans without probable cause. An invasion of privacy is only one of many unconstitutional violations which will result from the use of these drones.

- **March 13, 2012**

    The White House announced the creation of the **F.E.M.A. Corps**, described by F.E.M.A. as *"an innovative partnership between the Department of Homeland Security's Federal Emergency Management Agency and the Corporation for National and Community Service to establish a F.E.M.A.-devoted unit of 1,600 service corps members within Ameri-Corps' National Civilian Community Corps, which will be devoted to disaster preparedness, response, and recovery."* [281] The creation of the force reveals a fulfillment of Obama's statements made immediately prior to his election in 2008 of his designs to create a *"civilian national security force."* [282]

- **March 16, 2012**

  Obama's release of the liberty killing Executive Order No. 13603, **N**ational **D**efense
  Resource **P**reparedness [283] is yet another
  tactical media move. He releases it late on
  a Friday, avoiding the news cycle and the attention of the public. What happens next exploded on the scene. The following Monday
  morning, on March 19, 2012, a news story
  that was headed towards a month old case of
  the Trayvon Martin and George Zimmerman
  shooting, suddenly broke out of nowhere
  in Rwanda media style, driving tensions
  continuously and capturing the nation's attention in a suspect way. Media sources
  mysteriously gave no coverage of the huge
  news of Obama's Executive Order. The media's drive to keep the shooting case before
  the people, included doctoring several 911
  calls and video newscasts inciting passions
  for weeks which completely over shadowed
  Executive Order No. 13603 to such a degree that virtually no one heard of Obama's
  dangerous tyrannical E.O., as liberals and
  conservatives alike were all reacting to the

Trayvon Martin story. The Executive Order grants more unprecedented power to the President of the United States than is imaginable, thereby giving him authority over basically everything in the nation—energy, transportation, natural resources, labor, industry, health, private property, the food you eat, the water you drink, etc. It is important to understand Obama has authority over all the above and more.

Again, as the present administration and the 'powers that be' define the opposition that is rising up against the implementation of their plans as coming from anti-government extremists, then all of our founding fathers, being anti-big government, would be declared **hostiles** today. They would be classified as committing crimes of hostility, thereby stripped of their United States citizenship as the unconstitutional "Enemy Expatriation Act" mandates and they would finally be detained without a trial as terrorists under the N.D.A.A. Remember the leap from hostilities to terrorism is easy for the 'powers that be' just as in the case of Bernard von NotHaus who was labeled a terrorist for counterfeiting. The founders were acutely aware of all these possibilities and literally cemented protections into the Declaration, the Constitution, and the Bill of Rights against such tyranny.

Those who are behind the scenes who put Obama in power, those who will do whatever they have to, to keep him in power as their pawn, are doing their best to redefine who is behind their opposition. The rapid growing movement of those for a moral Judeo-Christian principled Constitutional government is being labeled by the 'powers that be' as anti-government and therefore, hostile to the State. The leap from being defined anti-government to hostiles, is not anymore of a distance than the leap of being defined hostiles to being terrorists. The way is then paved to squash like an ant, any objectors, conscientious or otherwise, in Obama's quest to march towards complete control over every aspect of life, over every belief, restricting freedom and liberty of all United States citizens. These are not opinions or theorics. It is the unlawful law of the land. Read it. It is there in the written executive orders and the invalid laws that have passed in rapid succession. It is in Obama's words before he was elected. It is in his actions after he was elected. He said he would literally fundamentally transform the United States of America, and he has. This consolidation and deposit of power is a growing evil which has a paper trail show-

ing it is what it says it is. No need to try and establish
a case, convince, or sell this as an interpretation, ideal,
or theory. If you do not see it so, go back over the last
few pages and re-read the previous dates, November
9, 2011, to March 16, 2012, of the executive orders and
unconstitutional laws again, if necessary, and prayerfully study them. If you look at an apple and someone
tells you it is an orange, and the next person tells you
the same thing, and all day long you hear this, it does
not change the shape, color, and character of the apple.
It is still an apple, no matter how many people tell you
it's an orange. The words of Obama's Executive Order,
National Defense Resource Preparedness, released
March 16, 2012, is what it says it is. It is Martial Law,
it is tyranny, imposed at any time of his choosing. The
Executive Order itself says it can be imposed in times
of 'non-emergency;' (Sec. 201 (b)) in time of peace (Sec
102, 103 (b), 310):

> *"...shall plan for and issue regulations to priori-*
> *tize and allocate resources and establish stan-*
> *dards and procedures by which the authority*
> *shall be used to promote the national defense,*
> ***<u>under both emergency and non-emergency con-</u>***
> ***<u>ditions</u>**...take appropriate action to ensure that*
> *critical components, critical technology items,*

*essential materials and industrial resources are available from reliable sources when needed to meet defense requirements **during peacetime, graduated mobilization**, and national emergency."*

Defense requirements will be interpreted, the defense of whatever Obama needs defending. As shown and stated, this pooling of power of the government will destroy the United States. The world will follow suit, as the giant wall will have been penetrated, that being the United States. Evil will reign quickly across all the nations of the earth. As Our Lady has said, **"Peace will not come through the presidents,"** but through prayer, and thereby, we will understand that peace comes not from the top down, the president, but from the bottom up, through 'we the people.' Thomas Jefferson wrote:

"The way to have good and safe government is not to trust it all to one, but to divide it among the many, distributing to everyone exactly the functions he is competent to. Let the national government be entrusted with the defense of the nation, and its foreign and federal relations; the State governments with the civil rights, laws, police, and administration of what con-

cerns the State generally; the counties with the local concerns of the counties, and each ward direct the interests within itself. It is by dividing and subdividing these republics from the great national one down through all its subordinations, until it ends in the administration of every man's farm by himself; by placing under everyone what his own eye may superintend, that all will be done for the best. What has destroyed liberty and the rights of man in every government which has ever existed under the sun? The generalizing and concentrating all cares and power into one body." [284]

Whether, we are speaking of the concentration of healthcare as Obama has done, or the federalization of local government, both are destructive to liberty. Just as every man has certain unalienable rights to manage and govern his affairs on his own plot of land and all the concerns that go with it, so too, the Catholic Bishops have total spiritual authority over Catholics and Catholic hospitals, schools and churches in the God-given authority dispensed to them through the Pope and Church in order that they may safeguard the truths and beliefs of our Christian faith and to carry out the Church's mission. When government is in contradiction with the Church, constitutionally the government must favor religious liberty. Any actions taken by the government to oppress the Church or make the Bishops, the Catholic faithful and other Christians comply against their consciences to an unjust law is unconstitutional and is to be defied.

We win. They lose. Nothing less.

We do not have to go to court to know what is Constitutional. Do not go to court. The plans of Obama, and the powers that surround him, are to greatly further and subjugate the courts to their rules, through expensive, exhausting, and lengthy lawsuits in which the liberal judges will be waiting as hungry lions in the coliseum. However, if we do not go by their rules, Obama and his administration cannot shut down our schools, hospitals, or takeover our private property, even though Obama's Executive Order says he can. The government is subjugated to the restraints of the Constitution for the protection of the unalienable rights of "we the people." It is not up to wayward judges, holding court, or any other authority to put itself higher than our Constitution. But how can we correct this? You wonder how? Our bleak situation will be addressed in future chapters. Catholic Bishops have not only spiritual authority but Constitutional authority over teaching what Catholics are to abide by and believe in following Biblical truth. A Protestant pastor has the same Constitutional protection of authority. Government does not have authority over the Bishops or heads of other Christian denominations in any matter concerning religious liberty and governing of "the affairs of their farms," as Jefferson states, paralleling to his meaning, the bishops and pastors and their governing authority of the Church. It is their right and no one can overrule the Constitutional protection afforded to them in their God-given right of authority. In regard to the religious liberty of Catholics and other Christians, the Bishop's management and authority of the Church or the people's right and authority to self-govern their affairs right down to a man ruling over his own farm or home, none can be usurped except by violation of the Constitution, if they all conform to our Constitutional Republic and all laws, Constitutional laws.

With the taking of total authority through Obama's March 16, 2012, Executive Order, and the other moves to strengthen the reach and consolidation of his power, one can see **"we've been had."** Obama's Executive Order, No. 13603 astoundingly even takes over authority. This is not addressing the issue of Obama designating his presidential authority to others, rather he is taking authority over authority. You will have to make it his authority. In other words, what you have under your authority is all subject to his authority. The Executive Order clearly makes *your* authority the president's authority. But not speaking only to the point of *what* you have authority over, which again Obama also has, but even more alarmingly, "authority itself." You don't believe the Executive Order means this? Study the actual Executive Order for yourself, Obama has taken authority from the United States Bishops and not only usurped it, but said to them, *"You, your institutions, your Catholic members will pay for abortions."* No matter if it was taken indirectly through the ruse of a tax. The Executive Order expands this to be clearly Biblical in proportion as to the great authority Obama has taken. As already quoted:

Revelation 13:2

> *"... and its mouth was like a lion's mouth. And to it the dragon gave his power and his throne and great 'authority'."*

We do not have to wonder if these actions are the anti-christ as did early Christians in their day who identified Nero as an anti-christ. Throughout history, we have had many. As time progresses they will grow in authority and will continue to grow until the final anti-christ system when the man-satan reigns. There is no question that Obama's inclination, his thinking, and his actions assail Christianity. He himself proves this by the evidence of his actions. An Illinois lobbyist, who in the scope of his work dealt with Obama, said:

> *"When I sat down with Senator Obama, it was eerie. It was as though you looked right through his eyes."*

The lobbyist added:

> *"When Senator Obama walked into a room, everyone became silent."*[285]

The lobbyist said it was *not a positive experience.* When asked if it was believed there was something evil behind it, he said: *"No. More than that."* When it was responded, *"No, really,"* to the lobbyist, the lobbyist responded that *"Obama is an anti-christ."* When it was responded back to the lobbyist, *"Really?"* The lobbyist stated, *"Yes, I'm serious. He is an anti-christ."* Is this too farfetched – an exaggeration of someone who has had direct dealings with Obama? Obama has great pride and is declared by many professionals who have studied him to be a narcissist, one who has an inordinate fascination with himself and excessive self-love. [286]

If this with all the other statements, facts and revealed actions of Obama presented in this book do not confirm and give credibility to such words, what are we to make of the Holy Virgin Mary's words:

August 2, 2011

> **"...you cannot stop the evil that wants to begin to rule in this world and to destroy it. But, according to God's will, all together, with my Son, you can change everything and heal the world..."**

The evil that wants to come to rule? How? With the National Defense Authorization Act and the slew of executive orders and policies enacted from November 9, 2011, to March 16, 2012, giving 'great' authority and even anti-christ type authority. Evil came to rule when?

February 2, 2012

> **"...pride has come to rule..."**

A narcissist would not be one if pride was not its source.

When Our Lady told us on August 2, 2011 that **"evil wants to begin..."** and then February 2, 2012 **"...has**

come to..." it is important to note the great significance of events of this span from August 2, 2011 to
March, 16, 2012, of the executive orders, policies, etc.
which gave Obama unprecedented power as no one
in the world before now has had. Do you realize the
significance of the dates? Our Lady tells us on August
2, 2011, that **"evil wants to rule."** Obama begins his
onslaught of passing new laws just a few months later
in November, 2011. Our Lady then tells us on February
2, 2012, **"pride has come to rule,"** and in the fullness
of pride, Obama signs the Executive Order stripping
every vestige of freedom away from the people. All the
while, Our Lady of Medjugorje was revealing a hidden
plan of darkness to rule, though no one knew what was
happening behind the scenes.

August 2, 1981, Our Lady of Medjugorje says:

> **"...A great struggle is about to unfold. A strug-
> gle between my Son and satan. Human souls are
> at stake."**

Exactly 30 years to the date, this struggle is referenced
in battle between darkness and light, when on August
2, 2011, Our Lady says:

> **"...evil that wants to begin to rule in this world
> and to destroy it..."**

Just three months after Our Lady's above message, Obama starts actions across the next five months,
setting up further his foundation to rule. In regards
to questioning Obama being given unprecedented
power as no one in the world before him, one could
say but emperors, kings, dictators, etc. have had ruthless power. Yes, but no one in history has had the high
tech *power over life* to control, keep track of, maintain,
dictate, keep up with etc., for good or for evil, as we
do today. Technology gives man today the ability to
control all aspects of life, presenting the possibility, as
never before in the history of the world, to mete out
retribution. In the book, Seal Target Geronimo, the
author, former Navy SEAL, Chuck Pfarrer tells of an
operation involving two Navy SEALs. Two men of
Navy SEAL Team 6 were secretly helicoptered in to
an undisclosed location in the Middle East under the
cover of night. They planted themselves in a hole in
a date grove and covered themselves with limbs from
the date trees. A group of houses 300 yards away was
their reason for being there. If one could view the wide
open landscape, they would never imagine anyone
could be hiding out with the equipment, plus the weapons the two men had. The Seals were watching one of
the houses on the end, where, through a tip from intelligence, bin Laden's Al Qaeda commander might be

hiding out. They laid still all day in the heat, speaking
no words, observing, with no one coming or leaving the
house. After night fell, they pointed a thermal imag-
ing scope at the thick, mud concrete house. They were
able to see the movement of someone and determined
those in the house slept during the day and moved
around at night. Several vehicles arrived and entered,
numbering about 14 men in the house. There was one
man on a cell phone. His voice was picked up and
sent halfway around the world. The voice was voice
printed and matched and word sent back to the two
Navy SEALs that they had their man. It was clear that
the 14 men were about to perform a terrorist attack
that night as they had brought many weapons into the
house. At this point, everything the SEALs did moved
at lightning speed with technology hardly imaginable.
Bin Laden's commander had only a minute and a half
to live. One SEAL pointed an invisible laser at the
second floor. Fixing the target, while way up near the
stratosphere, a drone scanned and located the infrared
laser on the house, and also detected the body heat of
the two Navy Seals a little more than 300 yards away.
With two hellfire missiles about to be fired, the SEALs
did not have box seats, nor front row seats, they were at
the stage. Chuck Pfarrer writes:

"A pair of missiles dropped from the drone's outboard pylons and silently fell away into the dark sky. Their rocket engines ignited, and the missiles started to spiral toward their target.

"The Hellfires quickly went transonic, then supersonic, traveling faster than the roar made by their rocket engines. The warheads homed unerringly on the laser beam. In the date grove, Drew and Johnny (the two Navy SEALS) waited for the sound of the rocket motors' ignition, a sort of muffled thud from the clouds above. They heard it, ten seconds after it happened, a sound like someone shaking dust from a rug, whump, whump. It meant the missiles were on their way.

"Even if Musab al-Zarqawi looked up and saw them coming, there was no place he could run. Johnny made sure that the laser was locked on the building. If Zarqawi (the Al Qaeda commander) jumped into a car, Johnny would put the laser on him. It was over.

"Zarqawi didn't show his face, but it didn't matter. The missiles found him. Moving too fast to see, the first Hellfire ripped through the roof of the house and detonated in a splash of orange-

white light. The initial explosion seemed to widen the walls and lift the roof. The second missile struck the courtyard just in front of the building, cratering it and destroying the three vehicles parked on the road. But then another blast tore through the building. It was what the SEALs called a secondary; the missiles had set off a cache of explosives – bomb-making materials Zarqawi had planned to use in his campaign of terror. This last explosion obliterated the structure, turning it upside down and inside out.

"The explosions echoed back from the riverbanks, and as they faded away, there came the sound of whizzing bits of concrete, the fluttering descent of shattered doors and roof tiles, the thuds made by bits of furniture, the clank of car parts, pots and pans, ammo crates and bits of glass. Also falling to earth were pieces of men.

"Drew remembered that after the blast, the night seemed impossibly still and quiet. For five minutes, not even the crickets sang. The two SEALs collected their equipment, checked their weapons and slipped back into the dump, over the crumbling wall toward their extract point. The mission was over, and now all they had to do was get out.

"Musab al-Zarqawi, Osama bin Laden's hand-picked deputy in Iraq, had killed thousands of people in an attempt to send the world back to the sixth century. In a fitting bit of irony, two operators from SEAL Team Six had killed him with an invisible laser beam and a flying robot."[287]

This is all well and good in the hands of those who are measured and are fighting for freedom, but if this kind of technology fell into the hands of a tyrant, what a very dangerous place the world would quickly become. With such technology to fight terrorists, **who** cannot be found, verified, and eliminated behind thick walls? What does this never before power to hunt down anyone, anywhere on earth, with no place to hide give the one who has such power at his command? If he be tyrannical, it gives him an oppressive power that can be exercised over the whole world as has never been known before; an anti-christ type power. Because of technological developments and modernism, there is now no place to hide, not even in caves in the wilderness.

Evil's ruling power is monitoring the rapidly growing movement from those of us Americans who aim to reset our nation back on the dreams of our forefathers. Those in power do not like it. Our Lady said:

August 25, 1994

"...I pray and intercede before my Son, Jesus, so that the dream that your fathers had may be fulfilled..."

When National Security is tethered by those who are in government, who become totalitarian, it falls upon the people to preserve their own National Security. By doing so, it is not the people who are terrorists, rather, the real terrorists are those who want to change the United States of America into who they are, as Obama said:

"We will stand up in this election to bring about the change that won't just win an election, but will ***transform America.*** *"* [288]

It is not a 'maybe' or a 'perhaps,' rather it is overwhelmingly evidential that **Obama is a threat to the National Security of the United States**.

With what you have read, and the maneuvers that were made and still are being made with this last Executive Order, there is <u>no hope</u> to stop the evil. It is not only about the destruction of the United States, but also the world. Our Lady tells us so:

January 25, 1991

"...satan is strong and wishes not only to destroy human life but also nature and the planet on which you live..."

The question begs to be asked, "But Obama has children, why would he want to destroy the United States?" He doesn't, satan does. Hitler did not want to destroy Germany, satan did. The difference today is not the destruction of just Germany, but the destroying of the whole world. satan uses tyrants who, blinded by pride, think their ideology will bring about utopia as it serves their ego. They progress in evil, incredulously becoming so blind in their pride to be the first on earth to achieve what thus far has been unachievable, that their name and life will be known until the end of time as a beloved benefactor having achieved what no man before them could accomplish. Rather, another principle will prevail over them, one which follows. The quote: *"Give me my Liberator or give me death."* The principle: *"Tyrants' reign will always end in disastrous defeat, ours in glory. We willingly give our life, while they unwilling pay with theirs."*

While Catholics and Christians are finally waking up and a massive number of people are growing in awareness that we must defy Obama's unconstitutional mandates, we must see the reality, that he with his co-horts know their steps are unlawful, and he is moving with lightning speed to quickly stop any resistance be-fore it grows too big to stop. We, therefore, are about to be checkmated by Obama and his total takeover, down to the food put on our plates and the water we drink,* which he will give you as long as you behave and don't teach about sin, as long as you don't oppose abortion, as long as you don't teach about abominables and all other moral wrongs, etc. But, though we are about to be checkmated and blocked by the devil in our moves by Obama's Executive Orders and uncon-stitutional laws and policies with no way out, can God show us a last minute move on the chess board that we can make? Will He, with prayer and fasting, give wis-dom to strategize, with great hope, our next move on the chessboard and defeat evil? Our Lady said:

March 28, 1985

> **"...In prayer you shall perceive the greatest joy and the way out of every situation that has no exit..."**

* Executive Order # 13603, Section 801 (e)

CHAPTER TWENTY-EIGHT

When all is Lost and There is no Way Out

In an art gallery in Europe hangs a painting titled, "Checkmate." On one side of the chessboard sits the devil full of laughter; his hand is poised, ready to make his next move. On the other side of the chessboard sits a shaking, frightened young man. Sweat covers his forehead, dripping down and mixing with a solitary tear on his cheek. The game is obviously drawing to a close, and the winner appears to have already been decided.

One day a chess champion from a far off country visited the gallery. Naturally, the painting caught his attention, inviting him to examine it for a long time. In fact, while others had moved on throughout the gallery, the chess champion remained fixated on the game and especially on the devil, who sat eagerly waiting for his next turn in which he planned to steal this man's soul, checkmating him. Minutes turned into hours as the chess champion studied the board from every possible angle. The sweat on the young man's forehead urged him to continue.

Finally, as the gallery was about to close, the chess champion found the proprietor of the gallery and asked him, "Sir, would you happen to have a chess board here?" After looking around in several of the offices, he located a chess board and brought it to the man. The chess champion laid the board out at the base of the painting precisely as it was in the painting. He made a move and then countered that move in the only way that the devil could avoid checkmate. He then made another move and countered it again, knowing that the devil would have to defend himself in his next move as well. The chess champion did this several more times, putting the devil on the defensive each and every time.

Eventually, a loud yell was heard throughout the gallery, as the chess champion cried out in relief, "I did it! I did it! I did it!" Turning to the painting, the chess champion lowered his voice and said, "Young man, your enemy miscalculated a very important move. I uncovered it and as a result you don't have to lose. You win!" The chess champion had discovered a way out, not only for the young man to escape, but also to checkmate the devil himself. [289]

By now, after reading to this point in the book, you see an ominous dark cloud looming over and about to descend down across the whole nation and the world. It is obvious we face checkmate on every move we can make. What is our move? Are we supposed to just wait, don't comply, and then go to prison? Are we to do nothing and let this darkness rule over us until our liberty is gone and we then obediently must walk right into the coliseum? If, as our bishops say, "we cannot, we will not comply with this unjust (unlawful) law," then what are we to do?

As already stated, victory will not come through the courts, protests, or trying to get more federal laws passed for protection. All this only increases the power of the government. Even if the United States Supreme Court was to throw out the healthcare bill as being unconstitutional, though the 'powers that be' will insure that it will not be thrown out, Obama's Executive Order No. 13603 has such totalitarian power, it can be reinstituted through the head of the Secretary of Health and Human Services who has full presidential authority *"with respect to health resources."*[*] They will implement it through federal regulation. The healthcare bill is important to the 'powers that be' because through the healthcare mandates, power is given to reach every aspect of life. That is the reason

---

* Section 201 (3)

for it. It is not that they are concerned that people have healthcare. So there is no victory with the Supreme Court overturning the healthcare laws. If anything, the battle over the healthcare mandate keeps our attention focused on this front to divert our attention away from another front in order for Obama to gain more time to amass in his arsenal more executive orders and actions to consolidate his power just as Hitler did.

The hope is not in the presidents or the United States Supreme Court or Congress. Avenues that have served us in the past for what was a representative government to make changes are not the moves to make unless you want to be checkmated. Do not follow the moves the Obama administration has anticipated for us through their strategies. "So what is left?" Most will respond, *"But there is no exit if we decline to make these moves!"* This is where we have been deceived for decades up until now. You make the moves your enemy expects and you are 'had' — d-e-a-d in the water. Just as the chessboard painting of the devil's victory over the young man showed. The question must be raised and answered clearly, "Even though the 'powers that be' will not allow it to be, what if the Supreme Court overturns the Obama Healthcare

Plan.* What if they reject the whole plan and it is no longer law? How is that not to be counted as a win?" If you do not grasp what is written to this point, you have missed the point. With the purpose of repetition to help instill the point in your heart, Obama and his strategists have run every scenario of 'if and what if's,' so that they will have something else to fall back on if one of their plans fails. Again review the following highlights of just five months of amassing power to rule, for the 'powers that be' to fall back on.

November 9, 2011:   First ever nationwide test of Emergency Alert System

November 18, 2011: Release of the Federal Emergency Management Agency's document of National Continuity Programs.

December 1, 2011:   National Defense Authorization Act (N.D.A.A.) bill passes in the Senate.

December 8, 2011:   White House releases Strategic Implementation Plan for Empowering **Local Partners** to Prevent Violent Extremism in the United States.

---

* This was written before the United States Supreme Court upheld the Healthcare law.

December 31, 2011: Obama signs into law the National
      Defense Authorization Act (N.D.A.A.)

February 14, 2012:   Obama signs into law H.R. 658,
      The Federal Aviation Administration Air Trans-
      portation Modernization and Safety Improve-
      ment Act of 2012.

March 13, 2012:   The Creation of the F.E.M.A. Corps.

March 16, 2012:   Release of Obama's Executive Or-
      der 13603, National Defense Resource Prepared-
      ness.

There is no possibility of Obama's healthcare being overturned by the courts, because it is immaterial
as his back up is his executive orders that already are
enacted as law. *He plans to use them.* So even if it
could be a loss for Obama on healthcare, it is only a
small lost battle for him. He is looking to win the war.
Before the Normandy invasion, we covertly wanted the
Germans to believe we would attack somewhere else.
We surprised the German force. Like the Germans being deceived, Obama's Supreme Court case leads us to
believe this is our counter attack. But, behind closed
doors, their laughter can be distinctly heard because
all of our energy and efforts have gone down the road
their "what if's" have strategized. Evil has enough

power to mandate anything and everything in peace time, in war time, in non-emergency, in a "created" crisis at the go of a simple order to do so! Do you not think the "what if" from every angle is not part of evil's strategy? Medjugorje visionary Ivan has said, *"The devil has a master intellect."* We must always pray for those who have masterminded this evil plan, as we also are sinners, but we are not to ignore them and their intentions of bad will. The devil's human minions do not have to be so smart, because it is he, satan, who guides these evil events with his master intellect. When he rules through them, he can even accomplish things unknown to his pawns. Therefore, the "what if" strategies can all be managed through Obama's other laws, policies and executive orders, even without the healthcare bill. Are you shocked at all the preceding? The Hutus gave plenty of warning of what was coming for the Tutsis. Did they not believe it? Or did they know it and just decided, "we will deal with it at the time it is a problem?" Are you shocked at many things in this book? Why? Obama has been saying these things as clear as he can. He told you before he was elected, the Supreme Court must break from the restraints the forefathers put in the Constitution. When the Warren Court acted radically to take some of these steps, Obama states the Warren Supreme Court was not radi-

cal enough. By this statement, Obama says he is a radical who wants radical changes. As you have already
read:

> *"…And to that extent as radical as I think people
> tried to characterize the Warren court, it wasn't
> that radical. It didn't break free from the essen-
> tial constraints that were placed by the founding
> fathers in the Constitution…"* [290]

Obama has expressed on many occasions, in his own
words explicitly, with clarity, his plans for the United
States of America.

- *"I'm in this race, not just to hold an office but together with you to **transform a nation**."* [291]

- *"We will stand up in this election to bring about
  the change that won't just win an election, but will
  transform America."* [292]

- *"It's not enough just to change parties in this election. If we hope to **truly transform** this country,
  we have to change our politics too. **It's time to
  turn the page**."* [293]

- *"We are five days away from **fundamentally
  transforming the United States of America**."* [294]

This is it. It is time. Everything is at the most opportune time for bringing about this transformational
change. While Obama is chasing an illusion, thinking
he is bringing about utopia just as past tyrants did,
the United States of America is in the crosshairs to be
fundamentally transformed for its ultimate destruction
by evil and thereby, the destruction of the world. But
this begs the question, "Fundamentally transformed
as a nation to what?" One of the milder aspects of
Obama's plan to transform America is to turn it into a
socialist state. The definition of a socialist state, defined
by one of its own, Albert Schaeffle:

> *"The Alpha and Omega of Socialism is the trans-*
> *formation of private and competing capitals into*
> *a united collective capital…In their places (**pri-***
> ***vate capital and competition**), we should have*
> *a state-regulated organization of national labor*
> *into a social-labor system, equipped out of col-*
> *lective capital: the state would collect, warehouse*
> *and transport all products, and finally would dis-*
> *tribute them to individuals in proportion to their*
> *registered amount of social labor, and according*
> *to a valuation of commodities exactly corre-*
> *sponding to their average cost of production."* [295]

Add to the above definition of transforming America, Obama's executive order of military occupation,[*] induction of youth into a youth corps, induction into national service outstanding and exceptional experts in their field "**without** compensation," and a hundred more "mandates" already made law, and you then will have not only a transformed United States of America into a socialistic state, but a fully transformed United States of America into a tyrannical state. Take a test.

Tyranny + Socialism = _____ (pick **only** one of the following letters for the line)

Select your answer:

    A. Loss of Liberty

    B. Loss of happiness

    C. Loss of freedom

    D. Loss of conscientious objection

    E. Loss of property rights

    F. Loss of self-determination

    G. Loss of free speech

    H. Loss of all of the above

[*] Section 308

I.   Loss of the above and more, and above all, the
     slavery of despotism.*

Pope Pius XI said:

> *"Socialism…cannot be reconciled with the teach-
> ings of the Catholic Church because its concept
> of society…is foreign to Christian truth."* [296]

Those who rule know that the Catholic Church
stands in its way and must at least be shackled in
chains, at best crushed. Evil must render Christianity
powerless to continue successfully its consolidation of
power to rule. Pope Pius XI also said:

> *"…Socialism and Christian Socialism are con-
> tradicting terms; no one can be at the same time a
> good Catholic and a true socialist."* [297]

Again, how can Obama be a Christian?

---

* Despotism means a system of government in which the ruler has unlim-
  ited power.

CHAPTER TWENTY-NINE

The David Answer

Winston Churchill said:

"If you will not fight for the right when you can easily win without bloodshed...

"If you will not fight when your victory will be sure and not too costly...

"You may come to the moment when you will have to fight with all the odds against you and only a precarious chance of survival.

"There may even be a worse case...

"You may have to fight when there is no hope of victory, because it is better to perish than live as slaves." [298]

As discussed in a previous chapter, what is very interesting in response to the *USA Today's* article, stating there is a "*'backlash' of growing anti-government sentiment,*"[299] is that this is a 'backlash' from those of us who

honor liberty and freedom against the backlash by an
evil surrogate group of people, who are against our nation's constitutional governing principles and who are
now in control. As already stated, to stand up today for
liberty and Godly principles and against growing government intrusion and abuse of our unalienable rights
is to be classified as anti-government "sovereigns."
This surrogate body of power has systematically and
uniformly transformed America, changing her to their
ideologies not in any way in line with our Constitution.
Once again, necessary repetition to remember what
Obama said just before he was elected president in
2008:

> *"We are five days from fundamentally transform-*
> *ing the United States of America."* [300]

The backlash against **"the surrogates"** who are
against our constitutional government is such that they
must classify and stereotype those who oppose them,
as stated earlier, using the verbiage "the sovereigns"
to divert attention away from their backlash against
the Constitution. At the same time, through these efforts they attempt to legitimize themselves as the good
guys while representing those who honor constitutional
rights, who have moral conscientious objections against
the immoral mandates, etc. as the bad guys. We must

constantly remind ourselves, "the surrogates" who have taken over have done so because of the weakness and sin of the church"ed". Evil thrives in fertile ground to grow where Christianity has stopped growing in convicting poor souls who are reprobates and/or those who do not know the love of God. Now we find ourselves face to face on the chessboard with evil, in which darkness is overwhelming us. Is there anything that can stop the checkmate we face with evil? Is there no way out? What can we do?

After reading to this point it is easy to be depressed. The situation is desperate and we can see there is no way out. This is exactly why Our Lady said:

March 28, 1985

"... In prayer you shall perceive the greatest joy and the way out of every situation that has no exit..."

We must realize without prayer there is **no** way out. We are checkmated. Yet, many have started praying and are beginning to put into their heart the following Bible verse:

"If my people, who are called by my name, shall humble themselves, and pray, and seek my

face, and turn from their wicked ways; then will
I hear from heaven, and will forgive their sin,
and will heal their land." 2 Chronicles 7:14

People are awakening, but is it too late? Yes, it is too late. Everything is already in place. That is why we have no way out. No hope for a way out. But…with prayer, with repentance, with "one tear of repentance," God will forgive us and we can find an exit, an exit where there is none. God, being God, will show us an exit that we do not know of or have not yet seen.

There is a glimmer of hope. Something most would never guess or imagine as a way out. In fact, it is such a "least likely" way out that you will be as surprised as Samuel the prophet was when he was told to go to Bethlehem to anoint with authority, Israel's chosen king. Samuel went to meet with Jesse, the Bethlemite, who had many sons. He knew out of these sons, one would be the anointed one. Each of Jesse's sons was called to stand before Samuel and one by one, Samuel said, *"The Lord has not chosen him."* After the seventh son was dismissed, Samuel, surprised not to have yet found the one who would be king, asked if these were all the sons he had. Jesse responded dismissively, *"There is still the youngest, but… he is guarding the sheep."* Jesse's son, David, a mere shepherd youth, was

summoned and to the astonishment of Samuel, the sons
and the father, Samuel declared that David was God's
chosen one. No one would have ever thought of the
youthful shepherd boy as king, yet it is often the most
unlikely whom God chooses, as history has proven time
and time again. Has God something of the like for us
today? Why not? Throughout history, this is the trait
of God. Is there somebody, like David, though he be
the most unlikely one to be chosen? One who has the
authority to defeat this evil assault against liberty and
to protect the constitution and us individually? Samuel
went through seven sons thinking each may be the answer for Israel's authority, before God indicated His
choice. Likewise, our rescue will not come through the
justices, the courts, the congress, the presidents—none
of these are chosen. We echo again Our Lady's words:

December 31, 1985

**"...You will not have peace through the presi-
dents..."**

Is there another son of the republic out somewhere
in the fields? All branches of government or "sons,"
who once governed our Constitutional Republic, are
being passed over to find the humble David, the shepherd who will defend the people against Goliath—that

evil surrogate group which is hourly taking away all liberty. It must again be reiterated that no one will rescue us without the repenting of our sins and the recognition of God as <u>our</u> "Sovereign" over our nation as indicated in the Declaration of Independence making our Constitution the supreme Sovereign law of our land. There is a need also for God's people to remember how God dealt with Israel when they sinned and how God dealt with Israel when they repented and put Him first, a principle that must be always in our heart in order for God to act on our behalf. When we repent, we are then to follow Our Lady's advice when She said:

April 17, 1986

"Pray, fast, let God act."

We must also remember another principle. We will not recover our unalienable rights solely by armaments and power. Those strengths, as shown through man's history, can be rendered useless when a people do not entrust themselves first to God by living His statutes. The principle to add to the above mentioned is, **"A people are not so much protected by their armaments as they are by their way of life."** * Our way of life must

---

* A Friend of Medjugorje has for years continually put forth this concept.

be a return to holiness, or no amount of armaments or strength is of use.

So where is the David who has the anointed authority to reinstate the Constitution and the unalienable rights written of in the Declaration of Independence against a Goliath? A David who will be a shepherd defending us against a federal anti-god wolf? To answer the question we must go back to a time not unlike the time of David when shepherds protected against wolf attacks, thieves and marauders. A time long ago, in which when we look back to it we will find a way out of our own situation, provided we as a people first turn back to God, acknowledging His sovereignty over ourselves, over everything we own, and over our nation. "The David Answer" is found when we go back one thousand years. One thousand years? Yes.

Two hundred years beyond one thousand years ago, in England, small groups of people lived in rural communities in groups of ten families. These "tuns," as they were called, lived, toiled and hunted across England. Over the next 200 years, these groups of ten grew into groups of 100 family units. A chief was set over each hundred group of families, and the chief was called a "reeve." By the time the new millennium dawned, around 1,000 A.D., groups of one hundred families

banded together with other hundreds, each several
miles apart and formed into a governing unit known
as a "shire." You might envision several small villages,
each with 100 families, located several miles apart from
each other but banded together to become a shire, each
with their own individual "reeve" or chief. It was the
King of England, by 871 A.D., who began appointing a
reeve for each group. The reeve, as the group's chief,
would be charged with keeping peace and order for the
100 family groups. To distinguish a reeve or chief who
was over a single 100 family group from a reeve appointed over all the 100 family groups united in a shire
of an area, the title "Shire"—"Reeve" was bestowed.
To the banded groups of 100's, the Shire Reeve became
the supreme peace-keeping authority for the people
in that area. Through time it evolved that people
elected this Reeve. He, therefore, was accountable to
the people and the people depended upon him for his
protection as their chief. In 1634, the first American
shires were established in Virginia. The banded together village in England that was called a shire, to us
in America became known as a "county." In Virginia
in 1651, the first reeve was elected. He became the
chief leader known as the Shire Reeve, or as would be
said today, shire/sher—reeve/iff. Or in other words, the

Shire Reeve is translated as the county chief or county *Sheriff.* [301]

We've been looking in the wrong places for our answer; our way out of our situation that has no exit is through prayer. And through prayer, we see peace won't come from the top, the presidents. The answer is in our own backyard and bigger still because we elect him, we are his boss while he is our keeper, with authority that will not only shock you of how far he can go to protect us from everything revealed in this book, but will also shock county sheriffs, themselves. Many county sheriffs do not know they are the supreme law keeping authority of their county, even when up against a Goliath, even if Goliath is the Federal government. When the government sends out its wolves to take away our liberty and our unalienable rights, the sheriffs have more authority. They have more authority than the President of the United States in their shire or county! To be clear, the county sheriff has total power to stand against the unconstitutional rulings, executive orders and unlawful rulings from the courts, the president and congress, even from state and local governments that violate constitutional rights. There are over 3,000 counties/shires in the United States with most counties having a local sheriff. We have checks and balances not just in our three branches of government in Washington, as we have always been taught, but in our own backyard, **and they are a part of the Executive Branch**. Sheriffs have enormous power when they use it, not only with more than a thousand years of history of common law behind them, but also backed by judicial precedents to this day! Along with the sheriffs, our whole nation needs to be informed of this. Do you feel hope? Do you feel joy?

March 28, 1985

> **"… In prayer you shall perceive the 'greatest joy' and the way out of every situation that has no exit…"**

But still, you find this hard to believe. Read on and you will believe. To begin to grasp this, first it must be understood how the County Sheriff is part of the three branches of government. In Article VI, paragraph 3 of the U.S. Constitution, it clearly states:

> *"…all executive and judicial officers, both of the United States and of the several States, shall be bound by oath or affirmation to support this Constitution…"*

In the book, The County Sheriff, America's Last Hope, written for county sheriffs and all peace-keeping officers (police) by Sheriff Richard Mack, he states (remember, he is addressing sheriffs):

> "Whether you like it or not, you have given your word through a solemn oath, to uphold, defend, support, and obey the United States Constitution. And, just in case you are wondering, sheriffs are part of the Executive branch of government. Along with the President, we are the executors of the law; and what is the supreme law of the land? The United States Constitution! Therefore, what is our supreme duty and responsibility? That's right! To protect and defend, the U.S. Constitution! There is nothing we could do, that could come even close to justifying any peace officer in this country failing to keep his oath of office. Keeping that oath is what makes our constitutional Republic unique and effective." [302]

Sheriff Richard Mack, who proved the chains binding "we the people" to federal whims, executive orders, regulations, confiscations, seizures of bank accounts, EPA regulations and many other imposed laws were only an illusion—illusions of federal, state and local chains we thought we were bound by, which all Ameri-

cans have been conditioned to believe to the point of
blindness. Now that our eyes are being opened, we are
realizing the chains were never there, rather only an illusion to make us believe them to be so.

Sheriff Joe Arpaio of Maricopa County in Arizona
is one of the few county sheriffs who, after learning
of and understanding his immense authority, has used
his power as the chief law officer of his county, standing down federal government officials. In his county,
he became famous for his stances on criminal justice
against federal laws and mandates. Sheriff Arpaio
writes of Sheriff Richard Mack:

> *"In 1994 Sheriff Mack took a courageous stand
> to defend the U.S. Constitution and the autonomy
> of Sheriffs against the Clinton administration.
> His lawsuit and subsequent victory at the Su-
> preme Court proved once and for all that the
> Sheriff is indeed the ultimate law enforcement
> authority in his county and in this country. He is
> not a bureaucrat and he does not answer to one.
> He answers to his boss, the citizens. The sheriff
> is the employee of the people and exists to serve
> and protect them in all matters.*

"This booklet (The County Sheriff: America's Last Hope) should be read by every citizen, police officer, and especially each sheriff of these United States, that we may become united in our service to the American people and dedicated to the preservation of those precious freedoms that so many have fought and died for. To uphold and defend the U.S. Constitution is our primary duty and our sworn responsibility." [303]

Sheriff Mack's father was a retired FBI agent, and Mack wanted to follow in his footsteps going into law enforcement. Sheriff Mack became a police officer in 1974 and said despite the fact that he considered himself a good person, he became a "by-the-number jerk" because of Utah's Provo Police Department who wanted numbers. He writes in his booklet, The County Sheriff: America's Last Hope:

"To acquire more manpower, more equipment, and of course, more money, we had to show the City Council that we were busy. And we were. We, as a police force, were all about road blocks, checking licenses, safety inspections, registrations, and anything else we could fish for. We had to write tickets and lots of them…We literally justified our existence, on the backs of the citizens." [304]

After going undercover for a year, Sheriff Mack was
disillusioned about his work. The undercover experience changed his life. He writes in his book,

> *"Is law enforcement really about public service
> or public harassment? To find answers to some
> of these questions I started reading and study-
> ing…My studies ultimately led me to the foun-
> dational principles of the making of America. I
> studied my oath of office—you know the one
> that every police officer swears to before he can
> start his job? It is an allegiance to <u>uphold the
> United States Constitution</u>. Given that, I decided
> to study the Constitution. I thought it might be
> worthwhile to study the document I swore to
> defend and obey. So I did and it amazed me. **It
> was beautiful and easy to understand.** Then I
> started reading about the Founding Fathers and I
> came to know and love them. It literally changed
> my life. These were men of principle who dedi-
> cated their lives to the well-being and freedom of
> their fellow men. I decided that I would never
> be on the wrong side of that document again. I
> was quick to gain a complete disdain for abusive
> government and became sickened with politi-
> cal correctness. I got fed up with the numbers*

*game in law enforcement and with the idea that
we, the police, were here to force people to wear
their seat belts, and to have their papers, driver's
license, registration, insurance, and state inspection, in order before they could freely go about
their lives. What I saw at the state capital and in
Washington DC made me even sicker. I looked
at the millions of laws being shoved down our
throats and I looked at the U.S. Constitution and
I saw very little resemblance." [305]*

Sheriff Mack moved to Arizona and in 1988 ran for county sheriff in Graham county. Later Clinton passed the Brady Bill. Sheriff Mack writes of this law:

*"This law literally forced each sheriff to become
a pawn for the Federal Government and to do
their bidding to promote gun control within our
jurisdictions. Even more astounding was the
fact that no funds were allocated for us to do this
work and the Brady Act contained a provision **to
arrest us if we failed to comply**. Wow! So here's
the U.S. Congress making an unconstitutional
gun control law, requiring a county official to
enforce it and pay for it, and then threatening to
arrest him if he refuses!" [306]*

Sheriff Mack filed a lawsuit over this bill and later six other sheriffs joined him in it. He writes,

> *"We ended up at the U.S. Supreme Court together on December 4, 1996. On June 27, 1997, the Supreme Court ruled that the Brady Bill was in fact unconstitutional and that the Federal Government could not commandeer state or county officers for federal bidding. This was more than monumental! Federal agencies could no longer do whatever they pleased. The ruling stated at least three times that the States were **'not subject to Federal direction.'** More importantly, the case proved that **'<u>local</u>'** officials have the right, the power, and the duty to **stand against** the far reaching incursions by our own Federal Government. In the ruling Justice Scalia wrote for the majority, stating, **<u>"The Federal Government may not compel the states to enact or enforce a federal regulatory program.</u>"** This means none... zero! They can't compel the states or the counties or local officials to comply with their regulations. Yes, the states can still go along voluntarily, and far too often, that is exactly what happens. But freedom won that day on June 27, 1997, and it started the snowball rolling for each sheriff in this*

*country to stand tall and to protect his constituents from 'all enemies **both** foreign and **domestic.'** This is the ultimate check and balance and it falls squarely on the shoulders of the county sheriff. The sheriff and police are indeed the last line of defense between the people and the criminals, both from the streets **and** from **the Federal Government**...(Sheriffs) you have the authority, the power, and the duty to be the ultimate check and balance for the American citizenry in your county and to defend them against all local and federal criminals."* [307]

Sheriff Mack, after reading and studying the Constitution, stated: ***"It was beautiful and easy to understand."*** We, as citizens, living with liberty in our own localities do not have to be lawyers to read and understand the Constitution. In fact, you will likely understand the Constitution better than a lawyer because you will be able to read and study it in more of the purity of the document than what law schools have "fogged" the Constitution into. While many states have laws requiring judges to be attorneys, the Constitution does not even require this of Supreme Court justices or for other federal judges. The only requirement placed in the Constitution for Supreme Court

judges is that they be of "good behavior." [308] We should
return to this, at the state level as well, by striking
down these laws, state by state. One with knowledge
of right and wrong based on the timeless statutes of
the Ten Commandments more than qualifies one as a
judge. Restricting this office only to lawyers has turned
it into an industry for lawyers. A person in command
of this knowledge and wisdom is qualified to rule on
law. Sheriff Mack's statement can now be understood
with greater significance about the Constitution as we
have left it up to others to tell us what it means. These
"others" are often corrupt in their understanding of the
Constitution or they purposely corrupt its meaning. It
is time and urgently important that we all begin reading and studying our nation's Constitution to learn ourselves of its beauty and how simple it is to understand.

Obama and the Federal Government, through their
many mandates, are unconstitutionally and rapidly expanding, immeasurably, their authority. With Obama's
executive orders, policies, and regulations, everything is
falling into a plan, as previously stated, for evil to consolidate its power. Sheriff Mack adds:

> *"Does it get any clearer than this? One of our*
> ***'structural protections of liberty'*** *is based on*
> *the notion and principle that 'different govern-*

*ments' will keep each other in check and by so
doing, provide a 'double security' to the rights
of the people. In this (Sheriff Mack's lawsuit
and victory) most monumental Tenth Amendment Supreme Court ruling, Justice Scalia stated,
'The power of the Federal Government would
be augmented immeasurably if it were able to
impress into its service—and at no cost to itself—
the police officers of the 50 States.' Scalia seemingly makes it clear that the federal government*
DOES NOT *have the power or authority to
'impress' the police from the states into federal
regulatory programs."*

*"On the other hand, the power of the Federal
Government would be 'augmented immeasurably' if the police from the 50 States went along
with or allowed the federal government to do
whatever it wanted. We do not have a lawful obligation to go along with them; in fact, documen-
tation would show quite the contrary.*

*"Finally, and most unambiguously, the Supreme
Court ruled repeatedly in this case 'state legislatures are not subject to federal direction.' So
when the Federal Government goes too far, we
should not only refuse to go along, but it is up to*

us to 'erect barriers' against such encroachments
and thus be found on the side of the people to
provide them with the protection they depend
on." [309]

Reckless officials at federal levels, by the federalization at state and local levels, have increased the loss of liberty through arrests and by threatening citizens for years with oppressive federal mandates and regulations. This is what now faces Catholics, with their 25 percent share of healthcare coverage. Through unconstitutional forced mandates, great pressure is being applied to force us and other Christians to comply or withdraw despite our conscientious objections. This tyranny, this evil, perpetuated by the surrogates, can be stopped cold in its tracks! It must be stopped **"at all cost."**

CHAPTER THIRTY

At All Cost!
Is it Possible the Answer is
in our own Backyard?

The county sheriff has supreme authority, the power needed to stop any unconstitutional actions "at his discretion" in upholding his oath. He can even forbid any officials from coming into his county to seize property, seize bank accounts or levy fines. He can stop federal and state officials from blocking the use of your private property. He can stop forced Federal regulations as well as the unconstitutional federalization of the counties and cities. And, in the case of an assault against religious liberty, he can protect it at all cost. He can go against the federal government, any federal agency, state and local governments, and the courts when they go AWOL against the United States Constitution with mandates that are unconstitutional. His oath is to the Constitution and not to the others listed above. We have a Constitutional Republic based on the rule of law, centered around the Constitution and the Bill of Rights, not a socialist republic as we are becoming. Sheriff Mack stated:

"We are focusing on the principal that the County Sheriff has the authority and the responsibility to protect our Constitution and to protect our rights against tyranny. People have gotten this brainwashed notion that the federal government can do anything it wants, and they cannot. And local and state governments can do anything they want, and they cannot. So the entire premise of our governments is basically based on this false notion that government can do anything it wants to us. That government can violate all our rights, violate the Constitution, even though they have sworn a sacred oath to uphold and defend the Constitution. They can violate the Bill of Rights, they can violate all the principles of freedom that our country was founded upon and then just put it back on us to prove in the courts that they can't do it. They can be ruthless, they can bully and destroy and confiscate homes and bank accounts, all without due process, all unconstitutionally, while in the meantime, we must go and prove in court that they cannot. Most of the courts are completely unreachable by most American citizens. They do not have the money; they do not have the time to go to court. It is very close to a full-time job. You don't just turn the case over to

your attorneys and say, "Sue the federal govern-
ment for me, or sue the state government for me,
or sue the county commissioners or sue the city
councils or the school board and I'll see you at
court when we finally go to win." It's not that way
at all. It's very time consuming; there are affida-
vits, there are depositions, there are interviews,
there are constant contacts with your lawyer. And
most people can't afford to do this, most people
can't afford to raise money to get a lawyer, and so
it's an inaccessible alternative for the American
people. So back to the answer then, is where is
the solution? And the solution is the bottom line,
county commissioners should be defending the
people, city councilmen should be defending the
people, the sheriff is the bottom line [not the top,
president] and he is absolutely the last line in the
sand for defense against tyranny and against the
federal government, local government, and state
governments by, for and of the people. We the
people. And the sheriffs intend to form a united
front in letting the federal government know
that." [310]

Can "The Davids" in each county across America stop
dead in its track the forcing of citizens to pay for abor-

tion against their conscience and their religious beliefs? In an interview for this book, April 16, 2012, Sheriff Mack responded to the following questions:

FOM*: *"Given the scenario, you are the sheriff of a county where a Catholic hospital is being forced to comply with the performing of and paying for someone else's abortion by way of Obama's Healthcare Federal Law, and the Catholic bishop of the county where the hospital is located states, "We cannot, we will not comply, with this unjust law." And the bishop adds to this statement that in addition, we will not close down our Catholic hospitals, nor cut back in anyway. What would be your position, Sheriff Mack?"*

Sheriff Mack: ***"We are not going to allow these hospitals to be shut down and that we will protect the God-given rights of freedom of religion, upon which our nation was founded.*** *The sheriff actually does have a responsibility and a duty to make sure that the Obama-care regulations and the bureaucratic regulations and policies of Washington D.C. do not supersede and never will supersede a church's right to conduct its affairs according to its own dictates and conscience."*

* A Friend of Medjugorje

FOM: *"Of course, this would play out for Catholic adoption centers and other agencies as well who refuse the mandate but, let's play out the hospital scenario: Say you are a county sheriff here in our county and St. Vincent's, the Catholic hospital here has been mandated to shut down for not complying because of conscientious objection. Let's say the federal government has a court order from the courts and because the bishop of the diocese stands with his guidance and refuses to shut down hospitals and not comply, the feds send in federal marshals. What actions at that point can you legally do and what actions would you take when the federal marshals come in to close the hospital for not complying with the mandates?"*

Sheriff Mack: *"What we're talking about here is actually a religious principle; the theory and doctrine of interposition, that the sheriff would actually put himself in the way. What I hope would happen is that the sheriffs nationally would let the federal government know there's certain things we are not going to allow you to do within our counties and jurisdictions. And as the duly elected, constitutionally elected sheriff, I represent the people of this county and we are not going to allow you to come in and shut down any hospitals. We are not going to allow you to fine churches or arrest anybody*

*out of the churches. Your Obamacare and your poli-
cies do not supersede the Bill of Rights. We put them on
notice that we are going to put ourselves in the way. In
response to such a scenario, I've even had reporters say,
'well that could cause an armed conflict between the
sheriff's office and federal agents.' I said, no it's going to
prevent armed conflict. And let me make this real clear:
if we get the sheriffs in this country, if we just get 10, 15,
20% of the sheriffs in this country to take this type of
a stand, it will stop it. So the Sheriff simply tells them
[federal marshals] they are not going to do it."*

FOM: *"We know there's got to be an invoking of the
Declaration of Independence, particularly the part which
states: 'Whenever any form of government becomes destructive of these ends, it is the right of the people to alter
or to abolish it, and to institute new government...it is
their right, it is their duty to throw off such government
and to provide new guards for their future security...,'
because somewhere along the line, this evil that's growing in its power and consolidating, is not going to stop.
So to just keep going with this hospital scenario, say the
courts send in 500 federal marshals, can you, like in the
old days, as the county sheriff in this modern day and
time, call a posse of 1000 to trump their 500?*

Sheriff Mack: *"If the sheriff has to form a posse, or whatever else he has to do to put himself in the way, then he does it and he takes action accordingly, even if he has to arrest United States Marshals...If we have sheriffs with that kind of guts and courage, then this whole thing is going to remain peaceful."*

FOM: *"Does the County Sheriff have authority to order citizens to form a posse?*

Sheriff Mack: *"Yes, a sheriff can call out every able-bodied citizen in his county to defend his county and to keep the peace."*

FOM: *"This is not an option. When you order this, your order must be complied with. Is this correct?"*

Sheriff Mack: *"Yes, the sheriff can order them. Yes. So what I would like to see is that the posse's get formed now."*

FOM: *"To be prepared?"*

Sheriff Mack: *"Yes, and that the organization of the posse, **be ready**. The posse really is the Minute Man of America. And let's make something else very clear here. It doesn't matter how you feel about the abortion is-sue...You still can't say that it's okay to take money from me to pay for somebody else's abortion. It's wrong and* *immoral for government to come in and say, well this person needs an abortion, so I'm going to forcibly take it from you, Christians, who don't believe in this and are forced to pay for this other person's abortion. This is explained by Thomas Jefferson:*

> *"To compel a man to furnish contributions of money for the propagation of opinions which he disbelieves, is sinful and tyrannical."*

It is tyranny and it is unconstitutional. It is unlawful and it is just absolutely sinful for government to be in that position."

FOM: *"When confronting such tyranny, as the hospital scenario, with a large posse as mentioned and they won't back down, what would you say?"*

Sheriff Mack: *"Well, I would say the calmer point first to be made* (to the federal marshals), *'I'm willing to get arrested at this point, are you?' Because somebody's going to get arrested and we are going to defend our land, and we are going to defend our rights and if need be, yes, to the death. But hopefully, that's not going to be the situation. This is not about violence, or even promoting violence. It's about preventing it. This is a peaceful solution. And I guarantee it will be."*

FOM: *"Well, if we're united, what can they do? They know they don't have the power and if it's just…"*

Sheriff Mack: *"If it's just one sheriff in one county here and there, they can win, but if there's hundreds, there's no way, there's no stopping our protecting the nation from tyranny. And that's what we've said with our Constitutional Sheriff Convention and movement, is that if we get several hundred sheriffs doing this, there is no way that it could ever be stopped."* [311]

End of Interview

With the law originating back 1200 years ago…

* followed by a continuous line of enforcement authority,

* that dates back before and through the birth of the United States unto this day,

* backed by legal common law,

* with a recent supporting Supreme Court ruling,

* of which it is a part of the three branches of government, the Executive Branch…

…it is a joy to find we don't have to believe change will come through the president, congress, or the courts.

Instead we go to the bottom and change everything
up. The sheriff is "The David Answer." The forgotten
shepherd in the field, guardian of the flock. We do not
have to place our hope on the one elected as president,
of which so much corruption is in place at that level. It
is far easier to focus locally and elect a constitutional
sheriff, where our voices and our votes still have power
of concentration because it's in our own backyard. We
can short-cut around the federalized positions of local,
county and state governments, along with the federal
government, and even the president, himself, when
they act unconstitutionally, or go meddling where they
do not belong—by going directly to the county sheriff
as the highest authority of law in the county.

The David Answer:

Sheriff for We the People.

We the People for the Sheriff.

The Sheriff, We the People, for the Constitution.

It is streamlining time. A time to "clean house"
throughout the government, to clean-up the enormous
clutter of regulations, unconstitutional laws, oppressive
action and communist-style monitoring of every aspect
of life. These range from random vehicle inspections

without probable cause as if a criminal, down to taking action against a teacher for calling a class to prayer or against a military chaplain for using the name of Jesus because of pressure from others to be politically correct. Yes, who would ever have guessed, who would ever have imagined a constitutional local sheriff, strong, courageous, with guts, is the way out of a situation that had no exit!! Now are you beginning to feel the great joy that comes out of every situation that has no exit!! Forget putting all your hope on a presidential election. Our answer is simple. Restore the Constitution. It is monumentally easier to educate a sheriff to become a Constitutional sheriff or else elect one who will be. When God grants you a solution, joy and its sweetness is yours, with the stipulation that you repent and live His Statutes. Leviticus 25:10:

> *"You shall make sacred by proclaiming liberty in the land for all its inhabitants. It shall be a jubilee for you, when everyone of you shall return to his own property."*

Everything will work out when God's people follow His ways because God always has a plan in the waiting. *If my people repent and mend their way, I will heal their land.* The grace will be given to see restored to us our "unalienable rights" first given by God, and now restored by Him.

CHAPTER THIRTY-ONE

Stories of the Davids

A sheriff is not a hired man. He is chosen by the people to protect them. With over a thousand years of history, a sheriff's duties are based on the principle functions of a shepherd who, through interposition, puts himself, even his life, between the threat and those he is to care for and protect. There are many sheriffs, but the preamble for "the Davids," a true Constitutional Sheriff, should read as the following Scripture passage:

> *"...A good shepherd lays down his life for the sheep. A hired man, who is not a shepherd and whose sheep are not his own, sees a wolf coming and leaves the sheep and runs away, and the wolf catches and scatters them. This is because he works for pay and has no concern for the sheep...I will lay down my life for the sheep...I have power to lay it down..."* John 10:11-18

As Sheriff Mack, who was previously quoted, spoke of how peace officers justified their existence off the backs of the citizens, a hireling does the same by abandoning his oath to protect and instead goes along with compromises or negotiates with the wolves. The wolves will have the sheep for dinner with the cooperation of the hireling shepherd. A quote from Sheriff Mack, a true David, is worth repeating:

> *"To acquire more manpower, more equipment, and of course, more money, we had to show the City Council that we were busy. And we were. We, as a police force, were all about road blocks, checking licenses, safety inspections, registrations, and anything else we could fish for. We had to write tickets and lots of them...We literally justified our existence, on the backs of the citizens."* [312]

What follows in this chapter are real life stories where the Davids have come to awareness of who they are and who they are supposed to protect. The Davids are not in office for the protection of city, county and state bureaucracies, or to see that these agency regulations are followed, or for federal government agencies and employees to do whatever they please. The Davids are to protect the rights of the people when these entities threaten the liberty and freedom of the people. Some sheriffs, who have realized that they have been more like hireling shepherds, have actually made public apologies. They have apologized to those they had not been protecting because of acting as extended hands for the mischief created by the federalization of local government agencies. Sheriffs across our nation are standing up against tyranny and are winning their battles without violence, without protests, without lawsuits. How? Because constitutional power is clear as to who holds the final authority in local areas. Not the President of the United States, not Congress, not the Supreme Court, but the local Sheriff holds the authority, and he is fast becoming the hero of the people.

In northern California, at the fairgrounds of Yreka, in October, 2011, a group of eight sheriffs, seven from California and one from Oregon, met to address a large gathering of concerned citizens. They were Constitutional Sheriffs who had banded together to support each other in living out their oath to the Constitution to protect the people. They came together on this day to help educate citizens as to their rights and to strongly encourage them to not buckle under threats and pressure of unconstitutional laws and regulations. These sheriffs said outright, they believed in their oath, they had sworn to protect their "flock," and they fully intended to do so by whatever means necessary.

Sheriff Dean Wilson Confesses — Del Norte County, California

Sheriff Dean Wilson was one of the eight sheriffs who spoke in northern California. He received the most enthusiastic applause for his honest confession of not understanding and living up to his oath of office in protecting the rights of the citizens in his county for most of the years he has been sheriff. He said, *"I had spent a good part of my life enforcing the penal code, but not understanding my oath of office. I was ignorant and naïve, but now I know of the assault against our people by the federal government."* [313] The people present were not only moved by Sheriff Wilson's humility in confessing his wrong, but by the transformation in him when he came to understand the oath that he took and the true role of a County Sheriff. Over the past year, he has worked hard in his county to protect the citizens under his care from unjust laws.

Sheriff Jon Lopey, Siskiyou County, California

Sheriff Jon Lopey, the host of the California gathering, spoke about the issues surrounding federal environmental intervention and regulations, in which people are losing their property rights under the guise of protecting the environment or endangered species. Sheriff Lopey has confronted both federal and local state agents saying, *"I have told federal and state officials over and over that, yes, we want to preserve the environment, but you care more about the fish, frogs, trees and birds than you do about the human race. When will you start to balance your decisions to the needs of the people?"* [314] He later told those gathered, *"We are right now in a fight for our survival,"* [315] admitting his belief that there is a real threat to our nation's survival by these forces that are chipping away at our freedoms, and that as a Sheriff, he is duty-bound to stand up to the threat.

The book, <u>Look What Happened While You Were Sleeping</u>TM, revealed that there are hidden agendas behind many of the policies the federal and state governments have instituted over the past 20–30 years, such as the U.N.'s Agenda 21. We know them as such programs as Smart Growth, Sustainable Development, Redevelopment, etc. What these programs translate into is the erasing of property rights, among many other abuses. Citizens all across the United States are now engaged in battles with government officials over their right to use their property as they see fit versus the government's environmental mandates that are directly opposed to citizen's use of their own property. Many city council members and county commissioners have been conditioned to approve of these mandates, with thinking such as all water, even in small creeks, belong to and are to be regulated by governmental or environmental groups. Water goes with the land when it is purchased unless water rights have been sold, which some states allow. In order to see these plans effectively grafted into the daily lives of U.S. citizens, the U.N. took on a motto that spoke of its goal: "Think of globalization locally," to enact global policies. In other words, a great deal of planning, time, money and effort was put forth to bring local authorities in line, literally brainwashing them with the "globalist" U.N. thinking that rejected the sovereignty of individual nations and worked towards a one-world government. They had to strategize in this way knowing that local officials would probably reject such U.N. initiatives. They end up accepting them, not fully realizing what they specified on a local level. The United States was particularly targeted as the U.N. plans could not be realized around the world without the United States being brought into subjugation.

However, what those pushing these agendas had hoped would not happen, is happening, and many Amer-

icans are beginning to rise up against the taking of their
rights, after educating themselves to what is in the Declaration of Independence, the Constitution, and what
our forefathers believed. The *Constitutional Sheriffs
and Peace Officers Association, C.S.P.O.A.,** was birthed
through one sheriff reading the Constitution, Sheriff
Mack, and learning that the power he holds as a sheriff
can stand up to federal and state agencies as well as any
Constitutional threat. At the California gathering, Sheriff Greg Hagwood of Plumas County, said:

>   ***"A giant has been awakened*** *and they didn't
>   count on that,"* [316]

speaking of the federal bureaucracy and other agencies.
When an unconstitutional law is applied to you, your
property or your Christian belief, you don't have to
make an emergency call to your congressman. Dial 911
to your county sheriff. He can protect you on the spot
without going to court and paying attorney fees!

Sheriff Gary Aman, Owyhee County, Idaho

Sheriff Gary Aman of Owyhee County in Idaho
began receiving complaints from local ranchers that
the federal agency, Bureau of Land Management, was

* See Resource page 831.

driving environmental agency employees across private
land, 'fishing' for grazing damage and looking for anything else they could discover. The Watersheds Project
and other radical environmental groups are striving to
end all lawful grazing off public land which would all
but destroy the primary economic base of the state, the
livestock industry, operated mostly by family owned
ranches. Questioned about the situation, Sheriff Aman
responded, *"In effect, the Bureau of Land Management was choosing sides in the biggest battle this county
has ever seen."* [317] He said, *"The nature of our western
county and the livelihood and traditions, common laws,
of our citizens, make it necessary that private property
rights be respected. Two recent incidents made it apparent to me that federal employees did not have that
respect. It was time to act."* [318]

Aman responded by declaring that **no** Bureau of
Land Management official was allowed to escort any
non-government person across private properties without both his own expressed permission <u>and</u> secondly,
the expressed permission of the landowner. According
to the dictates Sheriff Aman set down, they are now
required to give a five-day advance *written* notice to
the Sheriff of when they wish to cross private lands. It
is required of them to include in this notice the specific

management purpose of the crossing, the names of both federal and non-federal persons who would be crossing, and a statement of the specific status of any non-Bureau of Land Management employee. Other stipulations required include that access only allows for the movement across the private property to reach federal property. No other activity is allowed, including photographing or videotaping of the private property. He backed his words with the authority behind his badge that any violators of this policy would be arrested, the environmental activists along with federal workers. *"I was determined to not stand idly by while property rights were violated. The Bureau of Land Management employees are not above the law. They expect ranchers to obey the law. I expect the same of them."* [319]

A four-point agreement was written up by Sheriff Aman for the Bureau of Land Management to sign, and though they initially resisted, partly due to the pressure on them from angered radical environmental groups, they eventually agreed to all four points. Sheriff Aman stated of his relationship with the federal agents, *"We get along okay now, but nobody really thinks it's over. And I'll tell you what, it's still scary."* [320] Sheriff Aman has also set down strong policies for the Bureau of Land Management agents concerning impounding cattle found

on federal lands, and any investigations they wished to
do in his county. In both scenarios, they are not to act
independently, but are required to contact the Sheriff
department before any action is taken, and work under
the Sheriff's coordination efforts.

Everyone loves nature. Environmental groups have
capitalized on and taken advantage of this love that all
have for the mountains, the woods, nature, farms, etc.,
to put themselves between the people and the environment. If interposition is the sheriff's duty to the people,
environmentalists see that it is their duty to interpose
themselves between the people, their private property
and nature itself. God gave dominion to man over the
earth and its creatures, not to radical environmental
groups that plot in union with government agencies,
to lock away large portions of creation from men in
subjugation to animals and plants. However, this goes
deeper than what the environmentalists themselves
know, as they think of themselves as the do-gooders of
the earth. The 'powers that be' make use of their do-
gooder mentality to 'save the earth.' While they may
be sincere, most are unaware they are pawns used to
violate Constitutional rights of the land owners, violating God-given unalienable rights. Earth Day was
established on April 22, Vladimir Lenin's birthday. The

very first Earth Day, April 22, 1970 was on the 100th anniversary of Lenin's birth.[321] Is this not reminiscent of Obama naming May 1st, Loyalty Day, on this Communist "nationalist" day, inspired by Karl Marx? What does saving the earth have to do with Lenin? Much of the radical environmental agenda is directly connected to the "moving forward" of socialist plans in order to control the populations. Again, Look What Happened While You Were Sleeping™ is important to read to be educated about Agenda 21 and its global agenda that works locally against man's right to private property and his freedom of self-determination and liberty itself. The environmental "green" movement is part of this dangerous agenda, utilized by Obama and his gang. Do not buy into their justification for what they do. Through federalization of counties and cities, they impose regulations and restrictions so oppressive as to lock away unalienable rights to use your property because you "potentially" may do harm to the property you own. The property, through your vested interest, will do better under your care who will keep it up and improve it according to the needs of your land, your house and yourself. You are governor of your little republic. Even if you did do harm, it is ignored that the earth has incredible recovery ability. Look at creation and how it recovers even where not man, but nature it-

self inflicts incredible catastrophic environmental damage. Immediately actions programmed into creation by
its Creator begin to mend and heal the earth. This is
true, even while the catastrophe is still occurring.

Sheriff Billy McGee, Forrest County, Mississippi

Okay, sheriffs have authority, but what happens in
a confrontation with the military? What authority will
they have with the unconstitutional law of Obama's
National Defense Authorization Act when all of America can be declared a battlefield, given a military presence, even in a natural disaster?

Hurricane Katrina caused great havoc along the
Louisiana and Mississippi coast. The hurricane caused
power outages that went on for days, even weeks. Food
and medicine were in short supply in the days following
the devastation. The situation was deteriorating and
desperate. Sheriff Billy McGee had his hands full in
meeting the needs of all those living in his jurisdiction
of Forrest County. A federal shipment of six trucks of
ice was to arrive in Hattiesburg, but when only four arrived, Sheriff McGee went looking for the other two.
He found them being guarded by a few Army reservists
who refused to let the shipment go. When McGee tried

to secure the ice, he was told that he was not authorized to take the vehicles. When one of the Army soldiers refused to step down from his truck, preventing
McGee from being able to get the ice delivered to the
areas in need, Sheriff McGee had him handcuffed. To
this day, Sheriff McGee is known as The Ice Man.[322]

Another area of concern is the invasive pat-downs
and full body scans being imposed upon U.S. citizens
traveling on airplanes and now with public ground
transportation within the United States by government TSA agents. These can also be stopped by county
sheriffs. Federal mandates have no power in a state or
county where the citizens believe their rights are being
violated by such mandates—and their sheriffs are courageous enough to stand up for their rights.

What about protecting the religious liberties of the
citizens in their county? Do sheriffs have the authority to do so? We have already heard from Sheriff Mack
concerning the Obama healthcare bill. But there are
other sheriffs who know they are the guardian of the religious rights of their citizens and who are determined to
defend those rights, even in the face of opposition.

Sheriff Peter Mikkelson of Todd County, Minnesota

In a Minnesota Supreme Court ruling in the late 1980's, a case was decided that the Amish not only do not have to attach the fluorescent "Slow Moving Vehicle" sign on their buggies, but also black and white signs that are more in line with the simplicity of their life. The court decided that the Constitution prohibits forcing the Amish to do so, as it is an attack against their right to freedom of religion. Despite this ruling, the subject came up in discussions on TV, in newspapers and radio commentaries in the area, and often the sheriffs of districts the Amish are located in are criticized for not enforcing the signs. This criticism even comes from politicians and other people of influence. This drew one sheriff to answer these objections. Sheriff Mikkelson stated:

> *"As Chief Law Enforcement Officer and your county sheriff, it is my duty to protect all of the citizens of Todd County. This means protecting the safety of the citizens, protecting the Constitution, and protecting all from civil liability. That is what I have been doing. For that, I feel that I have been the subject of unfair criticism....Consulting with Legal Counsel Richard Hodsdon with the Minnesota Sheriff's Association, he said,*

'*in light of this decision that was decided based
upon the United States Constitution, if you (Law
Enforcement) did arrest, cite or otherwise take
enforcement action against an Amish person protected by the statute, you would face significant
civil liability…Once a court declares the matter
subject to First Amendment protections, should
you take enforcement actions against those covered by this case, you and the acting deputies
could face major civil liability.*' [However, if this
court ruled it unconstitutional, the sheriff could
stand it down.] *Hodsdon went on to explain that*
**if the county board ordered the sheriff's office
to take enforcement action, that county and
its board members could face a personal lawsuit for establishing a policy that violates the
constitutional First Amendment rights of these
persons**…*The law is clear…This is America
where all citizens have constitutional protections that grant each of us freedom of religion.
When I took my oath as sheriff I swore to defend
the Constitution, and I will stand by that sacred
oath.*"[323]

The question begs to be asked that if it is unconstitutional and against religious freedom to force the

Amish to display "slow moving signs" on their horse buggies, how can the federal government force Catholics to pay for someone else's abortion—a blatant and obvious violation of their religious beliefs? The government cannot do this without committing a grave injustice against the rights of Catholics guaranteed under the First Amendment of the Constitution. Sheriffs who have given a solemn oath to protect the Constitution, must protect the citizens in their counties from the abuses of federal power, just as Sheriff Mikkelson defends the religious freedom of the Amish as he is sworn to do, despite the fact that it is unpopular with some of the people.

Sheriff Dave Mattis, Big Horn, Wyoming

Not all federal officials are posing problems with Sheriffs. Some still believe in the Constitution. When Sheriff Mattis told the Feds that they could not come into his county without checking with him first with details of what business they had in his county, both the Attorney General and the head of the local FBI said this was entirely proper and they told Sheriff Mattis if he has any problems with federal agents, to let them know and they will deal with them. [324]

Any who are in federal regulatory positions who will review the Constitution can help transform the United States back to the land of the free and the home of the brave, by protecting the liberty and freedom of citizens by applying rules of conduct rather than carrying out their jobs with hostility against citizens. It would be extremely difficult for a federal department to fire someone who refuses to violate someone's Constitutional right of which occurs daily. This applies also to state and local officials.

Land issues, such as taking control of or regulating water on your land as if you do not own it, are not the only violations the Davids can take on. Governments are also interfering more and more in your food choices, even when you produce it. This is part of the conditioning to get people used to the mentality that the government knows better than you know. Why food? Globalist Henry Kissinger explains in a statement he made in 1970:

> *"Control oil and you control nations; control food and you control the people; control money, and you control the world."* [325]

Granted, there are many government authorities and law enforcement officials who do not know why

the issue of enforcement is wrong as they only enforce
through arrests or fines, mandates of the higher ups.
They are blind to the fact that they are part of the evil
tyranny when they come to arrest their neighbors, good
people who are simply exercising their unalienable
God-given rights. But even so, it's time law enforcement officials look in the mirror each morning and
question if their actions that day are serving the rights
of citizen's life, liberty and their pursuit of happiness,
or are they actively serving tyranny for the 'powers
that be,' veined down through federalization to the city
streets and rural areas, of which city councils and county commissioners often help institute. What follows is
an excellent example of one law enforcement official
who chose not to look the other way. What happens
when the Food and Drug Administration comes knocking at your door threatening to shut your farm operation down? This very situation happened recently to
an Amish dairy farmer in Indiana.

Sheriff Brad Rogers, Elkhart County, Indiana

Real life shepherds of old were not sissies. Does
one not think that David learned a lot about how to
protect his flock long before he met Goliath on the battlefield? King David's manly bravery, his skill in fight-

ing and his ability to face foes who meant to do harm to his sheep, be they thieves or wolves, all of these are rooted to his experiences of what made him into a good shepherd. It is not a job for weak, timid spirits.

The details of the following story will educate you to the complexity of how tyranny develops, takes on legitimacy, then implements its evilness. Often federal and local officials are unaware that what they are doing is participating in tyranny, and if questioned, would even argue, not so. But good shepherd, Brad Rogers, questioned and understood the tyranny and heroically stood against it.

An Indiana Amish farmer, David Hochstetler, sought out protection from his county Sheriff, Brad Rogers, when agents from the Food and Drug Administration repeatedly came to inspect his dairy farm without a warrant. Hochstetler distributes raw milk to people who buy into his herd of Jersey cows. The federal government has taken a strong stance against the selling of raw, unpasteurized milk, purporting that people are at risk from bacteria from raw milk, but the government is not justified in this. Industrialized dairies whose milk volume is filled with contaminants and must, therefore, be pasteurized up to four times, called "ultra pasteurization," lobbied and got Congress

to ban the sale of raw milk in 1987. The milk industry
knows raw milk is healthy and that man for thousands
of years has consumed raw milk without any negative
side affects. Therefore, these large volume milk production operations could not compete with the small
dairies and creameries across the nation. These large
industrial plants often collect milk from whole regions
from many different farmers batching it all together
making it almost impossible for the milk not to be
contaminated with things you would not like to even
know about. So, there is an unjust war being waged by
the milk industry against the growing raw milk movement in which the large industrial companies "pretend"
they want to "protect" the public from raw milk. This
feigning of "protection" uses the Feds to enforce and
violate the Constitutional rights of the producers who
in their freedom desire to produce raw milk products,
and the Constitutional rights of the buyers who wish to
purchase a healthier product. This war against raw milk
is growing as more people are discovering raw milk is
rich in vitamins, enzymes, good bacteria and other benefits. So, understanding this, you can grasp the aggression of the industrialized milk industry's yell of fear
for public health, falsely stating unpasteurized (raw)
milk is dangerous to public health. Often at the orders
of bureaucrats, federal officers swarm in with local

police, sometimes with more law enforcement as back-
ups, to go shut down and arrest a little old dairy man
that is simply doing what man has done for thousands
of years. This is what we have come to in a tyrannical society. With the growing interest of consumers to
eat healthier foods, there is a growing demand for raw
milk. Milk is a nutritionally loaded food product compared to ultra pasteurized milk that burns away most
all nutrition from milk, resulting in a product with little
or no nutritional value, except what is added artificially
which is often questionable to health. Pasteurizing
milk four times not only kills all the bad contaminants
but also the good and healthy bacteria you need. Pasteurization also alters enzymes and vitamins that can
actually lead to harmful effects in the body. In order to
get around the ban on raw milk, consumers buy shares
in cow herds. Deborah Stockton, executive director
of the National Independent Consumers and Farmers
Association, supports small farmers who want to sell
their agricultural products directly to the public. She
has the data to show that there are very few cited cases
where raw milk has been linked to people becoming ill.
And, in fact, the opposite is coming to light. It is not
raw milk that is a detriment to one's health. Scientific
evidence is mounting to show that there is a connection
between drinking "pasteurized" milk and developing

illnesses and other negative health problems. Despite all of these factors, the government continues to take a hardball approach to those who produce raw milk.

"Allegations" by the Food and Drug Administration that Hochstetler's farm was the source of a bacterial illness that broke out in Michigan in 2010 led to not only several inspections of his farm, but also a summons to testify before a federal grand jury in Detroit. Hochstetler, not trusting the government officials, had a sample of his milk sent to an independent lab and no contamination was found. It was at this point that a desperate and frustrated Hochstetler contacted Sheriff Rogers. Rogers was elected in 2010, with a campaign platform that he would be a **"Constitutional Sheriff."** He won by a wide margin. He found Hochstetler's operation to be clean and well managed upon his own inspection. But what Sheriff Rogers was most concerned with was whether the rights of David Hochstetler were being infringed upon by the federal government, and he determined they were. He said, *"This isn't about raw milk. It's about fundamental rights."* [326]   What he told Hochstetler is, *"I will protect you in Elkhart County, I can't protect you in Detroit."* Then he asked him, *"Are you ready for some sparks to fly?"* [327] Hochstetler said he was, and then refused to appear before the De-

troit grand jury, pleading the 5th Amendment. Things
continued to escalate in the battle of tyranny vs. Constitutional rights. Rogers sent an email to the Justice
Department's trial attorney. In part, it said:

> *"Any further attempts to inspect this farm without
> a warrant signed by a local judge, based on proba-
> ble cause, will result in Federal inspectors' removal
> or arrests for trespassing by my officers or I."* [328]

The federal agent who received the email, in Rogers' words, *"didn't take to that too well. He said the
federal government has precedence based on the Supremacy Clause. I* (Sheriff Rogers) *told him the federal
government is supreme if it has to do with the Constitution."* [329]

Rogers made it clear to the Justice Department
that he was not going to change his stance. This com-
munication between the two took place on a Friday. It
must have been a long weekend with multiple meetings
and communications from Goliath on what to do with
Little David. On the following Tuesday, Hochstetler
received a certified letter from the Department of Justice that they were withdrawing the subpoena. The
stone of David's sling hit its mark. Constitutional Sheriff Rogers' main objective in confronting the mammoth

FDA was to protect the Constitutional rights of all the citizens of his county. *"Due process is the important part of it,"* [330] he said in how Hochstetler was treated. He wants to see the federal agencies go through the court system and let the judge decide if there is enough evidence presented to justify a warrant for inspection. Rogers said:

> *"The thing is that if the FDA agents come in and they meet with the farmer and the farmer wants them to come in, I don't have a problem with that. But in this case Mr. Hochstetler did not want the agents there. This is an administrative rule of the federal government and I think people are tired of the federal government walking all over everybody and it is time to take a stand for states' rights."* [331]

> *"I want to protect citizens like Hochstetler. That stuff is not going to happen in my county."* [332]

Because of his efforts to protect Hochstetler, Sheriff Rogers was given an award, "For Meritorious Valor for Interposing Himself on Behalf of His Citizens." A shepherd puts himself between the danger and the sheep.

Since becoming **Sheriff, Rogers requires all his deputies to take three, two-day classes on the Constitution.**

Keeping the Constitution in mind gives clarity to sheriffs when they are confronted with situations that they must judge if the rights of their citizens are being compromised—from gun bans, to sobriety checkpoints, to imposing fines unconstitutionally, etc. There is an increasing awareness, though it is still very small, among sheriffs and the people that so many of the laws and regulations are not there for the sake of law and order. Yet, the underlying reason is understood by fewer still.

The unseen spirit of evil, of totalitarianism, as it rises in power, must gradually condition the citizens to accept the loss of liberty and freedom for the sake of public safety, national defense emergencies, and the welfare of the people. It's a deception. These threats that are made to look eminent are nothing of the sort. But the build up of power in this way always gives way to the Hitlers. The power will always be grabbed by who is at the top, who is there at the right place and at the right time. It is a given, evil will thrive in those who are possessed with the desire for power. Evil then finds a good vessel, open to possession, in those who have an inordinate desire for power. Hitler developed in his ideas, of becoming ruler of the world, and evil inspired him as he grew in power. We are on the exact path that was walked in the 1930's, as well as other periods of history when tyranny reigned. This is not good for anyone, because it creates an atmosphere where tyranny is gradually accepted as something good for reasons such as public safety, national emergencies, etc., and not recognized as tyranny until it is too late.

At this critical junction for the history of the United States of America, it is the Davids, the Constitutional Sheriffs, who have the highest authority in their counties that can protect the citizens when they are committed to stand against such regulations, laws, and tyrannies. The people who elect their protectors must enlighten their sheriffs in their own counties to encourage them to become a Constitutional Sheriff and if they will not, elect one who will commit to becoming one. We then must hope in God that He will act through the Catholic Bishops and other Christian pastors, united with "we the people" and the County Sheriff, for God "to heal our land" one county at a time.

The power of authority becomes immensely stronger when all energies can be focused and concentrated on electing the right sheriff on a county level, as opposed to the out of focus and diluted efforts, which spread our energies too thin to get the right president and congressmen and judges to protect Constitutional rights. We can mount our efforts on an achievable goal, focusing our votes, our money, our prayers, our unity on the local election of one single man that has strength to hold to our constitutional ground and "stand down the Goliaths," with the power of authority to stop all unconstitutional action! Be they federal or local extended hands of government who are implementing federal mandates, violating our religious liberties and freedoms, a Constitutional Sheriff has the authority to stop this encroachment in its tracks.

Sheriff Alderden, Colorado

The United States of America is unique among all the nations of the world. The Founding Fathers, aware of what happens in nations by governments, put into the Constitution the right to bear arms as the law of the land. This was not for the purpose of aggression or for hunting, it was for defense against the government if it shifted towards tyranny and the protection against criminals. Criminals can also be in the government. This uniqueness has preserved America. The United Nations recognizes the "right" to abortion, the "right" to abominables, reproduction "rights" and many more rights that are contrary to the moral order. One right, amazingly, the United Nations does not recognize is the right of self-defense. The Catholic Catechism is clear about this right to defend oneself, as well as Just War principles, as previously stated. The United Nations has led and covertly influences Congress, our courts, and many city and state officials to violate the right secured in the Second Amendment to bear arms. As also previously discussed in past chapters, the reason arms must be banned by evil is because tyranny cannot do as it wishes when a well-defended people are ready to stand against tyranny's reign.

The Second Amendment of the Constitution guarantees the right of citizens to bear arms. Yet, in February 2010, a gun ban was enacted at Colorado State University. In response to this unconstitutional act, Sheriff Alderden, whose jurisdiction the University falls under, stated:

> *"I have told the CSU (Colorado State University) police chief I will not support this in any way. If anyone with one of my permits gets arrested for concealed carry at Colorado State University, I will refuse to book that person into my jail. Furthermore, I will show up at court and testify on that person's behalf, and I will do whatever I can to discourage a conviction. I will not be a party to this very poor decision."* [333]

The Virginia Tech massacre could very well have been stopped had the university allowed its students to ex-

ercise their Constitutional Second Amendment right.
It is a statistical fact when good law abiding citizens
are armed, crime is decreased. It is statistically proven
criminals avoid those areas when it is known that people will defend themselves.

Sheriff Brett Barslou, Lemhi County, Idaho

It is common sense and common law that citizens
have the right to protect their livestock on their own
property against predators, even if the predator is listed
as an "endangered species." In many of the cases with
"endangered species," they are endangered only in a
specific region of the nation, but you will find them
doing quite well in their own native habitats. The "Endangered Species Act" is often used as another hidden
agenda to take control of private property and force
people off or restrict the use of their properties. Federal agents have brought great frustration and harm to
the livelihood of thousands of citizens who are forced
to watch, with their hands tied, the animals and livestock they make their living by, being attacked and
killed without being able to do anything about it. A
much greater number of citizens are forced to see the
dreams for their property die as they are not able to
build on their land because it would supposedly threat-

en wildlife, the environment, or a worm on their property. There is hardly any greater example of tyranny than when you must submit your private property to such radical dictates. However, the tide is changing.

The U.S. Fish and Wildlife Service sent three armed agents to serve a warrant for the arrest of a 74-year-old rancher who shot one of the abundantly populated "endangered gray wolves" which had killed one of his calves. County Sheriff Brett Barslou, when he learned of this, said that the federal agency's action was *"inappropriate, heavy-handed and dangerously close to excessive force."*[334] People all around are fed up with wolves repeatedly taking precedence over their rights to protect their means they live by. So it was no surprise a rally was held in the small towns of Challis and Salmon in which more than 500 people showed up to support Sheriff Barslou and the rancher. Their presence, in effect, said to the federal government, *"Back off."* [335]

Are we to remain helpless when federal agencies say "no" to a good for a community, against all logic and common sense, creating situations that place forced burdens on the backs of citizens because of their own agendas? Not if you have a Sheriff who knows the Constitution and is led by a true spirit of serving the people who elected him to his office for their help and protection.

The population of wolves has made a dramatic comeback while environmentalists have gone to court to keep
them on the endangered list. In fact, they have made
so much of a comeback the danger now is that they are
decimating whole elk and deer populations. The wolves
are so well fed and bored they are now sport killing!
Yes, they are chasing down herds killing them for fun,
leaving them dead and uneaten. And wouldn't you just
know it, attacks on humans by wolves are growing more
common. Environmentalists deny this, but one can research and find that stories of these attacks are increasing. And wouldn't you just know it, in Scripture it says
that living in God's Commandments, He will bless you:

Ezekiel 34:25

> *"I will make with them a covenant of peace*
> *and banish wild beasts from the land."*

Don't trust what is written here. Research for
yourself about the "wild beast," the wolf and what a
mess the 'federal' wolves have created for their human
brothers through their preferred adopted brother in
the wild in balancing the ecosystem. Along with courageous sheriffs, we should be motivated to live God's
statutes to **drive the wild beasts from our lands**, without
fear as to the size of the pack.

Sheriff Richard Mack, former Sheriff of Graham County, Arizona

Author of "The County Sheriff: America's Last Hope"

Is it tyranny when you are fined $1.00 a day? $10.00 a day? $10,000.00 a day? $50,000.00 a day? At what point does it turn into tyranny? The answer is when you can be fined unconstitutionally $1.00 per day. If it's not stopped there, what's a $50,000 fine per day to tyranny?

In Graham County, Arizona, residents traveled over a bridge to bring their children to school each day. One day the bridge was washed out. This forced parents to drive 26 miles out of their way to get their kids to school each day, when the school was only ½ a mile from the bridge. The bridge had been built by the U.S. Army Corps of Engineers. When they were contacted to fix the bridge, they said they first had to do an "environmental impact study." Why would a study have to be done on an area where a bridge had already been located for many years? After repeated prodding, in the end, the Army Corps of Engineers said it would take ten years before the bridge could be rebuilt. This is now standard procedure for agencies of the government and is a method outlined in Sustainable Develop-

ment, the United Nation's Agenda 21 plan, adopted
in nearly every county of the nation. In order to discourage rebuilding in areas there is a driven agenda to
cause delays and 'cited' other reasons for the agenda
to return areas back to nature. Often tactics include
ridiculously high fines until people finally throw up
their hands in frustration and give up. But again, in
essence, it is evil's unseen plans to destroy the infrastructure of the United States to turn our nation into a
third world country so evil can run rampant across the
world. Sheriff Richard Mack was Sheriff of Graham
County at this time. In his interview for this book, he
told how the Army Corps of Engineers' answer that it
would take ten years to rebuild the bridge wasn't good
enough for the people of Graham County. Sheriff
Mack decided to ignore the Army Corps of Engineers.
He states:

> *"We began fixing the washed out bridge and the*
> *Army Corps of Engineers came out and said,*
> *'You can't touch that bridge, it's not yours.' They*
> *said, 'We're the ones that put the bridge there.'*
> *We said, 'So, I've got news for you. This is Gra-*
> *ham County. We have a bridge there that people*
> *need to use to take their kids to school, and we're*
> *not going to allow you guys to come in and act*

*like you own the place.' The county tried to work
with them for over a year to get the bridge fixed
and they still wouldn't get it fixed so the county
voted unanimously to just fix the bridge. Then
the Army Corps of Engineers says, 'We will arrest
you.' They threatened to arrest the county com-
missioner. Then they said, 'We'll arrest all the
county employees who are fixing the bridge and
we're going to fine you* **$50,000** *a day.' They're
going to fine the county $50,000 a day for every
day that we're in violation! So I came in and told
the county commissioners that I would come in
and protect the workers at the scene, that I would
protect the county commissioners and anyone
else that we needed to, that I would call out the
posse if necessary. I said we would not charge
any overtime for the work that my deputies might
be doing 24 hours a day on this situation. Then
I called the Army Corps of Engineer heads into
my office, there were three of them. And I said,
'Look, I'm a real easy guy to get along with. I've
never been violent in my life. I've never even
hit anybody in 20 years of law enforcement; I've
never struck another human being. But...just
make sure...that you do not think I'm bluffing—*

if you guys come in here and try to arrest any-
body, I will arrest you.'

"And so let me tell you the bottom line: we fixed
the bridge, no one was arrested and we did not
pay one dime in fines." [336]

Sheriff Mack knows the power of the Office of
Sheriff. There are so many situations where citizens
are being forced to accept abuses in their lives that the
sheriff can simply put a stop to. Mack has explained
that county sheriffs across the country can even stop
medical mandates like forced vaccinations against
one's will. With the rapid increase of government mandated vaccinations, and the equally rapid increase of
autism, many are questioning if there is a connection
between the two. There are other issues rising up for
school children being forced to have mandatory vaccinations for the prevention of some venereal related
diseases. The sheriff's power supersedes federal regulatory programs, such as forced vaccinations, as sheriffs
are not agents of the federal government. Despite
grave concerns of evidence linking certain vaccinations
to the development of autism, seizures, and other mala-
dies, the federal government imposes strict enforcement of these vaccinations upon infants and children,
even over and despite parental objections. Sheriff

Mack states that your local sheriff has clear authority
to stop mandatory vaccinations, quarantines in detention facilities, checkpoints and anything that the Federal government mandates in your state, county and
locality. Some may think, "but public health is important." This is not what is being debated. What is being
debated is there is something else behind the government mandating these vaccinations. Is a crisis being
created by the 'powers that be' because of institutional
agendas having to do with population control, contraceptives, getting people conditioned to accept more
control over their lives, thrown in the batch for forced
mandates? Many are beginning to believe these issues
are driving forced vaccinations which are being done
for population control or, as euthanasia groups, such as
Texas Academy of Science in 2006, have proposed, for
depopulation. [337]

Sheriff Thomas Dart, Cook County, Illinois

It's not just from unjust and unlawful governmental
agencies that sheriffs can defend their people, but from
any corruption that strikes at the liberty of citizens.
During the crisis of the bank foreclosures of homes
over the past several years, one sheriff saw immediately
that many banks, who were guilty of creating the dire

situations people were finding themselves in, were benefitting financially at the expense of those who were losing their homes.

After receiving papers to foreclose on homes, what happens to a sheriff who finds himself standing in a living room with a battering ram looking like a swat team has been invited to dinner? What happens? A change of a hireling's heart to a Constitutional heart.

In 2009 and 2010, at the peak of bank foreclosures on homes taking place across the United States, Sheriff Thomas Dart and his deputies in the Chicago area were given the unpleasant task of evicting people from their homes in his county of jurisdiction. Time and time again, they would arrive at a house, and find the people were totally unaware that they were being evicted, having had no notification or warning. Sheriff Dart explained:

> *"I would go out with my deputies on these evictions and we would come into house after house where people were going about their normal day, having dinner, playing with their kids and here I am standing in their living room dressed in black with battering rams and they have no idea why I'm there, because in this reckless haste, that got*

us in this mess to start with, and it was all the
banks mind you, the recklessness that they did in
the first place, they wanted me to be just as reck-
less and just toss everyone into the streets, and so
after it became abundantly clear that person after
person had no idea that there was even a foreclo-
sure action going on, I just stopped doing fore-
closures altogether and said until they get their
act together, I'm not doing it anymore." [338]

Other times they would arrive at an address for an
eviction, only to find a deserted house. Sheriff Dart
said:

"One of the documents I got from a bank to go
conduct an eviction was a house that no longer
existed…the foundation had already become
overgrown with bushes because the house had
been missing for so many years, and that's where
I was supposed to go evict somebody." [339]

The banks Sheriff Dart came up against were giants
in the industry, including Bank of America, J.P. Morgan,
Chase and GMAC/Ally Financial. Employees of these
banks were signing off on foreclosure notices without
even reading them. *"This is so outrageous,"* said Sheriff
Dart,

"...these poor families are being put through this day in and day out by people that don't do their jobs. It's so hard for me to stomach these people [banks] because this isn't just their bike we're taking away or their car. It's their house."[340]

So Sheriff Dart simply stopped doing the evictions, and before he would resume these actions he began to require banks to sign affidavits under penalty of perjury stating they had done sufficient verifications and notifications necessary to warrant foreclosure and eviction. Though the bankers protested Sheriff Dart's action, the result of it was that the filings for foreclosure dropped from 300 to 170 per month. Sheriff Dart said,

*"All of a sudden the number of filings have gone down in our county, as well as one law firm pulled hundreds of cases out of the court system for reasons they wouldn't explain...We were finding messes there, so what **we've done now is we've opened up criminal investigations.**"[341]*

Sheriff Jim Singleton, Ohio

We end this chapter with a letter written by Sheriff Jim Singleton of the Ohio Oath Keepers Association, who wrote the letter in response to the passage of the National Defense Authorization Act by Congress, **N.D.A.A.,** and happily signed into law by Obama. It was written to oath keeping sheriffs as well as to civil officials. Sheriff Singleton's letter reflects how deeply Constitutional Sheriffs should feel about their nation and the duty they feel towards defending the Constitution and the citizens under their care, and the authority to stand down not just the Federal agents, but Congress and the President, himself, if it comes to that.

> *"It's unfortunate that I have to write this letter, however, in light of current events it is inevitable. Just days ago the United States Congress passed the National Defense Authorization Act (N.D.A.A.). This in itself was necessary. However, in this bill was an insidious piece of verbiage that for all intents and purposes destroys the foundation of everything we believe in and took an oath to uphold. To me the possibility of those citizens and others under my protection being spirited off in the middle of the night by agents of the military, then being summarily incarcerated without access to judge or jury are insufferable and intolerable acts.*
>
> *"It will be argued that this only applies to foreign persons or others suspected of terrorism, but*

*there are far too many avenues available to ap-
ply this to any group to which any administration
may take umbrage with. When growing up and
especially during our training in the academy
we are instructed that the constitutional rights
of all must be upheld at all times, as well as the
respect for all people we come in contact with or
represent. This section of the National Defense
Authorization Act attempts to remove those
rights which are enumerated and given to us by
our Creator, and places them in the hands of the
Office of the President of the United States to be
disregarded at his whim.*

*"And in those few words lies a conundrum, do
we as police officers, sheriffs, deputies and others
who have taken the oath to uphold and defend
the Constitution, now turn our backs on that very
oath? Do we now turn against the very same
people that entrusted us with a most sacred duty
to serve and protect them? If in fact we follow a
rule of law such as this bill enacts, it would mean
that the oath that we all took meant nothing. We
are obliged to follow all lawful orders given to
us, but we cannot do this blindly. History has
seen the result of these acts and has judged them*

*accordingly. I can only ask all of you to take
a moment to reflect upon all that we are taught
and hold dear, the people we serve deserve and
demand our highest respect for it is through them
and they alone that we were given this oath. Do
we simply turn a blind eye for the sake of political expediency and lose our respect? Is a few
pieces of silver so dear that we would sell our
honor for it? How will we explain to our friends
and loved ones why members of our community
were spirited away or how will they see us when
they realize, that when their time comes, we won't
be there for them?*

*"I believe that if and when those orders come, **I
cannot** **in good faith and in strict observance
to my oath,** allow myself to be a part of them
[accepting orders]. I would hope that members
of our military in accordance to the articles of
the Uniform Code of Military Justice, would also
refuse them as well. When that time comes I will
do exactly as I have sworn to do, I will serve and
protect those under my care, so help me God.*

Also I heard the voice of the Lord, saying,
Whom shall I send, and who will go for us?
Then said I, Here am I; Send me. *Isaiah 6:8*

Respectfully Submitted

James B. Singleton
Secretary Ohio Oath Keepers [342]

The above letter by a Sheriff, stating his commitment to protect all those who elected him, defined for all county sheriffs the path to liberty. This only works, however, when God's people put Him first in their hearts, by the principle that "the power behind the authority" is confirmed by God, who brings victory, when the people are living righteously. Remember also another principle already stated in this book: *a people are not so much protected by their armaments as they are by their way of life.* Sheriff Singleton puts into writing how his authority will be used **to stop a combination of Goliaths.**

The National Defense Authorization Act, a huge impacting law, passed by the United States Senate, passed by the United States House of Representatives, signed into law by the President of the United States of America, in effect, grants authority to treat the United States of America as a battlefield. If there is a 'crisis,' whatever that may be defined as, laws of war can be

applied through the N.D.A.A. giving Obama, or a future president, authority for the United States Army,
Marines, Air Force and more, to be used against United
States citizens. This is a monster of a Goliath that only
a 'David' who walks in the ways of God can strike
down because he can plan a preemptive strike against
any action that violates the unalienable rights of his
county's citizens that is committed through this unlawful law. Again, the N.D.A.A. is a law, which through
hook and crook is intended to give authority to treat
the United States as a battlefield, giving the military
authorization to whisk away United States citizens, taking away their rights, denying them a trial and having
them detained indefinitely just as if they were an enemy captured, such as on a battlefield in Afghanistan. In
Afghanistan and other war zones where our military is
fighting, there are no Constitutional rights for enemies.
Soldiers can stop and detain anyone and act in whatever is deemed necessary for what is being accomplished
in their rules of engagement. There are no Constitutional rights afforded to an enemy or the country's citizens when fighting in such situations for sound reasons.
This is war. So can this happen to American citizens?
Our forefathers framed within the Constitution and
the Bill of Rights protection for its citizens. And yet,
the National Defense Authorization Act violates these

rights. It is dangerous and it is unconstitutional despite congressional passage and a presidential signature.

The "Resolution of the Sheriff against N.D.A.A. 2012" is a document written for Patriotic, Constitutional, Oath-Keeping Sheriffs. It should be adopted and endorsed by every sheriff and every county in the United States, as well as by city councils, county commissions, and state legislatures.

As you read these pages, it is very important these facts are learned and burned in your heart to see the steps to total tyranny can be easily slid within one day's time. In a quick decision, a ruse can be used for a declared national emergency, or a peace time build up, as a necessary excuse for preparation for national defense, etc. All that has to happen is the use of an excuse or a created or made-up crisis in order to take control of every aspect of life. Who determines what is a National Emergency? Could a Hurricane Katrina, way down in the South, be declared a "National" Emergency, thereby, all resources, warehouses, travel, food, etc. be declared under the authority of the president through the Executive Order? Remember, evil will not let a crisis go to waste. Anything could be used as a National Emergency to "take control of every aspect of life." Therefore, a short review is given in a somewhat different example that you have absolute clarity of what the 'powers that be' are doing and how, with Constitutional Sheriffs, this can be confronted, anointed with God's power of authority. A section in the resolution of the Sheriffs against N.D.A.A. 2012 states: *"In essence what the N.D.A.A. accomplishes is applying a legal fiction to the United States that it is a 'battlefield' under the authority of the military and under the 'law of war.'"* [343] Stewart Richards and Richard Fry of Oathkeepers, who wrote the "Resolution of the Sheriff against N.D.A.A. 2012," further explained that battlefields are under the authority of the military and under the "law of war." As we know, if our house catches fire, the fire department will kick in our door and put out the fire. Due to the immediate emergency, they will not get a court order or even ask your permission. What the N.D.A.A. does is declares everyone's house is on fire. This is, of course, unconstitutional.

Even if the United States were a battlefield, such as during a "Rebellion or Invasion," the "law of war" still cannot be applied to United States citizens and lawful residing aliens.

CHAPTER THIRTY-TWO

"The Davids"
The People
The Turbo

Combustion engines can have varied horsepower from small to very powerful engines. To all these engines, an apparatus called a turbo charger can be added that easily adds more horsepower. An engine with an added turbo increases the air flow rammed in the engine, giving more combustion, with an appreciable increase in horsepower. You can understand this as a sailboat with a 20 mph wind blowing into the sail, powering it through the water. The sailboat, with an increase of an extra 10 mph wind to the 20 mph wind filling the sail, would be advantaged with more speed and power. An extra 10 mph wind in the sail is as a turbo on a combustion engine giving more speed and power to do the work it is designated for.

The Davids have everything they need to lawfully act. They can use their authority in a weak or powerful way according to their courage in using their authority. Nevertheless, sheriffs have the authority and, therefore,

the power to stand down <u>any</u> unconstitutional threat in
their county. But, as with a combustion engine in which
a turbo is added, there is something greater that can be
added, increasing the ability of the Sheriffs to act with
more speed and greater efficiency and power to stop
unconstitutional mandates—whether coming from local or federal government and everything in between.
The turbo, for true Constitutional Sheriffs, is

Nullification.

Nullification is simple: any federal law that violates
the Constitution is no law. It, instead, is a usurpation
of power. Matthew Spalding writes in an article titled,
"Idaho Draws the Constitutional Line,"

> *"The Constitution is the supreme law of the land
> —not the Supreme Court or the Federal govern-
> ment."* [344]

We have fallen into a false belief that to determine
the constitutionality of a law, executive order or action,
we must go to a court to tell us if it is constitutional or
unconstitutional. We submit ourselves to this meekly
as sheep led to the slaughter. These verdicts by the
judges of the courts, unconstitutional as they may be,
are accepted as if they, the judges are our shepherds.
These verdicts, instead, are from the hirelings who care

nothing for the sheep. Acceptance of these verdicts of
what is unconstitutional then runs through the veins of
state courts, commissions, city councils, agencies, etc.,
with everyone complying, following the false shepherd
judges, so much so that the people even accept to be
fined, jailed, or have their property taken away as if
there is nothing we can do. We must understand we do
not have to go to a hireling judge to determine, when
something is very clear, whether or not it is constitutional. We do not have to wait for any court to give an
answer where common sense has already granted the
verdict. The enemy <u>wants</u> you to go to court to expend
your money, your energies, and bury your motivation
to stand against what you know is wrong. They want
you to fight, "on their" managed damage control playing field. The healthcare mandate is blatantly unconstitutional. We, as individuals can give the verdict. We
are not to be mindless. A simple read of the Constitution shows Mr. Obama's law is null and void. We do
not have to comply, nor are we going to jail. If there
are those who want to force this compliance, it is those
in union with the Constitution who are to say to them,
you will not make us comply. We will not close down
any facility or church operational services helping people, and your attempts to make us will cost you your
own arrest. Everything is in place for *the Davids* to ar-

rest those who force enforcement of unconstitutional mandates for charges of trespassing to kidnapping (if federal officials come to arrest you) and more.

Through the Constitution, the federal government is very limited in its power over states and thereby, the people. Michael Boldin, founder of the 10th Amendment Center, states:

> *"Today we have a federal government that crosses the line almost constantly...The federal government believes it is authorized to tell us what size toilet we can have, what kind of light bulbs we can buy, what kind of plants we can grow and consume in our backyards... The Executive branch has overstepped its authority. Congress has overstepped its authority. The courts have overstepped their authority"* [345]

If the Constitution is the standard measurement to judge this overstepping, Boldin goes on to say:

> *"Many federal departments and agencies should not even exist..."* [346]

And also:

"The federal government (has) overstepped its constitutionally delegated power in massive ways."[347]

So what exactly is nullification? Boldin states:

"Nullification begins with a decision made in your state legislature to resist an unconstitutional federal law, (through passing a "nullification" state law) a refusal on the part of your state's government to cooperate with or enforce federal law deemed to be unconstitutional." [348]

We must break away from our being locked into the mentality that we have to go to courts to determine constitutionality in every case. It is not so. And any American who can read and has common sense can read the Constitution themselves and will know any blatant violations of Constitutional rights. Instead of to the courts, go to the Constitutional Sheriff to protect your unalienable rights.

Will states be on the side of the citizens and the Sheriffs? While states are not always "angels" and can in and of themselves be terrible because they also can pass regulations which are unconstitutional, the Davids have the power to keep them (states) in check as with the federal government. But when on the good side,

the states can *turbo charge* with nullification, backing
the Sheriffs who can more forcibly carry out actions,
stopping tyranny against county citizens. It is important to note: The people are the Sheriff's boss. They
elect him to be their guardian, and he can protect the
people with or without nullification. However, the turbo of nullification can make the federal government's
unconstitutional edicts begin to fall and shatter across
the United States of America like dust, a great victory.
Each state, through their legislature and their governor
signing it into law, can nullify each unconstitutional law.
This is more than a refusal to enforce unconstitutional
law within their state's border, because it actually
makes federal laws become no law in the state. But
this will happen only with us turning from our wicked
ways and being a repentant people, which in turn will
allow God to act with the "power of authority" in what
He promises in His Word, ***"I will heal their land."***
The importance of this is worth repeating. Again, to be
clear, a state nullifying a particular federal law, which
includes unconstitutional state laws, proclaims that
law void, non-effective within the state lines. Nullification is not new. In America, there is a long tradition of
when it has been invoked, going all the way back to our
nation's fathers.

In 2007, Maine passed a nullification against the "Real ID Act," declaring it null and void within the state lines. Following the initiative, twenty-five other states did the same. The Federal ID Law, still on the books, has become dormant, rendering it null and void because of massive state resistance. If one state stands against the president, congress, and courts, what can "federals" do? Not much of anything. If more states do likewise, the power that the government has unconstitutionally amassed, will crumble peaceably. The tiger is made out of paper and the 'wind' can blow it away. Yes, the Sheriff's authority alone can do so, but with the states' nullification, the power will give a "turbo wind," still blowing away the paper tiger, but making it happen all the more quickly and peaceably.

Aside from our losing our rights as a people, how have we gotten to this point that we must now take these steps? Is there an organized effort to destroy our Constitutional rights? Yes! Why? Because there are those who want to rule the United States with an evil tyranny and, thereby the whole world. Who is behind it?

There are several names and organizations which can be given because evil invisibly coordinates between physical entities. Even though these physical entities may be disconnected and working separately, they will eventually converge as their wicked plans evolve, becoming as one, by the simple fact of having the same goal. Evil's goal is for the destruction of what is good, in this case, Constitutional, in order to construct what is bad. This is the merry-go-round of tyranny throughout history. The difference today, in tyranny's consolidation to rule as opposed to past history of tyranny's reign, is that never before has evil had the means to monitor every action of men, seeing through walls, through infrared detection and other extraordinary technologies, as CIA director General David Petraeus said of today's spying capabilities, that they are *'diabolically clever'…"* [349] No "underground railroad,"* no ability for freedom fighters to resist tyranny such as what happened in World War II and throughout history. And, of course, never has evil tyranny reigned so broadly in a time with the ability to destroy the whole world. Our Lady said:

January 25, 1991

> **"…satan is strong and wishes not only to destroy human life but also nature and the planet on which you live…"**

---

* The Underground Railroad was a network of secret routes and safe houses used by 19th-century black slaves in the United States to escape to the North.

And as already quoted several times, Our Lady said:

August 2, 2011

> **"...you cannot stop the evil that wants to begin to rule in this world and to destroy it. But, according to God's will, all together, with my Son, you can change everything and heal the world..."**

Back to the question: What is behind the scenes that brought us to this point? Who is it driving the 'powers that be'? Why?

CHAPTER THIRTY-THREE

When? Who? Where? How? Why?

To understand 'one' part of the evil axis of the 'powers that be,' the questions must be asked: When? Who? Where? How? Why?

When? Into physical reality in 2005.

Who? The American Constitutional Society Conference called, "The Constitution in 2020," funded by multi-billionaire George Soros.

Where? Yale University Law School.

How? Through a coordinated effort to reorient people to think what they believe the Constitution means to be wrong and over time change the Constitution to mean something else.

Why? To have a supplanted United States Constitution by 2020 that will be a very radical, left, socialist reinterpreted Constitution.

Multi-billionaire globalist, George Soros, has used his billions to "dump" and "modify" the United States

Constitution, bringing the United States under international subjugation. It is amazing that one can go beyond
treason, using one's wealth to destroy many nations, as
he has done, and especially now, the United States of
America, that no one in the United States has brought
forth an investigation on Soros' criminal intentions of
insurrection and arrested him. This gives evidence of the
incredible network he has built around him. His actions
are not free speech. His goal is that the United States
Constitution will not be the Supreme Law of the Land,
rather that it will be subject to international laws and to
other nations. Of course, this goal brings about centralization, in order to implement internationalization of
each nation. It would allow for the first time for a leader
to lead from a central position globally with such power.
The Soros' gang called their movement "democratic
constitutionalism." [350] Somewhere along the line, a 'perfect model' of leftist ideals had to be found by the various 'greats,' leftist university professors and other im-
poverished spiritual souls. A mentor type perfect model
that the world could look upon in wonder and rave
about, holding it up for all to imitate and copy. In this
case, a constitution to strive for as the ultimate model
of what a constitution should be for all nations. United
States Supreme Court Justice Ginsburg is part of the
planned play to point to the model. All evidence shows

this "idolized" constitution was written by the 'powers that be.' They needed something they could later ooh and ahh over, as if they suddenly discovered something new, all the while they had precontrived it themselves for such a purpose. It follows the old tactics: go to the newspapers with several sources to get a story printed. Once your story is printed, shift from being the source, the one who gave the story to the newspapers, to now quoting the 'newspaper' that gave your story legitimacy. One can then state, "The New York Times reported that, '...*whatever statement you contrived to get into print...*'" This legitimizing tactic is a whole propaganda machine. It is used to get propaganda fed to other media, cited in other newspapers, slipped into school textbooks, etc. All the while the ones who created the story further their agenda. This can work also for preplanned documents which are put forth, 'precontrived' to make changes in society. The staged model that we are to be awed over and look to is South Africa's constitution. Ginsburg's preplanned strategized statement during an Egyptian television interview on January 30, 2012:

> *"I would not look to the United States Constitution if I were drafting a constitution in the year 2012. I might look at the constitution of South Africa..."* [351]

All of this is made to look natural and spontaneous, but one can understand and see clearly when one understands tyranny's intentions. Know your enemy. Anywhere liberty is under assault, you will find an enemy to those who cherish liberty. Ginsburg's statement is a clear rejection of the United States Constitution by a sitting judge on the Supreme Court! It is impossible for her to make verdicts on our Constitution without her interjecting what she wants the United States Constitution to be, rather than what the Constitution truly is and states. Has anyone questioned how a United States Supreme Court Justice can say such a thing and it not be considered treason? Ask yourself, where are the voices for her to be removed, impeached, for her actions? Why not? Because where evil begins its rule, its roots have been growing for some time in the ground. Once it begins to sprout, it is harder to pull up.

Who wrote South Africa's new constitution? George Soros began meddling with the overthrow of South Africa's apartheid government as early as 1979, and he has poured millions of dollars into efforts to build and maintain "the **infrastructure** and **institutions** of an open society." In 1993 he formalized his efforts in South Africa, just three years before the adoption of the country's final Constitution in 1996, by founding an institution

called the Open Society Foundation for South Africa.[352]
Remember, Sun-tzu taught to know your enemies, if you
want victory. The writing of the South African Constitution cannot be happen chance, rather it was planted stra-
tegically to be the "pointing star" for all to conform to
and the goal for all nations. Two key figures connected
to Soros, John Podesta and Cass Sunstein, participated in
the George Soros funded 2005 Yale Conference called,
"The Constitution in 2020." Podesta and Sunstein are
two of billionaire George Soros' yes men. Incredibly,
but not a coincidence, rather by strategy both men, after
the Yale Conference, ended up 'handling' Obama's campaign 'and' his presidential move into the White House,
arranging and rooting the 'powers that be' around
Obama. Do you need more "connect the dots" that
Obama is handled and is the stool pigeon for the Soros
gang? How does one, who was no one, become president except that one was handpicked to become president by the 'powers that be'? James Norell, contributing
editor of *American's First Freedom Magazine,* wrote:

> "...Soros' policy/influence machine (is) 'The
> Center for American Progress.' It has been a
> front of left-wing ideals that the Obama White
> House has turned into policy." [353]

Soros needed a president to implement his plans. The orchestrating of South Africa's constitution being written by the 'powers that be' fits in nicely in connecting the dots. 'Before' Supreme Court Justice Ginsburg made her strange and treasonous, even weird, statement about South Africa's constitution, Soros' man, Sunstein, Obama's presidential campaign advisor and transitioner into the White House, also made a statement about the South African constitution, saying that it is:

> *"the most admirable constitution in the history of the world." [354]*

Ginsburg makes a statement about a constitution Soros is behind and Sunstein has made another "awe" statement. Get these statements in the New York Times, or other major papers and then quote the paper/media and the statement is legitimized into 'being.' See the dots? Here are more dots.

In 2003, Mark Kende, now head of the Constitutional Law Center of Drake University Law School wrote an article titled, ***"Why the South African Constitution is better than the United States."*** Liberal and leftist professors from many universities came together for the Yale Conference in 2005. A second Yale Conference 'reconvened' in 2009, again paid for by billionaire George

Soros, and again called "The Constitution in 2020." The conference centered on a book authored by leftist professors who are planning a totally new United States Constitution by 2020. The book is their bible and the conference hailed it in a divine way as their holy book. The book's title is The Constitution in 2020. The cover even has the signers' names listed underneath the title to create an image, a semblance of something profound on the level of the United States Constitution, yet their goal is to keep this secret for now. It is apparent their goal is to fundamentally change America. Likewise, the South African constitution was manufactured for the purpose of gloriously holding it up, to take pieces of it to change our United States Constitution. Norell writes in his article:

"These people are not talking about replacing the United States Constitution with the South African Constitution out of hand. What they seek is to include key viral elements of that document, in a bit-by-bit infection that will ultimately transform the whole nature of our country." [355]

Is this not what also is happening in each of our 50 states? Have you also noticed in your own state and every state in the United States great effort and pressure being applied to rewrite each state's Constitution? Propaganda to do so is subtle, yet rampant over the last sev-

eral years. When you see in your local state media, "stories" about your state Constitution being inadequate to
address this or that issue, know the quoters are the ones
who drove the 'stories' into the media with the purpose
of building support to replace state constitutions. Why?
Because states' rights can trump federal. Why? Because
the United States Constitution says so and states' rights
model those God-given unalienable rights in their constitutions. So the tactic to change the United States Constitution includes state Constitutions. Why has this come
up spontaneously, without condemnation by "we the
people?" Because we are all busy making a living, keeping food on the table, while those at the Yale meetings
are busy toiling and creating evil schemes to rule and are
generously funded to keep food on their tables. Ask
yourself, why are state constitutions suddenly antiquated
like the United States Constitution? Sure they come
up with good arguments, but these arguments were contrived to be so, to not get opposition. Some states have
had their constitutions already rewritten. Evil moves in
the dark, in stealth, as in the 1930s until when the lights
come on, you find chains on your feet and hands in the
stockades that you knew not how they were placed there
while you were in the dark. Again, to get this in your
mind, to have it in your heart; are state constitutions being attacked because they are modeled on the United

States Constitution and protect unalienable rights given by God and not given by the state? Norell's article sheds light on the transformation of our founding documents by the Soros gang:

> "The 'progressive' movement to rewrite America's founding document on a global model (South Africa's Constitution), the guarantees of what the founders recognized as pre-existing God-given rights—among them, free speech, freedom to assemble, the Right to Keep and Bear Arms, the right against self-incrimination, the right to be protected against undue search and seizure—all of those most basic protections are considered (by those Soros bankrolls) 'negative rights.'

> "So what is it that these people find so attractive in the South African Constitution? In a phrase, the answer is something they call 'positive' rights." [356]

The United States Constitution must be portrayed like the states' constitutions, antiquated among other things, and therefore, a crisis that must be addressed. So, how are we to understand this? First of all, one must address the strategy of creating a crisis in need of an already pre-determined solution in order to implement that desired solution.

Ginsburg and Sunstein and other professors sing the glories of the South African Constitution that was written for a pre-determined purpose, to implement the solution. The Soros gang manufactured a tailor-made crisis in need of the pre-determined solution to bring about change for "The (United States) 'Constitution in 2020.'" Norell continued in his article:

> *"The most direct explanation of what they (those who want to destroy the United States Constitution), are going for was penned on the "Constitution in 2020" blog by Emily Zackin, now an assistant professor at Hunter College:*
>
> *'These rights (positive rights) obligate government to intervene in social and economic life, promoting equality rather than simply procedural fairness.'"*[357]

Norell comments on Emily Zackin's statement:

> *"So, fairness—the very basis of real blind justice in America—is to be replaced with social/cultural favoritism decided by a cadre of law school radicals."*[358]

How could the negative rights, positive rights, just grow into a spontaneous movement when Obama was making statements, before he was even President that negative rights must be countered and changed to positive rights, etc? Do you connect the dots? And South Africa ends up by random chance with a constitution by "fathers" of a new nation (South Africa) that is the most wondrous constitutional document in history? The United States Constitution is admired as the most important Constitution, ever to have been created, begetting and guiding a nation as never before in the world. The founders based much of it on the Bible, Jewish history, and drew from Leviticus and other parts of the Bible. The essence of what John Quincy Adams said on July 4, 1837, when he was speaking about the wonder of the American Revolution was that it:

> "...connected in one indissoluble bond, principles of civil government to the principles of Christianity."[359]

Is it, therefore, any surprise that when evil comes to rule, the document governing the nation, with references throughout to God's Word, must be destroyed, as well as the liberty that protects those who acknowledge their liberty comes from God and not man that is echoed in that founding document? Yet, a member of the Soros' gang, Sunstein, Obama's handler, in this statement, says of the South African constitution is:

> "the most admirable constitution in the history of the world." [360]

We would have to be blind in our reasoning ability not to see these dots connect in a vile, corrupt, dangerous, satanic way.

At the Soros money-driven "Constitution in 2020" Yale Conference in 2009, Professor Aziz Hug, of Chicago University Law School, Obama's Alma Mater, told the attendees how they would accomplish by 2020 their moves covertly:

> *"No constitutional movement ever got very far by admitting that it sought **innovation** (code word for 'changes') in the founding document. **Or by admitting that it was enabled** by the particular social/historical or doctrinal circumstances of the change that it urged.*

> *"Yet to be a credible movement for constitutional change—a credible social movement—that movement has to **'<u>deny</u>,'** in a sense, its ultimate goal."*[361]

It is plain. Her words clearly speak of a plan to subvert the United States into their socialist ideal, in opposition of its founding. Part of the pre-planned schedule of events is the use of culture warfare. We can learn from Rwanda and its culture war when division is propagated as the ultimate goal of evil, genocide is what follows. Norell writes of the ultimate goal of the 'powers that be' and what they are working towards, yet deny:

> *"And the deniable goal clearly is to supplant our rights, memorialized for Americans with our unique position as the freest people in the world, with a bizarre set of government-granted privileges masked as 'right' — a kind of leftist cultural affirmative action creating unprecedented social division: a constitutional caste system between the American people. It will be a reflection of President Obama's now ubiquitous cultural war."*[362]

And how has a leftist indoctrinated South African constitution fared its people? A document hailed as the most amiable in history should prove itself in the lives of its people. Yet, South Africa's homicide rate is seven times that of the United States. Their constitution says they have a positive right to food, housing, and healthcare, and yet they live in indescribable poverty. As Norell writes:

> *"South African citizens (are left) at the mercy of brutal, murderous, criminal violence."* [363]

The lives of the South African people are the proof and evidence as to the greatness or horror of their constitution.

Lastly, one more revelation: South Africa's constitution contains 61,000 words! To give a comparison, in the original United States Constitution with the Bill of Rights, including just the first 10 Amendments, the word count total was 5,172. If you include all amendments to date, there are 27, the word count goes up to 7,902 in the 225 years of its existence. This is one of the tactics of evil, add a lot of words like the Obama healthcare law and tyranny can use it in any form or fashion, interpreting it to mean whatever the government, 'the powers that be,' decides to whim out of it. In fact, at the Second Yale 2009 "Constitution in 2020" reconvened conference, **three tactics** were named in how to achieve the changing of the United States Constitution at its very core. One tactic is to make lengthy, wordy laws that no one could possibly read or understand. South Africa's constitution follows this pattern using 61,000 words. But also Obama's two healthcare laws, totaling 3216 pages, follows the same strategy.

James Madison, Father of the Constitution, as well as our other Founding Fathers understood the law must remain simple and uncomplicated if men were to place their confidence in it. W. Cleon Skousen, in his book, The 5000 Year Leap, stated:

"The Founders were sensitive to the fact that the people have confidence in the law only to the extent that they can understand it and feel that it is a rule of relative permanence which will not be continually changed. James Madison emphasized both of these points when he wrote:

'It will be little avail to the people that the laws are made by men of their own choice if the laws be so voluminous that they cannot be read, or so incoherent that they cannot be understood; if they be repealed or revised before they are promulgated, or undergo such incessant changes that no man, who knows what the law is today, can guess what it will be tomorrow. Law is defined to be a rule of action; but how can that be a rule, which is little known and less fixed?'

"Fixed in its original intent of meaning."

Most laws are simple, clear, one paragraph. God's Ten Commandments hardly amount to a paragraph, yet all true law is based upon it. God's ways are simple to follow. satan's words involve complexity, and masterfully makes grey what should be simple. It is not "yes" or "no", as the Bible says to be, **"Let your yes be yes and your no be no."** James 5:11 Instead, wordy laws can be

a yes or a no, applied to who you are and who you are
not with different results. Evil vs. "whoever it wants to
crush" with the law's application. Therefore, the tactic
to change the nation is to draw up big, complicated laws
that will take on the appearance of strength of the Constitution. Norell states:

> *"By what means do they alter the foundation of*
> *the nation? By what means do 'positive rights'*
> *creep into constitutional law?*
>
> *"Those questions were actually at the very core*
> *of the second Yale 2009 conference, The Constitu-*
> *tion of 2020. Among the back-door approaches*
> *discussed:*
>
> > *1. Enacting 'landmark' laws that are too big,*
> >   *too complicated and bring dramatic fun-*
> >   *damental change. These laws take on the*
> >   *force of the Constitution. (Healthcare, Na-*
> >   *tional Defense Authorization Act, etc.)*
> >
> > *2. Enacting international treaties that have*
> >   *the force of law. As one speaker at the*
> >   *2020 Conference put it, 'Once you have an*
> >   *Article II[*] treaty in place, it can undo state*

---

* Article II is the section of the Constitution that gives authority to make
treaties. According to Article II, the President has the power to make
treaties, but only if two-thirds of the Senate concurs. Therefore, a treaty

law that is contrary, and undo federal law that is contrary. [This item 2 is a huge lie, as you will understand as you read on].

3. *Creating administrative law [regulation] that the speaker [at the Yale 2009 Conference] claimed would be beyond the normal scope of judicial review.*

*"Yale law professor Jack Balkin, among the leaders of the "Constitution in 2020" movement, says under 'democratic constitutionalism', 'The basic way that the **Constitution changes over time is that people persuade each other that the way they thought about the Constitution and what it means isn't the right way of thinking about it...** "* [364]

What follows is a **very important** note concerning the above Number Two (2) statement that treaties signed by the United States trump and nullify all federal and state laws contrary to the treaty. But, before reading on, we suggest you return to pages 93–97, under the chapter title, *"If the Enemy Wanted to Take Over, How do They Make you Defenseless?,"* and familiarize

does not have to be adopted in law by the House of Representatives. The treaty only has to be ratified by two-thirds of the Senate to become law.

yourself with the information concerning the Second
Amendment so that you will fully appreciate what follows. There is tremendous international pressure to
disarm all Americans of guns. Switzerland's citizens
are all required to be armed. The nation's standing
army is its citizenry. Yet, it is the United States who the
'powers that be' want all guns owned by its citizens tak-
en away. They know they will have great resistance to
their evil agendas, if the U.S. citizens are armed. Therefore, the strategy and plans of the 'powers that be'
through the United Nations is to make an international
treaty to ban guns. By force of a treaty, disarm America. Their plan is to rule over the United States, taking
away our sovereignty. They want to make a treaty that
will overrule the guaranteed right of the citizens of the
United States to bear arms, that our forefathers saw
was so critical to a free people for us, and for all future
generations. The Second Amendment was designed
mainly to give citizens the right to protect themselves
from a government if it becomes tyrannical. Therefore,
without citizens having weapons, as the defenseless
Tutsis, the Hutus can have their way.

As you read on, you will see clearly what we have
been taught concerning international government treaties having authority that supersedes our Constitutional

rights is false. We have been taught for so long to believe this that it is now widespread belief that adopted
treaties overrule our nation's law. **No treaty can be
made which trumps the United States Constitution or
any part of the Constitution, period.** It is **not** true that
treaties can modify law when they do not conform to the
Constitution, and it is **not** true that treaties can change
the Constitution itself, even if ratified by the Senate.
This is not just a great lie. It is a **huge** lie. Only in very
rare cases, and only when in complete harmony and conformity with the Constitution, is it possible for treaties to
affect federal or state law. Practically all good and loyal
pro-Constitution citizens have fallen for this lie. We all
have because it has been drilled into us for decades, just
as leftist professor Jack Balkin said in item 3, of "Back
door approaches," to impact the Constitution:

> *"...people persuade each other that the way they
> thought about the Constitution and what it means
> isn't the right way of thinking about it..."* [365]

It is important to know how your enemy thinks.
While the Constitution in 2020 is the goal that was set
to achieve, it may result in a mentality by Christians
and others loyal to our founders that we have plenty
of time, at least until 2020. In fact, the pace of Obama
and the Soros gang's agenda is moving so fast that a

2020 target date may be a diversion making us think we have plenty of time to mobilize to counter. The year 2020 to Soros' people could just as easily mean 2015, or sooner. Sun-tzu would say: give disinformation that there is plenty of time to react, so the enemy (us) will not rise up urgently in a counter attack. We, not rising now in resistance, will enable those promoting the agenda to advance unimpeded in a much shorter time.

The tactic has already worked on us, thinking the Constitution means something it does not mean. The 2020 group plans to continue these lies we have fallen for. **Through this tactic, we have one of the biggest lies perpetrated against the Constitution — that being our Constitution can be changed by a treaty**. Reason it out. This is impossible. Article VI of the United States Constitution states:

> *"This Constitution, and the Laws of the United States which shall be made in Pursuance thereof; and all treaties made, or which shall be made, 'under' the authority of the United States, shall be supreme Law of the Land…"*

This means there are three things that make up the Supreme Law of the Land:

1. The Constitution itself.

2. The laws of the United States made in **pursu-
    ance** of the Constitution.

    > **Pursuance** means: A following; pros-
    > ecution, process or continued exertion
    > to reach or accomplish something; as in
    > pursuance **of the main design**. (The main
    > design is the Constitution).

    > Therefore, laws that follow the Constitu-
    > tion or laws made in consequence of the
    > Constitution.

3. Treaties made under the authority of the United
    States.

In regards to the wording in Article VI of the Constitution, in number 3, which states treaties made "under the authority of the United States," this has been
altered by revisionists and twisted around by those who
promote and teach that treaties can trump the Constitution. The enemies to the Constitution argue this
point in the following way:

1. Enemies of the Constitution say:

    > The Constitution does **not say that trea-
    > ties must be made in Pursuance of the
    > Constitution,** only that they are made un-
    > der the authority of the United States.

This, in fact, is not true...Pursuance of
the main design. The main design is
the Constitution. Therefore, all treaties must conform to and not contradict the Constitution.

2. Enemies of the Constitution say:

Treaties are part of the Supreme Law of
the Land.

This, in fact, is not true...Treaties are
not the Supreme Law of the Land, the
United States Constitution is. Treaties become law only when they conform to the Constitution.

3. Enemies of the Constitution say:

Congress makes new laws that validly
override previous laws, and therefore we
can make new treaties that override the
Constitution and take precedence as the
Supreme Law of the Land.

This, in fact, is not true...even though
Congress can make new laws that
override previous laws, they can**not**
make new laws that contradict the

Constitution, and by the same principles the Senate can**not** ratify* treaties proposed by the president that
contradict the Constitution.

Again, first reason it out. Could you ever really
think that our Founding Fathers, who knew tyranny
all too well, would spend so much effort to draft the
Constitution only to include a clause that would make
it possible for the entire document to be changed by
a treaty? This is exactly what is being attempted over
the United States at present. If treaties don't have to
"follow" the Constitution, then a treaty could, at any
time, be passed by Congress and completely wipe out
the entire Constitution. Does this make any sense at
all? Absolutely not! It is completely illogical.

It is absurd to think that our Founding Fathers ever
had it, as a figment of thought in their minds, to set the
United States up in this way. But if one still buys the
lie that a treaty can change the Constitution, just look
to what the Supreme Court has ruled on this issue for
over 150 years. The Supreme Court has ruled very explicitly in several cases that treaties must conform to
and cannot violate the Constitution.

---

* As noted previously, it is the president who makes treaties, but the treaties must be ratified by two-thirds of the Senate to become law.

In 1853, the US Supreme Court decided in Doe v. Braden:

> *"The treaty is therefore a law made by the proper authority, and the courts of justice have no right to annul or disregard any of its provisions <u>unless</u> **they violate** the Constitution of the United States."*[366]

In 1870, from a case titled, The Cherokee Tobacco:

> *"It <u>need hardly be said</u> that <u>a treaty cannot change the Constitution or be held valid if it be in violation of that instrument.</u>"* [367]

Therefore, a treaty in contradiction of the Constitution is to be "held invalid." In clear terms it is nullified by the Constitution. This is why internationalists **hate**, literally **HATE**, the United States Constitution and want it changed by 2020, if not before. Evil cannot run over the whole world until the United States Constitution is destroyed. Once that happens, Our Lady has told us what evil will do.

August 2, 2011

> **"...you cannot stop the evil that wants to begin to rule in this world and to destroy it..."**

If the United States falls, so will the world.

In 1890, the U.S. Supreme Court ruled in the case of Geofroy v. Riggs:

> *"It would <u>not</u> be contended that it [treaty power] extends so far as to authorize **what the Constitution forbids**..."* [368]

Some of the strongest language comes from one of the most recent cases. In 1956 in Reid v. Covert the Supreme Court ruled that:

> **"The obvious and decisive answer to this, of course, is that '<u>no</u>' agreement with a foreign nation can confer power on the Congress, or on any other branch of Government, which is free from the restraints of the Constitution..."** [369]

No treaty, no agreement, nothing can be made without being under the restraint of the Constitution, and this is obvious and decisive. Some still may argue that the language in Article VI of the Constitution does not require that treaties must be "pursuant" to the Constitution to be valid. The Supreme Court covered this as well in Reid v. Covert by stating that Article VI was intentionally worded this way so that treaties made by the nation before the Constitution was written would remain in effect and not be invalid under the Constitution. The United States Supreme Court, in 1956, said:

> *"There is <u>nothing</u> in this language [in Article VI]*
> *which intimates that treaties and laws enacted*
> *pursuant to them do not have to comply with*
> *the provisions of the Constitution…the reason*
> *treaties were not limited to those made in "pursu-*
> *ance" of the Constitution was so that agreements*
> *made by the United States under the Articles of*
> *Confederation, including the important peace*
> *treaties which concluded the Revolutionary War,*
> *would remain in effect."* [370]

So even though the Founders didn't write in the Constitution that treaties must be "pursuant" to the Constitution, these treaties clearly must still be in conformity with the Constitution. After clarifying this question about Article VI, the Supreme Court stated in the Reid v. Covert case:

> *"It would be <u>manifestly contrary</u> to the objec-*
> *tives of those who created the Constitution, as*
> *well as those who were responsible for the Bill of*
> *Rights—let alone alien to our entire constitution-*
> *al history and tradition—to construe Article VI as*
> *permitting the United States to exercise power un-*

der an international agreement without observing constitutional prohibitions." [371]

This should be understood by all, preached by all, practiced by all. This issue is decided by two things:

1. Common Sense — the Founders would never have conceived that all their work could be done away with by a treaty. Reason it out to truth. Isaiah says, ***"Come reason with me says the Lord."***

2. The Supreme Court, with 150 years of precedence.

One may say, "All this is new to me!" There is nothing new or unique about what is said here. It is new to you because revisionists have striven for decades over the last 2–3 generations to "persuade" and make people think over time, bit by bit, that the way they thought about the Constitution, and what it means, is not the right way of thinking about it. The enemies to the Constitution have been very successful in making everyone from law schools on down to the people on the streets believe that the Constitution means something other than what it really means. The Supreme Court finished this line of reasoning in Reid v. Covert with the following about the Supreme Court itself:

*"This Court **has regularly** and **uniformly recognized the supremacy of the Constitution over a treaty.**"* [372]

Can it be any more clear? While some of this can be complicated to fully understand, it is important that you do. Re-read the preceding if necessary. After learning this truth, we realize we've been duped. We have fallen into deception by accepting that our Forefathers wrote and believed that what is written in the United States Constitution is not Supreme when a treaty is in contradiction to the Constitution.

Stop. **Just Stop** for a moment. This is atomic impacting revelation about the Constitution. We have been taught bad doctrine in conflict with our forefathers' intent. This is a critical point to understand, for on this point all our rights are being readied to be swept away. We, with all those who believe in the Constitution, those of us who abide by the law, have believed **FALSELY** that any and all treaties trump any laws in conflict with the adopted treaty. Our belief that treaties trump the Constitution is how abortion will be protected, rights be given to abominables, the second amendment nullified by international law, etc. It is how all of Soros' goals will be achieved. The 2nd Amendment is globally under assault to be nullified by a treaty through the United Nations. We must reason out that there is no way, it is literally impossible, that our Forefathers ever in their original intent, not in the furthest stretch of interpretive imagination intended that a treaty would <u>ever</u> or could <u>ever</u> nullify the 2nd Amendment or any other for that matter. We must study what school textbooks teach our children and immediately change this lie we ourselves have adopted as truth. This lie must be broken open. Speak about this everywhere. Write about it. Teach your children about it. Reason it out. This one point cannot be left without a serious commitment to challenge every place, institution, school, etc., that teaches contrary to the fact that treaties cannot change our law when it is in conflict with the Constitution, nor can they alter our Constitution in any way. The Constitution is the Supreme Law that all treaties must conform to when they are adopted, otherwise these treaties are unconstitutional. Treaties can only change law when they are in accord with what the Constitution would allow.

A final point: Ask yourself about the Constitution vs. a treaty. One or the other is supreme and trumps the other. It is the treaty that contradicts and overrides the Constitution and, therefore the Constitution subjugates itself and conforms to the treaty—**Or it is**—the

Constitution that contradicts and overrides the treaty
and, therefore the treaty subjugates itself and conforms
to the Constitution. Common sense gives the answer,
therefore, no treaty can be constitutionally ratified if
not in accord to what is written in the United States
Constitution. Any aspect of treaties which are in conflict with the United States Constitution, those aspects
are, therefore, automatically nullified. We are not to
fall for Professor Balkin's trick of:

> *"The way ['we'] thought about the Constitution
> and what it means isn't the right way of thinking
> about it." 373*

That means—yes, the Davids—the Constitutional
Sheriff has the authority to stand down an adopted
treaty, when in violation of the Constitution, between
foreign nations and ours, as invalid when it is attempted
to be enforced in their local county. Who would have
ever thought when Our Lady said, **"peace will not come
through the presidents,"** that right in our back yard, the
people elected Constitutional Sheriff can impose himself
between another mighty nation and ours, through interposition, to protect our lives, our liberty, the pursuit of
our happiness, and all other unalienable rights!!! All that
from our patch of ground called the county. Thrilled?
You should be! Ready to join his posse?

CHAPTER THIRTY-FOUR

When You Are Ambushed Which Way do You Run?

Unless you have read this entire book, this and the next chapter will not be grasped as to the significance of what is written. If you skipped any previous part of this book, before going on to the next two important chapters, go back and read any parts skipped to make sure you progress in your understanding in order to grasp all the circumstances we face; to be open greater to the illumination of these two chapters and what follows in Part II.

Recently a sheriff told how in their Sheriff's department they had always passed religious messages to each other from car to car in some of their communications. They have always done this. But because of not being able to screen if one is a believer on their employment application, an atheist was hired. This is not said that atheists cannot be employed in thousands of jobs across the land. However, in positions where a sacred oath is required, how can someone be hired if he is an unbeliever since the oath requires a belief in God? Taking an oath is one of the qualifications for employment as a peace officer. Therefore, when a position requires such, how can an atheist be qualified to take the position? Every position has requirements. If someone lacks any required qualification, such as a degree, certification, a minimum number of years of expert experience, etc., another applicant is given the position instead. A sacred oath is every bit of a legitimate and necessary qualification for a law enforcement official to fulfill his duty to the citizens, a requirement that is also Constitutional. Can he take a secular oath? No. It would be an oath to self, therefore invalid, as an oath is beyond self to a higher accountability, so as cannot be violated without the knowledge of God of which in turn, is the incentive to keep the oath. (See Chapter 14, beginning on page 125 for more explanation)

When this newly hired atheist deputy received a religious message, he said he would sue the department if he got more such messages. He made nothing but a threat to sue the department, but the whole department had to make a policy change, in which all the religious messages from this point on could be sent only with a waiver stating, in essence, that the message being sent has religious material in it. So the atheist, and any others who come later, will have a *religious viewer discretion clause* so as to reject the messages. Of

course, this means that all the most important department information, the vital communications that must
be transmitted and read by all deputies to whom it
concerns can no longer include any religious content.
So comments such as, "God bless," at the end will be
blocked. So evil rules over God in this matter. We may
think a compromise worked out, for an *x-rated grad-
ing system warning of religious content for viewer discretion, is a win for us,* all the while we go backwards,
while we think we make a gain. Our Lady's words tell
us to be on the offense, for peace to reign. In other
words, **"that my Son may reign."** We do not have to
be on the defensive, apologizing in weakness, submit-
ting to atheists dictating to us what our public policy
is going to be. Recall and memorize the heart of John
Quincy Adam's July 4, 1837 speech, that the Revolution:

> *"...connected in one indissoluble bond, prin-
> ciples of civil government to the principles of
> Christianity."*[374]

Through those principles of civil government bonded "to" the principles of Christianity as one and indissoluble, we, therefore, must allow an atheist to choose
in his free will to be one. However, through these same
indissoluble bonded principles, we do not have to, mor-

ally or constitutionally, allow him to insert and normalize his beliefs of his **'god'** of atheism in what we allow in our public square. It is our God who reigns and while we are not to violate his personal free will, we can, however, be very pointed in keeping his personal decision of free will to be atheist, just that, a private, personal matter in need of healing of the heart. We, therefore, are to pointedly say, "No, the answer is no to you telling us no religious comments are allowed," whether we are speaking about from our police cars, to our highest skyscrapers, to every segment of society. The answer is simply "no." We do not have to say it with animosity or self-righteousness. We just say it with open honesty. "We will not comply," as the United States Bishops have said in regard to the healthcare mandate. Are believers imposing religion on the non-believers? No, he has free will to believe as he chooses. However, if we let public policies be formed to a non-believer belief, then it is their belief which is imposed. These beliefs cannot reign equally. One will reign; one will submit. Christianity cannot submit and comply with non-belief. Therefore, we choose the right, as our Forefathers did, that Christian principles prevail in the public square and our policies.

One may respond, but if a believer has a right to express in public religious expressions, should it not be that atheists also have to be afforded the same right? No.

Alliance Defending Freedom* is a non-profit organization who has an army of 1300 lawyers who protect religious liberty in court pro-bono, and educates the public and the government about Constitutional rights, especially concerning religious expression. One example follows of an atheist claiming an equal standing in the public square with Christians who were praying in public for a national event. An atheist demanded a simultaneous proclamation for all non-believers, when the mayor of a large city was observing prayer on the National Day of Prayer in his city. Michael Johnson, of the Alliance Defending Freedom's legal counsel, wrote to the mayor concerning the atheists' claim:

> "...patently absurd. Any similar demands upon
> you (mayor) or your city would have no basis
> in existing law and would run counter to well
> established right of government to accommodate
> religious expression." [375]

---

* Refer to the Resource Listing on page 831.

Supreme Court Justice Burger, in 1983, wrote of invoking prayer in legislative sessions, etc.:

> *"to invoke divine guidance on a public body...*
> *is simply a tolerable acknowledgement of belief*
> *widely held among the people of this country."* [376]

Michael Johnson adds that:

> *"Those beliefs help define who we are as a nation."* [377]

To be armed with the above understanding is crucial about what must be confronted now. If evil-minded men with darker intentions have put their crosshairs upon the United States Constitution in 2020 to destroy the United States, to destroy the world, should we not be reading it ourselves, studying what our Founding Fathers thought, and put into action what they did in building this great nation of liberty and freedom? Apply what those same forefathers believed—that one who was not a believer could not hold office since to give an oath requires a belief in God. By us being sheepish about holding true to Judeo-Christian standards, we have positioned ourselves for defeat. As with the atheist who was allowed to block religious messages, when the deputies accepted the restrictions, they took a step backwards, even though they found a way around the atheist's objection. In actual fact, wasn't it the atheist that won? A consent to a restriction on religious rights will always erode further, in the public square, as our religious liberty is taken away inch by inch.

So if you are ready to fight against the evil tyranny presently consolidating its power, what do you do when you are surprised and ambushed as with the healthcare legislation? Obama led many, including the Bishops, to believe that Catholics would be able to be exempt for conscientious objection. It was a trap in which Obama surprised and shocked with an ambush, attacking the religious liberty of those who trusted him. Those he deceived had no formalized plan of action except to retreat and figure out what the strategy was going to be, which means everyone was a day late and a dime short. All the while Obama sails on wistfully with his agenda while we go head long to an August 2012 or 2013 compliance date, according to the exemptions. These enemy ambushes, N.D.A.A., Executive Orders, Healthcare mandates, etc., have succeeded repeatedly, pushing us back for cover. What do we do? For decades, from the removal of school prayer to now, we have lost these battles, but time is now up. This is the hour of evil.

"We will not comply" must translate into *"This is what we change, beginning right now."* We need to apply some Sun-tzu tactics from our spiritual arsenal that will manifest physically. When ambushed, which way do you run to get cover? What does your instinct tell you to do to survive? How do you not lose and survive an ambush, with the enemy all around? Do you play dead and hope for an escape later? Ask yourself these questions. What would you do if you walked right into an ambush?

The book, We Got Him, about the capture of Saddam Hussein, was written by Lt. Col. Steve Russell.[378]* Russell was given command of one thousand plus troops who were looking for Hussein. He tells of one day being with a small brigade of troops who drove right into a trap. They were caught, surrounded in an ambush. These ambushes had been repeatedly happening, and the lives of American soldiers were being lost because of them. The first time this happened after Lt. Col. Russell took charge was while he was patrolling the streets in Iraq with just a few men and their military vehicles. A barrage of fire broke from surrounding buildings around them, and a hail of bullets. From street to roof level, Lt Col. Russell's men scattered,

* Note included in the endnote section.

running away to get cover. Their natural instinct took over. The mentality was if we scatter, they won't be able to shoot all of us. Some will survive, some will not. However, Lt. Col. Russell, seeing his men run, did just the opposite. He walked out in the middle of the street with his pistol and began firing. Bullets were landing on the pavement all around Lt. Col. Russell. He ordered his men to come and do the same. When his men saw his bravery, they followed suit. The enemy, though hidden, got so much gunfire back that they became disoriented and scattered or remained hidden. It was a major life lesson burned in the heart of his men that Lt. Col. Russell witnessed to them. Lt. Col Russell told his men later that when ambushed, the instinct is to run for cover, to run away from the ambush. "My men," he said, "will do just the opposite. You will run into the ambush and scatter them." Lt. Col. Russell's men began to be trained that when an ambush occurred on a patrol, they were to turn into the ambush, not run away from it. He instructed those who were blocks away from the shooting, whenever they heard the shooting, they also were to run and drive at top speed to go into the ambush. Russell's men became so successful at disbanding and pursuing these men who ambushed them, that after awhile the enemy stopped the ambushes almost completely from occurring. Lt. Col. Russell's men were not content to let the ambushers take cover. When ambushed, they did not settle for a hit and run. They went after their enemy and ended the matter right then and there. [379] Our Lady of Medjugorje said:

March 18, 2012

> **"...I desire to take you by the hand and walk with you in the battle against the impure spirit..."**

Our Lady wants to walk you into the battle just as Lt. Col. Russell "walked out into the street" with bullets flying to witness to his men how to run into the ambush to fight the battle.

We are no longer to allow a one man ambush by an atheist to change a whole county's law enforcement policy which in reality can be relayed as "common law practice." Common law is law. Our Lady's message today is to go into the ambush. New soldiers, being ambushed, naturally run to take cover, taken over by instinct to protect themselves, causing them to be scattered, not being able to form a strong offense. Ambushes for years against the moral order have caused us to scatter defensively while losing ground. The Lieutenant Colonel taught and witnessed to his soldiers, **"do not be afraid."** He went right into the middle of the ambush and told his men to follow him. In other words, his witness showed them, "I'll lead you, I'll hold your hand in this. Do not be afraid." What does Our Lady ask of us as Queen in Her orders to us?

April 2, 2012

> **"...great will be my joy when I see that you are accepting my words and that you desire to follow me. Do not be afraid. You are not alone. Give me your hands and I will lead you..."**

Lt. Col. Russell writes in his book of the bond and love between his men and himself, the care he had for them, yet he leads them into the streets while bullets are flying all around. The bond and love Our Lady has for us, does not stop Her from leading us right into the battle against evil.

August 2, 2011, Our Lady said:

> **"...you cannot stop the evil that wants to begin to rule in this world and to destroy it. But, according to God's will, all together, with my Son, you can change everything and heal the world..."**

You cannot win this war we are in, without Our Lady, without Jesus. Thinking we can fight secularism in the courts, in the "avenue" pre-laid out for us is an ambush, and we will be scattered, and the world destroyed. This is Our Lady's great joy, if we follow Her into the ambush and scatter evil. This message of **"...pride has come to rule...,"** is very much a call to be in an offensive position, not defensive. When Medjugorje visionary, Marija, was in Alabama in 2008, on July 4th to consecrate the United States of America, Our Lady told Marija, in regards to the Consecration prayer in the Field of Apparitions:

> **"Thank you for all your prayers, be my extended hands in this peaceless world."**

It is peace that is to rule and reign, not a rule of evil which has now come to reign. Our action must be done out of love and for peace. We live in a peaceless world. Are we to be content and let it continue? Our Lady tells us:

April 2, 2012

> **"...that peace may reign – that my Son may reign. When my Son will be the ruler in your hearts, you will be able to help others to come to know Him..."**

We can never bring a non-believer to know Him when our belief is so weak that his belief of non-belief prevails, subjugating the Christian faith and those who adhere to the Judeo-Christian principles to his belief system. Jesus was explicitly clear in some of His last instructions and words at His Ascension, calling his followers to go and witness 'Me' to the ends of the earth.

Matthew 28:19

> *"...Go therefore and make disciples of <u>all</u> the nations, baptizing them in the name of the Father and of the Son and of the Holy Spirit..."*

We are commanded to propagate Christianity, not retreat. We can do this and are supposed to do this as Jesus' words above say, if Jesus is to be the ruler of our hearts. Instead, we have let aspects of unbelief take over in the heart, no longer convicting others as is now manifesting more and more—non-belief out of the heart into the cultures and societies of the world. We have done this, all by seeking peace and satisfaction in the wrong places. We do not have to consign Jesus to second place, being put in a position of not ruling in the very heart of society. How do we change that? As Our Lady first preceded, and then gave birth 2000 years ago to Jesus in His first coming, She is sent to the world now to bear us into holiness in preparation for Jesus' second coming. Our Lady said:

March 25, 1990

> **"...As I bore Jesus in my womb, so also, dear children, do I wish to bear you unto holiness..."**

It is only proper that She is sent to the world for Jesus' Second Coming and precedes Jesus. Be it five years, 50 years, or 500 years from now, She is coming to prepare the world for Jesus' return.

He is to reign in our hearts and what is in the heart will manifest throughout society and the world. This is Our Lady's time and therefore, what is given to Her by Jesus will be given back to Jesus "magnified." It is through us that Her **Magnificat**, will triumph. His reign will come to the world when enough hearts run into the ambush. We do not have to sit around, while every vestige of Christianity is being removed from the public square. In fact, we cannot. To do so is to see the world destroyed before its designated time. That is how serious this time of life on earth is at this moment. It is Our Lady who said:

January 25, 1987

"...You are not able to comprehend how great your role is in God's design..."

To achieve where Jesus reigns first in society can only happen by Jesus reigning first in our hearts. This cannot happen if we do not think and go back to living the Christian ideals and principles, first in our lives and then in society, despite offending the many who will scream foul. Yet we must, with courage, reapply the bonds of principles of civil law back to being indissoluble bonds of Christian principles. Civil law must be rooted in God's Law, His Ten Commandments. When enough people live holiness and are true to His laws, we will defeat the anti-Christian assault winning against us at this moment. Things are no longer just progressing year by year or even week by week. We are now in the phase where things are changing hour by hour. We are very close to driving right into a huge ambush just around the corner, much bigger than the healthcare crisis. You need to know what to do, now that **they fired the first shot**, as we find ourselves in a great ambush. The healthcare mandate is the battle. We cannot accept it. The ambush must be turned upon those who fired the first shot. We cannot retreat, as it will be our end. There will not be another fight; we will not be able to mount another effort with strength enough to win. This is it. We will not survive if we are not prepared to stand and fight. If we continue to concede to non-belief, it is as running for cover from the ambush. To do so is to be slaughtered. Literally.

CHAPTER THIRTY-FIVE

This is the Battle Plan

The following chapter has over a quarter of a century of prayer and fasting behind it of what is our path out of the situation we find ourselves in. While a Friend of Medjugorje sees clearly that life as we know it is going to radically change, it is important what "we" change now in our actions, to be where God wills us to be when these changes occur. Chapters 35 through 43 will speak for themselves, but before proceeding, we recommend serious prayer to the Holy Spirit before entering into them.

Remember, the repetition threaded throughout this book, and especially in what follows in the coming chapters, is paramount for absorbing all that is found between the front and back cover of They Fired the First Shot 2012™. Repetition is a key foundation to learning. Without it, you will not know how to make decisions off the cuff.

Repetition is not just about learning facts, but through repetition, learned and applied principles become a part of the way you think. When these principles become "the way" you think, you will automatically have what is necessary for the choices and decisions you will make to navigate and set out into the future.

— The Publisher

This chapter is like getting a new model, bicycle, boat, or any desired product, car, etc. You want to use it immediately, but you do not want or do not relish reading the directions on how to put the bike together, the manual for the boat operation, etc. Reading directions

or the manual is not as exciting as riding the bike or
using and driving the boat. Yet, the manual is the most
important item to thoroughly cover in order to ride the
bike. To achieve religious liberty requires this section.
Set your mentality on pushing through the important
content of this chapter. Our problem, as Christians and
cherishers of liberty, is we all want to wish away what is
happening with our religious liberty. This is not going
to stop on its own, without a direction, any more than a
complex bicycle magically puts itself together without
a manual. Yes, once you put several bikes together,
you learn the way without the manual. But first you
must learn the way. Obama's healthcare is not going to
go away regardless of what the Supreme Court rules.[*]
In the next term, Obama's executive orders and new
laws, are not going to go away, nor is the direction tyranny is headed, going to turn around. Remember the
'powers that be' are patient. We must have a different
mentality about their plans. The 'powers that be' did
not set out to accomplish their goals just based on the
next election, rather with agenda's' by which in 2020
the Constitution will be changed in the way people
think about it. The 'powers that be' transcend who is
in office. Yes, they rapidly advance when their choice

---

* This was written just before the verdict in favor of the healthcare bill
  was given by the United States Supreme Court.

is president, but regardless, tyranny and its **forward march** will not stop advancing. As mentioned, Obama is not going to simply lose the election without great forces working behind the scenes to keep him in office, **with** or **without** enough votes. Therefore, we must continue to plan regardless of how things turn out.

What should be understood on this point in Obama's rise to power is that it was not within the natural realm. As already pointed out, Obama himself gave acknowledgement of this in the book he authored, <u>The Audacity of Hope</u>. Obama states:

> *"There was no point in denying my almost **spooky** good fortune."*[380]

"Spooky?" Obama **<u>will not</u>** be removed from office in the 2012 elections. If we know our enemy, we know our main enemy is unseen forces at play. The signature of darkness, it's thumbprint, is all over Obama's rise to power. **If** Obama is removed from office for this second term, **it will be only by the hand of God** who will decide it to be so. We are powerless on a human level to stop the evil that has come to rule, through our vote, through money, through influence…all is to no avail. This decision rests with God. God's decision is changed only by our way of life. Nineveh's future rested upon whether they would repent or not. God saw their repentance and relented from what He had planned for Nineveh. We also have arrived at a spiritual crisis point. Destruction by darkness or construction by Light. Our Lady's words again:

August 2, 2011

> **"...you cannot stop the evil that wants to begin to rule in this world and to destroy it. But, according to God's will, all together, with my Son, you can change everything and heal the world..."**

If we choose to ignore this direction to heal the world, God <u>will heal</u> the world through a purification, for our return back to Him. God's will is for us and our land to be healed. It is not God's will to do it through a purification. We decide which way our return will happen. It is, therefore, a reality that evil will not give up its authority through man's efforts. Obama will not be removed except if God is moved to do so by our lamenting, repentance and prayer.

A major change is coming. Of all the chapters of <u>They Fired the First Shot 2012</u>, these next three are the most important chapters. The people at the Yale Conference did not, and will not in the future, negate the importance of their instruction manual, "The Constitution in 2020," as has already been written about. Therefore, if we want to be victorious in restoring religious liberty, we cannot negate the following being a manual for a way out of a situation that has no exit. Read these directions with purpose and intent and turn these directions into physical manifestations across the United States of America. Yes, it will take effort, but those who are enemies of religious liberty spend 24/7 on their efforts. These poor souls believe stronger in working to implement their agenda than Christians believe in just having an agenda.

You must see that the war against your unalienable rights to life, liberty, and the pursuit of happiness began years ago against you. But for you, the engagement of war starts the second you finish this book. We are to take the offensive in this war and start dismantling what has, for decades, built up against Christians and against those who cherish liberty. As qualified before, we can hope for no success without first, having contrite hearts, tears of repentance, the living of God's statutes and constant prayer and fasting. Once that is established, then we must have a battle plan. Many believe we must protest. This is equivalent to running from the ambush. We do not protest. To do so, we have to get a permit for the Constitutional right of free assembly. That is the road laid out for us to take to manage our rights through permission forms, etc., the very principles of tyranny we are in opposition against. We, by doing so, allow ourselves to be lured into the conventional fighting arenas where we are always defeated. In essence, we are giving tyranny the power to come into our states, towns, and homes to ambush and scatter us.

In early May of 2012, Steubenville Catholic University dropped its student healthcare coverage.[381] This was their action not to be placed in a position to be forced into paying for contraceptives, abortions, etc. Many may applaud this action as a badge of honor. But now students who are forced to get their own insurance, are scattered by the ambush. Will they succumb to paying for the sins of others? Obama's mandate will require them to buy healthcare insurance or be fined by the I.R.S. This shutting down and scattering the flock in ambush is exactly what Obama and the 'powers that be' want. The Catholic Church and its institutions have great influential, temporal power in holding 25% of healthcare in the United States. *This is influence. This is power.* And we are just going to drop insurance and close hospitals and institutions as our response? We are just going to close shop? The Catholic Church has strength to be reckoned with. So what will we do when the Catholic Church no longer holds 25% of healthcare and its institutions any more?

When we vacate our position, we must understand they next will come after the Church itself. This is what the Mexican president did in 1927 after passing a new secular constitution ten years earlier in 1917. Immediately after the passing of the 1917 constitution, persecution began which included the confiscation of property. To take a religious vow became illegal. The persecution of the Church became more severe in 1926 with the passing of a new law that required uniform enforcement of anticlerical laws throughout the country. In 1927 the people began to take up arms and fight back. These combined events led to the martyrdom of many priests, religious, and laity and exile of many bishops. The churches were desecrated and countless blasphemies were made within these places of worship. Mexico birthed this ruthless campaign against the Church, martyring thousands by changing to a secular constitution, setting the stage less than a decade later to rid their nation of the Church. The Constitution in 2020 will set the stage for the same. We are not to give up our position of strength by closing shop. If we do,

President Reagan tells us in a speech given on July 17, 1980, what will happen:

> *"We know only too well that war comes not when the forces of freedom are strong, but when they are weak. It is then that tyrants are tempted."* [382]

Patrick Henry, before his "Give me liberty or give me death" statement, said:

> *"They tell us, sir, that we are weak, unable to cope with so formidable an adversary. But when shall we be stronger? Will it be the next week or the next year? Will it be when we are totally disarmed. Shall we gather strength by irresolution and inaction?...Sir, we are not weak, if we make proper use of those means which the God of nature hath placed in our power...we shall not fight our battles alone. There is a just God who presides over the destinies of nations, and who will raise up friends to fight our battles for us. The battle, sir, is not to the strong alone; it is to the vigilant, the active, the brave...There is no retreat but in submission and slavery!...The war is inevitable—and let it come! I repeat, sir, let it come!"*

*"It is in vain, sir, to extenuate the matter. Gentle-
men may cry, Peace, Peace, but there is no
peace...Why stand we here idle?...Is life so dear,
or peace so sweet, as to be purchased at the price
of chains and slavery? Forbid it, Almighty God! I
know not what course others may take, but as for
me, give me liberty or give me death."*[383]

Can we be so mindless to think that we will be stronger
later? When all is shut down, our institutions, hospitals, schools—that is when our strength will be such as
to lead us to victory? It is a grievous mistake to back
down when you have power at hand.

The students of Steubenville, who are attending
the University, are a committed group. The staff and
religious are the same. Just dropping healthcare, while
having all the prayers on the spiritual side, power of influence and the energy and enthusiasm of the students
on the temporal side, is a mistake. They missed the
point. They ran from the ambush. What will happen in
the next battle that will attack Christianity? Students
have **might**. They go to Steubenville by conviction
of their faith. The faith of the fathers of Steubenville
needs to be the leading force of the whole university.
They need to do what Lt. Col. Steve Russell did in

leading his soldiers right into the ambush, with their might. Our Lady said:

June 27, 1988

> **"...I give you might, dear children; with this might, you can bear everything. May this might make you strong in everything. You need it; that is why I give you might."**

We cannot abandon positions of strength in exchange for positions of weakness without heading down Mexico's 1927 path. Instead, we run into the ambush wherever unconstitutional laws force unconstitutional compliance, to close down hospitals, take your property, etc. As is shown through previous chapters, the selected and elected Constitutional Sheriff, with the power of a posse, can by imposition run into the ambush, disrupt tyrannical powers with the support of citizens and render those who violate their constitutional rights powerless. What if the whole university showed up on the doorsteps of the sheriff, telling him, "we want protection"? The university student population is 16% of the town of Steubenville's total population. This is a united block no one in Steubenville would likely ignore, nor in the population of the whole county. They, with local police, county sheriff, the bishop, pastors, and other citizens, can easily stand down the threat tyranny will throw at them. Our Lady said:

April 25, 1998

"...do not be afraid. I am with you..."

Will Our Lady abandon them for standing up for the faith? What can God do for Steubenville for just walking away and closing down their healthcare coverage? Yes, they do this instead of paying for abortion, etc., but what are the results? Still getting insurance and paying for abortions! Our Lady has said, **"do not be afraid."** Enter into the battle. Don't surrender and give up, or something worse will befall you. Steubenville's choice to surrender an unalienable right of religious liberty is a perfect example that we do not run away from the pressure of the ambush, rather, where there is pressure, turn and run into it, confronting it with full force. "We the people" have been ambushed for so long, running away when our victory is to go right into the ambush. Steubenville dropping healthcare puts the score at:

Obama 1   Steubenville/Catholic Church 0

Obama is not stopped in the least by Steubenville's actions. In fact he advances, eliminating one power of resistance that will be needed to protect the Church. The University of Steubenville has spiritual power because it is a faithful institution of the Church. On the temporal side, it has power because it is a small town and has the ability to unify its citizens. Lastly, it has power because it has a common spiritual conviction. This is the kind of power that Obama and the 'powers that be' want eliminated and are more than thrilled over the way Steubenville fizzled away on this mighty wrong. Obama has the victory and is celebrating Steubenville's decision. But, Steubenville doesn't have to be out of the fight. Steubenville can re-enter and do so with greater advantage than before because of now knowing their enemy and knowing themselves. Just as Sheriff Dean Wilson did by apologizing for not standing up as a powerful Constitutional Sheriff, and then became one.

We must battle, as Reagan conveyed, "from a position of strength," at Obama's doorsteps. Otherwise we will become weak, and they will bring the war to our Church steps.

Where do we begin the battle plan? First, understand in your local county when you set out, opposition may stop you at unlikely places. Sheriff Mack shows no matter who they are, get them to join you, and if they do not join you, ignore them, bypass them and continue. Mack states in his book, The County Sheriff America's Last Hope:

> *"The County Sheriff has no supervisor or boss, except for the people. He does from time to time receive 'legal advice' from the County Attorney. However, there is nothing that requires the sheriff to follow such advice and, for the most part, it is not legally binding. ... It would be nice and helpful to have the county attorney on the side of freedom, but it is not necessarily essential. It is hoped that he would keep his oath of office, also. However, most lawyers have been trained erroneously, that the 'supremacy clause' of the Constitution grants ultimate power and authority to the federal government. Regardless, this simply is not true. The supremacy clause reads: 'This Constitution and the laws of the United States which shall be made in pursuance thereof... The Constitution is the supreme law of the land... the County Sheriff has no obligation to go along with those who subvert the Constitution. Even if the County Attorney advises the sheriff to do so. And make no mistake; many of them will do just that. Thus, the sheriff is back at the*

beginning; his word, his oath, and his duty to
freedom…If we follow the Constitution and the
'supremacy' it entails, miracles will happen for
our citizens and maybe, just maybe the County
Attorney will see this and jump on board. We
fully invite him to be a part of this most worthy
cause. If he is reluctant to do so, we'll move for-
ward without him." [384]

Our Lady said on May 2, 2012:

"…do not waste time…"

There are three elements to align in order to build a foundation wall that the battering ram of tyranny will not defeat; a wall that no time can be wasted on building <u>now</u>.

The three elements consist of:

1. The Sheep

2. The Spiritual Shepherds

3. The Secular Shepherds

This power of authority is not to be built with an aim and focus on national change, but rather an aim and focus on local change. The center of focus is no broader than your own county. The power of authority that will be built around your county to protect it will be strong as a rock, a bulkhead seawall, breaking up harmlessly the mighty waves of tyranny that are constantly assaulting.

Again, it must be stated: forget protests, going to court, calling your congressman. Do you not see the leftists' radical plans as evidenced in the Yale Conference, "The Constitution in 2020," and their moving **forward** to implementation? They are busy contriving, instituting, and implementing while we protest, go to court, call our congressmen. They do not fall for these tactics that keep us locked into defeat and constant retreat. They have a game plan. It is simple. Tyranny wins and liberty loses. To have a rally, get steamed up, clap, go home, "we showed them," does nothing but give tyranny a laugh. While at their gatherings they are fundamentally, boldly, yet covertly changing things, while all we are doing is letting off steam, draining our energies. Tyranny is content with those of 'liberty' doing these things (protests, rallies, go to court, etc.) as it results in nothing that empowers those standing for liberty.

We have to wake up to the fact our actions have led to a continuous loss of ground, while tyranny gains ground. Our tactics do not work. Wake up to the fact that our efforts are being managed. We must turn our steam into a physical infrastructure. Think about the annual March for Life in Washington D.C. For 2012, over 400,000 people showed up, spent money, froze to death, and everyone went back home complaining that the media only reported on the ten pro-abortion protestors, ignoring the hundreds of thousands of anti-abortion protestors that were present. This may hurt some pro-life, moral, and patriotic feelings, but truth is truth. We must use common sense, look at our logic and change our mentality accordingly.

With 400,000 people in Washington, what if all that money spent on food, hotels, travel, loss of income for taking off work, etc., was instead spent on building an infrastructure in your local county. Just for the sake of example, to be conservative, if we figure only 250,000 attended and a very conservative average spending figure of only $150.00 each for the trip, this is over thirty-seven and a half million dollars. If we really want change, we must ask what could $37,500,000 do in building an infrastructure, aligning the three elements about to be discussed into an impenetrable wall of unity that can defeat all unconstitutional actions by tyranny? Your answer can be found in studying the enemy's three elements of action for a battle plan. Why do they achieve what they do when we **exceedingly** surpass them in numbers compared to their very small numbers. To explain it simply, they do what we do not.

1. They sit down, strategize the goal and patiently allow these strategies to grow into the goal.

2. They are unified.

3. They are focused.

The Soros gang has been at work for a long time. As a result, they have entered past the threshold of the home of liberty and are in the process of taking possession of the home of the brave. We are endangered, not with just a burglar in our homes, but a murderer, a murderer of Liberty, Justice, and Peaceable Living. If we do not come up with a plan, literally sit down in each and every of the 3000 counties across the United States, we will lose the United States. Does it matter who is in the White House this election? To some degree, but the Soros gang has set the stage, using Obama along the way, just as the 1917 secular constitution in Mexico set the stage for what came in 1927. It is not a maybe, it is a given, as They Fired the First Shot 2012 shows throughout the book.

If you study communist takeovers and dictatorships, you will see we are on this road. Mexico's history in the early part of the last century is proof. As in Mexico, the Catholic bishops, priests and religious in the United States will be among the first to be imprisoned or killed. Others will follow. The healthcare mandate first attacks the Catholic Church. Bishops, as the enemy sees them, are generals to be eradicated to scatter the flock and are the first that must be taken down. Don't want to believe it? Study history. Look at the French Revolution. The guillotines ran non-stop. Not possible in the United States? If there is not a radical stand now, "the guillotines," whatever that might be in the USA, will run non-stop. History clearly shows religion is first in line to be crushed and the first major blow to smash the Church is the healthcare mandate. There-fore, we must act while we can still stand with a plan that is simple to implement. We start with what has worked for our enemies. There are three elements of the battle plan to repulse the attack against our liberty that must be adopted:

1. Sit down and strategize the goal and patiently allow these strategies to grow into the goal.

2. Be unified.

3. Be focused.

Yes, it is what our enemies are doing. So, why not imitate what works? We must parallel the preceding three elements to build a unified impenetrable fort around your county and each of the 3000 counties throughout the United States to safeguard against tyranny. The above three elements (strategize, unity, focus) of action for the battle plan must then parallel the following three elements of an infrastructure:

1. The Sheep

2. The Spiritual Shepherds

3. The Secular Shepherds

The sheep and the Spiritual and Secular Shepherds must begin by building an infrastructure. Who are they?

1. The sheep are the citizens of the county.

2. The Spiritual Shepherd is a Catholic Bishop, with Protestant ministers.

3. The Secular Shepherd is the County Sheriff.

As you read, **'think <u>county</u>,' '<u>not nation.</u>'**

1. The **sheep**, being the Christians, receive **spiritual** strength and spiritual protection from their Shepherd.

   Eternal or **spiritual** powers are defined as:

   things that are not seen

   The **sheep**, being citizens, also receive **secular** temporal strength and protection from their secular Shepherd.

   Temporal or **secular** powers are defined as:

   things that are seen

   The sheep are covered by **spiritual** and **temporal** authority to live out the vocation as a Christian and citizen with the right to live in peace. Christian citizens make up the Church, **eternal**, and the county, **temporal**.

2. The **Spiritual Shepherd**, the **Catholic Bishop** is unique in that his strength of authority reaches within a diocese across several counties. As stated, twenty-five percent of all medical health

related care, totaling $100 billion, is under the spiritual authority and protection of the Catholic Church. This in itself is authority not to bargain with, but to mandate; not to request with, but to state: *"Our goal is we will not shut down. We will not relinquish our authority to the state. We will not go to jail."* Where does this put other Christian pastors? Are they minimized? No. A pastor of a church, or a mega-sized church or even a pastor of several churches must play an important role with the Catholic bishop. This is a fight for the continuance of the United States of America—as we all know, united we stand, divided we fall.

We must be in union in this fight for our religious liberty or we all will lose it. The Catholic Bishops and Protestant ministers joined together in California to successfully pass the traditional marriage amendment. We can do this across our land to stand united against tyranny. Catholic bishops have an advantage with their headship. There are 195 dioceses across the United States, with an average of approximately 91 churches per diocese, totaling about 17,745 churches under their authority.[385] This gives not only a spiritual strength of grace, but a unifying geographic advantage as well.

As a single shepherd, a bishop does not have to go through committees to act or enact directives for his diocese for every church within its boundaries. His position as a unifying shepherd is unique in the power of authority he holds in his diocese. He can bring hundreds of Catholic churches into oneness in taking a stand, numbering into hundreds of thousands, even millions of people. Of any one person in a local county, he, as a 'spiritual' shepherd, is equivalent to a sheriff in his (sheriff) 'secular' power, to act.

This, by no means, diminishes any other Christian pastor or church. All Christian pastors, within the geographic location of the county, when they join with a bishop in building the infrastructure of "the powers of authority" to affect civil government, immediately build and add to this authority with hundreds of churches and its people. It is why satan inspired Obama's executive orders to high-jack authority itself. Christian pastors who align with the bishop whose diocese is in their county are greatly increased in power to defeat tyranny.

Remember two of the three elements of the
Yale Conference is their **focus** and **unity**. You
cannot focus without unity. When you have
both, your efforts become constructive, and
the power of authority more formidable than
the 'powers that be' that act on a national level
while this force of spiritual authority will act
on a local level. So the spiritual Shepherd, as
the bishop, written here as one of the three elements, is not in any way intended to diminish
Protestant pastors' role in this fight. Rather, we
must simply recognize the geographic reality
and spiritual authority over so many.

With Catholic bishops holding authority over
25% of healthcare, not to mention holding au
thority over hundreds of other Catholic institutions, associations, Catholic colleges, etc., they
are placed in a key position of headship as one
of the three elements to defeat tyranny. These
thoughts should be kept in mind as one reads
on. Every time bishops are mentioned as the
Spiritual Shepherds, they should be aligned in
unity of effort with all others of legitimate spiritual authority. This is not a call for amalgama-
tion of the Christian faiths, but rather a call to

foster oneness that is essential if we are to face down and defeat tyranny.

3. The **Secular Shepherd**, the elected Constitutional **County Sheriff** over a single county also is unique. He is the highest law official over the county to safeguard the citizen's rights to liberty and to protect them from <u>every</u> unconstitutional law, regulation or abuse of power of authority. A Constitutional Sheriff is not to relinquish his authority to any agency of federal, state, or local control. He answers to the citizens. They appoint him for their protection from <u>all</u> elements which violate their Constitutional rights and unalienable rights. The power of authority is his from and by the people who invested this authority in him by election. This authority comes through common law precedence of over 1000 years. He has not the right to subjugate his authority to any unconstitutional action, whether it comes from inside or from outside the county. He is solely the highest law official in authority in the county.

CHAPTER THIRTY-SIX

This is the Battle Plan — Outline

The 3 Elements of Action of the Battle Plan, Paralleled with the Three Elements of Infrastructure, Should be Framed as Follows:

What is the purpose of an outline?

It is the first general sketch of any plan or design. What you've just read in "This is the Battle Plan" chapter will require study and will be the reference point for all your future actions. The outline that follows is both significant and important to refer to. Once you begin to take action and/or need to be "re-tuned" in your direction, you will have an outline to go to. The review it gives you now, through repetition, will add to more clear thinking of how to set out. The outline will conceive, in your thoughts and reasoning, concepts and steps that perhaps, at this moment, are not in your thinking. The outline and its categories follow:

1. Strategizing? The Sheep.

2. The Unity? The Spiritual Shepherd.

3. The Focus? The Secular Shepherd.

PART I

This is the Battle Plan—Outline

Who starts the strategy?

1. STRATEGIZING: STARTED BY THE SHEEP.

What is the goal?

> To restore first in your own heart, John Quincy
> Adams' following statement and then proac-
> tively implement the quote across the coun<u>ty</u>,
> not coun'<u>try</u>'. Local, not nation. John Quincy
> Adams, in essence, said:
>
> > The American Revolution"...*connected in
> > one indissoluble bond, principles of civil gov-
> > ernment '<u>**to the**</u>' principles of Christianity.*"[386]

"**...To the** principles of Christianity"—principles
which are bedrock, not moveable or changeable. It
is the principles of civil government that are to move
and change in order to be bonded **to** the principles of
Christianity. Thereby, these civil principles become
bedrocked, unshakable upon the solid foundation of
the principles of Christianity.

What is the first step?

A few people in a county connect, begin meeting and form a **Constitutional Small Prayer Group**. This first group is maybe 3 or 4 people, including its leader, to begin with. From there, the Constitutional Small Prayer Group can add a larger base group of 20 or even 50 people or more, to not only pray with, but use to help to implement what actions the core group of 3 or 4 set to take action on. This will not just be a prayer group that meets occasionally and goes home to life as normal after each session. Rather, its purpose is to grow in strength, fortified by repentance and prayer in order to be pro-active in changing this nation of the United States of America, county by county.

It is absurd to believe that God does not want Christians involved in government. We have vacated so many positions to the godless and now it is evident what that has resulted in. We have vacated our positions to rulers who are tyrants and godless and who, at the right moment will crush us. In regard to the United States continuing the path of vacating positions to the godless and to weak Christians, we must proclaim by action: this is over. Christians must demand to be the ones who guide and rule and direct government, based in Christian principles rooted to the Ten Commandments. Of course, this is fruitless if we, first, do not live fully our Christian walk turning it into a way of life.

The first step: In forming Constitutional Small Prayer Groups, the first rule is to be united. The first tool of satan is a wedge. With a wedge, he needs two who oppose each other. From there, satan will often align others into two opposing groups. This is a result of not building a clear and strong infrastructure where someone is in charge.

How do you protect the unity of the Constitutional Small Prayer Group from satan's wedge? You have a clear structure of authority. If you, through prayer, founded the Constitutional Small Prayer Group, you have the right of authority to lead it. But if formed by a mutual group of souls, a structure of authority should be established. Anyone who vies to be in authority is not worthy to be in authority. How do you avoid the cancer of competing for authority? Follow the apostles who elected two upright men as candidates to replace Judas as one of the Twelve Apostles. He was chosen after prayer and pleading with God to choose one of the two.

Acts 1:23–26

> *"And they put forward two, Joseph called Bar-sabbas, who was surnamed Justus, and Mat-*

thias. And they prayed and said, 'Lord, you know the hearts of all men, show which one of these two you have chosen to take the place in this ministry and apostleship from which Judas turned aside, to go to his own place.' And they cast lots for them, and the lots fell on Matthias, and he was enrolled with the eleven apostles."

This should not be done in a transient procedural way, rather nominate two or more to be prayed for, and spend the week praying not for who you want, but rather for who God wants.

Proverbs 16:33

"When the lot is cast into the lap, its decision depends entirely on the Lord."

Scripture scholars define the above verse as:

"The favorable or unfavorable result of chance depends on God. Deciding strifes and doubts by lot was practiced by the ancient Hebrews." [387]

As to those being prayed for to be nominated, if you are one of them, add your prayers and be resigned, asking God who is the one to be chosen. Those nominated, as well as the whole group, then should make a pledge of full support and follow the leadership of who is chosen. Which is better? To have a leader making final decisions with everyone united in effort with only a 70% best decision, producing 100% fruit because of unity. Or to have a 100% correct decision by a 'committee' making compromised decisions, arrived at through tension, debate, resulting in polarization which lingers on into the implementation of the strategy which will produce only 10% or 20% fruit because of disunity? St. Paul, chosen by God to spread Jesus' ways and teachings, in his letter to the Philippians said:

Philippians 2:2:

"Complete my joy by being of the same mind, having the same love, being in full accord and of one mind."

Support and stay behind the chosen leader, because the Constitutional Small Prayer Group, relied and trusted God to choose. A good leader can listen to input, but when a decision is made by the leader, all members should put 100% agreement into it. Even if you think it only 80% correct, it is important to agree with it. Remember, God can make the decisions produce 100%, even 110%, or greater fruit because of the grace of unity. **Do not turn the Constitutional Small Prayer Group into a committee**. You will expend all your energies debating and end up divided with a weak, watered down plan. Pray more than talk, and pray often for your Constitutional Small Prayer Group and its leader. The leader, specifically, is to be prayed for and more than just tokenism. These prayers should carry a certain gravity of importance because so many final decisions will be confirmed and determined by the leader. Beware of someone rising up in the prayer group informing the group that Jesus told them to do this or that. Many prayer groups have been destroyed by such people.*

This may seem too much detail, but if your foundation is not solid, you will be destroyed by "the wedge" between two people. Pressure will be placed on each member to choose a side to be on rather than, through prayer, just going in union with the established authority over the group. Supporting God's choice will be fruitful. Clear, defined leadership is a must if you are to take on the tyranny that faces your county.

A.   C.S.P.G. What are the strategies of the Constitutional **S**mall **P**rayer **G**roup?

(1.)   Form a larger base group of 20, even 50 people or more, with a purpose to:

---

* See the booklet "satan Wants to Destroy Medjugorje." in the Resource Listing beginning on page 831 or download free at mej.com. Click on "Downloads." under booklets, and search for the title.

(a.) Pray and fast. Our Lady said on April 17,
      1986:

"Pray. Fast. Let God act!"

(1.) Let God act does not mean to expect ev-
      erything to just fall down from Heaven.
      Rather it means God will act, when you
      pray and repent, and provide the moment.
      This is not a week or month commitment
      to prayer. It is long-term and consistent
      praying for yourself, your families, and
      your nation back to God. Constitutional
      Small Prayer Groups must seize the mo-
      ments God gives. The purpose of the
      Constitutional Small Prayer Group is not
      just to pray and be inactive, but be pro-ac-
      tive. Look at the enemy, they are always
      moving and looking forward. The Consti-
      tutional Small Prayer Group (C.S.P.G.) is
      to go backward to our roots and our Fore-
      fathers to refoundation our country, one
      county at a time, drawing closer to God.

(b.) Every member must have read <u>They Fired
      the First Shot 2012</u>_{TM} at least once. Also,
      within 30 days of joining, members must

have read <u>They Fired the First Shot 2012</u>_{TM} completely one more time and once more annually. The purpose of this is two fold. First, to act as a screening method to sift out those who would not be in one accord in their mentality and principles set forth with your Constitutional Small Prayer Group and the added larger base group. Second, to learn what is in the book so when you gather, there will be an advanced understanding bringing unity of purpose for the whole Constitutional Small Prayer Group and base group. This unity is critically important both in what you are praying for, and in what you begin to plan to implement. Remember, one mind, one heart. The book will help bring unity of thought and unity of prayer.

If others see differently, they should not belong to your Constitutional Small Prayer Group. Do not be timid in removing any who causes discord or who disagrees with the principles espoused. Do not debate. You want like-minded souls onboard. Those who could not except Jesus' teaching, He said to them: ***"Do you also want to leave?"*** Jn 6:67 Jesus gave everyone freedom to decide to stay with Him, but He was not willing to compromise His Way. Neither should you. All must be in accord to be powerful. If the C.S.P.G. is unified, and along with it, the base group, it will prosper in what it sets out to achieve. If not, it will falter. Do not mistake purification that God will send as faltering. Purification is to strengthen.

(c.) Every member must be committed to learning the truths contained in our nations founding documents, especially self-learning more about the Constitution.

(1.) Resources—see page 831

(2.) Educate people as to the path to standing down and defeating unconstitutional actions of every sort.

(a.) Methods to Educate:

(1.) Word of mouth

(2.) Printed material

(3.) Audio, etc.

(4.) Do not be tied to excesses of technology. The written word and witness in the end is most powerful.

(3.) Spread <u>They Fired the First Shot 2012</u>_™

(a.) One must walk away from conventional ways of battling threats against God-given unalienable rights. Just as you are thinking differently, in a new way, by what you've read, the easiest path for new converts to Constitutional protection in your county is to distribute and spread "the walk" in <u>They Fired the First Shot 2012</u>_™ to everyone. Especially send copies to **bishops, pastors, United States congressmen, to all state senators and members of the House of Representatives, county commissions, city councilmen, county sheriffs and deputies, mayors, police chiefs, and talk show hosts.** Anyone whose values and ideals would be fortified by <u>They Fired the First Shot 2012</u>_™.

Do not worry with sending the book to those public figures whose principles are opposed to what is written. This book will not change their mentalities and will waste your time. Send the book where you can harvest fruit or help one to clarify the conditions we are in. You can do this as a concentrated effort with the whole prayer group, and/or as an individual, in league with the broader C.S.P.G. base group, all of which is enlisted by the core **C**onstitutional **S**mall **P**rayer **G**roup (C.S.P.G.).

(4.) Stay Focused. Better to concentrate strong effort on a very few select things rather than many things and projects, spreading your efforts too thin, weakening the results. Focus on and accomplish your goals, building upon each one incrementally. Remember the Yale Conference people. Step by step they go "forward" toward socialism. They are patient, and content in taking one step at a time as long as they keep moving forward.

B.   Contact Your Bishop. Once formed as a group, with your path set, contact the Bishop within your diocese and county, or your Pastor if you are Protestant.

(1.) Meet and identify yourselves. Explain your intent to your bishop if you are Catholic, or pastor if Protestant. If Protestant, you can be part of a Constitutional Small Prayer Group working also with a bishop. Some may prefer this since a diocese covers several counties. A pastor in a Constitutional Small Prayer Group, may even wish to work with the bishop.

(a.) To explain the content of what is expressed
in <u>They Fired the First Shot 2012</u> will be
overwhelming.

    (1.) The goal: to convey there is a way out of
the assault on our Constitutional freedom
and religious liberty and you are part of a
group that wants to work closely with him
as bishop or pastor. Your meeting is generally an introduction to familiarize yourselves with the bishop or pastor. The best
way is for him to read fully <u>They Fired
the First Shot 2012</u> and then plan the next
meeting (after he reads the information.)
Give him a copy of the book.

    (2.) There are those cases where a few
bishops/pastors may not have a strong
objection to Obama's actions and the
healthcare bill, etc.. **The C.S.P.G. is not
seeking permission to form.** As baptized
Christians, you are given the commission
to evangelize. C.S.P.G. is seeking a working relationship of unity with the spiritual
authority. A blessing is important to have,
<u>but</u> if it is refused, continue on without
him and do not be daunted. Any move-

ment of God will be resisted. Stay in peace and persevere.

C.   **Contact Your County Sheriff.** Second step after your C.S.P.G. bishop/pastor path is set: County Sheriff

  (1.) Meet and identify yourselves. Explain your intent to the County Sheriff.

   (a.)   To explain the content of what is expressed in <u>They Fired the First Shot 2012</u>_{TM} will be overwhelming.

    (1.)   The goal: to show them there is a way out of the assault being made on our constitutional freedoms and on our religious liberty and you are part of a group that wants to work closely with him as County Sheriff. Your meeting is generally an introduction to familiarize yourselves with the sheriff. The best way is for him to read fully <u>They Fired the First Shot 2012</u>_{TM} and then plan the next meeting after he reads the information. Give him a copy of the book.

    (2.)   Over time, if there is potential for him to become a 100% Constitutional Sheriff, the **C**onstitutional **S**mall **P**rayer **G**roup

(C.S.P.G.), with the larger base group, will support him financially, raising funds and knocking on doors for his re-election, giving very committed and strong support. Spiritual prayer and "boots on the ground effort" comprises both eternal and temporal qualities that will be recognized as very powerful and valuable to the sheriff.

(3.) If a commitment is not made by the standing sheriff to be a Constitutional Sheriff, the leader and the Constitutional Small Prayer Group (C.S.P.G.) should immediately begin a search for a new candidate for sheriff. Out of a range of desired qualifications, the main qualification for a candidate must be that he would be courageously 100% committed to his oath of being a Constitutional Sheriff in order for C.S.P.G. to work for his election.

Do not think they must approach your C.S.P.G. (Constitutional Small Prayer Group) and leader. You can choose anyone who the C.S.P.G. believes may be a perfect candidate for a Constitutional Sheriff. You can tell him of your choice.

If he turns it down, good. It is all the more reason to convince him he is the choice. David was out in the field, content doing what he was doing. Do you think he was happy when he saw Goliath for the first time? He probably thought, "What did I get myself into?" But he was chosen, without ambition to be chosen.

Avoid inordinate emotional ties over who you nominate as a good sheriff. For example, if a member of the Constitutional Small Prayer Group (C.S.P.G.) nominates a family member or someone who is a close friend, emotional ties can cloud one's decisions. If the candidate strays from his commitment, such emotional ties would cause C.S.P.G. to be reluctant to fire him or do a recall election. It is not a popularity contest. It is a Constitutional moral qualification that has to be met 100%. You can know the sheriff, but you need to remember you are his boss and so the C.S.P.G. wants the best choice.

Again, the Constitutional Small Prayer Group can nominate several people. Pray and fast for several days. If necessary to narrow down the choices, choose by lots, pray and draw a name, as was already discussed, when the apostles replaced Judas by drawing lots. Once drawn, never test God by doing it a second time. If you do not like the choice and choose again, you will render the grace null and void to be able to do this again.

NEVER PLACE IN THE LAP OF GOD A DECISION, RELYING ON HIM TO CHOOSE BY LOT AND THEN RELY ON YOUR JUDGEMENT THAT GOD'S JUDGMENT WAS WRONG OR THAT PERHAPS HE DID NOT ANSWER YOU. YOUR C.S.P.G. COULD NEVER DO THIS AGAIN AND RECEIVE THE GRACE OF GOD'S CHOICE. It would be better to never have used this Biblical Old and New Testament method than to refuse to embrace and agree with 100% what was drawn. There should even be no second guessing in the heart about who or what issue was chosen. This is why you spend time (days, weeks, or even months) in preparation before, with a lot of prayer, that all can be confident God's choice is decisive.

Any who are divided by the choice should leave the C.S.P.G., as they will sow the seeds of a mortal division into the whole group, destroying its unity. Again, an individual in the running does not have to be a part of the process or even have knowledge that they are being considered. The **C**onstitutional **S**mall **P**rayer **G**roup not having strong emotional ties gives you freedom to 'fire' him in the next election, or a '<u>recall</u>' election before the regular election time if he fails to keep the task he is given.

We are not speaking here about the standard voting process mentioned earlier in <u>They Fired the First Shot</u>, in which we are 'given' candidates that we must choose from. You will gain little or no ground there. The current voting system is managed by the 'powers that be' with great influence and great money, often with altering of the rules. What we are speaking about here, is that *you*, the people through the C.S.P.G. and a broader group, choose the person, not the person you are given by the 'powers that be' aligned with the media choice.

D. **Spiritual and Secular Shepherds Unite:** Once you have your Constitutional Sheriff or candidate, join in meeting with the Bishop/Pastors and Constitutional Sheriff.

(1.) **Meet and Discuss:** The Bishop/Pastor, Constitutional Sheriff, and the leader, with the option of another member if desired by the leader, of the C.S.P.G. all meet together to discuss C.S.P.G. plans and implementation of C.S.P.G. strategies with the bishop to bring unity and the sheriff bringing focus of the strategies:

(a.) Strategize

(b.) Unify

(c.) Focus

(2.) **Recall Petition:** If your head sheriff now in office is of a contrary political persuasion, refusing to be a 100% Constitutional Sheriff, immediately begin looking for a worthy, 'principled' individual to hold the office of County Sheriff.

A commitment to the Constitution of who is elected is more important than having a lot of or even any police experience. The deputy sheriffs under him can do the expert policing. Good common sense is the greatest asset to possess. The county sheriff's greatest contribution will be to monitor that every action in his county is constitutional.

If your present sheriff is not interested in being 100% Constitutional, begin action of replacing him even if the election is years away. Do not hesitate to even do a recall election against a sheriff who is not willing to fulfill his oath of office to protect citizens' constitutional rights. A sheriff refusing to stand up and protect Constitutional rights is an issue that would make many citizens, when informed, willing to sign a petition to recall his election in order to replace him.

(a.) To do a recall usually requires collecting signatures in a petition. Usually only a small percentage of the vote count of the last election is required. You do not have to be a lawyer to do this. Research and check your election laws. Be decisive. Those who you

choose to appoint to office must understand
no politics. You are engaging in a battle to
rebuild your county on the quote of John
Quincy Adams that principles of civil government are to *"be indissolubly bonded to
Christian principles."*

(1.)   A recall petition is very achicvable.

PART II

This is the Battle Plan—Outline

Who holds the unity?

2. THE UNITY: THE BISHOP AND PASTORS IN UNION.

What is the goal?

> To restore first in your own heart John Quincy Adams' following quote and then proactively implement the quote across the coun<u>ty</u>, not coun'<u>try</u>'. John Quincy Adams, in essence, said:
>
>> The American Revolution *"…connected in one indissoluble bond, principles of civil government to the principles of Christianity."*[388]

"…To the principles of Christianity"—principles which are bedrock, not moveable or changeable. It is the principles of civil government that are to move and change in order to be bonded **to** the principles of Christianity. Thereby, these civil principles become bedrocked, unshakable upon the solid foundation of the principles of Christianity.

What is the first step for bishops?

> Uniting a group of like-minded leaders willing to pray and strive for the same goal of protecting religious liberty is necessary to achieve victory. The leader and C.S.P.G. can be invaluable to you as bishop to step out of the curtain of power that surrounds every power, which tends toward becoming sluggish, slow to react due to bureaucracy, even causing resistance. Ronald Reagan was resisted by practically everyone when he wrote in his speech of Russia being an "evil empire." His wife Nancy, his cabinet, state department, everyone with influence said he could not say this. It would hurt diplomacy and him politically.

Three times his speech writers scratched out "evil empire." Reagan would rewrite it back in. Reagan finally said, "You can scratch it out all you want, but you cannot stop me from saying it when I do my speech." Reagan did as he planned, calling Russia an "evil empire." The Communist newspaper *Provada* and others went ballistic, as did even the United States media, in condemning Reagan. They all were saying this set the relationship of the USA and Russia way back. Russia's communist media machine, *Provada,* put out propaganda with heavy condemnation of Reagan for calling Russia an evil empire. It was normal for prison guards to give brainwashing propaganda to political prisoners. They gave them *Provada's* newspaper articles in order for them to be against Reagan for condemning their Motherland.

One prisoner, who was beaten repeatedly and in prison for 18 years, read it with other prisoners. When they read the two short words, the two words everyone fought Reagan not to say, the prisoners began to violate every rule in the prison, even though they knew they would be beaten. They began to flush toilets, a violation because it was forbidden as it was used for a type of Morse code. They communicated to each other, spreading Reagan's speech through the prisons. Prisoners began jumping up and down in jubilation. This news spread all across Russia.

Prisoner Natan Sharansky said when they read those two words, **"evil empire,"** by a world leader, political prisoners, of which he was one, immediately claimed Reagan as their leader. They knew—they literally knew—Russia would fall. They knew Russia was so fragile that the courageously pronounced **"two**

words," evil empire, foretold the end of Russia. It had an effect like an exorcist, forcing a confrontation and driving evil to the surface, expelling the evil of communism out. It was not President Reagan's enemies who did everything to stop him from pronouncing these two words, "evil empire." It was his cabinet members, associates, friends, even his wife. Darkness often will use good people, close people to sway authority from doing what is right.

Reagan often pierced through the curtain of power to do what he knew in his heart was right despite his advisors. The leader and Constitutional Small Prayer Group should communicate directly to you as bishop. It is too important of a position to be delegated. This small group is key for the infrastructure, "the Navy Seal unit" to act. Streamline, as bishop, your power and spiritual authority directly to the front line of attack against those who fundamentally are making great advances in liberalizing youth's thinking about marriage, immorality, freedom of choice rights, etc. Break through committees, advisors, etc. and give personal time to research and investigate.

Use C.S.P.G. for parochial schools to do a Constitutional review of all textbooks in various subjects, teaching principles of religious freedom and that unalienable rights are from God, not government. Change the textbooks. Teachers teach by the books they have. Placement of books with anti-christian bias is not always detectable or seen for what it is. When communists planned to take over Hollywood in the 1950s, their goal was to plant the party line into only 5% of a movie. You cannot have 95% of a book filled with teachings and reflections on Christian principles or the principles of freedom, found in our Declaration of Independence and Constitution, but with 5% poison in them, and think that's not enough to cause damage. There must be 100% truth in the book or it must be rejected. Practice censorship. Censorship in the past was defined as the right of government ("authority") to protect the morals of the people. Students must be protected by censorship against redefining Judeo/Christian principles and morality.

Choosing not to put effort toward detecting and rooting out revisionists errors will leave a void. This void will be filled by those whose uncensored ideas will propagate a growing culture of death, thereby changing the future as students graduate with wrong ideas and move into positions of employment. Their daily decisions based in wrong ideologies will drive the

culture forward with the same ideas they were indoctrinated with. What kind of culture will it be? A pro-
death culture?

Are we talking about indoctrination on the part of
Christians? Yes, of course. Someone is going to do
it, why shouldn't we indoctrinate what is right and
proper thinking? We must learn from Reagan's
"evil empire" principle and without qualms say the
words, "We Censor." Yes, the devils will howl. Let
it be so. They always howl at an exorcism. The two
words **"we censor"** will bring on, just as the two
words "evil empire," the confrontation necessary
to purge revisionist doctrines ruling over students'
thinking. As bishop and pastors, one cannot be resigned for others or entrenched committees to do it.

Reagan bypassed obstacles that were often times
produced by those closest to him who advised
"compromise" and "caution" which was the order
of the day. Instead, Reagan struck out at problems
directly, dealing strongly with what was at hand.
Bishops can instantly pronounce, "we censor," and
act. Being resigned while evil indoctrinates our
youth while believing it is wrong to do the same
indoctrinating for good, is one of our errors that
has put us in the position we now find ourselves in.

Teaching is indoctrination. You <u>want</u> youth to learn what <u>you</u> are teaching.

A.   A Catholic bishop is an intricate key, holding the chair of unity.

(1.) Several counties are usually in one diocese.

(2.) This gives the advantage to unite in effort (not to be confused into centralization) several counties of a diocese together, each with a Constitutional Small Prayer Group to not only fortify each county, in union with pastors of other faiths, but it creates a block for greater protection of religious liberty and freedom to flourish.

B.   As bishop, with the power of spiritual authority, he aids in:

(1.) Helping build a unified infrastructure; a spiritual constitutional force, unified in strength with other pastors and with the leader and Constitutional Small Prayer Group of each county across the diocese.

C.   As bishop, the authority and infrastructure of his office can be used to institute educational

strategies, contradicting and contrasting the likes of Yale's, "The Constitution in 2020."

(1.)   A bishop countering the efforts of evil-minded men to fundamentally change the United States of America is not optional, but absolutely necessary so as not to allow our nation to fall into the darkness of full tyranny. Some of evil's tactics can be used by us in a moral way. If those who have perverted the "understanding of religious liberty" are not confronted by teachings contradicting their perversions which bishops could institute throughout the nation in parochial schools, we will have given over our nation to darkness by surrendering through "authority not used." Authority of God which could have acted but did not—a grave responsibility. Our Lady said:

June 2, 2012

> **"...My children, great is the responsibility upon you...you can do everything... Everyday I pray for the shepherds and I expect the same of you. Because, my children, without their guidance and strengthening through their blessing, you cannot do it. Thank you."**

(2.)   As bishop the power of spiritual authority, cou-
        rageously exercised, is enormous in effect and
        can strengthen the ability of all Christians and
        people of good will to defeat future assaults
        against religious liberty in the fight for liberty.

(a.)   To partially reiterate, led by a bishop, pa-
        rochial schools must, with no time wasted,
        institute urgently, teachings about the Dec-
        laration and Constitution and their 200 plus
        years of flourishing in this nation with liberty
        stories, court cases, examples illustrating how
        the Constitution is interpreted by Christians
        with a Biblical worldview, etc., as shown and
        applied by John Adams' words:

> *"Our Constitution was made **'only'**
> **for a moral** and **religious people.** It
> is **'wholly inadequate'** to the govern-
> ment of any other."* [389]

Youth need common sense teachings on the
level of each of their grades why the Constitution was made the way it was and that it can
only be used through a Biblical application
as opposed to secular humanism. Students in
every grade, year after year, need exposure to

these truths so to be grounded inside and out with teachings on liberty, unalienable rights, etc. through each of the 1–12 grades.

This should be seen in the light of an emergency because of the secular teaching of all grades that students in public and many private Catholic and Christian schools are receiving. There is a race to propagate a new way of thinking for a new socialistic Constitution by 2020, and we have not even begun to leave the starting line. A failure to utilize authority to implement counter teaching against a socialistic Constitution by 2020 will be the death of the United States of America. Afterward, the whole world will follow.

This is the agenda of the 'powers that be.' This threat will not go away, and will not cease to exist if one chooses not to believe it. The Soros, Obama and Yale gangs believe it. As earlier stated, the United States of America is the bulkhead to destroy, in order to destroy the whole world. Our Lady said evil has intentions to rule the world and destroy it. But if this is the case, then it must be a principle that will also work in an opposite way.

If the United States of America restores
what our Forefathers planned to be the indissoluble bond of civil principles to the principles of Christianity, by nullifying all laws
in contradiction to the Ten Commandments
and Christian principles, the United States of
America will be saved and the whole world
with it. In the name of Pope Benedict XVI
and the Church, the United States Papal Nuncio, Archbishop Carlo Maria Vigano, during a
speech at the Pontifical College Josephinum
in Columbus, Ohio, in April 2012 has said so:

> *"The Church in the United States*
> *should lead the entire Church in the*
> *world... This is a great task, but you*
> *have the determination and the grace*
> *to do it. This I know is the vision of*
> *the Holy Father regarding the Church*
> *in the United States."*[390]

The United States Papal Nuncio's call for
America to lead and change the world can
happen. Look at what Ronald Reagan's witness and the impact of his conviction sparked
on the secular side, while Blessed Pope John
Paul II's witness and the impact of his convic-

tion sparked on the spiritual side. Together, the two of them brought down an "evil empire." Now is the moment for the spiritual and secular shepherds to ignite the spark, one county at a time. Now is the hour.

(1.) Youth are targeted to be the first to radically think differently about what the Constitution means. As they grow to adulthood and become the ones sitting in positions of authority, they will exercise "The Constitution in 2020" thinking into their decisions.

Our Lady said on October 24, 1988

> **"...your Mother wants to call you to pray for the young of the whole world, for the parents of the whole world so they know how to educate their children and how to lead them in life with good advice. Pray, dear children; <u>the situation of the young is difficult</u>. Help them..."**

(2.) Bishops/pastors should courageously establish special courses on the Constitution as a 911 emergency. To negate what is presently happening to indoctrinate the youth through the educational system is to accept the loss of liberty, because of allowing the propagation of socialist, Marxist, anti-god policies. We will lose our youth, and with them, the United States of America. In contrast, bishops have thousands of parochial schools to help fundamentally change the face of America. No consulting with committees, principals, school boards, PTA's, is necessary except to expend energy and waste time. We have no time to waste. Remember Our Lady's words:

May 2, 2012

"...My children, do not waste time..."

To do nothing is to fall headlong into darkness. To act will lead back to the restoration of the "city on the hill," where freedom and a culture of life will flourish and the culture of death will die.

(3.)   Use the leaders and the Constitutional Small Prayer Group and broader groups of each county in the diocese to review all text books in parochial schools for "historic revisionism," a cancerous and rampant tactic stealthily implanted in all the schools, both public and private (including many Catholic). Use the leaders and the C.S.P.G. to bring in new fresh material and older constitutionally correct books on the Declaration of Independence, the Constitution, and the principles of our Republic, especially in teaching that our unalienable rights are not given by government or the Constitution, but by God. Understanding the principles of the Declaration and the Constitution is the Church's protection.

(b.) As Bishop, host Constitutional classes where your diocesan jurisdiction reaches. Require the attendance of all priests, religious, diocesan office personnel and teachers of parochial schools, just as Sheriff Rogers, from Elkhart County, Indiana, requires all his sheriffs to take. He requires three two-day courses on the Constitution.[*] If one thinks what has this got to do with the priesthood, remember St. Paul saved his head, at least for a while, by knowing his **social stud-**

---

[*] See Resource information, page 831

ies and claiming his Roman citizenship. Had he not known his "constitutional rights" and claimed them, we would not have eight books of the New Testament: [391] Ephesians, Philippians, Colossians, 1 Timothy, 2 Timothy, Titus, Philemon, and Hebrews. One recommended source to contact is The Constitution Institute. Their information is found in the Resource List at the back of the book, among other recommended sources, as well.

(c.)   Allow the Constitutional leaders of Constitutional Small Prayer Groups to organize with the larger broader base of each county to speak and distribute materials at every church in the diocese. Coordinate together in union with pastors for their churches to do the same.

(1.)   As Bishop/Pastors, financially support these meetings with support materials, by enlisting benefactors to fund them. George Soros funds his evil intentions. With authority and influence as bishops, evil can be countered. Bold times demand bold decisions by bold men. The Medjugorje visionaries, after seeing and observing Our Lady for 31 years, have said one of the traits the

Virgin Mary has is "a great spirit of decision." Bishops and other Christian pastors should make decisions according to what is right, **regardless of the consequences**. The weighing in of consequences will bring defeat. **Run into the ambush**.

D.   **Bishops can have a profound effect through directing priests for a full frontal assault to purify evil from your counties and places in need of purification, such as the following example:**

> *For decades, local Catholics had maintained a prayerful presence outside an abortion clinic in Rockford, Illinois, but the clinic remained open. According to Kevin Rilott of the Rockford Pro-Life Initiative, the tide began to turn in 2009 when **Bishop Thomas Doran** granted priests permission to recite prayers of exorcism outside the Northern Illinois Women's Center. At times, four priests would stand outside the four corners of the building and **recite the prayers together**. "Within two to three weeks of priests saying these prayers, the number of abortions began to drop," said Rilott. "Over a few months, the number of*

abortions was cut in half and the numbers
of women seeking our help probably dou-
bled. The clinic, which had been perform-
ing 25-75 abortions a week for years, also
reduced its days of business from three to
two." In late 2011, the State of Illinois tem-
porarily suspended the clinic's license; in
January, the clinic announced that it would
not reopen its doors.[392]

In **a great spirit of decision**, bishops can do
the same within their dioceses. Why would a
bishop, who with his spiritual authority, 'not'
call decisively upon his priests to do the same
in various places in his diocese? Not to do so
is to get no results, except to lose more ground.
To decide for these actions is to get results. Go
into the ambush, exercise authority through
exorcist prayers by priests. Spend, rather than
store spiritual gifts, what is at your command
in regards to authority. We are at war. It does
not matter how little support a bishop may have
for such action, even by some priests who may
resist. Ronald Reagan was not a priest or an exorcist, and satan did everything to stop Reagan
from pronouncing two dreadful words. Political prisoners said they knew Russia was over by

the bold pronouncement against evil—satan's empire. Across the whole of Russia these two words reverberated, as would the prayers of a priest performing an exorcism reverberate across the land. What would a frequently performed spiritual assault all across America against satan result in? The quaking of hell, shattering into pieces across our nation. **There can be no "non-believers" among those who have the authority, that it is of no value to use.** You have history of what only two words, **evil empire**, did.

Exorcism prayers recited by the four priests 'is running into the ambush,' exactly the strategy needed at this particular time. Standing on four corners of the Illinois abortion clinic, running into the battle, reciting prayers of exorcism, bishops can do as Bishop Thomas Doran did. Boldly, not only give permission, but command this to be duplicated in every part of the nation. Immediately a 911 reaction. As Our Lady has a great spirit of decision, a bishop does not have to wait for priests to come and make a request, rather give a directive to do so. It is no more optional than when a bishop decides a priest is to transfer to another parish and the priest willingly and obediently fulfills the bishop's directive. There should be no reason a bishop should accept any less when a directive is decisively given to run into the ambush. Lt. Col. Steve Russell went into the streets, bullets flying everywhere, and ordered his men to follow—a temporal order. Can it not be the same for an order of a spiritual nature to go into the ambush? Many plans, based on the Illinois example can be enacted, which should be battled continuously, with exorcising actions and exorcism prayers, until results are seen. The following locations are suggested:

(1.) Four corners of the White House

(2.) Four Corners of Congress

(3.) Four Corners of the United States Supreme Court

(4.) Four corners of each of the state legislatures

(5.) Four corners of each state Governor's Mansion or office

(6.) Four corners of each and every city council, and county commission offices

(a.) The Bishops' unique authority across 195 dio-
      ceses can institute these prayers of exorcism
      as no other spiritual leaders in the United
      States of America. As with the example
      of Bishop Doran and the four priests who
      won the battle in the Illinois abortion clinic,
      not to exercise this spiritual authority is to
      have results that add up to zero for good, all
      the while allowing the institutions who are
      ambushing Catholics and other churches to
      continue to scatter and weaken us across the
      land.

      An offensive run into the ambush must be
      daily strategized. **Utilizing God's grace, it
      is better we assault the gates of hell rather
      than let hell, assault the gates of the Church**.
      Even though the Scriptures say hell will not
      prevail against the Church, how many casu-
      alties will we suffer, by tyranny, in our fight
      to protect religious liberty at **our** gate, rather
      than **hell's** gate? Where are satan's gates?
      From what places is he bringing forth anti-
      christian edicts? Identify those gates and
      take the battle to their very steps, through
      fasting and the spiritual power of exorcism.

Think, use prayer coupled with common sense. We must stop letting our enemies bring the battle to us. We must bring the battle to them.

No one has more authority to begin such a wonderful, united, profoundly powerful assault than the Catholic Bishops. Not to, is to wait for a replay of 1927 Mexico, when in 1917, a chance to interrupt hell's advances against the Church was not taken, instead evil beings were allowed to advance forward in 1927 against the Church. Forget building new churches, adding on projects, or new programs, etc. We have one unified focus at hand. What is a new church if we do not act? How many churches in the past were turned into cow barns when they went face to face with tyranny, Mexico being just one example. The Constitution in 2020 is advancing. What will it be like? Answer: Mexico—1927.

E. One last special note, as bishop, for actions to immediately and decisively aid in changing our situation.

A special message was given by Our Lady for guidance in bringing healing to nations of the

West. Our Lady said in Medjugorje to heal the
West:

August 6, 1982

**"...Monthly Confession will be a remedy
for the Church in the West. One must
convey this message to the West..."**

As you already read, the following is worth
repeating. Prophecy or Private Revelation is
given not to forecast the future, but to move
us towards decisions which must be made in
the present in order to mitigate, or even avoid
altogether a future inherited from rejecting
God and His precepts, just as when Jonah went
through the city of Nineveh warning of its coming judgment. Listening to Jonah, the king down
to the lowest peasant repented, sacrificed and
ultimately avoided what was to be. Abraham,
looking for righteous souls to save the city, was
not so successful in Sodom.

If all bishops persistently and decisively sent out
pastoral letters calling for all priests to call everyone to monthly confession, and for priests to
be in the confessional before and/or after every
Mass, Our Lady tells us this is the way to cure

the West. Priests planning their daily scheduled times for Mass can accomodate more time before or after every Mass for confession. This will start Catholics thinking more about where they stand with God and the Church. Mass and Confession will be the two most important things on the priest's schedule for the day.

A bishop instituting a decisive and persistent call to Confession and his priests echoing this call will begin the Nineveh call. Timidness and pleasantries are over. The call is no longer optional for the crisis we face, rather pronounce at every Mass, everywhere and every time Mass is said, "Come to Confession a minimum of once a month." The people <u>will</u> respond through time. Again, as Reagan chose decisively to say what he knew was right not weighing out consequences of announcing the words "evil empire," priests may scoff at their bishop, not wanting to sit in the confessional before and after every Mass. **We are in war. Our Lady said it will cure the West. If one chooses not to accept the private revelations of Our Lady's words, what injury would occur by acting upon it anyway?** Only good can result.

Pope Benedict has made the call for renewal if we just give "one tear of repentance." Can this not be translated and wedded to Our Lady's call for one tear of repentance each month through confession? Constantly calling the Church membership to Confession and making it much more available, is the same philosophy behind, "You build it, they will come." Begin the "Nineveh call." The people will come to Confession when repeatedly called and told why this must be. Monthly Confession for all Catholics and a call for repentance for all Christian denominations must be the beginning call. Pope Benedict's full "one tear" quote:

> "Lord Jesus, open our eyes: Let us see the filth around us and recognize it for what it is so that a 'single' tear of sorrow can restore us to purity of heart and the breath of true freedom. Open our eyes." [393]

We cannot expect to escape the negative consequences of living through decades of error. But we, Catholics and Protestants, can repent and have hope of mitigating what is headed our way. If the people need a reason for monthly confession and repentance, **tell them, teach them**—**Rwanda is the reason!**

PART III

This is the Battle Plan—Outline

Who keeps the focus?

3. THE FOCUS: THE SECULAR SHEPHERD

What is the goal?

To restore first in your own heart John Quincy Adams' following quote and then proactively implement the quote across the county, not coun'try'. John Quincy Adams, in essence, said:

> The American Revolution "...*connected in one indissoluble bond, principles of civil government to the principles of Christianity.*"[394]

"**...To the** principles of Christianity"—principles which are bedrock, not moveable or changeable. It is the principles of civil government that are to move and change in order to be bonded **to** the principles of Christianity. Thereby, these civil principles become bedrocked, unshakable upon the solid foundation of the principles of Christianity. What is the first step?

A.   **Secular does not mean you, as sheriff, to be purely secular. As <u>They Fired the First Shot 2012</u> points out, without prayer, without being spiritually-minded and having a Biblical worldview, we are doomed.** As a County Sheriff, familiarize yourself with what it means to become a true David, a protector of those who you are obligated to protect, as your boss, because they hired you through their vote. Constitutional protection of their God-given rights, is your sole **focus**.

(1.)   Require Constitutional courses, as Sheriff Rogers of Elkhart County, Indiana requires of his deputies, for all your deputies.[*]

(2.)   Send deputies to all schools, public and private, giving a teaching on the Constitutional duty of the County Sheriff.

    (a.)   This is urgent to plan now as you will see enormous effects to be gained teaching students that sheriffs have Executive Branch power as the chief law officer, which will

[*] See Resource page 831

embolden them not to be afraid to freely exercise their God-given rights where an effort is mounted to try to stop them.

Not to teach these students about your authority as sheriff is to say good-bye to a thousand year history, as these students will later take positions on city councils, will become congressmen, bureaucrats, not to mention will begin voting their beliefs at the ballot box. They will illegally nullify the sheriff's rightful Constitutional and Common Law authority.

This is already beginning to happen in Delaware, where the 'powers that be' realizing that their wings of authority can be clipped by the County Sheriff and are making radical moves to legislate the County Sheriff's powers away. Other state legislatures in the northeast have reduced the duties of their sheriffs to simply serving papers, with no power to enforce law or power to arrest. These people know that all police chiefs, state troopers, and other law enforcement officers answer to bureaucrats and can thereby be controlled by them. The sheriff is the only peace officer that answers directly to the people, and he, therefore, empowers the people. The State of Connecticut has done away with the Office of Sheriff altogether— Connecticut has **no** sheriffs.

In a second interview with Sheriff Mack, he stated why there is a move to get rid of the County Sheriff. Mack stated, *"I don't find it any big surprise really when politicians don't want sheriffs answering to bureaucrats, or committees or other politicians who want to have the power to say what cops will do and what they won't do."*[395] You, as sheriff, must take the teachings to the classrooms and the people now. This means act 'yesterday' to build a teaching program to visit all schools to enlighten students.

As with Delaware, Connecticut and other states, where action is being attempted to de-power the sheriff's position, you not acting, instituting school programs, etc., will render powerless the sheriffs in the future. The residents of these states should begin to work immediately, fighting with their very lives, to restore back into their state law the real and necessary power of the Sheriff. This can be achieved with effort.

(3.) Every County Sheriff's office should institute this program of education immediately as a 9-1-1 emergency in every school in its county.

(4.) Tell students to inform parents of what they are being taught. Just as F.E.M.A. is using kids to become **change agents**, use these lessons for "truth agents" to reach parents about the authority of "the Davids."

B. **If you, as sheriff, are becoming aware of your authority and have not exercised it properly, formally apologize to county citizens and make a commitment to everyone in the county that you will keep your oath and become a Constitutional Sheriff.** Hold a news conference or take another public opportunity, even several opportunities to announce you are **becoming** a Constitutional Sheriff, and afterwards explain what it means to be one. It will help other sheriffs to also come out in the open, when they see others step forward. The people's admiration and support will only increase with such a move as they applauded Sheriff Dean Wilson[*] for his apology.

(1.) If you plan to run for the office as a Constitutional Sheriff, contact the Constitutional leader and **C**onstitutional **S**mall **P**rayer **G**roup to speak of your intentions and ask them to review you as a candidate. Contact Caritas of Birmingham to locate a Constitutional Small Prayer Group in your area. See also, the Resource Listing beginning on page 831 for additional information on C.S.P.G. and contact information.

With the three defined elements in place...

1. The Sheep
2. The Spiritual Shepherds
3. The Secular Shepherds

and with the parallel infrastructure in place...

1. Strategize
2. Unify
3. Focus

...the next step can be taken to stand down the threats against Constitutional violations, against God-given

---

[*] See Stories of the Davids, page 443

unalienable rights. The Bishop, with aligned pastors, sheriffs, and the **C**onstitutional **S**mall **P**rayer **G**roup can be a unified fortress, protecting the county against every Constitutional violation. This is where the field of battle is to be fought and will be won—one county at a time. **THINK, PLAN, IMPLEMENT AT THE COUNTY LEVEL**.

Simple clear plans, easy to implement are very achievable, very winnable—with a lot of prayer and work. Yes, it will take not only prayer, but a lot of work, but as already stated and worth repeating, as Benjamin Franklin said:

> *"They who can give up essential liberty to obtain a little temporary safety, deserve neither liberty nor safety."* [396]

CHAPTER THIRTY-SEVEN

This is the Battle Plan—Final Directive

Can we expect to only pray and God will rain down liberty from Heaven like manna? Manna sustained the Israelites but when God gave them the Promised Land, they had to fight for it. Prayer will bring down the manna of grace and that will give the opportunity of a promised land of liberty, but we too will have to fight for it and work to preserve it.

Who our president is, is a concern, but it is our least concern, for peace, as you know by these writings, will not come through the president. And if the president dictates against our well-being constitutionally, the three simple elements, through the Constitutional Sheriff, will nullify his edicts. When the three elements are foundationally built, the next level is to bring on board city council members and county commission members. The creating of small villages and hamlets across America is key. Part II that follows will be a cause of great excitement, in showing how small Christian incorporated Constitutional praying village communities, with all ordinances rooted to Christian principles and the Ten Commandments, can ignite a re-birth of what happened in 1776, with each village making a declaration of independence, signed by the citizens who will live in them. Once Constitutional Small Prayer Groups evolve into villages covering "this nation," city councils, county commissions, and state legislatures will follow. This will kill the anti-liberty federalization of each man's home, thereby, returning the home to a small moral republic, as Thomas Jefferson spoke of "the administration of every man's farm by himself; by placing under everyone what his own eye may superintend."[397]

Lastly, it is up to us to build an infrastructure where going the way of the courts can be greatly reduced, but we must stand down tyranny's assaults directly to its face.

Stop going to the courts? Do you **not** know what is Constitutional? Then, why go to court? Think differently. Scripture states:

Luke 12:57

> *"And why do you not judge for yourselves what is right?"*

Do what Scripture states in the next verse, Luke 12:58:

> *"If you are to go with your opponent before the magistrate, make an effort to settle the matter on the way."*

That is our mandate, we do not go to court. We are going to settle on the way to court and have our terms. These are the terms.

We win. Tyranny loses.

To do so we should look at Jesus' life and a side of Jesus many do not reason out. Jesus, with all His love and mercy, compassion and forgiveness, was no sissy. When contemplating Him, we should look at the entire scope and breath of His life from the God of Love…to the God of Sinai.

Love is best displayed through obedience to God and obedience to God must come first, rather than man's mandates of requiring us to violate laws against nature and nature's God. Jesus is God. He gave the witness of being peace, loving, meek, humble, merciful, compassionate, but He also was decisive, strong, convicting, authoritative, with no pretense, and was fearless in confronting evil. Likewise, in following the witness of the founder of Christianity; Christianity is not passive. It is, like its founder, meek and humble, but it is anything but passive. Did not Jesus drop the soldiers and guards of the temple to the ground when they were going to possibly arrest the apostles? Jesus complied with the laws, yet confronted the Sanhedrin on their imposed regulations which took on the form of law but were not. And throughout the history of Christianity, countless times God intervened in battles on behalf of nations to save them. Joan of Arc saving France is one of only many actions. No, passivity is over. We must go for victory. We will accept victory in meekness and humbleness. But it is turnaround time. 'Turn the tables over' time. We do not fully know the real Jesus because we see him only through our eyes. Our Lady said:

February 2, 2011

> **"...Wandering in darkness, you even imagine God Himself according to yourselves, and not such as He really is in His love..."**

These are times when, to achieve peace with God, we must **restore holiness**. Man cannot have peace with God, without holiness. Our Lady said on May 25, 2012:

> **"...I call you...to holiness..."**

We must love God's moral order. If you love God's moral order, you will keep His moral order. When you keep God's moral order, you will receive the power of authority of God's moral order. Only then can we turn the tables of tyranny upside down. The following is transcribed from a talk entitled, *"Change Now or Miss the Boat,"* with some added messages and Scripture for clarity.

"Jesus, if you really look at His personality, who He was as a man and as God, it's incredible to think really what He did. He stood for gentleness. He stood for pure love, pure love in the highest degree. There was no sin in Him, Who was God. No violations, nothing He did, ever, was wrong.

Now, picture this: make a whip. Get cords and fashion them together to make a real whip. If you were doing that, and you had premeditated intentions to beat something, it is a very serious thing, unless you were just making it for play. But if you had intentions to really use it, to do something with this, after you spent the time to make this whip, would you not then have a specific pre-meditated purpose for it? It was not a thoughtless shoot from the hip decision. Jesus did this. We already knew, in reading the Scripture, that He was upset. Now, here is Somebody Who is love, Who is sitting there, and I doubt if He snaps His finger and says, "Whip," and it's in His hand. In fact, I know He didn't do that, because He made it. So, he's there in the temple, premeditating what

He was going to do, twisting and making a whip. He's tying these cords together, and He fashions it, so He can strike. Love, He Who is Love, the King of Peace, the King of Love. Peace! Love! We tend to think love means, "You do what you want, I do what I want, we all love each other." No, this is not Jesus. He ran into the thick of battle [ambush] His whole ministry, crashing right into the Cross. Yet, He never sinned, never was against peace, yet Jesus has got this whip in His hand, and He's watching in the temple everything being sold. Was He just gonna act out a play with His whip?

> ***"In the temple precinct He came upon people engaged in selling oxen, sheep and doves, <u>and others seated changing coins</u>."***

Oxen, sheep, doves, 'others' are people.

> ***"He made a kind of whip of cords and drove the sheep and oxen 'alike' out of the temple, and knocked over the money changer's tables, spilling their coins."***

Now, our Jesus today, what's painted by many people who don't have the clear view of what real love is, say "Jesus was always gentle, He was always passively peaceful." Recall His Mother's words now:

February 2, 2011

"...Wandering in darkness, you even imagine God Himself according to yourselves, and not such as He really is in His love..."

*Zeal for His Father's house consumed Him. Zeal was His Love and Jesus, by the way the world judges, lost His peace! Did He? Or was His peace inflamed? He didn't go to a table and say, "Excuse Me, I don't want this to hit your toes, but I gotta turn this over because I want this to go in Scriptures, and I want to make an example. So I'm gonna just gently 'tump' this over and the coins, watch your toes, because with sandals you might get a black toenail. Just excuse me...and by the way, just a minute, and let me get this whip and let me drive these...****COME ON...****" Jesus was angry! Real anger! Love! It's not a game! "Oh no, I dropped this table on his toe! I'm Jesus. I shouldn't be doing that!" He beat the animals and drove them out. Jesus!! It doesn't say if He hit people, but I imagine it was pretty chaotic. This is the Man, who people model so much of Christianity today, as they* <u>imagine</u> *Him to be, yet* *not as He truly is. Which means that we can just let go of every moral principle and of everything we want to reject, and everybody can have their own relative truth and we just accept what everybody wants to do! No! This is not the real Jesus! We don't get upset about what is going on with the loss of religious liberty—but here we have Jesus Who has made a whip and He's beating animals, throwing things around, people stumbling, running away, the noise, yells of people, a riot in the temple. Jesus would be arrested today, if He did that now, for abuse of animals, causing a riot in public and criminal assault! And, of course, the real ironic charge against Jesus would be for disturbing the 'peace.' If you were to do that right now, you'd be arrested. So what is the truth? The truth is that love is not what we all understand it to be. We need to be 'disturbing some peace' for people whose plans are to destroy peace. Scripture relays Jesus became indignant. In John 2:17, Jesus said,* **"Zeal for my Father's house consumes me."**

And He turned what was violating the temple upside down. I didn't say that, the Bible said that. What is the Bible? God's Word. What is God's

Word? God's Word is the Truth!! We have lost common sense. Our Lady said:

December 2, 2007

"...God's Word which is the light of salvation and the light of common sense."

God's Word made flesh is Jesus. Jesus is the Light of Salvation. Therefore, Jesus is the Light of Common Sense. We have lost common sense. Because we have lost Jesus, the real Jesus, we have lost common sense. We do not know what action we should be willing to do to stand against tyranny. If Jesus turned the money-changers tables over because the Temple was being defiled, what must He think of the "selling" of abortion in the temple of the Holy Spirit—'the body'? And we are afraid to be seen as too radical in our response of exchanging our money to pay for someone's abortion?" Whether it be our tax money or direct money, it is the same. We are just going to close up shop and walk away? Cowards. No, that is not what we will be known as, rather more appropriately, chicken cowards. Christian cowards. Our enemy will shout when all Catholic institutions are shut down, "Weak is the God of the Christians!" Weak

*is the God of the chickens. But what of those early
Christians standing up to tyranny, being bravely
martyred in the coliseum, whose pagan spectators
left chanting "Great is the God of the Christians."
These impressed pagans left the coliseum, many
of them becoming Christians. How will you be
known? Weak is the God of the chickens, or Great
is the God of the Christians? Our Lady's call is
for the latter.*

A cowardly Christianity has prevailed over the Church. We must become a holy, humble, repentant people to reclaim the power of authority to change everything which assails us.

But first everything starts with the local county, the local village town, through the local Constitutional Small Prayer Groups. But we must never forget our efforts to stand down tyranny are nil unless we first purify ourselves with repentance, crying to God to heal this, our land. The elected sheriff, with a diocesan bishop, aligned with pastors, all unified with the county citizens, will defeat tyranny. And if we do not act? The answer is in evil's word, throughout this writing, as an epistle to you. Reread the book. You have not read this book if you have not read it twice.

United States Population:
314,000,000
Takes 5% of the Population to have a revolution
5% of the population
15,700,000
Constitutional Small Prayer Groups set out to find them

They fired the first shot in 2012.
Who fired the second shot in 2012?
The Woman did.*

July 3, 2012, the second shot was fired.

"Form and make prayer groups
through which we will pray for your healing
and the healing of this nation
to draw closer to God and to Me."

As you read on, you will understand the second shot fired.

---

* Genesis 3:15: *"...the <u>woman</u>, and enmity between your off-spring and hers."*

John 2:4: *"<u>Woman</u>...my time has not yet come."* *Jesus then performed His first miracle at the Woman's request.*

John 19:26: *"<u>Woman</u>, behold, your son."* *The Woman is given to all mankind.*

Revelation 12:1: *"...a <u>woman</u> clothed with the sun (Son),"* (*a great sign in the sky*).

PART II

Introduction — Part II

God is the same, yesterday, today and forever. He is Perfection. His thought is perfect. It is often being stated in the state-controlled media that we are living in a post-Christian era. However, the Church is being led towards a new springtime for Christianity. It is the reason why Our Lady has been appearing every day since June, 1981. How will this renewal take place? We have only to look at God's perfect thought in how He started the Church from the beginning. Jesus left behind just a handful of believers, just a very few seeds, when compared to the population of the earth. During Jesus' time on earth, geographically, He never traveled more than 200 miles from where He was raised. He spent His time within a geographical area that was no bigger than New Jersey. The Acts of the Apostles in the New Testament tell us that the "churches" became communities, though they were very small, as they often met in people's homes to break Bread and to hear

633

the Word. They were home churches. The 12 apostles were scattered out by the Holy Spirit to the farthest corners of the known world and following the example of Jesus, began forming small communities of believers in all of these various places. The potency of these seeds of Christ's teachings was such that the witness of the "way of life" of believers attracted nonbelievers who began leaving their pagan ways to join the Christians. Jesus called His believers out of pagan society, to begin building a new society built upon His precepts, similar to what God did when He called His people out of Egypt to lead them to the Promised Land. The Virgin Mary has been appearing for 31 years as of June 24, 2012. Our Lady has come to rebirth Christianity into the societies of all nations. In the decades following Jesus' life on earth, Christianity spread throughout all avenues of the Roman Empire, which, eventually, led all of Europe to become known as Christendom. The apostles could not have fully grasped, even though told by Christ, how that could happen from their small numbers.

It is the wrong mentality to think we can bring virtue out of a society that is so embedded with sin and evilness. We cannot. As stated and conveyed before this book, in the books and writings that have come through this mission, once hell establishes itself upon the earth, there is no possibility to redeem it except by its destruction through purification. God's plan was perfect the first time, therefore, we simply need to return to how He originally Christianized the world and follow in this way. We must separate from an immoral society, allowing it to decay on its own. Society needs us to keep it propped up. We do not need it. If we abandon a pagan system and government, it will fall, as there is no life or future apart from God. We are to establish Christ's ways in our own lives, small societies, small communities and villages. From there, it will replace the greater culture, which has cast judgement on itself, of its destruction, by its way of life without God.

A Friend of Medjugorje

A Friend of Medjugorje wrote the following letter on June 8, 2006. It actually was part of a personal letter. For the sake of the time frame of events, back in 2006, remember that no one had yet heard of the huge economic collapse which struck two years later on September 15, 2008, nor little or nothing of Obama, nor of the anarchy and rebellion that would take over sections of Europe. In fact, Europe's money, the Euro was still looked at with hope for a bright future. The American economy was daily making millionaires and billionaires, while the middle class was flourishing at the point of peaking out along with many other things that were not as today. Yet, there were those who were unsettled concerning the direction our nation was taking even with everything seemingly so good. Now, everyone can see our condition by what has transpired. As you will read, what was foretold in the following by A Friend of Medjugorje in June of 2006, before these conditions blatantly materialized, was right on target. A Friend of Medjugorje was writing in regards to the frustration and unpeace associated with a nation whose liberty and future were becoming more and more endangered because of immorality.

The Publisher

CHAPTER THIRTY-EIGHT

PART II—THE REVOLUTION

"...The Principles of Civil Government And its Indissoluble Bond To the Principles of Christianity."

June 8, 2006

The spirit of many Americans today, of the general citizenry itself, is one of unpeace and frustration. It is evolving into a readiness for what the Declaration of Independence called for, "to provide new guards for their future security." If a form of structure does not materialize that can lead to action towards this end, apathy will begin to permeate the heart, much like what prevails in Europe today, through the belief that "we the people" are powerless to affect change. The apathy in Europe has created fertile ground for governments to root more deeply and grow socialism within the fabric of their nations. The flourishing of the mentality that "nothing can be done" continues sowing seeds of hopelessness until a rupture of society takes place and rebellion and anarchy is embraced. The danger of this happening is that the wrong officials are raised to power, as we witnessed happen in the past century.

In America, for the prayerful and thoughtful, it is evident that our future society is gravely at risk by the present system of "guards." A system without integrity cannot elect someone with integrity, nor will it in the future. The present form of election is ingrained so deeply with its power structure and errors that the vote of the citizens is purchased, unknowingly to them. This happens through a system that has no traces of Godly virtues, principles or morals, through special interest groups of immoral principles who give to us the candidates of their choice, not ours.

Therefore, we arrive at a conclusion, through reason, that even those who are elected, who respect God's precepts will end up conforming or compromising to the immoral system and/or they will be rendered useless, even labeled fanatical for upholding their principles. In the system's present form, it cannot be otherwise. In a system of operation where God is absent, how can it be deduced that one will sanctify it? Abraham wanted to do it with Sodom. Moses tried to do it with Pharaoh. For the man with the biblical worldview, politics strikes an aversion in his heart. How then, can we put the right people in office in our present situation?

The gains the enemies of our nation have made to overturn our foundation has been made through education. While they navigated themselves for decades into positions of policy making, they have changed the heart of America. Simply put, we are in no position to enter into the present two party system and change anything. Any great institution which wants to rebirth itself, must return to its founding principles. As our Forefathers did in the beginning, so too, must we make a declaration to return to our founding. But what are words? Nothing but ink on paper. We can learn from the success of the enemies of our nation and realize we must change hearts, as they have.

It is known that a revolution is caused by 5% of the people. The rest of the 95% will follow. Founding Father, Samuel Adams, said:

> *"It does not require a majority to prevail, but rather an IRATE, TIRELESS MINORITY keen to set brush fires in people's minds."*[398]

To sum everything up, America needs two revolutions. The first revolution is needed in our Church by living the fullness of God's precepts. The second revolution is needed in our nation by the legal means of its original Declaration. We must discover what those means may be just as those discerned it in Williamsburg, Virginia in 1776.

I do not believe we can correct the corruption in our present government, nor, I believe would Thomas Jefferson, according to his statement below:

> *"When once a republic is corrupted, there is no possibility of remedying any of the growing evils but by removing the corruption and RESTOR-ING ITS LOST PRINCIPLES; every other cor-rection is either useless or a new evil."*[399]

This is the hour to call for a Declaration of Inde-pendence from the federalization of our states and local communities, and the growing influence from "internationalization" threading through our federal government. As Lincoln said:

> *"...their* (the founding fathers) *posterity might look up again to the Declaration of Independ-ence and take courage to renew that battle which their FATHERS began, so that truth...and Christian virtues might not be extinguished from the land...let me entreat you to come back...*

come back to the truths that are in the Declaration of Independence."[400]

The following words of John Adams, spoken on July 1, 1776, should be our rallying words today, now spoken as our own words as to our beliefs, principles and actions at this moment:

"Before God, I believe the hour has come. My judgement approves this measure, and my whole heart is in it. All that I have, and all that I am, and all that I hope in this life, I am now ready here to stake upon it. And I leave off as I began, that live or die, survive or perish, I am for the Declaration. It is my living sentiment, and by the blessing of God, it shall be my dying sentiment. Independence now, and Independence for ever!"[401]

The Declaration of Independence was the legal basis for American's "Revolutionary Rights." Those rights are still encoded in the Declaration for our time today. What was legal in our founding cannot be illegal in the present. A revolutionary right exists and can be exercised by Americans. There can be no duplicity in the Declaration of Independence of what was legal is now illegal.

****End of June 8, 2006 letter***

Is it worth it to drive one hour or even more to work each day if you can live in a place where you don't have to lock your doors, you can leave your keys in your car, and the whole village town is your 911 call, because everyone responds to whatever need must be met? A place where you can live and raise your children and then see their children raised along the same creeks and in the same woods and where each generation of your family is buried in your own small village cemetery? A place where one grows up and does not have to move away? A Constitutional village birthed by a prayer group? The Bible says you can achieve this:

2 Chronicles 7:14

> *"If my people who are called by my name humble themselves, and pray and seek my face, and turn from their wicked ways, then I will hear from Heaven, and will forgive their sin and heal their land."*

According to this Scripture passage, **"is"** it possible for God to heal a land if the people are not rooted to His statutes, the Ten Commandments? No, it is not. Therefore, the healing of our land will not come through the president, congress or the courts, but rather from the

other side of the spectrum of that authority. It will be
the people, the Christian citizens in their small hamlets,
in their counties, who will decide the future. Protection will come because of a return to living moral lives.
When the people rid their lives of everything not of
God, the people will be given good spiritual and secular shepherds and all three can then receive healing
and the power of authority and the protection necessary to safeguard their land. This protection is necessary for the revolution of the founding or "re"founding
of small Constitutional village hamlets to happen, praying towns where a moral republic is foundationed upon
connecting civil government principles indissolubly to
Christian principles. It is a real signing, with our lives,
a Declaration of Independence from the federalization
of our lives, homes and communities.

The best unit of government is when the governing
body is at the closest level to the people. The closer it
is to the people, the more it is the people who govern.
This is what Jefferson meant when he said the following statement which was quoted earlier in the book, but
is pertinent to this point and to be applied here as well:

> *"The way to have good and safe government is*
> *not to trust it all to one, but to divide it among*
> *the many, distributing to everyone exactly the*

functions he is competent to. Let the national government be entrusted with the defense of the nation, and its foreign and federal relations; the State governments with the civil rights, laws, police, and administration of what concerns the State generally; the counties with the local concerns of the counties, and each ward direct the interests within itself. It is by dividing and subdividing these republics from the great national one down through all its subordinations, until it ends in the administration of every man's farm by himself; by placing under everyone what his own eye may superintend, that all will be done for the best.

"What has destroyed liberty and the rights of man in every government which has ever existed under the sun? The generalizing and concentrating all cares and power into one body." [402]

A man is given authority by God to govern his affairs in his family and home, and over his lands and endeavors. The government's job is only to insure that protection of this God-given liberty is not restricted unduly by government. In other words, it is to stay out of the affairs of men when they are not government affairs. To do otherwise has and will lead to loss of liberty on every front of man's self-determination. One may argue, man cannot do whatever he pleases. It is not being advocated that man can do whatever he pleases. Self-determination must be in union and tempered by God's statutes. It works when Christian principles are promoted through society. It stops working when government usurps these principles and then tries to keep order through secular laws, which ultimately give way to more laws. Laws without God ultimately cannot keep order and, therefore, beget another law to correct what the first law was not able to achieve.

In regards to self-measured living, the key to peace is living a self-measured life. Being tempered means to live in peace with your neighbor and this is possible through living the Ten Commandments in all areas of life. The Ten Commandments were ordained by God for man to love Him and neighbor and to restrain man from, namely, his inordinate wants and passions. For the newly founded, or a rebirthed Constitutional prayer group village of an existing town, not to become rooted to God's Law is starting its beginning traveling down the same dead end road of anarchy and tyranny that the nation is traveling on now.

CHAPTER THIRTY-NINE

PART II—THE REVOLUTION

Tea Party Syndrome

For all the good within the Tea Party and the good it has done, it was destined to lose its momentum. Why? When the Tea Party first rallied, we at Caritas, saw a glimmer of hope. It was a seize the moment in reconnecting the civil principles of government indissolubly to Christian principles. A day and a half before one of their first major local events, we called and offered our personal time for the event. What did they need, we asked? They had little printed material. There was a void of direction in understanding what the Tea Party had to grow into. It had to have something other than tax issues for it to be victorious—victorious, first in being graced with God's blessing. God's blessing would then bring victory in all other battles. At least 30 of us worked around the clock coming up with patriotic posters, patriotic Christian principles and statements, books reflecting the same, patriotic themed materials explaining the need for the civil government to be bonded to Christian principles. The event was very heavily attended and the enthusiasm of the people was high. We were told it would not have been what it was without our effort and we witnessed this result as well. Another event was immediately planned, but when we called to help, though an acknowledgement was given of how great our help had been to make things turn out so well in the last event, they no longer needed such help, so "thanks, but no thanks." Not wanting to let go of helping form the people's sentiments in the right direction we called and spoke again. Finally we were told, the Tea Party's only focus was about being anti-taxes and anti-big government. In essence, through the conversation we understood, they did not want to bring religion into it. Yes—God, family and country was on t-shirts and in the rhetoric, but little more. It was obvious to us that this political correctness that many, unknowingly, were falling into, would ultimately cause the Tea Party to "teeter" out. While the movement continued to grow with the initial momentum, its limiting or absenting out God, ordained it to falter and fade. A **fatal** mistake. Our Lady just gave a message:

July 25, 2012

"Dear children! Today I call you to the 'good'. Be carriers of peace and goodness in this world. Pray that God may give you the strength so that hope and pride may always reign in your heart and life because you are God's children and carriers of His hope to this world that is without joy in the heart, and is without a future, because it does not have its heart open to God who is your salvation..."

We are not to practice Quietism. We are to be proud of being in God's family. We are not to apologize or keep silent about re-connecting our government back into an indissoluble bond with Christian principles, because of fear of offending someone. This mentality killed what the Tea Party movement could have been. Again, this is not to deny that there are Tea Party candidates who are being placed in office. However, it's time to be honest with ourselves. Since the Tea Party began, we still have lost <u>a lot,</u> a lot of ground. The Tea Party did not die — it's still alive. It just kind of fades away like a sunset, dooming itself with the false mentality that if it can stay in the right, it can stay in the light. But darkness trails every sunset and where light "was", God is no longer, while darkness envelops it. We know some, maybe many, will disagree with us that the Tea Party movement has fizzled. Some say it has just taken on a different form. There are now Tea Party candidates who are winning elections, etc. But ask yourself, what is the Tea Party doing to stop the advancement of tyranny? Is it stopping Obama from putting through his Executive Orders or the healthcare mandates? It could have. It *would* have. But when you say no to God, God will allow you to go forward without Him.

The Tea Party movement chooses to drive on without God's blessing by this exclusion. Yes, there was token acknowledgement about God, but God is not satisfied with tokenism. He's looking to empower those who understand a future without Him is no future. It's not enough for the Tea Party to say our rights come from God. We have to be wedded to the principles that were birthed with our Savior. This is what the Tea Party avoided doing. John Quincy Adams, who was the sixth president of the United States, on **July 4**, 1847, sixty-one years after the Declaration was signed did not avoid saying this. He unabashedly and incredibly stated:

"Why is it that, next to the birthday of the Savior of the World, your most joyous and most vener-

ated festival returns on this day?...Is it not that, in the chain of human events, the birthday of the nation is indissolubly linked with the birthday of the Savior? That it forms a leading event in the Progress of the Gospel dispensation? Is it not that the Declaration of Independence first organized the social compact on the foundation of the Redeemer's mission upon earth? That it laid the cornerstone of human government upon the first precepts of Christianity and gave to the world the first irrevocable pledge of the fulfillment of the prophecies announced directly from Heaven at the birth of the Savior and predicted by the greatest of the Hebrew prophets 600 years before."[403]

Take time to really study this statement in prayer. What is it saying? Our enemies know what it is saying better than we do and it is their greatest fear and their greatest goal to keep us from this knowledge. They know if we were to really grasp what it says and act upon it, their defeat would be impending. The essence of John Quincy Adams' statement is that what our founding fathers did in creating the United States of America was that the American Revolution:

"...connected in one indissoluble bond, principles of civil government to the principles of Christianity."[404]

The Tea Party movement waned and will continue to do so, rather than becoming a great force to fight tyranny, out of fear of driving away numbers who would not want to be associated to Christ's name. We act as if we are embarrassed to bring God into what we do. People say a blessing over their food at home but are reluctant to do so in public at a restaurant. We have allowed ourselves to be manipulated into being so politically correct, even though many would not describe themselves as being so, that we, ourselves, consider it not nice to cause alienation by putting forth our beliefs in what we do and say.

And yet, everyone took notice when a single company gave witness through a biblical statement made by its owner that literally drove hundreds of thousands of people to their drive-in and walk-in restaurants to show their support for standing up for Christian principles. The numbers that turned out for Chick-fil-A's Day of Appreciation were astounding and that was with only a nine day notice after Governor Mike Huckabee called for people to stand in solidarity with Chick-fil-A's actions. This should speak to the Tea

Party movement as to what is most important in this battle against tyranny. Taxes and big government are only symptoms of a much greater problem and threat. This is not said to demean the Tea Party movement because its ideal is good, but rather to bring it and all of us to reality. **Without Jesus, we have no future.** The Virgin Mary is coming to tell us that the world, at this time, is under judgement. This period of time is given to us as a grace period to decide for Jesus or against Him; to decide for God, or against Him. The Tea Party's example of being focused only on taxes and big government is a tomb stone, R.I.P. statement. What we are fighting, in the tyranny that faces us, is helped along and fortified by satan himself. And we think we are going to fight, by ourselves, this cunning deadly being who has a master intellect? We're going to engage in a fight without God, with only human strength? How pitifully stupid we must be before God, even in His love for us. Excusing ourselves from God in what we partake in is part of the wickedness we need to turn away from if we want our land to be healed. As the Bible relays, what is absolutely necessary for God to heal our land is that man must "turn from his wicked ways." This is the answer.

So, in looking at the example of Nineveh in the
Bible, when looking at establishing a village, the people
must first humble themselves, repent, turn from their
wicked ways and pray. These villages and towns then
must nullify <u>all</u> laws without apology or fear in rejecting political correctness and reinstitute ordinances
and laws only rooted to God's Law. If this is not done,
there is **'<u>no</u>'** hope to escape the judgment we are now
under as God withdraws. Where God is not wanted,
to the degree God withdraws and is absent, is to the
same degree hell will descend upon villages, cities and
nations. One may think, on first thought, that nullifying all ordinances of existing village towns when re-
founding them is radical. To man—yes! To God—no!
Scripture is clear and unapologetic that the <u>only</u> future
is with God. Rather than go through law after law,
tear down the whole Tower of Babel of laws. You may
find it surprising to know that this is exactly what our
founding fathers did once they made the decision to
break from England's laws and government.

> *"It will be recalled that Thomas Jefferson re-*
> *signed from Congress in 1776 to hasten back to*
> *Virginia and volunteer for the task of rewriting*
> *the state laws so that, when independence had*
> *been won, the people would have a model system*

*of legal principles which they could understand
and warmly support. The complex codes of laws
and regulations in our own day could be greatly
improved through a similar housecleaning."*[405]

Once all civil laws are nullified, rewrite only what is
necessary, derived from the principles of Christianity, rooted to the Ten Commandments and what the
Church and Scripture teaches. We are not speaking of
instituting a theocracy.* We are instituting civil government and its ordinances connecting indissolubly to the
principles of Christianity. The villages should take on
a Christian principled character. This is how our nation first grew and the majority of those making up the
groups of both saints and sinners understood this as a
good for society. If some get upset with basing villages
and towns on the principles of Christianity, let it be so.
Some were also upset with Chick-fil-A and the throngs
that came out in support of the owner whose biblical
character was forged into his company's principles.
This is what won the admiration of so many and fond-
ness of him for his stance.

Those who govern these small village towns, out of
the fear of the Lord, are to never dare enact laws or

---

* Theocracy — a form of government in which God or a deity is recognized as the supreme civil ruler. The laws, based in God or a deity, are
  interpreted by the ecclesiastical authorities.

take actions that are contrary to Scripture or the Ten Commandments. Those same governing individuals are to be sensitive to the Church, holding great respect for Judeo-Christian principles. They are to never dare trespass against the right of the Church and her pastors to hold citizens accountable to moral Christian principles. This means not only all statutes and ordinances are to hold to Christian principles, of which all civil decisions are to bind themselves, but the officials personally must be men of faith and hold to Judeo/Christian principles, as well. The ideal is not to expend a lot of energy in electing individuals for office but rather appoint them after there has been enough prayer to create a strong unity in the group so that there is no need to have someone oppose them in running for the town councils of these small villages. If one goes astray, act immediately. Recall procedures is the order of the day.

The mentality the council should have is not of an active governing body, rather a proxy for its citizens to govern themselves. They should not be paid. Some state laws require such. The office holders should donate their funds back to the village. In addition, the council is not there to move forward their plans and ideas but to represent the complete will of the people of the village. There is to be no governing from the top down, rather governing from the bottom up. This means very little governing at all. A good council meeting would be opening up the meeting, move to the order of business, seeing that there is none to discuss, close the meeting. In other words, the village council's function is simply to protect the natural rights of all the villagers. That is its umbrella purpose. In essence, it is a return to what our nation thrived upon, what was responsible for its growth and the increasing strength of its Christian citizens, that helped make it the freest most powerful nation in the world. Respect "we the people" and leave them alone and in peace.

CHAPTER FORTY

PART II—THE REVOLUTION

Churches of the Colonies Played the Major Part in the American Revolution

With respect to the Church and civil officials, in the past, it was not without reason that towns and their officials did not build any structures higher than the church steeple. David Alfredo wrote of why this was in *"The Reason for Church Steeples."*

> *"The steeple's main purpose during the middle ages was to make the church visible from any part of a town. At that time, everything from civil institutions to education revolved around the church. It was essentially the heart of any European town. The steeple was thus built to be the tallest structure in town, clearly there for all to see and be reminded of the Church's importance in their lives."*[406]

Wisdom knew that if it were allowed that other buildings could be built higher than the church, civil authority would become arrogant and rule over religious authority. It was a sign of respect for God that men dare not overshadow the Church, otherwise the god of humanism would come to be represented in these idol towers and the people would fall into worshipping them, voluntarily, or by force, which is the position we find ourselves in now.

In the past, in many early towns and villages when the church was strong, living near the church, being close to the place of worship, made real-estate more valuable. In most regions, the church was the focal point and was part of the town center. This blessing of valuable real-estate became a curse when men began to segregate the Church from the governing of their daily lives and began to worship the dollar. Men then thought nothing of building skyscrapers on the valuable real estate, near the churches that made the real estate valuable in the first place, thereby diminishing the church and its ground. After the blessing of the church and its formation of the people, satan is always ready to bring in a curse to reverse the blessing. As we can now see, where the buildings overshadow the church, darkness of crime and many other evils flourish. In Paris, for example, Notre Dame Church, built in the 13th century was the highest point in the city. One hundred years after the French Revolution, in 1889, during a time when a war of ideas between the Church and secular humanism, was fighting over Paris to gain dominance, those against the Church came up with the idea to build the Eiffel Tower to hang the flag of the republic. It would rise higher than Notre Dame, which was the desire—that the immoral republic would be above the Church. Around the same time, a new ba silica began to be built, the Church of the Sacred Heart. The site chosen for the church was on the highest hill in Paris. Upon its completion, Adoration of Jesus within the Basilica was instituted and has taken place for over 100 years continuously to this day. Those who carried the spirit of humanism purposely built the Eiffel Tower to rise above the Church. Jesus, in the Blessed Sacrament, should be King over the city, but for most, He is forgotten and the people continue to reject Him.

When one looks at France today, it is obvious that secular humanism is the god of many and flourishes. The most important thing for the security of liberty in villages and the self-governing of communities in the pursuit of happiness and freedom is the heart set upon Christian principles that is aided in its formation through the Church and its buildings. If you lose sight of this principle, if you lose sight of Whose house it is, then civil buildings become the source of your liberty. Not accepting this principle you will lose the **protection** of the unalienable rights of life, liberty and the pursuit of happiness. Therefore, nullification of all former laws and starting over, enacting laws to be bonded to the principles of Christianity along with prayer is the only cure for our land. Again, an applicable quote to the point, Jefferson said:

> *"When once a republic is corrupted, there is no possibility of remedying any of the growing evils but by removing the corruption and RESTOR-ING ITS LOST PRINCIPLES; every other correction is either useless or a new evil."*[407]

This will be the beginning of breaking from the shackles of the federalization of towns; towns which have enslaved themselves to godlessness for money. Federal funds passed to state funds, passed to counties, passed to cities and towns has resulted in a suffering producing the bad fruit of crime, brokenness, and no peaceable living. These federalized local places have become in and of themselves promoters and protectors of wickedness. It must be recognized that what local, state, and federal governments do in propagating wickedness, is still under God's Law, not just civil law, and will incur the judgement and wrath of God. Founding father, George Mason, said:

> *"As nations cannot be rewarded or punished in the next world, they must be in this. By an inevitable chain of causes and effects, Providence punishes national sins by national calamities."*[408]

It, therefore, is not just man that can break the laws of God, but governments also are guilty. Radical environmental policies and laws adopted through regulations, etc., have taken away citizen's rights to their own private property through the local and federal government's support. This is a violation of the Eighth Commandment—"Thou shalt not covet thy neighbor's goods." Just because a council of elected officials pass an ordinance saying it is now law, does not mean it is a valid law. For example, a law saying that the government may establish green areas, severely restricting the use of property against the will of the citizens who own that land, or to even take the land away unconstitutionally in an abuse of eminent domain,* does

* Eminent domain means a right of a government to take private property for public use. Because of this power, officials **regularly abuse** such powers and are in violation of at least one of the Ten Commandments, thou shall not covet thy neighbors goods. Officials, when they vote for such illicit things, such as buying below value or condemning private property to give over to private development are thieves; corrupt men in suits.

not give immunity from the consequences of breaking this Commandment. Consequences of sin show up in several ways. It contributes to why we have the deterioration of societies in cities across the land. Not only is this coveting a neighbor's authority to decide how to use his own property, **it is stealing**. Judge Janice Brown, in an eminent domain case, in her dissenting decision, caustically came out on the side of truth and God's Law. She stated:

> *"Once again a majority of this court has proved that if enough people get together and act in concert, they can take something and not pay for it... But theft is still theft. Theft is theft even when government approves of thievery... Turning a democracy (a republic) into a kleptocracy* does not enhance the stature of thieves; it only diminishes the legitimacy of government."*[409]

Justice Brown's use of the world "kleptocracy" is actually inferring that in this situation the taking of land is no different than being a "kleptomaniac," a neurotic that is overcome with persistent impulses to steal. Even burdensome restrictions forcing home and land owners to comply to oppressive regulations put in place by Agenda 21 Sustainable Development is a dis-

---

* In addition, do not be deceived by what federalized city councils and federalized county boards call 'redevelopment.' It is a nice name for eminent domain.

guise for stealing or coveting a neighbor's goods. The purpose of these regulations, in the words of the zoning ordinances themselves, is to make it so costly as to discourage even the building of an addition onto a house. Or in the case of land improvement, it forces the owner to develop where the federalized cities or counties want them to develop. This is called Smart Growth. But it is still stealing because owners are required to spend large sums of money as a penalty to build where they desire on their own property. But, if instead they build where Smart Growth zoning ordinances designate for them to, they are "rewarded" with only having to pay small fees. Many have to sell the land they purchased for their homestead because of built in high cost fees and costly commercial development forces them to go where the incentive of lower costs makes their choice for them. This is exactly what Smart Growth was designed to do. This is raw theft. They call this and spell it out as Smart Growth but in the reality of stealing it should be spelled satan's **G**rowth.

If you research it you will see these concentrated population zoning areas that people are being forced into are called "infill" zones. Because these areas are more concentrated with people, there is more crime and other problems that are grown with Smart Growth.

State, county and city officials who pass these policies and enforce them through regulations often are not aware of how they are being used. However, if one contemplates these actions and ordinances, it will become clear it is tyranny over the citizens. This tyranny does not originate with the states, counties or cities rather, it originates through the federal government which for decades now, has been influenced by international*ism* and transferred, through internationali*zation* of the federal government and its bureaucracy to the local government, to the citizens.

The simplest definition of internationalization is *"to make international; to place under international control."* In terms of this writing, we would define this as the action of any group acting internationally to influence by pressuring nations to conform to their ideologies and agendas. This is done through a system of control where regulations, laws, treaties and penalties are utilized to force the nations to comply, which forces the states to comply, down to the local governing bodies. Everything dealing with human life is brought under the management of internationalization and their ideologies. Internationalization is not about nations cooperating with each other, as internationalism is defined, but rather is about control and forcing nations to comply with a central, international agenda. This happens through the compliance of the states when they agree to federal mandates in exchange for funds from the federal government which are then passed down from the state to the counties, to the cities. This is how the federal government has found its way not only in our backyards but in our very homes, telling you what kind of light bulb you can use and what kind of toilet you can have, etc. The growing danger today is that the evil brought in through internationalization of our federal government has now taken possession of it spreading federalization, making a bigger demon which will be brought to your door steps in the form of localization. Smart Growth, Agenda 21 is from the United Nations. Just think for a moment on the values that Obama and the 'powers that be' hold. These values, through internationalization, though federalization, and now through localization are being placed in our schools, brought into our neighborhoods, and now even under the roofs of our homes.

CHAPTER FORTY-ONE

PART II—THE REVOLUTION

New Villages not by a Method but by Prayer

Part II—the Revolution of <u>They Fired the First Shot 2012</u>_{TM} is about locating small village towns already in existence but with a minimum population and declaring them Constitutional Christian principled village hamlets. These village towns are to be fortified by continual active prayer, and re-founded upon the indissoluble bond of civil government to the principles of Christianity. This is stated with no apology or practice of Quietism. These principles are founded upon the teaching and witness of Christ and the beginning Church. If you want to attempt any rebirth, any renewal and be detached from God, your efforts are destined and doomed to failure. Time for theories is over. The future is only given for those who accept truth. The Constitution and prayer will be their foundation formed out of Christian principles, with a Declaration of Independence away from federalization. In many cases these small village communities are close enough

to larger cities making it possible for people to re-lo-
cate there and have a suitable distance and time frame
to go back and forth from work while at the same time
being able to build an infrastructure in the new community for a more agrarian way of life. With prayer, it
will evolve into a new way of life. If you already live
in a small, low populated town, you can start a Constitutional Small Prayer Group and immediately enter
into a period of prayer to establish a Constitutional
village following the steps as shown in the next pages.
If this does not describe your situation, then look to
establish a Constitutional Small Prayer Group with
just a few families, or through a large church where
one can solicit 5, 10, 15, or 20 families who may feel a
calling through prayer to relocate, or to begin a village.
A whole church, with its pastor, can even relocate or
found your own village and have its own "Early American Colony." This will, of course, scare and horrify the
devils, but you will know who they are when they howl
in opposition to such a move. A Constitutional praying
village can be established in just a matter of months,
followed by elections and nullifications. A re-ordered
town based in a moral republic, independent of federalization will give protection over your life, liberty
and the pursuit of happiness. Your world in your self-
governing town can be defederalized, re-moralized and

with your heart set out for Christ, be healed which in turn means being blessed. You can, in a matter of a few months time, be dwelling in a Constitutional praying village, rooted in principles to God's laws to bring you and the village into compliance of God's requirement to heal our land.

Will there be resistance? When God's people are on the move towards righteousness and God is ready to heal their land, expect satan to work to block it in every way. It does not matter what demons howl about it. Either you believe God's Scripture from 2 Chronicles 7:14, *"If my people who are called by my name..."* or you don't. If you set out to accomplish in your life what He instructs you to do, then you trust that He will make a way for what He promised to happen, through His Word. If you do not, nothing changes. If you are obedient to His inspirations and you change your life, it must then reflect into the town ordinances of the village God has given you and your group. You then, through being tried by fire and purification, will begin to experience God's blessings of being healed and you will experience a new springtime for your new Constitutional small prayer group village community. Yes, the whole of hell will bring forces of tremendous resistance against you but you are not asking hell's permission.

You are asking forgiveness and seeking repentance for God to heal you and your land. There then must be a correlation of the Christian principles you have established in your life to be reflected in the laws of your village. However, when man is living God's laws there is a minimal need for civil law. It is important not to have a lot of laws. Why? Because every law is a restriction of man's freedom. God gave man Ten Commandments. If those ten laws are lived there will be few other laws we need. A supporter of Caritas spoke truth in a quote he sent in, spoken by one of our founding fathers, with a small alteration:

"If Men be Saints, no government be necessary."

When you begin meeting with others, through the Constitutional Small Prayer Groups, and then begin establishing the broader group, you will, through prayer, begin to yearn for community, a village type of life. **This will not happen by following a method in a legalistic way.** Not through human strength, but in a spirit of prayer of the heart, God will lead you through the method. Many people are already on this path after praying for years. They have been waiting for the next steps to be revealed as to how these villages can begin to form after following the way of life shown through Our Lady's messages, through the Community of Caritas, a small village. This can be done in several ways. The shortest path is to identify an already small incorporated town in an area you and your group could locate to and establish your homes. Many of these towns have a very small population. The numbers you bring into this town will give you the ability to establish the civil government of the town upon the Declaration and Constitution through prayer. You are not going to a town to take over, though it may be a dead or dying town. You are going to birth anew a flourishing village not for growth and expansion, but for a way of life for the young, middle-aged and old alike. Many yearn for a sane yesterday. It can be had in a few tomorrow's time.

But what about the non-believer or atheist who may be a resident of the existing town? "Whatta bout 'em?" Does he object to civil government principles being based on Judeo/Christian principles?

- Does he not want his spouse to commit adultery? — Thou shalt not commit adultery.

- Does he not want to be murdered? — Thou shalt not kill.

- Does he not want his car stolen out of his driveway? — Thou shalt not steal.

- Does he not want to live in peace? — Thou shalt love thy neighbor as thyself.

- Does he not want his child's respect? — Thou shalt honor thy father and thy mother.

You get the point!

Ask the question, does an atheist fare better in quality of life and liberty under a Christian principled society or not? Six decades or so ago, a non-believer <u>wanted</u> to live within a Christian society and appreciated the fruits of such a society. Today, as we move more toward atheism, you are not even safe in a movie theater in Colorado.* It is simple. God blesses what is of God. God does not bless what is not of Him. Through Constitutional Small Prayer Groups, your village will become a fortress with the might and blessing of God. There is no political correctness offered here. We either change into Constitutional praying villages, connecting their laws to God's statutes, or we go to the coliseum. We have followed the devil's instructions too long. **It is the hour to follow God and His statutes, first, in our hearts, through tears of repentance, fasting, and supplication and then through your Constitutional Small Prayer Group and broader group or other struc-**

---

* Around midnight, on July 20, 2012, in a Colorado movie theater, a young man went on a shooting rampage, killing 12 people.

ture. Select one village out of more than 'six thousand' village towns shown across the United States of America (State Map section). If you reside in one of these, begin your Constitutional Small Prayer Group and set out to establish your village on Christian principles and the Constitution.

One note of caution. One must be very prudent in these beginning steps. Many people, even good people, will be suspect and ruffled about new people coming into "their" village or town. The human condition grows to be content and complacent of its situation and will often choose to put up with a bad situation rather than having someone come in who can make things better. Remember, the Jews were ready to go back and be slaves in Egypt because the challenges of where God was leading them was too high a price. One must be very prudent and thoughtful, fortified with prayer, penance, fasting and peace before any attempt should be made to head towards a town to lead it towards a better way to live. If you do not take these initial steps with a lot of prayer and be unassuming, you will be stopped. satan will incite good people against your efforts. As Constitutional Small Prayer Group members, no matter what, you are going to have problems. Don't make them bigger through imprudence. But do not be so overly prudent that you stop yourself from taking steps. Just be prayerfully calculated. The Bible explains it this way, ***"Be wise as serpents and innocent as doves."*** Matt 10:16

Once Constitutional praying villages are formed and newly created, or can be made so by already living in one of the ones listed under the State maps, what has begun to grow in your hearts in holiness and obedience will then manifest into the civil laws of your village. If you heed God's Commandments, Deuteronomy 11:11-15 states:

> ***"The land into which you are crossing for conquest is a land of hills and valleys that drinks in rain from the heavens, a land which the Lord, your God looks after; his eyes are upon it continually from the beginning of the year to the end. If, then, you truly heed my commandments which I enjoin on you today, loving and serving the Lord, your God, with all your heart and all your soul, I will give the seasonal rain to your land, the early rain and the late rain, that you may have your grain, wine and oil to gather in; and I will bring forth grass in your fields for your animals. Thus you may eat your fill."***

But if you cross over into the land and do not act in your town to change the laws* to heed God's Commandments, Deuteronomy continues saying:

> *"But be careful lest your heart be so lured away that you serve other gods and worship them. For then the wrath of the Lord will flare up against you and he will close up the heavens, so that no rain will fall, and the soil will not yield its crops, and you will soon perish from the good land he is giving you."*

If your heart is thumping fast in excitement on when and how to form a village, we will be hosting the first of several "How to Begin a Constitutional Praying Village" Conference, December 6–7, 2012. These villages can evolve from Constitutional Small Prayer Groups. Information will be given at the end of the book.

---

* There are many unbiblical laws against God's Commandments, not only the healthcare mandates but many others such as what has been mentioned already under Agenda 21's environmental Smart Growth laws, unnatural laws and laws against nature. Just as the Israelites purified themselves of idols across Israel so must one's lands be purified of these laws against God's Commandments.

What To Do For Now?

Forget the Supreme Court, the President's Executive Orders, and other actions of the federal government. They have skipped centuries of lawful and common law precedence and have cited false and contrived precedences for instituting unconstitutional laws. They have created a lineage of fake precedents of only a few decades old, all of which must be nullified, first on a town level, so to turn the tide against wickedness, otherwise we perish. We can only be healed if we repent, live God's Law, and re-establish our laws on the truths of the Ten Commandments.

Following is a relief scene carved in stone, showing Moses holding the Ten Commandments before the people. This relief is found at the step entrance to the United States Supreme Court building showing the tablets Moses is holding, the Ten Commandments, as the central and supreme basis of all western laws through its history. This image, being the center piece of law, speaks to the fact that all laws emanating from underneath this roof must be derived from Divine Law and is never to be in conflict with laws of nature's God, or God's statutes, namely His Ten Commandments. When we as a people allow laws to be made that are contrary to the truths contained in the Ten Commandments we come under judgement and see our land grow sicker and sicker and sicker still, until we come back to God and His laws. Or otherwise we will be destroyed by our own making. How does this work? Deuteronomy 11 states how it works:

Deuteronomy 11:26-29, 31-32

> *"I set before you here, this day, a blessing and a curse: a blessing for obeying the Commandments of the Lord, your God, which I enjoin on you today; a curse if you do not obey the Commandments of the Lord, your God, but turn aside from the way I ordain for you today, to follow other gods, whom you have not known. When the Lord, your God, brings you into the land which you are to enter and occupy, then you shall pronounce the blessing...For you are about to cross...to enter and occupy the land which the Lord, your God, is giving you. When therefore, you take possession of it and settle there, be careful to observe all the statutes and decrees that I set before you today."*

Think a few moments on the above biblical passage and the United States Supreme Court relief, of Moses and the Ten Commandments of why we must pray and decisively come back to God's Laws in order to cross over and to dwell in a blessed and healed land.

CHAPTER FORTY-TWO

PART II—THE REVOLUTION

Change What is immediately at Hand

In meditating on Moses and the Ten Commandments as the center of law, as shown our U.S. Supreme Court Building, do not get puffed-up, thinking we have the high ground and the wicked do not. They, being wicked, are the grade we received on the test we failed because of not convicting them by our lives. Rather, be humble for it is we, as Christians, who are to blame for what it is we suffer. Not through pride, not through arrogance, but through humility, and a solid, committed, firm decision you can, in less than a year, change the world that surrounds you in your little Constitutional Small Prayer Group birthed village. You can go back to the United States of America as our fathers dreamed of it and founded it upon the principles of Jesus Christ. As Our Lady said:

August 25, 1994

"...pray...that the dream that your fathers had may be fulfilled..."

Do not focus on changing the nation. Focus on changing that which is immediately at hand that affects your daily comings and goings of your life. Pray, be in unity. God will bring you together through a Constitutional Small Prayer Group, turning it into a community of liberty—living and thriving by God's blessing. Consecrate it to Our Lady that She may guide it, make it holy and give it to Her Son. The prayer group is to evolve into a community and is to turn into a small village. These villages are to root across America, bringing healing to the nation. When the United States is healed, the whole world will be led by the United States to healing. When America's exceptionalism is spoken of, this is not the same things as nationalism. America's exceptionalism is the recognition that no other nation in the world has been blessed as we have been. America's exceptionalism becomes complete when we understand we must pass this blessing on to the other nations of the world. Being blessed, we are to share this blessing, that by our recognition of God's favors, other nations may hope for the same. Is this not why immigrants continuously have come to America in fulfillment of their dream for freedom? Is this not what has kept political prisoners alive, while being tortured in prison, with hope for their beloved fatherland, while also claiming America as their second fatherland? Yes, America's exceptionalism is the recognition, "God has shed His grace on thee," and we are to spread the blessings of life, liberty, and the pursuit of happiness to all other lands. As Patroness of our nation, Our Lady wants us to realize this grace from Her Son.

One may think this is all about Mary. But, Mary is all about Jesus. No one ever had in this life more intimacy with Jesus than Mary. No one in Heaven will experience the intimacy with Jesus as Mary. For Jesus will not be excelled in living the commandment to honor His Mother and Father—Mary, the Mother, God the Father. It is simple, for those who love and keep the commandments, to understand how God could honor His Mother, sending Her to the Earth a second time, in preparation for His coming a Second time. Through Her, we had Him and through Her we will have Him again. It is the decision of God Himself:

November 2, 2009

> **"...Also today I am among you to point you
> to the way that will help you to come to know
> God's love, the love of God Who permitted you**

to call Him Father and to perceive Him as Father...Invoke the Father, He is waiting for you. Come back to Him. I am with you because He, in His mercy, sends me..."

We have wandered in the desert since June, 1981, when the Virgin Mary first appeared in Medjugorje, in what was then Yugoslavia. She told the people, "You have forgotten God." When we begin to draw back to Him, He will respond. God wants us to find the Promised Land. No one understood what was playing out in Medjugorje in those beginning months and years of the apparitions because there was little physical reality to give evidence of what was happening.

Our Lady has been pointing out a way of life through Her messages. There has been constant and repeated mocking and persecution of the initiatives of spreading this way of Her messages, as applied to all facets of life, especially over the last few years. Those who now are following this direction are coming to understand it more and more, helped along by the physical deterioration of our society that Our Lady foretold. These physical realities, like the crippled economy, genetic modifications of all life—plants, animals and humans, among other dangerous scientific advancements promoting the culture of death, the birth of a redirectioned family life consisting of everything from normalization of abominables to normalizing dysfunctional families, etc., now give evidence of why Our Lady was sent and has stayed for so long. These realities were hidden in prophecy in Our Lady's messages. But, so also was the remedy to counter the advancement of the culture of death by reestablishing the culture of life. Yet, how to do this could not be seen except for whom Our Lady wished to show it to, and She did so in order to have Her messages put into a practical form so that they could be lived. Her messages were transformed into a way of life, and a witness was created for those who follow this way, thereby, Our Lady's children could begin to understand by that witness of what to do.

What could not be seen by Our Lady's children is now manifesting, aided by physical evidence by the world's direction which is opening the eyes more fully of many of those who have followed this direction. Life is going to change. Where do you want to be spiritually and where do you want to be physically when events unfold? We are in great debt of the wages of decades of sin. Embedded sins give way to embedded ordained consequences. We cannot hope to avoid a correction, but we can hope to mitigate it by changing life's direction now. We must become a holy people and we must now cross over into Constitutional prayer based small villages across the land, a land promised to all those who will keep God's statutes without compromise or rationalization. Joshua gathered and addressed the Israelites:

Joshua 24:2, 11-13

> *"Thus says the Lord the God of Israel:*
>
> *"Once you crossed the Jordon...the men of Jericho fought against you...I sent the hornets ahead of you which drove them out of the way, it was <u>not your sword or your bow.</u>"*

It will not be **by our sword or by our bow**. It is through Jesus and Jesus alone that we, as Christians, will have a future, as Our Lady has said repeatedly of Jesus in Her apparitions. What good are armaments of **"swords and bows,"** if there is not a holy way of life established? It is a holy way of life more than armaments that protect us. This is not saying not to have armaments. Where one is armed, that area is avoided by marauders and those of criminal intent. In Switzerland, every male receives training, serves one or two years in the military, and then is required to keep their gun and ammunition when they go home. They are able to maintain peace and order in their own towns. Because of this, Switzerland has a very low crime rate. Its citizens are its protectors. On May 1, 1982, the city of Kennesaw, Georgia *"unanimously passed a law requiring 'every head of household to maintain a firearm together with ammunition.'"*[410] Since the passage of this law, Kennesaw has the lowest crime rate in the nation for a city its size (35,000). They have a *"virtually non-existent murder rate."* [411] Tim Brown in his article, "Mandated Gun Ownership: A Tale of Two Cities," stated:

> *"There were three murders in 2010 committed by the same man in what is described as a 'school safety zone'* (banning guns), *an area extending 1,000 feet from any school, including adult colleges and technical schools. This means that even though Kennesaw has the most* (lenient) *gun laws in the United States, employees at the facility where the murders were committed could not have a gun on the premises."*[412]

Tim Brown continues that Kennesaw is:

> *"one of Family Circle's '10 best towns for families' where the rights of individuals protecting themselves with a firearm are encouraged and even mandated."*[413]

Kennesaw promotes the Second Amendment. They made a little Switzerland where its citizens are peace officers. Crime has literally stopped, dropping to just shy of a 90% decrease.[414] Yet, still our first reliance is not on armaments, rather, our first reliance is upon God's protection by living a holy way of life. However, a moral way of life is not just going to happen without difficulty. When you decide to establish a holy way of life, you can count on efforts to stymie or stop your establishing this way of life, even confrontation, but if you hold fast to living God's statutes, you will experience what Joshua expressed when he continued to address the Israelites:

Joshua 24: 13-14:   Thus says the Lord...

> *"I gave you a land which you had not tilled and cities which you had not built, to dwell in; you have eaten of vineyards and olive groves which you did not plant. Now, therefore, fear the Lord and serve him completely and sincerely."*

How does Joshua tell the Israelites to serve God completely and sincerely? Joshua says to God's people:

Joshua 24:14-15

> *"Cast out the gods...and serve the Lord. If it does not please you to serve the Lord, decide today whom you will serve..."*

Joshua then makes **his declaration of independence** away from the tyranny of many idols the Israelites were following, as our founding fathers made their Declaration of Independence from the tyranny that was bringing this land of the colonies to ruin. He states:

Joshua 24:15

"As for me and my household, we will serve the Lord."

To save our land, to find a way out of wandering through the desert, to enter the Promised Land, we must identify what and why tyranny has strengthened its hold over us. Just as the Israelites, we must be purified, casting out all gods.

What are the gods in your life? What do you spend more time occupied with that prevents your thoughts from being upon God? Are there not competing gods with God in your life? What dictates and directs your day? How do the minutes of your day pass? Is it with God or is it with your god? What do you do within your world that is without value, that takes away from your time each day for praying, reading Scripture, living out your Christian life, or just being able to live virtuously and in holiness? There are many things that one may not even recognize as gods in one's life because satan has disguised them. They are disguised by satan to make you think they are tools to help you, yet they have an addictive hold on your heart and intellect and hold the first place in your life — a place that is to be reserved only for God.

The members of the Church, in a world filled with little gods, have forsaken Christ without even believing or realizing they have done so. So we respond, as the people did to Joshua.

The people responded back to Joshua:

Joshua 24:16–18

> *"Far be it from us to forsake the Lord for the service of other gods...for the Lord God, who brought us...out of the state of slavery...Therefore, we also will serve the Lord for He is our God."*

Joshua then tells the Israelites that it will not be easy to serve God because stained and imprinted in their mentalities and made weak by following false gods, they may not be able to do what God expects. Joshua responds to their statement of *"we will not forsake God,"* with a warning:

Joshua 24:19–20

> *"You may not be able to serve the Lord for He is a Holy God; He is a jealous God who will not forgive your transgressions or your sins if after the good He has done for you, you forsake the Lord and serve strange gods, He will do evil to you and destroy you."*

Joshua knew the people, as the above Scripture states, **"might not be able to,"** because fidelity to God's service is not easy. The people who take such solemn obligations personally must be ever-vigilant against human weakness.

Even with this warning, the people then answered Joshua:

Joshua 24:21

> *"We will still serve the Lord."*

At this point, Joshua resigned himself to their wish and responded, that they are their own witnesses and tells them:

Joshua 24:23

> *"Now, therefore, put away the strange gods that are among you and turn your heart to the Lord, the God of Israel."*

Joshua then made a renewal of the Covenant with the people's promise to forsake idols and obey God.

Joshua 24:25–27

> *"So Joshua made a covenant with the people that day and made statutes and ordinances for them at Shechem, which he recorded in the book of the Law of God. <u>Then he took a large stone and set it up there under the oak [tree] that was in the sanctuary of the Lord.</u> And Joshua said to all the people, '<u>This stone</u> shall be our witness <u>for it has heard all the words which the Lord spoke to us.</u> It shall be a witness against you, should you wish to deny your God."*

Before the last presidential election in 2008, Medjugorje visionary Marija came to Caritas for a gathering of "we the people" to give the United States of America to Our Lady in consecration to Her on the birthday of our nation. This was repeated in July 2009, in Our Lady's presence again. Because of the critical hour we find ourselves in, Marija returned this year, July, 2012, for a third reconsecration of the United States. On July 3, 2012, the eve of our nation's birth, Our Lady appeared and responded to the plea of the people to intercede to Her Son Jesus, to heal our nation. Christ's Mother said during the apparition:

"Form and make prayers groups through which we will pray for your healing and the healing of this nation to draw closer to God and to Me."

The stone of Our Lady's statue under the pine tree, stands as witness of what these stones have heard. They testify to what has happened originally there since 1988. Our Lady, in that time, indicated to Marija for a Community to be established. It began with a prayer group within a family, with love for our homeland and the liberty it was founded upon, before the 1988 apparitions. It later broadened to a community. Our Lady brought into being a community that was birthed through the family prayer group. Through prayer and fasting, the small family prayer group began identifying and ridding itself of idols it did not even realize were idols.

Later, following the witness, the newly formed Community was led, following the messages, in a direction and walk that inspired them to embrace a new way of life shown by God. The Community was led with prayer, fasting, sacrifice, and the resulting purifying fire of tribulation and became: TV free, home computer free, cell phone free and newspaper free. This purging included much music, books and magazines as well. It was a purifying of hearts and the heart of the home, where all the gods in this world of today's home steal the place that should be reserved for God alone. Because these things have taken first place in man's life, they hold man's heart close to its idolism. The Community of Caritas is a sign of a walk with God, where the Virgin Mary, Our Lady, appeared in the family bedroom* of a home and a nearby field. The home testifies through Our Lady's words and actions, that holy families make up holy villages, which make up holy nations. Man must turn away from the gods holding him sway, entertaining him with glitter, captivating his interests so that there is little time or interest for God. As Joshua renewed the covenant with God's people and placed a large stone under a great tree as testimony and witness to that covenant, Our Lady came with words, appearing under a great tree to renew the covenant and to

---

* At these two sites, over the past nearly 25 years, there have been 167 apparitions of the Virgin Mary to Medjugorje visionary Marija Lunetti. The primary site of the apparitions has been in the Bedroom of a "beloved home," with 134 apparitions in this room, which is the heart of a group called the Caritas Community, a community similar to the first Christian communities 2,000 years ago. The Field was consecrated to Our Lady for the conversion of our nation. The two sites were connected in that the Bedroom represents the family, "the home," and the Field, our nation. We cannot hope to heal our nation without first healing the family home. Our Lady has come to convert and heal individuals. Individuals make up families. In turn, converted and healed families bring peace to nations, thereby, bringing peace to the world.

give instruction of how to return our land back to God. Under that tree is a stone altar and a stone statue. The statue sits upon a pile of stone rocks that marks a spot. This was the site of Our Lady's first apparition in the Field, November 24, 1988. It was a day Our Lady chose to appear on this spot, the only day designated specifically and officially by the United States to give thanksgiving to God—Thanksgiving Day. Our Lady appeared there to call our nation back to its Christian roots. On that day part of what Our Lady said was:

"...I am here to help you..." Nov. 24, 1988

From that first apparition in the Field, Our Lady brought forth what happened under this tree to fruition 24 years later on July 3, 2012.

- After leading us to turn away from idols and false gods;

- On the eve of our nation's birthday, at 10:00 at night;

- Seconds after we had just re-consecrated the United States of America to Our Lady;

Marija and the stones alone heard and gave testimony to 3000 counties across our nation, and to the whole world, what to do to re-establish with God His covenant with His people. What blossomed into words that holy night, the Eve of the 4th of July, 2012, was a Christmas hope to birth and receive Holy Jesus back into our hearts, into our homes, into our villages and throughout **"this nation,"** to heal us. When we are healed, our nation will then lead the whole world back to the only One who can save it—Our Lord Jesus Christ. The very stones shout out the words of Our Lady after hearing them spoken beneath the tree at the place, as Joshua says **"in the sanctuary of the Lord,"** and Our Lady says, July 3, 2012, from Her heart to ours in **"this sanctuary of the Lord,"** the Bedroom and the Field:

**"Form and make prayer groups
through which we will pray for your healing and the
healing of this nation
to draw closer to God and to Me."**

July 3, 2012

CHAPTER FORTY-THREE

PART II—THE REVOLUTION

Prophetically New Villages Springing Up Across the Land

You now have everything you need to know to go into the ambush. Yet, still there is something more to strengthen your faith. Though you may have read the following in previous writings, do not skip it, as it is vital to understanding the points about it. It was re ported, appearing in the National Tribune, Vol. 4, #12 in December 1880, and was told by Anthony Sherman in 1859 to Wesley Bradshaw.

George Washington was in his tent at Valley Forge and had ordered his aide not to disturb him. Suddenly, before him appeared a woman of such beauty he could not describe. He also saw a distinctly different being which was clearly an angel. He felt he was in some kind of state he had never experienced. The beautiful woman showed George Washington three perils and their outcome that would assail the United States of America on its own land. The first was the American Revolution. The second was the Civil War. And the third has yet to be fulfilled. Are we in the midst of it coming true now? Was the most beautiful woman the Virgin Mary? The publishing of this article in 1880 did not at that time lend itself to fantasy. The date, just after the prophesied second peril had come, and the character involved, George Washington, alone gives credibility to this event. A portion of Washington's vision is given here to shed light on the republic and villages springing forth across the land in defeating its enemy. The third and worst peril will be the attacking of the very foundation of the United States. The reporter, Wesley Bradshaw, began speaking of his interview:

> *"The last time I saw Anthony Sherman was on the Fourth of July, 1859, in Independence Square. He was then ninety-nine years old, and becoming feeble. But though so old, his dreaming eyes rekindled as he gazed up Independence Hall, which he came to visit once more.*

> *"Let us go into the hall," he said. "I want to tell you an incident in Washington's life—one which no one alive knows except myself; and, if you live, you will before long, see it verified.*

"From the opening of the Revolution we experienced all phases of fortune, now good and now ill, one time victorious and another time conquered. The darkest period we had, I think, was when Washington, after several reverses, retreated to Valley Forge, where he resolved to pass the winter of 1777. Ah! I have often seen the tears course down our dear commander's careworn cheeks, as he would be conversing with confidential officers about the condition of his poor soldiers. You have doubtless heard the story of Washington's going to the thicket to pray. Well, it was not only true, but he used often to pray in secret for aid and comfort from God, the interposition of whose Divine Providence brought us safely through the darkest days of tribulation.

"One day—I remember it well—the chilly wind whistled through the leafless trees, though the sky was cloudless and the sun shone brightly. He remained in his quarters nearly all afternoon alone. When he came out I noticed that his face was a shade paler than usual, and there seemed to be something on his mind of more than ordinary importance. Returning just after dark, he dispatched an orderly to the quarters of an of-

ficer, who was presently in attendance. After a preliminary conversation of about half an hour, Washington, gazing upon his companion with that strange look of dignity which he alone could command, said:

'I do not know whether it is owing to the anxiety of my mind, or what, but this afternoon, as I was sitting at this table engaged in preparing a dispatch, something seemed to disturb me. Looking up, I saw standing opposite a singularly beautiful female. So astonished was I, for I had given strict orders not to be disturbed, that it was some moments before I found language to inquire the purpose of her presence.

'A second, a third, even a fourth time did I repeat my question but received no answer from my mysterious visitor, except a slight raising of her eyes. By this time I felt strange sensations spreading through me. I would have risen, but the riveted gaze of the being before me rendered volition impossible. I essayed once more to address her, but my tongue had become useless. Even thought itself had become paralyzed. A new influence, mysterious, potent, irresistible, took possession of me. All I could do was to gaze steadily, vacantly

at my unknown visitor. Gradually the surrounding atmosphere filled with sensations and grew luminous. Everything about me seemed to rarefy, the mysterious visitor herself becoming more airy and yet more distinct to my sight than before. I now began to feel as one dying, or rather to experience the sensation which I have sometimes imagined accompanies dissolution. I did not think, I did not reason, I did not move. All, alike, were impossible. I was conscious only of gazing fixedly, vacantly, at my companion.

'Presently I heard a voice say, 'Son of the Republic, look and learn!'[415]

The beautiful woman then showed Washington the first two perils,[*] the American Revolution and the Civil War. The following describes the third and worst peril:

'Then my eyes beheld a fearful scene: from each of these countries arose thick black clouds that were soon joined into one. And throughout this mass there gleamed a bright Red Light, by which I saw hordes of armed men, who, moving with the cloud, marched by land and sailed by sea to

---

[*] See "American History You Never Learned." Download free on mej. com or see Appendix III for the two perils which were edited out of this section.

America; which country was enveloped in the volume of cloud.

'And I saw dimly these vast armies devastate the whole country and burn the villages, towns, and cities that I beheld springing up (after the first peril was over).

'As my ears listened to the thundering of the cannon, the clashing of swords, and the shouts and cries of millions in mortal combat, I again heard the mysterious voice say, 'Son of the Republic, look and learn.' As the voice ceased, the shadowy figure of the angel, for the last time, dipped water from the ocean and sprinkled it upon America. Instantly the dark cloud rolled back, together with the armies it had brought, leaving the inhabitants of the land victorious.[416]

Washington continues:

'Once more I beheld villages, towns and cities springing up where I had seen them before; *while the bright angel, planting the Azure Standard he had brought in the midst of them, cried in a loud voice, 'While the stars remain and the heavens send down dew upon the earth, so long shall the Union last.' And taking from her brow* *the crown on which was blazoned the word, 'Union,' she placed it upon the Standard, while people kneeling down, said, Amen.*

'The scene instantly began to fade away, and I saw nothing but the rising curling vapor I had at first beheld. This also disappeared, and I found myself once more gazing upon the mysterious visitor, the beautiful female, who said, 'Son of the Republic, what you have seen is thus interpreted. Three great perils will come upon the Republic. The most fearful is the third, but the whole world united shall not prevail against her. __Let every child of the Republic learn to live for God, his land, and the Union.__' With these words the angel vanished from my sight.'

"Such, my friend," concluded the narrator, "were the very words I heard from Washington's own lips; and America will do well to profit by them."[417]

A Sign in the Beginning

A second major event to strengthen your faith, to encourage you to begin your steps, is an event that happened in Medjugorje in the beginning days which incredibly and prophetically speaks to us today. Again, though you may have read, in a previous writing, what follows, it is still important to read this in the context of what has already been revealed.

> In Medjugorje, sometime in the beginning days, many saw a strange occurrence on Cross Mountain, during the daytime.* Some even saw it from afar. One of those who witnessed it was Medjugorje visionary Marija's brother, Andrija. He said that he and others saw the whole of the sky over Cross Mountain, covered in what looked like a white veil, except one could see through it. Through the veil, they could see up in the sky a small church with four or five houses around it. The four or five houses were surrounded with green fields. Then there was another church with four or five houses around it, surrounded by green fields. And then another and another repeat of the scene. When Andrija was asked how many, he said hundreds of churches were surrounded the same way. How long did the vision last? Fifteen minutes. Did they just stay in the sky? No, the little village churches were descending to the earth

---

* A large cement cross was erected in 1933 on top of this mountain overlooking Medjugorje for the 1900th Anniversary of Christ's death and resurrection. In the beginning days of the Medjugorje apparitions, Our Lady would often appear there to the Medjugorje visionaries.

(on Cross Mountain) very slowly. Through
the years, Andrija was asked about this several
times, and what he thought it meant. He would
say, "It meant what I saw."

What did Marija's brother see? How should
we understand it? The Community of Caritas
is a prophetic community, a "prototype" of
what the future will look like. How can that
be said? The following is taken from the book
Words From Heaven₀.

December 13, 1988

*When Our Lady appeared, She conveyed to
Marija Her desire to start a community at the site.
Marija turned to the host in whose house she was
living and said to him immediately after the apparition, somehow it was indicated that,*

"Our Lady wants to start a community here."

*The husband and wife were deeply struck by
these words.*

The resulting Community of Caritas continues
to evolve in present time to show and point
the way for a future time. Our Lady, through
Marija's apparitions, has continually formed and

shaped Her community with Her words and actions, especially in Her apparitions when Marija stays in the home in the community in Alabama.

What Andrija, Marija's brother, saw was small villages in numbers where people could be community. [418]

George Washington seeing villages and towns springing up. Andrija, seeing many small villages—each made up of houses surrounding a church—were descending from the sky upon the land. All cannot be but an impulse for you to change your future. As you launch and "set out into the future":

–   already living in a listed village town or

–   searching your state or other states, or

–   to found your own village township with others,

...remember Our Lady's words of June 22, 2012:

"...decide for Jesus. Decide and set out together with Him into the future..."

They Fired the First Shot 2012 is a mandatory immediate second read. Do not deceive yourself that you grasped all that is written. You might think, "I got it," but once you get into your second read, you will see how much you did not grasp on the first read and that a third read is necessary. The Constitution in 2020 is hailed as their content book of study, their declaration book. They Fired the First Shot 2012 is your manual of understanding and direction to heal a nation through a Constitutional Small Prayer Group taking back, through Christian citizens, possession of federalized counties. They Fired the First Shot 2012 is the light of Christ's common sense, through the messages of the Virgin Mary who is leading the world back to Jesus Christ. The Constitution in 2020 is the anti-book. These two books are in direct opposition, each with an agenda. One is Biblical; one is anti-biblical. The middle ground is vaporizing. They Fired the First Shot 2012 is a book resulting from millions of prayers, through novenas and gatherings of prayer groups for over 25 years, not only through all 50 states, but many foreign countries as well. One must learn everything in it to possess wisdom for decisions today for your future and your children to have a land, sacred, holy and safe in peace to dwell in with liberty for the mor'all', not just the immoral.

New Communities
It is the Hour
Take Action

A Declaration of Independence

from

Federalization of Our States, Counties, Cities, Village Towns

and

Our Very Selves

Begin the Revolution

For years many have asked the question and told us, "We want to start a community, can you help us?" Here is the answer.

Take action:

For the five following "you cans:" Make a declaration of independence from federalization by transforming towns back into Constitutional village towns that are rooted and bonded indissolubly in law to the principles of Christianity and the Ten Commandments, incorporating traditional Judeo-Christian values. We do not have to rewrite a new declaration, we already have one. Its truth is what we must declare a return to. **To initiate:** Organize a reading through your C.S.P.G. of the original Declaration preceded with the words:

"A Declaration of Independence from Federalization of our States, Counties, Cities, Village Towns and Our Very Selves."

Add to the original reading, 2 Chr 7:14: *"If My people...* and a lot of prayers, like the Patriotic Rosary,* meditations and others prayers familiar to your faith.

---

* See Resource Listing for "The Patriotic Rosary," at the back of the book, beginning of page 831.

Do not read as a shallow formality, rather do so in the same spirit our Forefathers had. Prepare beforehand, with many weeks and months of prayer. You can contact Caritas of Birmingham for patriotic promotional materials.

The following are five steps to take for different approaches.

You can:

1. **Live in a Village:** If you are already living in a listed small village town (see page 729), form a Constitutional Small Prayer Group and discover what God's will is for your group. Make a declaration of independence from federalization of your town, its

> **Remember,** your Constitutional Praying Village, and a David, have the power to face down and nullify the healthcare laws, the National Defense Authorization Act, the Enemy Expatriation Act, the Executive Orders, induction of you or your children in the Civilian National Security Force—any unconstitutional act or action. **What is being declared and proclaimed to "we the people" is, the Davids have the might and authority to stand down the President of the United States, Congress, the Supreme Court, international ratified treaties, even all combined together, when unconstitutional.** Your village might need to raise a posse, but if your David calls for it, people from across the Nation will come to your aid. Be on guard against the efforts of those who will try to clip the wings of the Davids, namely through state legislators. Be ready to fight these efforts with all your might.

grounds, your homes and lands, businesses, churches
and schools. Explore solutions in <u>They Fired the
First Shot 2012</u>ₜₘ to return your village town back
to a Constitutional Christian principled foundation,
implemented through prayer and repentance. Apply nullification as number two below shows.

2. **Select A Village:** Form a Constitutional Small
    Prayer Group according to the guidelines and sug-
    gestions in <u>They Fired the First Shot 2012</u>ₜₘ. Begin
    prayerful research, if you are not already in a vil-
    lage, to select a village town. Or if you relocate to
    a small village, form a Constitutional Small Prayer
    Group in the village. Set out to transform and re-
    turn it to a Constitutional Christian principled foun-
    dation through nullification of all its current laws.
    Pass new laws with civil principles of government
    indissolubly bonded to principles of Christianity.
    Solidly set your village, through prayer and repen-
    tance, back upon those same Christian principles as
    also found in our Declaration of Independence and
    in the United States Constitution. Explore other
    solutions in the book to help you achieve and dis-
    cover what God's will is for your prayer group.

3. **Incorporate a Village:** Form a Constitutional Small
    Prayer Group, explore solutions found in <u>They</u>

Fired the First Shot 2012~TM~. Research state law to found and create a Constitutional new village town based upon the Constitution and the principles of Christianity, as the village's foundation. Implement this foundation with prayer and repentance. As with all these five listed **"you cans,"** sign a declaration of independence from federalization of your village and your very self. Carry everything through even if it takes years.

4. **Second Home in a Village:** Those who have the financial means, but cannot relocate at this moment can establish a second home, helping to foundation and transform a village town, by bringing back Constitutional principles based in Christian principles. Form a Constitutional Small Prayer Group according to the guidelines and suggestions in They Fired the First Shot 2012~TM~. Explore

> The goal of all five of the **"you cans"** is to establish a Constitutional new village town connecting in one indissoluble bond, principles of civil government to the principles of Christianity, as the village's foundation. Implement with prayer and repentance through the Constitutional Small Prayer Group. After the village comes into being, continue always to pray and be repentant to keep it strong and its people blessed.

other solutions in the book to help you achieve and discover what God's will is for your prayer group.

With this second home, or "fall back upon house,"
one could have the security of an agrarian life. By
changing one's mentality of what is an investment,
one will have the vision to see and understand that
an agriculturally based, subsistence living is an
investment for your future, surpassing in importance any other investment. Simply said, get your
food from your ground to your mouth. This is the
best security one can have when the economy and
infrastructure of a nation collapses. What better
investment could you have? The payback of your
investment will be a roof over your head,[*] food,
and protection with others who have shared values
and faith, and most importantly a strong community
prayer life. Do not believe protection is solely with
armaments. Protection is first through a way of life
based in no shame of putting God first in everything. Likewise, as with armaments, money will not
achieve a home, or a place of peace to live. Prayer,
repentance and living God's statutes achieves this
goal. Money can help establish it and armaments
can help protect it, but only through a life rooted
in principles of holiness will it bear the fruit of a
peaceable way of life. Holiness is simply doing

---

[*] See the book, It Ain't Gonna Happen[TM]. about why you must have no
debt and what to do for the future. See resource page 831.

God's will in everything in your life. As to money,
when, what many feel in the heart begins to happen,
what good is a lot of investments? You will not be
able to eat money. Use it now that God may bless it
into the fruit of helping to achieve one of these five
listed **"you cans"** for yourself and others.

5. **Secede:** Different neighborhoods and or regional
   areas can secede from the large cities and form
   their own self-governing Constitutional Christian
   principled villages. Implement with prayer and
   repentance. Begin a Constitutional Small Prayer
   Group and explore solutions found in <u>They Fired
   the First Shot 2012</u>_{TM}. Research state laws to find
   out how to secede. Accept no obstacles. If necessary
   work to pass state law to allow secession from the
   mega federalized city which refuses to give your
   area the right and liberty to self-government. Remember Our Lady said on March 28, 1985:

   > **"...In prayer you shall perceive the great-
   > est joy and the way out of every situation
   > that has no exit..."**

   What of funding? The county sheriff can still give
   police protection. The citizens, themselves, as
   well. Basically, all you will have to pay for would

be garbage pickup and that would be much cheaper than city taxes. Do not worry about these things, as they can be worked out much better under a close, self-governing body than a federalized city council. Otherwise, "shake the dust from your sandals of the city" and refer back to numbers 1-4. This number five is a more difficult path, but not impossible with prayer, sacrifice and time.

Can you expect to be successful?
Yes!
Why?

What did God promise?

"If My people who are called by My name humble themselves, and pray and seek My face, and turn from their wicked ways, then I will hear from Heaven, and will forgive their sin and heal their land." 2 Chronicles 7:14

What did Our Lady promise?

July 25, 2010

"...I desire to lead all of you to my Son, your Savior. You are not aware that without Him you

do not have joy and peace, nor a future or eternal life…"

6. **Go to www.TheyFiredtheFirstShot2012.com/ther-evolution.html[*] to:** (see item E)

    A.   Connect with others in your area.

    B.   Search a village or town and see pictures of existing village towns listed in each state.

    C.   Find history of existing towns and villages.

    D.   See much more to come.

    E.   Though this website is not fully operational at the time of this first publishing, check the home page at www.TheyFiredtheFirstShot2012.com for updates on the finished construction of the website. To have access to this chapter and more, type www.TheyFiredtheFirstShot2012.com/ther-evolution.html into your web browser and view maps, towns, villages etc. Websites can be inexpensive or very expensive. This website will contain a demand for constant research from a staff of employed people. This type of website development is costly and time consuming, requiring

---

[*] Do not share this link or the contents with anyone who has not read the book. It is important that the book be read completely before this part is revealed.

a whole staff to build and maintain full-time. It will not be done without the support of your donation and prayers. If it is not financially supported, it cannot launch. It therefore depends on you. Donations can be made through the website, www.TheyFiredtheFirstShot2012.com, or by mailing your donation to:

They Fired the First Shot 2012
Caritas of Birmingham
100 Our Lady Queen of Peace Drive
Sterrett, AL 35147

See page 719 about the first conference on starting your new communities. It will be a "How To" Conference on setting out to making a Constitutional village based in Christian principles, prayer, repentance and seeking God's face.

719

"Villages Springing up Across the Land"

Contact us when you form your **Constitutional Small Prayer Group** to be placed on the C.S.P.G. mailing list. We are gathering information concerning small village stories and "How they did it." Will connect others to your C.S.P.G. and much more to come as well as inform you of events continuing to help Constitutional Small Prayer Groups spread and flourish.

To Sign Up:

Write: **Caritas of Birmingham**

100 Our Lady Queen of Peace Drive

Sterrett, Alabama 35147 USA

Or Call: **205-672-2000, ext. 333**

Or Go Online:

Theyfiredthefirstshot2012.com

STATE
MAPS

Special Note

In referencing "villages," "hamlets," "small towns," etc., it is best viewed in the light of a population of a small number. Better to have three villages in an area than all three villages becoming one village. The larger it grows, the more bureaucracy grows. The more bureaucracy grows, the more there is a need for funds. The more need for funds, the greater the temptation for the village to sell its soul to federalization. What will follow from there is the loss of protection for unalienable rights. What is the best number for the population? In the book the Tipping Point, it explains that when the number of people in any venture, organization, community, etc., reaches 150, it is the tipping point. What this means is that even before reaching that number, cliques have begun to form, division

can set in and cohesiveness is lost. Therefore, a good
maximum number for your village is 100. This is why
military companies stay at around 100. Cohesiveness,
the unity necessary to be effective, begins to wane after
100. Less than 100 is still a good number. A village
may be only 20-30 people when you begin to transform
it. The Hutterites, a long lasting religious community,
with foundations located in Europe and the United
States, observed this principle in their own experience as well. Spanning hundreds of years, these self-
sufficient agrarian-based colonies, once their numbers
reach 150 in a colony, will divide into two groups of 75.
One half will stay where they are, and the other half
will form another community in the area. This practice
has contributed to the Hutterites continuation. When
Our Lady came to Medjugorje in 1981, there were five
small villages circled within the mountains surrounding
Medjugorje. The Tipping Point, by Malcolm Gladwell,
is important to read in understanding this concept.

What follows in this section is a map of all 50 states
in which all the towns highlighted are with very small
populations. Establish your Constitutional Small
Prayer Group and begin praying for guidance in your
selection of a small town to establish a Constitutional
village with an indissoluble bond of principles of civil

government to the principles of Christianity, implemented through prayer and repentance, maintained and continued by prayer and repentance. May God grant the grace for the reconciling of ourselves, our families and our nation back to God, one village at a time.

Lastly, before reviewing the maps, it is important to understand the definition of liberty. [See the following page.]

IT IS IMPORTANT TO DEFINE LIBERTY AS OUR FOUNDERS OF THE UNITED STATES OF AMERICA UNDERSTOOD IT.

LIBERTY

The state of being free; freedom or release from bondage or slavery; freedom from arbitrary or despotic government, or, often, from other rule or law **other than that of a self-governing community**; freedom from external or foreign rule; freedom from control, interference, obligation, restriction, hampering conditions; Natural liberty consists in the power of acting as one thinks fit without any restraints or controls except from the laws of nature. Natural liberty is only (lessened) and restrained as is necessary and expedient for the safety and interest of the society, government or nation. A restraint of natural liberty not necessary or expedient for the public is tyranny or oppression.[419]

Notes

726

<u>Notes</u>

Notes

728

Notes

State Listings

Alabama

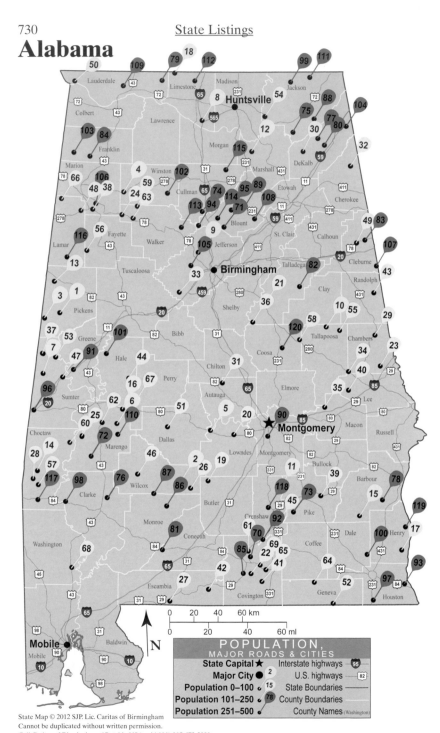

POPULATION,
MAJOR ROADS & CITIES
State Capital ★   Interstate highways
Major City ●   U.S. highways
Population 0–100   State Boundaries
Population 101–250   County Boundaries
Population 251–500   County Names (Washington)

State Map © 2012 SJP. Lic. Caritas of Birmingham
Cannot be duplicated without written permission.
Call Caritas of Birmingham: (Outside USA add **001**) **205-672-2000**
or write: **Caritas of Birmingham**
100 Our Lady Queen of Peace Drive
Sterrett, AL 35147 USA

	City, State	Population			City, State	Population
1.	McMullen, Alabama	10		61.	Gantt, Alabama	222
2.	Oak Hill, Alabama	26		62.	Providence, Alabama	223
3.	Memphis, Alabama	29		63.	Kansas, Alabama	226
4.	Natural Bridge, Alabama	37		64.	Coffee Springs, Alabama	228
5.	Benton, Alabama	49		65.	Horn Hill, Alabama	228
6.	Dayton, Alabama	52		66.	Detroit, Alabama	237
7.	Emelle, Alabama	53		67.	Union town, Alabama	237
8.	Mooresville, Alabama	53		68.	McIntosh, Alabama	238
9.	Cardiff, Alabama	55		69.	Sanford, Alabama	241
10.	Goldville, Alabama	55		70.	Heath, Alabama	254
11.	Petrey, Alabama	58		71.	County Line, Alabama	258
12.	Union Grove, Alabama	77		72.	Sweet Water, Alabama	258
13.	Ethelsville, Alabama	81		73.	Goshen, Alabama	266
14.	Needham, Alabama	94		74.	Colony, Alabama	268
15.	Blue Springs, Alabama	96		75.	Langston, Alabama	270
16.	Faunsdale, Alabama	98		76.	Fulton, Alabama	272
17.	Haleburg, Alabama	103		77.	Shiloh, Alabama	274
18.	Lester, Alabama	111		78.	Bakerhill, Alabama	279
19.	Ridgeville, Alabama	112		79.	Anderson, Alabama	282
20.	Lowndesboro, Alabama	115		80.	Pine Ridge, Alabama	282
21.	Bon Air, Alabama	116		81.	Repton, Alabama	282
22.	Libertyville, Alabama	117		82.	Waldo, Alabama	283
23.	Cusseta, Alabama	123		83.	Fruithurst, Alabama	284
24.	Eldridge, Alabama	130		84.	Hodges, Alabama	288
25.	Myrtlewood, Alabama	130		85.	Carolina, Alabama	297
26.	Pine Apple, Alabama	132		86.	Beatrice, Alabama	301
27.	Pollard, Alabama	137		87.	Vredenburgh, Alabama	312
28.	Toxey, Alabama	137		88.	Dutton, Alabama	315
29.	Five Points, Alabama	141		89.	Rosa, Alabama	316
30.	Lakeview, Alabama	143		90.	Gordonville, Alabama	326
31.	Billingsley, Alabama	144		91.	Boligee, Alabama	328
32.	Gaylesville, Alabama	144		92.	Dozier, Alabama	329
33.	North Johns, Alabama	145		93.	Gordon, Alabama	332
34.	Waverly, Alabama	145		94.	West Jefferson, Alabama	338
35.	Franklin, Alabama	149		95.	Nectar, Alabama	345
36.	Talladega Springs, Alabama	166		96.	Cuba, Alabama	346
37.	Geiger, Alabama	170		97.	Madrid, Alabama	350
38.	Gu-Win, Alabama	176		98.	Coffeeville, Alabama	352
39.	Banks, Alabama	179		99.	Hytop, Alabama	354
40.	Loachapoka, Alabama	180		100.	Napier Field, Alabama	354
41.	Onycha, Alabama	184		101.	Akron, Alabama	356
42.	Riverview, Alabama	184		102.	Arley, Alabama	357
43.	Woodland, Alabama	184		103.	Vina, Alabama	358
44.	Newbern, Alabama	186		104.	Mentone, Alabama	360
45.	Glenwood, Alabama	187		105.	Maytown, Alabama	385
46.	Yellow Bluff, Alabama	188		106.	Twin, Alabama	399
47.	Epes, Alabama	192		107.	Ranburne, Alabama	409
48.	Beaverton, Alabama	201		108.	Highland Lake, Alabama	412
49.	Edwardsville, Alabama	202		109.	St. Florian, Alabama	413
50.	Waterloo, Alabama	203		110.	Thomaston, Alabama	417
51.	Orrville, Alabama	204		111.	Pleasant Groves, Alabama	420
52.	Black, Alabama	207		112.	Elkmont, Alabama	434
53.	Gainesville, Alabama	208		113.	Sipsey, Alabama	437
54.	Paint Rock, Alabama	210		114.	Hayden, Alabama	444
55.	Daviston, Alabama	214		115.	Fairview, Alabama	446
56.	Belk, Alabama	215		116.	Kennedy, Alabama	447
57.	Gilbertown, Alabama	215		117.	Silas, Alabama	452
58.	Kellyton, Alabama	217		118.	Rutledge, Alabama	467
59.	Nauvoo, Alabama	221		119.	Shorter, Alabama	474
60.	Pennington, Alabama	221		120.	Rockford, Alabama	477**

* Town populations and incorporated cities reflect data taken from the 2010 U.S. Census. Before acting upon this information it is very important to verify the accuracy of all the information represented, including current population, incorporated status, location of cities and counties, etc.

**This state has more cities to research under 500 population to view the full listing go to our website
TheyFiredtheFirstShot2012.com/therevolution.html

Alaska

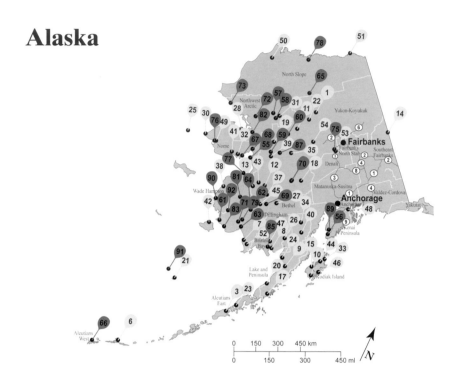

State Capital ★

Major City ●

Anchorage

Fairbanks

State Map © 2012 SJP. Lic. Caritas of Birmingham
Cannot be duplicated without written permission.
Call Caritas of Birmingham: (Outside USA add **001**) **205-672-2000**
or write: **Caritas of Birmingham**
        100 Our Lady Queen of Peace Drive
        Sterrett, AL 35147 USA

	City, State	Population
35.	Ruby, Alaska	166
36.	Coffman Cove, Alaska	176
37.	Holy Cross, Alaska	178
38.	Nunam Iqua, Alaska	187
39.	Kaltag, Alaska	190
40.	Newhalen, Alaska	190
41.	White Mountain, Alaska	190
42.	Mekoryuk, Alaska	191
43.	Grayling, Alaska	194
44.	Port Lions, Alaska	194
45.	Upper Kalskag, Alaska	210
46.	Old Harbor, Alaska	218
47.	Aleknagik, Alaska	219
48.	Whittier, Alaska	220
49.	Teller, Alaska	229
50.	Atqasuk, Alaska	233
51.	Kaktovik, Alaska	239
52.	Goodnews Bay, Alaska	243
53.	Anderson, Alaska	246
54.	Tanana, Alaska	246
55.	Shaktoolik, Alaska	251
56.	Seldovia, Alaska	255
57.	Ambler, Alaska	258
58.	Shungnak, Alaska	262
59.	Nulato, Alaska	264
60.	Huslia, Alaska	275
61.	Nightmute, Alaska	280
62.	Lower Kalskag, Alaska	282
63.	Eek, Alaska	296
64.	Russian Mission, Alaska	312
65.	Anaktuvuk Pass, Alaska	324
66.	Adak, Alaska	326
67.	Elim, Alaska	330
68.	Koyuk, Alaska	332
69.	Akiak, Alaska	346
70.	McGrath, Alaska	346
71.	Napakiak, Alaska	354
72.	Kiana, Alaska	361
73.	Kivalina, Alaska	374
74.	Hydaburg, Alaska	376
75.	Nenana, Alaska	378
76.	Brevig Mission, Alaska	388
77.	St. Michael, Alaska	401
78.	Nuiqsut, Alaska	402
79.	Napaskiak, Alaska	405
80.	Saxman, Alaska	411
81.	Marshall, Alaska	414
82.	Buckland, Alaska	416
83.	Chefornak, Alaska	418
84.	Gustavus, Alaska	442
85.	Manokotak, Alaska	442
86.	Angoon, Alaska	459
87.	Galena, Alaska	470
88.	Thorne Bay, Alaska	471
89.	Kachemak, Alaska	472
90.	Scammon Bay, Alaska	474
91.	St. Paul, Alaska	479
92.	Nunapitchuk, Alaska	496

	City, State	Population
1.	Bettles, Alaska	12
2.	Kupreanof, Alaska	27
3.	False Pass, Alaska	35
4.	Kasaan, Alaska	49
5.	Port Alexander, Alaska	52
6.	Atka, Alaska	61
7.	Platinum, Alaska	61
8.	Clark's Point, Alaska	62
9.	Pilot Point, Alaska	68
10.	Akhiok, Alaska	71
11.	Hughes, Alaska	77
12.	Shageluk, Alaska	83
13.	Anvik, Alaska	85
14.	Eagle, Alaska	86
15.	Larsen Bay, Alaska	87
16.	Pelican, Alaska	88
17.	Chignik, Alaska	91
18.	Nikolai, Alaska	94
19.	Koyukuk, Alaska	96
20.	Port Heiden, Alaska	102
21.	St. George, Alaska	102
22.	Allakaket, Alaska	105
23.	Cold Bay, Alaska	108
24.	Egegik, Alaska	109
25.	Diomede, Alaska	115
26.	Ekwok, Alaska	115
27.	Chuathbaluk, Alaska	118
28.	Deering, Alaska	122
29.	Tenakee Springs, Alaska	131
30.	Wales, Alaska	145
31.	Kobuk, Alaska	151
32.	Golovin, Alaska	156
33.	Ouzinkie, Alaska	161
34.	Nondalton, Alaska	164

* Town populations and incorporated cities reflect data taken from the 2010 U.S. Census. Before acting upon this information it is very important to verify the accuracy of all the information represented, including current population, incorporated status, location of cities and counties, etc.

Arizona

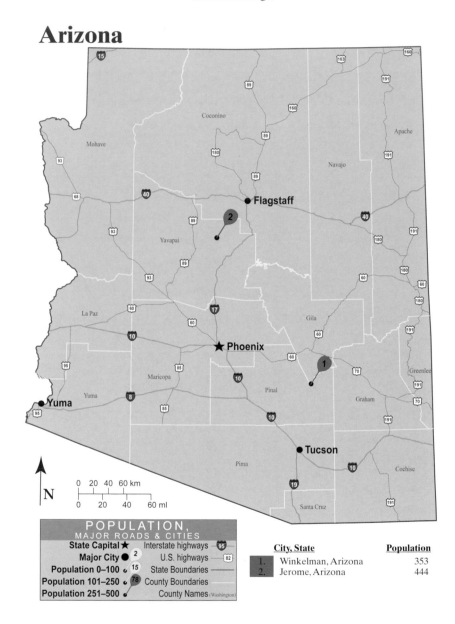

City, State	Population
1. Winkelman, Arizona	353
2. Jerome, Arizona	444

According to the 2010 Census, there were only two incorporated towns in Arizona with a population under
500.* Visit the Arizona Secretary of State website to research other laws for incorporation in Arizona. Explore
in greater detail solutions discussed in this book, such as
the nullification of laws. Find out how you can take back
already incorporated towns, returning them to a Constitutional Christian foundation.

Early Beginnings: How It Was Done

It was one man, a Franciscan missionary, who in 1539
paved the way for others to bring the Gospel to Arizona. The 48th state in the Union, Arizona's road to state-
hood is the story of perseverance and faith. The early
communities settling in Arizona struggled for decades
to establish a way of life in the desert. "Ditat Deus,"
meaning "God enriches," was chosen as the state motto
and undoubtedly expresses what was in the hearts and
minds of these early communities; that of gratitude and
trust in God. Despite persecution, missionaries continued to bring Christian principles to the existing communities of the new territory, teaching them a way of life
built on Biblical principles.**

---

* Town populations and incorporated cities reflect data taken from the 2010 U.S. Census. Before acting upon this information it is very important to verify the accuracy of all the information represented, including current population, incorporated status, location of cities and counties, etc.

** *Arizona,* Unsigned, The Encyclopedia Britannica, 11th Edition, Volume I-II, The Encyclopedia Britannica Company, 1910, pp 547-548; *Arizona,* George F. Herrick, The Encyclopedia Americana, Volume II, Americana Corporation, 1956, pp.251, 256

Arkansas

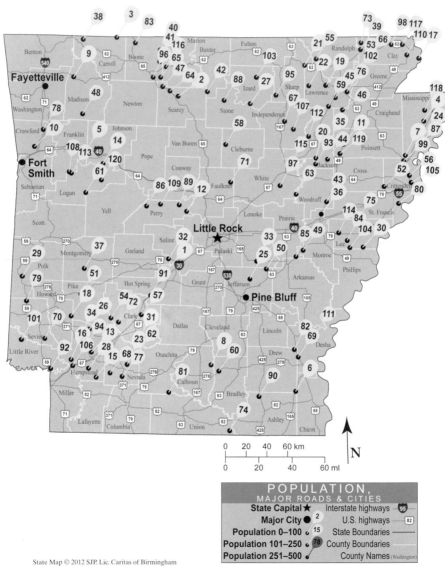

0   20   40   60 km
0   20   40   60 ml

N

POPULATION,
MAJOR ROADS & CITIES

State Capital ★	Interstate highways
Major City ●	U.S. highways
Population 0–100	State Boundaries
Population 101–250	County Boundaries
Population 251–500	County Names (Washington)

	City, State	Population		City, State	Population
1.	Magnet Cove, Arkansas	5	61.	Blue Mountain, Arkansas	124
2.	Gilbert, Arkansas	28	62.	Bluff City, Arkansas	124
3.	Blue Eye, Arkansas	30	63.	Georgetown, Arkansas	124
4.	Victoria, Arkansas	37	64.	St. Joe, Arkansas	132
5.	Wiederkehr Village, Arkansas	38	65.	Everton, Arkansas	133
6.	Jerome, Arkansas	39	66.	Peach Orchard, Arkansas	135
7.	Birdsong, Arkansas	41	67.	Moorefield, Arkansas	137
8.	Tinsman, Arkansas	54	68.	Bodcaw, Arkansas	138
9.	Hindsville, Arkansas	61	69.	Reed, Arkansas	141
10.	Rudy, Arkansas	61	70.	Ben Lomond, Arkansas	145
11.	Waldenburg, Arkansas	61	71.	Mount Vernon, Arkansas	145
12.	Fourche, Arkansas	62	72.	Okolona, Arkansas	147
13.	Oakhaven, Arkansas	63	73.	Success, Arkansas	149
14.	Morrison Bluff, Arkansas	64	74.	Felsenthal, Arkansas	150
15.	Patmos, Arkansas	64	75.	Haynes, Arkansas	150
16.	McNab, Arkansas	68	76.	Sedgwick, Arkansas	152
17.	Nimmons, Arkansas	69	77.	Willisville, Arkansas	152
18.	Corinth, Arkansas	70	78.	Chester, Arkansas	159
19.	Powhatan, Arkansas	72	79.	Gillham, Arkansas	160
20.	Weldon, Arkansas	75	80.	Anthonyville, Arkansas	161
21.	Williford, Arkansas	75	81.	Louann, Arkansas	164
22.	Smithville, Arkansas	78	82.	Winchester, Arkansas	167
23.	Cale, Arkansas	79	83.	Omaha, Arkansas	169
24.	Marie, Arkansas	84	84.	Aubrey, Arkansas	170
25.	Sherrill, Arkansas	84	85.	Ulm, Arkansas	170
26.	Ozan, Arkansas	85	86.	Casa, Arkansas	171
27.	Guion, Arkansas	86	87.	Bassett, Arkansas	173
28.	Spring, Arkansas	87	88.	Fifty-Six, Arkansas	173
29.	Vandervoort, Arkansas	87	89.	Houston, Arkansas	173
30.	LaGrange, Arkansas	89	90.	Fountain Hill, Arkansas	175
31.	Whelen Springs, Arkansas	92	91.	Friendship, Arkansas	176
32.	Lonsdale, Arkansas	94	92.	Ogden, Arkansas	180
33.	Coy, Arkansas	96	93.	Tupelo, Arkansas	180
34.	McCaskill, Arkansas	96	94.	Washington, Arkansas	180
35.	Amagon, Arkansas	98	95.	Sidney, Arkansas	181
36.	Fargo, Arkansas	98	96.	Valley Springs, Arkansas	183
37.	Black Springs, Arkansas	99	97.	West Point, Arkansas	185
38.	Beaver, Arkansas	100	98.	McDougal, Arkansas	186
39.	Datto, Arkansas	100	99.	Gilmore, Arkansas	188
40.	South Lead Hill, Arkansas	102	100.	Burdette, Arkansas	191
41.	Zinc, Arkansas	103	101.	Winthrop, Arkansas	192
42.	Big Flat, Arkansas	105	102.	O'Kean, Arkansas	194
43.	Hunter, Arkansas	105	103.	Franklin, Arkansas	198
44.	Beedeville, Arkansas	107	104.	Rondo, Arkansas	198
45.	Minturn, Arkansas	109	105.	Sunset, Arkansas	198
46.	Egypt, Arkansas	112	106.	Fulton, Arkansas	201
47.	Pindall, Arkansas	112	107.	Magness, Arkansas	202
48.	St. Paul, Arkansas	113	108.	Ratcliff, Arkansas	202
49.	Roe, Arkansas	114	109.	Adona, Arkansas	209
50.	Allport, Arkansas	115	110.	Greenway, Arkansas	209
51.	Daisy, Arkansas	115	111.	Watson, Arkansas	211
52.	Jennette, Arkansas	115	112.	Jacksonport, Arkansas	212
53.	Delaplaine, Arkansas	116	113.	Caulksville, Arkansas	213
54.	Antoine, Arkansas	117	114.	Moro, Arkansas	216
55.	Ravenden Springs, Arkansas	118	115.	Russell, Arkansas	216
56.	Jericho, Arkansas	119	116.	Pyatt, Arkansas	221
57.	Gum Springs, Arkansas	120	117.	Pollard, Arkansas	222
58.	Higden, Arkansas	120	118.	Dell, Arkansas	223
59.	Alicia, Arkansas	124	119.	Fisher, Arkansas	223
60.	Banks, Arkansas	124	120.	Scranton, Arkansas	224 **

* Town populations and incorporated cities reflect data taken from the 2010 U.S. Census. Before acting upon this information it is very important to verify the accuracy of all the information represented, including current population, incorporated status, location of cities and counties, etc.

**This state has more cities to research under 500 population to view the full listing go to our website
TheyFiredtheFirstShot2012.com/therevolution.html

California

City, State	Population
1. Vernon, California	112
2. Amador City, California	185
3. Industry, California	219
4. Sand City, California	334
5. Trinidad, California	367
6. Tehama, California	418
7. Point Arena, California	449

State Map © 2012 SJP. Lic. Caritas of Birmingham
Cannot be duplicated without written permission.
Call Caritas of Birmingham: (Outside USA add **001**) **205-672-2000**
or write: **Caritas of Birmingham**
                100 Our Lady Queen of Peace Drive
                Sterrett, AL 35147 USA

According to the 2010 Census, there were only seven incorporated towns in California with a population under 500.* Visit the California Secretary of State website to research laws for incorporation in California. Explore in greater detail solutions discussed in this book, such as the nullification of laws. Find out how you can take back already incorporated towns, returning them to a Constitutional Christian foundation.

Early Beginnings: How It Was Done

It is widely known California was settled by Catholic missionaries and the establishment of missions which spread Christian principles throughout the territory with the creation of small religious communities, also known as missions. It was the Franciscan missionaries who began founding small religious communities first in 1769. By 1823, a total of 21 mission communities had begun through the Christian missionaries. Over 80,000 were converted to Christianity through the witness and life of the people in these 21 small communities. As converts grew, so did the size of these communities, which soon evolved into plantations. These plantations were large in scale and allowed these communities to sustain themselves by raising large herds of cattle, planting orange and olive trees, and growing wheat.**

---

* Town populations and incorporated cities reflect data taken from the 2010 U.S. Census. Before acting upon this information it is very important to verify the accuracy of all the information represented, including current population, incorporated status, location of cities and counties, etc.

** *California*, Unsigned, The Encyclopedia Britannica, 11th Edition, Volume XIII The Encyclopedia Britannica Company, 1910, pp 16-17;
California, Unsigned, The Universal Standard Encyclopedia, Volume 4, Universal Standard Encyclopedia, 1956, pp.1299-1300

Colorado

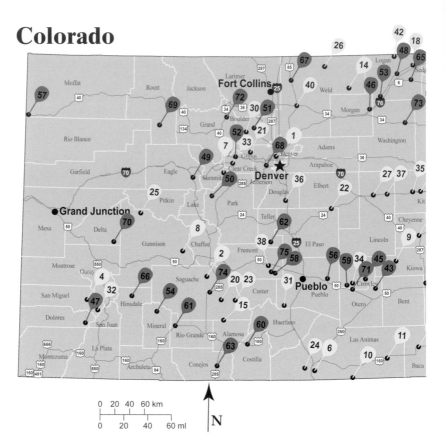

0 20 40 60 km
0 20 40 60 ml

N

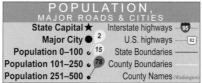

POPULATION,
MAJOR ROADS & CITIES
State Capital ★   Interstate highways 95
Major City ● 2   U.S. highways 82
Population 0–100 15   State Boundaries
Population 101–250 78   County Boundaries
Population 251–500   County Names (Washington)

	City, State	Population
25.	Marble, Colorado	131
26.	Grover, Colorado	137
27.	Genoa, Colorado	139
28.	Pritchett, Colorado	140
29.	Sedgwick, Colorado	146
30.	Ward, Colorado	150
31.	Rye, Colorado	153
32.	Ophir, Colorado	159
33.	Silver Plume, Colorado	170
34.	Crowley, Colorado	176
35.	Seibert, Colorado	181
36.	Larkspur, Colorado	183
37.	Arriba, Colorado	193
38.	Brookside, Colorado	233
39.	Kit Carson, Colorado	233
40.	Garden City, Colorado	234
41.	Bethune, Colorado	237
42.	Peetz, Colorado	238
43.	Cheraw, Colorado	252
44.	Eckley, Colorado	257
45.	Sugar City, Colorado	258
46.	Hillrose, Colorado	264
47.	Rico, Colorado	265
48.	Iliff, Colorado	266
49.	Red Cliff, Colorado	267
50.	Alma, Colorado	270
51.	Jamestown, Colorado	274
52.	Empire, Colorado	282
53.	Merino, Colorado	284
54.	City of Creede, Colorado	290
55.	Ovid, Colorado	318
56.	Boone, Colorado	339
57.	Dinosaur, Colorado	339
58.	Coal Creek, Colorado	343
59.	Olney Springs, Colorado	345
60.	Blanca, Colorado	385
61.	South Fork, Colorado	386
62.	Victor, Colorado	397
63.	Romeo, Colorado	404
64.	Wiley, Colorado	405
65.	Fleming, Colorado	408
66.	Lake City, Colorado	408
67.	Nunn, Colorado	416
68.	Morrison, Colorado	428
69.	Yampa, Colorado	429
70.	Crawford, Colorado	431
71.	Manzanola, Colorado	434
72.	Grand Lake, Colorado	471
73.	Otis, Colorado	475
74.	Saguache, Colorado	485
75.	Rockvale, Colorado	487

	City, State	Population
1.	Lakeside, Colorado	8
2.	Bonanza, Colorado	16
3.	Paoli, Colorado	34
4.	Sawpit, Colorado	40
5.	Two Buttes, Colorado	43
6.	Starkville, Colorado	59
7.	Montezuma, Colorado	65
8.	Pitkin, Colorado	66
9.	Haswell, Colorado	68
10.	Branson, Colorado	74
11.	Kim, Colorado	74
12.	Hartman, Colorado	81
13.	Sheridan Lake, Colorado	88
14.	Raymer (New Raymer), CO	96
15.	Hooper, Colorado	103
16.	Vona, Colorado	106
17.	Campo, Colorado	109
18.	Crook, Colorado	110
19.	Vilas, Colorado	114
20.	Moffat, Colorado	116
21.	Black Hawk, Colorado	118
22.	Ramah, Colorado	123
23.	Crestone, Colorado	127
24.	Cokedale, Colorado	129

* Town populations and incorporated cities reflect data taken from the 2010 U.S. Census. Before acting upon this information it is very important to verify the accuracy of all the information represented, including current population, incorporated status, location of cities and counties, etc.

Connecticut

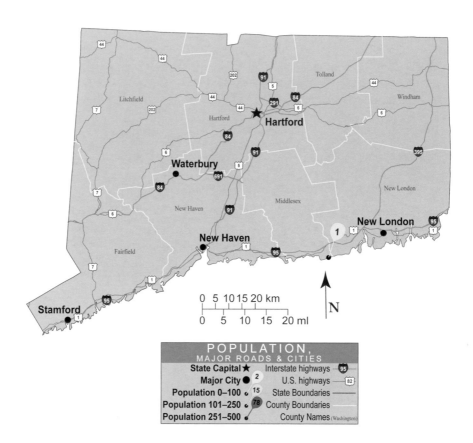

City, State	Population
1. Fenwick Borough, Connecticut	43

According to the 2010 Census, there is only one incorporated town in Connecticut with a population less than 500.* Fenwick, considered a borough, is somewhat unique in its relationship to other incorporated towns and was established by a special act of the Connecticut legislature in 1899. Visit the Connecticut Secretary of State website to research other laws for incorporation, including special acts regarding the incorporation of boroughs. Explore in greater detail solutions in this book, such as the nullification of laws, and find out how you can take back already incorporated towns, returning them to a Constitutional foundation.

Early Beginnings: How It Was Done

It was 1633, when word came to three religious men from three separate towns in Massachusetts that a new valley laden with resources had been discovered. Each of these men rallied those in their villages to flee the absolutist government imposed on them and set out toward this new land. Five years later, a second group of Puritans came from Boston and settled in the area now known as New Haven. This community of people created a "plantation covenant," with a vision of founding this new town on sacred Scriptures, desiring God's principles as the supreme guide for all civil and religious decisions. This vision was realized a year later when a formal declaration was made stating that "the rules of Scripture should determine the ordering of the church, choice of magistrates, making and repeal of laws," etc., adding that "only church members would be eligible for becoming officials of the colony." These officials would choose twelve men, along with seven others, and together organize the church and civil government for the colony. In 1644, the general court of the New Haven colony declared, "the judicial laws of God, as they were declared by Moses," should be the rule for all courts, "until they be branched out into particulars hereafter." This first community established a theocratic character within their government, and built their foundation on God's principles. One such principle made into a law of the land regarded the strict observance of the Sabbath.**

---

* Town populations and incorporated cities reflect data taken from the 2010 U.S. Census. Before acting upon this information it is very important to verify the accuracy of all the information represented, including current population, incorporated status, location of cities and counties, etc.

** *Connecticut*, Unsigned, The Encyclopedia Britannica, 11th Edition, Volume V-VI, The Encyclopedia Britannica Company, 1910, pp 954-957

Delaware

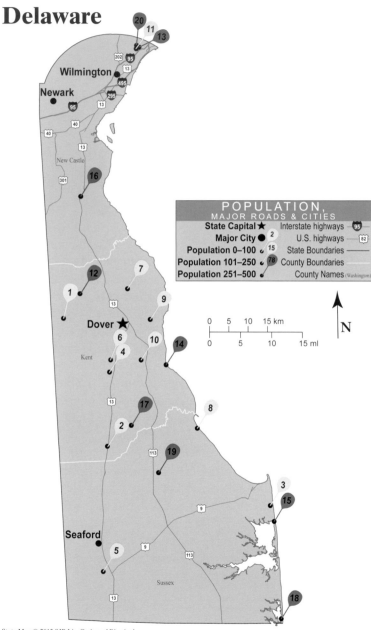

Wilmington

Newark

New Castle

Dover ★

Kent

Seaford

Sussex

POPULATION,
MAJOR ROADS & CITIES

State Capital ★	Interstate highways
Major City ●	U.S. highways
Population 0–100	State Boundaries
Population 101–250	County Boundaries
Population 251–500	County Names (Washington)

0   5   10   15 km

0   5   10   15 ml

N

	City, State	Population
1.	Hartly, Delaware	74
2.	Farmington, Delaware	110
3.	Henlopen Acres, Delaware	122
4.	Viola, Delaware	157
5.	Bethel, Delaware	171
6.	Woodside, Delaware	181
7.	Leipsic, Delaware	183
8.	Slaughter Beach, Delaware	207
9.	Little Creek, Delaware	224
10.	Magnolia, Delaware	225
11.	Ardencroft, Delaware	231
12.	Kenton, Delaware	261
13.	Ardentown, Delaware	264
14.	Bowers, Delaware	335
15.	Dewey Beach, Delaware	341
16.	Odessa, Delaware	364
17.	Houston, Delaware	374
18.	Fenwick Island, Delaware	379
19.	Ellendale, Delaware	381
20.	Arden, Delaware	439

* Town populations and incorporated cities reflect data taken from the 2010 U.S. Census. Before acting upon this information it is very important to verify the accuracy of all the information represented, including current population, incorporated status, location of cities and counties, etc.

Florida

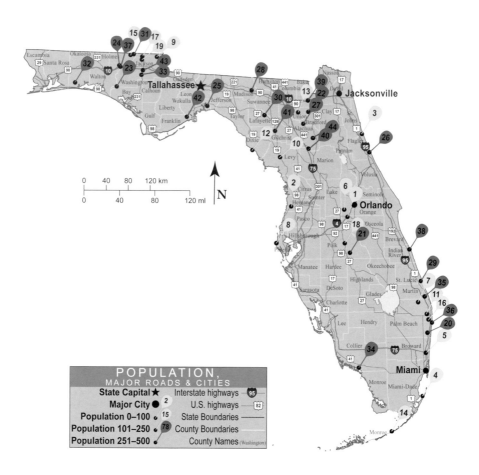

POPULATION,
MAJOR ROADS & CITIES

State Capital ★	Interstate highways	95
Major City ●	2	U.S. highways	82
Population 0–100	15	State Boundaries	
Population 101–250	78	County Boundaries	
Population 251–500		County Names (Washington)	

	City, State	Population
1.	Lake Buena Vista, Florida	10
2.	Weeki Wachee, Florida	12
3.	Marineland, Florida	16
4.	Islandia, Florida	18
5.	Lazy Lake, Florida	24
6.	Bay Lake, Florida	47
7.	Indian Creek, Florida	86
8.	Belleair Shore, Florida	109
9.	Bascom, Florida	121
10.	Otter Creek, Florida	134
11.	Cloud Lake, Florida	135
12.	Horseshoe Beach, Florida	169
13.	Worthington Springs, Florida	181
14.	Layton, Florida	184
15.	Noma, Florida	211
16.	Glen Ridge, Florida	219
17.	Campbellton, Florida	230
18.	Highland Park, Florida	230
19.	Jacob City, Florida	250
20.	Golf, Florida	252
21.	Hillcrest Heights, Florida	254
22.	Raiford, Florida	255
23.	Ebro, Florida	270
24.	Westville, Florida	289
25.	St. Marks, Florida	293
26.	Beverly Beach, Florida	338
27.	Brooker, Florida	338
28.	Lee, Florida	352
29.	Ocean Breeze Park, Florida	355
30.	La Crosse, Florida	360
31.	Esto, Florida	364
32.	Cinco Bayou, Florida	383
33.	Wausau, Florida	383
34.	Everglades, Florida	400
35.	Jupiter Inlet Colony, Florida	400
36.	Manalapan, Florida	406
37.	Caryville, Florida	411
38.	Orchid, Florida	415
39.	Glen St. Mary, Florida	437
40.	McIntosh, Florida	452
41.	Bell, Florida	456
42.	Sopchoppy, Florida	457
43.	Alford, Florida	489
44.	Hampton, Florida	500

* Town populations and incorporated cities reflect data taken from the 2010 U.S. Census. Before acting upon this information it is very important to verify the accuracy of all the information represented, including current population, incorporated status, location of cities and counties, etc.

Georgia

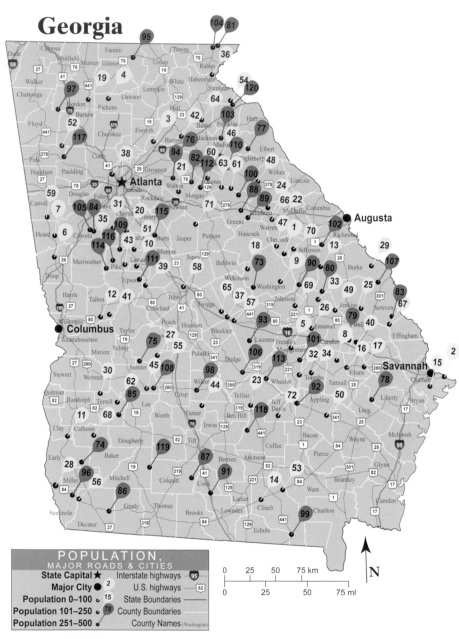

	City, State	Population		City, State	Population
1.	Edge Hill, Georgia	24	61.	Maxeys, Georgia	224
2.	Riverside, Georgia	35	62.	Bronwood, Georgia	225
3.	Rest Haven, Georgia	62	63.	Lexington, Georgia	228
4.	Talking Rock, Georgia	64	64.	Gillsville, Georgia	235
5.	Tarry, Georgia	87	65.	Danville, Georgia	238
6.	Gay, Georgia	89	66.	Norwood, Georgia	239
7.	Lone Oak, Georgia	92	67.	Oliver, Georgia	239
8.	Manassas, Georgia	94	68.	Morgan, Georgia	240
9.	Riddleville, Georgia	96	69.	Kite, Georgia	241
10.	Aldora, Georgia	103	70.	Avera, Georgia	246
11.	Bluffton, Georgia	103	71.	Shady Dale, Georgia	249
12.	Geneva, Georgia	105	72.	Denton, Georgia	250
13.	Vidette, Georgia	112	73.	Oconee, Georgia	252
14.	Du Pont, Georgia	120	74.	Damascus, Georgia	254
15.	Vernonburg, Georgia	122	75.	Andersonville, Georgia	255
16.	Bellville, Georgia	123	76.	Carl, Georgia	255
17.	Daisy, Georgia	129	77.	Carlton, Georgia	260
18.	Deepstep, Georgia	131	78.	Gumbranch, Georgia	264
19.	Ranger, Georgia	131	79.	Pulaski, Georgia	266
20.	Sunny Side, Georgia	134	80.	Midville, Georgia	269
21.	Jersey, Georgia	137	81.	Sky Valley, Georgia	272
22.	Camak, Georgia	138	82.	Good Hope, Georgia	274
23.	Jacksonville, Georgia	140	83.	Newington, Georgia	274
24.	Sharon, Georgia	140	84.	Turin, Georgia	274
25.	Rocky Ford, Georgia	144	85.	Sasser, Georgia	279
26.	Nunez, Georgia	147	86.	Climax, Georgia	280
27.	Dooling, Georgia	154	87.	Ellenton, Georgia	281
28.	Jakin, Georgia	155	88.	Siloam, Georgia	282
29.	Girard, Georgia	156	89.	White Plains, Georgia	284
30.	Parrott, Georgia	158	90.	Bartow, Georgia	286
31.	Woolsey, Georgia	158	91.	Cecil, Georgia	286
32.	Alston, Georgia	159	92.	Graham, Georgia	291
33.	Summertown, Georgia	160	93.	Rentz, Georgia	295
34.	Santa Claus, Georgia	165	94.	Between, Georgia	296
35.	Haralson, Georgia	166	95.	Morganton, Georgia	303
36.	Tallulah Falls, Georgia	168	96.	Iron City, Georgia	310
37.	Allentown, Georgia	169	97.	Plainville, Georgia	313
38.	Buckhead, Georgia	171	98.	Pitts, Georgia	320
39.	Culloden, Georgia	175	99.	Fargo, Georgia	321
40.	Register, Georgia	175	100.	Woodville, Georgia	321
41.	Junction City, Georgia	177	101.	Higgston, Georgia	323
42.	Talmo, Georgia	180	102.	Keysville, Georgia	332
43.	Meansville, Georgia	182	103.	Ila, Georgia	337
44.	Rebecca, Georgia	187	104.	Dillard, Georgia	339
45.	De Soto, Georgia	195	105.	Sharpsburg, Georgia	341
46.	Hull, Georgia	198	106.	Chauncey, Georgia	342
47.	Mitchell, Georgia	199	107.	Hiltonia, Georgia	342
48.	Rayle, Georgia	199	108.	Cobb, Georgia	351
49.	Garfield, Georgia	201	109.	Williamson, Georgia	352
50.	Surrency, Georgia	201	110.	Arnoldsville, Georgia	357
51.	Orchard Hill, Georgia	209	111.	Yatesville, Georgia	357
52.	Taylorsville, Georgia	210	112.	Bostwick, Georgia	365
53.	Argyle, Georgia	212	113.	Scotland, Georgia	366
54.	Avalon, Georgia	213	114.	Molena, Georgia	368
55.	Lilly, Georgia	213	115.	Jenkinsburg, Georgia	370
56.	Brinson, Georgia	215	116.	Concord, Georgia	375
57.	Montrose, Georgia	215	117.	Braswell, Georgia	379
58.	Payne, Georgia	218	118.	Ambrose, Georgia	380
59.	Roopville, Georgia	218	119.	Sale City, Georgia	380
60.	Bishop, Georgia	224	120.	Martin, Georgia	381 **

* Town populations and incorporated cities reflect data taken from the 2010 U.S. Census. Before acting upon this information it is very important to verify the accuracy of all the information represented, including current population, incorporated status, location of cities and counties, etc.

**This state has more cities to research under 500 population to view the full listing go to our website
TheyFiredtheFirstShot2012.com/therevolution.html

Hawaii

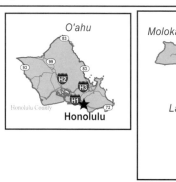

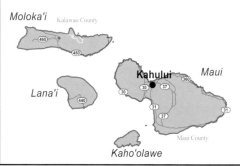

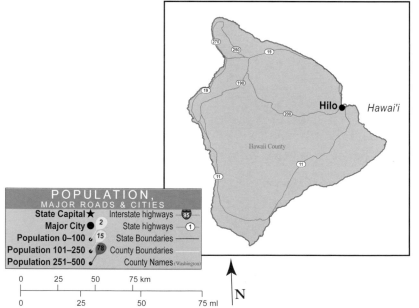

POPULATION,
MAJOR ROADS & CITIES

State Capital ★	Interstate highways 95
Major City ● 2	State highways 1
Population 0–100 ₒ 15	State Boundaries
Population 101–250 ₒ 78	County Boundaries
Population 251–500 ₒ	County Names (Washington)

0   25   50   75 km

0   25   50   75 ml   N

Call Caritas of Birmingham: (Outside USA add **001**) **205-672-2000**
or write: **Caritas of Birmingham**
   100 Our Lady Queen of Peace Drive
   Sterrett, AL 35147 USA

The state of Hawaii is made up of 5 counties that also operate as incorporated municipalities in and of themselves. Four of those counties have a population greater than 50,000,* while the fifth county, Molokai, which was once a leper colony, has a very small population. Visit the Hawaii Secretary of State website for more information on Hawaii. Find out how you can take back already incorporated towns, and counties returning them to a constitutional Christian principle foundation.

Early Beginnings: How It Was Done

Our Lady often calls us to be "missionaries" of Her messages, bringing them to the whole world. In 1820, a farmer, a printer, a physician, two teachers and two clergymen, with their wives, along with three Hawaiians arrived on the shores of Honolulu, met by a pagan people. They were Christian missionaries from America and their task was to permeate the culture with Christian principles. They set to work incorporating Christian values into their way of life as they taught the people how to read and write. In just five years, a revolution occurred, with large numbers converting to Christianity that resulted in the Ten Commandments being recognized by the King as the basis of a code of laws.**

---

* Town populations and incorporated cities reflect data taken from the 2010 U.S. Census. Before acting upon this information it is very important to verify the accuracy of all the information represented, including current population, incorporated status, location of cities and counties, etc.

** *Hawaii,* Unsigned, The Encyclopedia Britannica, 11th Edition, Volume XIII The Encyclopedia Britannica Company, 1910, pp 90-93

Idaho

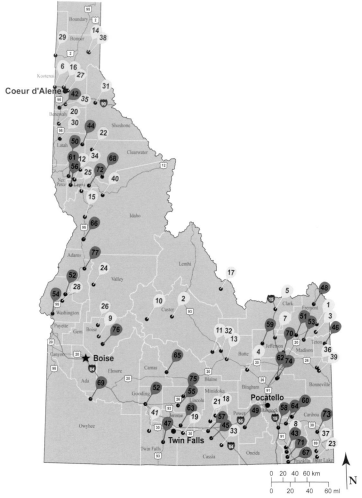

0 20 40 60 km
0 20 40 60 ml

N

POPULATION,
MAJOR ROADS & CITIES

State Capital ★	Interstate highways 95
Major City ●	U.S. highways 82
Population 0–100	15
Population 101–250	
Population 251–500	78
	County Names (Washington)
	State Boundaries ———
	County Boundaries ———

	City, State	Population		City, State	Population
1.	Warm River, Idaho	3	61.	Culdesac, Idaho	380
2.	Clayton, Idaho	7	62.	Basalt, Idaho	394
3.	Drummond, Idaho	16	63.	Eden, Idaho	405
4.	Atomic City, Idaho	29	64.	Lava Hot Springs, Idaho	407
5.	Spencer, Idaho	37	65.	Fairfield, Idaho	416
6.	State Line, Idaho	38	66.	Riggins, Idaho	419
7.	Hamer, Idaho	48	67.	Weston, Idaho	437
8.	Oxford, Idaho	48	68.	Weippe, Idaho	441
9.	Placerville, Idaho	53	69.	Grand View, Idaho	452
10.	Stanley, Idaho	63	70.	Lewisville, Idaho	458
11.	Lost River, Idaho	68	71.	Dayton, Idaho	463
12.	Reubens, Idaho	71	72.	Nezperce, Idaho	466
13.	Butte City, Idaho	74	73.	George, Idaho	476
14.	Hope, Idaho	86	74.	Firth, Idaho	477
15.	White Bird, Idaho	91	75.	Richfield, Idaho	482
16.	Huetter, Idaho	100	76.	Idaho City, Idaho	485
17.	Leadore, Idaho	105	77.	New Meadows, Idaho	496
18.	Minidoka, Idaho	112			
19.	Murtaugh, Idaho	115			
20.	Tensed, Idaho	123			
21.	Acequia, Idaho	124			
22.	Elk River, Idaho	125			
23.	St. Charles, Idaho	131			
24.	Donnelly, Idaho	152			
25.	Ferdinand, Idaho	159			
26.	Crouch, Idaho	162			
27.	Fernan Lake Village, Idaho	169			
28.	Midvale, Idaho	171			
29.	Old, Idaho	184			
30.	Onaway, Idaho	187			
31.	Wardner, Idaho	188			
32.	Moore, Idaho	189			
33.	Malta, Idaho	193			
34.	Peck, Idaho	197			
35.	Harrison, Idaho	203			
36.	Swan Valley, Idaho	204			
37.	Bloomington, Idaho	206			
38.	East Hope, Idaho	210			
39.	Irwin, Idaho	219			
40.	Stites, Idaho	221			
41.	Castleford, Idaho	226			
42.	Worley, Idaho	257			
43.	Clifton, Idaho	259			
44.	Bovill, Idaho	260			
45.	Albion, Idaho	267			
46.	Tetonia, Idaho	269			
47.	Hollister, Idaho	272			
48.	Island Park, Idaho	286			
49.	Rockland, Idaho	295			
50.	Kendrick, Idaho	303			
51.	Parker, Idaho	305			
52.	Bliss, Idaho	318			
53.	Newdale, Idaho	323			
54.	Cambridge, Idaho	328			
55.	Dietrich, Idaho	332			
56.	Winchester, Idaho	340			
57.	Declo, Idaho	343			
58.	Arimo, Idaho	355			
59.	Mud Lake, Idaho	358			
60.	Bancroft, Idaho	377			

* Town populations and incorporated cities reflect data taken from the 2010 U.S. Census. Before acting upon this information it is very important to verify the accuracy of all the information represented, including current population, incorporated status, location of cities and counties, etc.

Illinois

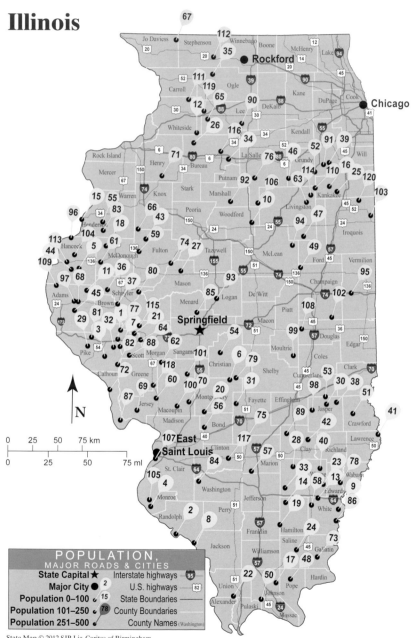

State Map © 2012 SJP. Lic. Caritas of Birmingham
Cannot be duplicated without written permission.
Call Caritas of Birmingham: (Outside USA add **001**) **205-672-2000**
or write: **Caritas of Birmingham**
100 Our Lady Queen of Peace Drive
Sterrett, AL 35147 USA

	City, State	Population		City, State	Population
1.	Valley City, Illinois	13	61.	Tennessee, Illinois	115
2.	Kaskaskia, Illinois	14	62.	Scottville, Illinois	116
3.	Time, Illinois	23	63.	Emington, Illinois	117
4.	Fults, Illinois	26	64.	Lynnville, Illinois	117
5.	Bentley, Illinois	35	65.	Harmon, Illinois	120
6.	Wenonah, Illinois	37	66.	St. Augustine, Illinois	120
7.	Florence, Illinois	38	67.	Nora, Illinois	121
8.	Rockwood, Illinois	42	68.	Mound Station, Illinois	122
9.	Phillipstown, Illinois	44	69.	Otterville, Illinois	126
10.	Panola, Illinois	45	70.	Eagarville, Illinois	127
11.	La Prairie, Illinois	47	71.	Bishop Hill, Illinois	128
12.	Deer Grove, Illinois	48	72.	Hamburg, Illinois	128
13.	Burnt Prairie, Illinois	52	73.	Junction, Illinois	129
14.	Belle Prairie City, Illinois	54	74.	Liverpool, Illinois	129
15.	Gulf Port, Illinois	54	75.	Vernon, Illinois	129
16.	Union Hill, Illinois	58	76.	Leonore, Illinois	130
17.	Simpson, Illinois	60	77.	Naples, Illinois	130
18.	Sciota, Illinois	61	78.	Browns, Illinois	134
19.	Macedonia, Illinois	63	79.	Ohlman, Illinois	135
20.	Walshville, Illinois	64	80.	Browning, Illinois	137
21.	Exeter, Illinois	65	81.	New Salem, Illinois	137
22.	Mill Creek, Illinois	65	82.	Pearl, Illinois	138
23.	Golden Gate, Illinois	68	83.	Raritan, Illinois	138
24.	Muddy, Illinois	68	84.	Venedy, Illinois	138
25.	Irwin, Illinois	74	85.	Cantrall, Illinois	139
26.	New Bedford, Illinois	75	86.	Maunie, Illinois	139
27.	Topeka, Illinois	76	87.	Brussels, Illinois	141
28.	Johnsonville, Illinois	77	88.	Glasgow, Illinois	141
29.	El Dara, Illinois	78	89.	Iola, Illinois	141
30.	Rose Hill, Illinois	80	90.	West Brooklyn, Illinois	142
31.	Bingham, Illinois	83	91.	Wilmington, Illinois	142
32.	Detroit, Illinois	83	92.	La Rose, Illinois	144
33.	Keenes, Illinois	83	93.	Broadwell, Illinois	145
34.	Hollowayville, Illinois	84	94.	Anchor, Illinois	146
35.	Adeline, Illinois	85	95.	Muncie, Illinois	146
36.	Camden, Illinois	86	96.	Pontoosuc, Illinois	146
37.	Ripley, Illinois	86	97.	Coatsburg, Illinois	147
38.	Yale, Illinois	86	98.	Wheeler, Illinois	147
39.	Symerton, Illinois	87	99.	Allenville, Illinois	148
40.	Mount Erie, Illinois	88	100.	Dorchester, Illinois	151
41.	Russellville, Illinois	94	101.	Standard City, Illinois	152
42.	Sailor Springs, Illinois	95	102.	Longview, Illinois	153
43.	Ellisville, Illinois	96	103.	Iroquois, Illinois	154
44.	Basco, Illinois	98	104.	Ferris, Illinois	156
45.	Columbus, Illinois	99	105.	Maeystown, Illinois	157
46.	Kinsman, Illinois	99	106.	Dana, Illinois	159
47.	Strawn, Illinois	100	107.	Sauget, Illinois	159
48.	Eddyville, Illinois	101	108.	Garrett, Illinois	162
49.	Foosland, Illinois	101	109.	Lima, Illinois	163
50.	Belknap, Illinois	104	110.	Reddick, Illinois	163
51.	Stoy, Illinois	104	111.	Coleta, Illinois	164
52.	East Brooklyn, Illinois	106	112.	Ridott, Illinois	164
53.	Hidalgo, Illinois	106	113.	Elvaston, Illinois	165
54.	Jeisyville, Illinois	107	114.	Campus, Illinois	166
55.	Media, Illinois	107	115.	Concord, Illinois	167
56.	Old Ripley, Illinois	108	116.	Dover, Illinois	168
57.	Walnut Hill, Illinois	108	117.	Huey, Illinois	169
58.	Springerton, Illinois	110	118.	Rockbridge, Illinois	169
59.	Marietta, Illinois	112	119.	Nelson, Illinois	170
60.	Fidelity, Illinois	114	120.	Papineau, Illinois	171 **

* Town populations and incorporated cities reflect data taken from the 2010 U.S. Census. Before acting upon this information it is very important to verify the accuracy of all the information represented, including current population, incorporated status, location of cities and counties, etc.

**This state has more cities to research under 500 population to view the full listing go to our website
TheyFiredtheFirstShot2012.com/therevolution.html

Indiana

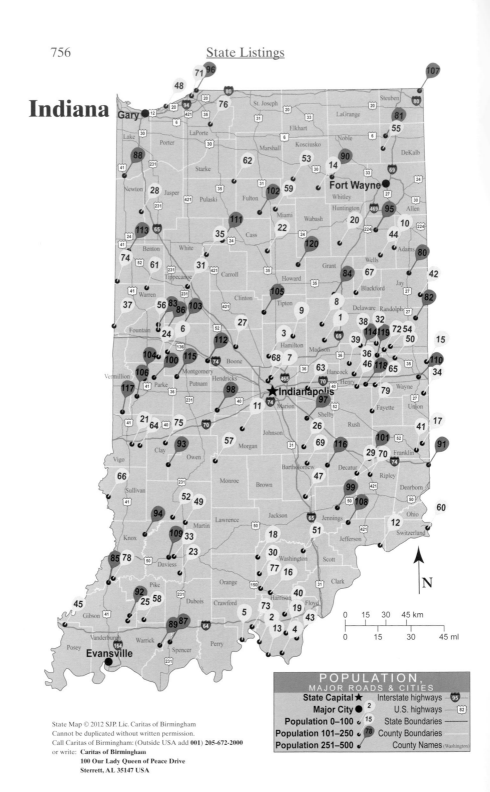

POPULATION,
MAJOR ROADS & CITIES

State Capital ★	Interstate highways
Major City ●	U.S. highways
Population 0–100	State Boundaries
Population 101–250	County Boundaries
Population 251–500	County Names (Washington)

	City, State	Population		City, State	Population
1.	River Forest, Indiana	22	61.	Pine Village, Indiana	217
2.	New Amsterdam, Indiana	27	62.	Monterey, Indiana	218
3.	North Crows Nest, Indiana	45	63.	Spring Lake, Indiana	218
4.	Laconia, Indiana	50	64.	Riley, Indiana	221
5.	Alton, Indiana	55	65.	Straughn, Indiana	222
6.	Alamo, Indiana	66	66.	Merom, Indiana	228
7.	Crows Nest, Indiana	73	67.	Shamrock Lakes, Indiana	231
8.	Country Club Heights, Indiana	79	68.	Wynnedale, Indiana	231
9.	Woodlawn Heights, Indiana	79	69.	Clifford, Indiana	233
10.	Vera Cruz, Indiana	80	70.	Napoleon, Indiana	234
11.	Bethany, Indiana	81	71.	Pottawattamie Park, Indiana	235
12.	Brooksburg, Indiana	81	72.	Losantville, Indiana	237
13.	Mauckport, Indiana	81	73.	Leavenworth, Indiana	238
14.	Sidney, Indiana	83	74.	Ambia, Indiana	239
15.	Whitewater, Indiana	83	75.	Center Point, Indiana	242
16.	Fredericksburg, Indiana	85	76.	Kingsbury, Indiana	242
17.	Mount Carmel, Indiana	86	77.	Hardinsburg, Indiana	248
18.	Saltillo, Indiana	92	78.	Decker, Indiana	249
19.	New Middle, Indiana	93	79.	Glenwood, Indiana	250
20.	Mount Etna, Indiana	94	80.	Bryant, Indiana	252
21.	Spring Hill, Indiana	98	81.	Corunna, Indiana	254
22.	Onward, Indiana	100	82.	Saratoga, Indiana	254
23.	Alfordsville, Indiana	101	83.	Newtown, Indiana	256
24.	Wallace, Indiana	105	84.	Fowlerton, Indiana	261
25.	Mackey, Indiana	106	85.	Hazleton, Indiana	263
26.	Mount Auburn, Indiana	117	86.	Wingate, Indiana	263
27.	Ulen, Indiana	117	87.	Gentryville, Indiana	268
28.	Mount Ayr, Indiana	122	88.	Schneider, Indiana	277
29.	Millhousen, Indiana	127	89.	Tennyson, Indiana	279
30.	Livonia, Indiana	128	90.	Larwill, Indiana	283
31.	Indian Village, Indiana	133	91.	West Harrison, Indiana	289
32.	Blountsville, Indiana	134	92.	Somerville, Indiana	293
33.	Cannelburg, Indiana	135	93.	Switz City, Indiana	293
34.	Boston, Indiana	138	94.	Edwardsport, Indiana	303
35.	Yeoman, Indiana	139	95.	Uniondale, Indiana	310
36.	Greensboro, Indiana	143	96.	Michiana Shores, Indiana	313
37.	State Line City, Indiana	143	97.	Fairland, Indiana	315
38.	Springport, Indiana	149	98.	Stilesville, Indiana	316
39.	Cadiz, Indiana	150	99.	Vernon, Indiana	318
40.	Crandall, Indiana	152	100.	Marshall, Indiana	324
41.	Cedar Grove, Indiana	156	101.	New Point, Indiana	331
42.	Salamonia, Indiana	157	102.	Fulton, Indiana	333
43.	Elizabeth, Indiana	162	103.	New Richmond, Indiana	333
44.	Poneto, Indiana	166	104.	Bloomingdale, Indiana	335
45.	Griffin, Indiana	172	105.	Kempton, Indiana	335
46.	Dunreith, Indiana	177	106.	Mecca, Indiana	335
47.	Jonesville, Indiana	177	107.	Clear Lake, Indiana	339
48.	Dune Acres, Indiana	182	108.	Dupont, Indiana	339
49.	Crane, Indiana	184	109.	Montgomery, Indiana	343
50.	Economy, Indiana	187	110.	Spring Grove, Indiana	344
51.	Little York, Indiana	192	111.	Burnettsville, Indiana	346
52.	Newberry, Indiana	193	112.	New Ross, Indiana	347
53.	Burket, Indiana	195	113.	Earl Park, Indiana	348
54.	Modoc, Indiana	196	114.	Mount Summit, Indiana	352
55.	Altona, Indiana	197	115.	Russellville, Indiana	358
56.	Mellott, Indiana	197	116.	Hartsville, Indiana	362
57.	Stinesville, Indiana	198	117.	Universal, Indiana	362
58.	Spurgeon, Indiana	207	118.	Lewisville, Indiana	366
59.	Macy, Indiana	209	119.	Mooreland, Indiana	375
60.	Patriot, Indiana	209	120.	Amboy, Indiana	384 **

* Town populations and incorporated cities reflect data taken from the 2010 U.S. Census. Before acting upon this information it is very important to verify the accuracy of all the information represented, including current population, incorporated status, location of cities and counties, etc.

**This state has more cities to research under 500 population to view the full listing go to our website
TheyFiredtheFirstShot2012.com/therevolution.html

Iowa

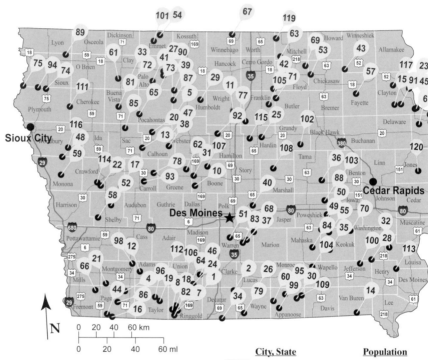

City, State	Population
1. Beaconsfield, Iowa	15
2. Le Roy, Iowa	15
3. Durango, Iowa	22
4. Hepburn, Iowa	23
5. Pioneer, Iowa	23
6. Bankston, Iowa	25
7. Delphos, Iowa	25
8. Maloy, Iowa	29
9. Millville, Iowa	30
10. Berkley, Iowa	32
11. Galt, Iowa	32
12. Carbon, Iowa	34
13. Yetter, Iowa	34
14. Mount Sterling, Iowa	36
15. Elkport, Iowa	37
16. Blanchard, Iowa	38
17. Aspinwall, Iowa	40
18. Benton, Iowa	41
19. Conway, Iowa	41
20. Jolley, Iowa	41

POPULATION,
MAJOR ROADS & CITIES

State Capital ★   Interstate highways 95
Major City ● 2   U.S. highways 82
Population 0–100 ● 15   State Boundaries ——
Population 101–250 ● 78 County Boundaries ——
Population 251–500 ●   County Names (Washington)

0   20   40   60 km
0   20   40   60 ml

Call Caritas of Birmingham: (Outside USA add 001) 205-672-2000
or write: **Caritas of Birmingham**
            100 Our Lady Queen of Peace Drive
            Sterrett, AL 35147 USA

City, State	Population		City, State	Population
21. Coburg, Iowa	42		61. Rossie, Iowa	70
22. Buck Grove, Iowa	43		62. Dana, Iowa	71
23. Clayton, Iowa	43		63. Orchard, Iowa	71
24. Ellston, Iowa	43		64. Shannon City, Iowa	71
25. Owasa, Iowa	43		65. Varina, Iowa	71
26. Millerton, Iowa	45		66. Imogene, Iowa	72
27. Rodman, Iowa	45		67. Scarville, Iowa	72
28. Coppock, Iowa	47		68. Swan, Iowa	72
29. Hardy, Iowa	47		69. Colwell, Iowa	73
30. Udell, Iowa	47		70. Kinross, Iowa	73
31. Beaver, Iowa	48		71. Aredale, Iowa	74
			72. Greenville, Iowa	75
			73. Plover, Iowa	77
			74. Struble, Iowa	78
			75. Chatsworth, Iowa	79
			76. Graf, Iowa	79
			77. Popejoy, Iowa	79
			78. Ralston, Iowa	79
			79. Clio, Iowa	80
			80. Spragueville, Iowa	81
			81. Truesdale, Iowa	81
			82. Redding, Iowa	82
			83. Ackworth, Iowa	83
			84. Keomah Village, Iowa	84
			85. Nemaha, Iowa	85
			86. Yorktown, Iowa	85
			87. Bradgate, Iowa	86
			88. Hartwick, Iowa	86
			89. Matlock, Iowa	87
			90. Cylinder, Iowa	88
			91. Garber, Iowa	88
32. Cotter, Iowa	48		92. Webster City, Iowa	88
33. Gillett Grove, Iowa	49		93. Willey, Iowa	88
34. Pleasanton, Iowa	49		94. Craig, Iowa	89
35. Hayesville, Iowa	50		95. Rathbun, Iowa	89
36. Vining, Iowa	50		96. Sharpsburg, Iowa	89
37. Sandyville, Iowa	51		97. Zwingle, Iowa	91
38. Rinard, Iowa	52		98. Grant, Iowa	92
39. Ottosen, Iowa	55		99. Numa, Iowa	92
40. Valeria, Iowa	57		100. Pleasant Plain, Iowa	93
41. Curlew, Iowa	58		101. Gruver, Iowa	94
42. Dougherty, Iowa	58		102. Morrison, Iowa	94
43. Jackson Junction, Iowa	58		103. Luzerne, Iowa	96
44. Northboro, Iowa	58		104. Chillicothe, Iowa	97
45. Osterdock, Iowa	59		105. Hansell, Iowa	98
46. Thayer, Iowa	59		106. Arispe, Iowa	100
47. Knierim, Iowa	60		107. Fraser, Iowa	102
48. Rodney, Iowa	60		108. St. Anthony, Iowa	102
49. Gibson, Iowa	61		109. Unionville, Iowa	102
50. Guernsey, Iowa	63		110. Andover, Iowa	103
51. Spring Hill, Iowa	63		111. Oyens, Iowa	103
52. Kirkman, Iowa	64		112. Cromwell, Iowa	107
53. Bassett, Iowa	66		113. Mount Union, Iowa	107
54. Dolliver, Iowa	66		114. Arion, Iowa	108
55. Thornburg, Iowa	67		115. Buckeye, Iowa	108
56. Balltown, Iowa	68		116. Oto, Iowa	108
57. Randalia, Iowa	68		117. St. Olaf, Iowa	108
58. Tennant, Iowa	68		118. Baldwin, Iowa	109
59. Turin, Iowa	68		119. Carpenter, Iowa	109
60. Plano, Iowa	70		120. Center Junction, Iowa	111 **

* Town populations and incorporated cities reflect data taken from the 2010 U.S. Census. Before acting upon this information it is very important to verify the accuracy of all the information represented, including current population, incorporated status, location of cities and counties, etc.

**This state has more cities to research under 500 population to view the full listing go to our website
TheyFiredtheFirstShot2012.com/therevolution.html

Kansas

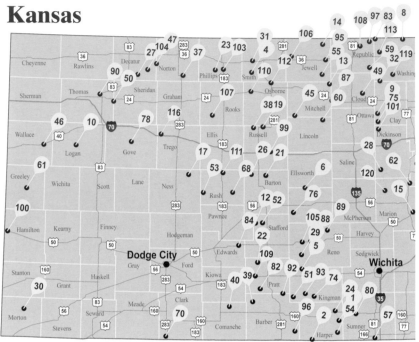

	City, State	Population			City, State	Population
1.	Freeport, Kansas	5		27.	Dresden, Kansas	41
2.	Waldron, Kansas	11		28.	Carlton, Kansas	42
3.	Bassett, Kansas	14		29.	Langdon, Kansas	42
4.	Cedar, Kansas	14		30.	Richfield, Kansas	43
5.	Penalosa, Kansas	17		31.	Athol, Kansas	44
6.	Frederick, Kansas	18		32.	Vining, Kansas	45
7.	Latimer, Kansas	20		33.	Coyville, Kansas	46
8.	Hollenberg, Kansas	21		34.	Hamlin, Kansas	46
9.	Oak Hill, Kansas	24		35.	Matfield Green, Kansas	47
10.	Russell Springs, Kansas	24		36.	Leona, Kansas	48
11.	Lone Elm, Kansas	25		37.	Edmond, Kansas	49
12.	Radium, Kansas	25		38.	Paradise, Kansas	49
13.	Scottsville, Kansas	25		39.	Sun City, Kansas	53
14.	Webber, Kansas	25		40.	Wilmore, Kansas	53
15.	Cedar Point, Kansas	28		41.	Huron, Kansas	54
16.	Mildred, Kansas	28		42.	Earlton, Kansas	55
17.	Brownell, Kansas	29		43.	Elmdale, Kansas	55
18.	Dunlap, Kansas	30		44.	New Albany, Kansas	56
19.	Waldo, Kansas	30		45.	Hunter, Kansas	57
20.	Bushong, Kansas	34		46.	Wallace, Kansas	57
21.	Susank, Kansas	34		47.	Clayton, Kansas	59
22.	Byers, Kansas	35		48.	Parkerville, Kansas	59
23.	Speed, Kansas	37		49.	Aurora, Kansas	60
24.	Danville, Kansas	38		50.	Menlo, Kansas	61
25.	Willis, Kansas	38		51.	Nashville, Kansas	64
26.	Galatia, Kansas	39		52.	Seward, Kansas	64

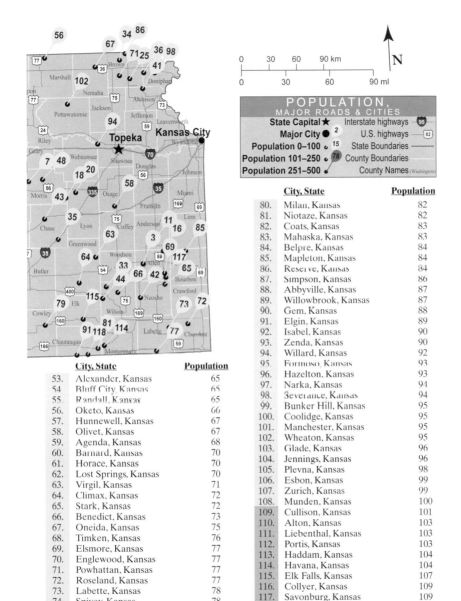

POPULATION,
MAJOR ROADS & CITIES

State Capital ★	Interstate highways	95
Major City ● 2	U.S. highways	82
Population 0–100 ● 15	State Boundaries	
Population 101–250 ● 78	County Boundaries	
Population 251–500 ●	County Names (Washington)	

City, State	Population
80. Milan, Kansas	82
81. Niotaze, Kansas	82
82. Coats, Kansas	83
83. Mahaska, Kansas	83
84. Belpre, Kansas	84
85. Mapleton, Kansas	84
86. Reserve, Kansas	84
87. Simpson, Kansas	86
88. Abbyville, Kansas	87
89. Willowbrook, Kansas	87
90. Gem, Kansas	88
91. Elgin, Kansas	89
92. Isabel, Kansas	90
93. Zenda, Kansas	90
94. Willard, Kansas	92
95. Formoso, Kansas	93
96. Hazelton, Kansas	93
97. Narka, Kansas	94
98. Severance, Kansas	94
99. Bunker Hill, Kansas	95
100. Coolidge, Kansas	95
101. Manchester, Kansas	95
102. Wheaton, Kansas	95
103. Glade, Kansas	96
104. Jennings, Kansas	96
105. Plevna, Kansas	98
106. Esbon, Kansas	99
107. Zurich, Kansas	99
108. Munden, Kansas	100
109. Cullison, Kansas	101
110. Alton, Kansas	103
111. Liebenthal, Kansas	103
112. Portis, Kansas	103
113. Haddam, Kansas	104
114. Havana, Kansas	104
115. Elk Falls, Kansas	107
116. Collyer, Kansas	109
117. Savonburg, Kansas	109
118. Chautauqua, Kansas	111
119. Palmer, Kansas	111
120. Durham, Kansas	112 **

City, State	Population
53. Alexander, Kansas	65
54. Bluff City, Kansas	65
55. Randall, Kansas	65
56. Oketo, Kansas	66
57. Hunnewell, Kansas	67
58. Olivet, Kansas	67
59. Agenda, Kansas	68
60. Barnard, Kansas	70
61. Horace, Kansas	70
62. Lost Springs, Kansas	70
63. Virgil, Kansas	71
64. Climax, Kansas	72
65. Stark, Kansas	72
66. Benedict, Kansas	73
67. Oneida, Kansas	75
68. Timken, Kansas	76
69. Elsmore, Kansas	77
70. Englewood, Kansas	77
71. Powhattan, Kansas	77
72. Roseland, Kansas	77
73. Labette, Kansas	78
74. Spivey, Kansas	78
75. Longford, Kansas	79
76. Raymond, Kansas	79
77. Bartlett, Kansas	80
78. Gove City, Kansas	80
79. Cambridge, Kansas	82

* Town populations and incorporated cities reflect data taken from the 2010 U.S. Census. Before acting upon this information it is very important to verify the accuracy of all the information represented, including current population, incorporated status, location of cities and counties, etc.

**This state has more cities to research under 500 population to view the full listing go to our website
TheyFiredtheFirstShot2012.com/therevolution.html

Kentucky

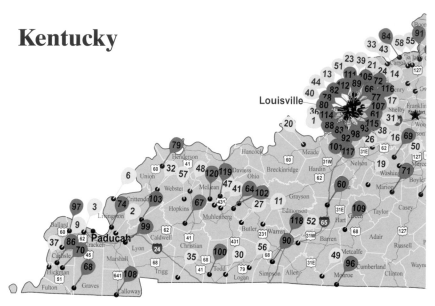

City, State	Population		City, State	Population
1. South Park View, Kentucky	7		31. Sycamore, Kentucky	160
2. Dycusburg, Kentucky	26		32. Wheatcroft, Kentucky	160
3. Concord, Kentucky	35		33. Prestonville, Kentucky	161
4. Foster, Kentucky	44		34. Buckhorn, Kentucky	162
5. Blaine, Kentucky	47		35. LaFayette, Kentucky	165
6. Carrsville, Kentucky	50		36. Mockingbird Valley, Kentucky	167
7. Gratz, Kentucky	78		37. Columbus, Kentucky	170
8. Booneville, Kentucky	81		38. Cambridge, Kentucky	175
9. Blandville, Kentucky	90		39. Thornhill, Kentucky	178
10. California, Kentucky	90		40. Maryhill Estates, Kentucky	179
11. Woodbury, Kentucky	90		41. South Carrollton, Kentucky	184
12. Sardis, Kentucky	103		42. Lakeview Heights, Kentucky	185
13. Ten Broeck, Kentucky	103		43. Worthville, Kentucky	185
14. Smithfield, Kentucky	106		44. Glenview Manor, Kentucky	191
15. Kenton Vale, Kentucky	110		45. Allen, Kentucky	193
16. Fairfield, Kentucky	113		46. Mentor, Kentucky	193
17. Hickory Hill, Kentucky	114		47. Bremen, Kentucky	197
18. Blackey, Kentucky	120		48. Slaughters, Kentucky	216
19. Raywick, Kentucky	134		49. Fountain Run, Kentucky	217
20. Ekron, Kentucky	135		50. Mackville, Kentucky	222
21. Meadowbrook Farm, Kentucky	136		51. Crossgate, Kentucky	225
22. Monterey, Kentucky	138		52. Oakland, Kentucky	225
23. Manor Creek, Kentucky	140		53. Livingston, Kentucky	226
24. Hills and Dales, Kentucky	142		54. Woodlawn, Kentucky	229
25. Fairview, Kentucky	143		55. Sparta, Kentucky	231
26. Lincolnshire, Kentucky	148		56. Corinth, Kentucky	232
27. Rochester, Kentucky	152		57. Nebo, Kentucky	236
28. Germantown, Kentucky	154		58. Sanders, Kentucky	238
29. Wallins Creek, Kentucky	156		59. Dover, Kentucky	252
30. Allensville, Kentucky	157		60. Bonnieville, Kentucky	255

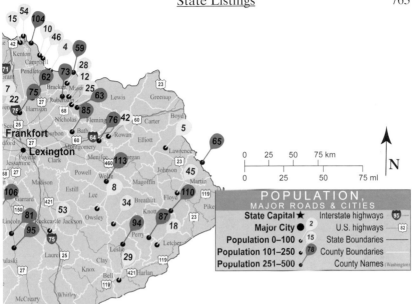

City, State	Population		City, State	Population
61. Wildwood, Kentucky	261		93. Meadowview Estates, Kentucky	363
62. Berry, Kentucky	264		94. Hyden, Kentucky	365
63. Ewing, Kentucky	264		95. Norwood, Kentucky	370
64. Rockport, Kentucky	266		96. Gamaliel, Kentucky	376
65. Warfield, Kentucky	269		97. Kevil, Kentucky	376
66. Broeck Pointe, Kentucky	272		98. Kingsley, Kentucky	381
67. St. Charles, Kentucky	277		99. Grand Rivers, Kentucky	382
68. Water Valley, Kentucky	279		100. Trenton, Kentucky	384
69. Williebburg, Kentucky	282		101. Hunters Hollow, Kentucky	386
70. Spring Mill, Kentucky	287		102. McHenry, Kentucky	388
71. Bradfordsville, Kentucky	294		103. Fredonia, Kentucky	401
72. Goose Creek, Kentucky	294		104. Melbourne, Kentucky	401
73. Mount Olivet, Kentucky	299		105. River Bluff, Kentucky	403
74. Smithland, Kentucky	301		106. Hustonville, Kentucky	405
75. Sadieville, Kentucky	303		107. Richlawn, Kentucky	405
76. Salt Lick, Kentucky	303		108. Hazel, Kentucky	410
77. Creekside, Kentucky	305		109. Center, Kentucky	423
78. Druid Hills, Kentucky	308		110. Wayland, Kentucky	426
79. Waverly, Kentucky	308		111. Moorland, Kentucky	431
80. Brownsboro Village, Kentucky	319		112. Briarwood, Kentucky	435
81. Eubank, Kentucky	319		113. Campton, Kentucky	441
82. Glenview Hills, Kentucky	319		114. Norbourne Estates, Kentucky	441
83. Bellewood, Kentucky	321		115. Forest Hills, Kentucky	444
84. Ghent, Kentucky	323		116. Riverwood, Kentucky	446
85. Sharpsburg, Kentucky	323		117. Fox Chase, Kentucky	447
86. Arlington, Kentucky	324		118. Plum Springs, Kentucky	453
87. Vicco, Kentucky	334		119. Island, Kentucky	458
88. Strathmoor Manor, Kentucky	337		120. Sacramento , Kentucky	468 **
89. Old Brownsboro Place, KY	353			
90. Woodburn, Kentucky	355			
91. Glencoe, Kentucky	360			
92. Poplar Hills, Kentucky	362			

* Town populations and incorporated cities reflect data taken from the 2010 U.S. Census. Before acting upon this information it is very important to verify the accuracy of all the information represented, including current population, incorporated status, location of cities and counties, etc.

**This state has more cities to research under 500 population to view the full listing go to our website
TheyFiredtheFirstShot2012.com/therevolution.html

Louisiana

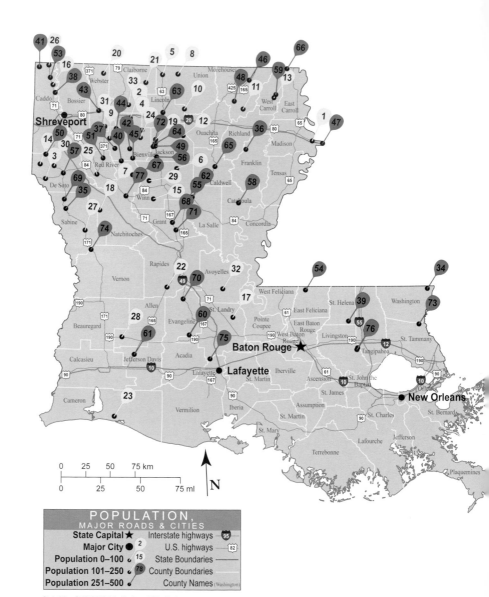

0 25 50 75 km
0 25 50 75 ml
N

POPULATION,
MAJOR ROADS & CITIES
State Capital ★   Interstate highways 95
Major City ●   U.S. highways 82
Population 0–100   15   State Boundaries
Population 101–250   78   County Boundaries
Population 251–500   County Names (Washington)

State Map © 2012 SJP. Lic. Caritas of Birmingham
Cannot be duplicated without written permission.
Call Caritas of Birmingham: (Outside USA add **001**) **205-672-2000**
or write: **Caritas of Birmingham**
       100 Our Lady Queen of Peace Drive
       Sterrett, AL 35147 USA

	City, State	Population		City, State	Population
1.	Mound, Louisiana	19	61.	Fenton, Louisiana	379
2.	Mount Lebanon, Louisiana	83	62.	Tullos, Louisiana	385
3.	Stanley, Louisiana	107	63.	Vienna, Louisiana	386
4.	Bryceland, Louisiana	108	64.	North Hodge, Louisiana	388
5.	Lillie, Louisiana	118	65.	Columbia, Louisiana	390
6.	Sikes, Louisiana	119	66.	Kilbourne, Louisiana	416
7.	Powhatan, Louisiana	135	67.	Goldonna, Louisiana	430
8.	Spearsville, Louisiana	137	68.	Dry Prong, Louisiana	436
9.	Jamestown, Louisiana	139	69.	Converse, Louisiana	440
10.	Downsville, Louisiana	141	70.	Turkey Creek, Louisiana	441
11.	Oak Ridge, Louisiana	144	71.	Pollock, Louisiana	469
12.	Eros, Louisiana	155	72.	Hodge, Louisiana	470
13.	Pioneer, Louisiana	156	73.	Sun, Louisiana	470
14.	Longstreet, Louisiana	157	74.	Hornbeck, Louisiana	480
15.	Atlanta, Louisiana	163	75.	Cankton, Louisiana	484
16.	Gilliam, Louisiana	164	76.	Springfield, Louisiana	487
17.	Palmetto, Louisiana	164	77.	Clarence, Louisiana	499
18.	Robeline, Louisiana	174			
19.	Quitman, Louisiana	181			
20.	Shongaloo, Louisiana	182			
21.	Lisbon, Louisiana	185			
22.	McNary, Louisiana	211			
23.	Creola, Louisiana	213			
24.	Bienville, Louisiana	218			
25.	Edgefield, Louisiana	218			
26.	Ida, Louisiana	221			
27.	Fisher, Louisiana	230			
28.	Reeves, Louisiana	232			
29.	Calvin, Louisiana	238			
30.	Grand Cane, Louisiana	242			
31.	Heflin, Louisiana	244			
32.	Plaucheville, Louisiana	248			
33.	Athens, Louisiana	249			
34.	Angie, Louisiana	251			
35.	Noble, Louisiana	252			
36.	Baskin, Louisiana	254			
37.	Castor, Louisiana	258			
38.	Belcher, Louisiana	263			
39.	Montpelier, Louisiana	266			
40.	Ashland, Louisiana	269			
41.	Rodessa, Louisiana	270			
42.	Lucky, Louisiana	272			
43.	Dixie Inn, Louisiana	273			
44.	Dubberly, Louisiana	273			
45.	Saline, Louisiana	277			
46.	Bonita, Louisiana	284			
47.	Delta, Louisiana	284			
48.	Collinston, Louisiana	287			
49.	East Hodge, Louisiana	289			
50.	Keachi, Louisiana	295			
51.	Hall Summit, Louisiana	300			
52.	Evergreen, Louisiana	310			
53.	Hosston, Louisiana	318			
54.	Norwood, Louisiana	322			
55.	George, Louisiana	327			
56.	Dodson, Louisiana	337			
57.	South Mansfield, Louisiana	346			
58.	Harrisonburg, Louisiana	348			
59.	Forest, Louisiana	355			
60.	Chataignier, Louisiana	364			

* Town populations and incorporated cities reflect data taken from the 2010 U.S. Census. Before acting upon this information it is very important to verify the accuracy of all the information represented, including current population, incorporated status, location of cities and counties, etc.

Maine

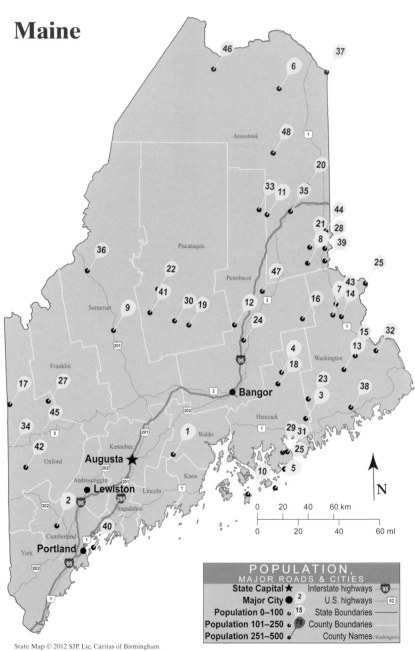

POPULATION,
MAJOR ROADS & CITIES

State Capital ★	Interstate highways 🛡95
Major City ● 2	U.S. highways 82
Population 0–100 ● 15	State Boundaries ——
Population 101–250 ● 78	County Boundaries ——
Population 251–500 ●	County Names (Washington)

	City, State	Population
1.	Hibberts Gore, Maine	1
2.	Frye Island, Maine	5
3.	Beddington, Maine	50
4.	Great Pond, Maine	58
5.	Frenchboro, Maine	61
6.	Westmanland, Maine	62
7.	Talmadge, Maine	64
8.	Bancroft, Maine	68
9.	Caratunk, Maine	69
10.	Isle au Haut, Maine	73
11.	Hersey, Maine	83
12.	Maxfield, Maine	97
13.	Wesley, Maine	98
14.	Waite, Maine	101
15.	Crawford, Maine	105
16.	Lakeville, Maine	105
17.	Upton, Maine	113
18.	Aurora, Maine	114
19.	Bowerbank, Maine	116
20.	Hammond, Maine	118
21.	Haynesville, Maine	121
22.	Beaver Cove, Maine	122
23.	Deblois, Maine	124
24.	Edinburg, Maine	131
25.	Vanceboro, Maine	140
26.	Cranberry Isles, Maine	141
27.	Byron, Maine	145
28.	Orient, Maine	147
29.	Northfield, Maine	148
30.	Willimantic, Maine	150
31.	Cooper, Maine	154
32.	Meddybemps, Maine	157
33.	Mount Chase, Maine	201
34.	Gilead, Maine	209
35.	Dyer Brook, Maine	213
36.	Moose River, Maine	218
37.	Hamlin, Maine	219
38.	Whitneyville, Maine	220
39.	Weston, Maine	228
40.	Long Island, Maine	230
41.	Shirley Mills, Maine	233
42.	Stoneham, Maine	236
43.	Topsfield, Maine	237
44.	Amity, Maine	238
45.	Hanover, Maine	238
46.	Allagash, Maine	239
47.	Woodville, Maine	248
48.	Masardis, Maine	249

* Town populations and incorporated cities reflect data taken from the 2010 U.S. Census. Before acting upon this information it is very important to verify the accuracy of all the information represented, including current population, incorporated status, location of cities and counties, etc.

Maryland

City, State	Population
1. Port Tobacco Village, Maryland	13
2. Eldorado, Maryland	59
3. Brookview, Maryland	60
4. Eagle Harbor, Maryland	63
5. Luke, Maryland	65
6. Highland Beach, Maryland	96
7. Barclay, Maryland	120
8. Church Creek, Maryland	125
9. Brookeville, Maryland	134
10. Galestown, Maryland	138
11. Templeville, Maryland	138
12. Marydel, Maryland	141
13. Henderson, Maryland	146
14. Burkittsville, Maryland	151
15. Hillsboro, Maryland	161
16. Barnesville, Maryland	172
17. Queen Anne, Maryland	222
18. Goldsboro, Maryland	246
19. Glen Echo, Maryland	255
20. Vienna, Maryland	271
21. Rosemont, Maryland	294
22. Kitzmiller, Maryland	321
23. Accident, Maryland	325
24. Betterton, Maryland	345
25. Mardela Springs, Maryland	347
26. Laytonsville, Maryland	353
27. Clear Spring, Maryland	358
28. Deer Park, Maryland	399
29. East New Market, Maryland	400
30. Midland, Maryland	446
31. Barton, Maryland	457
32. Friendsville, Maryland	491
33. Sudlersville, Maryland	497

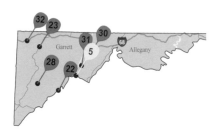

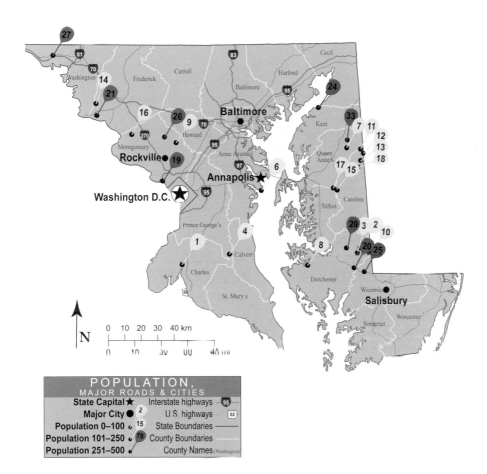

* Town populations and incorporated cities reflect data taken from the 2010 U.S. Census. Before acting upon this information it is very important to verify the accuracy of all the information represented, including current population, incorporated status, location of cities and counties, etc.

Massachusetts

	City, State	Population
1.	Gosnold town, Massachusetts	75
2.	Monroe town, Massachusetts	121
3.	Mount Washington town, MA	167
4.	New Ashford town, MA	228
5.	Aquinnah town, Massachusetts	311
6.	Tyringham town, Massachusetts	327
7.	Hawley town, Massachusetts	337
8.	Rowe town, Massachusetts	393
9.	Tolland town, Massachusetts	485
10.	Alford town, Massachusetts	494

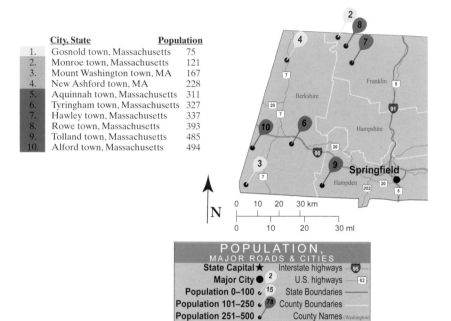

Michigan

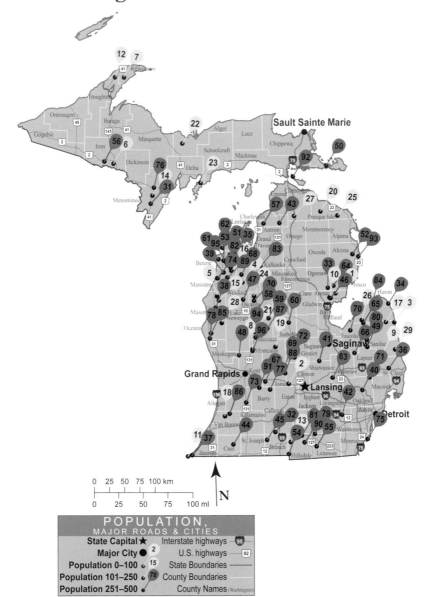

0 25 50 75 100 km

0 25 50 75 100 ml

N

POPULATION,
MAJOR ROADS & CITIES

State Capital ★	Interstate highways	95
Major City ●	2	U.S. highways	82
Population 0–100	15	State Boundaries	
Population 101–250	78	County Boundaries	
Population 251–500		County Names (Washington)	

	City, State	Population		City, State	Population
1.	Turner, Michigan	114	61.	Elberta, Michigan	372
2.	Eagle, Michigan	123	62.	Empire, Michigan	375
3.	Forestville, Michigan	136	63.	Gaines, Michigan	380
4.	Harrietta, Michigan	143	64.	Whittemore, Michigan	384
5.	Free Soil, Michigan	144	65.	Gagetown, Michigan	388
6.	Alpha, Michigan	145	66.	Otter Lake, Michigan	389
7.	Ahmeek, Michigan	146	67.	Clarksville, Michigan	394
8.	Pierson, Michigan	172	68.	Mesick, Michigan	394
9.	Melvin, Michigan	180	69.	Hubbardston, Michigan	395
10.	Twining, Michigan	181	70.	Akron, Michigan	402
11.	Michiana, Michigan	182	71.	Leonard, Michigan	403
12.	Copper City, Michigan	190	72.	Perrinton, Michigan	406
13.	Allen, Michigan	191	73.	Martin, Michigan	410
14.	Carney, Michigan	192	74.	Onekama, Michigan	411
15.	Fountain, Michigan	193	75.	Estral Beach, Michigan	418
16.	Copemish, Michigan	194	76.	Powers, Michigan	422
17.	Minden City, Michigan	197	77.	Woodland, Michigan	425
18.	Breedsville, Michigan	199	78.	Rothbury, Michigan	432
19.	McBride, Michigan	205	79.	Cement City, Michigan	438
20.	Millersburg, Michigan	206	80.	Kingston, Michigan	440
21.	Stanwood, Michigan	211	81.	Hanover, Michigan	441
22.	Chatham, Michigan	220	82.	Thompsonville, Michigan	441
23.	Garden, Michigan	221	83.	Fife Lake, Michigan	443
24.	Tustin, Michigan	230	84.	Kinde, Michigan	448
25.	Posen, Michigan	234	85.	New Era, Michigan	451
26.	Owendale, Michigan	241	86.	Bloomingdale, Michigan	454
27.	Wolverine, Michigan	244	87.	Mecosta, Michigan	457
28.	Walkerville, Michigan	247	88.	Pewamo, Michigan	469
29.	Applegate, Michigan	248	89.	Kaleva, Michigan	470
30.	Le Roy, Michigan	256	90.	North Adams, Michigan	477
31.	Daggett, Michigan	258	91.	Freeport, Michigan	483
32.	Burlington, Michigan	261	92.	Mackinac Island, Michigan	492
33.	Prescott, Michigan	266	93.	Harrisville, Michigan	493
34.	Port Hope, Michigan	267	94.	Morley, Michigan	493
35.	Lake Ann, Michigan	268	95.	Benzonia, Michigan	497
36.	Emmett, Michigan	269	96.	Sand Lake, Michigan	500
37.	Grand Beach, Michigan	272			
38.	Custer, Michigan	284			
39.	Bear Lake, Michigan	286			
40.	Lake Angelus, Michigan	290			
41.	Oakley, Michigan	290			
42.	Barton Hills, Michigan	294			
43.	Boyne Falls, Michigan	294			
44.	Vandalia, Michigan	301			
45.	Sherwood, Michigan	309			
46.	Omer, Michigan	313			
47.	Luther, Michigan	318			
48.	Casnovia, Michigan	319			
49.	Clifford, Michigan	324			
50.	De Tour Village, Michigan	325			
51.	Honor, Michigan	328			
52.	Lincoln, Michigan	337			
53.	Beulah, Michigan	342			
54.	Montgomery, Michigan	342			
55.	Clayton, Michigan	344			
56.	Gaastra, Michigan	347			
57.	Ellsworth, Michigan	349			
58.	Hersey, Michigan	350			
59.	Barryton, Michigan	355			
60.	Rosebush, Michigan	368			

* Town populations and incorporated cities reflect data taken from the 2010 U.S. Census. Before acting upon this information it is very important to verify the accuracy of all the information represented, including current population, incorporated status, location of cities and counties, etc.

Minnesota

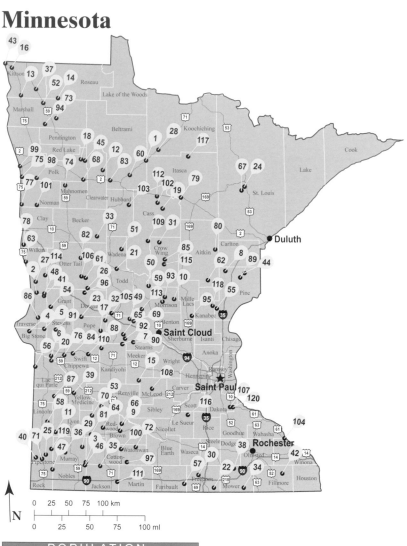

0   25   50   75   100 km
0   25   50   75   100 ml

N

	City, State	Population		City, State	Population
1.	Funkley, Minnesota	5	61.	Vining, Minnesota	78
2.	Tenney, Minnesota	5	62.	McGrath, Minnesota	80
3.	Kinbrae, Minnesota	12	63.	Kent, Minnesota	81
4.	Barry, Minnesota	16	64.	Wanda, Minnesota	84
5.	Johnson, Minnesota	29	65.	Spring Hill, Minnesota	85
6.	Correll, Minnesota	34	66.	Evan, Minnesota	86
7.	Regal, Minnesota	34	67.	Iron Junction, Minnesota	86
8.	Denham, Minnesota	35	68.	Lengby, Minnesota	86
9.	Cobden, Minnesota	36	69.	St. Anthony (Stearns Co.), MN	86
10.	Hillman, Minnesota	38	70.	Seaforth, Minnesota	86
11.	Florence, Minnesota	39	71.	Trosky, Minnesota	86
12.	Leonard, Minnesota	41	72.	La Salle, Minnesota	87
13.	Donaldson, Minnesota	42	73.	Holt, Minnesota	88
14.	Strathcona, Minnesota	44	74.	Bejou, Minnesota	89
15.	Cedar Mills, Minnesota	45	75.	Nielsville, Minnesota	90
16.	Humboldt, Minnesota	45	76.	Holloway, Minnesota	92
17.	Sedan, Minnesota	45	77.	Perley, Minnesota	92
18.	Trail, Minnesota	46	78.	Comstock, Minnesota	93
19.	Boy River, Minnesota	47	79.	Zemple, Minnesota	93
20.	Louisburg, Minnesota	47	80.	Tamarack, Minnesota	94
21.	Aldrich, Minnesota	48	81.	Revere, Minnesota	95
22.	Myrtle, Minnesota	48	82.	Richville, Minnesota	96
23.	Farwell, Minnesota	51	83.	Solway, Minnesota	96
24.	Leonidas, Minnesota	52	84.	Danvers, Minnesota	97
25.	Hatfield, Minnesota	54	85.	Trommald, Minnesota	98
26.	Urbank, Minnesota	54	86.	Dumont, Minnesota	100
27.	Doran, Minnesota	55	87.	St. Leo, Minnesota	100
28.	Mizpah, Minnesota	56	88.	Sunburg, Minnesota	100
29.	Dovray, Minnesota	57	89.	Bruno, Minnesota	102
30.	Manchester, Minnesota	57	90.	Roscoe, Minnesota	102
31.	Manhattan Beach, Minnesota	57	91.	Alberta, Minnesota	103
32.	Westport, Minnesota	57	92.	Lake Henry, Minnesota	103
33.	Wolf Lake, Minnesota	57	93.	Lastrup, Minnesota	104
34.	Taopi, Minnesota	58	94.	Viking, Minnesota	104
35.	Wilder, Minnesota	60	95.	Bock, Minnesota	106
36.	Hadley, Minnesota	61	96.	Milleryille, Minnesota	106
37.	Halma, Minnesota	61	97.	Odin, Minnesota	106
38.	Sargeant, Minnesota	61	98.	Beltrami, Minnesota	107
39.	Hazel Run, Minnesota	63	99.	Squaw Lake, Minnesota	107
40.	Ihlen, Minnesota	63	100.	Darfur, Minnesota	108
41.	Tintah, Minnesota	63	101.	Borup, Minnesota	110
42.	Whalan, Minnesota	63	102.	Federal Dam, Minnesota	110
43.	St. Vincent, Minnesota	64	103.	Laporte, Minnesota	111
44.	Kerrick, Minnesota	65	104.	Minneiska, Minnesota	111
45.	Gully, Minnesota	66	105.	West Union, Minnesota	111
46.	Dundee, Minnesota	68	106.	Clitherall, Minnesota	112
47.	Kenneth, Minnesota	68	107.	New Trier, Minnesota	112
48.	Nashua, Minnesota	68	108.	Biscay, Minnesota	113
49.	St. Rosa, Minnesota	68	109.	Chickamaw Beach, Minnesota	114
50.	Fort Ripley, Minnesota	69	110.	De Graff, Minnesota	115
51.	Nimrod, Minnesota	69	111.	Alpha, Minnesota	116
52.	Strandquist, Minnesota	69	112.	Bena, Minnesota	116
53.	Delhi, Minnesota	70	113.	Elmdale, Minnesota	116
54.	Norcross, Minnesota	70	114.	Foxhome, Minnesota	116
55.	Henriette, Minnesota	71	115.	Riverton, Minnesota	117
56.	Nassau, Minnesota	72	116.	Heidelberg, Minnesota	122
57.	Walters, Minnesota	73	117.	Effie, Minnesota	123
58.	Arco, Minnesota	75	118.	Quamba, Minnesota	123
59.	Genola, Minnesota	75	119.	Woodstock, Minnesota	124
60.	Turtle River, Minnesota	77	120.	Miesville, Minnesota	125 **

* Town populations and incorporated cities reflect data taken from the 2010 U.S. Census. Before acting upon this information it is very important to verify the accuracy of all the information represented, including current population, incorporated status, location of cities and counties, etc.

**This state has more cities to research under 500 population to view the full listing go to our website
TheyFiredtheFirstShot2012.com/therevolution.html

Mississippi

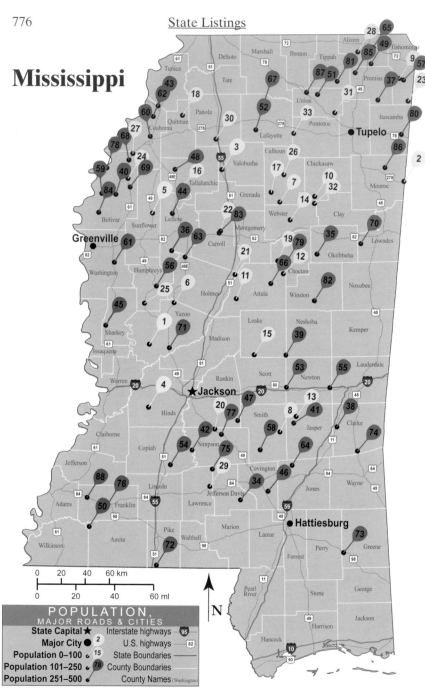

	City, State	Population			City, State	Population
1.	Satartia, Mississippi	55		61.	Arcola, Mississippi	361
2.	Gattman, Mississippi	90		62.	Coahoma, Mississippi	377
3.	Tillatoba, Mississippi	91		63.	Cruger, Mississippi	386
4.	Learned, Mississippi	94		64.	Soso, Mississippi	408
5.	Doddsville, Mississippi	98		65.	Glen, Mississippi	412
6.	Eden, Mississippi	103		66.	Ethel, Mississippi	418
7.	Slate Springs, Mississippi	110		67.	Abbeville, Mississippi	419
8.	Sylvarena, Mississippi	112		68.	Duncan, Mississippi	423
9.	Paden, Mississippi	116		69.	Merigold, Mississippi	439
10.	Woodland, Mississippi	125		70.	Artesia, Mississippi	440
11.	Sallis, Mississippi	134		71.	Bentonia, Mississippi	440
12.	McCool, Mississippi	135		72.	Osyka, Mississippi	440
13.	Montrose, Mississippi	140		73.	McLain, Mississippi	441
14.	Walthall, Mississippi	144		74.	Shubuta, Mississippi	441
15.	Lena, Mississippi	148		75.	New Hebron, Mississippi	447
16.	Glendora, Mississippi	151		76.	Meadville, Mississippi	449
17.	Big Creek, Mississippi	154		77.	D'Lo, Mississippi	452
18.	Falcon, Mississippi	167		78.	Gunnison, Mississippi	452
19.	French Camp, Mississippi	174		79.	Weir, Mississippi	459
20.	Braxton, Mississippi	183		80.	Tremont, Mississippi	465
21.	West, Mississippi	185		81.	Dumas, Mississippi	470
22.	Carrollton, Mississippi	190		82.	Noxapater, Mississippi	472
23.	Golden, Mississippi	191		83.	North Carrollton, Mississippi	473
24.	Winstonville, Mississippi	191		84.	Benoit, Mississippi	477
25.	Louise, Mississippi	199		85.	Jumpertown, Mississippi	480
26.	Pittsboro, Mississippi	202		86.	Hatley, Mississippi	482
27.	Alligator, Mississippi	208		87.	Myrtle, Mississippi	490
28.	Kossuth, Mississippi	209		88.	Roxie, Mississippi	497
29.	Silver Creek, Mississippi	210				
30.	Pope, Mississippi	215				
31.	Blue Springs, Mississippi	228				
32.	Mantee, Mississippi	232				
33.	Toccopola, Mississippi	246				
34.	Bassfield, Mississippi	254				
35.	Sturgis, Mississippi	254				
36.	Morgan City, Mississippi	255				
37.	Marietta, Mississippi	256				
38.	Pachuta, Mississippi	261				
39.	Sebastopol, Mississippi	272				
40.	Pace, Mississippi	274				
41.	Louin, Mississippi	277				
42.	Georgetown, Mississippi	286				
43.	Lula, Mississippi	298				
44.	Schlater, Mississippi	310				
45.	Cary, Mississippi	313				
46.	Seminary, Mississippi	314				
47.	Puckett, Mississippi	316				
48.	Sumner, Mississippi	316				
49.	Rienzi, Mississippi	317				
50.	Crosby, Mississippi	318				
51.	Snow Lake Shores, Mississippi	319				
52.	Taylor, Mississippi	322				
53.	Lake, Mississippi	324				
54.	Beauregard, Mississippi	326				
55.	Chunky, Mississippi	326				
56.	Silver City, Mississippi	337				
57.	Tishomingo, Mississippi	339				
58.	Mize, Mississippi	340				
59.	Beulah, Mississippi	348				
60.	Lyon, Mississippi	350				

Missouri

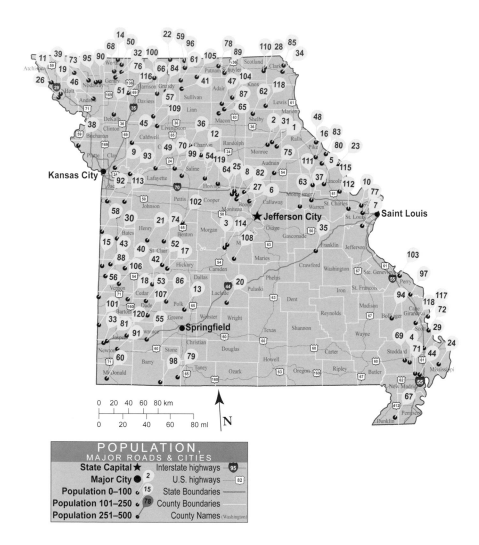

0   20 40 60 80 km

0   20   40   60   80 ml   N

POPULATION,
MAJOR ROADS & CITIES

State Capital ★	Interstate highways 95
Major City ●	U.S. highways 82
Population 0–100	State Boundaries ———
Population 101–250	County Boundaries ———
Population 251–500	County Names (Washington)

	City, State	Population		City, State	Population
1.	Florida, Missouri	0	61.	Harris, Missouri	61
2.	Goss, Missouri	0	62.	Leonard, Missouri	61
3.	Lakeside, Missouri	0	63.	McKittrick, Missouri	61
4.	Baker, Missouri	3	64.	Wooldridge, Missouri	61
5.	Cave, Missouri	5	65.	Ethel, Missouri	62
6.	Three Creeks, Missouri	6	66.	Brimson, Missouri	63
7.	Peaceful Village, Missouri	9	67.	Rives, Missouri	63
8.	McBaine, Missouri	10	68.	Worth, Missouri	63
9.	River Bend, Missouri	10	69.	Penermon, Missouri	64
10.	Champ, Missouri	13	70.	Grand Pass, Missouri	66
11.	Corning, Missouri	15	71.	Catron, Missouri	67
12.	Dalton, Missouri	17	72.	Commerce, Missouri	67
13.	Goodnight, Missouri	18	73.	Arkoe, Missouri	68
14.	Irena, Missouri	18	74.	Tightwad, Missouri	69
15.	Stotesbury, Missouri	18	75.	Vandiver, Missouri	71
16.	Tarrants, Missouri	22	76.	Gentry, Missouri	72
17.	Gerster, Missouri	25	77.	Country Life Acres, Missouri	74
18.	Milford, Missouri	26	78.	Livonia, Missouri	74
19.	Bigelow, Missouri	27	79.	Coney Island, Missouri	75
20.	Evergreen, Missouri	28	80.	Whiteside, Missouri	75
21.	La Due, Missouri	28	81.	Dennis Acres, Missouri	76
22.	South Lineville, Missouri	28	82.	Pierpont, Missouri	76
23.	Annada, Missouri	29	83.	Paynesville, Missouri	77
24.	Pinhook, Missouri	30	84.	Tindall, Missouri	77
25.	Huntsdale, Missouri	31	85.	Revere, Missouri	79
26.	Fortescue, Missouri	32	86.	Aldrich, Missouri	80
27.	Lupus, Missouri	33	87.	Elmer, Missouri	80
28.	Granger, Missouri	34	88.	Deerfield, Missouri	81
29.	Lambert, Missouri	34	89.	Worthington, Missouri	81
30.	Passaic, Missouri	34	90.	Clyde, Missouri	82
31.	Stoutsville, Missouri	36	91.	Ritchey, Missouri	82
32.	Denver, Missouri	39	92.	Riverview Estates, Missouri	82
33.	Cliff Village, Missouri	40	93.	Levasy, Missouri	83
34.	Arbela, Missouri	41	94.	Glen Allen, Missouri	85
35.	St. Cloud, Missouri	41	95.	Guilford, Missouri	85
36.	Triplett, Missouri	41	96.	Lucerne, Missouri	85
37.	Pendleton, Missouri	43	97.	Old Appleton, Missouri	85
38.	Iatan, Missouri	45	98.	Arrow Point, Missouri	86
39.	Quitman, Missouri	45	99.	Mount Leonard, Missouri	87
40.	Harwood, Missouri	47	100.	Mount Moriah, Missouri	87
41.	Osgood, Missouri	48	101.	Waco, Missouri	87
42.	Umber View Heights, Missouri	48	102.	Ionia, Missouri	88
43.	Metz, Missouri	49	103.	Lithium, Missouri	89
44.	North Lilbourn, Missouri	49	104.	Millard, Missouri	89
45.	Elmira, Missouri	50	105.	Pollock, Missouri	89
46.	Rea, Missouri	50	106.	Milo, Missouri	90
47.	South Gifford, Missouri	50	107.	South Greenfield, Missouri	90
48.	Ashburn, Missouri	52	108.	Brumley, Missouri	91
49.	Randolph, Missouri	52	109.	Mooresville, Missouri	91
50.	Allendale, Missouri	53	110.	South Gorin, Missouri	91
51.	Amity, Missouri	54	111.	Truxton, Missouri	91
52.	Vista, Missouri	54	112.	Weldon Spring Heights, Missouri	91
53.	Arcola, Missouri	55	113.	Baldwin Park, Missouri	92
54.	Arrow Rock, Missouri	56	114.	Bagnell, Missouri	93
55.	Hoberg, Missouri	56	115.	Chain of Rocks, Missouri	93
56.	Burgess, Missouri	57	116.	McFall, Missouri	93
57.	Lock Springs, Missouri	57	117.	Dutch, Missouri	94
58.	Merwin, Missouri	58	118.	Newark, Missouri	94
59.	Powersville, Missouri	60	119.	Franklin, Missouri	95
60.	Ginger Blue, Missouri	61	120.	Reeds, Missouri	95 **

* Town populations and incorporated cities reflect data taken from the 2010 U.S. Census. Before acting upon this information it is very important to verify the accuracy of all the information represented, including current population, incorporated status, location of cities and counties, etc.

**This state has more cities to research under 500 population to view the full listing go to our website
TheyFiredtheFirstShot2012.com/therevolution.html

Montana

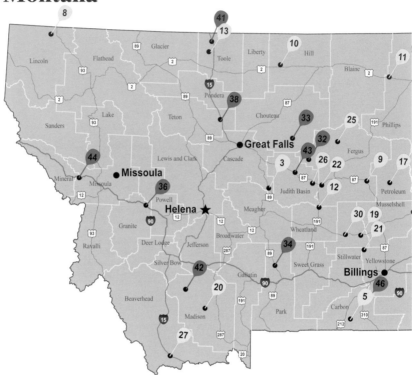

	City, State	Population			City, State	Population
1.	Ismay, Montana	19		21.	Broadview, Montana	192
2.	Outlook, Montana	47		22.	Moore, Montana	193
3.	Neihart, Montana	51		23.	Saco, Montana	197
4.	Flaxville, Montana	71		24.	Bainville, Montana	208
5.	Bearcreek, Montana	79		25.	Winifred, Montana	208
6.	Opheim, Montana	85		26.	Hobson, Montana	215
7.	Melstone, Montana	96		27.	Lima, Montana	221
8.	Rexford, Montana	105		28.	Medicine Lake, Montana	225
9.	Grass Range, Montana	110		29.	Fort Peck, Montana	233
10.	Hingham, Montana	118		30.	Ryegate, Montana	245
11.	Dodson, Montana	124		31.	Brockton, Montana	255
12.	Judith Gap, Montana	126		32.	Denton, Montana	255
13.	Kevin, Montana	154		33.	Geraldine, Montana	261
14.	Plevna, Montana	162		34.	Clyde Park, Montana	288
15.	Westby, Montana	168		35.	Nashua, Montana	290
16.	Richey, Montana	177		36.	Drummond, Montana	309
17.	Winnett, Montana	182		37.	Hysham, Montana	312
18.	Froid, Montana	185		38.	Dutton, Montana	316
19.	Lavina, Montana	187		39.	Ekalaka, Montana	332
20.	Virginia City, Montana	190		40.	Jordan, Montana	343

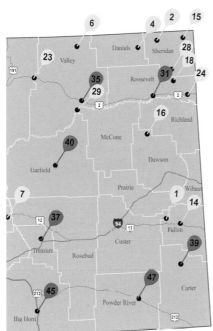

City, State	Population
41. Sunburst, Montana	375
42. Twin Bridges, Montana	375
43. Stanford, Montana	401
44. Alberton, Montana	420
45. Lodge Grass, Montana	428
46. Fromberg, Montana	438
47. Broadus, Montana	468

* Town populations and incorporated cities reflect data taken from the 2010 U.S. Census. Before acting upon this information it is very important to verify the accuracy of all the information represented, including current population, incorporated status, location of cities and counties, etc.

Nebraska

City, State	Population		City, State	Population
1. Monowi, Nebraska	1	29.	Clinton, Nebraska	41
2. Gross, Nebraska	2	30.	Lorton, Nebraska	41
3. Anoka, Nebraska	6	31.	Norman, Nebraska	43
4. Burton, Nebraska	10	32.	Surprise, Nebraska	43
5. Brewster, Nebraska	17	33.	Huntley, Nebraska	44
6. Nenzel, Nebraska	20	34.	Stockham, Nebraska	44
7. Nora, Nebraska	21	35.	Cotesfield, Nebraska	46
8. Sholes, Nebraska	21	36.	Tarnov, Nebraska	46
9. Lamar, Nebraska	23	37.	Saronville, Nebraska	47
10. Obert, Nebraska	23	38.	Belvidere, Nebraska	48
11. Barada, Nebraska	24	39.	Emmet, Nebraska	48
12. Hendley, Nebraska	24	40.	Harbine, Nebraska	49
13. Stockville, Nebraska	25	41.	Elyria, Nebraska	51
14. Preston, Nebraska	28	42.	Foster, Nebraska	51
15. Bazile Mills, Nebraska	29	43.	Garrison, Nebraska	54
16. Strang, Nebraska	29	44.	Smithfield, Nebraska	54
17. Cowles, Nebraska	30	45.	Burr, Nebraska	57
18. Lushton, Nebraska	30	46.	Hamlet, Nebraska	57
19. Verdel, Nebraska	30	47.	Magnet, Nebraska	57
20. Cushing, Nebraska	32	48.	Julian, Nebraska	59
21. Gandy, Nebraska	32	49.	Virginia, Nebraska	60
22. Moorefield, Nebraska	32	50.	Primrose, Nebraska	61
23. Seneca, Nebraska	33	51.	Steele City, Nebraska	61
24. Cornlea, Nebraska	36	52.	Thayer, Nebraska	62
25. McLean, Nebraska	36	53.	Ong, Nebraska	63
26. Crab Orchard, Nebraska	38	54.	Royal, Nebraska	63
27. Ragan, Nebraska	38	55.	Wood Lake, Nebraska	63
28. Gilead, Nebraska	39	56.	Johns, Nebraska	64

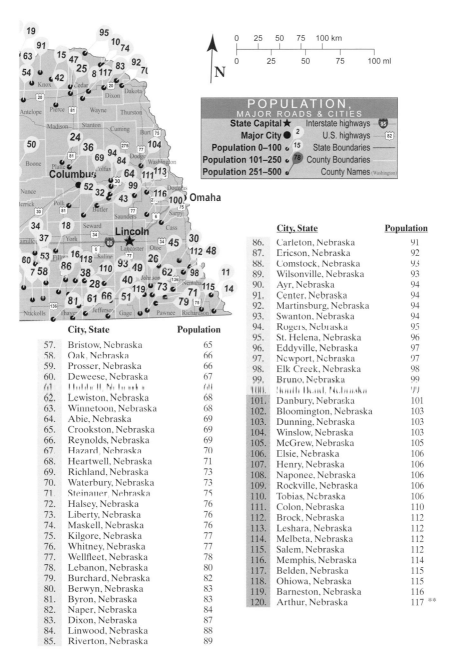

City, State	Population
86. Carleton, Nebraska	91
87. Ericson, Nebraska	92
88. Comstock, Nebraska	93
89. Wilsonville, Nebraska	93
90. Ayr, Nebraska	94
91. Center, Nebraska	94
92. Martinsburg, Nebraska	94
93. Swanton, Nebraska	94
94. Rogers, Nebraska	95
95. St. Helena, Nebraska	96
96. Eddyville, Nebraska	97
97. Newport, Nebraska	97
98. Elk Creek, Nebraska	98
99. Bruno, Nebraska	99
100. South Bend, Nebraska	99
101. Danbury, Nebraska	101
102. Bloomington, Nebraska	103
103. Dunning, Nebraska	103
104. Winslow, Nebraska	103
105. McGrew, Nebraska	105
106. Elsie, Nebraska	106
107. Henry, Nebraska	106
108. Naponee, Nebraska	106
109. Rockville, Nebraska	106
110. Tobias, Nebraska	106
111. Colon, Nebraska	110
112. Brock, Nebraska	112
113. Leshara, Nebraska	112
114. Melbeta, Nebraska	112
115. Salem, Nebraska	112
116. Memphis, Nebraska	114
117. Belden, Nebraska	115
118. Ohiowa, Nebraska	115
119. Barneston, Nebraska	116
120. Arthur, Nebraska	117 **

City, State	Population
57. Bristow, Nebraska	65
58. Oak, Nebraska	66
59. Prosser, Nebraska	66
60. Deweese, Nebraska	67
61. Halsted, Nebraska	68
62. Lewiston, Nebraska	68
63. Winnetoon, Nebraska	68
64. Abie, Nebraska	69
65. Crookston, Nebraska	69
66. Reynolds, Nebraska	69
67. Hazard, Nebraska	70
68. Heartwell, Nebraska	71
69. Richland, Nebraska	73
70. Waterbury, Nebraska	73
71. Steinauer, Nebraska	75
72. Halsey, Nebraska	76
73. Liberty, Nebraska	76
74. Maskell, Nebraska	76
75. Kilgore, Nebraska	77
76. Whitney, Nebraska	77
77. Wellfleet, Nebraska	78
78. Lebanon, Nebraska	80
79. Burchard, Nebraska	82
80. Berwyn, Nebraska	83
81. Byron, Nebraska	83
82. Naper, Nebraska	84
83. Dixon, Nebraska	87
84. Linwood, Nebraska	88
85. Riverton, Nebraska	89

* Town populations and incorporated cities reflect data taken from the 2010 U.S. Census. Before acting upon this information it is very important to verify the accuracy of all the information represented, including current population, incorporated status, location of cities and counties, etc.

**This state has more cities to research under 500 population to view the full listing go to our website
TheyFiredtheFirstShot2012.com/therevolution.html

Nevada

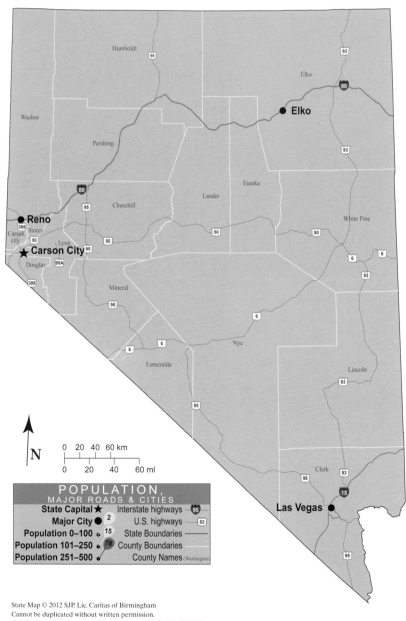

Humboldt
93
95
Elko
80
● **Elko**
Washoe
Pershing
93
80
Eureka
95
Lander
● **Reno**
395
Storey
White Pine
Carson
city
50
Lyon
50
50
50
50
★ **Carson City** 95
6
6
95A
Douglas
93
395
Mineral
95
6
Nye
6
6
Esmeralda
Lincoln
95
93

N

| 0 | 20 | 40 | 60 km |
| 0 | 20 | 40 | 60 ml |

Clark
93
95
15
Las Vegas ●

95

POPULATION,
MAJOR ROADS & CITIES

State Capital ★	Interstate highways	95
Major City ●	2	U.S. highways	82
Population 0–100 ⌂	15	State Boundaries ———
Population 101–250 ⌂	78	County Boundaries ———
Population 251–500 ⌂	County Names (Washington)

State Map © 2012 SJP. Lic. Caritas of Birmingham
Cannot be duplicated without written permission.
Call Caritas of Birmingham: (Outside USA add **001**) **205-672-2000**
or write: **Caritas of Birmingham**
100 Our Lady Queen of Peace Drive
Sterrett, AL 35147 USA

According to the 2010 Census, there are no incorporated towns in Nevada with a population less than 500. *
Visit the Nevada Secretary of State website to research laws on how to incorporate an **un**incorporated area in Nevada and explore solutions in this book, such as nullification of current laws. Find out how you can take back already incorporated towns, and counties returning them to a constitutional Christian principle foundation.

How They Did It: Incorporation

Nevada's state motto is *"All for our country,"* its nickname is "Battle Born State," fitting names, although not what you would expect from a state whose first European settler was a Franciscan. Giving their all to gain freedom, the settlers in this area held the first public meeting on November 12, 1851, discussing the means of protecting their way of life and property. The closest territorial government was in Utah and too far away to quickly respond on their behalf. In 1858 the boundaries for Carson City were laid out. A year later, they met to choose delegates who would draft their constitution in only 10 days. The people voted, adopted the constitution and state officers were chosen. The beginnings of a state were established. After years of perseverance, Nevada entered the Union on October 31, 1864, through a declaration by President Abraham Lincoln.**

---

* Town populations and incorporated cities reflect data taken from the 2010 U.S. Census. Before acting upon this information it is very important to verify the accuracy of all the information represented, including current population, incorporated status, location of cities and counties, etc

** *Nevada*, Unsigned, The Encyclopedia Britannica, 11th Edition, Volume XIX The Encyclopedia Britannica Company, 1911, pp 455–456

New Hampshire

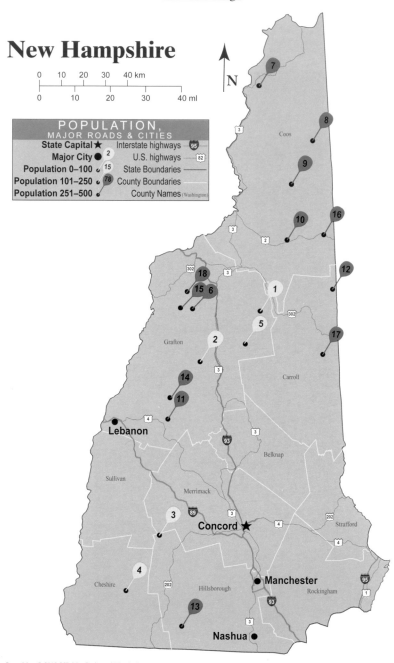

POPULATION,
MAJOR ROADS & CITIES

State Capital ★   Interstate highways [95]
Major City ●   [2]   U.S. highways [82]
Population 0–100   [15]   State Boundaries ———
Population 101–250   [78]   County Boundaries
Population 251–500   County Names (Washington)

	City, State	Population
1.	Livermore, New Hampshire	0
2.	Ellsworth, New Hampshire	83
3.	Windsor, New Hampshire	224
4.	Roxbury, New Hampshire	229
5.	Waterville Valley, NH	247
6.	Easton, New Hampshire	254
7.	Clarksville, New Hampshire	265
8.	Errol, New Hampshire	291
9.	Dummer, New Hampshire	304
10.	Randolph, New Hampshire	310
11.	Orange, New Hampshire	331
12.	Chatham, New Hampshire	337
13.	Sharon, New Hampshire	352
14.	Dorchester, New Hampshire	355
15.	Benton, New Hampshire	364
16.	Shelburne, New Hampshire	372
17.	Eaton, New Hampshire	393
18.	Landaff, New Hampshire	415

New Jersey

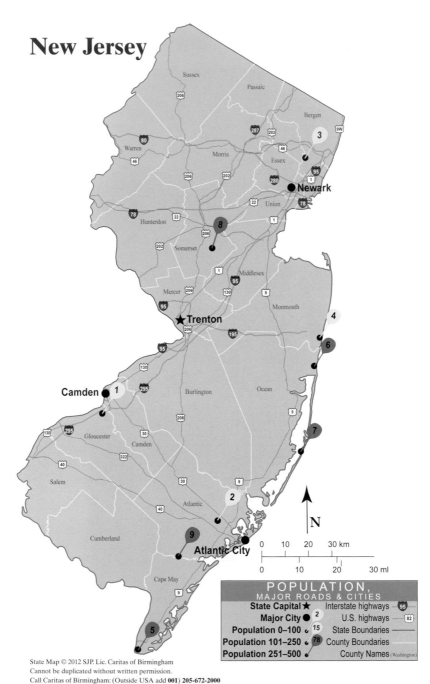

State Map © 2012 SJP. Lic. Caritas of Birmingham
Cannot be duplicated without written permission.
Call Caritas of Birmingham: (Outside USA add **001**) **205-672-2000**
or write: **Caritas of Birmingham**
100 Our Lady Queen of Peace Drive
Sterrett, AL 35147 USA

	City, State	Population
1.	Tavistock, New Jersey	5
2.	Pine Valley, New Jersey	12
3.	Teterboro, New Jersey	67
4.	Loch Arbour, New Jersey	194
5.	Cape May Point, New Jersey	291
6.	Mantoloking, New Jersey	296
7.	Harvey Cedars, New Jersey	337
8.	Millstone, New Jersey	418
9.	Corbin City, New Jersey	492

New Mexico

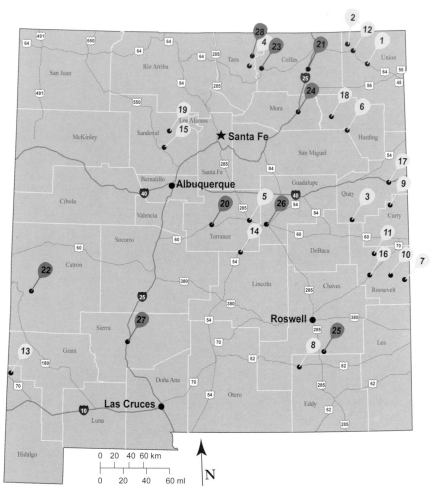

0   20   40   60 km

0   20   40   60 ml

N

	City, State	Population
1.	Grenville, New Mexico	38
2.	Folsom, New Mexico	56
3.	House, New Mexico	68
4.	Taos Ski Valley, New Mexico	69
5.	Encino, New Mexico	82
6.	Mosquero, New Mexico	93
7.	Causey, New Mexico	104
8.	Hope, New Mexico	105
9.	Grady, New Mexico	107
10.	Dora, New Mexico	133
11.	Floyd, New Mexico	133
12.	Des Moines, New Mexico	143
13.	Virden, New Mexico	152
14.	Corona, New Mexico	172
15.	San Ysidro, New Mexico	193
16.	Elida, New Mexico	197
17.	San Jon, New Mexico	216
18.	Roy, New Mexico	234
19.	Jemez Springs, New Mexico	250
20.	Willard, New Mexico	253
21.	Maxwell, New Mexico	254
22.	Reserve, New Mexico	289
23.	Eagle Nest, New Mexico	290
24.	Wagon Mound, New Mexico	314
25.	Lake Arthur, New Mexico	436
26.	Vaughn, New Mexico	446
27.	Williamsburg, New Mexico	449
28.	Red River, New Mexico	477

·

* Town populations and incorporated cities reflect data taken from the 2010 U.S. Census. Before acting upon this information it is very important to verify the accuracy of all the information represented, including current population, incorporated status, location of cities and counties, etc.

New York

	City, State	Population
1.	Dering Harbor, New York	11
2.	Saltaire, New York	37
3.	West Hampton Dunes, New York	55
4.	Ocean Beach, New York	79
5.	Herrings, New York	90
6.	Ames, New York	145
7.	Galway, New York	200
8.	Burke, New York	211
9.	Smyrna, New York	213
10.	Gainesville, New York	229
11.	Turin, New York	232
12.	Constableville, New York	242
13.	Ellisburg, New York	244
14.	Laurens, New York	263
15.	Hammond, New York	280
16.	Barneveld, New York	284
17.	Grand View-on-Hudson, New York	285
18.	Cove Neck, New York	286
19.	Lodi, New York	291
20.	Prospect, New York	291
21.	Deferiet, New York	294
22.	Madison, New York	305
23.	Argyle, New York	306
24.	Dresden, New York	308
25.	Meridian, New York	309
26.	Millport, New York	312
27.	Sagaponack, New York	313
28.	Lisle, New York	320
29.	Richville, New York	323
30.	Speculator, New York	324
31.	Cold Brook, New York	329
32.	Rensselaer Falls, New York	332
33.	Esperance, New York	345
34.	Clayville, New York	350
35.	Castorland, New York	351
36.	Fleischmanns, New York	351
37.	Fabius, New York	352
38.	Mannsville, New York	354
39.	Jeffersonville, New York	359
40.	Bemus Point, New York	364
41.	Franklin, New York	374
42.	Ellicottville, New York	376
43.	Delanson, New York	377
44.	Farnham, New York	382
45.	Limestone, New York	389
46.	Morristown, New York	395
47.	Gilbertsville, New York	399

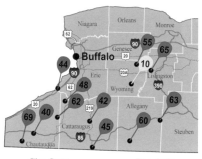

	City, State	Population
48.	Perrysburg, New York	401
49.	Hewlett Bay Park, New York	404
50.	Altmar, New York	407
51.	Centre Island, New York	410
52.	Milford, New York	415
53.	Bloomingburg, New York	420
54.	Hermon, New York	422
55.	Wyoming, New York	434
56.	Edwards, New York	439
57.	Hobart, New York	441
58.	Hewlett Neck, New York	445
59.	Parish, New York	450
60.	Richburg, New York	450
61.	Holland Patent, New York	458
62.	Cherry Creek, New York	461
63.	Almond, New York	466
64.	Valley Falls, New York	466
65.	Leicester, New York	468
66.	Bridgewater, New York	470
67.	Brushton, New York	474
68.	Munnsville, New York	474
69.	Panama, New York	479
70.	Fort Ann, New York	484
71.	Fort Johnson, New York	490
72.	Riverside, New York	497

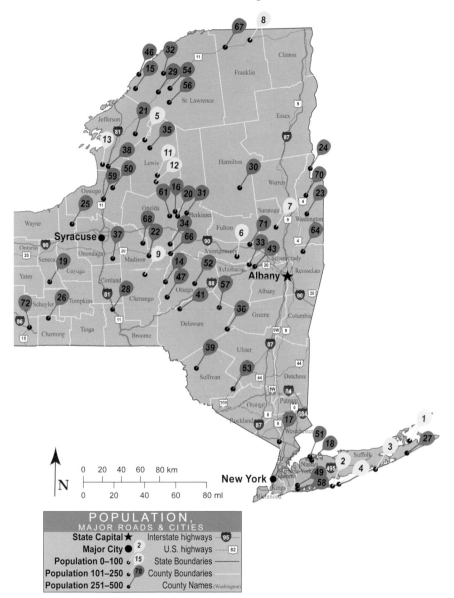

POPULATION,
MAJOR ROADS & CITIES

State Capital ★	Interstate highways 🛡95
Major City ●	U.S. highways 🛡82
Population 0–100 • 15	State Boundaries —
Population 101–250 • 78	County Boundaries —
Population 251–500 •	County Names (Washington)

0 20 40 60 80 km

N

0 20 40 60 80 ml

* Town populations and incorporated cities reflect data taken from the 2010 U.S. Census. Before acting upon this information it is very important to verify the accuracy of all the information represented, including current population, incorporated status, location of cities and counties, etc.

North Carolina

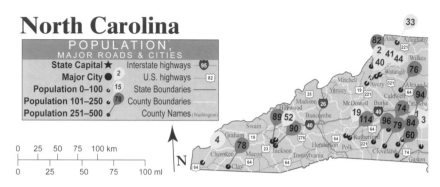

POPULATION,
MAJOR ROADS & CITIES

State Capital ★	Interstate highways — 95
Major City ● 2	U.S. highways — 82
Population 0–100 ◔ 15	State Boundaries —
Population 101–250 ◕ 78	County Boundaries —
Population 251–500 ◕	County Names (Washington)

0   25   50   75   100 km

0   25   50   75   100 ml

N

	City, State	Population		City, State	Population
1.	Dellview, North Carolina	13	41.	Seven Devils, North Carolina	192
2.	Grandfather, North Carolina	25	42.	Autryville, North Carolina	196
3.	Spencer Mountain, North Carolina	37	43.	Eureka, North Carolina	197
4.	Lake Santeetlah, North Carolina	45	44.	Sugar Mountain, North Carolina	198
5.	Leggett, North Carolina	60	45.	Harrells, North Carolina	202
6.	Raynham, North Carolina	72	46.	Colerain, North Carolina	204
7.	Bear Grass, North Carolina	73	47.	Cerro Gordo, North Carolina	207
8.	Speed, North Carolina	80	48.	Walstonburg, North Carolina	219
9.	Hassell, North Carolina	84	49.	Mesic, North Carolina	220
10.	Centerville, North Carolina	89	50.	Momeyer, North Carolina	224
11.	Love Valley, North Carolina	90	51.	Seagrove, North Carolina	228
12.	Como, North Carolina	91	52.	Dillsboro, North Carolina	232
13.	Orrum, North Carolina	91	53.	Halifax, North Carolina	234
14.	Lumber Bridge, North Carolina	94	54.	Roxobel, North Carolina	240
15.	Falkland, North Carolina	96	55.	Askewville, North Carolina	241
16.	Harrellsville, North Carolina	106	56.	Bath, North Carolina	249
17.	Seven Springs, North Carolina	110	57.	Kelford, North Carolina	251
18.	Indian Beach, North Carolina	112	58.	Vandemere, North Carolina	254
19.	Chimney Rock, North Carolina	113	59.	Falcon, North Carolina	258
20.	McDonald, North Carolina	113	60.	Earl, North Carolina	260
21.	McFarlan, North Carolina	117	61.	Sandy Creek, North Carolina	260
22.	Proctorville, North Carolina	117	62.	Castalia, North Carolina	268
23.	Tar Heel, North Carolina	117	63.	Goldston, North Carolina	268
24.	Macon, North Carolina	119	64.	Creswell, North Carolina	276
25.	Lasker, North Carolina	122	65.	Powellsville, North Carolina	276
26.	Linden, North Carolina	130	66.	Severn, North Carolina	276
27.	Middleburg, North Carolina	133	67.	Parmele, North Carolina	278
28.	Norman, North Carolina	138	68.	Stonewall, North Carolina	281
29.	Godwin, North Carolina	139	69.	Sims, North Carolina	282
30.	Bolivia, North Carolina	143	70.	Cameron, North Carolina	285
31.	Boardman, North Carolina	157	71.	Trenton, North Carolina	287
32.	Bald Head Island, North Carolina	158	72.	Turkey, North Carolina	292
33.	Lansing, North Carolina	158	73.	Conetoe, North Carolina	294
34.	Everetts, North Carolina	164	74.	Casar, North Carolina	297
35.	Milton, North Carolina	166	75.	Atkinson, North Carolina	299
36.	Marietta, North Carolina	175	76.	Cedar Rock, North Carolina	300
37.	Pantego, North Carolina	179	77.	East Laurinburg, North Carolina	300
38.	Danbury, North Carolina	189	78.	Hayesville, North Carolina	311
39.	Watha, North Carolina	190	79.	Mooresboro, North Carolina	311
40.	Crossnore, North Carolina	192	80.	Pollocksville, North Carolina	311

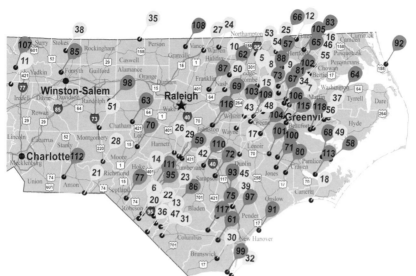

City, State	Population		City, State	Population
81. Oak City, North Carolina	317		113. Minnesott Beach, North Carolina	440
82. Beech Mountain, North Carolina	320		114. Ruthfordton, North Carolina	440
83. Gatesville, North Carolina	321		115. Grimesland, North Carolina	441
84. Waco, North Carolina	321		116. Micro, North Carolina	441
85. Bethania, North Carolina	328		117. Sandyfield, North Carolina	447
86. Dublin, North Carolina	338		118. Washington Park, North Carolina	451
87. Bunn, North Carolina	344			
88. Hobgood, North Carolina	348			
89. Webster, North Carolina	363			
90. Forest Hills, North Carolina	365			
91. Topsail Beach, North Carolina	368			
92. Duck, North Carolina	369			
93. Teachey, North Carolina	376			
94. Brookford, North Carolina	382			
95. Rennert, North Carolina	383			
96. Bostic, North Carolina	386			
97. St. Helena, North Carolina	389			
98. Staley, North Carolina	393			
99. Caswell Beach, North Carolina	398			
100. Cove City, North Carolina	399			
101. Dover, North Carolina	401			
102. Hamilton, North Carolina	408			
103. Saratoga, North Carolina	408			
104. Hookerton, North Carolina	409			
105. Cofield, North Carolina	413			
106. Simpson, North Carolina	416			
107. Ronda, North Carolina	417			
108. Stovall, North Carolina	418			
109. Fountain, North Carolina	427			
110. Salemburg, North Carolina	435			
111. Parkton, North Carolina	436			
112. Peachland, North Carolina	437			

* Town populations and incorporated cities reflect data taken from the 2010 U.S. Census. Before acting upon this information it is very important to verify the accuracy of all the information represented, including current population, incorporated status, location of cities and counties, etc.

North Dakota

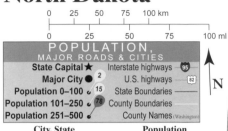

0   25   50   75   100 km

0   25   50   75   100 ml

POPULATION,
MAJOR ROADS & CITIES

State Capital ★	Interstate highways 95
Major City ● 2	U.S. highways 82
Population 0–100 ● 15	State Boundaries ——
Population 101–250 ● 78	County Boundaries ——
Population 251–500 ●	County Names (Washington)

N

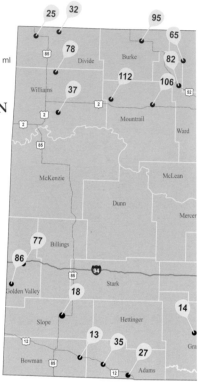

	City, State	Population
1.	Ruso, North Dakota	4
2.	Bergen, North Dakota	7
3.	Grano, North Dakota	7
4.	Loraine, North Dakota	9
5.	Perth, North Dakota	9
6.	Venturia, North Dakota	10
7.	Churchs Ferry, North Dakota	12
8.	Hansboro, North Dakota	12
9.	Pillsbury, North Dakota	12
10.	Kief, North Dakota	13
11.	Bantry, North Dakota	14
12.	Hannah, North Dakota	15
13.	Gascoyne, North Dakota	16
14.	Leith, North Dakota	16
15.	Loma, North Dakota	16
16.	Ayr, North Dakota	17
17.	Overly, North Dakota	18
18.	Amidon, North Dakota	20
19.	Calvin, North Dakota	20
20.	Leal, North Dakota	20
21.	Mylo, North Dakota	20
22.	Braddock, North Dakota	21
23.	Hamberg, North Dakota	21
24.	Calio, North Dakota	22
25.	Fortuna, North Dakota	22
26.	Conway, North Dakota	23
27.	Haynes, North Dakota	23
28.	Ludden, North Dakota	23
29.	York, North Dakota	23
30.	Elliott, North Dakota	25
31.	Knox, North Dakota	25
32.	Ambrose, North Dakota	26
33.	Balfour, North Dakota	26
34.	Antler, North Dakota	27
35.	Bucyrus, North Dakota	27
36.	Cayuga, North Dakota	27
37.	Springbrook, North Dakota	27
38.	Egeland, North Dakota	28
39.	Sarles, North Dakota	28
40.	Gardena, North Dakota	29
41.	Kramer, North Dakota	29
42.	Lawton, North Dakota	30
43.	Sibley, North Dakota	30
44.	Luverne, North Dakota	31
45.	Wales, North Dakota	31
46.	Berlin, North Dakota	34

	City, State	Population
47.	Alsen, North Dakota	35
48.	Brinsmade, North Dakota	35
49.	Monango, North Dakota	36
50.	Wolford, North Dakota	36
51.	Robinson, North Dakota	37
52.	Fairdale, North Dakota	38
53.	Landa, North Dakota	38
54.	Alice, North Dakota	40
55.	Voltaire, North Dakota	40
56.	Dickey, North Dakota	42
57.	Bathgate, North Dakota	43
58.	Cathay, North Dakota	43
59.	Regan, North Dakota	43
60.	Clifford, North Dakota	44
61.	Canton City, North Dakota	45
62.	Courtenay, North Dakota	45
63.	Fredonia, North Dakota	46
64.	Rogers, North Dakota	46
65.	Tolley, North Dakota	47
66.	Hampden, North Dakota	48
67.	Inkster, North Dakota	50
68.	Nekoma, North Dakota	50
69.	Woodworth, North Dakota	50
70.	Barney, North Dakota	52

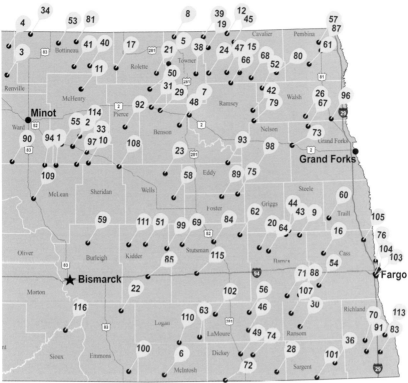

City, State	Population	City, State	Population
71. Kathryn, North Dakota	52	94. Benedict, North Dakota	66
72. Forbes, North Dakota	53	95. Flaxton, North Dakota	66
73. Niagara, North Dakota	53	96. Ardoch, North Dakota	67
74. Fullerton, North Dakota	54	97. Butte, North Dakota	68
75. McHenry, North Dakota	56	98. Pekin, North Dakota	70
76. North River, North Dakota	56	99. Pettibone, North Dakota	70
77. Sentinel Butte, North Dakota	56	100. Hague, North Dakota	71
78. Alamo, North Dakota	57	101. Havana, North Dakota	71
79. Brocket, North Dakota	57	102. Jud, North Dakota	72
80. Milton, North Dakota	58	103. Briarwood, North Dakota	73
81. Souris, North Dakota	58	104. Prairie Rose, North Dakota	73
82. Donnybrook, North Dakota	59	105. Gardner, North Dakota	74
83. Great Bend, North Dakota	60	106. Palermo, North Dakota	74
84. Pingree, North Dakota	60	107. Fort Ransom, North Dakota	77
85. Dawson, North Dakota	61	108. Martin, North Dakota	78
86. Golva, North Dakota	61	109. Coleharbor, North Dakota	79
87. Hamilton, North Dakota	61	110. Lehr, North Dakota	80
88. Nome, North Dakota	62	111. Tuttle, North Dakota	80
89. Grace City, North Dakota	63	112. White Earth, North Dakota	80
90. Douglas, North Dakota	64	113. Dwight, North Dakota	82
91. Mantador, North Dakota	64	114. Karlsruhe, North Dakota	82
92. Balta, North Dakota	65	115. Cleveland, North Dakota	83
93. Warwick, North Dakota	65	116. Solen, North Dakota	83 **

* Town populations and incorporated cities reflect data taken from the 2010 U.S. Census. Before acting upon this information it is very important to verify the accuracy of all the information represented, including current population, incorporated status, location of cities and counties, etc.

**This state has more cities to research under 500 population to view the full listing go to our website
TheyFiredtheFirstShot2012.com/therevolution.html

Ohio

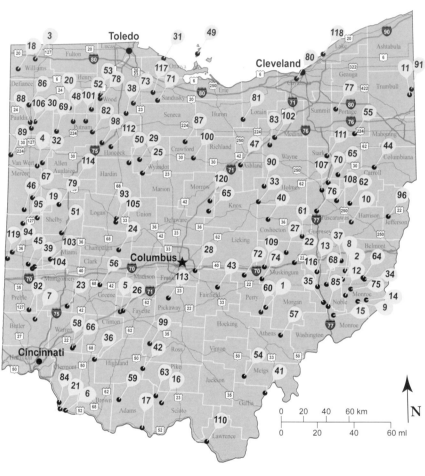

State Map © 2012 SJP. Lic. Caritas of Birmingham
Cannot be duplicated without written permission.
Call Caritas of Birmingham: (Outside USA add **001**) **205-672-2000**
or write: **Caritas of Birmingham**
              100 Our Lady Queen of Peace Drive
              Sterrett, AL 35147 USA

	City, State	Population		City, State	Population
1.	Rendville, Ohio	36	61.	Plainfield, Ohio	157
2.	Miltonsburg, Ohio	43	62.	Leesville, Ohio	158
3.	Holiday City, Ohio	52	63.	Rarden, Ohio	159
4.	Elgin, Ohio	57	64.	Jerusalem, Ohio	161
5.	Octa, Ohio	59	65.	Sparta, Ohio	161
6.	Chilo, Ohio	63	66.	Butlerville, Ohio	163
7.	Jacksonburg, Ohio	63	67.	Montezuma, Ohio	165
8.	Batesville, Ohio	71	68.	Sarahsville, Ohio	166
9.	Graysville, Ohio	76	69.	Cloverdale, Ohio	168
10.	Deersville, Ohio	79	70.	Zoar, Ohio	169
11.	Yankee Lake, Ohio	79	71.	Burgoon, Ohio	172
12.	Stafford, Ohio	81	72.	Glenford, Ohio	173
13.	Fairview, Ohio	83	73.	West Millgrove, Ohio	174
14.	Antioch, Ohio	86	74.	Fultonham, Ohio	176
15.	Lower Salem, Ohio	86	75.	Lewisville, Ohio	176
16.	Otway, Ohio	87	76.	Stone Creek, Ohio	177
17.	Rome, Ohio	94	77.	Sugar Bush Knolls, Ohio	177
18.	Blakeslee, Ohio	96	78.	Custar, Ohio	179
19.	Yorkshire, Ohio	96	79.	Kettlersville, Ohio	179
20.	New Bavaria, Ohio	99	80.	Linndale, Ohio	179
21.	Neville, Ohio	100	81.	Rochester, Ohio	182
22.	Norwich, Ohio	102	82.	Gilboa, Ohio	184
23.	Centerville, Ohio	103	83.	Congress, Ohio	185
24.	Mutual, Ohio	104	84.	Moscow, Ohio	185
25.	Marseilles, Ohio	112	85.	Macksburg, Ohio	186
26.	Milledgeville, Ohio	112	86.	Cecil, Ohio	188
27.	Adamsville, Ohio	114	87.	Chatfield, Ohio	189
28.	Brice, Ohio	114	88.	Latty, Ohio	193
29.	Kirby, Ohio	118	89.	Wren, Ohio	194
30.	Broughton, Ohio	120	90.	Nashville, Ohio	197
31.	Harbor View, Ohio	123	91.	Orangeville, Ohio	197
32.	Venedocia, Ohio	124	92.	West Elkton, Ohio	197
33.	Gann, Ohio	125	93.	Zanesfield, Ohio	197
34.	Wilson, Ohio	125	94.	Palestine, Ohio	200
35.	Dexter City, Ohio	129	95.	Rossburg, Ohio	201
36.	St. Martin, Ohio	129	96.	Bloomingdale, Ohio	202
37.	Salesville, Ohio	129	97.	Harpster, Ohio	204
38.	Bairds, Ohio	130	98.	Mount Cory, Ohio	204
39.	Castine, Ohio	130	99.	South Salem, Ohio	204
40.	Nellie, Ohio	131	100.	North Robinson, Ohio	205
41.	Cheshire, Ohio	132	101.	West Leipsic, Ohio	206
42.	Sinking Spring, Ohio	133	102.	Burbank, Ohio	207
43.	West Rushville, Ohio	134	103.	Ludlow Falls, Ohio	208
44.	Summitville, Ohio	135	104.	Gordon, Ohio	212
45.	Ithaca, Ohio	136	105.	Valley Hi, Ohio	212
46.	New Weston, Ohio	136	106.	Haviland, Ohio	215
47.	Mifflin, Ohio	137	107.	Parral, Ohio	218
48.	Miller City, Ohio	137	108.	Roswell, Ohio	219
49.	Put-in-Bay, Ohio	138	109.	Gratiot, Ohio	221
50.	Patterson, Ohio	139	110.	Hanging Rock, Ohio	221
51.	Lockington, Ohio	141	111.	Hills and Dales, Ohio	221
52.	Belmore, Ohio	143	112.	Jenera, Ohio	221
53.	Milton Center, Ohio	144	113.	Darbyville, Ohio	222
54.	Wilkesville, Ohio	149	114.	Uniopolis, Ohio	222
55.	Limaville, Ohio	151	115.	Vinton, Ohio	222
56.	Clifton, Ohio	152	116.	Belle Valley, Ohio	223
57.	Amesville, Ohio	154	117.	Helena, Ohio	224
58.	Pleasant Plain, Ohio	154	118.	Lakeline, Ohio	226
59.	Cherry Fork, Ohio	155	119.	Hollansburg, Ohio	227
60.	Hemlock, Ohio	155	120.	Chesterville, Ohio	228 **

* Town populations and incorporated cities reflect data taken from the 2010 U.S. Census. Before acting upon this information it is very important to verify the accuracy of all the information represented, including current population, incorporated status, location of cities and counties, etc.

**This state has more cities to research under 500 population to view the full listing go to our website
TheyFiredtheFirstShot2012.com/therevolution.html

Oklahoma

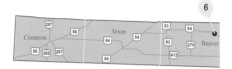

	City, State	Population			City, State	Population
1.	Lotsee, Oklahoma	2		51.	Erin Springs, Oklahoma	87
2.	Shady Grove, Oklahoma	2		52.	Sweetwater, Oklahoma	87
3.	Cardin, Oklahoma	3		53.	Hitchita, Oklahoma	88
4.	Hoot Owl, Oklahoma	4		54.	Lake Aluma, Oklahoma	88
5.	Lambert, Oklahoma	6		55.	Strang, Oklahoma	89
6.	Knowles, Oklahoma	11		56.	New Alluwe, Oklahoma	90
7.	Jefferson, Oklahoma	12		57.	Leon, Oklahoma	91
8.	Renfrow, Oklahoma	12		58.	Maramec, Oklahoma	91
9.	Loveland, Oklahoma	13		59.	Etowah, Oklahoma	92
10.	Cooperton, Oklahoma	16		60.	Gate, Oklahoma	93
11.	Oak Grove, Oklahoma	18		61.	Greenfield, Oklahoma	93
12.	Stidham, Oklahoma	18		62.	Headrick, Oklahoma	94
13.	Foraker, Oklahoma	19		63.	Elmer, Oklahoma	96
14.	Picher, Oklahoma	20		64.	Centrahoma, Oklahoma	97
15.	Capron, Oklahoma	23		65.	Horntown, Oklahoma	97
16.	Friendship, Oklahoma	24		66.	Kildare, Oklahoma	100
17.	Fallis, Oklahoma	27		67.	Shamrock, Oklahoma	101
18.	Putnam, Oklahoma	29		68.	Fair Oaks, Oklahoma	103
19.	Grainola, Oklahoma	31		69.	Manchester, Oklahoma	103
20.	Rosston, Oklahoma	31		70.	Armstrong, Oklahoma	105
21.	Douglas, Oklahoma	32		71.	Albion, Oklahoma	106
22.	Macomb, Oklahoma	32		72.	Castle, Oklahoma	106
23.	Byron, Oklahoma	35		73.	Terlton, Oklahoma	106
24.	Texola, Oklahoma	36		74.	Tullahassee, Oklahoma	106
25.	Amorita, Oklahoma	37		75.	Dacoma, Oklahoma	107
26.	Meridian, Oklahoma	38		76.	Blackburn, Oklahoma	108
27.	May, Oklahoma	39		77.	Smithville, Oklahoma	113
28.	Sugden, Oklahoma	43		78.	Addington, Oklahoma	114
29.	Strong City, Oklahoma	47		79.	Bridgeport, Oklahoma	116
30.	Clearview, Oklahoma	48		80.	Gerty, Oklahoma	118
31.	Hollister, Oklahoma	50		81.	Ratliff City, Oklahoma	120
32.	IXL, Oklahoma	51		82.	Hillsdale, Oklahoma	121
33.	Skedee, Oklahoma	51		83.	Hitchcock, Oklahoma	121
34.	Lima, Oklahoma	53		84.	Loco, Oklahoma	122
35.	Mutual, Oklahoma	61		85.	Mead, Oklahoma	122
36.	Webb City, Oklahoma	62		86.	Hallett, Oklahoma	125
37.	Brooksville, Oklahoma	63		87.	Pensacola, Oklahoma	125
38.	Oakwood, Oklahoma	65		88.	Wann, Oklahoma	125
39.	Ashland, Oklahoma	66		89.	Hoffman, Oklahoma	127
40.	Smith Village, Oklahoma	66		90.	Moffett, Oklahoma	128
41.	Rosedale, Oklahoma	68		91.	Rentiesville, Oklahoma	128
42.	Hickory, Oklahoma	71		92.	Bradley, Oklahoma	130
43.	Atwood, Oklahoma	74		93.	Deer Creek, Oklahoma	130
44.	Grand Lake Towne, Oklahoma	74		94.	Slick, Oklahoma	131
45.	Yeager, Oklahoma	75		95.	New Woodville, Oklahoma	132
46.	Valley Park, Oklahoma	77		96.	Peoria, Oklahoma	132
47.	Hendrix, Oklahoma	79		97.	Bearden, Oklahoma	133
48.	Loyal, Oklahoma	79		98.	Kemp, Oklahoma	133
49.	Carrier, Oklahoma	85		99.	Fairmont, Oklahoma	134
50.	Paradise Hill, Oklahoma	85		100.	Phillips, Oklahoma	135

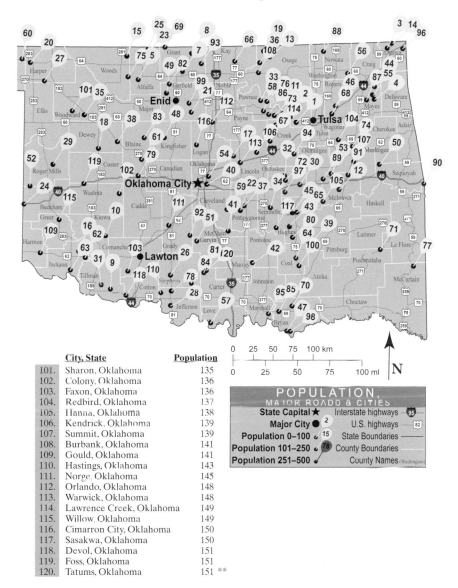

	City, State	Population
101.	Sharon, Oklahoma	135
102.	Colony, Oklahoma	136
103.	Faxon, Oklahoma	136
104.	Redbird, Oklahoma	137
105.	Hanna, Oklahoma	138
106.	Kendrick, Oklahoma	139
107.	Summit, Oklahoma	139
108.	Burbank, Oklahoma	141
109.	Gould, Oklahoma	141
110.	Hastings, Oklahoma	143
111.	Norge, Oklahoma	145
112.	Orlando, Oklahoma	148
113.	Warwick, Oklahoma	148
114.	Lawrence Creek, Oklahoma	149
115.	Willow, Oklahoma	149
116.	Cimarron City, Oklahoma	150
117.	Sasakwa, Oklahoma	150
118.	Devol, Oklahoma	151
119.	Foss, Oklahoma	151
120.	Tatums, Oklahoma	151 **

POPULATION,
MAJOR ROADS & CITIES

State Capital ★	Interstate highways	95
Major City ●	2	U.S. highways	82
Population 0–100	15	State Boundaries
Population 101–250	78	County Boundaries
Population 251–500		County Names (Washington)

* Town populations and incorporated cities reflect data taken from the 2010 U.S. Census. Before acting upon this information it is very important to verify the accuracy of all the information represented, including current population, incorporated status, location of cities and counties, etc.

**This state has more cities to research under 500 population to view the full listing go to our website
TheyFiredtheFirstShot2012.com/therevolution.html

Oregon

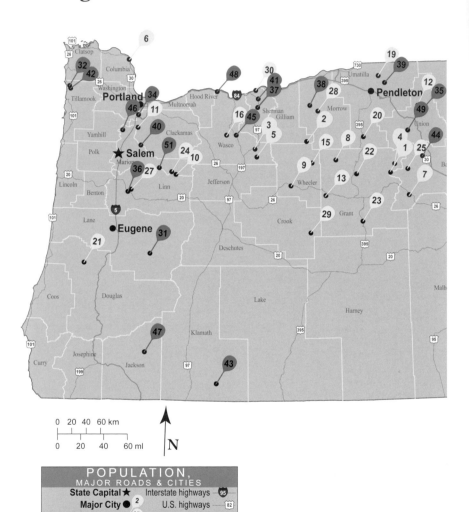

	City, State	Population
1.	Greenhorn, Oregon	0
2.	Lonerock, Oregon	21
3.	Shaniko, Oregon	36
4.	Granite, Oregon	38
5.	Antelope, Oregon	46
6.	Prescott, Oregon	55
7.	Unity, Oregon	71
8.	Monument, Oregon	128
9.	Mitchell, Oregon	130
10.	Idanha, Oregon	134
11.	Barlow, Oregon	135
12.	Summerville, Oregon	135
13.	Dayville, Oregon	149
14.	Richland, Oregon	156
15.	Spray, Oregon	160
16.	Grass Valley, Oregon	164
17.	Adrian, Oregon	177
18.	Jordan Valley, Oregon	181
19.	Helix, Oregon	184
20.	Ukiah, Oregon	186
21.	Elkton, Oregon	195
22.	Long Creek, Oregon	197
23.	Seneca, Oregon	199
24.	Detroit, Oregon	202
25.	Sumpter, Oregon	204
26.	Lostine, Oregon	213
27.	Waterloo, Oregon	229
28.	Lexington, Oregon	238
29.	Paisley, Oregon	243
30.	Rufus, Oregon	249
31.	Westfir, Oregon	253
32.	Nehalem, Oregon	271
33.	Halfway, Oregon	288
34.	Rivergrove, Oregon	289
35.	Imbler, Oregon	306
36.	Sodaville, Oregon	309
37.	Moro, Oregon	324
38.	Ione, Oregon	329
39.	Adams, Oregon	350
40.	Scotts Mills, Oregon	357
41.	Wasco, Oregon	410
42.	Wheeler, Oregon	414
43.	Bonanza, Oregon	415
44.	Haines, Oregon	416
45.	Maupin, Oregon	418
46.	St. Paul, Oregon	421
47.	Butte Falls, Oregon	423
48.	Mosier, Oregon	433
49.	North Powder, Oregon	439
50.	Huntington, Oregon	440
51.	Gates, Oregon	471

* Town populations and incorporated cities reflect data taken from the 2010 U.S. Census. Before acting upon this information it is very important to verify the accuracy of all the information represented, including current population, incorporated status, location of cities and counties, etc.

Pennsylvania

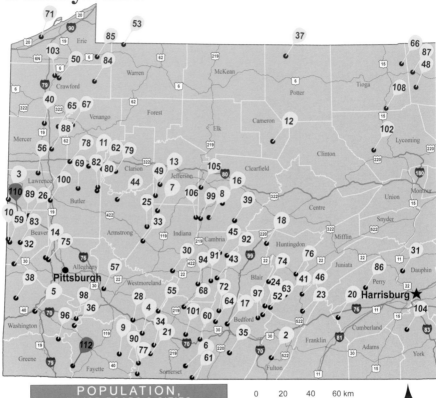

	City, State	Population		City, State	Population
1.	Centralia, Pennsylvania	10	16.	Lumber City, Pennsylvania	76
2.	Valley-Hi, Pennsylvania	15	17.	St. Clairsville, Pennsylvania	78
3.	S.N.P.J., Pennsylvania	19	18.	Birmingham, Pennsylvania	90
4.	Seven Springs, Pennsylvania	26	19.	Mount Carbon, Pennsylvania	91
5.	Green Hills, Pennsylvania	29	20.	Newburg (Clearfield County), PA	92
6.	Callimont, Pennsylvania	41	21.	Casselman, Pennsylvania	94
7.	Smicksburg, Pennsylvania	46	22.	Jeddo, Pennsylvania	98
8.	New Washington, Pennsylvania	59	23.	Shade Gap, Pennsylvania	105
9.	Ohiopyle, Pennsylvania	59	24.	Coalmont, Pennsylvania	106
10.	Glasgow, Pennsylvania	60	25.	Atwood, Pennsylvania	107
11.	Cherry Valley, Pennsylvania	66	26.	Homewood, Pennsylvania	109
12.	Driftwood, Pennsylvania	67	27.	Friendsville, Pennsylvania	111
13.	Worthville, Pennsylvania	67	28.	Donegal, Pennsylvania	120
14.	Haysville, Pennsylvania	70	29.	Eagles Mere, Pennsylvania	120
15.	New Morgan, Pennsylvania	71	30.	Armagh, Pennsylvania	122

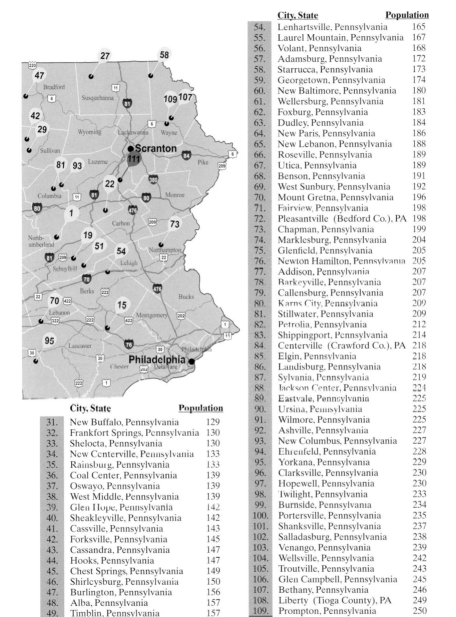

	City, State	Population
54.	Lenhartsville, Pennsylvania	165
55.	Laurel Mountain, Pennsylvania	167
56.	Volant, Pennsylvania	168
57.	Adamsburg, Pennsylvania	172
58.	Starrucca, Pennsylvania	173
59.	Georgetown, Pennsylvania	174
60.	New Baltimore, Pennsylvania	180
61.	Wellersburg, Pennsylvania	181
62.	Foxburg, Pennsylvania	183
63.	Dudley, Pennsylvania	184
64.	New Paris, Pennsylvania	186
65.	New Lebanon, Pennsylvania	188
66.	Roseville, Pennsylvania	189
67.	Utica, Pennsylvania	189
68.	Benson, Pennsylvania	191
69.	West Sunbury, Pennsylvania	192
70.	Mount Gretna, Pennsylvania	196
71.	Fairview, Pennsylvania	198
72.	Pleasantville (Bedford Co.), PA	198
73.	Chapman, Pennsylvania	199
74.	Marklesburg, Pennsylvania	204
75.	Glenfield, Pennsylvania	205
76.	Newton Hamilton, Pennsylvania	205
77.	Addison, Pennsylvania	207
78.	Barkeyville, Pennsylvania	207
79.	Callensburg, Pennsylvania	207
80.	Karns City, Pennsylvania	209
81.	Stillwater, Pennsylvania	209
82.	Petrolia, Pennsylvania	212
83.	Shippingport, Pennsylvania	214
84.	Centerville (Crawford Co.), PA	218
85.	Elgin, Pennsylvania	218
86.	Landisburg, Pennsylvania	218
87.	Sylvania, Pennsylvania	219
88.	Jackson Center, Pennsylvania	224
89.	Eastvale, Pennsylvania	225
90.	Ursina, Pennsylvania	225
91.	Wilmore, Pennsylvania	225
92.	Ashville, Pennsylvania	227
93.	New Columbus, Pennsylvania	227
94.	Ehrenfeld, Pennsylvania	228
95.	Yorkana, Pennsylvania	229
96.	Clarksville, Pennsylvania	230
97.	Hopewell, Pennsylvania	230
98.	Twilight, Pennsylvania	233
99.	Burnside, Pennsylvania	234
100.	Portersville, Pennsylvania	235
101.	Shanksville, Pennsylvania	237
102.	Salladasburg, Pennsylvania	238
103.	Venango, Pennsylvania	239
104.	Wellsville, Pennsylvania	242
105.	Troutville, Pennsylvania	243
106.	Glen Campbell, Pennsylvania	245
107.	Bethany, Pennsylvania	246
108.	Liberty (Tioga County), PA	249
109.	Prompton, Pennsylvania	250
110.	Darlington, Pennsylvania	254
111.	Bear Creek Village, Pennsylvania	257
112.	Greensboro, Pennsylvania	260 **

	City, State	Population
31.	New Buffalo, Pennsylvania	129
32.	Frankfort Springs, Pennsylvania	130
33.	Shelocta, Pennsylvania	130
34.	New Centerville, Pennsylvania	133
35.	Rainsburg, Pennsylvania	133
36.	Coal Center, Pennsylvania	139
37.	Oswayo, Pennsylvania	139
38.	West Middle, Pennsylvania	139
39.	Glen Hope, Pennsylvania	142
40.	Sheakleyville, Pennsylvania	142
41.	Cassville, Pennsylvania	143
42.	Forksville, Pennsylvania	145
43.	Cassandra, Pennsylvania	147
44.	Hooks, Pennsylvania	147
45.	Chest Springs, Pennsylvania	149
46.	Shirleysburg, Pennsylvania	150
47.	Burlington, Pennsylvania	156
48.	Alba, Pennsylvania	157
49.	Timblin, Pennsylvania	157
50.	Woodcock, Pennsylvania	157
51.	Landingville, Pennsylvania	159
52.	Coaldale (Bedford County), PA	161
53.	Bear Lake, Pennsylvania	164

* Town populations and incorporated cities reflect data taken from the 2010 U.S. Census. Before acting upon this information it is very important to verify the accuracy of all the information represented, including current population, incorporated status, location of cities and counties, etc.

This state has more cities to research under 500 population to view the full listing go to our website **TheyFiredtheFirstShot2012.com/therevolution.html

Rhode Island

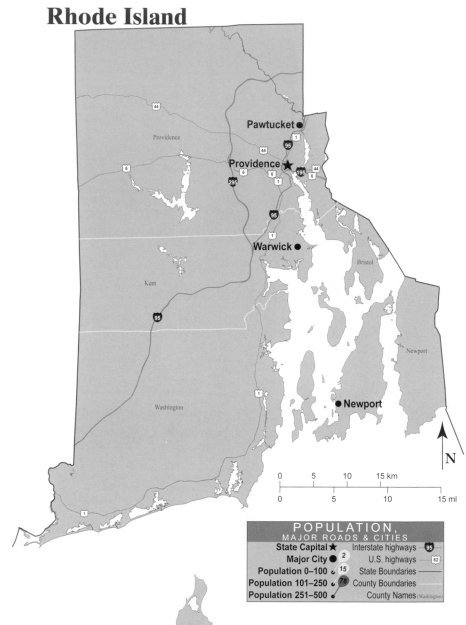

Pawtucket

Providence

Providence

Warwick

Kent

Bristol

Newport

Washington

Newport

N

| 0 | 5 | 10 | 15 km |
| 0 | 5 | 10 | 15 ml |

POPULATION,
MAJOR ROADS & CITIES
State Capital ★   Interstate highways
Major City ●   U.S. highways
Population 0–100   State Boundaries
Population 101–250   County Boundaries
Population 251–500   County Names (Washington)

According to the 2010 Census, there are no incorporated towns in Rhode Island with a population less than 500.* Visit the Rhode Island Secretary of State website to research laws on how to incorporate an **un**incorporated area in Rhode Island and explore solutions in this book such as the nullification of laws. Find out how you can take back already incorporated towns, and counties returning them to a constitutional Christian principle foundation.

Rhode Island: A Window for the Future

It was done once, now it can be done again. The foundation of this state began in June of 1636 when one man settled in Providence after fleeing religious persecution in Massachusetts. A second settlement was established in 1638 by two men and one woman, just three people. The cities of Newport and Warwick were founded a few years later. From there, the "founding fathers" united these towns together. It was the people of these small towns who struggled for independence, formed militias, and defended themselves against the British. Rhode Island became one of the first communities in the world advocating religious freedom. These people became a light and witness for others seeking religious freedom in their homeland.**

---

* Town populations and incorporated cities reflect data taken from the 2010 U.S. Census. Before acting upon this information it is very important to verify the accuracy of all the information represented, including current population, incorporated status, location of cities and counties, etc

** *Rhode Island*, Unsigned The Encyclopedia Britannica, 11th Edition, Volume XXIII The Encyclopedia Britannica Company, 1911, pp 251–253

South Carolina

City, State	Population
1. Smyrna, South Carolina	45
2. Jenkinsville, South Carolina	46
3. Peak, South Carolina	64
4. Govan, South Carolina	65
5. James, South Carolina	72
6. Tatum, South Carolina	75
7. Cope, South Carolina	77
8. Plum Branch, South Carolina	82
9. Ulmer, South Carolina	88
10. Pelzer, South Carolina	89
11. Ward, South Carolina	91
12. Troy, South Carolina	93
13. Pawleys Island, South Carolina	103
14. Parksville, South Carolina	117
15. Williams, South Carolina	117
16. Lodge, South Carolina	120
17. Windsor, South Carolina	121
18. Smoaks, South Carolina	126
19. Luray, South Carolina	127
20. Lowndesville, South Carolina	128
21. Rockville, South Carolina	134
22. Salem, South Carolina	135
23. Livingston, South Carolina	136
24. Blenheim, South Carolina	154
25. Hodges, South Carolina	155
26. Silverstreet, South Carolina	162
27. Waterloo, South Carolina	166
28. Cordova, South Carolina	169
29. Vance, South Carolina	170
30. Starr, South Carolina	173
31. Pomaria, South Carolina	179
32. Sycamore, South Carolina	180
33. Paxville, South Carolina	185
34. Woodford, South Carolina	185
35. Elko, South Carolina	193
36. Mount Croghan, South Carolina	195
37. Reevesville, South Carolina	196
38. Trenton, South Carolina	196
39. Kline, South Carolina	197
40. Lowrys, South Carolina	200
41. Scotia, South Carolina	215
42. Central Pacolet, South Carolina	216
43. Sellers, South Carolina	219
44. Perry, South Carolina	233
45. Monetta, South Carolina	236
46. Furman, South Carolina	239
47. Stuckey, South Carolina	245
48. McConnells, South Carolina	255
49. Olar, South Carolina	257
50. Snelling, South Carolina	274
51. Richburg, South Carolina	275

City, State	Population
52. Gifford, South Carolina	288
53. Little Mountain, South Carolina	291
54. West Union, South Carolina	291
55. Rowesville, South Carolina	304
56. Eutawville, South Carolina	315
57. Ridgeway, South Carolina	319
58. Atlantic Beach, South Carolina	334
59. Bethune, South Carolina	334
60. Norway, South Carolina	337
61. Donalds, South Carolina	348
62. Patrick, South Carolina	351
63. Ruby, South Carolina	360
64. Nichols, South Carolina	368
65. Lynchburg, South Carolina	373
66. Neeses, South Carolina	374
67. Salley, South Carolina	398
68. Summit, South Carolina	402
69. Edisto Beach, South Carolina	414
70. Cameron, South Carolina	424
71. Carlisle, South Carolina	436
72. Greeleyville, South Carolina	438
73. Hickory Grove, South Carolina	440
74. Hilda, South Carolina	447
75. Briarcliffe Acres, South Carolina	457
76. Hemingway, South Carolina	459
77. Bonneau, South Carolina	487
78. Lockhart, South Carolina	488
79. Sharon, South Carolina	494
80. McClellanville, South Carolina	499

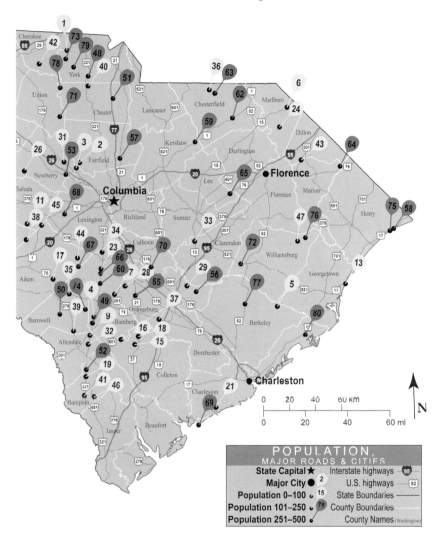

South Dakota

	City, State	Population
1.	Hillsview, South Dakota	3
2.	White Rock, South Dakota	3
3.	Lily, South Dakota	4
4.	Verdon, South Dakota	5
5.	Lowry, South Dakota	6
6.	Wetonka, South Dakota	8
7.	Artas, South Dakota	9
8.	Cottonwood, South Dakota	9
9.	Farmer, South Dakota	10
10.	Onaka, South Dakota	15
11.	Roswell, South Dakota	15
12.	Albee, South Dakota	16
13.	Virgil, South Dakota	16
14.	Butler, South Dakota	17
15.	Bancroft, South Dakota	19
16.	Vilas, South Dakota	20
17.	Chelsea, South Dakota	27
18.	Broadland, South Dakota	31
19.	Long Lake, South Dakota	31
20.	Rockham, South Dakota	33
21.	Altamont, South Dakota	34
22.	Marvin, South Dakota	34
23.	Tolstoy, South Dakota	36
24.	Dolton, South Dakota	37
25.	Seneca, South Dakota	38
26.	Naples, South Dakota	41
27.	Akaska, South Dakota	42
28.	Nunda, South Dakota	43
29.	Erwin, South Dakota	45
30.	Vienna, South Dakota	45
31.	Hetland, South Dakota	46
32.	Lebanon, South Dakota	47
33.	Turton, South Dakota	48
34.	Ward, South Dakota	48
35.	Belvidere, South Dakota	49
36.	Raymond, South Dakota	50
37.	Lake City, South Dakota	51
38.	Garden City, South Dakota	53
39.	Grenville, South Dakota	54
40.	Quinn, South Dakota	54
41.	Lane, South Dakota	59
42.	Fairview, South Dakota	60
43.	Ravinia, South Dakota	61
44.	Ree Heights, South Dakota	62
45.	Wood, South Dakota	62
46.	Camp Crook, South Dakota	63
47.	Orient, South Dakota	63
48.	Fruitdale, South Dakota	64
49.	Bushnell, South Dakota	65
50.	Ortley, South Dakota	65
51.	Utica, South Dakota	65
52.	Morristown, South Dakota	67
53.	La Bolt, South Dakota	68
54.	Twin Brooks, South Dakota	69
55.	Mound City, South Dakota	71
56.	Bradley, South Dakota	72

	City, State	Population
57.	Strandburg, South Dakota	72
58.	Stratford, South Dakota	72
59.	Olivet, South Dakota	74
60.	Agar, South Dakota	76
61.	Claire City, South Dakota	76
62.	Brentford, South Dakota	77
63.	Sherman, South Dakota	78
64.	New Witten, South Dakota	79
65.	Wasta, South Dakota	80
66.	Draper, South Dakota	82
67.	Dante, South Dakota	84
68.	Davis, South Dakota	85
69.	Fairburn, South Dakota	85
70.	Wallace, South Dakota	85
71.	Eden, South Dakota	89
72.	Andover, South Dakota	91
73.	Fulton, South Dakota	91
74.	Hazel, South Dakota	91
75.	Hitchcock, South Dakota	91
76.	Interior, South Dakota	94
77.	Cresbard, South Dakota	104
78.	Canova, South Dakota	105
79.	Glenham, South Dakota	105
80.	Herrick, South Dakota	105
81.	Badger, South Dakota	107
82.	Brandt, South Dakota	107

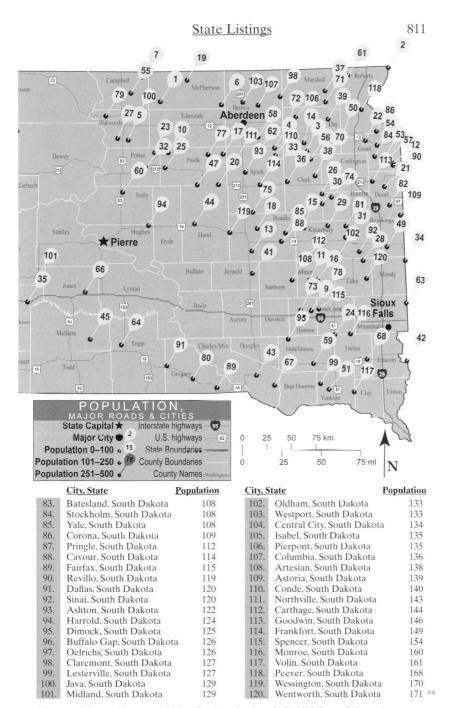

City, State	Population		City, State	Population
83.	Batesland, South Dakota	108	102.	Oldham, South Dakota	133
84.	Stockholm, South Dakota	108	103.	Westport, South Dakota	133
85.	Yale, South Dakota	108	104.	Central City, South Dakota	134
86.	Corona, South Dakota	109	105.	Isabel, South Dakota	135
87.	Pringle, South Dakota	112	106.	Pierpont, South Dakota	135
88.	Cavour, South Dakota	114	107.	Columbia, South Dakota	136
89.	Fairfax, South Dakota	115	108.	Artesian, South Dakota	138
90.	Revillo, South Dakota	119	109.	Astoria, South Dakota	139
91.	Dallas, South Dakota	120	110.	Conde, South Dakota	140
92.	Sinai, South Dakota	120	111.	Northville, South Dakota	143
93.	Ashton, South Dakota	122	112.	Carthage, South Dakota	144
94.	Harrold, South Dakota	124	113.	Goodwin, South Dakota	146
95.	Dimock, South Dakota	125	114.	Frankfort, South Dakota	149
96.	Buffalo Gap, South Dakota	126	115.	Spencer, South Dakota	154
97.	Oelrichs, South Dakota	126	116.	Monroe, South Dakota	160
98.	Claremont, South Dakota	127	117.	Volin, South Dakota	161
99.	Lesterville, South Dakota	127	118.	Peever, South Dakota	168
100.	Java, South Dakota	129	119.	Wessington, South Dakota	170
101.	Midland, South Dakota	129	120.	Wentworth, South Dakota	171 **

* Town populations and incorporated cities reflect data taken from the 2010 U.S. Census. Before acting upon this information it is very important to verify the accuracy of all the information represented, including current population, incorporated status, location of cities and counties, etc.

**This state has more cities to research under 500 population to view the full listing go to our website
TheyFiredtheFirstShot2012.com/therevolution.html

Tennessee

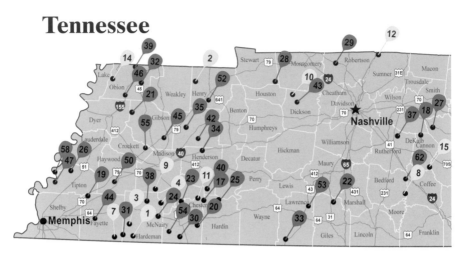

	City, State	Population		City, State	Population
1.	Saulsbury, Tennessee	81	34.	Parker's Crossroads, Tennessee	330
2.	Cottage Grove, Tennessee	88	35.	McLemoresville, Tennessee	352
3.	Hickory Valley, Tennessee	99	36.	Copperhill, Tennessee	354
4.	Silerton, Tennessee	111	37.	Dowell, Tennessee	355
5.	Orme, Tennessee	126	38.	Toone, Tennessee	364
6.	Viola, Tennessee	131	39.	Woodland Mills, Tennessee	378
7.	La Grange, Tennessee	133	40.	Sardis, Tennessee	381
8.	Normandy, Tennessee	141	41.	Ridgeside, Tennessee	390
9.	Medon, Tennessee	178	42.	Clarksburg, Tennessee	393
10.	Slayden, Tennessee	178	43.	Vanleer, Tennessee	395
11.	Enville, Tennessee	189	44.	Williston, Tennessee	395
12.	Mitchellville, Tennessee	189	45.	Gibson, Tennessee	396
13.	Oakdale, Tennessee	212	46.	Hornbeak, Tennessee	424
14.	Samburg, Tennessee	217	47.	Burlison, Tennessee	425
15.	Center, Tennessee	243	48.	Baileyton, Tennessee	431
16.	Parrottsville, Tennessee	263	49.	Townsend, Tennessee	448
17.	Milledgeville, Tennessee	265	50.	Stanton, Tennessee	452
18.	Auburn, Tennessee	269	51.	Watauga, Tennessee	458
19.	Braden, Tennessee	282	52.	Henry, Tennessee	464
20.	Stantonville, Tennessee	283	53.	Ethridge, Tennessee	465
21.	Yorkville, Tennessee	286	54.	Guys, Tennessee	466
22.	Lynnville, Tennessee	287	55.	Gadsden, Tennessee	470
23.	Finger, Tennessee	298	56.	Duck, Tennessee	475
24.	Hornsby, Tennessee	303	57.	Beersheba Springs, Tennessee	477
25.	Saltillo, Tennessee	303	58.	Gilt Edge, Tennessee	477
26.	Garland, Tennessee	310	59.	Baneberry, Tennessee	482
27.	Liberty, Tennessee	310	60.	Calhoun, Tennessee	490
28.	Cumberland City, Tennessee	311	61.	Cumberland Gap, Tennessee	494
29.	Cedar Hill, Tennessee	314	62.	Bell Buckle, Tennessee	500
30.	Ramer, Tennessee	319			
31.	Grand Junction, Tennessee	325			
32.	Rives, Tennessee	326			
33.	Iron City, Tennessee	328			

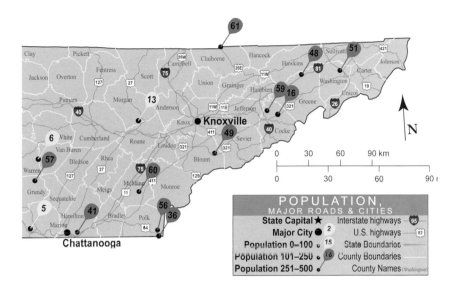

POPULATION,
MAJOR ROADS & CITIES
State Capital ★   Interstate highways 95
Major City ●   U.S. highways 82
Population 0–100 ·   State Boundaries
Population 101–250 ·   County Boundaries
Population 251–500 ·   County Names (Washington)

* Town populations and incorporated cities reflect data taken from the 2010 U.S. Census. Before acting upon this information it is very important to verify the accuracy of all the information represented, including current population, incorporated status, location of cities and counties, etc.

Texas

#	City, State	Population
1.	Mustang, Texas	21
2.	Corral City, Texas	27
3.	Impact, Texas	35
4.	Quintana, Texas	56
5.	Sun Valley, Texas	69
6.	Rocky Mound, Texas	75
7.	Toco, Texas	75
8.	Round Top, Texas	90
9.	Toyah, Texas	90
10.	Dayton Lakes, Texas	93
11.	Domino, Texas	93
12.	Putnam, Texas	94
13.	Uncertain, Texas	94
14.	Spofford, Texas	95
15.	Neylandville, Texas	97
16.	Mobeetie, Texas	101
17.	O'Brien, Texas	106
18.	Lakeview, Texas	107
19.	Todd Mission, Texas	107
20.	Springlake, Texas	108
21.	Aquilla, Texas	109
22.	Dodson, Texas	109
23.	Edmonson, Texas	111
24.	Seven Oaks, Texas	111
25.	Petronila, Texas	113
26.	Pyote, Texas	114
27.	Mertens, Texas	125
28.	Kirvin, Texas	129
29.	Emhouse, Texas	133
30.	Marietta, Texas	134
31.	Valentine, Texas	134
32.	Powell, Texas	136
33.	Novice, Texas	139
34.	Cuney, Texas	140
35.	Oak Ridge (Cooke Co.), Texas	141
36.	Estelline, Texas	145
37.	Austwell, Texas	147
38.	Dorchester, Texas	148
39.	Miller's Cove, Texas	149
40.	Cool, Texas	157
41.	Sanford, Texas	164
42.	Adrian, Texas	166
43.	Jolly, Texas	172
44.	Weinert, Texas	172
45.	Carl's Corner, Texas	173
46.	Opdyke West, Texas	174
47.	Leona, Texas	175
48.	Melvin, Texas	178
49.	Mullin, Texas	179
50.	Round Mountain, Texas	181
51.	Cottonwood, Texas	185
52.	Mobile City, Texas	188
53.	Bishop Hills, Texas	193
54.	Browndell, Texas	197
55.	Penelope, Texas	198

#	City, State	Population
56.	Bynum, Texas	199
57.	Windom, Texas	199
58.	Goodlow, Texas	200
59.	Dish, Texas	201
60.	Moore Station, Texas	201
61.	Creedmoor, Texas	202
62.	Goree, Texas	203
63.	Megargel, Texas	203
64.	Pecan Gap, Texas	203
65.	Wellman, Texas	203
66.	Broaddus, Texas	207
67.	Woodloch, Texas	207
68.	Ravenna, Texas	209

#	City, State	Population
69.	Forsan, Texas	210
70.	Navarro, Texas	210
71.	La Ward, Texas	213
72.	Caney City, Texas	217
73.	Hays, Texas	217
74.	Ackerly, Texas	220
75.	Anderson, Texas	222
76.	Knollwood, Texas	226
77.	Midway, Texas	228
78.	Taylor Landing, Texas	228
79.	Douglassville, Texas	229
80.	Roaring Springs, Texas	234
81.	Mingus, Texas	235
82.	Millican, Texas	240
83.	Progreso Lakes, Texas	240
84.	Barry, Texas	242
85.	Thompsons, Texas	246
86.	North Cleveland, Texas	247
87.	Streetman, Texas	247
88.	Carmine, Texas	250
89.	Westbrook, Texas	253
90.	Wixon Valley, Texas	254
91.	Goldsmith, Texas	257
92.	Benjamin, Texas	258
93.	Fayetteville, Texas	258
94.	Marquez, Texas	263
95.	Richland, Texas	264
96.	Woodson, Texas	264

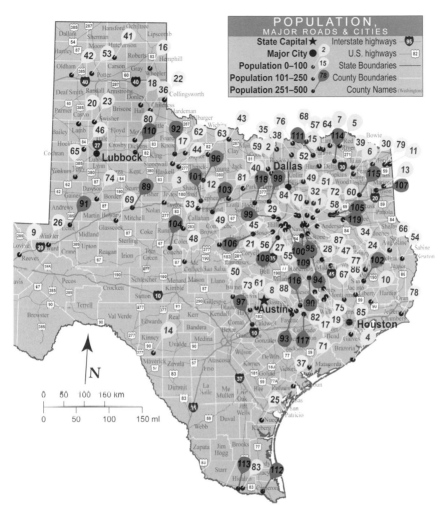

City, State	Population		City, State	Population
97. Staples, Texas	267		109. Tehuacana, Texas	283
98. Cross Timber, Texas	268		110. Dickens, Texas	286
99. Covington, Texas	269		111. Bailey, Texas	289
100. Malone, Texas	269		112. Rangerville, Texas	289
101. Moran, Texas	270		113. Granjeno, Texas	293
102. Goodrich, Texas	271		114. Tira, Texas	297
103. Carbon, Texas	272		115. Warren City, Texas	298
104. Paint Rock, Texas	273		116. Burton, Texas	300
105. Coffee City, Texas	278		117. Industry, Texas	304
106. Cranfills Gap, Texas	281		118. Brazos Bend, Texas	305
107. Nesbitt, Texas	281		119. Poynor, Texas	305 **
108. Ross, Texas	283			

* Town populations and incorporated cities reflect data taken from the 2010 U.S. Census. Before acting upon this information it is very important to verify the accuracy of all the information represented, including current population, incorporated status, location of cities and counties, etc.

**This state has more cities to research under 500 population to view the full listing go to our website
TheyFiredtheFirstShot2012.com/therevolution.html

Utah

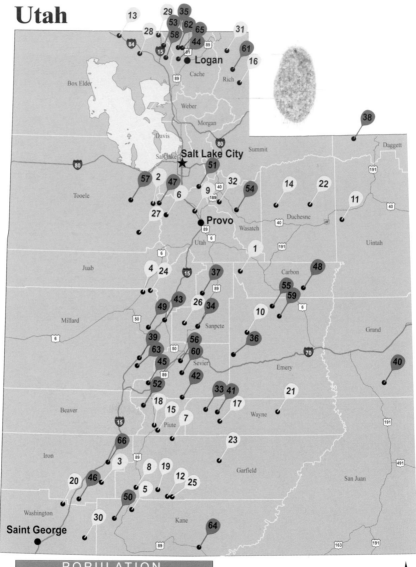

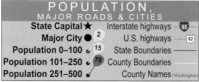

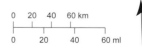

	City, State	Population			City, State	Population
1.	Scofield, Utah	24		61.	Randolph, Utah	464
2.	Ophir, Utah	38		62.	Trenton, Utah	464
3.	Brian Head, Utah	83		63.	Kanosh, Utah	474
4.	Lynndyl, Utah	106		64.	Big Water, Utah	475
5.	Alton, Utah	119		65.	Amalga, Utah	488
6.	Fairfield, Utah	119		66.	Paragonah, Utah	488
7.	Antimony, Utah	122				
8.	Hatch, Utah	133				
9.	Vineyard, Utah	139				
10.	Clawson, Utah	163				
11.	Independence, Utah	164				
12.	Cannonville, Utah	167				
13.	Snowville, Utah	167				
14.	Tabiona, Utah	171				
15.	Kingston, Utah	173				
16.	Woodruff, Utah	180				
17.	Torrey, Utah	182				
18.	Junction, Utah	191				
19.	Bryce Canyon City, Utah	198				
20.	New Harmony, Utah	207				
21.	Hanksville, Utah	219				
22.	Altamont, Utah	225				
23.	Boulder, Utah	226				
24.	Leamington, Utah	226				
25.	Henrieville, Utah	230				
26.	Fayette, Utah	242				
27.	Vernon, Utah	243				
28.	Howell, Utah	245				
29.	Portage, Utah	245				
30.	Rockville, Utah	245				
31.	Lake, Utah	248				
32.	Wallsburg, Utah	250				
33.	Lyman, Utah	258				
34.	Sterling, Utah	262				
35.	Cornish, Utah	288				
36.	Emery, Utah	288				
37.	Wales, Utah	302				
38.	Manila, Utah	310				
39.	Meadow, Utah	310				
40.	Castle Valley, Utah	319				
41.	Bicknell, Utah	327				
42.	Koosharem, Utah	327				
43.	Scipio, Utah	327				
44.	Deweyville, Utah	332				
45.	Joseph, Utah	344				
46.	Kanarraville, Utah	355				
47.	Cedar Fort, Utah	368				
48.	Sunnyside, Utah	377				
49.	Holden, Utah	378				
50.	Glendale, Utah	381				
51.	Alta, Utah	383				
52.	Marysvale, Utah	408				
53.	Plymouth, Utah	414				
54.	Charleston, Utah	415				
55.	Elmo, Utah	418				
56.	Sigurd, Utah	429				
57.	Rush Valley, Utah	447				
58.	Fielding, Utah	455				
59.	Cleveland, Utah	464				
60.	Glenwood, Utah	464				

* Town populations and incorporated cities reflect data taken from the 2010 U.S. Census. Before acting upon this information it is very important to verify the accuracy of all the information represented, including current population, incorporated status, location of cities and counties, etc.

Vermont

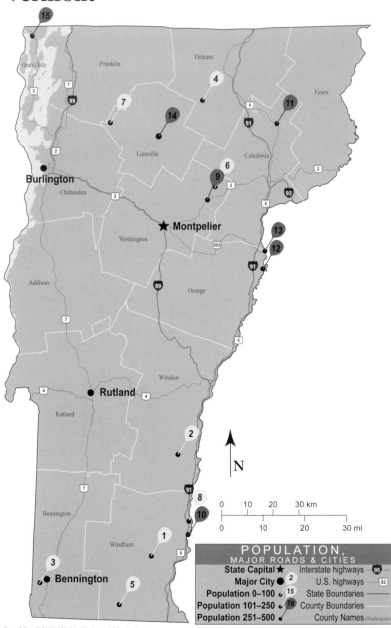

	City, State	Population
1.	Newfane, Vermont	118
2.	Perkinsville, Vermont	130
3.	Old Bennington, Vermont	139
4.	Albany, Vermont	193
5.	Jacksonville, Vermont	223
6.	Cabot, Vermont	233
7.	Cambridge, Vermont	236
8.	North Westminster, Vermont	247
9.	Marshfield, Vermont	273
10.	Westminster, Vermont	291
11.	West Burke, Vermont	343
12.	Newbury, Vermont	365
13.	Wells River, Vermont	399
14.	Hyde Park, Vermont	462
15.	Alburg, Vermont	497

* Town populations and incorporated cities reflect data taken from the 2010 U.S. Census. Before acting upon this information it is very important to verify the accuracy of all the information represented, including current population, incorporated status, location of cities and counties, etc.

Virginia

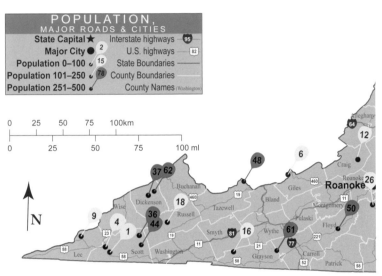

	City, State	Population		City, State	Population
1.	Clinchport, Virginia	70	27.	Saxis, Virginia	241
2.	Hillsboro, Virginia	80	28.	Surry, Virginia	244
3.	Columbia, Virginia	83	29.	Toms Brook, Virginia	258
4.	Duffield, Virginia	91	30.	Dendron, Virginia	272
5.	Branchville, Virginia	114	31.	Clifton, Virginia	282
6.	Glen Lyn, Virginia	115	32.	Alberta, Virginia	298
7.	Scottsburg, Virginia	119	33.	Brodnax, Virginia	298
8.	Port Royal, Virginia	126	34.	Eastville, Virginia	305
9.	St. Charles, Virginia	128	35.	Newsoms, Virginia	321
10.	Washington, Virginia	135	36.	Dungannon, Virginia	332
11.	Monterey, Virginia	147	37.	Clinchco, Virginia	337
12.	New Castle, Virginia	153	38.	Ivor, Virginia	339
13.	Virgilina, Virginia	154	39.	White Stone, Virginia	352
14.	Capron, Virginia	166	40.	Fincastle, Virginia	353
15.	Keller, Virginia	178	41.	Goshen, Virginia	361
16.	Trout Dale, Virginia	178	42.	Stanardsville, Virginia	367
17.	Stony Creek, Virginia	198	43.	Claremont, Virginia	378
18.	Cleveland, Virginia	202	44.	Nickelsville, Virginia	383
19.	Hallwood, Virginia	206	45.	Montross, Virginia	384
20.	The Plains, Virginia	217	46.	Bloxom, Virginia	387
21.	Pamplin, Virginia	219	47.	Iron Gate, Virginia	388
22.	Phenix, Virginia	226	48.	Pocahontas, Virginia	389
23.	Madison, Virginia	229	49.	Melfa, Virginia	408
24.	Painter, Virginia	229	50.	Floyd, Virginia	425
25.	Wachapreague, Virginia	232	51.	Boydton, Virginia	431
26.	Boones Mill, Virginia	239	52.	Troutville, Virginia	431

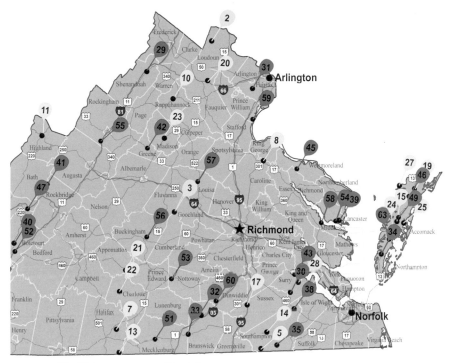

City, State	Population
53. Burkeville, Virginia	432
54. Irvington, Virginia	432
55. Mount Crawford, Virginia	433
56. Dillwyn, Virginia	447
57. Mineral, Virginia	467
58. Urbanna, Virginia	476
59. Quantico, Virginia	480
60. McKenney, Virginia	483
61. Fries, Virginia	484
62. Haysi, Virginia	498
63. Nassawadox, Virginia	499

Washington

	City, State	Population		City, State	Population
1.	Krupp, Washington	48	17.	Washtucna, Washington	208
2.	Lamont, Washington	70	18.	Conconully, Washington	210
3.	Hatton, Washington	101	19.	Creston, Washington	236
4.	Waverly, Washington	106	20.	Nespelem, Washington	236
5.	Starbuck, Washington	129	21.	Elmer City, Washington	238
6.	Farmington, Washington	146	22.	Metaline Falls, Washington	238
7.	Hartline, Washington	151	23.	Spangle, Washington	278
8.	Metaline, Washington	173	24.	Riverside, Washington	280
9.	Index, Washington	178	25.	Almira, Washington	284
10.	Latah, Washington	183	26.	Springdale, Washington	285
11.	Marcus, Washington	183	27.	Endicott, Washington	289
12.	Kahlotus, Washington	193	28.	Union, Washington	294
13.	Skykomish, Washington	198	29.	Northport, Washington	295
14.	Malden, Washington	203	30.	Beaux Arts Village, Washington	299
15.	Wilson Creek, Washington	205	31.	Hamilton, Washington	301
16.	Cusick, Washington	207	32.	LaCrosse, Washington	313

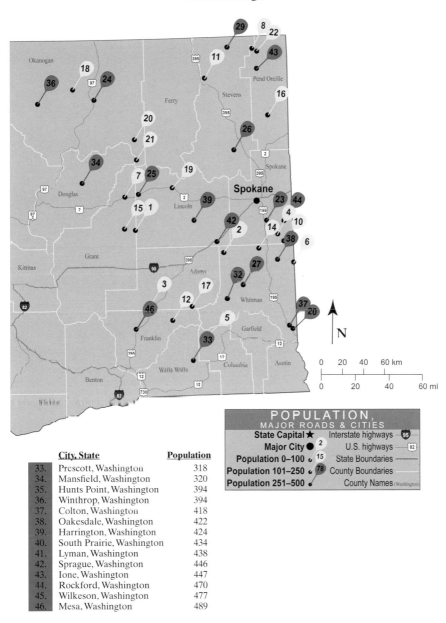

POPULATION,
MAJOR ROADS & CITIES

State Capital ★   Interstate highways
Major City ●   U.S. highways
Population 0–100   State Boundaries
Population 101–250   County Boundaries
Population 251–500   County Names (Washington)

* Town populations and incorporated cities reflect data taken from the 2010 U.S. Census. Before acting upon this information it is very important to verify the accuracy of all the information represented, including current population, incorporated status, location of cities and counties, etc.

West Virginia

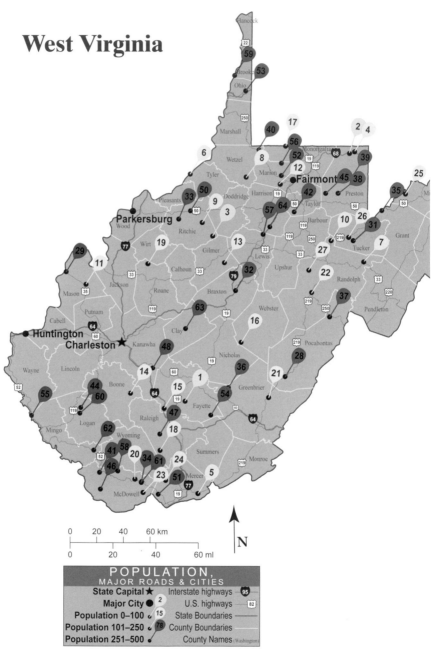

0   20   40   60 km

0   20   40   60 ml

N

	City, State	Population		City, State	Population
1.	Thurmond, West Virginia	5	33.	Cairo, West Virginia	281
2.	Bruceton Mills, West Virginia	85	34.	Keystone, West Virginia	282
3.	Auburn, West Virginia	97	35.	Bayard, West Virginia	290
4.	Brandonville, West Virginia	101	36.	Quinwood, West Virginia	290
5.	Oakvale, West Virginia	121	37.	Durbin, West Virginia	293
6.	Friendly, West Virginia	132	38.	Tunnelton, West Virginia	294
7.	Harman, West Virginia	143	39.	Albright, West Virginia	299
8.	Smithfield, West Virginia	145	40.	Hundred, West Virginia	299
9.	Pullman, West Virginia	154	41.	Iaeger, West Virginia	302
10.	Montrose, West Virginia	156	42.	Flemington, West Virginia	312
11.	Leon, West Virginia	158	43.	Hedgesville, West Virginia	318
12.	Worthington, West Virginia	158	44.	Mitchell Heights, West Virginia	323
13.	Sand Fork, West Virginia	159	45.	Newburg, West Virginia	329
14.	Sylvester, West Virginia	160	46.	Bradshaw, West Virginia	337
15.	Pax, West Virginia	167	47.	Lester, West Virginia	348
16.	Camden-on-Gauley, West Virgina	169	48.	Handley, West Virginia	349
17.	Blacksville, West Virginia	171	49.	Capon Bridge, West Virginia	355
18.	Rhodell, West Virginia	173	50.	Ellenboro, West Virginia	363
19.	Reedy, West Virginia	182	51.	Bramwell, West Virginia	364
20.	Kimball, West Virginia	194	52.	Farmington, West Virginia	375
21.	Falling Spring, West Virginia	211	53.	Valley Grove, West Virginia	378
22.	Huttonsville, West Virginia	221	54.	Meadow Bridge, West Virginia	379
23.	Anawalt, West Virginia	226	55.	Kermit, West Virginia	406
24.	Matoaka, West Virginia	227	56.	Fairview, West Virginia	408
25.	Elk Garden, West Virginia	232	57.	Jane Lew, West Virginia	409
26.	Hambleton, West Virginia	232	58.	Davy, West Virginia	420
27.	Womelsdorf (Coalton), West Virginia	250	59.	Windsor Heights, West Virginia	423
28.	Hillsboro, West Virginia	260	60.	West Logan, West Virginia	424
29.	Henderson, West Virginia	271	61.	Northfork, West Virginia	429
30.	Wardensville, West Virginia	271	62.	Gilbert, West Virginia	450
31.	Hendricks, West Virginia	272	63.	Clay, West Virginia	491
32.	Flatwoods, West Virginia	277	64.	Lost Creek, West Virginia	496

* Town populations and incorporated cities reflect data taken from the 2010 U.S. Census. Before acting upon this information it is very important to verify the accuracy of all the information represented, including current population, incorporated status, location of cities and counties, etc.

Wisconsin

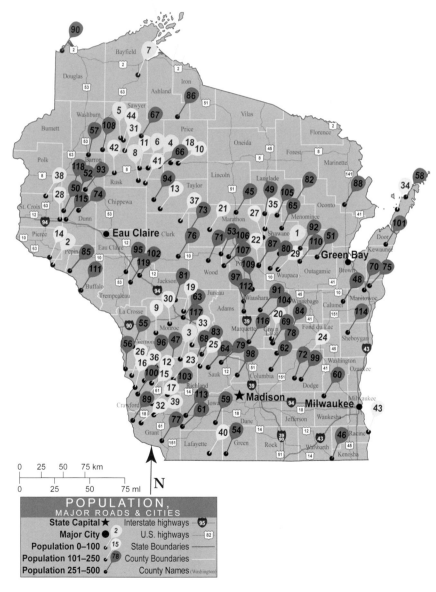

0   25   50   75 km
0   25   50   75 ml   N

	City, State	Population		City, State	Population
1.	Big Falls, Wisconsin	61	61.	Rewey, Wisconsin	292
2.	Stockholm, Wisconsin	66	62.	Doyles, Wisconsin	297
3.	Yuba, Wisconsin	74	63.	Oakdale, Wisconsin	297
4.	Ingram, Wisconsin	78	64.	Loganville, Wisconsin	300
5.	Couderay, Wisconsin	88	65.	Bowler, Wisconsin	302
6.	Glen Flora, Wisconsin	92	66.	Hawkins, Wisconsin	305
7.	Mason, Wisconsin	93	67.	Winter, Wisconsin	313
8.	Conrath, Wisconsin	95	68.	Cazenovia, Wisconsin	318
9.	Melvina, Wisconsin	104	69.	Kingston, Wisconsin	326
10.	Catawba, Wisconsin	110	70.	Kellnersville, Wisconsin	332
11.	Tony, Wisconsin	113	71.	Arpin, Wisconsin	333
12.	Bell Center, Wisconsin	117	72.	Lowell, Wisconsin	340
13.	Lublin, Wisconsin	118	73.	Unity, Wisconsin	343
14.	Maiden Rock, Wisconsin	119	74.	Wheeler, Wisconsin	348
15.	Steuben, Wisconsin	131	75.	Maribel, Wisconsin	351
16.	Lynxville, Wisconsin	132	76.	Granton, Wisconsin	355
17.	Woodman, Wisconsin	132	77.	Tennyson, Wisconsin	355
18.	Kennan, Wisconsin	135	78.	Friesland, Wisconsin	356
19.	Wyeville, Wisconsin	147	79.	Rock Springs, Wisconsin	362
20.	Marquette, Wisconsin	150	80.	Scandinavia, Wisconsin	363
21.	Fenwood, Wisconsin	152	81.	Warrens, Wisconsin	363
22.	Nelsonville, Wisconsin	155	82.	White Lake, Wisconsin	363
23.	Boaz, Wisconsin	156	83.	La Valle, Wisconsin	367
24.	Kekoskee, Wisconsin	161	84.	Fairwater, Wisconsin	371
25.	Lime Ridge, Wisconsin	162	85.	Nelson, Wisconsin	374
26.	Ferryville, Wisconsin	176	86.	Butternut, Wisconsin	375
27.	Elderon, Wisconsin	179	87.	Amherst Junction, Wisconsin	377
28.	Wilson, Wisconsin	184	88.	Pound, Wisconsin	377
29.	Ogdensburg, Wisconsin	185	89.	Bagley, Wisconsin	379
30.	Hustler, Wisconsin	194	90.	Oliver, Wisconsin	399
31.	Exeland, Wisconsin	196	91.	Lohrville, Wisconsin	402
32.	Patch Grove, Wisconsin	198	92.	Embarrass, Wisconsin	404
33.	Union Center, Wisconsin	200	93.	Dallas, Wisconsin	409
34.	Egg Harbor, Wisconsin	201	94.	Gilman, Wisconsin	410
35.	Eland, Wisconsin	202	95.	Pigeon Falls, Wisconsin	411
36.	Mount Sterling, Wisconsin	211	96.	Reads, Wisconsin	415
37.	Curtiss, Wisconsin	216	97.	Hancock, Wisconsin	417
38.	Deer Park, Wisconsin	216	98.	Merrimac, Wisconsin	420
39.	Mount Hope, Wisconsin	225	99.	Clyman, Wisconsin	422
40.	Gratiot, Wisconsin	236	100.	Eastman, Wisconsin	428
41.	Sheldon, Wisconsin	237	101.	Forestville, Wisconsin	430
42.	Weyerhaeuser, Wisconsin	238	102.	Hixton, Wisconsin	433
43.	North Bay, Wisconsin	241	103.	Blue River, Wisconsin	434
44.	Radisson, Wisconsin	241	104.	Neshkoro, Wisconsin	434
45.	Brokaw, Wisconsin	251	105.	Mattoon, Wisconsin	438
46.	Genoa, Wisconsin	253	106.	Junction City, Wisconsin	439
47.	Ironton, Wisconsin	253	107.	Rudolph, Wisconsin	439
48.	Potter, Wisconsin	253	108.	Birchwood, Wisconsin	442
49.	Aniwa, Wisconsin	260	109.	Almond, Wisconsin	448
50.	Downing, Wisconsin	265	110.	Bear Creek, Wisconsin	448
51.	Nichols, Wisconsin	273	111.	Cochrane, Wisconsin	450
52.	Ridgeland, Wisconsin	273	112.	Coloma, Wisconsin	450
53.	Milladore, Wisconsin	276	113.	Cobb, Wisconsin	458
54.	Brown, Wisconsin	280	114.	Glenbeulah, Wisconsin	463
55.	Chaseburg, Wisconsin	284	115.	Knapp, Wisconsin	463
56.	De Soto, Wisconsin	287	116.	Endeavor, Wisconsin	468
57.	Haugen, Wisconsin	287	117.	Kendall, Wisconsin	472
58.	Ephraim, Wisconsin	288	118.	Prairie Farm, Wisconsin	473
59.	Hollandale, Wisconsin	288	119.	Taylor, Wisconsin	476 **
60.	Lac La Belle, Wisconsin	290			

* Town populations and incorporated cities reflect data taken from the 2010 U.S. Census. Before acting upon this information it is very important to verify the accuracy of all the information represented, including current population, incorporated status, location of cities and counties, etc.

**This state has more cities to research under 500 population to view the full listing go to our website
TheyFiredtheFirstShot2012.com/therevolution.html

Wyoming

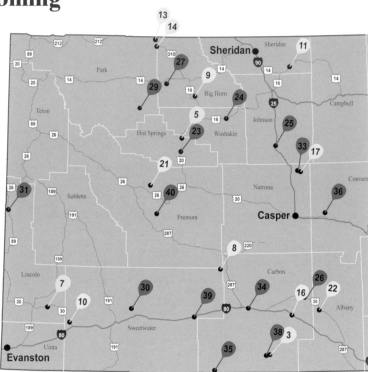

POPULATION,
MAJOR ROADS & CITIES

State Capital ★	Interstate highways	95
Major City ●	U.S. highways	82
Population 0–100	State Boundaries	
Population 101–250	County Boundaries	
Population 251–500	County Names (Washington)	

State Map © 2012 SJP. Lic. Caritas of Birmingham
Cannot be duplicated without written permission.
Call Caritas of Birmingham: (Outside USA add **001**) **205-672-2000**
or write: **Caritas of Birmingham**
                100 Our Lady Queen of Peace Drive
                Sterrett, AL 35147 USA

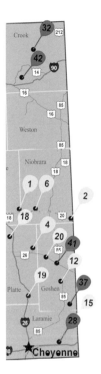

	City, State	Population
1.	Lost Springs, Wyoming	4
2.	Van Tassell, Wyoming	15
3.	Riverside, Wyoming	52
4.	Hartville, Wyoming	62
5.	Kirby, Wyoming	92
6.	Manville, Wyoming	95
7.	Opal, Wyoming	96
8.	Bairoil, Wyoming	106
9.	Manderson, Wyoming	114
10.	Granger, Wyoming	139
11.	Clearmont, Wyoming	142
12.	Yoder, Wyoming	151
13.	Frannie, Wyoming	157
14.	Deaver, Wyoming	178
15.	Albin, Wyoming	181
16.	Elk Mountain, Wyoming	191
17.	Edgerton, Wyoming	195
18.	Glendo, Wyoming	205
19.	Chugwater, Wyoming	212
20.	Fort Laramie, Wyoming	230
21.	Pavillion, Wyoming	231
22.	Rock River, Wyoming	245
23.	East Thermopolis, Wyoming	254
24.	Ten Sleep, Wyoming	260
25.	Kaycee, Wyoming	263
26.	Medicine Bow, Wyoming	284
27.	Burlington, Wyoming	288
28.	Burns, Wyoming	301
29.	Meeteetse, Wyoming	327
30.	Superior, Wyoming	336
31.	Thayne, Wyoming	366
32.	Hulett, Wyoming	383
33.	Midwest, Wyoming	404
34.	Sinclair, Wyoming	433
35.	Baggs, Wyoming	440
36.	Rolling Hills, Wyoming	440
37.	La Grange, Wyoming	448
38.	Encampment, Wyoming	450
39.	Wamsutter, Wyoming	451
40.	Hudson, Wyoming	458
41.	Lingle, Wyoming	468
42.	Pine Haven, Wyoming	490

* Town populations and incorporated cities reflect data taken from the 2010 U.S. Census. Before acting upon this information it is very important to verify the accuracy of all the information represented, including current population, incorporated status, location of cities and counties, etc.

Resource Listing and
Recommended Reading

Other books by A Friend of Medjugorje:

For over 25 years, A Friend of Medjugorje has been writing in a convicting way that literally transforms the way people think. With readership across the world, his books, booklets and other writings number into the hundreds and have deeply impacted millions and led them to decide for serious changes in a return to living a holy way of life. Few write with the power that moves people to sell their homes, change the level of their lifestyles, stop divorce, change their lives in radical ways as tens of thousands have testified in doing after reading A Friend of Medjugorje's writings. Bringing to life what he writes in words, changes not only those who read his writings, but so many others who are changed by the witness of those who are changing their lives.

- **Words From Heaven**_{TM} – The definitive and most widely used book on the messages of Our Lady of Medjugorje. For research or reference, this is the handbook for the Medjugorje phenomenon.

- **It Ain't Gonna Happen**_{TM} – For those who think life will continue as normal, and that the wild swing and tumbling stock markets will recover, that bailouts will work, and that everything will return as previous, guess what?

- **Look What Happened While You Were Sleeping**_{TM} – To change America...change America's mentality. Global warming, gun control, abortion, education, etc., looking at everything through a Biblical worldview.

- **<u>How To Change Your Husband</u>**_{TM} – The owner's manual for the family.
- **<u>I See Far</u>**_{TM} – What do you have in your home that allows evil to come and go as it pleases?
- *American History You Never Learned*
- *Two America's*
- *As Go God's People, So Goes the World*
- *Patriotic Rosary*
- *Changing History*
- *How the Early Church Learned*
- *Judge with Right Judgment*
- *Our Lady's Formula for Victory: Pray, Pray, Pray*
- *Quietism*
- *Readying for the Storm*
- *Why So Many Disasters*
- *satan Wants to Destroy Medjugorje*

Caritas *Radio WAVE* programs, especially the weekly *Mejanomics* programs with A Friend of Medjugorje often cover topics connected to beginning a new way of life—spiritually, materially, and economically. All past programs can be downloaded free on the Caritas website, Medjugorje.com, or can be ordered from Caritas. Call for recommended titles.

<u>www.Medjugorje.com</u>– Caritas of Birmingham's official website, the most extensive Medjugorje website in the world.

Contact Caritas of Birmingham for Other Resources, Books & Booklets:

- **Caritas of Birmingham** – for more information on Medjugorje and A Friend of Medjugorje's writings and materials.
  100 Our Lady Queen of Peace Drive
  Sterrett, AL 35147
  Phone: 205-672-2000

www.TheyFiredTheFirstShot2012.com– Official web site of They Fired the First Shot 2012 and Caritas Constitutional Small Prayer Groups (CSPG), where you will be able to look up state listings and connect with others in a CSPG. New functionality has been added

Recommended Reading:

Our highest recommendation to understanding the content of They Fired the First Shot 2012_{TM}, is to begin studying the original writings of our Founding Fathers. Before the Revolutionary War, a great many of the citizenry of the colonies were involved in studying what was law, and the foundation of law. This was invaluable education for becoming "we the people," government for the people, of the people and by the people. America's founding documents, the Declaration of Independence, the United States Constitution, un-revisionist renditions of the lives of the founders, the history of the United States, etc., will more and more release the fire of liberty in the soul just as it did in 1776 in those who found the will and courage to break away from tyranny and begin a new nation in which in one indissoluble bond, the principles of civil government were connected to the principles of Christianity.

Important for Spreading the Information and What Not to Do

As you read They Fired the First Shot 2012, you will be motivated to begin to spread the information in the book. However, it is important for each person to have the proper philosophy in understanding the answer, and why the answer contained in the book is God's solution. **Do not fall for the mistake** of giving out smaller sections of this book to your sheriffs or any other people for fear that they won't read it. They Fired the First Shot 2012 is a complete book, it builds to bring the reader to a full understanding of how dire our situation is, and in giving the proper spiritual philosophy *before* revealing the answer. **It is important the order in which you spread the information.** Everyone should get a copy of this book, <u>They Fired the First Shot 2012,</u> **first**. After the person has received the understanding of what <u>They Fired the First Shot</u> educates one to, then giving them Sheriff Mack's booklet, *The County Sheriff: America's Last Hope,* would **then** be beneficial in a greater way. This first and second process is critical and important for each reader to go through these steps in order to engage them in wanting to be a part of the solution - a solution they cannot understand without having first read <u>They Fired the First Shot 2012</u>. Your enthusiasm, encouragement and persistence will move them to read the book. If they are reluctant because of the size, challenge them to do so. Once they read <u>They Fired the First Shot 2012</u>, then and **only then**, send them other materials covering some topics included in the book, for example books about Agenda 21, or Sheriff Mack's book about county sheriffs, etc., so that they have a greater understanding and formation for what they may read in other books.

- *The County Sheriff: America's Last Hope —* Sheriff Richard Mack

- *Unraveling Federal Jurisdiction within a State —* Sheriff Gil Gilbertson

- **<u>The 5000 Year Leap: The 28 Great Ideas That Changed the World</u>** – W. Cleon Skousen

- **<u>Original Intent</u>**—David Barton

- **<u>The Tipping Point</u>** – Malcolm Gladwell

- **<u>Hurtling Toward Oblivion: A Logical Argument for the End of the Age</u>**—Richard A. Swenson, M.D.

- **<u>The War Against Population: The Economics and Ideology of World Population Control</u>**—Jacqueline Kasun

- **The Encyclopedia Britannica: A Dictionary of Arts, Sciences, Literature and General Information. Eleventh Edition, Volumes 1-12, Copyright 1910.** – It is important to find a good set of older

encyclopedias as they will be more accurate, free from revisionists, and pure in their information than newer editions in regard
to the principles of our nation's founding, the states' founding,
and the proper mentality toward the principles that built "this
nation." Search online, check garage sales, etc. in order to find a
quality set.

Recommended Associations & Speakers:

- **A Friend of Medjugorje** — passionate and authoritative
writer and witness to the events surrounding the apparitions of
Medjugorje, foundationed on 26 years of experience in living
Our Lady's messages. A Friend of Medjugorje is the founder of
the the second largest non-profit organization in Alabama, Caritas of Birmingham, which is the largest Medjugorje center worldwide. He has written more on the messages of Medjugorje than
anyone in the world and shares with audiences around the world
how his success was achieved through living out Our Lady's messages in his own life and in the life of the Community of Caritas,
of which he also founded. He is the author of They Fired the
First Shot 2012 and is receiving many requests to come and share
his understanding on how to implement the plan in the book.

- Constitutional Sheriffs and Peace Officers Association –
C.S.P.O.A. – Equipping Sheriffs, Peace Officers, and public officials to carry out their duties in accordance with their Oaths
of Office. www.cspoa.org/

- **County Sheriff Project** — Supporting Peace
Officers in uniting to end State and Federal tyranny.
www.CountySheriffProject.org

- **KrisAnne Hall** – Missionary and fiery advocate for the
Constitution. KrisAnne is an attorney, teacher, and author. As a ministry she travels to speak and teach about the

Constitution and threats to our liberty in the United States.
Her presentations are excellent and powerfully delivered.
KrisAnne@KrisAnneHall.com.

- **Don Casey** – Don is a national speaker who exposes the insidious nature of Sustainable Development/Agenda 21, social
  justice, and the efforts to abolish property rights. Don seeks
  to raise public awareness of our God-given unalienable rights,
  which is the only true avenue of combating the process of globalization. Much through Don's efforts with a core group of
  people, a huge victory against Federalization was won when
  Agenda 21/Sustainable Development was made illegal in the
  State of Alabama in 2012.

- **Alliance Defending Freedom (formerly Alliance Defense
  Fund) — A.D.F.** – a powerful organization coordinating
  very successful legal efforts against attacks on religious liberty in the United States and abroad. Phone: 800-835-5233,
  www.alliancedefendingfreedom.org.

- **Liberty Council** — An international non-profit organization
  utilizing litigation, education, and public policy to advance religious freedom, the sanctity of life and the family. Phone: 800-
  671-1776, www.lc.org

- **Thomas More Foundation** — A national non-profit law center
  fighting for religious freedom, family values and the sanctity of
  life through litigation, media, and education. Phone: 734-827-
  2001, www.thomasmore.org

- **Institute on the Constitution** — An educational effort to recon-
  nect Americans to the history of the American Republic and
  to their heritage of freedom under law. The Institue on the
  Constitution offer classes, speaking engagements, etc., for this
  purpose. Phone: 866-730-9796, www.theamericanview.com

- **The Constitution Institute** — The Constitution Institue provided Constitutional classes to the Sheriff's office of Elkhart County, Indiana as discussed in this book. Phone: 812-459-7813, www.constitutioninstitute.org.

Recommended Sources for Village and Agrarian Life:

- **Acres USA** – Books, monthly publications, good information on agricultural topics.
  Phone: 800-355-5313, www.acresusa.com

- **Stockman Grass Farmer** – Monthly publications, good information on livestock.
  Phone: 800 748-9808, www.stockmangrassfarmer.com

- **Joel Salatin: Polyface Farms** – Good books on small to mid-size farming (you can order Joel's books through Acres USA).
  Phone: 540-885-3590, 540-887-8194, www.polyfacefarms.com

- **Gerald Fry** – Beef & dairy cattle consultant: genetics, feeding, breeding, selection, and animal health.
  Phone: 501-454-3252, www.bovineengineering.com

- **Greg Judy** – Author of Comeback Farms. Good information on grazing animals with no input costs.
  www.greenpasturesfarm.net

- **Agri Dynamics** – Supplier of feeds, supplements, and health products for livestock. Phone: 877-393-4484
  www.agri-dynamics.com

- **Erath Earth** – Consultant for compost tea (a natural fertilizer) and equipment supplier: soil fertility for crops, gardens and pastures. Phone: 254-485-3560 www.erathearth.com

- **Seed Savers** – Vegetable, herb and flower seeds. Phone: 563-382-5990, www.seedsavers.org

- **Southern Exposure** – Vegetable, herb and flower seeds. Phone: 540-894-9480, www.southernexposure.org

APPENDIX I

More of the Forward Chapter

As you see this devastating picture emerging, consider these words of Our Lady:

August 25, 1994

> **"Dear children, today I am united with you in prayer in a special way, praying for the gift of the presence of my beloved Son in your home country... I pray and intercede before my Son, Jesus, so that <u>the dream that your fathers had may be fulfilled</u>. Pray, little children, in a special way because satan is strong and wants to destroy hope in your heart. I bless you..."**

The dream your fathers had? What dream? In the United States of America we speak of our founding "fathers" and the "dream" they had of founding a nation based upon the principles of Jesus Christ. Some call it the Great Experiment, but in reading their own words, it was more than an experiment—it was a dream, their greatest hope, their greatest longing for all of mankind. Though Our Lady's messages will always

mean different things to different people, and this is as
true with the message above as any other, there can be
no doubt that She was speaking of the United States
when She spoke these words. James Madison, who was
known as the "Father" of the Constitution said:

> *"Whatever may be the judgment pronounced on
> the competency of the architects of the Constitu-
> tion, or whatever may be the destiny of the edifice
> prepared by them, I feel it a duty to express my
> profound and solemn conviction…that there
> never was an assembly of men charged with a
> great and arduous trust who were more pure in
> their motives, or more exclusively or anxiously
> devoted to the object committed to them, than
> were the members of the Federal Convention of
> 1787 to the object of devising and proposing a
> constitutional system which should…best secure
> the permanent liberty and happiness of their
> country."[420]*

But James Madison also said:

> *"The happy union of these states is a wonder;
> their Constitution **is a miracle;** their example the
> hope of liberty throughout the world. **Woe to the**

ambition that would meditate the destruction of either!"[421]

What is coming to light in this chapter of "Forward" is that there is, as Madison said, woe to an *"ambition meditating the destruction"* of the United States as our founding fathers dreamed it to be. But what is most frightening about this "meditation" is that there are "dreams of **a** father" that are wanting to supplant the dreams of "**our** fathers." Obama, who was fatherless growing up, took on the dreams of Frank Marshall Davis and made them his own. But, he also did this with his own biological father. In Dinesh D'Souza's book, The Roots of Obama's Rage, it very clearly reveals that Obama took on the dreams of his own father.

"We are today living out the script for America and the world that was dreamt up not by Obama but by Obama's father. How do I know this? Because Obama says so himself. Reflect for a moment on the title of his book: it's not Dreams of My Father but rather Dreams from My Father. *In other words, Obama is not writing a book about his father's dreams; he is writing a book about the dreams that he got from his father.*

"Think about what this means. The most pow-erful country in the world is being governed according to the dreams of a Luo tribesman of the 1950's — a polygamist who abandoned his wives, drank himself into stupors, and bounced around on two iron legs (after his real legs had to be amputated because of a car crash*), raging against the world for denying him the realization of his anti-colonial ambitions. This philander-ing, inebriated African socialist is now setting the nations' agenda through the reincarnation of his dreams in his son. The son is the one who is making it happen, but the son is, as he candidly admits, only living out his father's dream. The invisible father provides the inspiration, and the son dutifully gets the job done. America today is being governed by a ghost."[422]

But, it is more than a ghost. Is it not unseen princi-palities at work that Obama has opened himself up to, to be filled by evil's *"ambition meditating on the destruction"* of the United States. Frank Marshall Da-vis and Obama's father had the same dream, a dream that came from the Father of Communism. This is the

---

* Obama's father was involved in many car accidents because of his drinking. He died in one such accident when his car went off the road and slammed into an old tree stump.

"dream of your fathers" that is being lived out in the White House today. And the goal is to bond indissolubly the principles of civil government to the principles of an anti-freedom, anti-God system. The actions of satan always "opposite" the actions of God. In contrast, Our Lady wants us to see the dream of our Father in Heaven, *"If my people, who are called by my name, shall humble themselves, and pray, and seek my face, and turn from their wicked ways; then I will hear from Heaven, and will forgive their sin, and will heal their land,"* through the great Healer, Jesus, Himself. Our Lady tells us this so clearly:

"...I pray and intercede before my Son, Jesus, so that the dream that your fathers had may be fulfilled..."

We have in the White House the influence of satan leading it. In Medjugorje, we have the influence of Jesus' Mother leading those who hear Her voice to follow Her Son. Which Father's dream is going to be fulfilled?

APPENDIX II

More Stories of the Davids

The following are more stories of the Davids:

Sheriff Ken Jones, Eureka County, Nevada

When Federal Badge VS. Local Badge

"They despise me,"[423] said Sheriff Ken Jones of Eureka County in Nevada regarding how federal officials from the U.S. Bureau of Land Management feel about him. Sheriff Jones has been on the job for 17 years, the longest-serving sheriff of his county and also the senior officer by service in the entire state of Nevada. Jones has said, *"Local people have come to me again and again about horse gathers or cattle seizures or property rights and asked me to defend them from their own government. I can't blame them. Sometimes, the government scares me, too."* [424] Sheriff Jones has refused state and federal funds to set up checkpoints on holidays because he sees this as entrapment. Sheriffs are starting to stop these checkpoint inspections because there is no probable cause involved, therefore, it is unconsti-

tutional and results in harassment of law abiding citizens who are detained without doing anything. Sheriff Jones has only a four-deputy force to cover the 4,000 square miles of his county, but he has turned down the government's offer to expand and modernize, preferring not to have federal strings attached to his authority.

Conflicts have also arisen in Sheriff Jones' county over federal agents attempting to seize cattle or horses that were grazing on federal lands, circumstances that have always been lawful until recent years. Every federal attempt to take the cattle was met with protests, until one day a man set himself on fire and charged at the federal agents. Sheriff Jones offered no support to the federal agents, when the man was charged with assaulting a federal officer. *"They asked me what I was going to do with him. I said, 'Nothing, it was you guys he was after, you do something."* [425]

In response to a suggestion by an agent with Bureau of Land Management telling Sheriff Jones that a "stronger liaison be set up between federal agents and his division," Jones commented, *"He* (of the Bureau of Land Management) *suggested we could deputize the Bureau of Land Management agents and whatever citations they wrote would bring all the revenue to Eureka*

County." Sheriff Jones responded, *"Oh, you mean like you guys* (from the Bureau of Land Management) *see a hay truck without a taillight or something?"* The agent responded back to the Sheriff, *"Yeah, traffic stuff, things out of hand..."* Jones answered back rather pointedly, *"I told him to have his agents find the nearest payphone and dial 911, and I'd give them the same authority as everybody else in the county."* [426]

Sheriff Gary Penrod, San Bernardino, California

Sheriff Gary Penrod, from San Bernardino, California, implemented a similar policy in his jurisdiction, as Sheriff Aman did against radical environmental groups, when he set down strong policies, restricting or stopping the Bureau of Land Management. Sheriff Penrod, after experiencing numerous problems with Bureau of Land Management officials over the private property of citizens in his county, revoked all local law enforcement authority from the federal government over the 20,000 square miles of his county. Sheriff Penrod told the Bureau of Land Management that concerning any action they wish to take on private property, they must first consult him. Penrod was led to this decision partly because of radical environmentalists who were working with the Bureau of Land Management wanting to prove that cattle was endangering the habitat of the desert tortoise. Federal agents were causing confusion on county roads and Penrod grew frustrated with how these agents were *"challenging the livelihood of people who have lived in the desert for generations."*[427] A better relationship between the federal agents and himself resulted from Penrod taking such a strong stance. He concluded, *"I think we've been able to send out the message that we're not going to be run over by Big Brother."*[428] For too long, sheriffs have "proxied" their authority to federal, state and even local tyranny, thinking it was right to do so or that they had to comply with their directives. When sheriffs understand it is not so, instead, it's the people who are their boss and he is to serve them with protection, everything begins to change and liberty reigns. Parallel these actions, recognizing God's sovereignty over us, and the country will be refreshed with peace and freedom.

Sheriff Glenn E. Palmer, Grant County, Oregon

"I am not a government employee. I am a public servant."

Sheriff Palmer of Grant County, Oregon is another sheriff that refused to renew his county's contract

agreement with the Forest Service, willingly forgoing
significant revenue that the Forest Service had provided in the past because of not wanting to be under
the control of federal agencies. Sheriff Palmer stated
in a letter to the U.S. Forest Service of many concerns
he had with their policies that were against the Constitutional rights of the citizens in his county. Sheriff
Palmer said, *"I have sent at least two requests to the
U.S. Forest Service asking for information that pertains
to where the U.S. Forest Service gets its Constitutional
authority to have law enforcement officers within Grant
County. Your jurisdiction, as I see it, is limited in nature
to the Federal Building in John Day (Oregon). I want
to remind you that all policing within the external borders of Grant County are the exclusive responsibility of
the Grant County Sheriff's Office and enforcement of
all laws shall rest with the County Sheriff and his designees."* [429]

Sheriff Palmer spoke at an informational meeting in California with other sheriffs to inform citizens
of their Constitutional rights and the responsibility
of sheriffs to uphold those rights in their own various
counties. In his presentation, Palmer said, *"I am not
a government employee. I am a public servant. I serve
the people who elected me...**I take a stand against bad***

*government...I have a duty and obligation to keep you from bad government when you are in my county...It is up to you folks to hold us accountable...Don't give up your **water rights** or your **mining rights**...Stand up and defend what you believe in!"* Palmer also added, *"If an elected official has not taken an oath of office, he does not belong in office."* [430] Wherever you live in the United States of America, your county sheriff can exercise authority to do as Sheriff Palmer states, support you in *"standing up and defending what you believe in."* [431]

Sheriff Phil Barney, Utah

Learning that a citizen in his county had cattle taken from him by the Bureau of Land Management, Utah Sheriff Phil Barney, courageously and heroically drove a couple of hundred miles to recover the cattle impounded by federal agents in the Escalante region and return them to their owner.[432]

Sheriff Tony DeMeo, Nye County, Nevada

Wayne Hage owned the Pine Creek cattle ranch in Nye County, Nevada. Federal agents began illegally seizing Hage's cattle off federally owned land. He chronicled his experience in a book entitled, "Storm

Over Rangelands, Private Rights in Federal Lands."
Sheriff Tony DeMeo finally put a stop to the confiscation by requiring all federal agents to contact him before they take any action in his county.

National and State Parks are another area of con-
tention between sheriffs and government agents. In recent years, moves have been made by federal workers
to assume law enforcement authority in Parks which,
constitutionally, doesn't exist. Sheriffs are coming
against the usurping of their own authority by federal
and state officials. Sheriffs have full authority of law enforcement in Parks that fall in the jurisdiction of their
own county.[433]

Sheriff Dennis Spruell, Montezuma County, Colorado

When it was made known to Sheriff Spruell that the
U.S. Forest Service had closed certain roads to "off-road
vehicles" in the San Juan National Forest, he threatened
to cut locks on the gates and ticket any Forest Service
agent who was caught enforcing the closures.[434]

Sheriff Gil Gilbertson, Josephine County, Oregon

Because of confiscations of private property and
violations of county citizen's Constitutional rights and
dreaming up regulations such as "Monument Status"
that prevent citizens from being able to use their private property, in his county of Josephine, Oregon Sheriff, Gil Gilbertson, found it necessary to write to the
U.S. Forest Service. It is important to realize the Forest Service has become a pawn for the environmental
agenda.

> *"...I am concerned that information is withheld
> from this Office. This uncooperative posture ap-
> pears to present a challenge of authority. Frank-
> ly, I was somewhat taken aback by your legal
> department's position advising you to not discuss
> issues with me. I am further aghast to the sug-
> gestion I must file a Freedom of Information Act
> (FOIA) to find out what your agency is doing in
> regards to the citizens of this county.*

> *"As the Chief Law Enforcement Officer of this
> County, elected by the citizens, saddled with the
> expectation and responsibility to safeguard their
> rights I fully intend to uphold the laws against
> any threat, inappropriate or unlawful actions*

against them. The citizens of this County are complaining about unfair treatment and harassment by the federal government law enforcement officers.

"The issues of illegal road closures, grazing, logging, minerals, taking land under the auspices of "Monument" status, citizen complaints against your law enforcement agents, high unemployment and other socio-economic issues we all face today; coupled with the uncooperative nature presented by the U.S. Forest Service are causing me great concern about our relationship and future cooperation..."[435]

Do to the continued conflicts arising between policies of the federal agencies and his department, Sheriff Gilbertson began to research the origin and extent of federal power within a state. This resulted in a 13-page report entitled, <u>Unraveling Federal Jurisdiction within a State</u>, and has been very helpful in providing the legal justification to resist federal expansion in states. Gilbertson said of his report:

"This paper is a result of a clash with the federal law enforcement (from the Forest Service) in this county, from citizens complaining of what can

only be described as harassment and violations
of their rights. The first time I approached the
U.S. Forest Service the door closed regarding any
discussion. The Forest Service advised me to file
a Freedom of Information request."[436]

Eventually, Gilbertson was able to sit down and
discuss his concerns with the Forest Service. Of this
meeting he said, *"Most of my questions were answered*
except for one: **Where does the U.S. Forest Service's**
authority come from?*"* [437] It was this question that he
wanted answered, and in the end, he discovered the
authority that these agencies are taking come from no
legal entity. So it is that they had no more authority
than a man on the street. The United States Forestry
Department is only one of many government bureaucracies which has created aspects of its authority out
of air, with a basis that does not exist. This is the paper
tiger's Achilles heel. For decades, whether you are talking the Eastern, Northern, Southern or Western states,
or states across middle America, the authorities imposing ridiculous and oppressive zoning of areas, taking
control and ruling over citizen's use of private property,
and even parent's rights over their own children—
many of these authorities are not in authority, except
by regulation. They have taken liberties contrary to the

Constitution's protection of liberty! The local elected
sheriffs, the Davids, are in authority and the citizens are
their boss. Consequently, millions of dollars of fines
and the unconstitutional taking of private property has
occurred, resulting in wrecked lives of many who have
done nothing in violating a law, rather only a regulation, and often unconstitutional ones at that. When
Sheriff Gilbertson was asked why he decided to take
on this battle with the U.S. Forest Department, he said:

> *"My duty lies in the oath that I took to protect
> and serve the people of Josephine County, state
> law and the Constitution, and their (federal gov-
> ernment) agencies are infringing on all of the
> above. It's that simple.*

> *"Look, much suffering occurred and many lives
> were sacrificed to make this great country what
> it is today; many sadly take this horrific loss for
> granted. A Republic form of government can
> be long-term but only if we maintain a system of
> checks and balances.*

> *"Once we allow a runaway centralized govern-
> ment to weaken and/or erode the rights enumer-
> ated in our Constitution and Bill of Rights, we
> risk losing it all. Our government is rapidly ap-*

proaching a socialistic posture; and seemingly,
changing our life, as we knew it, through 'feder-
ally imposed REGULATIONS'."[438]

These federally imposed regulations are made without
authority to do so, yet they are applied with the force
of law.

Sheriff Joe Baca, Sierra County, New Mexico

The power of the Davids is shown of what can be
done when the federal government takes over jurisdictions by slipping in new regulations and acting upon
them as if they were law.

The Gila National Forest is located in Sierra County in New Mexico. The U.S. Forest Service manages
approximately 378,700 acres of the more than 3,000,000
acres that make up the National Forest. A contract
existed between the sheriff's department and the Forest Service in which sheriffs were compensated $16,000
annually for patrolling and enforcing laws in the Gila
Forest. In 2011, the Western States Sheriff's Association received notice that the U.S. Forest Service had
proposed rule changes to the code of federal regulations granting themselves greater power and authority
in law enforcement areas. Being in disagreement with
these changes, Sheriff Joe Baca made the decision not

to renew the contract between the sheriffs and the Forest Service. The Western States Sheriff's Association said the proposed rule changes *"exhibit an absolute disregard for the sovereignty of the individual States, show a disregard for the authority of the Office of Sheriff, and a continued inability of the Forest Service to understand the mission and function of its law."* [439] Baca, speaking on behalf of the Western States Sheriffs Association stated, *"The Forest Service has added stipulations that we do not agree with. We sheriffs have jurisdiction in the forest if the land is within our county, and I won't take money for doing what I already get paid to do by the residents of Sierra County."* [440] Sheriff Baca and the other sheriffs of his region who refused to continue the $16,000 contract from the Forest Service made a clear statement that they would not allow federal agencies to mandate what they can and cannot do. In another area of contention, the Forest Service has been drawing up a plan in which they would be closing 1,000 or more miles of roads in the Gila National Forest. This plan drew significant opposition locally, as the roads are public and if closed would prevent access to some public lands. Sheriff Baca publically stated that he and his department would not enforce any federal regulations that would prevent citizens from accessing public lands. Sheriff Baca stated, *"It might make some people mad, but I want to do what's right, not what's required by the Forest Service, violating the U.S. Constitution or state statutes."* [441]

Sheriff Benny House, Otero County, New Mexico

The county commission of Otero County, New Mexico, voted to establish an 80,000 acre plan to manage forest overgrowth. The mountain villages of this county are surrounded by forests and when the villagers wanted to cut fire breaks in the trees to protect their homes, because of the new zoning plan, adopted locally by the orchestration of the United Nations' Agenda 21 Sustainable Development plan, they were told "no". Knowing their homes would be threatened without the fire breaks, the residents sent word that they were going to defy the order and create the fire-breaks anyway. The Forest Department sent word that if trees were cut down there would be arrests made. To that threat, Sheriff Benny House told the federal agents that anyone who made arrests, would be arrested themselves for false arrest. The trees did come down, and Republican congressman Steve Pearce was on hand to level the first one. In the end, no opposition was raised by Forest Service officials.[442]

Sheriff Makita, El Paso, Texas

In communist Russia, a man could be walking down the street and have his papers checked, go to the next street corner and have his papers checked again, and so forth. Checkpoints are normal in military zones. But in Croatia today, though it is a free nation, a mentality held over from communist days accepts that people can be randomly pulled over for no reason except for a fishing expedition to find something wrong. In America's past, when we lived by the Constitution, this could not be done. But with our loss of freedom in the last decades there is a growing acceptance of what is unacceptable constitutionally.

So are roadside checkpoints, in which every vehicle is stopped, to find those who are driving under the influence of alcohol constitutional? According to a Supreme Court decision, the answer is yes, but according to more and more sheriffs who have participated in these checkpoints and who are questioning the Constitutional legality of such a search, they are becoming increasingly uncomfortable with the action. Sheriff Makita from El Paso, Texas, has altogether stopped these checkpoints in his county as unconstitutional.

"I'm not going to continue to be bribed at the state level or the federal level, by money, to do something that I think is inappropriate. That's how you live... your oath of office and even if the Supreme Court says its okay, we still have the opportunity to decide, yes, we will or no, we won't. Because this is not what our forefathers had in mind when they spoke of freedom."[443]

Why would Sheriff Makita take such a stance when the Supreme Court ruled its okay to do? A review of a 2012 audit in California will shed light on how police checkpoints are a fishing expedition in which everyone's rights are abused—the innocent as well as the guilty. The audit showed that in seven hours, 949 cars passed through a San Diego sobriety checkpoint on a Saturday night. You can safely estimate that in those seven hours, roughly 1900 people were detained without probable cause. What did the checkpoint flush out? Just 15 citations were issued, and none of them were for drunk driving! In Fresno, in 10 hours, 348 cars were stopped, about 700 people, at a checkpoint and there were 33 citations given. Five of those were for under the influence while driving, 15 for unlicensed vehicles, 12 for suspended or revoked driver's licenses, and one miscellaneous.[444] While it is good to catch a

DUI or snag a criminal, it cannot justify constitutionally the detaining and searching of innocent people
without probable cause. The risk of growing more and
more into a police state as what happened on Russian
streets is why our Forefathers restricted search and sei-
zure without probable cause, even with the possibility
of catching a lawbreaker or two. They, in their wisdom,
saw the greater danger not in the criminal slipping
through the cracks but rather the loss of freedom and
liberty for the greater society. They knew, inevitably,
this would evolve to greater loss of liberty. What the
audit revealed is that the checkpoints without probable cause are having little impact in making our roads
safer, but that they are benefiting the revenue of city
departments and court fees who utilize them, at the
expense of lost Constitutional rights of the citizenry
of our nation. It is for this reason that more and more
sheriffs are coming to the same conclusion as Sheriff
Makita and will no longer hold roadside checkpoints in
their counties.

What if there is a threat of bodily harm to citizens
that stems from the religious beliefs of another people?
Do these citizens have the right of protection given in
the First Amendment?

Sheriff Robert Arnold, Rutherford County, Tennessee

As sheriffs begin to understand their Constitutional duty and power invested in them to protect the citizens in their specific counties, more of them are taking pro-active steps to be prepared for any threat or danger. Tennessee Sheriff Robert Arnold hired former FBI agent and outspoken critic of Islam and Sharia law, John Guandolo, to train his deputies. Guandolo has stated that many of the local mosques are front orga-nizations for the Muslim Brotherhood, and as such, he has said, *"They do not have a First Amendment right to do anything."* [445] Questioned about his move to hire Guandolo, Sheriff Arnold said:

> *"There are not many classes out there for any-thing when it comes to Muslims…but this train-ing isn't just about that, it has many other compo-nents to it. My stance is and my office's stance is we are not here to pick sides.*[446]

As even discussing potential Islamic threats from extremist groups falls in the category of political-incorrectness, federal and state agencies have no con-tingency plans in case of an attack. This is the case, even though extremist groups are very vocal and pub-lic about threatening such future attacks and there is much evidence to show that terrorists are being formed in these mosques within our own borders. Sheriff Arnold, knowing he was elected to protect and defend his county under oath, believes it to be his moral obligation to educate his deputies to potential threats from extremist groups and be prepared to defend the citizens of his county if a situation arises to warrant protection. In order to protect, one must know and study the mind of those who would wish to do harm. In an action that would make him a target for the liberal press, Sheriff Arnold willingly takes hits simply because, as he said, *"I am here to protect the people of this county, and I am never going to waiver from that."*[447]

We must never forget that we are a Christian nation based in law that is indissolubly foundationed in Christian principles. Our founding fathers who spoke and wrote of freedom of religion were addressing the point from Judeo-Christian values and principles. Of the Constitution John Adams said:

> *"Our Constitution was made only for a moral and religious people. It is wholly inadequate to the government of any other."* [448]

One has a right to be a Muslim in this nation, but not the right for public policies to be formed upon Is-

lam's beliefs and ways. This is wholly reserved for Judeo-Christian principles of all Christian denominations
and foundations in our public squares and policies, just
as Islam is in Muslim countries.

APPENDIX III

Was Washington's life preserved by God for special plans of Our Lady?

The following was taken from the booklet *"American History You Never Learned."* In this appendix the full acount of George Washington's dream of the three perils is given.

> *"The last time I saw Anthony Sherman was on the Fourth of July, 1859, in Independence Square. He was then ninety-nine years old, and becoming feeble. But though so old, his dreaming eyes rekindled as he gazed up Independence Hall, which he came to visit once more.*
>
> *"Let us go into the hall," he said. "I want to tell you an incident in Washington's life—one which no one alive knows except myself; and, if you live, you will before long, see it verified.*
>
> *"From the opening of the Revolution we experienced all phases of fortune, now good and now ill, one time victorious and another time con-*

quered. The darkest period we had, I think, was when Washington, after several reverses, retreated to Valley Forge, where he resolved to pass the winter of 1777. Ah! I have often seen the tears course down our dear commander's careworn cheeks, as he would be conversing with confidential officers about the condition of his poor soldiers. You have doubtless heard the story of Washington's going to the thicket to pray. Well, it was not only true, but he used often to pray in secret for aid and comfort from God, the interposition of whose Divine Providence brought us safely through the darkest days of tribulation.

"One day—I remember it well—the chilly wind whistled through the leafless trees, though the sky was cloudless and the sun shone brightly. He remained in his quarters nearly all afternoon alone. When he came out I noticed that his face was a shade paler than usual, and there seemed to be something on his mind of more than ordinary importance. Returning just after dark, he dispatched an orderly to the quarters of an officer, who was presently in attendance. After a preliminary conversation of about half an hour, Washington, gazing upon his companion with

that strange look of dignity which he alone could command, said:

'I do not know whether it is owing to the anxiety of my mind, or what, but this afternoon, as I was sitting at this table engaged in preparing a dispatch, something seemed to disturb me. Looking up, I saw standing opposite a singularly beautiful female. So astonished was I, for I had given strict orders not to be disturbed, that it was some moments before I found language to inquire the purpose of her presence

'A second, a third, even a fourth time did I repeat my question but received no answer from my mysterious visitor, except a slight raising of her eyes. By this time I felt strange sensations spreading through me. I would have risen, but the riveted gaze of the being before me rendered volition impossible. I essayed once more to address her, but my tongue had become useless. Even thought itself had become paralyzed. A new influence, mysterious, potent, irresistible, took possession of me. All I could do was to gaze steadily, vacantly at my unknown visitor. Gradually the surrounding atmosphere filled with sensations and grew luminous. Everything about me seemed to rarefy,

*the mysterious visitor herself becoming more airy
and yet more distinct to my sight than before. I
now began to feel as one dying, or rather to experience the sensation which I have sometimes
imagined accompanies dissolution. I did not
think, I did not reason, I did not move. All, alike,
were impossible. I was conscious only of gazing
fixedly, vacantly, at my companion.*

*'Presently I heard a voice say, 'Son of the Repub-
lic, look and learn!' while at the same time my
visitor extended her arm eastwardly. I looked
and beheld a heavy white vapor rising, at some
distance, fold upon fold. This gradually dis-
sipated, and I looked upon a strange scene. Before me lay spread out in one vast plain all the
countries of the world — Europe, Asia, Africa,
and America. I saw rolling and tossing between
Europe and America, the billows of the Atlantic
Ocean, and between America and Asia lay the
Pacific. 'Son, of the Republic,' said the mysterious voice as before, 'look and learn.'*

*'At that moment I beheld a dark, shadowy be-
ing, like an angel, standing, or rather floating in
mid-air between Europe and America. Dipping
water out of the ocean with his right hand, he*

cast it upon America, while that in his left hand went upon the European countries. Immediately a cloud arose from these countries, and joined in mid ocean. For awhile it remained station- ary, and then it moved slowly westward, until it enveloped America in its folds. Sharp flashes of lightning gleamed through at intervals; and I heard the smothered groans of the American people. A second time the angel dipped water from the ocean and sprinkled it as before. The dark cloud was then drawn back to the ocean, in whose heaving billows it sank from view. A third time I heard the mysterious voice say, 'Son of the Republic, look and learn.'

'I cast my eyes upon America and beheld vil- lages, towns and cities springing up one after another until the whole land, from the Atlantic to the Pacific, was dotted with them. Again I heard the voice say, 'Son of the Republic, the end of the century cometh. Look and learn.'

'And with this the dark, shadowy figure turned its face southward, and from Africa an ill-omened specter approached our land.

'It flitted slowly over every town and city of the land. The inhabitants presently set themselves in battle array against each other. As I continued to look I saw a bright angel, on whose brow rested a crown of light on which was traced the word, 'Union,' place an American flag between the divided nation, and say, 'Remember, ye are brethren.' Instantly, the inhabitants, casting from them their weapons, became friends once more, and united around the National Standard.

'Again I heard the voice say, 'Son of the Republic, look and learn!' At this, the dark, shadowy angel placed a trumpet to his mouth and blew three distinct blasts; and taking water from the ocean he sprinkled it upon Europe, Asia, and Africa.

'Then my eyes beheld a fearful scene: from each of these countries arose thick black clouds that were soon joined into one. And throughout this mass there gleamed a bright Red Light, by which I saw hordes of armed men, who, moving with the cloud, marched by land and sailed by sea to America; which country was enveloped in the volume of cloud.

'And I saw dimly these vast armies devastate the whole country and burn the villages, towns, and cities that I beheld springing up.

'As my ears listened to the thundering of the cannon, the clashing of swords, and the shouts and cries of millions in mortal combat, I again heard the mysterious voice say, 'Son of the Republic, look and learn.' As the voice ceased, the shadowy figure of the angel, for the last time, dipped water from the ocean and sprinkled it upon America. Instantly the dark cloud rolled back, together with the armies it had brought, leaving the inhabitants of the land victorious.

'Once more I beheld villages, towns and cities springing up where I had seen them before; while the bright angel, planting the azure standard he had brought in the midst of them, cried in a loud voice, 'While the stars remain and the heavens send down dew upon the earth, so long shall the Union last.' And taking from her brow the crown on which was blazoned the word, 'Union,' she placed it upon the Standard, while people kneeling down, said, Amen.

'The scene instantly began to fade away, and I saw nothing but the rising curling vapor I had at first beheld. This also disappeared, and I found myself once more gazing upon the mysterious visitor who said, 'Son of the Republic, what you have seen is thus interpreted. Three great perils will come upon the Republic. The most fearful is the third, but the whole world united shall not prevail against her. Let every child of the Republic learn to live for God, his land, and the Union.' With these words the angel vanished from my sight.'

"Such, my friend," concluded the narrator, "were the very words I heard from Washington's own lips; and America will do well to profit by them."[449]

* * * * *

Endnotes

Chapter One

1 *"Why: The Killing Fields of Rwanda,"* Nancy Gibbs, Time Magazine, May 16, 1994

2 Ibid.

3 "Leave None to Tell the Story: Genocide in Rwanda." Human Rights Watch Report (Updated April 1, 2003)

4 Diamond, Jared. "Collapse", Penguin Books, New York, NY, 2005, pp 316

5 Gerard Prunier, *The Rwanda Crisis: History of a Genocide* (London: Hurst, 1995); rpt. In "Rwanda & Burundi: The Conflict", *Contemporary Tragedy, The Holocaust: A Tragic Legacy*

6 "Leave None to Tell the Story: Genocide in Rwanda." Human Rights Watch Report (Updated April 1, 2003)

7 Mark Doyle, "Ex-Rwandan PM reveals genocide planning," BBC News, March 26, 2004

8 "RWANDA: No consensus on genocide death toll", *Agence France-Presse*, iAfrica.com, April 6, 2004

9 Linda Melvern, *Conspiracy to Murder: The Rwandan Genocide* Verso, 2004, ISBN 1-85984-588-6, p. 49

10 "Part 1: Hate media in Rwanda&#149 Call to genocide: radio in Rwanda, 1994: International Development Research Centre" Retrieved August 30, 2010

11 Staff, "Burundi," Prevent Genocide International

12 "French probe finds missile fire from military camp downed Rwandan president's plan in 1994", *Washington Post*, 11 January 2012

13 "Part 1: Hate media in Rwanda&#149 Call to genocide: radio in Rwanda, 1994: International Development Research Centre," Retrieved August 30, 2010

Chapter Two

14 Immaculee Ilibagiza, <u>Our Lady of Kibeho</u>, Hay House, Inc., 2008, pp. 149

15 Gerard Prunier, *The Rwanda Crisis: History of a Genocide* (London: Hurst, 1995); rpt. In "Rwanda & Burundi: The Conflict", *Contemporary Tragedy, The Holocaust: A Tragic Legacy*

16 Jared Diamond, Collapse: How societies choose to fail or survive, page 318

Chapter Three

17 *"191 Bishops have Spoken Out Against Obama/HHS Mandate,"* Thomas Peters, Catholic Vote, June 23, 2012.

18 Joint letter for the Catholic diocese of Alabama (Mobile and Birmingham) written by Rev. Thomas J. Rodi, D.D. Archbishop of Mobile and Rev. Robert J. Baker, S.T.D., Bishop of Birmingham in Alabama, February 3, 2012

19 *"Catholic Politicians Who Attack Church Should Remember God's Judgment,"* David Kerr, Catholic News Agency, February 13, 2012.

20 Bishop Jenky's Pastoral Letter of February 10, 2012 – Peoria, Illinois

21 *Catholic Politicians Who Attack Church Should Remember God's Judgment,"*

David Kerr, Catholic News Agency, February 13, 2012.
22 Ibid.

Chapter Four

23 Abraham Lincoln: *The Works of Abraham Lincoln, Speech and Debates,* Jon *H.
      Clifford, Editor (new York, The University Society Inc. 1908), fol. III, August 17,
      1858, p. 126-127*
24 Ibid.

Chapter Six

25 Foundation for Moral Law, Inc., Introduction to Commentaries of the Laws of
      England; Birmingham, Alabama
26 Ibid.
27 Ibid.
28 Ibid.
29 Ibid.

Chapter Seven

30 *"Cardinal Lopez Trujillo: Family Being Destroyed 'Brick by Brick' in Spain,"*
      Catholic News Agency, April 25, 2005
31 The Works of John Adams, Second President of the United States, Vol. 9,
      Charles Francis Adams, Boston, Little, Brown, and Com., 1856.
32 Revolutionary Services and Civil Life of General William Hull, Maria Campbell,
      D. Appleton and Company, New York, 1848, pg. 266
33 The Works of John Adams, Second President of the United States, Vol. 9,
      Charles Francis Adams, Boston, Little, Brown, and Com., 1856.

Chapter Eight

34 Fraternitas Sacerdotalis Sancti Petri, Fr. Eric Flood, FSSP, North American
      District Superior
35 Raymond Arroyo Interview with Archbishop William Lori, March 17, 2012.
36 Ibid.

Chapter Ten

37 Letter of Cardinal Timothy Dolan, Archbishop of New York, President of the
      United States Conference of Catholic Bishops, to the United States Bishops,
      March 2, 2012
38 The Collected Works of Abraham Lincoln, Ed. Roy P. Busler, Volume VII,
      "Reply to New York Workingmen's Democratic Republican Association." Pp.
      259-260.

Chapter Eleven

39 Letter of Cardinal Timothy Dolan, Archbishop of New York, President of the
    United States Conference of Catholic Bishops, to the United States Bishops,
    March 2 2012
40 Ibid.
41 Ibid.
42 Look What Happened While You Were Sleeping, A Friend of Medjugorje
43 General William Sherman Monument in Washington D.C., D.C. Memorials
44 Catechism of the Catholic Church, #2263-2265
45 *"Address of His Holiness Benedict XVI to the Bishops of the United States of
    America on their "Ad Limina" Visit,"* Librreria Editrice Vaticana, January 19,
    2012, © 2012
46 Ibid.
47 Ibid.
48 Ibid.
49 Ibid.
50 Ibid.
51 Ibid.

Chapter Twelve

52 George Washington's Farewell Address, 1796,
53 *"Florida Man Guilty of DUI Manslaughter Sues Victim,"* Edward Lovett, ABC
    News, January 18, 2012.

Chapter Thirteen

54 Original Intent, David Barton, pg. 336
55 Ibid.
56 Ibid., pg. 337
57 Cites by Topic: Democracy, Chris Hansen, 2004
58 Ibid.
59 Original Intent, David Barton, pg. 335
60 Ibid.
61 Cites by Topic: Democracy, Chris Hansen, 2004
62 Ibid.
63 Original Intent, David Barton, pg. 335
64 Cites by Topic: Democracy, Chris Hansen, 2004
65 Original Intent, David Barton, pg. 337-338
66 Cites by Topic: Democracy, Chris Hansen, 2004

Chapter Fourteen

67 Fraternitas Sacerdotalis Sancti Petri, Fr. Eric Flood, FSSP, North American
    District Superior
68 John Locke, Treatise of Civil Government and a Letter Concerning Toleration,

Chas Sherman ed., (NY) Appleton-century, 1937, pp. 212-213
69 Look What Happened While You Were Sleeping, A Friend of Medjugorje
70 Original Intent, David Barton, pg. 38
71 Ibid.

Chapter Fifteen

72 *"Voter Identification Requirements,"* National Conference of State Legislatures,
    June 5, 2012
73 Fox News, *"Michelle Obama takes Heat for Saying She's 'Proud of My Country'*
    or the First Time," February 19, 2008
74 Thomas Jefferson, The Jeffersonian Cyclopedia, Ed. John P. Foley, Funk &
    Wagnalls Company, 1900, pg. 663

Chapter Sixteen

75 *"Obama Overturns 'Mexico City Policy' Implemented by Reagan,"* Tapper,
    Miller, and Khan. ABC News, January 23, 2009.
76 *"Obama Backs Bill to Repeal Defense of Marriage Act,"* David Nakamura.
    Washington Post, July 19, 2011.
77 *"Obama Ends 'Don't Ask, Don't Tell' Policy,"* Elisabeth Bumiller. The New
    York Times, July 22, 2011.
78 The New York Times, Microphone Catches a Candid Obama, March 26, 2012
79 "Obama: 'They Cling to Guns or Religion,'" Sarah Pulliam Bailey, Christianity
    Today, April 13, 2008
80 "Obama to Lift 'Conscience' Rule for Health Care Workers," Aliza Marcus,
    Bloomberg, February 17, 2009;
81 "Jesus Missing From Obama's Georgetown Speech," Jim Lovino, NBC News,
    April 17, 2009
82 "Vatican Vetoes Barack Obama's Nominees for US Ambassador," The
    Guardian, April 14, 2009.
83 "Obama ends Bush-era National Prayer Day Service at White House," Andrew
    Malcolm, Los Angeles Times, May 7, 2009.
84 "Obama Continues to Omit 'Creator' From Declaration of Independence,"
    Meredith Jessup, The Blaze, October 19, 2010.
85 *"History of 'In God we Trust.'"* United States Department of the Treasury
86 "Feds Sued by Veterans to Allow Stolen Mojave Desert Cross to be Rebuilt,"
    Red State, January 14, 2011.
87 "Amid Criticism, President Obama moves to Fill Vacant Religious Ambassador
    Post," Marianne Medlin, Catholic News Agency, February 9, 2011.
88 "Obama Administration Changes Bush Conscience Provision for Health
    Workers." Sarah Pulliam Bailey, Christianity Today. February 18, 2011.
89 *"ENDA Passage Effort Renewed with Senate Introduction,"* Chris Johnson,
    April 15, 2011.
90 "HHS's New Health Guidelines Trample on Conscience," Chuck Donovan, The
    Heritage Foundation, August 2, 2011.
91 "Obama Administration Opposes FDR Prayer at WWII Memorial," Todd

Starnes, Fox News, November 4, 2011.

92 "Remarks in Recognition of International Human Rights Day," Hillary Clinton, U.S. Department of State, December 6, 2011

93 "Church Wins Firing Case at Supreme Court," Ted Olsen, Christianity Today, January 1, 2012.

94 "Obama Administration Deletes Religious Service for Student Loan Forgiveness," Audrey Hudson, Red State, February 15, 2012.

95 "Houston Veterans Claim Censorship of Prayers, Including Ban on 'God' and 'Jesus,' Fox News, June 29, 2011.

96 "Air Force Suspends Ethics Course that used Bible Passages to Train Missile Launch Officers," Jason Ukman, The Washington Post, August 2, 2011.

97 "Maintaining Government Neutrality Regarding Religion," Memorandum from General Norton A. Schwartz, Air Force Chief of Staff, September 1, 2011.

98 "U.S. Military to Rescinds Policy Banning Bibles at Hospitals," Todd Starnes, Fox News, December 2, 2011

99 "Air Force Academy Backs Away From Christmas Charity," Todd Starnes, Fox News, November 4, 2011.

100 "Air Force Academy Adapts to pagans, druids, witches, and wiccans," Jenny Deam, Los Angeles Times, November 26, 2011.

101 "General Boykin Blocked at West Point," Ken Blackwell, Cybercast News Service, February 1, 2012.

102 "Air Force Unit Removes 'God' from Logo; Lawmakers warn of 'dangerous precedent,'" Geoff Herbert, Syracuse.com, February 9, 2012.

103 "Army Silences Catholic Chaplains," Todd Starnes, Fox News, February 6, 2012.

Chapter Seventeen

104 Transcribed from an audio of interview with Obama on January 18, 2001 on Chicago Public Radio WBEZ.FM

105 The Poem of the Man-God, Vol. 3, Maria Valtorta, Centre Editoriale Valtortiano, © 1989, pg. 583

106 Transcribed from an audio of interview with Obama on January 18, 2001 on Chicago Public Radio WBEZ.FM

107 The Fiscal Times, "Obama Risks $100 Billion if Catholic hospitals Close," by Edward Morrissey, March 1, 2012

108 The American Life, Ronald Reagan, © 1990, pg. 226-227

Chapter Eighteen

109 The Blueprint For Change, Barack Obama's Plan for America 2008.

110 Transcript of Obama's Acceptance Speech on November 4, 2008, the Guardian.

111 Jean-Hugho Lapointe, "Socialism and the Corruption of Words and Language" Le Quebecois Libre, February 5, 2006, #165

112 Ibid.

113 Inside Politics, "New Obama Slogan has Long Ties to Marxism, Socialism," by Victor Morton, April 30, 2012

114 The Blueprint For Change, Barack Obama's Plan for America 2008.

115 The New York Times, February 5, 2008, Barack Obama's Feb. 5 Speech
116 Ibid.
117 The Chronicle of Philanthropy, *"Obama Unveils Ads and Web Site to Promote Community Service"*, May 11, 2012
118 CNN Politics, *"Powell Endorses Obama Service Initiative,"* January 10, 2009
119 Barack Obama's Inaugural Address, January 21, 2009. The White House blog.
120 Ibid., p. 2
121 Ibid., p. 3
122 *"Remarks by the President on a New Strategy for Afghanistan and Pakistan"*, March 27, 2009. The White House.
123 "Statement by the President on H.R. 1540," The White House, Office of the Press Secretary, December 31, 2011.
124 USA Today, *"Obama Announces Pentagon Budget Cuts"*, by Aamer Madhani, January 5, 2012
125 *"We Can't Wait: The White House Announces Federal and Private Sector Commitments to Provide Employment Opportunities for nearly 180,000 Youth."*, January 5, 2012. The White House.
126 Audio Recording and Transcript of Obama's speech given in Colorado Springs, Colorado on July 2, 2008, World Net Daily.
127 Ibid.
128 Ibid.
129 Ibid.
130 *"September 11th National Day of Service and Remembrance,"* May 11, 2012, United We Serve.
131 *"National community Service Initiative Launched, Leveraged by Organizations Across the Country,"*Philanthropy News Digest, June 24, 2009
132 Barack Obama's Inaugural Address, January 21, 2009,The White House Blog.
133 The Communist. Frank Marshall Davis: The Untold Story of Barack Obama's Mentor, Paul Kengor, Threshold Editions/Mercury Ink, © 2012, pg. 12.
134 Ibid., pg.15
135 Ibid., pg. 10
136 Ibid., pg.1
137 Ibid.
138 Ibid., pg. 250
139 Ibid. pg. 250
140 Ibid., pg 257
141 Ibid., pg 251-252
142 Ibid., pg
143 Ibid. pg 251
144 Ibid., pg 253
145 Ibid.,
146 Ibid., pg 259
147 Ibid., pg. 254
148 Ibid., pg 293
149 Barack Obama's Speech given after winning the Democratic Presidential Nomination, February 5, 2008, recorded by the New York Times.

Chapter Nineteen

150 H.R. 4872, "The Reconciliation Act of 2010," United States Congress, pgs. 1016-1018.

151 *"Remarks Delivered by Director David H. Petraeus at the In-Q-Tel CEO Summit,"* Central Intelligence Agency, March 1, 2012.

152 Ibid.

153 Ibid.

154 Ibid.

155 Mark Doyle, "Ex-Rwandan PM reveals genocide planning," BBC News, March 26, 2004

Chapter Twenty

156 *"In Crisis, Opportunity for Obama,"* Capital Journal, Wall Street Journal, November 21, 2008.

157 Memoirs of the Life and Writings of Benjamin Franklin, Vol. I, Benjamin Franklin, pg. 270

158 Revolutionary Services and Civil Life of General William Hull, Maria Campbell, D. Appleton and Company, New York, 1848, pg. 266

159 *"Enemy Expatriation Act Would Strip Americans of Citizenship for 'Hostilities Against the United States,'"* Mac Slavo, January 17, 2012.

160 Ibid.

161 Ibid.

162 Transcribed from of audio of interview with Obama on January 18, 2001 on Chicago Public Radio WBEZ.FM

Chapter Twenty-One

163 *"NBC News Apologizes for Error in Editing of Trayvon Martin Story,"* Mytheus Holt, The Blaze, April 3, 2012.

164 *"Did ABC News Purposely use Unnecessary Chyron to Cover Up Zimmerman's Head Bruise?"* P.J. Gladnick, Newsbusters, March 30, 2012.

165 Executive Order #13603 - National Defense Resource Preparedness.

166 *"Enemy Expatriation Act Would Strip Americans of Citizenship for 'Hostilities Against the United States,'"* Mac Slavo, January 17, 2012.

167 American Thinker, *"Obama's Second Term Transformation Plans,"* Steve McCann, May 8, 2012

168 Ibid.

169 *"Barack Obama and the Comfort Room; Exclusive: Jill Stanek relates exchange she had with senator about live aborted babies,"* Jill Stanek, World Net Daily, June 18, 2008

170 Ibid.

171 Ibid.

172 Interview with Jill Stanek by a Friend of Medjugorje, August 1, 2012

173 *"Barack Obama and the Comfort Room; Exclusive: Jill Stanek relates exchange she had with senator about live aborted babies,"* Jill Stanek, World

Net Daily, June 18, 2008

174 *"Understanding Why Obama Lies What's behind the president's obvious and unprecedented dishonesty?"*, David Kupelian, Whistlebolower, July 2012

Chapter Twenty-Two

175 The American Life, Ronald Reagan, © 1990, pg. 226-227
176 *"The Third Amendment,"* Revolutionary War and Beyond.
177 Ibid.
178 Ibid.
179 Transcript of Barack Obama, Final Primary Night at St. Paul, MN, June 3, 2008, The New York Times

Chapter Twenty-Three

180 The History Place, World War II in Europe, *"Hitler's Enabling Act"*
181 Statement by the President on H.R. 1540, The White House Press Office, December 31, 2011.
182 Ibid.
183 Ibid.
184 The History Place, Hitler Youth, *"Prelude to War."*
185 Ibid.
186 Ibid.
187 Ibid.
188 Ibid.
189 Ibid.
190 *"Hitler Youth,"* Leo Heska.
191 Ibid.
192 Some sources indicate eight basic needs proposed by Erich Fromm (i.e. "Erich Fromm," Path to Well Being. www.asheham.wordpress.com/authors-teachers/erich-fromm), other sources indicate Fromm proposed only six basic needs (Engler, Barbara. Personality Theories, p. 137. Boston: Houghton Mifflin Harcourt Publishing Company, 2008.), and still others only five. A simple, common sense look at needs 6, 7 and 8, "Excitation," "Unity," and "Effectiveness," as listed and described in the text, clearly identifies them as basic needs regardless of the varying interpretations as to the exact number of needs proposed by Fromm.
193 Fromm, Erich. Escape from Freedom, pp. 35-36. Henry, Holt and Company, LLC, 1941.
194 Audio Recording and Transcript of Obama's speech given in Colorado Springs, Colorado on July 2, 2008, World Net Daily
195 The Audacity of Hope: Thought on Reclaiming the American Dream, Barack Obama, Vintage Books-Random House, (c) 2006

Chapter Twenty-Four

196 National Association of Broadcasters, FEMA, Additional Campaign Elements,

"Emergency Preparedness Live Announcer Copy."
197 Audio Recording and Transcript of Obama's speech given in Colorado Springs, Colorado on July 2, 2008, World Net Daily
198 Ibid.
199 Ibid.
200 *"AP Newsbreak: Marine Critical of Obama faces Charges."* Julie Watson, Associated Press, San Antonio Express News, March 24, 2012
201 Ibid.
202 *"Koran Burning at U.S. Base Sparks Afghan Protests,"* Aleem Aghn, ABC News, Feb. 21, 2012; *"Military Burns Unsolicited Bibles Sent to Afghanistan,"* CNN, May 22, 2009
203 *"AP Newsbreak: Marine Critical of Obama faces Charges."* Julie Watson, Associated Press, San Antonio Express News, March 24, 2012
204 Ibid.
205 Chuck Pfarrer, Seal Target Geronimo, St. Martin's Press, © 2011, pg. 51
206 Audio Recording and Transcript of Obama's speech given in Colorado Springs, Colorado on July 2, 2008, World Net Daily
207 United States Declaration of Independence, 1776 A.D.
208 Audio Recording and Transcript of Obama's speech given in Colorado Springs, Colorado on July 2, 2008, World Net Daily
209 Ibid.
210 Ibid.
211 Ibid.
212 Ibid.
213 Ibid.
214 *"Top Army General Backs Plan to Cut 80,000 Troops,"* Reuters, NBC News, January 27, 2012.
215 Audio Recording and Transcript of Obama's speech given in Colorado Springs, Colorado on July 2, 2008, World Net Daily

Chapter Twenty-Five

216 A Friend of Medjugorje, Look What Happened While You Were Sleeping, © 2007, pg. 232
217 Nazi Conspiracy and Aggression, Vol. I, Chapter VII, The Nizkor Project, pg. 320.
218 A Friend of Medjugorje, Look What Happened While You Were Sleeping, © 2007, pg. 332-333
219 *"Ensuring Brighter Futures for Youth Through Federal Mentoring Programs,"* Federal Mentoring Council, June 23, 2012
220 The Communist. Frank Marshall Davis: The Untold Story of Barack Obama's Mentor, Paul Kengor, Threshold Editions/Mercury Ink, 2012
221 *"Barack Obama's Plan for Universal Voluntary Citizen Service,"* BarackObama.com
222 The Audacity of Hope: Thought on Reclaiming the American Dream, Barack Obama, Vintage Books-Random House, (c) 2006
223 Ibid.

224 *"New FEMA – AmeriCorps Partnership Strengthens Response, Recovery Efforts Following Disasters,"* FEMA, March 13, 2012

225 Transcript of Obama's speech given in Colorado Springs, Colorado, July 2, 2008, World Net Daily.

226 Ibid.

227 Ibid.

228 Ibid.

229 *"We Can't Wait: The White House Announces Federal and Private Sector Commitments to Provide Employment Opportunities for Nearly 180,000 Youth,"* The White House, Office of the Press Secretary, January 5, 2012.

230 Ibid.

231 USA Today, *"Obama Announces Pentagon Budget Cuts"*, by Aamer Madhani, January 5, 2012

232 *"An Innovative Cost-Saving Partnership to Strengthen Disaster Response and Expand Opportunities for Young People,"* FEMA Corps, March 13, 2012

233 *"Announcing the Creation of FEMA Corps,"* , March 13, 2012, FEMA Blog, pg. 2

234 *"New FEMA-AmeriCorps Partnership Strengthens Response, Recovery Efforts Following Disasters,"* March 13, 2012, FEMA.

235 Ibid.

236 Audio Recording and Transcript of Obama's speech given in Colorado Springs, Colorado on July 2, 2008, World Net Daily

237 *"Announcing the Creation of FEMA Corps,"* , March 13, 2012, FEMA Blog, pg. 2

238 Ibid.

239 Ibid.

240 *"FEMA Individual and Community Preparedness Division – Youth Preparedness Council: Frequently Asked Questions,"* Citizen Corps, March 27, 2012.v

241 Ibid.

242 Youth Preparedness: Implementing a Community Based Program - *"Introduction, 1.2 Strengths Youth Bring to Preparedness,"* FEMA.

243 Youth Preparedness: Implementing a Community Based Program - *"Introduction, 1.4 Benefits,"* FEMA.

244 Nazi Conspiracy and Aggression, Vol. I, Chapter VII, The Nizkor Project, pg. 320.

245 The History Place, *"Hitler Youth: Prelude to War 1933-1939,"* pg. 3.

246 *"Barack Obama's Plan for Universal Voluntary Citizen Service,"* Obama'08, BarackObama.com

247 *"Barack Obama's Plan for Universal Voluntary Citizen Service,"* Obama'08, BarackObama.com

248 *"Obama's Civilian National Security Force,"* Lee Cary, American Thinker, July 20, 2008.

249 *"Barack Obama's Plan for Universal Voluntary Citizen Service,"* Obama'08, BarackObama.com

250 The Plan: Big Ideas for Change in America, Rahm Emanuel and Bruce Reed, page 57, Paperback edition, Public Affiars, 2006

Chapter Twenty-Six

251 The History Place, *"Hitler Youth: Prelude to War 1933-1939,"* pg. 5

252 Transcript of Obama's speech given in Colorado Springs, Colorado, July 2, 2008, World Net Daily.

253 *"Welcome to Generation Obama,"* https://go.barackobama.com/page/content/gohomepage.

254 Transcript of Obama's *"This is Your Victory"* speech November 2008, Chicago, Illinois, CNN Politics.

255 H.R. 1388, Serve America Act, United States Congress

256 Ibid.

257 Executive Order #13603 - National Defense Resource Preparedness, Sec. 601 (a)2

258 *"ATK Secures .40 Caliber Ammunition Contract wtih Department of Homeland Security, U.S. Immigration and Customs Enforcement (DHS,ICE),"* March 12, 2012, ATK Press Release

259 Department of Homeland Security, "EEO Complaints and Adjudication," December 23, 2011

260 "DOD Meeting Small and Medium Calilber Ammunition Needs, but Additional Actions are Necessary," Report by the U.S. Government Accountability Office to the House of Representatives Committee on Appropriations, July 2005

261 *""ATK Secures .40 Caliber Ammunition Contract wtih Department of Homeland Security, U.S. Immigration and Customs Enforcement (DHS,ICE),"* March 12, 2012, ATK Press Release

262 Audio Recording and Transcript of Obama's speech given in Colorado Springs, Colorado on July 2, 2008, World Net Daily

263 Ibid.

264 Ibid.

Chapter Twenty-Seven

265 Alabama State Constitution, Section 35.

266 Barnhill, John Basil. Barnhill-Tichenor Debate on Socialism, As It Appeared in the National Rip-Saw. Saint Louis: The National Rip-Saw Pub. Co., c1914. 63 pp. Pamphlet B262 .B3 1914, pg. 34

267 *"Can the County Sheriff Save the Constitution?"* Patrick Krey. The New American, September 30, 2009.

268 *"Texas Standoff is Emblematic of the Nation's Growing Anti-Government Sovereign Movement,"* USA Today, March 30, 2012

269 United States Declaration of Independence, 1776 A.D.

270 Hitler's speech before the passing of the Enabling Act, March 23, 1933

271. Inside The Third Reich, Albert Speer.

272 Ibid.

273 Ibid.

274 "RAND at a Glance," RAND Corporation, April 10, 2012

275 *"Understanding Homeland Security: Session 4 – Times of Crisis: Ensuring*

Government Continuity in Emergencies," John E. Peters, RAND Corporation

276 H.R. 1540, National Defense Authorization Act for Fiscal Year 2012, United States Congress

277 Ibid.

278 Ibid.

279 Strategic Implementation Plan For Empowering Local Partners to Prevent Violent Extremism in the United States, p. 1. Executive Office of the President, National Security Staff.

280 H.R. 658: FAA Modernization and Reform Act of 2012. United States Congress.

281 "FEMA Corps - An Innovative Cost-Saving Partnership...," March 13, 2012. FEMA.

282 *"Obama's Civilian National Security Force,"* Lee Cary. American Thinker, July 20, 2008.

283 Executive Order: National Defense Resource Preparedness. The White House Press Office. March 16, 2012.

284 The Writings of Thomas Jefferson Edited by Andrew A. Lipscomb and Albert Ellery Bergh. Washington: Thomas Jefferson Memorial Association, 1905.

285. This information was verified by Caritas of Birmingham, but the source will remain confidential for protection.

286 Webster's New Collegiate Dictionary, 1980

287 Chuck Pfarrer, Seal Target Geronimo, 2011, pg. 15-16

288 *"Obama: We'll 'Transform America,'"* Angela Galloway. Seattle PI, December 11, 2007.

Chapter Twenty-Eight

289 Victory in Spiritual Warfare, Tony Evans, © 2011, pp. 11-12

290 Transcribed from an audio interview with Obama on January 18, 2001 on Chicago Public Radio WBEX.FM

291 *"Obama's Campaign Commitments to Active Citizenship,"* Peter Levine. A Blog for Civic Renewal, June 1, 2009.

292 *"Obama: We'll 'Transform America,'"* Angela Galloway. Seattle PI, December 11, 2007.

293 Remarks of Senator Barack Obama, "Take Back America 2007." Transcript by Federal News Service, June 19, 2007.

294 *"Thousands Cheer Obama at Rally for Change,"* Hayley Tsukayama and Liz Lucas. The Missourian, October 30, 2008.

295 The Quintessence of Socialism, Dr. Albert Schaffle, Swan Sonnenschein & Co., London, 1891. pgs. 20 and 45.

296 Encyclical *Quadragesimo Anno*, May 15, 1931, n. 117

297 Ibid., n. 120

Chapter Twenty-Nine

298 Winston Churchill, The Second World War, Volume 1: The Gathering Storm (1948), pg. 312

299 *"Texas Standoff is Emblematic of the Nation's Growing Anti-Government Sovereign Movement,"* USA Today, March 30, 2012

300 *"Thousands Cheer Obama at Rally for Change,"* Tsukayama and Lucas. The Columbia Missourian, October 30, 2008.

301 Sheriff Richard Mack, The County Sheriff America's Last Hope, pg. 23-24

302 Ibid.

303 Ibid., pg. 6

304 Ibid., pg 7-8

305 Ibid., pg 9

306 Ibid., pg 9-10

307 Ibid., pg. 8

308 United States Constitution, Art.III Sec. 1

309 Sheriff Richard Mack, The County Sheriff America's Last Hope, pg. 16-17

Chapter Thirty

310 Interview with Sheriff Mack by A Friend of Medjugorje, April 16, 2012

311 Ibid.

Chapter Thirty-One

312 Interview with Sheriff Mack by A Friend of Medjugorje, April 16, 2012

313 Sheriff Richard Mack, The County Sheriff America's Last Hope, pg. 6

314 U.S. Sheriffs Rise Up Against Federal Government: Sheriff Threatens Feds with SWAT Team – Grass Roots Take Charge!, November 14, 2011

315 Ibid.

316 Ibid.

317 Range Magazine, *"Badge vs. Badge, Local Lawmen Bump Heads with Feds on the Range,"* by Tim Findley

318 Liberty Matters, *"Sheriff Issues BLM Trespass Policy,"* by Fred Kelly Grant, November 2000

319 Ibid.

320 Range Magazine, *"Badge vs. Badge, Local Lawmen Bump Heads with Feds on the Range,"* by Tim Findley

321 "A Memento Mori to the Earth," Time Magazine, May 4, 1970.

322 Gun Owners of America, Sheriffs Standing with the People Against the Feds by Larry Pratt, January 4, 2012

323 Dairyland Peach, Sauk Centre, Minnesota, Posted January 4, 2012, by Peter J. Mikkelson, "Sheriff's legal counsel confirms High court Ruling"

324 Audio recording of Sheriff Mattis speaking at the January 30-31, 2012 Constitutional Sheriffs and Peace Officers Association Convention

325 The Looming Food Crisis, 2012 Truth

326 *"Middlebury Dairy Farmer, Sheriff Stand up to FDA,"* Goshen News, by Roger Schneider, December 17, 2011

327 *"How's This for a Change of Pace: Sheriff who Challenged Feds for Amish Raw Dairy Farmer…",* David Gumpert, The Complete Patient, February 1, 2012

328 *"Amid Sheriff – D of J Warnings, Pullback in Grand Jury Investigation of IN*

Dairy Farmer; Raw Milk Freedom Riders Push Further on Interstate Milk Prohibition," David Gumpert, The Complete Patient, December 7, 2011.

329 *"How's This for a Change of Pace: Sheriff who Challenged Feds for Amish Raw Dairy Farmer…",* David Gumpert, The Complete Patient, February 1, 2012

330 *"Middlebury Dairy Farmer, Sheriff Stand up to FDA,"* Goshen News, by Roger Schneider, December 17, 2011

331 Ibid.

332 *"How's This for a Change of Pace: Sheriff who Challenged Feds for Amish Raw Dairy Farmer…",* David Gumpert, The Complete Patient, February 1, 2012

333 *"The County Sheriff: Powers, Duties, and You!",* Butler County Sheriff Brigade, March 12, 2012

334 "The Sheriff – More Power Than the President," Alan Stang, News With Views, March 20, 2009

335 Ibid.

336 Interview with Sheriff Mack by A Friend of Medjugorje, April 16, 2012

337 Forest M. Mims III, "Meeting Doctor Doom," *The eco-logic Powerhouse,* May 2006, p. 16-17

338 *"Local Sheriff Takes on the Banks, fighting for the Middle Class,"* CNN interview with Sheriff Tom Dart, Cook County, Illinois, April 21, 2011

339 Ibid.

340 Ibid.

341 Ibid.

342 Oath Keepers, county Sheriffs, Marxism, The Constitution, January 16, 2012

343 *"NDAA Resolution for Sheriffs,"* Stewart Rhodes & Richard Fry, Oath Keepers, 2012.

Chapter Thirty-Two

344 Matthew Spalding, *"Idaho Draws the Constitutional Line"*

345 Michael Boldin, founder of 10th Amendment Center, Speaks up for States Rights, Washington Times, February 6, 2012

346 Ibid.

347 Ibid.

348 Ibid.

349 "Remarks Delivered by Director David H. Petraues at the In-Q-Tel CEO Summits," March 1, 2012. Central Intelligence Agency.

Chapter Thirty-Three

350 *"Roe Rage: Democratic Constitutionalism and Backlash,"* Robert C. Post and Reva B. Siegel, January 1, 2007

351 Supreme Court Justice Ruth Bader Ginsburg, Egyptian television interview, January 30, 2012

352 There are numerous sources that indicate or state outright that George Soros has a heavy hand in manipulating governments around the world, especially in Africa. Rather than quote these varied sources, we find it most valuable and most telling to review Soros' own words as well words from South Africa's government.

As mentioned in the main text, according to Soros, he became involved with the overthrow of the South African government as early as 1979. (*The Capitalist Threat,* George Soros; The Atlantic Monthly; *February 1997; Volume 279, No. 2; pages 45-58.*) Just one year before drafting of the country's final Constitution began in 1994 and just 3 years before the adoption of the final South African Constitution in 1996, Soros founded an organization called the Open Society Foundation for South Africa (1993), "to promote the **ideal** of an **open society** in Africa; an **ideal** which includes **democracy...a strong civil society... tolerance** for divergent opinions." The foundation "will encourage new approaches and ideas which will contribute to the creating of an open society in South Africa" (Open Society Foundation for South Africa, "How Do We Operate?" 2012). This society reports that Soros has poured hundreds of millions of dollars into funding these aims in many countries including South Africa (Open Society for South Africa, "The Philanthropist," 2012). Soros also published a book in 1991 titled, <u>Underwriting Democracy</u>. Though this book deals primarily with his work in creating "open societies" in Europe, the title of the book and his efforts in this arena give much evidence to help one "know your enemy."

Turning to words from South Africa: South Africa's Parliament maintains a website and states the following about their constitution, which is strikingly familiar to the schemes of Soros through his foundation. The South African Parliament states, "Our constitution lays the foundation for an **open society** based on **democratic values, social justice** and **fundamental human rights...**" As noted above, Soros has made many covert moves to create the **"ideal,"** that the South African Constitution is the standard, the model that other nations are to look to. In step, as puppets on a string, the South African Parliament is handled by Soros. The Parliament echoes a scripted line that all look to their constitution which they promote **"is hailed worldwide..."** (Parliament of the Republic of South Africa, "Our Constitution.").

Again, these are only a few of the strongest sources that indicate Soros' heavy involvement in the overthrow of South Africa and the setting up of its Constitution as a "pointing star." Why would Soros do this? As you read previously in this chapter, Soros' goal is "centralization, in order implement internationalization of each nation. It would allow for the first time for a leader to lead from a central position globally with such power" (see page 500).

353 James Norell, *"The Movement to Torch the United States Constitution,"* American's 1st Freedom Magazine, May 2012, pg. 34
354 Ibid., pg. 34
355 Ibid., pg. 61
356 Ibid., pg. 61
357 Ibid., pg. 61
358 Ibid., pg. 61
359 *The American Covenant,* Marshall Foster and Mary-Elaine Swanson, The Mayflower Institute, 1992, p. 18

360 James Norell, *"The Movement to Torch the United States Constitution,"* American's 1st Freedom Magazine, May 2012, pg. 34

361 Professor Aziz Huq of the University of Chicago Law School, lead-off speaker at the Constitution of 2020 Conference at Yale University, Oct. 2, 2009

362 James Norell, *"The Movement to Torch the United States Constitution,"* American's 1st Freedom Magazine, May 2012, pg. 61

363 Ibid., pg. 63

364 Ibid.

365 Ibid., pg. 63

366 Doe v. Braden, 57 U.S. 657 (1853)

367 The Cherokee Tobacco, 78 U.S. 620 (1870)

368 Geofroy v. Riggs, 133 U.S. 267 (1890)

369 Reid v. Covert, 354 U.S. 16 (1956)

370 Ibid.

371 Reid v. Covert, 354 U.S. 17 (1956)

372 Ibid.

373 America's First Freedom, *The Movement to Torch the United States Constitution,* James Norell, May 2012, pg. 63

Chapter Thirty-Four

374 *The American Covenant,* Marshall Foster and Mary-Elaine Swanson, The Mayflower Institute, 1992, p. 18

375 Alliance Defense Fund, J Michael Johnson, March 31, 2010, pg. 4

376 Ibid., pg. 3

377 Ibid.

378 This story, taken from We Got Him! by Lt. Col. Steve Russell, was compiled from a couple of sections from the book. Though it speaks of a specific incident, what is evident throughout the whole book is an important principle that we must all take hold of when facing our enemies. Some description has been added to the original story to bridge and emphasize the point being made with Russell's way of commanding.

379 Ibid.

Chapter Thirty-Five

380 The Audacity to Hope, Barack Obama, Vintage Books, © 2006

381 *"Catholic University Stops Providing Student Health Insurance Over Birth Control Mandate."* Nap Nazworth, Christian post, May 16, 2012.

382 Ronald Reagan, Republican National Convention, July 17, 1980

383 Patrick Henry's speech before the Virginia House of Congress at St. John's Church, March 23, 1775, as recorded by the National Center for Public Policy Research

384 Richard Mack, The County Sheriff: American's Last Hope, © 2009

385 *"Frequently Asked Church Statistics."* Center for Applied Research in the Apostolate. 2012

Chapter Thirty-Six

386 *The American Covenant,* Marshall Foster and Mary-Elaine Swanson, The Mayflower Institute, 1992, p. 18
387 The New American Bible, Collins Publishers, © 1970
388 *The American Covenant,* Marshall Foster and Mary-Elaine Swanson, The Mayflower Institute, 1992, p. 18
389 The Works of John Adams, Second President of the United States, Vol. 9, Charles Francis Adams, Boston, Little, Brown, and Com., 1856
390 Catholic News Herald, *"Pope wants US Catholics to lead worldwide Church revival, nuncio says,"* Diocese of Charlotte, April 25, 2012.
391 *"Chronology of Apostle Paul's Journeys and Epistles,"* Matthew McGee, 1998
392 The Company of St. Joseph, Exorcism Prayers Preceded Closing of Illinois Abortion Clinic, February 20, 2012
393 Look What Happened While You Were Sleeping, A Friend of Medjugorje, © 2007, pg. 111
394 *The American Covenant,* Marshall Foster and Mary-Elaine Swanson, The Mayflower Institute, 1992, p. 18
395 Interview with Sheriff Richard Mack, August 13, 2012
396 Memoirs of the Life and Writings of Benjamin Franklin, Vol. I, Benjamin Franklin, pg. 270

Chapter Thirty-Seven

397 The Writings of Thomas Jefferson Edited by Andrew A. Lipscomb and Albert Ellery Bergh. Washington: Thomas Jefferson Memorial Association, 1905.

Chapter Thirty-Eight

398 "Samuel Adams: Quotes," American History Central, Digital Encyclopedia. © 2012.
399 Ibid.
400 Abraham Lincoln: *The Works of Abraham Lincoln, Speech and Debates,* Jon H. Clifford, Editor (New York, The University Society Inc. 1908), Vol. III, August 17, 1858, p. 126-127
401 John Adams, The Debate on the Declaration, Revolutionary War and Beyond, July 1, 1776
402 The Writings of Thomas Jefferson Edited by Andrew A. Lipscomb and Albert Ellery Bergh. Washington: Thomas Jefferson Memorial Association, 1905.

Chapter Thirty-Nine

403 An oration delivered before the Inhabitants of the Town of Newbury Port, at their request, on the sixty-first Anniversary of the Declaration of Independence, July 4, 1837, John Quincy Adams
404 *The American Covenant,* Marshall Foster and Mary-Elaine Swanson, The Mayflower Institute, 1992, p. 18

405 The 5,000 Year Leap, W. Cleon Skousen, National Center for Constitutional Studies, 1981

Chapter Forty

406 *"The Reason for Church Steeples,"* David Alfredo, eHow.com
407 "Thomas Jefferson on Politics and Government," Family Guardian. © 2009
408 The Papers of James Madison, Voume III, Publixhed by Henry Gilpih by direction of the Joint Library Committee of Congress, J&H.G. Langley, New York, 1841
409 Understanding Sustainable Development - Agenda 21: Guide for Public Officials, Freedom 21 Santa Cruz.

Chapter Forty-Two

410 *"Mandated Gun Ownership: A Tale of Two Cities,"* Tim Brown, July 25, 2012.
411 Ibid.
412 Ibid.
413 Ibid.
414 Ibid.

Chapter Forty-Three

415 *"American History You Never Learned,"* A Friend of Medjugorje, (c)
416 Ibid.
417 Ibid.
418 It Ain't Gonna Happen, A Friend of Medjugorje, SJP (c) 2010

State Maps

419 Look What Happened While You Were Sleeping, A Friend of Medjugorje, SJP (c) 2007

Appendix I

420 The 5000 Year Leap: A Miracle that Changed the World, W. Cleon Skousen, National Center for Constitutional Studies, © 1981
421 Ibid.
422 The Roots of Obama's Rage, Dinesh D'Souza, Regnery Publishing, Inc. © 2010

Appendix II

423 Range Magazine, Badge vs. Badge, Local Lawmen Bump heads with Feds on the Range, Tim Findley, Winter, 2003
424 Ibid.
425 Ibid.

426 Ibid.
427 Ibid.
428 Ibid.
429 *"Grant County Sheriff Palmer Stands Against 'Bad Government'*, February 22, 2012, Reclaim Baker's County
430 Ibid.
431 Ibid.
432 Ibid.
433 "Badge vs. Badge: Local Lawmen Bump Heads with Feds on the Range," by Tim Findley, Range Magazine, Winter, 2003
434 376 *"Constitutional Sheriff Tony DeMeo,"* Cassandra Anderson, Morph City, July 30, 2010.
435 Richard Mack, The County Sheriff: American's Last Hope, © 2009
436 U.S. Observer; "Gil Gilbertson Sheriff of and for the People, April 23, 2012,
437 Political Vel Craft, "Oregan Sheriff Gil Gilbertson Continues Stand Against Federal Government
438 U.S. Observer; "Sheriff: This Land is Our Land, Feds Have No Jurisdiction!", by Ron Lee
439 Ibid.
440 "Sheriff Baca Won't Renew Forest Service Agreement", Sierra County Sentinel, February 3, 2012, by Etta Pettijohn
441 Ibid.
442 Ibid.
443 *"New Mexico Law and Local Sheriff Trump the Feds,,"* The Tenth Amendment Center, November 7, 2011
444 San Diego Reader, "Sheriff's Sobriety Checkpoint Yields No DUIs, Least Revenue, Auditor Says", by Matt Potter, February 17, 2012
445 Ibid.
446 *"Tennessee County Sheriff's Office Brings in Anti-Muslim Speaker to Train Officers about Muslim Culture,"* Amanda Beadle, Think Progress, February 15, 2012
447 Ibid.
448 Revolutionary Services and Civil Life of General William Hull, Maria Campbell, D. Appleton and Company, New York, 1848, pg. 266

Appendix III

449 Look What Happened While You Were Sleeping, A Friend of Medjugorje, SJP (c) 2007

INDEX

"It is when a people forget God that tyrants forge their chains. A vitiated state of morals, a corrupted public conscience, is incompatible with freedom. No free government, or the blessings of liberty, can be preserved to any people but by a firm adherence to justice, moderation, temperance, frugality, and virtue; and by a frequent recurrence to fundamental principles."

—Patrick Henry

★ Why have unbelievers, today, been allowed to get in positions to turn our laws upside down, destroying our Nation?

★ Why are the unbelievers in offensive positions, while we, Christians, find ourselves in defensive positions?

★ Why do individual States have to pass amendments to defend marriage?

★ Why can't we get Godly leaders in office?

★ Why have we lost authority over wickedness?

★ Why do the godless proudly parade their unmentionable and illicit lifestyles that cannot even be described in these writings, their abortions, their decadence, all the while imposing them forcibly upon society as the norm, flaunting in our faces that *"You cannot stop us!"*?

Find out how you can help change this Nation by reading the book,
Look What Happened While You Were Sleeping™

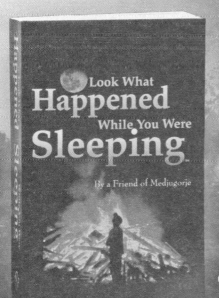

I SEE FAR

By a Friend of Medjugorje

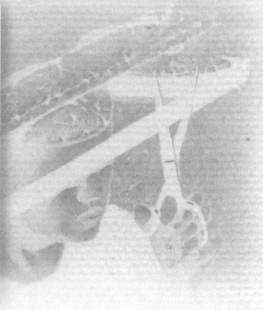

Never authoring a book that is a let-down, A Friend of Medjugorje's writing, <u>I See Far</u>™, is strongly connected to Our Lady's apparitions in Medjugorje. A book of surprises, worth buying as a gift, that will quake the soul and make life radically different, fruiting into happiness few people experience in today's society. A book which convicts and motivates one to a more richer and happier life. Testimony after testimony repeats that <u>I See Far</u>™ is one of the most impacting and life-changing books they have ever read.

> *"I applaud the book, "I See Far," The book put into words something I have suspected for a long time…I quit watching the tube a long time ago, believing it to be a waste of one's life. Kids should run in the woods, swing from trees, swim in the creek down the road, and play "hide and seek" half the night with the other kids in the neighborhood."*
>
> *Davison, Michigan*

**TO ORDER call Caritas: 205-672-2000 twenty-four hours
OR ORDER on mej.com,**

TO ORDER See below order form
OR CALL Caritas of Birmingham **205-672-2000** ext. **315 twenty-four hours**
ORDER NOW on **mej.com** click on mejmart
OR ORDER thru **amazon.com** OR thru Barnes & Noble on **bn.com**

They Fired the First Shot 2012.
SOFT COVER BOOK BF110

~~$28.50 each~~ Sale Price For Promotion
$15.00

Qty	Books	S&H	Total
☐ 1	$15.00 +	$7.50 =	**$22.50**

Give Away to Save America!!!

Special Case Pricing $5.00/Book
16 Books $80.00 + $30.00 S&H = $110.00

Cases	Qty	Total
☐ 1	16	**$110.00** (includes S&H)
☐ 3	48	**$330.00** (includes S&H)
☐ 5	80	**$550.00** (includes S&H)
☐ 10	160	**$1,100.00** (includes S&H)
_____	Other	(**$110.00** ea) (includes S&H)

These rates are normal postal delivery
We recommend calling us for faster
trackable delivery (UPS) 205-672-2000
Call for pallet pricing (512 books)

$5.00 Each!!! **+ S&H**

Below Cost!!!

Case of Soft Cover Books

☎ Ph: **205-672-2000 ext. 315** (24 hours)

📠 Fax: **205-672-9667 24 hrs.**

✉ Mail: **Caritas of Birmingham**
100 Our Lady Queen of Peace Drive
Sterrett, AL 35147-9987 USA

WARNING! See Box Below:

*The United States Postal Service (U.S.P.S., the "Post Office") is in degeneration. We have had very many problems with cases shipped via the United States Postal Service – lost and destroyed cases, delivery taking up to 6 weeks, and even other propaganda materials being inserted inside of books. Perhaps some individuals within the U.S.P.S. are opposed to some of the principles contained within Caritas materials. Therefore, we HIGHLY RECOMMEND choosing United Parcel Service (U.P.S.) for shipping your case. If you still choose to ship via United States Postal Service, Caritas cannot be held responsible for books that are lost, destroyed, delayed, etc. We will not be able to replace your books for free. Again, we highly recommend calling Caritas for United Parcel Service (U.P.S.) pricing on cases of books. This is not a blanket statement against all post office workers. Our own local postmaster provides very good service. We do, however, experience many problems nationwide which is why we find it necessary to make this recommendation.

They Fired the First Shot 2012. Soft Cover (price includes shipping) BF110	$
Donation for the Promotion of <u>They Fired The First Shot 2012</u>™	$
TOTAL:	$

Enclose in remittance envelope or call in your order and donation
24 hours a day! 205-672-2000 ext. 315

The Federal Tax Exempt I.D. # for Caritas of Birmingham is 63-0945243.

Ship to:

Name (please print) _____ I.D. # _____

Address _____

City _____ State _____ Zip Code _____

Country _____ Birthday _____

Phone # _____(if an international number, include all digits)

Credit Card type (circle one) ☐ VISA ☐ MasterCard ☐ Discover

Credit Card Number ☐☐☐☐ ☐☐☐☐ ☐☐☐☐ ☐☐☐☐

Expiration date: ☐☐-☐☐ e-mail: _____

Phone (hm): _____ (wk): _____

ABOUT THE AUTHOR

The author of this book is also the author of the books <u>Words From Heaven</u>®, <u>How to Change Your Husband</u>™, <u>I See Far</u>™, <u>Look What Happened While You Were Sleeping</u>™, <u>It Ain't Gonna Happen</u>™, <u>They Fired the First Shot 2012</u>™ hundreds of booklets, and other publications such as the *Words of the Harvesters* and the *Caritas of Birmingham Newsletter*. He has written more on Medjugorje and its messages than anyone in the world, producing life-changing writings and spiritual direction to countless numbers across the world, of all nationalities. He wishes to be known only as "A Friend of Medjugorje." The author is not one looking in from the outside regarding Medjugorje, but one who is close to the events — many times, right in the middle of the events about which he has written; a first-hand witness.

Originally writing to only a few individuals in 1987, readership has grown to over 250,000 in the United States, with additional readers in over one hundred thirty foreign countries, who follow the spiritual insights and direction given through these writings.

The author, when asked why he signs only as "A Friend of Medjugorje," stated:

> *"I have never had an ambition or desire to write. I do so only because God has shown me, through prayer, that He desires this of me. So from the beginning, when I was writing to only a few people, I prayed to God and promised I would not sign anything; that the writings would have to*

carry themselves and not be built on a personality.
I prayed that if it was God's desire for these
writings to be inspired and known, then He could
do it by His Will and grace and that my will be
abandoned to it.

"The Father has made these writings known and contin-
ues to spread them to the ends of the earth. These
were Our Lord's last words before ascending: ***"Be a***
witness to the ends of the earth." *These writings give*
testimony to that desire of Our Lord to be a witness
with one's life. It is not important to be known. It is
important to do God's Will."

For those who require "ownership" of these writings by the
author in seeing his name printed on this work in order to
give it more credibility, we state that we cannot reconcile the
fact that these writings are producing hundreds of thousands
of conversions, if not millions through grace, and are
requested worldwide from every corner of the earth. The
author, therefore, will not take credit for a work that, by proof
of the impact these writings have to lead hearts to conversion,
have been Spirit–inspired with numbers increasing yearly,
sweeping as a wave across the ocean. Indeed in this case,
crossing every ocean of the earth. Our Lady gave this author
a direct message for him through the visionary, Marija, of
Medjugorje, in which Our Lady said to him to witness not
with words but through humility. It is for this reason that he
wishes to remain simply "A Friend of Medjugorje."

— Caritas of Birmingham

Don't Miss a Visit to the Caritas Mission House

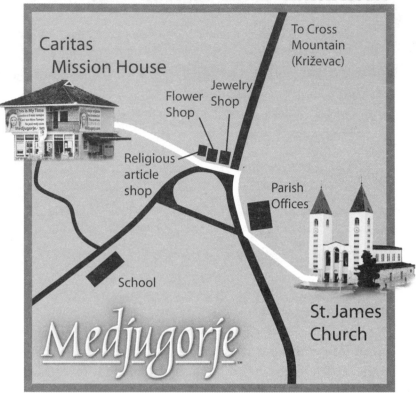

Located just over one block from the church.

Facing the front of St. James Church from outside—exit the courtyard to the LEFT.

Walk past the Parish Offices to the main road and turn RIGHT.

Follow the sidewalk a brief distance to the next road and turn LEFT, crossing the road at the crosswalk. You will see a jewelry shop on the corner. The jewelry shop and a flower shop will be on your right as you pass it.

Follow STRAIGHT on the sidewalk a very short distance.

At the first road next to a religious article shop bear slightly RIGHT.

Follow this road past a row of Pansions until you reach the Caritas of Birmingham Mission House.

Look for the **St. Michael statue** and **"This is My Time" Signs**.

Caritas of Birmingham Mission House is operated by the Community of Caritas.

The Mother house is located at: **100 Our Lady Queen of Peace Drive Sterrett, Alabama 35147 USA**

Mej.com *Fastest growing Medjugorje website in the world. Extensive up-to-date information on Medjugorje as it happens.*